MW00809653

THE BARRIER

CREATED WITH THE
BODY OF A FALLEN GOD
THE BARRIER SEPARATES
THE KNOWN WORLD
FROM THE
FORGOTTEN LANDS

THE KNOWN WORLD

UNCHARTED WATERS

MORO ISLAND

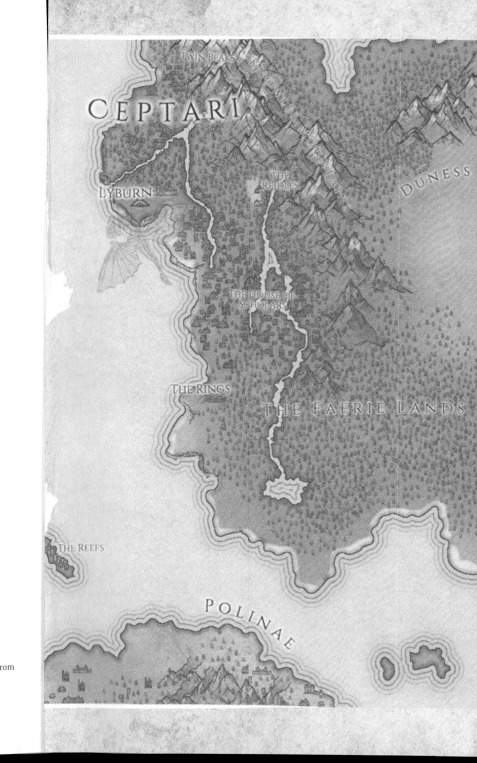

Sea of F...

Anneliese Peters

For my first reader.

I hope you found your wings.

CONTENTS

Pronunciation Guide

characters

Elarie Crosha— el-LA-ree CRO-sha

Calix Lathin— CAL-ix LATH-in

Kaelum Metar— KAY-lum MET-tar

Terry— terry

Grey/Greilor— grey/GREY-lor

Terisa— ter-ISS-sa

Rol— roll

Jamison— jam-I-son

Red— red

Tran— tran

Lester— LESS-ter

Lione— LEE-own

Masha— MA-sha

Greenie— Green-EE

Finnal— FINN-al

Gee— 'G'

Retch— W-retch

The Messenger— the messenger

Damila— da-MIL-la

Will- will

John— john

Johnson— JOHN-son

Ryd Lathin— reed LATH-in

Marcella Lathin— mar-SELL-a LATH-in

Queen Vienn Lathin— queen VEE-en LATH-in

King Ritan Lathin— king RITE-tan LATH-in

Dina— DEE-na

ANNELIESE PETERS

Enid— EE-nid

Rosette Metar— ro-Z-ette MET-tar

Macri Fengge— ma-CREE FEN-g

Bobo— BO-BO

Rint— rin-T

Moy— moy

Styd— st-EED

Renci— ren-CEE

Tahra— TAH-rah

Kolto— KOL-toh

Brin— Brin

from the past

Matian— ma-TEE-an

Ritker Crosha— rit-KER CRO-sha

Cammie Crosha—KA-me CRO-sha

Ashter Crosha— ASH-ter CRO-sha

Danien Crosha— dan-I-an CRO-sha

Ave— AY-ve

Trion— TREE-on

dragon species

Great Dragon— great dragon

Skeep— SK-eep

Jitter—JI-ter

Windryd— WIND-reed

Gurin— gur-IN

Dindaruo— din-DA-ru-oh

Fyndall— FIN-dall

Kretton— Kret-TON

SEA OF FLAMES

places

The Reefs (Gerton)— the reefs (GUR-tun)

Moro Island— MOR-oh island

The Rings— the rings

Lyburn— LIE-burn

Ceptari— SEPT-tar-ee

North/South Reidle— north/south REY-del

Duness— dune-NESS

Trec— tr-EK

Polinae— pol-LIN-ay

The Forgotten Lands—the forgotten lands

The Muntaiins— the MOON-tains

Twin Peaks— twin peaks

Eneblood- en-NE-blood

creatures

Jiiver— Ji-ver

Fae— fey

Faerie— fairy

Frei— FR-ey

Yaerling— YAR-ling

Parind— PAIR-ind

Metarina— met-tar-EE-na

PART ONE

THE SEA

Chapter One

Elarie

Elarie thought of the golden dragon in her dreams as she watched Terisa walk across the board to a large ship. The old seer was allowed to take her time unlike any other—no point in wasting whatever price they paid for her.

The golden dragon continued to fly through her mind as Terisa was helped to the dock of the *Greyscale* by a young looking pirate. Its body twisted and turned with the changes of the wind, high in the sky at sunrise. The sun's light bathed its scales in a glow so unmatchable any king would be shamed for his crown. Elarie closed her eyes for a moment. The dragon in her dreams tended to mean something. Something was happening or was going to happen. And this was true, of course, because Captain Rol's slaves were being bought by this young, fresh looking pirate.

He looked no older than twenty three. His skin was dark and smooth. A light stubble covered his jaw, though it was controlled as if he kept up with it and his tightly cut hair. The pirate boy-captain laughed as he shook hands with Rol. Their business was finished. He began following Terisa over the board connecting their ships, placing a hand on the back of who Elarie assumed was his second. This man seemed to be the same age, with sharp eyes like he missed nothing and black, silky hair that fell to his neck. The pair of them took the board together while their crew began disconnecting the ships from one another.

A booming roar sounded from above them when they were pulling the board from its position. Many looked up in fear. Light colored clouds dotted the sky as they reflected off the rising sun. Elarie again thought of her golden dragon in the sunrise as her eyes moved upward. Again, a dragon roared. The sound sent a chill running from the top of her head downward. Long ago her brother called the feeling her 'coming down to earth.' She spent far too much time in the clouds, and this strange feeling of dread put her feet back on the ground.

Elarie watched a large dark grey dragon drop from the clouds. He landed carefully on a deck full of screaming slaves and calm pirates. He roared for their attention, such a narcissistic beast. Elarie sank to her knees, her chains clanking together. She watched smoke and sparks blow from the mouth of the Great Dragon. A rider slid off his back, running a hand over his grey scales.

"Greilor?" Elarie whispered.

The dragon's head snapped to her, the sharp jaw closing. He looked at the ship of frozen and curious people, black eyes searching. They fell to Elarie. At first, the dragon was just as frozen as the humans and faeries. He didn't seem to know what to do. Smoke huffed nervously from his nostrils and he shook his head around. Elarie breathed a quiet sob as she watched him. Thousands of years of torment and pain were wiped away from her for just a moment. Only a moment and that was all Greilor needed to cry out sharply and nearly capsize his rider's ship to get closer. He reached out and latched onto Rol's *SeaDaisy* with his sharp claws, dragging it toward him.

A spark of flame built in the back of his throat. Those around Elarie ran for cover before Greilor bathed her in hot magic flame. Elarie laughed as it kissed her skin and melted her chains, burning only what she wanted. Tears streamed from her eyes, alight on her cheeks even as the Dragonflame burned away evidence of dirt and bloody grime. They remained. She wanted him to see.

As the fire dissipated, Elarie could hear the screams of shock. She paid no mind to it as she stood. Greilor leaned over the ship, tilting both to the sides and making things roll over the wood as well as ruining the balance of even the most experienced of the pirates. Elarie fell against him, digging her nails under his scales. The dragon began to speak in her mind for the first time in a few millenniums. *I missed you desperately,* he told her in the gentle rumble of his voice, *I searched for so long but I could not get into the Keep to find you.* Elarie nodded. She'd been outside it when the Keep went down. It was the rest of her family that had been trapped, not her. *Come. You must come,* he insisted, raising his big head.

Elarie looked back at Captain Rol. The pirate, fiercest on the water, was not afraid. He was curious. And, in Elarie's experience, he needed payment. She turned to Greilor, "open your mouth, I need your teeth." The Great Dragon obliged, willing to give anything to have his Elarie back. He was even willing to have a few teeth pulled. Elarie held three fresh dragon teeth in her hand, walking up to the captain.

"Buying your freedom with teeth?" He asked, sneering. It made the brand on his cheek—a curved letter *M*—twist into something else. Rol had been a slave once. The story went that he killed nearly everyone for his freedom and, with the help of what now made up his crew, he stole a slaver's ship and escaped. Only it seemed that the slave missed the trade and became a slaver.

"They're more valuable than gold if you sell them to the right people," Elarie told him. "If you can read I suggest finding a novel by Netirn Kalis, she wrote about the usefulness of different parts of a dragon's body. You won't get it in Ceptari, the book was banned from the country." She dropped the teeth at the feet of the pirate, not caring that they began to make their own slide to the port side. "And I am free."

He said, "I haven't accepted your payment."

Elarie looked back at Greilor and replied, "tell him you haven't." She walked back to the dragon, wrapping her hand around the horn at the tip of his nose. Rol said nothing as Greilor lifted her into the air and released his hold on the *SeaDaisy*. He carried her across the calm sea and deposited her next to his rider, a man close to her age with light brown skin and a ring of blue in his otherwise dark eyes.

The dragon flew into the air and set fire to Rol's sails. The pirates aboard scrambled to put it out as Greilor soared into the sky, turning his great wings and grabbing onto the *Greyscale's* bowsprit. He began to drag it out to the west. It was as if he was taking them home, but only for a moment before he decided he'd had enough carrying. Looking back, the *SeaDaisy* was small and on fire. They wouldn't be able to follow them for at least some time. Greilor landed with a satisfied *thud* and purred against Elarie. He pushed her close to his new rider, already insisting she get comfortable with him.

"So," the rider said. He shifted uncomfortably, perhaps not liking the attention being placed upon him. "He knows you."

Elarie swallowed nervously. She'd been faced with riders of dragons that had taken an interest in her. Oftentimes it led to a decent conversation, sometimes more, but facing down *this* rider particularly was far more daunting than anything else. Greilor's rider. The one he chose after years and years of being parted from her. Elarie cleared her throat and glanced at the dragon. "I am Elarie," she said tightly.

He picked up on her discomfort quickly. "Calix. That's me," he tried for a smile. It was easy for him, it spread slowly over his whole face. A voice came into her mind saying, *he's sweet, you might like him.* Elarie smiled, too, both because of Greilor and because of Calix.

"Prince Calix?" Elarie asked.

"What? No, no that's not me," he stuttered. Elarie felt her smile grow slightly, feeling a laugh come from the dragon in the form of a low hum. "Why, is it because of the name?" Calix reached up to rub the back of his neck. Already Elarie could tell he was someone that would be easy to befriend. Perhaps that was why Greilor chose him as a rider. The dragon was usually so particular.

She said, "I have been to Lyburn, you know. Even if sightings of the kingdom's prince are scarce in the capital, that doesn't mean I haven't seen him."

"Well, maybe but the prince does take pride in the fact that he looks like many of his subjects," he countered.

"Except the eyes," she said, looking at the pretty color. A lovely brown, a ring of blue.

Calix blinked quickly, fluttering his thick lashes. "The eyes? What about—"

"Lathin blue?" Elarie quirked a brow. He seemed to blush, a chuckle bouncing through his chest as he looked away.

"Lathin blue," he repeated with a joking resentment, "how'd you know about Lathin blue?"

Elarie felt herself laugh, "it is a lovely color, Your Highness."

"Right, thanks."

"Don't expect me to bow," she looked at Greilor, petting him gently. His skin was so thick she was never sure if she actually felt it. The dragon *told* her he could, but he told her many things as a child that turned out to be little white lies to spare her feelings.

Calix shook his head, "of course not. I don't expect that of anyone." Elarie glanced at him. He rocked on his feet, "so you and Grey..."

"*Grey?*" Elarie asked, her eyes a little wide. Her pale brows rose on her head, "how'd you come up with that?"

"Well," he rocked again. The prince was agitated. Nervous. Perhaps he didn't like having to defend his naming choices. "I sort of... I don't know—first off he *is* grey and black." She laughed. "Come on," Calix joined in her laughter, "I'm not sure how it happened. I was with him and talking to him, asking what I should call him. It was the first thing that came to mind. So he's Grey and I'd appreciate you not teasing me about it."

She grinned.

"I already got shit from my little sister for it," he added, "but he seemed to like it. That's what matters."

Elarie inquired, "your sister?"

He said, "Marcella. She's seven and is highly opinionated."

"Is it just Marcella or do you have other siblings?" She continued, moving up Greilor's face to hold onto the horn like she did as a child.

"I have a little brother named Ryd," he followed her to the horn, "he's four. The quietest of all three of us." Calix smiled fondly, "I adore that kid. And you? Do you have any siblings?"

Greilor made a noise of mourning. Another hum. Elarie doubted anyone but she would be able to tell the difference between the sounds. The dragon lowered to a lying down position, sighing. Elarie said, "I did." A familiar sense of pity now spread over the prince's face, replacing his soft smile. "Four siblings, two older and two younger. They and my parents passed a few years ago." The dragon between them thanked her for her honesty. He wanted her to know him and to be known by him. This, according to the dragon, was the first step to a friendship. *Share with him, let him share with you. Please,* Greilor added. And he hardly ever said please.

"I am sorry," Calix said, nothing but sincerity in his tone. "How did they pass? If you don't mind sharing that."

Share, Greilor said. His head turned slightly. Elarie felt warmth adjust at her back, causing her to turn. Two men were there, the captain and his first mate, and both seemed shocked she knew they'd stopped where they were. Elarie's eyes darted from one person to the other. They both stared right back.

It was Calix that ended their silent assessment. He said, "guys, this is Elarie. Elarie, that's Captain Kaelum and his first mate, Terry."

Her eyes moved for the first time. The ship was active, many men in the man-only crew dutifully going about their tasks while also keeping an ear or an eye trained on the newcomer. Not the other slaves, but Elarie. Strange, though it was Elarie who came onto the ship without permission hanging off the horn of a Great Dragon. Elarie saw these men, but she also saw the slaves without their chains. She saw Terisa making a young pirate laugh. "You free them," she realized, her eyes going back to the young captain. "You don't sell them?"

"We are pirates that pirate slaves," Kaelum said, pushing down a smile. He must've enjoyed saying it. Elarie reached for her wrist, rubbing her thumb over the inside of it. "Except for you," the captain said, noticing her action. "A dragon freed you."

"Would you like to tell us about that?" His first mate asked. Terry. Up close Elarie could see a worldly knowledge in his sharp eyes. He'd experienced much for someone so young. He had sharp features, like his eyes, with defined cheekbones and a long jaw. Terry kept his face shaven and it looked like he wasn't very good at keeping it even. Small cuts were on his jaw from the blade. Looking at his hands, they had a tremor to them. That and something familiar to Elarie. A brand.

Calix shifted suddenly on her left side, taking her focus off of the first mate. Greilor moved as well, breathing out the steam Elarie used to stick her face in. She liked the smell. The dragon shook out his head and she smiled, watching as he moved to a more comfortable position, though her smile quickly dropped. "What is that?" She asked both him and his rider, looking at a strap under his arm. "What is *that*?" Elarie walked across the deck and grabbed the leather. She whipped around to Calix, "you put a *saddle* on him?"

He stuttered, "he let me!"

"Of course he let you!" She threw her arms up, "he's your dragon! Every dragon has to say yes to a saddle for the comfort of their riders!"

"Then what's wrong with him having a saddle if he wants me to be comfortable?" His eyes were wide and defensive. Calix took a step forward. His two friends shifted nervously, unable to judge how defensive of the prince they should be given the topic of discussion.

"Gods, of course you would ask that," Elarie rolled her eyes and looked at Greilor, "and you, 'O Ancient One, don't tell me you let the prince give you baths as well?" Greilor chuffed a laugh. Elarie climbed onto his back to inspect the dark leather. It was a seat that was strapped over him, going around his front arms and the base of his grand wings. Someone had taken great care of the craftsmanship, that was obvious. Not only was it well built, but flowers were embroidered into the front with vines twisting up to the horn. "Saddles," Elarie muttered.

She dropped off of Greilor's back and landed in front of Calix. The prince looked at the part of the saddle that he could see, then Elarie. "Do you not approve?" He asked.

"Of course not," she rolled her eyes, "and even if you are his current rider, I've been on his back since before I could walk so I simply cannot stand for this."

"Since before you could walk?" Calix repeated as he walked around her, "and you never sat in a saddle?"

"He isn't a horse, Your Highness," she turned. Elarie smiled when he unbuckled the thick leather strap on the dragon's arm. Calix climbed on to fix the wing, then slid off and ducked around to the other side. The saddle loosened. Her smile brightened as she watched it slide off his large body. Calix came back dragging it behind him.

He said, "this is a very expensive saddle, you know," and dropped it in front of her.

"I love the embroidery," Elarie replied.

"Thank you," he smiled. Calix looked at Greilor, watching the dragon stretch out without the chafing of the saddle. His wing almost hit a sail. A pirate hanging from boom above them yelped and held tight. Greilor, only in Elarie's mind, called them all scared children.

Teach him how to ride bareback, Elarie, he told her when neither of them said another word. Calix was calm, at ease next to his dragon and shockingly next to Elarie. She moved her eyes down the foremast and dragged them slowly to Calix. He wanted her to say it just as much as Greilor did. "I can teach you," she managed. Elarie kicked the fine leather, "how to not need this."

"I'd be happy to learn," Calix said with a fresh smile, one that meant he got what he wanted without needing to ask. "So what's his name? Grey," he motioned to the dragon behind him.

"Greilor," she answered.

He laughed, "*Grey*-lor! Where did you come up with that?"

Elarie ignored the two pirates completely as she walked to Greilor's head, again holding the horn. Calix followed. The part of her mind that desired attention over everything else wanted to say he was mesmerized or fascinated by her. "That has been his name for longer than time can say," she said fondly. Elarie leaned back, using the dragon to hold her. She gazed at Greilor, smiling faintly. "He is a Great Dragon, one of the last of his kind. His age is unknown to us."

Calix opened his mouth, most likely to ask another question, but a young voice cried out and caused every head to turn toward him and the old woman he was holding. She'd fainted.

"How inconvenient," Elarie said and walked to the pair of them.

CHAPTER TWO

ELARIE

"What's wrong with her?" The young pirate asked. He seemed to be the youngest on the ship, with a face far too kind for pirating. His worried dark eyes, his creased brow, his flared nostrils. What was a boy like this doing around pirates and slaves? "Will she be all right?"

Elarie nodded, placing Terisa's head in her lap, "she's just having an intense vision."

The young pirate rested back on his heels. He was still nervous, but at least having an explanation for Terisa's problem gave him some semblance of comfort. He then looked from the aging woman to Elarie and his eyes went wide, "you're the girl Grey lit on fire."

"My name is Elarie," she said, reaching over to take his hand. He tensed for a moment, then began to move like he'd shake with her, but she put his fingers against Terisa's cheek. "I'm too warm," she explained. In reality, she wasn't, but the kid took up the task like he needed one.

He nodded, looking at her hand on his. "You are," he agreed. He left his hand as it was when she let go. "I'm Jamison, by the way," he added with a blush, "I'm the one that does all the cleaning."

"It's nice to meet you, Jamison," Elarie smiled, looking behind her at Calix. The prince was speaking to the captain and the first mate, but upon making eye contact with Elarie he excused himself and crossed the deck. Greilor watched closely, his black eyes following everything. He said nothing when Elarie knew he wanted to. She knew they needed to have a long conversation and she knew it would hurt so badly she would explode with her bottled emotions spilling from her body. But for now, there was this, and most likely plenty in between.

Calix knelt awkwardly next to her. Luckily for Elarie, Terisa awoke before he had the chance to say anything. Elarie looked down at her. Her golden eyes were clouded as they processed her vision. Terisa had told her it was as if she was lost in a thick fog in the first moments after the vision was through. All she could do was walk and hope she was going in the right direction. She was reminded of the house of the gods, a place Elarie often went to for their little mind games. It was surrounded by a thick fog that so many things seemed to lurk in. Maybe Terisa was one of them.

"Anything interesting?" Elarie asked, removing Jamison's hand from her face. He placed it in his lap, gripping a baggy part of his pants.

"Monsters are coming," she told her, the distance in her eyes growing nearer. Terisa moved slowly, needing aid to sit up. She did not look away from Elarie. "Large encrusted bodies, skin thin enough to reveal a fast heart." Such worry engulfed her. Such pity. "It will be another end for you."

Elarie no longer felt dread when it came to Terisa predicting her death. They'd known each other for seven long months on the *SeaDaisy* and the seer had told Elarie of two deaths she'd face. One was an illness that had spread because of a dying merchant and the other had been dehydration. Elarie's 'generosity' would kill her. She'd been giving others her water and not drinking enough to sustain herself. The first time, the first prediction, left Elarie restless in a way she hadn't felt in years. Now, looking at Terisa's pity-filled face, Elarie felt nothing.

"Were the monsters following a storm?" She asked her, "did they walk with the legs of a crab?"

"A horrible end," she whispered, "and not the only one for you on this journey."

Elarie attempted not to roll her eyes. "Can you tell me how soon?" She pressed. Thunder crackled to the south in answer. Elarie stood sharply and watched massive black clouds curl and twist together along the horizon. She touched Calix's shoulder gently as a strike of lightning arched toward them. Turning around, Elarie shouted, "fly!" In her familiar, natural dragon tongue. She hadn't spoken it in years and she doubted Greilor had heard anyone speak it to him in just as long. She switched to Ceptareei for Jamison and Terisa, telling him to get her below, but was again in her first language when she looked at Greilor. "Fly now!" She threw her arm up, pointing to the white clouds that dotted the part of the sky unmarred by an oncoming monster. "Disappear until I call you again," Elarie walked across the deck. Greilor groaned but sensed in her tone that she would retaliate if he didn't do as she said.

The ship lurched and swayed when the dragon took to the skies. Calix grabbed Elarie's arm and twisted her around. "Why did you do that? What did you say?" He questioned. Elarie looked at his hand on her arm, her heart jumping at how tightly he was holding her. She was not afraid of monsters the way she was afraid of men she did not know. Calix released her. "Elarie?" His eyes were wide.

"Just come with me," she said and led him to the captain and his first mate. They both seemed just as confused as Calix and only a little less worried. After all, Greilor was *Calix's* dragon and Elarie just ordered him to fly away. What else could she get him to do? "Do you know what a Jiiver is?" She asked them.

They looked at each other, all three of them with their heads moving back and forth like gulls for fish. "No," Kaelum finally answered, "should I?"

Elarie said, "you should, actually. They're monsters that live beneath the Barrier and eat magic users. They use storms like that one," she motioned to the one building behind her. The wind around them picked up. The ship rocked on unsteady waves. "To disorient passengers so hunters can come aboard to kill the people that aren't magic users while the storm takes us to the Barrier for a live meal."

"So we should tie down everything, prepare for a storm," Terry nodded, "and get the magic users below. Everyone else fights them—"

"You can't fight them," Elarie shook her head, "that is the mistake most people make. The Jiivers cannot attack unless they are provoked."

Calix asked, "why did you send Grey away? He could fight them."

"The Jiivers are quicker than they look. They'd cut his wings off and feast on his fire," she looked at him. "Letting him stay would kill him. Now I can—" Lightning struck with the thunder on its tail.

She looked at the captain, "I can get rid of them, you just need you get everyone below."

"Terry, get us prepped for a storm. Lower the sails." Captain Kaelum turned to his ship, "if you are not a member of my crew I need you to get below!" He shouted. Many of the rescued slaves were already on their way below, having no desire to be caught in the storm. Terry began shouting orders to tie everything down, saying the storm looked like a nasty one.

Before Kaelum could walk away Elarie moved in front of him, "I know going below with the others might be a bit embarrassing, but you aren't going to stay up here, are you?"

The rain hit them first coming from the edges of the dark clouds. It pelted at them sideways, loud enough to be deafening. Kaelum shifted so he wasn't being hit in the face by it. "I'm not a magic user," he said.

Elarie blinked a few times. She hadn't expected him to completely deny it. "You... what do you mean? You're a Metar."

"Kaelum Metar, yes it's my last name," he nodded, beginning to move again, "not a user."

"Wait, you really can't feel your magic?" Elarie intercepted him again just as he was about to yell something. "Kaelum, you can feel it, can't you? I can feel it, the Jiivers will be able to as well."

He tightened his jaw. Kaelum looked around before lifting his hand between them. She took it, taking note of how intensely Terry was watching her from paces away. She flattened his left hand, lightly touching the black line on his palm. "It started hurting a year ago," he said, his tone clipped. He had no desire to share this with her. "I don't know what I feel, I just know I need it to stop."

Stop? Oh, how that must hurt his ancestors to hear. Elarie let go of him as pirates confirmed the sails had been reduced and everything was secure. Terry commanded everyone below. Only he, Kaelum, Calix, and the man at the helm remained. The first mate walked to Elarie, going as far as to try to step between her and Kaelum. "Now how are you supposed to get rid of monsters if even a dragon can't?"

"I will help you with this," Elarie told Kaelum. He said and did nothing. It was Terry that seemed to want to interrogate her for more information. Elarie ignored him and stood in front of Calix. The prince was just as silent as his captain friend, though there was much more than forced indifference in his Lathin eyes. The storm was above them, but the darkness swirling in the clouds did not seem to dim the bright color. "Can you call him? Greilor, have you learned how to do that?" He shook his head, not moving when she held onto his belt and wrapped her hand around the handle of his dagger. She pulled it from its sheath and said, "I can teach you how."

To this, the prince nodded. "I'd like that," he said over the rain. She backed up.

"None of you do anything!" Elarie shouted, wanting to be heard by the three around her and the one braving the crashing waves while trying to keep the ship steady at the helm. The ocean sprayed over them, leaving nothing dry, and by the struggle it looked like the man was putting up, the sea may have wanted to capsize them as well. Elarie walked to the center of the ship with her eyes on the thick fog slowly crawling toward them. A wave crashed over them and knocked someone down, but Elarie stayed on her feet as a clicking sound came through the rain.

She'd never faced Jiivers before. Perhaps that was why she was going to die—inexperience. The first of them stepped one clawed leg onto the deck, scurrying over the railing like a crab. Its lower half was as black as night, though marred with scars turning it grey, and six legs sprouted from the body. Where the waist began, transparent, slimy skin rose to a long and flat torso. Its arms were long, clawed, and four-fingered. The claws shined with every strike of lightning. Another crawled over, moving along the ship's edge. They intended to surround the four of them. A third stood on the stairs that led to the quarterdeck.

The storm around them quieted. Elarie walked forward, distancing herself from the three men, but ensuring she was also the center of attention. "*Tru-ni ak f'tina p-rean,*" she said. She lifted her hand and Calix's blade. Elarie sliced a small cut in the heel of her hand and allowed blood to drip over the deck, "*pantru mer-tgna, breyn xae laeio-rn.*" She was most likely butchering the saying—on my blood, leave this place. Elarie didn't like the language. It was ancient and most ancient things were too dead to help her practice, but the gods had cursed her with a perfect memory so it came back to her easily.

The Jiiver she'd been speaking to chuckled. The hoarseness of its voice made it seem more like a cough. It clicked toward her, tilting its pale head, and spoke in Ceptareei. It was something Elarie was hoping to avoid, but there wasn't any going back from it. "An ancient custom long forgotten," it said.

"It was worth a shot," Elarie replied quietly. No matter how tall she was, she still had to crane her neck to see the face of the creature. Its small black mouth twisted into a smile. "I am still going to have to insist you crawl back down into your sea and leave this ship and its passengers—"

The Jiiver wrapped a long clawed hand around her throat and lifted her into the air. "You would make demands of me?" It laughed.

"Look into my eyes," Elarie whispered. She watched the Jiiver do as she told it to. Even with the lack of features like eyebrows, she could see the realization cross its face. There was nothing truly special about Elarie's eyes—not in the way Calix's Lathin blue ring revealed his heritage. They were just green. Bright and lively, but just green. It was the power the Jiiver was looking at. "Now put me down," she demanded. The Jiiver lowered Elarie back onto the deck and scuttled back a few steps.

"*Metar*," another Jiiver clicked. Elarie turned her head. This one was closer to the three humans and its black eyes were set on Kaelum. It breathed in through its slitted nose, the gills on its neck wiggling excitedly. "*Metar*," it repeated, the crab legs piercing small holes in the wood below it.

Elarie threw the dagger. The sharp blade sunk into the deck as if it were nothing but a soft dessert and the handle lit to flames. "My Metar," Elarie hissed. It hissed right back. "I've already claimed him. His magic is mine to feast on, not some Jiiver—"

The four black claws of the Jiiver she'd made demands of suddenly appeared in front of her. Elarie looked down at them. They protruded from her chest and glinted with red blood. *Huh*, she thought, *how fitting.* Her ancestors had once sworn to protect the Metars with their lives, now she was doing just that. The Jiiver lifted Elarie into the air. She grunted, coughing up blood as gravity caused her to slide back on the claws.

"Now he is our Metar," said the Jiiver.

Elarie was already in water before she was thrown overboard.

Chapter Three

Elarie

The first time Elarie died it was on her birthday and it had been quite confusing. One moment, she'd been with the love of her life. She'd been guessing that the gift he planned to give her just before midnight, the last gift of the day, was to be a wedding ring. The next moment, she was cresting the hill and looking at the Dragon Keep, where her entire family was eating breakfast anticipating a ceremony that would take all morning to prepare, right up to the heat of the highest sun. Another moment a blast of yellow magic knocked her backward, sending her back down the hill, and snapping her neck.

Elarie knew there was an afterlife. She'd seen it. She'd died when the blast hit and awoken in the clear waters of the afterlife. Yet she'd only seen, never touched, for as soon as she tried to swim to the white sand beach she was yanked back into the clear waters and sent back into her body. The gods healed the injury that killed her and forced her to continue.

So surfacing in the crystal, beautiful blue water one moment then being pulled to a body slowly falling to the depths of the wild black sea was not surprising. Elarie simply kicked her feet and gulped down cold, salty air. The waves moved her unsteadily, but the control she had over them didn't allow them to force her under again. They surged beneath her, carrying her in the direction she wished to go. Elarie rose on it, allowing her anger to fuel her energy. Adrenaline pumped through her hot veins.

She gripped the side of the ship and dug her nails into the railing. Lifting herself over was easy, it was preventing her knees from shaking that was difficult. Dying had become such a normal thing for Elarie. It was practically second nature. Still, sometimes she felt the weakness that went with the painful death she experienced. When the Jiiver impaled her it had torn into her heart and through her lungs, which caused her chest to ache and her body to long for rest. Elarie used to be a napper. She enjoyed sleeping more than many other things, and dying tended to remind her of that.

Elarie faced the Jiivers and the three humans. Calix was looking right at her, the first to notice she was alive. Steam rose from her body, hissing in the air. He mouthed her name, both horrified and intrigued. Because of this, a Jiiver turned. Its transparent body was temporarily pelted with rain, looking like a bit of sheer fabric slowly being soaked through to reveal what was underneath. It calmed the wind once again, stilling everything around it. Even the rain stopped, though the hissing surrounding Elarie did not.

"*Ig-gnrjé*," the Jiiver that killed her straightened, even taking a step back from the humans. Immortal. Elarie's nostrils flared. She felt like hissing at them, even growling.

"Get away from my humans," She said instead. One Jiiver had a clawed hand hovering over Kaelum's head ready to stab down. The five Jiivers that had boarded the ship were meant to only be hunters, but they would not share the Metar with the rest of their clan. To taste the stars? No, not one Jiiver would share with hundreds. That Jiiver, with its hand still over the petrified, still human, chuckled a hissing, clicking laugh. Elarie's hand lit to flames, hot and as red as her anger. "I will not ask again," she said.

Elarie could kill the five Jiivers but had no desire to. Killing the Jiivers may anger the rest of the clan. They would search for the magic that caused the deaths of their hunters and she'd have to deal with the hundreds rather than the five.

None of the Jiivers moved. Elarie took a long, deep breath. She rolled her shoulders and walked forward. "Fine," Elarie said and the Jiiver lit to flames. It screamed and thrashed, the rough edges of its voice making it sound much more gruesome. Elarie had her eyes on the one that killed her. She presumed it to be the leader. While its friend writhed on the deck with fire seeping through its thick black shell, the Jiiver shuffled nervously. "You will leave," she told it, "and take your burned friend with you."

The fire went out and left the Jiiver crying for the pain to cease.

Elarie grabbed Kaelum by the collar with her hand still aflame. She shoved him to his knees and looked at Calix. He sunk, staring up at her. Terry followed his lead. "Because you understand what I am. You can see," she faced the Jiiver leader. Even with her having to look up at it, she could see the tension in its expression. The wariness. The fear. Ages ago, she lived on that fear. "What makes my fire so different."

"*Ig-gnrjé,*" it repeated quietly.

"Very good," Elarie said. Lightning struck above them and the Jiiver clicked nervously.

It said, "we need magic to take, you expect us to go with nothing?"

Elarie stepped to the side and grabbed the dagger out from its embedded position in the deck. She gripped the handle and the weapon burned red. It glowed for a moment, shining in the darkness around them. She handed it to the Jiiver, who inspected it by sniffing it through its slitted nose and licking it with a forked tongue. It spoke in its clicking ancient language, hissing commands while its burned comrade demanded justice for its pain. The Jiiver was lifted by two others while the leader addressed Elarie. Its eyes were on her chest, where the bloody holes in her shirt were.

"*Gner rego-aepi taeri'n, ig-gnrjé,*" it said—we will not forget this, immortal.

"I will not either," she replied, "now leave me and the humans I have claimed."

Elarie watched as they hissed to each other. The burned Jiiver moaned painfully. They went across the deck the way they came. Only the leader looked back at her. It made a point of licking red blood off of its claws before crawling down the side of the ship. Elarie stared at the place they'd gone, half expecting the monsters to come back, laugh, and use the speed Elarie might not have been able to keep up with to kill all of them anyway. All they had to do with Elarie was keep killing her. Over and over and over every time she woke up.

"Elarie?" Calix asked, his voice thick with fear and nearly drowned out by the rain despite its beginning to calm. The storm around them was settling. "Elarie," he repeated.

"You can stand," she managed. Elarie looked at him, watching him rise. He moved in the same awkward manner, one leg sticking out oddly.

"What are you?" Terry asked. There was nothing but a cold calm in his tone. It didn't seem that he was hiding anything, nor did it seem he was curious. He was demanding the answer and had no desire to learn anything beyond it. Not yet, anyway.

Elarie rubbed her face and dragged her fingers through her hair. She continued looking at Calix, dropping her arms to her side. "I'd appreciate it if you let me take Greilor for a ride," she said, looking him over. His shirt stuck to his skin and his jacket was soaked through. Why he wasn't in one made of leather, she didn't know. Perhaps this was warmer.

"Tell me about Kaelum and then yes," he nodded to his friend. Elarie took note of his priorities. Of course he'd want to know what she was just as much as Terry did, but his first thought was his friend.

"He is a Metar," she answered. He grit his teeth, already having that answer. "A very rare magic user. They started out as Fae," she glanced at Kaelum, "but the bloodline is too thin to really consider him one now. Some would. I don't."

Kaelum asked, "why not?"

"You don't have pointy ears," Elarie said. It wasn't her true answer, but it was the one she'd give. "Kaelum, you are the most powerful magical being on any continent, in any kingdom, at any time. Given time, you will be able to do amazing things."

"But I'm not—"

"The pain in your hand? I assume you've been having trouble sleeping, perhaps you feel more active at night?" She asked, taking a step back. The rain turned to a drizzle and the sky brightened as the clouds broke apart. Kaelum glanced at Terry. "You are a creator, Kaelum," she told him, "and the first thing you will make is a star."

Elarie walked away even as he stepped closer, "wait—"

"I answered your questions," she threw over her shoulder before putting both of her smaller fingers into her mouth and whistling sharply. She held the note as she climbed the stairs to the quarter-deck. She ignored the red haired pirate at the helm completely.

It was Calix that reached her first. The sky had broken blue behind him and Elarie could see Greilor flying toward them at his leisure. "Just..." Calix swallowed. Elarie looked at him. He said, "just come back. You'll come back, right?"

"Every time," she nodded.

He held his hand out. "Swear it, Elarie," he insisted. She wasn't sure where this was coming from and was unable to recall if she said something implying she wouldn't return. Hadn't she said she would teach him how to call his dragon? Still, Elarie took his hand. His grip was firm.

"I swear every time I leave with him I will come back," she obliged. Elarie shook once before pulling her hand away. He was cold to the touch, especially at his fingertips. She hesitated, her brow furrowing. Calix was silent. The prince was obviously unsure of her. He did see her die, after all, and had seen a display of power not many possessed.

Greilor was waiting, circling the ship. His great wings spread wide. Elarie had waited thousands of years to see them again.

"Just once," Elarie decided softly. She stepped close to the prince, who remained as still as ever, and put her hand at the center of his chest. "Trust me," she told him. She didn't have to look up at him because they were the same height, so his eyes were straight on hers. Steam rose between them. It engulfed him. She could feel Calix tense. The muscles in his chest tightened and a tremor ran through him.

Elarie slid her hand off of him as he shook his arms out, finding himself completely dry. "Thanks," Calix said, his voice a higher pitch. Elarie nodded tightly. She didn't *have* to do it, so why had she done it? She gained nothing from drying him off.

Greilor came to the port side and Elarie climbed onto the railing, dropping onto his wing. He beat into the air and she grinned, walking toward his back. The dragon began to move forward, not remaining in his hovered position, and the wind aided him in keeping steady. Elarie's eyes burned. Centuries and millenniums could have passed and she would not forget how to walk on his wings. All the time in the world could fly by and she would not lose the joy she had when kneeling on the dragon's back. He had been hers so long ago. Not the way she had wanted, but in the way that could be.

Once he found her to be settled, Greilor pulled away from the ship and took off high into the sky.

Chapter Four

Elarie

Her mind was still in the clouds, her eyes on the islands they circled. Even in her newfound position in one of the chairs that dotted the captain's quarters. Calix was next to her, silent. He seemed bored, but also like he didn't want to be the first to speak. Elarie was content with the silence. When he fidgeted, however, she brought herself back to where she was. They were in the corner to the left of the door. Her chair twinned with his. They were both tall backed and leather with their own holes and rips. A spring was sticking out of Calix's. Every so often he'd reach up to pull on it. There was a short table in front of them that had been bolted to the floor. Under it was a black bag that hadn't been buttoned. Elarie could see a blue string of yarn sticking out of it.

"Does Kaelum knit?" She asked, reaching for the bag.

"No, that's me," Calix shifted once again, although he didn't seem nervous about this. "I find it calming." He watched her lift the latest thing he'd been working on—a little plush toy meant for a child. It was a red and blue dragon. The only thing left to complete was the tail. "It's for Ryd," he said, "he's got a collection going." Elarie smiled, setting it back inside and sliding the bag to its original place. "I made this for you," Calix pulled a tightly braided bit of blue yarn out of his pocket. "For your hair," he told her, "so it doesn't whip in my face when we go riding."

She took the blue yarn, smiling at it. It had been ages since someone had given her a sort of gift, the last time being a glass flower from a boy who liked to be called a giver. He'd gifted it to her and that night she'd been informed that it was he, the giver, that turned her in to the Rings because he knew of her power.

But this circle of yarn was lovely and innocent. "Thank you," Elarie said. She moved her hair over her shoulder, leaning back while she braided her hair. "*When* we go riding," she repeated as if she'd just heard him. Elarie looked over at Calix, "when?"

"You can't teach me to ride without a saddle if we aren't together," he informed her, tilting his head just slightly. Calix then looked away, searching the room for something else to focus on. Elarie did as well. It was a spacious cabin despite how small it actually was. The walls to Elarie's left and right were half covered in windows and the back was only glass. The ocean splashed behind the quick-moving ship. Kaelum's bed was against the right wall. It was large with two ruffled pillows. Another table was in the center of the room with papers weighed down by rocks and shells.

Elarie tied her hair with the yarn and showed it to Calix. The prince smiled. "So did you try riding bareback before you chose to have a saddle commissioned or did you have him measured straight away?" She asked.

Calix sighed, "both, I suppose. I never actually got into the air with him. I couldn't find a good position to get into."

She allowed her eyes to move down his body. "And why is that? It's the same position as a horse, really, just wider and on your knees."

"That would be the issue," he said. Calix leaned down and began rolling up his left pant leg. "I don't have a knee," he said. Elarie leaned forward, her chest pressed against the chair arm as she looked at the fake leg attached to him. He knocked on the wooden part of it. Calix had a thigh. The prosthetic fit around the stump. Calix said, "the saddle helped relieve the pressure on my leg."

Elarie reached out, pausing to look at him with her hand hovering over it. "Is this all right?" She asked, "if I…"

"Sure," Calix said easily. He even adjusted so she didn't have to reach so far. "I was born without it so this really isn't that big of a deal. When people find out they tend to get curious." When Elarie said nothing, his nerves seemed to set in. She ran her fingers along the thin piece of metal on the side of the fake calf. Little designs had been hammered into it. "So," he cleared his throat, "do you think you can teach me to ride?"

"Of course I can," Elarie waved that away. She stood, "kneel." He gaped for a moment, his mouth open. Elarie snorted and moved away from the table, "I need to see how it's moving."

He blinked away his shock, his thick eyelashes fluttering. "You know, I've never met a girl that demanded I kneel before," he said as he got off the chair.

"Did you like it?" She raised a brow, on her knees as well, and the prince went silent. Elarie looked at the prosthetic. "Spread your legs more. I'm going to touch you, so you know," she said. Calix laughed out loud, swiping a hand over his face and hair. She looked at him and asked, "how old are you?" With a shake of her head.

"Twenty one," he answered as if he didn't understand the meaning behind her question, "and you?"

"Twenty," she rolled her eyes and pushed the rolled up part of his pants. "Is the pain around the stump or is it your whole thigh? And does it hurt now or because you're in the same position for too long?"

He blew a hard breath out from between pursed lips. Elarie pulled on the straps securing the leg to his body. She could feel the magic helping support it as well. Calix shifted a little, "when I sit like this for too long it starts to hurt up my whole leg, but right now just the stump."

Elarie pushed on his shoulders, "sit." He did, extending the leg under the table while keeping the other bent with his knee in the air. Elarie was on the left side of his leg, moving it to the side. "Perhaps the prosthetic is the problem."

"This is my newest one," he leaned back against his chair.

"And how does it feel?"

Calix shrugged, "mostly the same as the others. It feels more sturdy. I have more support."

She looked at it. "I like the designs," she said, running her finger down the metal line again. They were little swirls that sort of made flowers.

"Terry did that," he told her, "took it when I was sleeping and stamped them on. I didn't notice until he told me."

Elarie smiled faintly. She lifted his leg and bent it, watching the prosthetic.

"Elarie," Calix said, a twinge of nervousness in his tone. She put his leg down and faced him. Judging by the look on his face, she knew what the next part of their conversation would be about. Calix didn't seem to want to ask, but she wouldn't say anything until he did. "You died," he decided to state. She nodded. "And you came back." Again, she nodded. "How is that possible?"

She thought back to her ride with Greilor. Elarie had no desire to talk to him about Calix. She wanted him to tell her of his new adventures the way he used to tell her of his old ones. She wished to know of the dragons he shared caves with, what villages he'd burned, and if there had been any other humans he rode with. But no, he wished to tell her about the prince she was now sitting with. Greilor wished for him to trust her and for her to trust him. He thought the latter would take longer, but Elarie had more experience in losing people's trust rather than gaining it and keeping it.

"He loves you," Elarie told the prince, avoiding the subject of her resurrection. She'd avoid it for as long as she could. "Greilor."

Calix switched from his nervousness to a tentative curiosity. His eyes trailed her up and down. "How do you know?" He asked.

"I can speak to dragons," she said. Calix sat bolt upright. He shook his head, about to tell her that no one could, but she said, "he wanted me to tell you that. And to prove it he said to say that you sleepwalk." His jaw dropped. She continued, "you once went out half naked and barefoot with your eyes closed and climbed onto his leg like it was his back and told him to fly you to the moon so you could piss on it."

He stared at her. And stared. "That's amazing," he finally said. Calix laughed, "you can talk to him? That's amazing—how? Is there some sort of magic you can do?"

"No, I inherited the ability," Elarie answered and watched a bit of light go out in his eyes. She knew he probably dreamed of being able to have actual conversations with his dragon, not just the one-sided rants Greilor told her about. "My ancestors were the ones that created dragons," she told him, "and as such, every one of their descendants has the ability to communicate with them."

His dark brow slowly furrowed, "are you saying the gods did not create dragons?"

"That is exactly what I am saying," she said as she stood. Elarie held her hand out, "and I can show you why they never would."

Calix took her hand.

CHAPTER FIVE

CALIX

Elarie waited until he'd rolled his pant leg down to open the door. From that point on, she didn't wait for him. Calix smiled faintly as he shut the door behind him. It was a straight walk down the stairs and across the deck to where Grielor's large body was waiting and eating something large and slimy looking. Elarie ignored everyone as she made her way to him.

"Did she tell you?" Kaelum asked as Calix walked to the stairs. He was at the helm with Terry and Lester, all three of them looking ready to start steering the ship with how close they were.

"No," Calix said, "but did you know that the gods didn't make dragons?" He smiled when Kaelum rolled his eyes and scoffed. "I'll get her to talk, I just have to get her to trust me first." He stepped down, "did you really think she'd answer the first time I asked?"

The captain was silent because he knew Calix was right, so the prince left the quarterdeck. Calix moved out of the way of Jamison as he swabbed the deck. The kid said nothing, he just took all of it in. Calix could see him looking over at the old woman that Elarie knew, and that old woman was looking at Elarie. Her eyes were golden, Calix could see that from where he was, and to him that meant she was some sort of magical. She had predicted the Jiivers appearing, after all, and Elarie dying.

"Calix," Elarie said. His attention went to her. She had yet to change out of the ratty slave clothes she'd been in for the gods knew how long, but she still looked relatively clean. No dirt was on her, anyway. Her fair hair could've used a proper wash, though. "Here," she held her hand out.

He cringed at the piece of a fish she was holding out to him. Elarie had another piece in her other hand. It had come from whatever Grey was eating. "Shark?" He asked, tilting his head at the very large sea creature. "Is this a shark?"

"Half of a whale shark," Elarie answered, "he left the rest for a nesting water dragon. *Here.*"

Calix took the piece of shark because she was so insistent. "Why?"

"Eat it," she answered and took a bite of hers. Elarie's piece was steaming.

"Yours is cooked," he pointed. "And why would I eat this?"

She rolled her eyes the way Kaelum had, "you have to take the first bite raw and I'll cook it for you after. And you eat it because you've been riding for three years and you haven't shared a single one of his catches. It's a 'thing' for dragons."

Calix looked at the piece of bloody white meat, then looked at Grey. He was blowing steam out of his nose pleasantly, his eyes alight with what might've been a smile. "What sort of... 'thing' is this?" He asked, trying to hide his cringe now that he could see the dragon was enjoying this. Or that he wanted it, perhaps. Calix had never thought to take a piece of his food.

"You know how cats bring their humans dead animals?" She asked before taking another bite. Elarie chewed as he nodded. Calix became aware of the people staring at the three of them. She didn't seem to care even if she noticed. "This is similar. It doesn't have to be a big piece, Calix," she picked off a small piece of her own shark and showed it to him. "Just swallow."

"What if I vomit?"

"How sensitive is your stomach that you'll vomit after a tiny bite of it?" Elarie raised a brow, calling him an idiot without words. At least that's what it seemed. Calix just shook his head, then looked at the shark chunk. The skin was still on it, though he doubted he'd have to eat it if Elarie wasn't. The piece was a little bigger than his hand.

He used his front teeth to tear off a piece, cringing at the texture. Calix didn't chew, he swallowed it like nasty medication. When his eyes went to Elarie, approval shined on her face. "I don't think I like shark," he admitted.

Elarie laughed and the shark warmed in his hand. Calix watched it cook from the inside out. "It would be better with a bit of seasoning," she said, "but it's not awful. This is one of Greilor's favorite meals." She walked around the dragon, "come on." Elarie finished her shark and wiped her hands on her pants before climbing onto Grey's back. Calix took a bite of cooked shark. She'd been right—it needed seasoning.

Calix looked behind him at Kaelum, Terry, and Lester. Their expressions weren't completely clear from where he stood, but they were watching.

"Come up here, Calix," Elarie demanded from the back of the dragon. Calix sighed and climbed on. It was difficult with one hand, but he managed. He'd been riding for three years, after all, and had conquered climbing a dragon in difficult positions. He slid next to Elarie, who was sitting with her legs crossed waiting for him. "Do you actually want to eat that?" She asked him, her voice softening. Calix shook his head and she snatched it from him, tearing off a big bite.

"Hungry?" He laughed.

Elarie's eyes lifted to his. She swallowed some of what was in her mouth and asked, "where was I before this?"

His smile fell. Elarie took another bite. "Elarie, why were you there at all? You have rare, powerful magic. You could've escaped at any time, so why didn't you?"

She wiped her mouth with the back of her hand. "I wasn't planning on staying and had planned on just killing everyone, taking the ship, and figuring out how to sail everyone back to Trec. But I also knew Rol would eventually take us to Polinae."

"The slave trade kingdom."

Elarie nodded. She said, "I decided to stay and wait it out until I got to Polinae so I could burn it all down."

Calix straightened slowly, looking at her indifferent position. "You were going to burn down a whole island?" She nodded and took another bite of the shark. "How could you do something like that? Not everyone on that island is guilty, you can't just kill everyone."

She tilted her head at him, chewing silently. Calix waited for her to speak. Burning everyone and everything on an island? That was horrific. It was barbaric. "We aren't going to come to any sort of agreement regarding right and wrong," she said, "so we might as well move on in conversation."

They stared at each other as if it were a contest to see who would speak next. Calix looked into her bright green eyes trying to find a murderer. She was presenting her decision as if she'd done it before. How many times? Was she a killer?

"Fine," he swallowed. Elarie went back to eating. When she finished and threw the skin overboard, she again wiped her hands on her pants. Calix looked at the ocean. She'd thrown *skin* that far?

Elarie got to her knees. "I'm not going to show you anything about riding right now, that can wait until we're on land that way I have more room. However, I can show you this." She shuffled to the center of Grey's back. She was closer to him than before, close enough to smell. Elarie looked at him. "What?" She asked with a lightness in her tone, "do I smell that bad?"

He shook his head faintly and tried to wipe whatever expression caused her to notice he was smelling her, "no, you smell like a bonfire. You don't even smell like sweat at all." It was very strange. He could tell that she did sweat because of the stains on her back and under her arms, but she smelled like nothing but a warm fire. Calix looked at Elarie's face again. Her brow was furrowed, although it didn't look like it was because she was uncomfortable. "Sorry," he said.

Elarie looked away from him with something far more distant in her eyes than he'd seen before. "I—" she started, then her eyes went wide, "Greilor don't you dare—get off," she pushed on Calix's shoulder as Grey got up. "We are not flying with you right now—" the dragon disagreed. Calix's eyes went wide as they moved to the edge and he flapped his powerful wings, taking off with a great leap into the air. Calix yelped, grabbing Elarie's upper arm as she cursed at both Grey and Calix as if he had anything to do with wanting to fly with her. Or fly at all. Elarie stood, pushing Calix's hands off of her with strength he hadn't expected.

"Elarie," he said, choosing to dig his fingernails into Grey's scales. She walked up Grey's back and stomped on it, speaking another language rather than the one he knew. "Elarie," he said again, louder this time. She was yelling at Greilor, pointing behind her to where he assumed the ship was. Calix did not want to turn his head. "Elarie!" He shouted. This time she did look at him.

"Shit," she said bluntly in Ceptareei, a hint of an accent breaking through. Elarie walked toward him. "It'll be fine," she told him, "I'm going to pull you to a safer place." Calix felt ready to throw up the bite of shark he had. Perhaps he did have a weak stomach for raw meat. "I will help you, Calix, I promise." Elarie then held onto the crook of his left elbow, then the back of his right knee. "Ready?"

"Shit," he said and nodded. Calix hated himself suddenly. He was looking at Elarie, who was standing and *walking* on Grey, and Calix was being dragged with his legs raised across his back to a 'safer place.' He was like a child to her. Calix was a child compared to her.

When she stopped, Elarie knelt between his legs. They were spread. She had room. "Look at me," Elarie said, "look at me. You can hold on to me." Calix looked at her extended arms, then at the gentleness on her face. "I won't let you fall, just keep looking at me."

CHAPTER SIX

He was a pathetic excuse for a dragon rider and he desperately hoped Elarie never mentioned it to anyone. She was seated between his legs with her legs crossed and he was holding her arms now memorizing what she looked like because he had no desire to look at anything else.

"You aren't pathetic for needing to do this," she told him while he stared at the lower half of her face. He'd already gone through every part of her forehead, her light brows, her eyes, and now he was looking at a cluster of freckles on her crooked nose by a faint white scar. "Everyone gets scared," she continued. He liked the sound of her voice when she was fighting the wind. How raised it was, how there was a gravelly sound at the back of it. "And this doesn't make you a bad rider," Elarie said while Calix was looking at her lips. They were chapped and peeling. "Calix?" She asked, "can you speak?" He looked into her eyes. "Fine, would you like me to keep speaking?"

Calix glanced out at the ocean. He'd been over it more times than he could count—he lived right next to it for the gods' sake, so what was bothering him now? He was secure on the dragon in the place Elarie told him was the safest and he was holding onto her. There shouldn't have been any issue with this.

"This is something you've never done before," Elarie told him as if she could sense his feelings. "Would you like me to tell you about the first time I rode Greilor by myself? It went poorly, so that might make this worse..." she paused for a moment and looked around. Elarie moved without any reason to fear while Calix sat hunched like a child. *Pathetic.* "Greilor wants me to tell you so many things," she said, once again facing him. A distant look grew in her eyes, the same one Calix found after he said she smelled like a bonfire. "See, you are his rider, but I was once the same. Well, not exactly the same. I suppose this is what it was like before."

"That doesn't make any sense," Calix managed, making her laugh.

Elarie moved her legs to a more comfortable position, which inadvertently brought her closer. She tilted her head with the slightest of smiles, perfectly calm. He tried to focus on that, on how calm she was. Perhaps it would rub off on him. "Very good," she said softly. "Just breathe, all right? Greilor will find an island so we can yell at him to his face."

"I don't want to yell at him," he said.

Her eyes darted over his face. She seemed like she knew everything. She held herself like she did, even with her shoulders hunched and her body weak. It was in her face. In her eyes. Elarie had something he didn't recognize, something that made her different. "All right, we won't yell," she said in a gentle voice he hardly heard.

"What are you? You can distract me with that," he suggested. Calix couldn't find a way to make himself sound casual, as if it was a mere proposal. He watched her force down a smirk and look away from him. "Some sort of Fae?"

"Gods no," she snapped. Elarie winced, glancing at him. "Look, I don't want to talk about it," she shook her head, "it's not something I advertise, and no matter how much Greilor wants me to share every aspect of myself with you and vice versa, you don't get to know. Just... tell everyone I'm a human that was cursed or something."

Calix watched her calm herself once again, choosing against pushing the topic while atop a dragon flying bareback over the ocean for the first time. "Wait, vice versa?" He asked. She nodded, still not looking at him. He watched some of her hair get pulled from her braid and wave through the air. "Why?"

"We are the two most important people in his life," she answered. Grey dipped, moving to the right, and Calix saw a large island full of greenery and surrounded by white sand beaches. Elarie said, "it's about a connection he wants us to have."

"A connection?" He repeated.

The smooth ride switched to a landing. Grey's wings flapped strongly and Calix gripped Elarie's arms tighter. He bent one leg to put his foot flat on the dragon's back, which bent Elarie's upward. She didn't seem bothered by any of it. When Grey's great body landed on the sand Calix heaved a strong breath. Elarie laughed, "come on, I want to teach you a word in the dragon language." She stood and pulled him with her with inhuman strength. Calix's legs were shaking as he climbed off after her.

Elarie took a few staggering steps forward. Calix watched as her knees buckled and she landed gracelessly. Her hands buried themselves in the sand. She gripped it. Calix walked toward her and got down in front of her. "How long were you on Rol's ship?" He asked, trying to stay as gentle as she had been before.

Grey hummed behind them and laid down, placing his head in the sand to Elarie's left. Her eyes were filled with tears, though nothing streaked down her pale cheeks. She shook her head and sniffed, "seven months." She pulled sand toward her and lifted both of her hands up, watching it fall through her fingers. She did it again.

Calix looked around. The island was beautiful. They were at an inlet. In the water, there were pieces of sand above the lapping waves. It must've been low tide, he imagined they'd be covered otherwise. Tropical plants lined the land to their left. Calix stood and wiped sand off his legs as he walked around Grey. Elarie and the dragon did not pay any attention to him. Grey was moving closer to Elarie, who was still playing with sand. Calix glanced back at them when he picked up a ripe coconut. At least he hoped so.

"I don't have a way of opening this, but," Calix said as he approached Elarie once again. She looked up at him, then at the coconut. Her eyes lit up, which brought an intense satisfaction into Calix's chest. He sat again and handed it to her. "So what's the word?"

"*Matealn*," she answered and, with the utmost ease, tore the top of the coconut off. "Ma-tee-aln," Elarie sounded out for him while ripping off pieces of the shell. Greilor growled a little as she brought the coconut up to drink from it.

"Matealn," he repeated to the best of his ability. "What's it mean?"

She handed the coconut to him and he drank. The water spilled off his chin and onto his shirt. "It means fool."

"And why did you want me to learn it?"

She said, "just in case you decide to say it to Greilor for this little adventure," with a smile that said she called him a fool often. Calix smiled, looking at the dragon. He didn't say it and Grey groaned, getting up to go sit in the minimal shade. "He's going to take a nap, we're stuck here until he wakes," Elarie translated.

Calix picked off some of the coconut meat. He stared at it, popped it in his mouth, and looked again at Elarie. Her head was turned and staring at Grey. "What happened that made you lose him?"

Her eyes darted back and forth and her brow slowly furrowed. Elarie whispered, "come this way," and stood. Calix watched her walk to the water, where she sat once again. He set the coconut down and followed. Her feet were touched by the whitewater every time a wave came ashore and Elarie said nothing when he sat next to her and only took one shoe off to put a bare foot in the path of the ocean. She pulled the yarn out of her hair and ran her hands through it, saying, "you know this is one of the things he's dying for me to tell you."

"Already dying for it?" He joked, "we just met."

She smiled, "right. But Greilor has always been impatient. He's... he means well, I suppose. He knows I haven't had a friend in a long time just as much as he knows you want to be sure you can have a real one."

Calix blushed, glad she wasn't looking at him. "I don't know what you mean," he said.

Elarie nudged him, "Kaelum and Terry. Greilor was trying to convince me to talk to you while we were riding. He said that you talk about not being sure if they think of you as *prince* or *friend* first. And that it hurts more with Kaelum, who was your friend first."

"Wow," he breathed, "damn. Are you going to tell me something personal to make up for that breach of privacy?"

She laughed. "How about why I don't have any friends?" She suggested. Calix shrugged, squinting out at the water. It was a perfect blue, almost shiny. Elarie began braiding her hair again. "The last friend I had," she sighed, "found out about my magic. How much of it I have." Elarie looked at him, "and he sold me out. I went to meet with him, he said he was going to take me to a show, and when I got there I was... ambushed, I guess."

"Who did he sell you to?" Calix asked. He looked at her this time.

"The Rings," she answered softly. Elarie pulled her knees up and rested her arms against them. She shook her head and mumbled, "five years."

Five, Calix repeated inwardly. He knew what the Rings were, of course. Calix fought with his father about them once before the subject was shut down. The Rings were an illegal slave pit for magical individuals. Fae or otherwise. Owners brought their fighters and put them in a cage to face off for money. It was Calix's understanding that those who weren't willingly there were drugged too much to understand what was going on. He and his father had fought about demolishing it. Calix wanted to, his father disagreed. Even with the morality in question, the king believed that it wasn't the best thing at the time.

The argument had been six years ago when the prince had first discovered it. Calix hadn't forgotten it. The look on his father's face when Calix told him he believed getting the slaves out was just as important, if not more, as any other order he wished to give was not one he'd soon forget. Half of the Rings was on their land—what would be Calix's soon.

"I won't sell you to the Rings," he told her, choosing to nudge her as she'd done to him before. If he'd insisted, if he'd convinced his father and they launched an attack on the Rings, they might've freed Elarie. "How did you get out? Did you pay your way?"

She laughed. "No, no I didn't buy my freedom."

"So you killed everyone," he concluded.

Elarie shook her head. "I only killed enough to escape. Revenge wasn't my priority at the time. I just needed out."

A wave of silence passed between them, long enough for Calix to push down morality and replace it with sincerity. "I'm sorry you were there at all," he said.

A great sigh moved her whole body. "I'm hungry," she said, "are you hungry?" Elarie stood, wiping her pants off as she looked around.

"Hey," he grunted and put his hand out. Elarie lifted him easily. He practically weighed nothing to her. "Please no fish," he said. She smiled and started off toward the trees, forcing him to follow with one shoe hanging from his hand. Elarie picked up the coconut and set it in the shade before slowing. "Can you hunt?" Calix asked her quietly.

She moved around sticks and leaves. "No," she replied. Calix followed her as quietly as he could manage until she stopped, her fingers dancing at her sides. She seemed to be buzzing with energy, ready to kill and eat something. Her eyes moved quickly on what was around her, falling on a butterfly for a moment. Calix looked as well, smiling. It was small and yellow with rounded wings. The butterfly landed on a tall blade of grass.

Elarie leaned forward and stuck her finger out, holding very still. The butterfly fluttered, moving up and down on the grass. Calix held his breath when it landed on her finger. He thought of his wings, of the thing that made him dream of dragons. He recalled his tutor telling him how important that was. *Only those who dream of wings will have a chance with a dragon.* Calix's wings, the first he'd seen that made him desperate to fly, had been butterfly wings. They were yellow, bigger than the one Elarie had poised on her finger, and the wings were pointed with black tips.

He'd been dreaming of dragons for years and years before Grey showed up at a terrible time in his life. Calix had *needed* Grey before knowing it. And now he was a boy who dreamed of wings turned into a man that rode a dragon.

Did Elarie have wings? What were they? Would she tell him? Calix had never told anyone of his butterfly, even his own mother. He kept it close to his heart. How close did she keep hers?

The yellow butterfly flew away and Elarie turned to look at Calix, grinning. He found himself smiling softly. Elarie turned back to the tropical forest around her, somehow attuned to it. She was still, more still than he'd seen her in his single day of knowing her.

Elarie flicked her hand out and sparks of red fire flew around her fingertips. A bird fell from the trees, landing on the ground with a *thunk* that made Calix grimace. Elarie walked toward it and picked up the large macaw by its yellow tail. "Still hungry or have I made you lose your appetite?" She asked him teasingly. Elarie looked around her and collected a few sticks that seemed perfect for a spit. How she found them so easily, Calix didn't know. He'd be stupidly searching until the sun went down. "Come on," she cocked her head in the direction of the beach, already walking.

"How did you even see the bird?" He asked as he followed, "you weren't looking." She shrugged and stopped in the shade next to the dragon. Grey was snoring. It always made Calix laugh when he did because he somehow managed to sound like a human. There was a snort at the back of his steaming nostrils. Elarie dug a pit in the cool sand. "Do you want me to collect something for the fire?" He asked.

She blinked a few times, looking up at him, "oh. No, I don't need anything," she stabbed sticks into the ground. The macaw lit on fire as Calix sat.

"Convenient," Calix muttered. He rolled up his pant leg and watched her pick up the now featherless bird. She easily went about stabbing her third stick straight through it from the mouth to the rear. She then put the bird on the two sticks. Her hand sparked with the fire and a ball of it lit to life. "Wow."

Elarie smiled with half her face, crossing her legs. "Feel free to compliment," she said with the same smile, though Calix could see a hint of blush on her face. "Or tell me it's terrifying. It goes either way."

"Well it is *fire* magic," he said, "everyone knows how rare that is." Elarie nodded, waiting for something. "And dangerous," he added, "which is why it's so rare—"

"That's not why," she shook her head. Calix quirked a brow, now the one to be waiting. Elarie said, "fire is the gods' least favorite element. They rarely give it to people."

He watched her turn the bird a little. It was most likely to distract herself. Calix wondered when the last time she had a conversation about things like this was. With the man who betrayed her and sold her out? And then she was at the Rings for five years... there may have been time in between that and Rol, but she was there for seven months and Calix doubted she openly spoke about dangerous magic to anyone on that ship.

"And they gave some to you," he said, pressing her just a bit.

Elarie said, "quite a bit, actually." She looked at her hands, "my mother said I was blessed with it once. That to be such a powerful fire elemental was a wonderful thing."

"And?" He asked, "is it?"

"Like you said," her shoulders moved up and down, "it's dangerous. And wild and destructive and..." her brow furrowed as she looked for another word. "Angry."

Calix looked at the fire she created to slowly cook the macaw. "What makes fire angry?"

"I do," she admitted. Shame crossed her face. Her eyes also darted to the flames in front of her. "I'm an angry person." Calix pulled his wooden leg off and set it aside. She breathed in, "tell me something to make up for my confession?"

"You'd like me to confess something?" He asked. She nodded, turning the macaw. Calix pushed air out through parted lips as he thought. "I hate to admit I'm not a very interesting person with many things to confess," he said. Elarie sighed and began to play with her hair, again removing it from its tie. He watched her. "I like to braid," he admitted as her fingers moved through the knots. "My mother taught me first with her hair and my aunt on my father's side taught me how to braid my sister's hair."

She looked at him. "Is there a difference?"

Calix laughed out loud, but turned it into a cough quickly. Elarie smirked. He said, "like the difference between my hair and your hair."

"Ah, your mother isn't dark. You could've just said that." A small, coy smile spread over her face and she continued pulling the small knots from her hair. "You'll be glad to know I love having other people's hands in my hair, so whenever you feel like it," she flipped her hair over her shoulder suggestively. Calix rolled his eyes.

CHAPTER SEVEN

CALIX

He wanted to give in. She hadn't done anything other than flip her hair over her shoulder and play with the yarn circle she'd put around her wrist, but that was enough to have it stay on his mind. Calix loved braiding. Elarie looked at him over the fire like she could tell he was thinking of her. The flames lit up her features as the sun moved across the sky, turning her green eyes a paler shade the later in the day it got. She went back down to the macaw. Elarie ripped off a leg.

"Good?" He nodded to it, not even commenting on how easily she was holding the obviously hot piece of meat. Elarie leaned over and held it out for him. "It's a little hot for me," he informed her. Calix could smell it, though, and that was fine. He'd have to remind himself to cook something well-seasoned for Elarie when she came to Lyburn with them. He doubted she'd ever leave Grey again, so her joining him at the castle seemed likely.

"Oh right," she pulled it back with a lightly furrowed brow. Calix watched her fingers sort of glow like small embers before the steam lessened. "Try this," she held it out again.

Calix took it from her, blowing on it as he picked the skin off and put it in her fire. "That must be so convenient," he said to the food she'd cooked on a fire she didn't need wood or brush to make. Elarie ripped off the other leg. "How do you do with cold things?"

She tore off a bite and shook her head, speaking with the food tucked in her cheek, "horribly." She chewed the macaw, looking at him as he tried his cooled down version. He cringed a bit, again at the texture.

"How does it go? Does everything melt before you can touch it?" He bit off another piece. This one was easier to chew. When he looked up, Elarie had finished her leg and was taking a wing.

"No I'm not that hot," she laughed. Elarie ripped off another bite. She finished the wing quickly. "I just don't like it. I get cold differently than you do—well," she cringed, "I'm not really sure. But I'm not hot enough to melt everything around me just by standing there."

Calix finished his leg as she finished her confused short ramble. "How hot can you make yourself?" He asked.

Elarie sucked juice off her thumb. Calix waited. He liked this better than a lot of the conversations that involved waiting. Elarie was far too interesting to get bored of it. Everything she said had something about it that made him want to hear more and he would wait for it.

She glanced around her, then back at Grey. "Calix," she faced him, "I do want to trust you. I know that I can because Greilor wouldn't be with you otherwise. Now, you trusting *me* is very different, but that's not exactly what I'm worried about."

He didn't need to wait to come to his conclusion. "Kaelum and Terry?"

"And everyone else, but yes," she admitted, her shoulders moving inward as if she was ashamed to admit it, or perhaps that she was afraid of his reaction to telling him how she felt.

Calix looked behind her at Grey. The sleeping, snoring dragon they both mutually loved. "I don't have to tell them everything," Calix decided. She tried not to perk up at this statement. He said, "they want to know what you are. Terry isn't very trusting and he has bad experiences with people and Kaelum wants what's best for everyone." His eyebrows flicked up and down, "he'll probably scold me for going off with you." Calix reached up and rubbed the back of his neck. "But I can just tell them what you told me. That you're a human that's been cursed. I don't believe you, but that's what you said."

"And when they ask what you've been doing with me this whole time?"

He shrugged, "eating chewy macaw while we wait for Grey to wake up."

Elarie slowly smiled. "All right, promise."

"I promise," he nodded, "powerful secrets are safe with me."

The smile turned to a grin. "You can stay here, then," she said and went down to the beach. The sun was at her back. Calix wanted it to set. He would much rather be sleeping on the beach than on a rocking boat. Even if that worried everyone. Then again—who would attack someone while a dragon was sleeping right next to them? And Elarie? Calix was already deciding she was harmless to him. He watched her turn around, shouting, "are you ready?"

"Absolutely!" He shouted back and watched her back up. She was at the shoreline backing into the water. Steam rose behind her. Calix straightened, trying to see her feet from his position. She kept walking and the steam only got thicker. He could see a smile on her face. She was at waist level and no water was touching her at all, it was evaporating before it could reach her.

"Ready?" She asked again, now at chest level.

"There's more than that?" He asked, quickly grabbing his leg. She wasn't doing anything, perhaps waiting for him to stagger to his feet and move closer.

She asked, "did you think all I was going to do was melt a little water?"

A little water? She was melting a hole in the ocean. "I mean..." he stopped when she motioned for him to. Calix took a small step backward as Elarie closed her eyes. She was smiling, enjoying what she was about to do. Calix imagined her melting the whole beach behind her. He'd be even more curious about her magic after that. How much power was there? How much could she do?

Her veins began to change color. There was no strained effort on her face, this was simple for her. Calix's lips parted. Her skin brightened. He wanted to move forward, to inspect the hot molten glow traveling up her arms and into her rolled up sleeves. Instead, he took another step back. *Gods.* He could feel it.

Calix had been to a volcanic island to study it once. He recalled rowing toward it on a ship lined in magic that hopefully held up against the lava spewing slowly into the water. Calix thought he was back on that island for a moment. She was hot enough to sear off his eyebrows, and even then... this was too easy for her. What sort of magic would come out of her if she put in the effort? No wonder people were terrified of fire magic. How much damage would she be able to do at her best?

Elarie pushed her hands downward toward the sand and let a great wave cover her. Calix stumbled backward with wide eyes. It was an explosion of steam and the bright red of a too-powerful burning flame. The sea tried to engulf it, to swallow it, but it didn't stand a chance against her.

She swam through the steam and it followed, coming off of her in waves. Elarie was beaming at him—thankfully without glowing. "Come here," she grinned and grabbed his hand. He tensed. Elarie stopped and dropped his hand just as quickly as she took it, "sorry."

"No, I just..." he took it again, rubbing his thumb over her skin, "how did you cool down so quickly?"

She was smiling again, though hesitantly. She was waiting for him to turn on her, then. "I've had a lifetime to regulate temperature. It was the first thing I needed to learn and that was hard on everyone in my family."

"How?" He questioned, now holding her hand and following the flow of her veins with his fingers. She was warm—too warm for a human that wanted to not die of a fever—but she wasn't burning him.

"Well take a moment to think about how hot an upset baby with no ability to control her little emotions can be," Elarie suggested. He looked into her eyes. "I've been told breastfeeding one can be *quite* difficult." Calix laughed suddenly, able to feel the tension in her decrease. "Come on, Your Highness," she pulled him to the water. "Ready?" She looked back at him. The ocean was still steaming.

He looked at it, then her, "to go in?"

"I promise I won't let you burn," she pulled on his hand, "but you don't have to come."

"I was just making sure," he swallowed. Elarie chuckled and led him *into* the ocean. She'd warmed up a little, or perhaps that was the hot air around them. "Holy gods," Calix said. He looked back at the path she created and ran into her when she stopped.

"Amazing." He couldn't see anything through the steam around them, just the wall of hot water that went to his shoulders. It was like the thick hot springs in the north only without the smell. Calix breathed in, the salt itching his nose and clearing his sinuses.

"Ta-da," she said, motioning in front of her. Calix looked.

Elarie had created obsidian. She created a rock and managed to make a shape out of it. A dragon in flight. She sculpted obsidian that she created in only a few seconds, then managed to regulate her temperature before she even reached the beach again. And he didn't think that was as powerful as she could actually go, this was just a display. "How did you..."

"Magic," she wiggled her fingers on her free hand and sparks flew from them. "Do you want it?" Elarie motioned to the sculpture.

"Do I..."

"You aren't as smart as you look," she told him.

He choked a bit. "I am too as smart—" Calix stopped to clear his throat. "I've just never seen anything like this, forgive me for being a bit slow."

"Fine, I forgive you," she sighed. "Do you want the sculpture? The dragon. I can take it out of the ocean for you, otherwise I'm going to break it to pieces."

"Why would you do that?"

She shrugged, "if someone tried swimming over this they'd hurt themselves and I doubt even a boat would be safe. So you can either take it home with you and display it in your princely bedroom to always be reminded of me," she took a deep breath, "or I can destroy it."

"I am utterly amazed by you," he mumbled as he looked at the dragon.

"Aw, and we've only just met," Elarie said, "imagine how much more amazed by me you can be as time goes on."

Calix laughed, "gods. Yes. Yes, I want it. How are you going to get it out?"

She let go of his hand and he looked around, half expecting the ocean to cave in on him, but it remained as it was. Calix watched her wrap her hand around the bottom part while she held the sculpture with the other. Her left hand glowed and she snapped the sculpture off the top. Elarie held the dragon in her arms with both hands. She placed her foot on the bottom of the obsidian sculpture. It warmed. She kicked it and it shattered.

"Shit," Calix whispered, bending to pick up a chunk of it. "It's so realistic, practically authentic," he said as he observed it.

Elarie breathed a laugh through her nose. "Come on," she said and began walking out of the water. He followed at her heel, still inspecting the magic obsidian. "It isn't exactly the same," Elarie looked back at him as she went, "actual obsidian is stronger. Denser, too."

"I'll have to compare it with a piece I have at home," he walked up the beach. Behind them, the ocean crashed back to where it was supposed to be. "Is it just obsidian or can you make other things with your fire?"

"Regular glass," she shrugged. Elarie set the dragon down. Calix sat in front of it. She'd managed to sculpt scales into the piece. "Are you still hungry?" She asked.

"No, thank you," Calix merely glanced at her before extending his leg comfortably. He ran his hand over the wing. The sculpture was large, which was all the more impressive. "So is this supposed to be Grey?" It didn't exactly look like him. This dragon was longer, its wings had sharp pointed ends, and a slimmer head. It could've been him, but it wasn't exact.

Elarie took the macaw off the spit, "no. I don't sculpt dragons I know."

"Don't want to make anyone jealous?" Calix smiled. Elarie didn't reply.

"Can you whistle?" Elarie asked. She was lying down with her eyes closed, the partially burned bird lying on her left. "Please tell me you can."

He said, "I can."

"Good," she sighed. Elarie threw her arm over her eyes and sighed again. "That's how I call the dragons. What you do is whistle with the intention of bringing the dragon to you. You need to focus solely on him. You want to picture where he is or where you think he is and imagine him hearing you. Then you call him to you."

"You made that sound easy," he said. *The dragons*, she had said, dragons plural. There were more? She knew more? She'd ridden more? "'Just go whistle for them' you say, and when I do it I'll look like an idiot."

"*Matealn*," she mumbled. "Go down the beach and whistle to him. If he hears your intent he'll wake up, otherwise you'll just be whistling. If it doesn't work just keep trying."

Calix looked at Grey as he stood. The dragon was still fast asleep. They'd been on the island for hours and he hadn't moved once. He wouldn't wake to just any whistle. "I've got this," he mumbled to himself. Elarie cheered him on faintly. He looked over at her, "are you going to sleep too?"

"I miss being able to nap," she said. "Just tell me if you need something, I'll be there wide awake, otherwise focus on calling Greilor. Being able to see him now will make things easier."

He nodded despite the fact that she wasn't looking and made his way down the beach. *Think about him, about where he is, and whistle.* Calix blew off a few practice whistles as he walked.

"And be loud!" Elarie shouted.

"I am—" he turned, but waved her off before arguing. She was still lying down, arm over her eyes, and didn't know what Calix was doing. So he kept walking. Calix got far enough away that the curve of the island was ahead. Her fire was too small to make out. Once he was sure of the distance, he looked at Grey. The giant black and grey body, the massive wings. He knew this dragon and this dragon knew him. So this should've been easy, right? Calix rolled his shoulders. He doubted he'd get it first try. Going into the task anticipating failure was a good start, wasn't it?

How did Elarie do it? He'd seen her whistle and Grey had come for her, but apparently it wasn't just a whistle. She could see him in her mind the way Calix could see him now.

He took a deep breath.

Calix whistled.

Nothing happened. Not even Elarie giving encouragement. Did he need encouragement? No. Well, it would be nice, but he didn't *need* it. Calix breathed in again and whistled for a second time. Elarie shot up to a sitting position. He squinted at her. "What?" Calix took a small step forward. She got up and walked toward him with her hands in her hair again. She was shaking out sand. "Elarie?" He hesitated.

She stopped in front of him. "Don't ever do that again," she said and shivered, "that felt so wrong."

"What did?"

"I didn't even know you *could* call people," she shivered again, waving her hands through the air, "never ever do that again. Never again."

His brow furrowed, "wait I was focused on Grey."

"Evidently not," she looked around, her eyes landing on something behind Calix. "Your friends are here," she nodded to the ship. He looked back, almost disappointed. "Look, you may have thought you were focused on Greilor, but you were thinking about me so when you whistled I felt it and that was *extremely* uncomfortable so," she held his shoulder, aiming his body to face Grey without her obstructing his view. "This is your dragon. He is your dragon, you are his rider. You want to be with him. All you're doing is getting him to come to you."

"Does this work long distances?" He asked.

She stepped back, "not very well."

Calix breathed in.

"Stop," she put her hand up. He rolled his eyes. "Don't focus on the whistle. You aren't preparing to whistle."

His brow furrowed, "I was just breathing in. Is this how you teach everyone?"

"No, I'm much nicer to children. Would you like me to treat you like a child?" She crossed her arms.

"You know what, yes," he faced her, also crossing his arms.

Elarie looked at him for a moment before she burst into a fit of laughter. She covered her mouth and apologized. Elarie ran her fingers through her hair. "You know how you whistle to call a dog?" He nodded. "It's like that. It's supposed to be easy and loud. The only difference is that most of the time Greilor is supposed to hear you when he isn't near you."

"So calling a dog when that dog is nowhere in sight," he concluded.

"Exactly," she faced the dragon and he followed suit, "the magic is in your connection to him. The one you have with him now isn't the best—"

"Why?"

"You're having flight issues, now," she pointed to Grey, "just whistle." He did. "Good, can you hold the note?" Calix breathed in hoping she didn't comment on him 'focusing on the whistle' and did it again, only looking at Grey as he did. "Now whistle like you want him to look at you."

Calix rubbed his fingers together and tried again.

Grey stirred, groaning in his sleep. Elarie clapped softly. "Try again. Louder."

He whistled again.

Grey opened his eyes and Elarie cheered, putting her arms in the air as she did. Calix grinned as the dragon lifted his head. Elarie shouted something to him in the dragon language and he got up, stretching his wings as he walked over.

Chapter Eight

Kaelum

The pain in his hand was unbearable. How such a small line in his palm created such unending pain he now longed to know. He held a fist as he helped drag his rowboat up the shore to a safe place. There were seven boats. Most of the crew decided to stay aboard. Apparently there was something *off* about this island, so only some of them plus most of the rescued chose to touch land.

Kaelum looked around. It was sunset now, the light shining on the other side of the island which sent dusk and shadows falling heavily around them. Even through it, he found Calix. Grey was hovering over him and Elarie, wings outstretched only making him look more massive than he was.

He walked over, feeling Terry follow silently. His first mate was only steps away from him most of the time, even less when they were alone. It sent chills crawling up Kaelum's spine to think about. "Calix," he called to distract them. The prince turned, adjusting the leg of his pants. "You all right?"

"Yeah," he said, "I just have some sand stuck in the leg. How did you find us so quickly?" His tone was nervous, Kaelum couldn't tell why. Like he was hiding something. He glanced at Elarie. She stood off to the side, watching with her arms wrapped around her body in a protective stance.

"It was Jamison," Kaleum answered. "He's still figuring out the magic, but he did well. Hated being close to the helm, though."

Elarie looked over at the group. Kaelum cleared his throat and squeezed his hand, following her eyes. The twenty three of those that had come ashore were setting up a small camp, drawing straws to see who would take watches already. A large fire was being built for dinner as well. Tran, the best cook Kaelum knew, had brought all his favorite ingredients. He just needed someone to catch a few fish. But Elarie wasn't looking at them, she was looking at Jamison.

Then the old woman. Jamison had informed Kaelum, Terry, and Lester that her name was Terisa. They'd known she was a seer upon purchase, but had already gotten evidence of it when she saw the Jiivers and predicted Elarie's sudden death.

"Elarie," Calix said. She looked at him. He nodded to Kaelum.

Her eyes went to the captain. "What?" She asked. "Oh, actually I need to speak to you." She pointed to him, then to Terry, "and you... and anyone else that knows about your magic or anything about what you've been feeling. Now excuse me," she said before walking away. They saw her run her fingers through her hair and pull it into a knot at the back of her head before she disappeared into the trees.

"I like her," Calix said pleasantly. Terry sighed. "What? She's nice and actually pretty funny."

"She could be dangerous," Terry told him in his deadpanned matter-of-fact tone. Kaelum loved it when he spoke low the way he was. He looked over at his first mate as he said, "we have no idea what she is—"

Calix said, "human. She told me as much. I couldn't tell if she was lying or not, but she said she was a human who was cursed. I guess the curse is not dying." He turned his head back to the trees.

"I bet she's lying," Terry shook his head and met eyes with Kaelum. Kaelum stared back. He'd memorized Terry's face, so the setting sun did nothing to take the lines of Terry away. His hard, sharp jaw, his deep-set and narrow eyes, the mole at the edge of his hairline, and his thick black eyebrows... Kaelum knew all of it. All of him.

The prince was looking between them awkwardly. "You aren't doing anything inappropriate and I still feel like I walked in on something," he said. It made Terry blush. Kaelum laughed softly. "What's for dinner?"

"Something with fish," Kaelum answered. Calix rubbed his stomach. "Have you eaten?"

"Elarie cooked a macaw," he said. When he turned again, she was on her way back. Her head was turned to the party. She stopped next to Calix. "Everything all right?" He asked.

She nodded. "I have much against the Fae," she muttered. Elarie looked away from them, now addressing Kaelum. "Does anyone else know about your magic?" He nodded. "Then bring them here," she motioned as if she were annoyed he didn't follow her instructions the first time.

Kaelum shouted, "Lester get over here! Jamison you too!" Elarie was snapping, causing little fires to spark. She muttered something in another language, her green eyes trained on the four Fae Kaelum had rescued while Lester and Jamison left the fire to answer Kaelum's call. "This is Elarie," he motioned to her, "Elarie, this is Jamison and Lester. They, Terry, and Calix are the only people that know about my hand." He waited. She was still staring at the Fae. "Elarie?" One of them was making eye contact with her.

"Elarie, you wanted to talk to them," Calix said gently. He was looking from her to the Fae, as was everyone. The Fae, a tall and broad male, smirked and spit onto the sand. He called something out to her in one of the many faerie dialects. His comrades, another male and two females, laughed. "Elarie, come on," he said and grabbed her arm before she could move toward them.

"Fine," she grunted, turning when he pulled. She faced the group. Calix let go and Grey got up. He stretched and walked away. "He's going hunting," she said dully, "no whale shark." Elarie looked at each of the men, her expression softening when she looked at Jamison. Good, she had a soft spot. Terry would be glad to know that.

Elarie glanced back at the Fae. All four of them were looking at them.

A fire burned in a line between them and who she was standing with. Lester inched back as it popped and cracked. "It's not going to hurt you, I just need something they won't be able to hear over," Elarie said. She took a deep breath. "Right. Kaelum," she looked at him, "I cannot stress the importance of no one else knowing what you have. The pain, the stars, the line in your hand, *no one else* can know about it. If the wrong person hears it could be the death of you."

Kaelum looked at the four people around him. "I trust these men more than anyone in the world." Aside from his mother. Kaelum would go home and tell her right away without hesitation. "Anything you tell me, they can know, too. No one else."

Elarie stepped toward him, her hand out. "Give it to me," she said, "I won't hurt you." Kaelum put his hand out and she took it with both of hers. "The Metars," she said as she flattened his hand, "are the only Fae to ever have been granted magic. Beyond nature, the Fae have nothing special about them, but the *Metars*," she said with complete admiration. Elarie shook her head, "the Metars are the greatest creations. The only creation that a god and nature worked together to make."

"Why haven't we heard of them, then?" Calix asked. He walked closer.

She smiled sadly and put her hand over Kaelum's. "Because most of them are dead and the rest would prefer to be kept secret. The Metars were killed off by Fae after their magic. Taking magic is the only thing Fae are good at."

Kaelum asked, "are you going to take some?"

She snorted. Elarie ran her middle finger along the line. "I'm going to teach you to control your gift," she said, "because if you don't have control many people could die."

"What?" He pulled his hand away with his eyes wide.

"And you think fire magic is dangerous," she wiggled her fingers around, showing sparks, "I wouldn't want to go near yours on a bad day."

It was Lester who asked, "what do you look like on a bad day?"

She sighed. Her wall of crackling flames went out when she backed into Calix. Elarie stepped to the side and looked up. "Every day is a bad day," she squinted. The sky was a deep blue, though some bright stars were already peeking out. She laughed softly.

"Every day?" Calix asked, "what about today?" Elarie turned her head and looked at him. Her head was still tilted back so Kaelum figured it was an odd angle to look at her. Neither of them said anything at first, they just looked at each other. "Check out what she did," Calix snapped his fingers, which made her straighten and watch him go to get something. He then grunted and cursed, "Elarie, how did you lift this thing?"

Elarie said, "with my knees," then blinked a few times, "shit, sorry." Lester laughed as she went over to Calix. "I'll do it. Greilor would kill me if you hurt yourself." They heard Calix sigh and Elarie squatted to lift whatever black thing they couldn't see clearly.

"Oh wow," Lester stepped forward as the thing she'd created came into view. "This is impressive."

Calix nudged Elarie, "he's a sculptor."

"How did you get the obsidian? This is obsidian, right?" Lester lowered himself down as Elarie set the dragon sculpture on the sand. "Amazing."

"I made it," Elarie told him. "If you'd like some I can make a block for you. But it's not real obsidian," she tapped on the black rock with a nail.

Calix said, "Still extremely impressive."

"You *make* obsidian?" Lester looked up at her.

She nodded, though now she seemed nervous. Kaelum doubted she wanted the attention to be placed on her about the sculpture, he guessed she would've wanted Calix to introduce it when she wasn't there—perhaps even on the ship—so that she wouldn't have to answer questions about it. "Anything that can be made with extreme temperatures, I can do it," she said and again looked at the further blackened sky. "Just not now..." Elarie tilted her head. "Where are we?"

"On an island," Terry joked. A rarity for him. Kaelum smiled. "We were thrown off course when the Jiiver storm hit so this is the furthest west we've ever gone, but it'll be corrected in the morning."

"And then what?" She looked at him.

Kaelum allowed the answer. He nodded to Terry even though his first mate didn't seem remotely pleased. "We're going to the Reefs."

She straightened. "The Reefs," Elarie looked at Kaelum, "to what? Continue your quest of rescuing slaves?" He nodded. Her shoulders seemed to relax. Elarie moved to rest her body weight on one leg a lot like how Calix was standing. The prince was looking at her with a worried brow. Her eyes grew just the slightest bit distant before she looked at Calix. They mirrored each other and it made Kaelum's stomach churn. "Do you want to practice calling him from further away or are there too many people to embarrass yourself in front of?"

"You are so very mean," he shook his head.

"No then?" She smirked at him. He rolled his eyes. Elarie backed up and whistled sharply the way she had before. Kaelum turned to where she was looking. It was only moments before the shadow of a dragon carrying something rather large with him flashed over the bright moon. "Oh my..." Elarie grabbed Calix's wrist and pulled him forward as Grey landed with enough force to shake the ground. He roared, flapping his great wings.

Calix looked at her. Their backs were to everyone else now, so all Kaelum could see was the two of them standing in front of a massive, angry looking dragon. "What?" The prince asked her.

She turned around suddenly and brought him back to the group. Elarie looked at each of them with the same amount of seriousness she had when she was talking about Kaelum's magic. "A wyvern is not a dragon," she said, "do you understand? A wyvern is not a dragon."

"Isn't it though?" Jamison's brow furrowed, "I mean, it's just the legs that are different, otherwise they're the same..."

He trailed off as she shook her head. Calix chuckled. "Don't tell a dragon *or* a wyvern that," she said. Calix still laughed. She looked at him, "you get to eat it."

His smile dropped. "What? I thought that was just one time."

"No," she said, "you get to eat a wyvern." Elarie then looked at the group once again, "don't let anyone say the dragon is eating a dragon. Dragons take great offense to it."

"Right, Jamison will you spread the word?" Kaelum asked.

He nodded, muttering, "but they *are* the same," and walked toward the camp full of people trying to get a good look at them and what the dragon was eating.

Elarie again pulled Calix to the dragon, but this time they were followed. Lester was cursing under his breath, as he often did. Kaelum was sure there was something in his past that haunted him about it. Perhaps a parent or some other adult told him not to curse and now as an adult, it was all he did.

"So you fought him?" Elarie asked. She let go of Calix's wrist. Grey tore into the spiked back of the wyvern. It really did look like a dragon, just without the two front legs. "Yes, Calix and I are very proud," she continued and Calix nodded. His hands were in his pockets. He didn't know what to do, whereas Elarie was inspecting the kill. "Can we have the head?"

"To eat?" Calix hissed, his eyes wide. She waved him off. "Elarie, I am not eating the head—"

"You aren't eating the head, be quiet," she snapped and Grey got his jaws around the neck and crunched down. He gnawed on it like a dog with a bone for a moment before the head popped off. "Excellent," Elarie said. "Calix, grab a horn and help me move it down the beach."

He moved to the other side of the wyvern head. "Why?"

"Firm sand," she answered, grabbing two of the many horns on the head. Kaelum cringed, staring at the thing. Its eyes were still open, red as a ruby, and its tongue was sticking out. "It's a gift," she said, "now lift."

"Oh shit," Calix grunted as he lifted. Elarie's side of the wyvern head was much higher off the ground than his. Calix shuffled to where Elarie wanted and dropped it with shaking arms. "A gift for who?" He asked, gasping for breath despite the short walk.

She pointed to Kaelum. He tensed. "Come here," she moved her finger, arching it toward herself. "Do you know how valuable the stuff that's in this head is?" She asked as he, Terry, and Lester approached with caution. "Some of it more than a dragon."

Grey lifted his head and growled.

"Everyone knows you are the most valuable dragon alive, Greilor, this is just a vague generalization," she said. The dragon shook his big head and growled again. "Calix can choose."

"I can what?" His head whipped to her.

She took the dagger off Kaelum's belt, leaving him gaping at how quickly she'd taken it. "Go cut off some of the wyvern," she handed it to him. Calix looked like he might vomit. She quieted, "go for the leg, ask him to break the skin for you, and take some of the meat. He'll love how active you're being with his likes and interests and I promise you don't have to eat this raw."

"Are you going to eat it raw?" He asked.

"Gods no," she shook her head and pushed him. "Go." Calix shivered at her, but did as she told him to. "Kaelum," Elarie turned to him. Again, he tensed. "I realize you are getting all of your money from Calix so you don't need it—"

He took a small step, "that's not exactly what we're doing."

"Sure," she nodded. Kaelum's brow furrowed. She didn't believe him. "Now there are many things about a wyvern head that people would give horrifyingly large amounts of money for. Teeth, tongue, saliva, eyes, blood, brain matter—all of it. So I wanted to give it to you. I can preserve it for as long as you need."

"Oh," Kaelum looked at the nasty head. "Well..."

"You don't have to take it," she said, "although I would at least consider the teeth, those are worth much."

Terry said, "like how you used dragon teeth to buy your freedom from Rol?"

"Yes," she nodded, otherwise silent. She wouldn't even look at him. Kaelum turned his head to Terry, who held an expression he hadn't seen in his first mate in some time. He was conflicted. "Well," Elarie cleared her throat, "if you don't want the head I can get rid of it."

"I don't have anywhere to put the whole thing, but the teeth would be good to have. You never know when you might need them."

The wyvern head lit on fire.

CHAPTER NINE

ELARIE

Greilor seemed to think that Elarie needed more than one friend. *Why not a whole pirate ship?* He had asked. And Elarie replied, "why not just the prince?" Still, she didn't want to upset him. Greilor and she had been separated far too long to fight over how many friends she made.

The wyvern head had a little to do with that. For Greilor and for Calix, whom Elarie would be spending much more time with for the foreseeable future. It was better to be seen making an effort of friendship, or giving a gift, than to ignore the pirate giving her odd looks in his attempt to surmise how dangerous she was to both the prince and the people.

But he seemed to like the teeth. Kaelum was bent over them with Terry. They'd laid them out on a jacket and were organizing them by size. Elarie could hear them whispering about prices and worth. What they could buy with wyvern teeth, how many people would know them to be wyvern teeth, how to barter, and blah, blah, blah.

Elarie turned her attention to Calix. He'd expressed not wanting to eat the wyvern—which according to him smelled much better than the shark so it *might* be good—until he'd seasoned them. Calix had gone without seasoning for too many meals. So Elarie sat against Greilor's wing and waited with the piece of wyvern in her hands.

Apparently, this was the closest Greilor had gotten to sitting with the crew and its rescued for as long as they'd been together. He was behind Elarie holding the wyvern carcass and slowly tearing off every last bit of meat and fat from the bones. Usually, when he was eating, and even most of the time, he was separate. Now because he wanted to stay with Elarie while simultaneously wanting Elarie to 'make friends' with people, he was willing to sit closer.

"Here we are," Calix said as he sat. In his hands were two plain shells of the same size. "Smell," he held one out. Inside was a pile of different spices he'd selected and put together into a colorful blend he seemed very proud of.

"Do you like to cook?" Elarie sniffed the spices. She wasn't adept when it came to naming ingredients, but there were obvious notes of chili. Most of what she could smell was *spicy.*

Calix shrugged and held out the other shell, "I prefer eating."

She put the piece of meat in her lap and slipped both shells out of his hands. She sifted the spices around. "Do you prefer cooking your own food or having it made for you?" Elarie sniffed the one that smelled more like chilies again. "This one," she held it out.

His hand covered the back of hers as he smelled her choice. "Excellent, now give me one moment," he smiled largely before getting up again with the other shell. Elarie laid back and watched, now holding the seasoning and the thing they could've eaten long before if he hadn't insisted on taking advantage of the cook's plentiful selection of spices. Elarie would only pretend to mind, though, because she couldn't remember the last thing she ate that had any sort of flavor on it at all.

I like having things made for me, Greilor said in her mind. He shifted, forcing Elarie to lean forward. The dragon got up with the carcass hanging from his mouth and turned around. *I'll eat with you.*

"Joining us for dinner, Grey?" Calix asked. He turned his body to face both the dragon and Elarie, sitting happily.

Elarie held the shell of seasoning out for the prince. "He wants you to cook for him," she said, shaking it a little.

"We're both cooking," he said and excitedly flattened out a spot of sand between them. "Not on a spit because I am starving," he added. Calix then set down a piece of wood meant to act as a plate and a bottle of something. Elarie placed the piece of meat on the plate and picked up the skinny dark bottle. "Olive oil," he said as she uncorked it and smelled, "from the orchard on the grounds."

I've been, Greilor told her, *Calix has many different things growing in his gardens. Lots of butterflies.*

"Butterflies?" Elarie repeated. She handed the bottle and cork to Calix. He drizzled the oil on the wyvern chunk and rubbed it in. "Calix, do you have a butterfly garden?"

"Butterfly garden," he mumbled shyly, "no, I don't have a 'butterfly garden.'"

She looked at Greilor, then at the prince once again, "yes you do. Greilor says you do." Elarie leaned forward and held the spice shell out for him to pinch some off and put it on their dinner. "Calix?" He hummed, not looking at her. She whispered, "were your wings a butterfly?"

His head snapped up to hers. His eyes were wide, "how did you—did Grey tell you—"

"No he didn't betray you like that," she said, "I was just guessing."

Calix looked around shamefully, his voice low as he said, "don't tell anyone."

"Mine were too," she said. Calix seemed to relax slightly. His eyes went to hers. With the firelight shining on his left side, only half of his face was defined, the other was shrouded in shadow. His eyes as well. Calix had one lovely, bright, brown and blue Lathin eye. The other was black, only a shine of light to reflect in his iris. "We have that in common," Elarie said.

He was far too shy about his wings to discuss the details of the experience. Elarie was glad for it—she had no desire to share hers either. Greilor would whine and groan about this, but it was her decision. Elarie's wings were important to her, especially after so long. They were hers and only hers. Her butterfly, one no one else would ever see.

She'd been born with dragons, many would say that when it came to the members of her family, the dragons were their first wings. They were Elarie's. She'd fallen in love with them the moment she saw them and they with her. It was a common story that was told on her birthday, how Greilor shocked everyone by storming into the entry hall and breaking the doors the day she was born. He refused to leave, insisting that he wait until Elarie's mother was ready so that he may be the first dragon to greet the first daughter. The fire elemental.

But it was their traditions that made it so that Elarie had to wait to find her wings before she could ride her own dragon. Wings beyond that of their ancestors' creations. *Dragons are our birthright, but wings are our gateway to them.* It was the beginning of a great

connection and a path for dragons to choose a rider. They all needed wings to fly, after all.

Calix wiped his hands on the bottom of his pant leg. It was
extended toward Elarie, and the movement brought her out of
her tunneling thought process. The day she found her wings.
Her brother's reaction. Her father's reaction. "How do you cook a
wyvern?" He asked her.

The wyvern began to cook. She charred it a bit on the outside
and let it cook through on the inside. Elarie would usually prefer
something that wasn't so well done, but wyvern was like chicken.
If it wasn't cooked all the way through they'd be sick. "Like that,"
she said.

The prince watched her the way Greilor did. He assessed her.
"Are you all right?" He asked. Calix had quieted. They weren't as
close to the crew as even the Fae were, but still, he was sure to lower
his voice as she had when asking about his wings.

"Just thinking," she moved closer, wiping sand off her hand
before ripping off a piece of the wyvern. "Here, give this to Greilor.
Put it on his tongue and he'll taste it."

Calix took the meat from her. Greilor moved his head and
opened his mouth pleasantly. He was smiling in his own dragon
way, especially because this was the first time Calix had ever done
something like this. He was glad Elarie was willing to show him
new things, he was glad she was there, he was glad Calix was
accepting of her. He was a glad dragon, apparently. Greilor named
off what he was thankful for as his rider put the piece of wyvern on
his thin tongue. He left his mouth open. They watched the piece
sizzle, flavor collecting on the pink muscle.

He hummed.

"A lovely choice of spices," Elarie translated. Calix grinned.

He said, "I've never done that before."

"There are many things you've never done," she agreed as he sat back in his place. They both took a piece of the wyvern. "And I can teach you if you'd like."

Calix held up the wyvern as if it were a glass and they were toasting something. "I'd very much like that." They cheered like kids and both took a bite of the wyvern at the same time.

CHAPTER TEN

CALIX

He was forced to admit that the wyvern was delicious, he just had to get past the *what it is* part of the experience. Elarie had smiled like she won some game he didn't know they were playing. It only slightly bothered him. Calix wasn't one that usually lost. Still, seeing Elarie relaxed again was nice. She'd been tense since the ship showed up, only trying to hide it.

"You keep looking at them," Calix mumbled to her. The wyvern plate was gone from between them and Elarie had moved to a much closer position. It gave her room to lay her head and shoulder against Grey, who had also finished. The wyvern bones were discarded off to the side. Now Calix's leg was extended in front of him. He faced the ocean and Elarie was on his right side. She seemed content, and so did Grey. Like all either of them needed was a good meal.

"At who?" Elarie asked. She held her hand out and he gave a clear bottle to her. The only water brought to the beach at all. No one else was drinking it.

He gave her a look. She knew. Elarie drank slowly, brows raised. "The Fae," he answered despite this. She lowered the bottle, again looking at them. The four of them sat together drinking with everyone else. They seemed personable. It appeared they made good company. Everyone else seemed to be enjoying their conversation—the parts they could understand. Often, they slipped back into their own tongue. One of the many faerie languages Calix wanted to know. He thought it would be good to learn the most common one.

It seemed that Elarie knew it. She tended to look up when they were speaking it and stopped when they joined back in everyone else's conversation.

"Why don't you like them?" Calix whispered. She handed the water back to him and he took a drink.

"Magic stealing bastards," she muttered. Calix looked back at them. The four were laughing, talking, and eating. Not stealing magic. He then looked at Kaelum. The captain was sitting with Terry and Lester. Terry was telling them a story and Kaelum was hitting his first mate's leg every time he laughed. Would the Fae try to take Kaelum's magic, whatever it may be?

He looked at her once again, "can I ask you something?" She only nodded and he caught her trying not to look at the Fae again. Calix asked, "what are the things you don't want to talk about with me?"

Elarie seemed taken aback by this. She blinked rapidly and shifted, then looked at Grey. "Well Greilor wants me to tell you everything," she said. Elarie was quiet for some time, considering. He imagined her going through her life, trying to find the things that were too close to her chest that she couldn't share them. "I am trying to be open with you. Maybe we should just play it by ear."

Her eyes moved over him. "And you? Are there things you don't want me to bring up?"

He shook his head. "I'm an open book. It's you I'm worried about."

"I just don't like having important conversations around people," she took the water back from him.

Calix looked at her for a time. A nervous expression crawled up on her face. "Then let's go for a walk," he decided and pushed himself to his feet. He held his hand out. "I want to see how much I can learn about you in the single day we've known each other."

She snorted just a little. Calix wiggled his fingers. Elarie looked at them, then at him, and caved. She took his hand and let him pull her up. "As long as we're both sharing," she pointed accusingly at him and backed up, not even glancing at the group. She ran her hand along Grey's neck and wing, going all the way down his body. Calix began to follow, turning to look at Kaelum. His brow was furrowed warily. Terry just looked pissed.

Calix gave them a thumbs up and followed Elarie. He jogged to catch up to her, stating, "I'll go first. Shall we start small?" She just smiled. "I prefer my mother over my father."

"I preferred my father over my mother," she said. "I have a favorite sibling, do you?"

"I do."

Elarie sighed. She pulled on her hair and began playing with it again. "My second eldest brother, Cammie. He..." she trailed off, breathing slowly and quietly. Elarie looked around before saying, "he was the one I thought loved me the most. Not even my father loved me the way he did."

Calix said, "my little brother Ryd. He's quiet and I think he's very thoughtful. He draws, too. Ryd has his own little room for all his art things and I go in to sit with him. Sometimes he lets me use his pencils or brushes, but mostly I just sit and read. It's nice, like a peaceful bubble."

"It does sound nice," she agreed. "I am not remotely artistically talented. In any way other than the glass sculpture and that took years to get right."

"Did you live by the beach?" He asked.

She nodded, "for a while."

"Would it be obvious to say that I live by the beach?" Calix smiled a little. Grey came to their sides walking silently. He wondered if he was saying anything. Confessing as they were.

"It would be," Elarie nodded. She tilted her head back as the ocean breeze picked up. "Something you love?"

He answered, "dragons."

"Dragons," she agreed. They continued on their way. Grey seemed pleased. "But what else? Other than dragons and knitting and braiding and the like."

"Specificities," he muttered. Calix looked up at the moon. It was almost full and bright in a suddenly completely cloudless sky. "Reading. I love reading."

Elarie pulled on his elbow and led him gently further down the beach. "Take your shoe off," she urged and stood in the water. She hummed pleasantly and wiggled her toes. Calix removed the shoe. It was a bit awkward with the lack of a shoe heel, but the beach wasn't exactly flat either. He adjusted to it. Freezing water hit his foot, making him hiss and back up. "What sort of reading do you do?" She inquired.

He stepped up to the water again as she kicked it around, continuing their walk. Calix said, "I enjoy many genres. Fantasy, romance, history."

"Romance, really?" She asked, not to tease him. Calix recognized it as pure curiosity. "Authors like Lialan Cos and Pewtra Gogn or like Dan Fredin and L.L. Craci?"

Calix rolled his eyes, "no question, L.L. Craci." She stopped where she was. He began to laugh at her, watching her face heat. "Gods, L.L. Craci?" He laughed again, "and Dan Fredin should never be allowed to write another romance book after the obscene objectification of his female characters—not to mention the completely unnecessary rape scene in his latest novel to make the love interest seem more like a hero. I wrote him a very strong letter after that." He cleared his throat to stop the laughter. "Sorry," he said to her, "I got you, though."

"My view of you would have completely changed," she told him. Elarie walked once again. "I've never read a truly good romance by a man. They always get something wrong."

"Female expression?" Calix suggested. Elarie laughed a little, kicking some more water. "I have actually read a book by a man that was truly good." She turned her head to him, enticing him to go on. "It was by my father, he wrote it for my mother as a gift for their twentieth anniversary. He called it *His Heart's Arrow*. Not the best of titles, but the way he wrote it was beautiful."

Elarie smiled, "was it about them?"

He nodded. "How they met from his perspective. My mother lived in the south, her parents were librarians at the House of Scholars. Ironically she was never big on books. My father went to visit the library to get away from his father. He made up some strategy study excuse and rode off as fast as he could." Calix smiled faintly. It was in this one story that he felt any sort of similarity and connection to his father. "My mother was carrying a stack of books in both arms with her needlepoint and a cup of tea balanced on the top."

"They ran into each other?" She asked, suddenly excited by it.

Calix said, "no, actually, some kid on a field trip to the House put his foot out and tripped her."

"What a little asshole."

"If it wasn't for that little asshole I would have never been," he put his hand over his heart solemnly. They both laughed. "Anyway, the books and my mother were on their way to the floor, yes? And in comes my father trying to lose the guards following him so he can get a bit of peace. He slips on her tea and lands on his ass right in front of her."

Elarie said, "fate."

"Absolutely." Calix felt a lightness in his chest. He'd never spoken to anyone about this and she was turning out to be the perfect person to talk to about anything. What else could he share without judgment? What could *she* share? He said, "while my mother was telling the child's teacher that it was fine, nothing was broken, my father was staring at her. She hadn't even noticed him."

"Oh, that is the best."

The lightness grew. "When a guard came in running after the prince still starstruck on the floor, everyone saw him then, but he only looked at my mother. He called it love at first sight on his end and apprehension on hers."

"How old were they?" Elarie asked.

"Same age as us, I suppose. Father spent all his time trying to get her attention in the library—and it worked because when her parents offered to send her up to Lyburn on some sort of errand she grappled for the opportunity. That was after my father had gone back to the capital," he added. "They wrote to each other, father still has all the letters in a jewelry box that belonged to my grandmother."

So sweet, she mumbled under her breath.

Calix grinned at Grey, who seemed to nod at him. "So my mother went north. At this point, they'd been writing for months. He asked her to marry him as soon as she got out of the carriage."

"She said yes?"

"In public, yes, but in private no. According to the book she smacked him upside the head and told him that if the ring he proposed with wasn't the ring that belonged to her mother then she would not marry him," he said, "so while she *would* say yes, she also wouldn't. He had to ask my grandmother for permission and for her ring."

Elarie was laughing softly. "I think I adore your mother."

"How did your parents meet, then?"

She sighed animatedly. "Quite romantically, actually. They were *betrothed.*"

"There has to be more than that," Calix argued. He tucked the idea of a betrothal into the back of his mind, storing it with the *what is Elarie* question. Could peasants have betrothals? Was that classist of him to assume otherwise?

"I don't know," she said, "I don't remember ever being told about how they met or really even about their wedding. I do remember them being in love." Her brow slowly furrowed. "They used to share seats. They kissed a lot."

"And had five children," he added, "so..."

Elarie stopped and faced him, getting him to turn to her. She put her hands on his upper arms and began running them down the fabric of his sleeves. Her warm touch heated his skin despite the layers between them. Calix didn't know what she was doing, but he could very distinctly see pain in her green eyes. "I think she resented me for it," she said. Her hands held his wrists. Elarie blinked quickly, the flash of the determination to share disappearing. "I've never told anyone that. Other than Matian, but," she shook her head.

He had two questions, but chose the first one to come up. "Why would your mother resent you for her children?"

Behind him, Grey let out a low, mournful hum. It caused her to change somehow. The warmth on his wrists flickered between hot and cold as Grey's words flushed through her. Elarie stepped closer to Calix and put her head against his collar. Her head was warmer than her hands. "She had so many miscarriages before she had me. And I think," she swallowed thickly, he could hear it like he could hear the ragged breath she brought in after, "I think after I stopped being a baby all she could see was what she went through to have me and she stopped liking me."

"I'm sure that's not true," Calix found himself saying, though he seriously doubted it. How would he know better than her?

"When she had my brothers everything was different," she shook her head, "I could see how much she loved them and I could feel how little she loved me."

He sighed a little. Calix put his head against hers. "Do you want a hug? I'm quite good at them."

"Stay like this," she whispered, "don't put your arms around me."

"All right," he said. Calix stared at the ocean. It still seemed to shine a little, not in the way moonlight reflected off of it. "Who's Matian?" He asked to move on from the topic of neglectful mothers. He couldn't relate to it, even when it came to his father. His father loved him. They weren't as close as he was with his mother, but never once did he make Calix feel unloved or unwelcome.

She groaned just a bit. He felt it against his collarbone. Elarie took a step back and the absence of her sent a chill over his body, especially in the places she'd touched. Suddenly the beach was freezing. "He was," Elarie wiped her eyes, "the love of my life. We met when we were children. It was one of those 'will they, won't they' things where there were so many times I could've or he could've."

"I suppose one of you did?"

"We did. Fifteen year old Elarie got very jealous seeing him with another girl. She confronted him and he called her a matealn," she smiled sadly. "It was awkward for a while. We didn't really talk about what it was for another year, even after kissing him."

Calix nodded. He'd never had an awkward situation with a woman. Calix liked to think of himself as very confident, so this was yet another thing he couldn't relate to.

"I was going to marry him," she said softly. Again, Grey moaned sadly. "Now he's dead. Everyone is." Calix was about to say something when her hands slipped into his, "can we not talk about it?" She asked, looking at him like his yes or no answer would change the way she saw him in an instant. "Just sit with me for a while?"

He nodded. "Sure, yeah," he said. Calix backed up so they wouldn't be sitting in the damp sand.

Chapter Eleven

Kaelum

A sharp, long whistle startled him to wake when the sun was just rising. Kaelum grabbed for his sword, instead taking hold of Terry's arm. It had been outstretched toward him. Kaelum let go in an instant and sat up to his knees. It had been Calix who whistled and he was doing it again. The sharp sound broke apart. He'd awoken everyone, yet paid no mind to them. Calix was standing in front of Grey, now pushing on him, but the dragon wouldn't wake.

"What's wrong?" Kaelum stood. He looked around. The crew watched closely, plenty of them worried. They'd all lived and sailed with Grey for years. If there was something wrong with the dragon, everyone would want to know.

Calix turned to him desperately. "Elarie is gone, so are the Fae, and Grey isn't waking up," he said, motioning to both the dried circle of blood on the ground and the empty place the Fae used to sit. "And the footprints? There have to be people living on this island we didn't know about and they took her."

He was breathing heavily. Desperately. Kaelum looked around. His eyes trailed the many footprints—and the drag marks, which must've been Elarie—into the woods. He saw Jamison looking at them as well. "All right," Kaelum scratched sand off his jaw. "All right!" He shouted to get everyone's attention. "Get to the boats, everyone back to the ship. Leave one boat for me, Calix, Terry, Jamison, and Elarie."

Jamison perked up nervously.

"Lester have everything ready to sail once we get there," he nodded to him. "I don't know how long this is going to take so try to be patient."

"I'll do my best, Captain," he bowed his head jokingly. "What about Grey?" Lester looked at the dragon. Turning around, Kaelum saw that Calix was still pushing on him, shaking him trying to get him to wake up. "Has he been spelled or something?"

Kaelum tried not to shrug. His heart ached as he looked at the worry on Calix's face. It reflected in his whole body. He was breaking down. *What if he never woke up?* "We will figure it out. I'm sure Elarie will know what to do. Now everyone get to the ship," he looked to his crew and the rescued that had previously been enjoying their time on land. "Jamison."

The kid stood and walked over slowly. "You want me to track her, don't you?" He asked, glancing around. His eyes settled on Calix. It was the prince he was worried about. Jamison and he got along just fine, they were good together and shared many laughs, but now Calix was looking at his dragon with a horrible sense of loss and it was up to Jamison to find Elarie so she could fix it. *What if he failed?*

It was a horrible question Kaelum didn't want to entertain. "I do. And you can do it, I know it."

Jamison looked at the trail to the woods as people dragged themselves or hurried themselves to get off the island. They had to assume it was Fae living on the island if the four Kaelum had rescued were gone as well as Elarie. There was no evidence that they'd struggled either, nothing like the blood that looked to be enough for Elarie to be dead. Or have died and come back.

"It'll be fun," Terry clapped Jamison on the back. He then handed Kaelum's cutlass over. "Humans in a Fae-infested jungle looking for some kind of undead being? What could possibly go wrong."

Calix shot a terrible look at Terry. "Finding her is my top priority. I don't care what she is and I never will if she can wake up my dragon."

Terry nodded shortly, a tightness in his jaw. He looked at Jamison and said, "can you find her?"

The kid shrugged, "I can try." His head turned and he looked at Terisa. The old woman nodded with a sure smile. "Yeah, I can," he said and breathed in slowly. "I can do it, I can do it."

Sometimes Kaelum wasn't sure he made the right decision by letting Jamison aboard. The kid was seventeen and looking for an adventure. Kaelum knew that having someone younger on the ship would help everyone, keep people calm, and give them someone to keep sane and hopeful. And it was working especially with the rescued. Because he was young he was more personable and easier to accept. But still, Jamison was a kid. A *good* kid. A few times Kaelum had considered letting him go. He was attached, however. Too attached.

Jamison walked along the footprints with Calix being the first to follow. His head stayed turned to the dragon, inwardly begging him to wake. But the dragon didn't, and when they reached the woods the prince looked away.

"So what do you think she is, Calix?" Terry asked. He'd always been straight to the point. He'd always asked questions at the wrong time because he couldn't hold back when he wanted to know something. It was the same when he was telling people things. He needed to finish, even if he just whispered it to Kaelum. "If you think she's lying about being a cursed human."

He glanced back, looking at both Terry and Kaelum, then went back to looking ahead. "I don't know. She looks human, she acts human," he shrugged, "maybe she is. The *cursed* part is what I'm trying to figure out. If I believe she's human then I believe her when she says the gods cursed her, now I just need to figure out why."

He's lying. Kaelum could see it from where he was. He could see it in his shoulders. They'd been friends since they were children, did Calix really think Kaelum wouldn't be able to tell? No, Calix knew something he didn't want to share. She told him something. What she was? Probably not. But something.

Kaelum said nothing. He didn't look at Terry, he just looked at where he was stepping. Jamison walked silently ahead of them, tracking better than anyone Kaelum had ever worked with. At seventeen, too. He was unsure of himself, unsure of his ability, but gods was he great at it. Tracker magic wasn't rare. There were two other trackers on his ship of varying levels. It was a gift Fae possessed as well, one of the few, so humans having it wasn't all that special. It was only useful because trusting a Fae with something like tracking a person wasn't the best idea for humans.

"Terisa says she's good," Jamison said suddenly. Each of them looked at him. He didn't turn, he just stepped over a log and picked up a piece of her light hair. Blood was on it. He put it down. "She says that Elarie just needs someone to give her a chance and she thinks that it's Calix that will."

"I'm already giving her a chance," Calix said.

"Not now," he turned a little and they turned with him. This was the best way to get him to track something—distracted. When he was thinking of something else he tended to let his ability lead him. "Something is going to happen that will change everything. If Calix accepts her she'll stay good."

Calix looked back at them. "And if I don't?"

"She never said," Jamison looked back. "It doesn't seem like she's giving you much of a choice, though, huh?"

He shook his head, "not really, no."

"Maybe you should ask Terisa to elaborate," Jamison suggested before continuing his walk. It lasted hours. Hours in complete silence because Calix seemed far too preoccupied with his thoughts and Terry seemed preoccupied trying to guess what those thoughts were. Kaelum's head was just spinning. He was attempting to concentrate on one thing at a time, but everything he tried to focus on made his hand hurt. His hand hurting brought him to Elarie and the way she held it the night before. Tenderly, gently. She knew what he was and seemed ready to protect him with her life. Her life, which it seemed was never ending. But she also was going to teach him about it.

At least he had an excuse to want to find her. Other than Calix, who he'd do anything for.

Jamison stopped. "That's a lot of blood," he said.

They gathered around it. Yes, it was a lot of blood. It wasn't fresh and it had soaked into the ground. "I suppose this means she died?" He looked at Calix.

"They would've left her here if she didn't come back to life," he said with a hard jaw. He was worried about her beyond just wanting his dragon back.

"You care about her already," Terry realized, speaking Kaelum's mind. He'd never say that out loud—at least not right now, and yet there was Terry. Speak or stew Terry. "Without knowing how dangerous she could be?"

Calix said, "she's not dangerous to me."

Terry was ready to contradict him, probably to say he couldn't be sure after a day and a nice stroll on the beach, but he was cut off by a chilling scream. Each of them looked in the direction it had come from. They were by a field of light, long grass, with a few hills in the distance. Once they walked out of the tree line they could see a village on one of the hills. It was large with sturdy stone houses. There was even a square. Down the hill, following a path of stone was a temple. It looked much older than most of the village and was in the process of being renovated. Poles and stones were stacked outside it, even glass was rested against the wall near broken windows.

It was Elarie screaming and she screamed again, this time sounding much more angry than the first time.

Calix ran down the hill without any thought to his own safety or the possibility of there being more Fae around that weren't in the temple. He just ran and the rest of them were forced to follow. Calix tripped as he went down, able to catch himself by hopping a few times. Slowing was difficult. Kaelum and the others had reached him before he was against the temple wall.

They looked through the furthest window from the dais where a shirtless, sickly pale Fae was standing. Kaelum prayed silently that no one saw them. From his position, he could see that the temple held many strong and capable Fae that would kill the much slower, much weaker humans at a moment's notice.

Elarie was cursing in another language. Blood covered her back. It was caked into her hair. At her wrists was a line of tightly wrapped thorns. Fresh blood was on her hands.

She was dragged toward the dais unable to free herself from two large male Fae. Elarie skidded against the uneven stones and stopped in front of the shirtless Fae. She spit in his face. The Fae only wiped her spit away and motioned for her to be turned to the front and put on her knees.

Next to Kaelum, Calix put his hands over his mouth and whistled softly, soft enough to hopefully not be heard, and he was looking at Elarie as he did it. She lurched forward unintentionally and her eyes moved.

The Fae began to speak, addressing his crowd of followers. There was enough to be every Fae in the village. The numbers included the four Kaelum rescued. They were off to the side, standing proudly. They looked at Elarie and the Fae as if they were the cause of all of this, as if they deserved praise.

Elarie's eyes swept the Fae males, females, children, and elderly, and they landed on Calix. She sobbed without tears on her face and managed to look betrayed as she forced her gaze away. Elarie mumbled words under her breath as the Fae spread his arms wide. There was a curved blade in his hand.

Another Fae came up to the dais, this one with long brown hair and a scar on his jaw. A stick was on fire in his pale hands. There were still two holding onto Elarie. This Fae had to move around one to get behind her while the shirtless one shouted something that made Elarie flinch.

He lifted a piece of her hair from the top of her head and used the curved blade to cut it off. This new Fae took it. The shirtless one held his hand under the long strands as the new Fae lit the hair aflame.

Elarie closed her eyes. The first tear fell.

They watched ash fall into the Fae's open hand, though that shouldn't have been possible. The burning stick was discarded once the task was completed and Elarie's mouth was forced open. The newest Fae held her jaw while the leader scraped the ash into her mouth. It was shut again, now with a hand over it.

The leader began speaking again.

Elarie watched the leading Fae drag the curved blade over the dirt coming through the cracks in the ground. It seemed like he was explaining something. His hand moved the way a tutor's would when explaining something complicated. And with the dirt he'd gotten on the blade, he dragged his thumb over it. It collected on his finger.

The Fae with the long hair forced her mouth open again and the leader wiped his thumb along the inside of her cheek and had her mouth shut once again.

"Elements," Jamison whispered. The kid was on the other side of the window, closer to the dais, and looking through a little hole in the glass. "Fire, earth... air," he said and they watched the Fae wave the blade around. The male held it under Elarie's nose as well, waiting for her to breathe on it. When she did he shouted the same words that made her flinch like the first time.

"This is why she hates the Fae," Calix breathed. He whispered, "'magic stealing bastards.' That's what she called them. They're going to take her magic."

Kaelum looked at the Fae in the temple. Many looked uncomfortable. A few children were crying. Most of their faces were passive, only watching and listening to the temple leader. He must've been an elder or someone highly respected in the community.

He had a clay bottle in his hand. The Fae broke the neck with the blade, splashing water over the dais. He turned to Elarie, saying something to her that caused her to squirm, but not fight. Kaelum expected more of the cursing and jerking around she'd been doing before. But she didn't fight any of them as the Fae thrust the bottle into her mouth. He had her head tilted back. She choked on it, but she did nothing.

Water soaked her front. The clay bottle was broken, discarded below her, and the Fae was moving around her. The male with the long hair got up and left. Her mouth no longer needed to be covered. Had she swallowed the dirt and ash?

The Fae leader stood behind her with her hair wrapped around his fist. He spoke reverently, imploring his people to listen. Elarie cried silently with blood now dropping down her chin from her lip. The curved blade was placed against her throat. She looked at Calix once again.

"Oh gods, she's going to kill everyone for this," he realized. He'd known her for a day and he could already read her? Or was the resolved expression something Kaelum should've seen as well?

The blade dragged across her throat, cutting deep and clean. Her blood sprayed over the ground. It hit a few people in the front row. Elarie choked and coughed. Her face turned white.

She was dead before the Fae dropped her.

Chapter Twelve

CALIX

"How is she supposed to come back?" Terry asked. They stood around Elarie, all staring and expecting her to wake. "It was quick with the Jiivers," he looked around at them. "So?"

Calix shrugged. "I assumed she'd just... wake up."

"Same," Kaelum sighed. It was dark out, the captain had expressed his annoyance that this was taking so long. He wanted to leave. Terry and he were planning where they were going next while they waited for the area to be clear of any murderous Fae. Kaelum knelt at her back and tilted his head. "What kind of plant is this?" He asked, "why didn't they use rope?"

He pulled out his short dagger and grabbed her arm. Calix moved to the ground. The parts of the ground that were still wet with her blood began to soak into his pants. Kaelum grunted and cursed. "What?" Calix asked without looking up.

"The shit tried to wrap around me," he said. He waved his hand through the air and inspected it further. "It's digging into her skin. Maybe it's some kind of magic thorn keeping her from coming back?"

Terry asked, "then how do we get it off? Did the dagger work?" He shook his head.

"We can peel it by hand," Jamison suggested nervously. "Maybe someone that doesn't have any magic ability should be the one to do it, just in case whatever it is can sense that sort of thing."

"I will," Terry stepped over her body and knelt next to Kaelum. "Shit," he said when he got a good look at it.

Calix touched her face. "She's still warm," he said, "how is she still warm?" He turned her chin and cringed at the deep cut across her throat. The blade had cut to the bone.

"Got it," Terry said. He pulled the thorns off of her with blood on his fingers and watched them shrink to a portable size. Terry looked at Elarie, then Calix. They made eye contact as he slipped the thorns into the small bag at his belt where he kept his spyglass. He buckled it shut.

Tearing his eyes away, Calix looked down at Elarie. Her eyes had cleared from the once foggy glasslike color they were before and the slash along her throat was gone. All that was left of it was a clean white line, and even that was difficult to see. As if it had healed and faded in a matter of seconds. He watched her blink. "Elarie?" Calix asked. He wasn't sure if touching her was the best idea, so he climbed down from the dais and tilted his head. "Elarie?" He asked again.

She stared at him for a moment, distant but able to tell it was Calix, before she gagged. Elarie coughed, gasping as she turned onto her stomach. Her body trembled. She grabbed her throat and pressed her forehead against the stone below her. Elarie heaved and spit dripped from her open mouth.

Calix looked at Kaelum and Terry, who were both still behind her. Jamison was off to the side with his dark eyes wide. He hadn't seen her come back before, as the three of them had on the ship. This was new for him.

When she relaxed she was still breathing heavily. Calix looked at the spit below her. She'd coughed up dirt. Some of what they made her swallow came back out of her, even some of the water. She closed her eyes and wrapped an arm around her stomach.

"Elarie?" Calix asked tentatively, "are you all right?"

She pushed herself onto her knees. Elarie's expression was blank. Empty. Her head turned slowly to where the noise of celebrating Fae was coming from. The village. They'd left after the temple leader had finished explaining something to crying children. He'd assured them somehow and after what felt like hours of it, they finally walked as a group back to their village. While Calix, Kaelum, Terry, and Jamison went into the temple, the sounds of a great party echoed down the hill toward them.

And now toward Elarie.

"Elarie, I need your help," Calix said. He wasn't at her level anymore, he was looking up at her. "Look at me, please, there's something wrong with Grey."

She slid off the dais and swayed, catching herself before she hit the ground. Elarie blinked rapidly as if she were struggling to adjust to the gravity of the world.

Calix got up, glancing at his friends. He stood at her side. "Elarie—"

"Wait," she said faintly.

"What?" His eyes widened, "no, he's been on the beach asleep all day you have to fix him. I know you can wake him—"

She looked at him. "Just wait," Elarie said. There were two things he could read behind her eyes. Pain and rage. Calix anticipated she'd choose between one of the two to feel in the next few moments, and it was likely to be rage.

"You don't have to kill anyone," he found himself saying. This must've been what Terisa meant. That *something* that would happen that he'd have to accept her for and ensure she 'stayed good.' But this was wrong. Killing people wasn't right, how was he supposed to accept that?

"Wait," she said once again before walking away from him. Elarie went down the aisle she'd been dragged down just hours before.

Calix followed, his friends coming right after him. "Elarie, please," he caught up with her quickly, "we can just go to the beach and Grey and it can be over."

"Over?" She snapped. When she turned around, a wave of heat blew toward them that made him step back. Only then did she hesitate. She calmed slightly. "I died *three times*, Your Highness, it's over when they've died, too."

He watched her walk away again. Three times? First on the beach, then in the woods where Jamison found too much blood for her to have survived, then again when they killed her on the dais. There was no way he'd be able to stop her from enacting her own form of justice, even if it was murder.

Elarie moved along the path. She wasn't quick, but Calix still had trouble keeping up with her as they climbed the hill. They were at the edge of the village. It seemed that everyone was at its center. Most of the homes were vacant and noiseless. Calix wasn't sure what time it was, but the moon was high and they were loud. Their joyous songs were lively, their chanting was too.

Until all the light in the village went out at once. Not even smoke singed in the air as it would have if the candles were blown out. Light just... disappeared. The Fae screamed, no longer in the celebratory, carefree mood as Elarie walked down the main path. When a Fae staggering drunkenly saw her he turned white. He fainted, knocking over a barrel that began to roll loudly down the path.

When Elarie passed a spot that once had light, the flame returned.

"Has she done this before?" Terry whispered. He was right next to Kaelum, Jamison next to him. "This has to have been planned."

Calix looked back at them and shook his head, mouthing for them to shut up. He couldn't think his way out, he couldn't argue his way out or prevent her from killing, but he could ensure that she didn't react negatively to the interruption.

The more Fae she passed the more light she returned until she was in the square. They were screaming, not chanting. Crying, not singing. Before, many of them had been passive or indifferent, but now they were terrified. Elarie stood silently, staring across a fire she hadn't lit at the temple leader who had slit her throat. He was just as pale as he had been on the dais, only now it seemed that he was shaking. Even from the distance they were at and the lack of light around them, Calix could see he was fighting a tremble.

Elarie spoke in their Fae language. She stepped forward, tilting her head at the male as she spoke. Calix was cursing himself for not trying to learn a faerie language when the thought first came to him. What if it had been this one he chose? Then he'd know what threat she was spouting at them.

"If I was forced to have an audience for my death," she said in Ceptareei. The male seemed to understand. "Then you shall have an audience for yours."

Walls of fire erupted behind the group of once happy Fae. They screamed, moving away from the heat. They pushed together, crying and shouting.

Elarie didn't care. She just wanted people to watch. Why had she said it in a language the humans understood? What was the point? She spoke again, casually and without feeling, while turning to the very humans she'd switched languages for. Elarie looked at Calix. There was no remorse on her face. She walked toward him. "We can still leave," he whispered, "it's not too late."

"The only way you would ever come close to understanding what I feel right now," she slid his sword out of its sheath, "is if it was Kaelum on that dais and not me. You, Terry, every pirate on that stupid ship would tear this village to pieces for him." Elarie stepped back. The sword hung loosely at her side. "But it's just me," tears formed in her eyes, "so I will tear apart what I see fit."

She pushed the tears away and threw the sword across the courtyard. A Fae dove for it—one of the four. The female held it with both of her hands. She hissed, rocking from one foot to the other in a fighting stance.

Did she stand a chance? Calix had never seen Elarie fight. Fae were supposed to be faster, stronger, and more agile, so maybe the female would put up a good fight. She'd lose, Calix knew that much. He could tell by the way Elarie was holding herself. The times that she'd died he was now sure she'd been caught off guard. She knew she'd win any fight thrown at her.

She walked toward the female and the female charged. She yelled as she did, the sword in position for a good clean swing. Her fangs were out and shining. Calix wouldn't want to face that. *That* was desperation. The female didn't want to die, but if she had to go she'd be fighting.

Elarie didn't even dodge. She just grabbed. Her hand wrapped around the female's slender throat. The sword fell when her palm turned red with a burn Elarie had given her. She'd thrown a sword down as bait.

The female scratched at her hand with unkempt nails, gagging and gasping while Elarie simply moved the hold she had...

And snapped.

Jamison joined the group of screaming Fae. Calix looked back. He was covering his mouth with both hands.

One of the other rescued simply walked toward her, resigned to his coming death. She moved past him and he dropped. It was the same way of dying as the bird. He simply died. What had she done to make it so? Elarie did it two more times. She was finished with the ones she'd been on Rol's ship with, she wanted the ones directly involved.

Two of them had heads facing the wrong way. One of them didn't have a face.

"I'm going to vomit," Jamison whispered when the Fae with the long hair—the one who forced her mouth open and closed—stumbled around blindly, flailing his arms in front of him screaming before Elarie killed him. "Gods, I'm going to—"

And he did. Calix cringed and looked away quickly. He walked forward, seeing Elarie stop and turn her head. She was looking right at him. Her eyes moved over him, resting on his own as he bent to retrieve his sword. They drifted and he straightened, holding the sword at his side while he looked at her. Elarie was in front of the leader. The Fae wasn't hiding the shaking now. He was alone, no one was going to defend him against her.

Elarie's hand went into the Fae's chest empty.

Her hand came out holding a heart.

Calix would have the sound of screaming forever seared into his eardrums.

She turned, throwing the warm heart up into the air and catching it again. Elarie sort of smiled at it before tossing it into the pyre. The flames came to life around it and the walls of fire were gone.

Chapter Thirteen

Calix

She kept rubbing her fingers together. Elarie was silent and she hardly looked where she was going. She didn't need to, though, because the same wave of heat Calix had felt before was in front of her. It pushed aside plants and burned away sticks so she didn't have to step over anything.

And she kept rubbing her fingers together. Blood dripped off her hand while she rubbed her fingers in it. Calix stared at her hand. He tripped a few times because he couldn't stop looking at it. Elarie could just burn it off of her, yet she was playing with it. The blood of someone whose heart she just ripped out.

They reached the sand where the camp used to be. The ship was in the distance waiting for them. And there was Grey. "Elarie," Calix stood next to her. "Can you fix him?" He asked, moving to be in her line of sight. She was facing Grey, but her eyes weren't looking at anything. "Elarie," he pressed, "fix him."

She focused on him for a moment. The rage he'd seen before was ebbing away. Her shoulders were getting heavier. Her lips pulled into a thin line, but she nodded and Calix managed to let out a deep breath as she walked around him. Elarie put her hands on Grey's snout and a flash of fire sparked over his large body. He snorted and thrashed. Elarie stepped back. Her shoulder hit Calix.

Grey shook his head around and scratched his scales. Elarie said something to him in the dragon language that made him stop. Grey looked at her. She spoke again, holding up the hand covered in drying blood. It sounded like she was explaining something to him as Grey bent his head and licked some of the blood away. Calix listened to her speak fluently. There were no breaks, he couldn't hear any hint of an accent. It was as if this beautiful, complex sounding language was her first, only he'd never heard it. A dragon language? Calix would know about something like that—something like that wouldn't fade from every history book.

Elarie's hand lit to flames for a few seconds and the blood burned away leaving only clean skin behind. She said something else in the dragon language, then said Calix's name. It sounded strange given the language—she didn't drop the smooth, warm tone when she spoke his name. It managed to flow with whatever she was saying, but it was still strange to hear.

Calix looked over at Kaelum and Terry. Jamison had walked down the beach toward the boat already. He was ready to leave, that was for certain. As was the captain and his first mate. Calix eased away from Elarie, backing up from behind her. She didn't move. He went down the beach and waited for the two pirates to follow. "I'm going to stay," he said when they did.

"Stay?" Kaelum hissed, "are you out of your mind?"

"She's not going to hurt me," Calix said, "and I think maybe I can get some information from her now while she's vulnerable." It wasn't a total lie, but it felt like one. Calix had no desire to interrogate Elarie while she was visibly distressed, even after everything she did. He might get a few good questions in, but he doubted he'd press. At least not when she was shaking the way she was.

Terry was shaking his head.

"Look, Grey might not even be able to fly right now and Elarie might not be able to be around other people," the prince argued further, "so we're staying. Can you get some clothes picked out for her? And I have some soap hidden in my knitting bag—"

Kaelum put a hand up to stop him. "You hid soap in your knitting bag?"

"Yes," Calix tried not to blush.

"Why? Wait, which soap?" The question was formed like a make-or-break in their years long relationship.

He said, "the lemon one."

Kaelum sort of gasped. It was a strangled sound in his throat. "The manly lemon? You've had that this whole time?"

Terry asked, "have you used it?" His nostrils flared like he was trying to smell Calix from the distance they were at.

"No, I didn't want you to give me shit for using it," he said.

Kaelum scoffed, "shit for using it..." He shook his head. "I'm taking a chunk of it and giving you shit for not sharing."

"All right, fine," Calix rubbed his brow. He glanced back at Elarie, who was still in the same shaking position that she had been in before. "Just," he faced the two of them again, "make sure Elarie has some."

Terry snorted, "she could use it."

"She could?" Calix asked before he could stop himself. He looked back at her again, then returned to their confused faces.

"You're too polite," muttered Kaelum, "the girl wreaks. We'll see you tomorrow, right?" He clasped Calix's arm. The prince nodded. "Right. Goodnight."

Calix moved back toward Elarie. "Row safe," he said. Kaelum threw a curse at him as they pushed the boat out. Calix watched them struggle against the incoming surf for a moment before he had to squint to see them. He turned to Elarie and stared. Calix breathed in deeply, only smelling the ocean and some fire. Like the fireplace in his mother's study. Could a person smell like that?

"Where do you think you will go when you die?" Elarie asked faintly. "What do you believe?"

He assumed this had to do with her dying and decided not to dwell on his answers if it meant getting some from her. "The after-life. I believe that is where we all go." He waited for her to elaborate and give a reason for asking, but she didn't. He asked, "is it?"

Elarie nodded slowly. "I see it when I die."

"Is it as beautiful as they say?" Calix questioned. He rocked his foot, looking from her to Grey. The dragon was silent. Watching. Calix took this as a sign he should be paying as much attention to her as he was.

Again, she nodded slowly. "It's a paradise. All... big trees and shade and paths to walk on," her brow furrowed. She sniffed, "Some sort of perfect for each sort of person." Elarie trailed off as she loosed a breath. "May I see your hand, Calix?" She asked. She faced him and not the dragon. Calix held it out for her and she took it in the clean, now bloodless one. "I won't hurt you," she told him.

"I know," he said.

Elarie brought his hand up to her throat, where she touched his fingers to the left side of the white scar. "If it is given," she whispered and dragged his fingers along the line, "so it will be." When she finished speaking, she was on the other side of the scar. Elarie then spoke in the Fae language.

"That was what he was saying?" Calix asked.

She nodded. A tear dropped down her cheek and she said, "Calix, I am a sacrifice. Like a pig or a goat, I am a sacrifice." Calix brushed his thumb over her neck. "It's happened three times in my lifetime." She pulled his hand down but still held it, seemingly trying to explain everything at once.

"You've never told anyone this before," he realized.

Elarie breathed a laugh, trying to brush it off. She wiped her face. "I can't," she started. Elarie looked away from him. "I don't want you to hate me or... or resent me for what I did in response to what was done to me."

"Tell me why you did it," he said, "and not like it was some revenge thing or because you were angry. I want to know *why*."

"What if I was just angry?" She asked. Elarie stared off toward the ocean behind him. "What if I just wanted to hurt someone?"

He took a step back from her. Elarie looked at him when he took his hand away. Calix raised his brows. "I don't think you were," he said.

She glanced at the dragon on her right. Grey only watched. He was confident in both of them, he knew they'd work through whatever was between them. This was a drama to him. Calix wondered if he'd seen Elarie this way with anyone else. A sibling or a parent or a friend.

Elarie took a step toward him that brought them to the same position as before. They were a little further away from the dragon now. He wasn't sure what the point of the closeness was, even if she wanted to take his hand again. He was sure, however, that she did not wreak. The fact that she didn't smell was clouding part of his mind even as she lifted his hand and placed it against her chest. Calix could feel her heart beat strongly beneath his touch.

"When I die," she said, "I am steps from paradise. I see it for only a moment before I am pulled back into my body by the gods." He felt her breathe in deeply, "but when I am sacrificed," she said, "I don't go there."

"Then where do you go?" Calix asked. He imagined her just remaining in her body and watching things pass before her eyes. Trapped.

She said, "I relive the moment every member of my family died. Over and over again until the faerthorne is taken off and I wake up."

He nodded, looking at his hand on her chest. "So you killed the Fae because of that?" Calix recognized it was traumatizing, but it didn't justify killing. She killed them, some even brutally.

Elarie swallowed, shifting closer. "You have a family," she whispered, "a beautiful, probably complicated family. What do you think you would do if you were ritually sacrificed and made to relive the memory of them dying again and again? You wouldn't be angry? Vengeful?"

"You ripped out someone's heart," Calix shook his head, "I understand your anger—or I want to, at least—but you taunted them and killed them and probably traumatized every child you forced to watch," he hesitated at his own words. Elarie let go of his hand and stepped back.

She was putting a wall up between them, Calix could practically see it. Elarie's lip shook, but she was visibly hardening herself to him. She was pushing it all down so he wouldn't see it.

"No, don't do that," he said, "Elarie, I want to understand but you can't fault me for my reaction." Calix touched her elbow, wrapping his hand gently around it to get her to look at him, "Elarie."

"I was a child," she whispered, her eyes burning intensely into him. "I was a child, I was a girl with people who loved me and dreams of weddings and love and I watched them die. Everything and everyone. And now I'm... I-I'm this angry person cursed by the gods that humans praise to be a sacrifice. I won't fault you for your reaction to me killing but you cannot fault me for doing it."

His eyes softened. "I am sorry, Elarie," he said. Calix watched shock float over her face. Grey hummed appreciatively and pushed Elarie into his chest. Calix didn't move as she put her head on his shoulder. He expected her to pull away, but she didn't. She just stood there, her warm breath heating his skin. Calix reached up and held her shoulder. "I'll try to understand."

Elarie tensed, her arms moving. When he put his head against hers he felt her hand on his side. It slid around and went to the middle of his back. Every movement was stiff, as if it were a struggle to wrap an arm around him. When she did, she let out a shaking breath and shuffled even closer. Calix stared at the sand below them, his brow furrowed. How difficult could it be for someone to be held? He moved his other hand to her shoulder, keeping both hands in a safe place. She put her other arm around him. Such a small thing that seemed to be a great feat. Elarie pressed her face into his neck and he felt the wetness of tears against his skin. "I have lived such a terrible life," she whispered.

His eyes darted back and forth. He lifted them to Grey. He hummed and a hot breath blew from his nostrils. He nodded his head. *Talk to her*, he seemed to say. Calix squeezed her shoulder. "I think it'll get better," he tried, "it already has, hasn't it?" She said nothing, though he could feel her eyelashes blink against him. He took that as a sign she was listening. "After all, you're safe. You have Grey back. You've made a friend."

"You're my friend? Truly?" She shifted, moving her head back. "Even after what I did to the Fae?"

"Are you going to do something like that again?" He asked.

She pulled her lower lip into her mouth to bite it, shrugging her shoulders slightly before saying, "probably."

Calix sighed. He looked at Grey. The dragon only nodded. "I suppose even then?" He looked at her. Elarie smirked a little before putting her face back where it had been before. "Even then," he mumbled. Gods, what was he getting himself into? Was this wrong? It didn't *feel* wrong, and yet his gut churned.

CHAPTER FOURTEEN

KAELUM

He breathed in the smell of the lemon soap while Terry poured cold water into a low basin. His first mate lit candles around it. "Don't you have a stash of that at home?" He asked, looking back. Terry smiled at him.

Kaelum brought the soap to the table full of maps and tools. He grabbed a sharp blade. "It's running low," he said with a smirk as he cut the soap in half. "I keep meaning to go to the castle to steal some, but..." he smelled it again. "Busy, busy." Kaelum walked to Terry. He was standing against the wall hovering over the basin. "I want to try something before we do anything," he said.

"What did you have in mind?" He wiggled his brows. Terry faced him while Kaelum went into his belt and opened the bag holding his spyglass. "Ah," he said, taking out the vine. His captain set the soap down. "You want me to prick you?"

Kaelum held his hand between them.

Terry took the hand and ran his thumb over the mark on his palm. "This is probably going to hurt very badly," he said. Terry adjusted his hold on the vine of thorns and positioned one over the edge of his hand. "Ready?" He looked at Kaelum, whose jaw was tight. He nodded. There was nothing slow or ceremonious about the way Terry stabbed Kaelum with the thorn, nor was there anything quiet about the shout of pain that burst from Kaelum.

Pain flooded from his hand. It engulfed him. Kaelum cursed, falling against the table the basin was on. His blood pumped in his ears. One of the candles toppled to the ground, its flame winking out. "Out!" He shouted and Terry yanked it free. Kaelum shrunk down, holding his shaking hand. Terry dropped the thorns and knelt in front of him.

"What can I do? Is there anything I can do?" He was asking, touching Kaelum's face.

Kaelum could still feel it. It soaked into his hand and made his fingers shake. "Holy gods," he breathed, "holy gods."

Terry cursed and got up, snatching a bottle of rum off the table and popping the cork. Kaelum took it gratefully, swallowing down gulp after gulp until his mind fogged over and his stomach protested. He set the bottle at his side, mouth open as he looked at Terry. "It's awful," he told him, "so terrible." He felt like crying. His body was numb, yet the pain was still there. Terry ran his thumb over Kaelum's cheek before reaching up to take the basin off the table. Some of the water spilled onto the floor and he set the basin in the small puddle. "And she had the whole thing..." he stared at the thorns, "it must've been agony."

His first mate only glanced at the thorns again before soaking a rag in the lukewarm water and lathering it in the soap. He set it on the lip of the basin. "Still hurts?" He asked gently, lifting Kaelum off the table leg to remove his jacket. Their faces were close. For a moment all Kaelum could do was look at him. Terry blushed under his gaze.

"You are so beautiful," he mumbled in his freshly drunken state. Terry played with the ties on his shirt while Kaelum stared numbly at his dark eyes. "There has never been a more beautiful person."

Terry chuckled. "I beg to differ."

Humming, Kaelum shook his head. He helped get his loose shirt off and sat up a bit, offering the rum to him. Terry took it, swallowing. Kaelum watched his throat bob. He leaned forward and kissed his windpipe. He breathed against Terry's soft, tan skin and kissed him again.

Terry held his jaw and brought Kaelum's mouth to his own, pressing a rum tasting kiss to his lips. Kaelum groaned, "I want to see you naked," in such a way that he was sure he wouldn't have said it before the alcohol. Like a fool in love. And while he was in love, Kaelum did not want to think of himself as a fool.

Chuckling, Terry pushed him back, shrugging off his jacket, then his shirt. Kaelum smiled at his sculpted body. All else melted away. Even the pain. Only Terry remained in his head. He reached out and ran his fingers down Terry's torso the way he liked so much. Terry took his arm, squeezing out the excess water before dragging the rough rag over his skin.

"Is the feeling mutual?" Kaelum asked. He hid the nerves, yet Terry seemed to find them anyway.

He moved closer, letting Kaelum's arm fall. He rested his hand against his pants. "Very much," he said, getting more of the manly lemon soap and rubbing it over Kaelum's chest. "Always," Terry scrubbed lightly at the small dark hairs on his chest. Kaelum moved his hand smoothly over the fabric, the friction sending them both into a spiral. Terry groaned and leaned in, pecking his jaw while the soap traveled downward. "I thought you wanted to bathe," he said, lips still against his skin. He pushed the soap under the waistband of his pants and the belt around it.

Kaelum cursed colorfully, dragging Terry's face to match his. "That can wait," he said before he kissed him. Kaelum pushed into him, ridding the soap from Terry's hand. He wasn't sure where it had gone, nor did he care. Kaelum held him with both hands, moaning as he lifted himself off the table and tipped Terry's head back.

"The soap was so important only minutes ago," Terry argued while allowing Kaelum to straddle him.

"You are the most important thing," he gasped. Kaelum pulled Terry's belt off. "And you will be for the rest of my life."

He mumbled, "drunken words," while also preparing to be rid of Kaelum's pants. "Aren't they meaningless?"

"Gods, you are my afterlife," Kaelum said, slowing to brush his nose against Terry's. This was what he loved. The single moment before everything went further. Kaelum was too close to Terry to truly see his eyes, but he knew what they were saying. He could feel what Terry wanted like their hearts were attached, twinned together by some sort of string.

"And you are mine," Terry replied. The drunken words were nowhere near meaningless. Not for either of them. "Kiss me, afterlife," he whispered. Kaelum did, slowly. He moved his right hand into Terry's pants.

Kaelum asked, "can we go to the bed?"

"Of course," Terry nodded. "Just kiss me first."

He laughed and tilted Terry's chin, now looking down at him. "Afterlife," he muttered, touching his thumb to Terry's lips even if the injury on his hand demanded he stop suddenly. He stroked Terry. Kaelum leaned down, wishing to devour him. Terry opened his mouth for it, accepting anything Kaelum did at any moment. The kissing lasted. And lasted. Terry wouldn't want it to stop. They'd get to the bed eventually.

CHAPTER FIFTEEN

ELARIE

It had been years since she'd woken up with someone. At first, she didn't know how to act. It seemed that neither did he, because he was just staring at her. Calix had a slight furrow to his brow. He wasn't really frowning, but it looked like it. "Morning," he said, his breath moving over her face. Elarie almost hated that it didn't stink as any other man's breath would. She smiled for him a little. "Sorry, my hand is kind of numb," he motioned.

"Sorry," Elarie sat up. She'd been lying on his forearm. When that had happened she wasn't sure. Elarie rubbed her crusty eyes while he flexed his hand and shook it.

"Wow, you have a lot of sand..." Calix reached forward and picked up her long hair. He waved it around and the sound of sand falling came from behind her. "How's mine?" He laughed. Elarie looked at him as he brushed his hand over his head and stretched. Silence formed between them. "What now?" He asked to clear it.

Elarie again rubbed her eyes. She breathed in slowly with her hands against her face. "I'd like to bathe. Use the... manly lemon soap?"

He cursed, "shit, you heard that?" Elarie nodded with a smile. "Gods, how embarrassing."

"You have a favorite soap?"

Calix nodded, "I do. Who doesn't?"

Greilor grunted and stood. He stretched like a cat before walking off. Elarie smiled as she watched him. Calix's words came back to her. That maybe her life might've been taking a turn for the better. She had Greilor. She had a friend.

She stared at the ship. Calix nudged her, "I'll be back." She nodded and laid back down as he stood up. The sky was a clear blue. Perfect. Like it had been when everything went wrong. There hadn't even been dragons in the sky, they were all in the nest waiting for her. Dragons didn't believe in birthdays, yet they knew that day had been the most important day for her. That day she became their queen, they were all there to celebrate.

Elarie recalled being told that they'd wait all day and night if they had to. They'd hunted enough food to last them the day and the hatchlings would be entertained. Mothers would hover over their eggs in the hopes that one or two would hatch to share the day.

She stood. Elarie walked down the beach. The memories always began with her walking up the hill, so she walked down the beach. It haunted her. *Hills* haunted her, how pathetic was she? Elarie stood on the wet sand. Ocean water kissed her toes as she stared at the blue. Her home had been on a cliff. She'd grown up by the ocean, flying over it, swimming in it, befriending water dragons. It used to be her comfort.

"Are we going to head back to the ship?" Calix asked as he walked toward her. Elarie looked back at him. He stopped at her side nervously. "Elarie?" He looked her up and down. "You're steaming."

Elarie looked at her feet and the wet sand. "Oh, sorry," she mumbled, stepping to the side. "It happens sometimes."

"Is everything all right?"

She nodded, changing the subject. "Yes, when Greilor comes back. He might eat first, I'm not sure, but he'll fly us to the ship, I'll use the manly lemon soap—" he interrupted with a laugh, "and I need to fly on my own."

Calix slid his hands into his pockets. "For how long?" He asked, jealousy and nervousness ringing in his tone.

"Until it stops," Elarie answered.

He looked her up and down, his Lathin eyes attempting to know everything about her in such a short amount of time. "What stops?"

"The flashbacks," she said quietly. Elarie wished she could look away from him, but she'd frozen in place. "The day it happened... I see it. Pieces. It doesn't usually take very long for it to stop, you don't have to worry about that."

"I'm not worried about you being gone for a long time," he shook his head, "I'm worried about you."

She looked away from him.

"Maybe talking about it would help?" He suggested.

Elarie shook her head slightly, "I need to scream." Before he could ask about it she said, "it's a release thing that I do." She held up a hand between them, "I have so much in me..." Elarie's brow furrowed at the faint orange glow shining under her skin.

Calix braved reaching for her hand. He held the tips of her fingers. "And you're a very angry person," he said, stepping closer. He held her arm next. Elarie stared at him while he traced his thumb over an orange vein. "You know I am not an angry person. We'd make a good pair, don't you think?" She saw him smile just a bit, hesitance and joking both gleaming on his face. "You can be angry for me and I can be calm for you," he closed her hand into a fist and placed his knuckles against hers.

"You just want me to tell you what happened," she said, pushing on his fist. He pushed back.

"Didn't you say that you would?" Calix met her eyes.

Elarie glanced in the direction Greilor had gone before saying, "I did. I just can't right now, I don't want to hurt you."

"I know you won't," he said, sounding like he wasn't going to pry for much longer. Elarie pulled her hand away from his, the color of her skin returning to normal. He let his hand fall to his side.

She moved past him and went to Greilor, feeling the prince following behind. Elarie brushed her hand over his scales as she made her way to his back and climbed on. A specific ache made its way into her heart as she waited for Calix to climb on after her. It was yet another reminder that Greilor was never hers and never would be. First it was her father, then her brother, and now Calix who kept a distance between them.

"How should I do this?" Calix asked, once again taking her from her mind.

Elarie led him to the best place to sit. "I'll keep you steady," she said, "we can just do this same thing as before until we can figure something else out."

"Sure," he said as he sat, legs extended. Elarie sat between them.

※

She didn't care about anyone staring at her but Terisa. The old woman's golden eyes bore sharply into her, causing a headache at the back of Elarie's mind. One she was determined to ignore. Terisa would want to talk about what happened, perhaps tell her of some new dream she'd had, but Elarie was desperate to distance herself from her. She was going mad.

Elarie walked up the steps to the quarterdeck in shoes that were a size too big for her. The boots scraped across the deck. "It does smell nice," she said to Calix, who pushed down a smile. "I'll be back, all right?"

"Take your time," he said with a nod before turning to Kaelum and the others easily. Kaelum's eyes followed her as she moved to the edge. The ship was moving quickly over the water, it splashed up toward her as she whistled for Greilor. He'd been hunting while she bathed.

"Elarie," Terry called. She turned. "Have you ever been to Moro Island?"

"Once," she answered, "why, are we going?"

Greilor roared in the distance. Terry said, "yes, just want to know if it's friendly enough for you. No Fae that will kill you."

Her eyes darkened as she climbed onto the railing. "Nothing but judgmental locals," she replied before dropping onto Greilor's wing. The wind pushed against her as she walked up to his back as she had before. The dragon moved away from the ship and she looked behind her, finding Calix looking right back. She'd have to teach him how to walk on wings, given the way he was looking at her. Elarie knelt on Greilor's back. She looked away from him.

They took off into the sky, the wind freeing the tension from her shoulders. Elarie waited until they were covered by clouds to collapse against Greilor.

It'll be all right, he moaned melancholically.

She sobbed.

You have a friend now! He reminded her. Greilor flew up to where the air was thin. *Tell him.*

No, not then. Not when everything was so close to boiling over. "I was going to see you," she told him, sitting up. Elarie crawled closer to his neck, saying, "I left breakfast early, mother was giving Danien and Ashter cake, and like a child I was upset." She swallowed thickly, her tears flying off her face, "so I was going to see you."

Were you on your way when it happened?

"No," she wrapped her arms around herself, "no, mother cut me off, she was so mean and I just wanted to escape everything."

Elarie recalled waking up with a need to see Matian. She had a plan. There had always been a plan for her birthday. Wake up. Breakfast. Spend time with her family. Wait and wait until the ceremony.

And yet she wanted to see Matian. She'd decided against wearing her morning dress because she wanted to wear his favorite shirt. Elarie had found herself leaving to see him. She found herself leaning against their tree on their hill with him. She had found herself on the grass with him over her. His mouth, his hands, his skin.

If she had stayed with her family, she'd be dead. If Elarie had done as she planned, she'd be dead.

And after years of wondering *why*, she'd discovered it was the gods' doing. They needed her to stay alive so they put him in her head. They did it. She was alive because they put him in her head.

Oh, how she wished she was dead.

Chapter Sixteen

Calix

There were more benefits to Moro Island than it seemed there previously had been. The fee to dock the ship was low, no questions asked. And the dragons. There were so many dragons. Calix moved next to Elarie, who walked at the front of the group headed for the docks. "You didn't tell me about the dragons," he said, reading the sign written in bold lettering 'Do Not Pet The Wildlife!' in one of six languages.

"Slipped my mind," she mumbled, watching one. They were small and feathered, cawing like birds with long, toothy beaks.

"Are you going to continue avoiding me for the rest of the trip?" Calix inquired, leaning into her. She didn't move away, at least. "I thought we could have lunch."

Again, she mumbled, "sure."

They were off the dock when he pulled her aside. Elarie tripped in the shoes that were too big for her, using him to catch herself before falling to the stone walkway. "Please stop whatever you're doing," he said, holding her elbow.

Elarie said, "I'm not doing anything."

"Yes, you are. I'm not stupid, Elarie, I can feel you avoiding me."
When he said it her eyes met his. It was the first time in days. "I
know that island was hard, I can't imagine how difficult it was for
you. And I don't know, maybe I went too far asking about what
happened to your family, but please stop whatever this is."

She looked away from him, her green eyes moving over the
green trees behind him and the ground below them. They darted
to where the main town started, where noises and smells floated
toward them. "I'm not good at this," she finally said. Her eyes met
his once again.

"Maybe not, but I am," he insisted, "and you're doing the friend
thing wrong."

Elarie glared at him, though it fell away as she accepted he was
right. She was terrible at being a friend. "So what do I do?"

"Tell me you don't want to talk about your family so we can
move on to talk about something else," he suggested, shrugging.
Calix let go of her arm. "Have lunch with me, maybe?"

She pursed her lips. He could see her biting on the inside of her
cheek. "I do not wish to talk about my family and I would like to
have lunch with you," she managed to get out. He smiled at how
difficult she made it before turning and facing the town. "I can tell
you about the dragons," she suggested as they walked.

"I would love that," he nodded. Calix again looked up and saw
one. Its features were white. It dove through the air for something
a seller had on a tray. The seller swatted at it, cursing it. They
moved further into town, where a lively sound began to play all
around them. The plucking of instruments, the soft voice of a man
standing in the middle of a band. He sang in another language,
serene pleasure on his face as he did.

Calix moved his hand into his pocket to fish out coin for them, but Elarie stopped him. "You have to wait for the song to finish if you want to give them money," she told him, motioning to a few people waiting with coin in their hands. "It's considered rude to do otherwise."

"Right," he said, taking his hand out of his pocket. They stopped to listen. "Do you like music?" Calix asked. He looked away from the band to Elarie, who was nudging one of the small dragons away from her with the toe of her boot. He whispered, "you aren't allowed to touch them."

She rolled her eyes. Elarie said, "he says hello."

"Hello," Calix greeted in kind. Elarie smiled brightly at him. It faded quickly when someone else said her name. It was in a questioning tone, shocked and unsure. Elarie looked around for it as her name was said again.

An older woman came into view. Grey streaked her fair, curly hair and wrinkles moved around her eyes like the feet of crows. She smiled. "Elarie," she said again. Elarie glanced at Calix. "You always said you'd look the same if we ever saw each other again," the woman said. She wasn't speaking Ceptareei, but Calix had no trouble with the language change. His father called it the language of the Dunes. Duness, his neighboring kingdom.

Elarie looked nervously at Calix once before allowing a smile to break over her nervous face. She spoke the Dune language, probably hoping that Calix didn't know what she was saying. "It's good to see you, Ave. I hope you aren't too shocked by it."

"Truthfully I didn't believe you before," the woman named Ave said. She reached out and touched Elarie's face. Her skin was smooth and clean, unlike this woman. "How long has it been?" Ave asked her faintly. "What I wouldn't give to look like this again."

"And what I wouldn't give to look like you," Elarie replied. She took Ave's hand and squeezed it. "Are you still with Trion?"

Nodding, Ave swallowed. "He's off on a beach somewhere. Damn locals, huh?" There was such longing on her face. Was it for Elarie specifically or for the youth she no longer possessed? A stretch of silence passed between them until she cleared her throat, seeming to be forcing herself out of whatever memory she'd trapped herself in. It had to do with Elarie, who stood nervously still holding Ave's hand. "And is this your newest human companion?" She nodded to Calix. "Didn't expect a man from you."

She laughed. Elarie shut her mouth quickly. "This is Calix, he's my friend. Calix is from Ceptari, he rides an Ancient."

"Ah, impressive," Ave said appreciatively. She looked at Calix, "I apologize I do not speak Ceptareei, but I hope Elarie expresses to you how grateful I am that she has found another person to ride with."

Calix opened his mouth to reply, though it got caught in his throat. "Sorry," he said in the Dune language. He looked from her to Elarie. "I never learned."

"It's all right," Elarie told him, "she's saying that you riding an Ancient is very impressive. They don't let people ride them often. This is Ave, she rides a Kretton."

He nodded, "I've studied those. Aren't they explosive?"

"Yes, that's why Ave wears armor spelled to keep her safe while riding," Elarie answered.

"That's amazing," he said to Ave, smiling pleasantly.

Ave was looking at Elarie. Her eyes were soft. Loving. Calix wondered what their story was—the one Elarie would lie about. They knew each other years ago, perhaps they loved one another. Ave had said companion. Human companion, which only reiterated

Elarie not being human. And she didn't age. That opened a few things up for him. He'd have to begin a timeline.

"I've missed you," Ave said, "I think of you often."

Elarie stared at her warily. She stepped forward, giving Ave the opportunity to wrap her arms around her in a tight embrace. Her arms loosened after a moment, but she still hung on. Elarie stood the way Calix imagined she did when they hugged. Stiff and with her hands placed awkwardly. Calix looked at the two of them. Visibly, the age difference made them out to look like mother and daughter. There had to be thirty years between them.

"You were the best thing to happen to me," Ave whispered. Her wrinkled hand moved into Elarie's hair and she brushed it down. "I was so heartbroken when you left."

"I'm sorry," he heard Elarie mumble.

Ave squeezed her once before pulling away. "I forgave you a long time ago, I hope you know that." Elarie nodded. "And I prayed to the gods you felt nothing but happiness since we parted. Tell me it's true?"

"So much happiness," Elarie blatantly lied. Still, Ave didn't take it as one. Instead, she beamed.

"I'm so glad I saw you here today," she said, again placing her hand on Elarie's cheek. It was clear that Ave loved Elarie once, and perhaps the feelings were mutual. Calix then tried to imagine Ave younger. Their age, not the age of their parents. His parents, at least. He'd never been one for age gaps, so he chose to see Ave as a young dragon rider before he attached any romance to the relationship.

"It was good to see you as well," Elarie replied, though her tone was far less loving and more clipped than Ave's. The rider didn't catch on. She looked at Calix, her eyes moving over his face. Elarie said, "I wouldn't tell Trion you found me, he might come looking."

Ave laughed, "yes, he would. Well..." she sighed. Her light brows crinkled. Ave kissed Elarie's cheek and turned to Calix, bringing him into a short hug. She placed her hand on his shoulder, her eyes shining with tears. "Take care of her," she said with a sad smile. Ave then clicked her tongue and embraced him again. Calix looked at Elarie with wide eyes. She seemed to distance herself once again just with a look. "She'll probably tell you I said something different than this, but," he felt her sigh before pulling away from her completely. "Don't let her run away from you."

She looked at Elarie one last time and, without a goodbye word, she left. Ave did not look back. Elarie stared until she lost sight of her, then turned to Calix. "She said goodbye," she lied easily, though her throat was tight.

"Long goodbye," he said.

Elarie nodded. She pushed hair behind her ear and ran her fingers through it nervously. "Lunch now?" She suggested, breathing in deeply.

Calix motioned, sure to put a few coins in the cup in front of the band as they passed. "So how do you know Ave?" Her words moved through him, flashing in his mind as if he'd only just processed them. *Don't let her run away from you*, Ave had said. So Elarie, probably years ago, had run. Without a goodbye most likely.

"She is the mother of a friend that passed away a few years ago," Elarie answered. Calix led her into an open pub that didn't look too busy despite the warm afternoon. They weaved through tables to the back, where he pulled out a chair for her at a table meant for four. "Well, more than a few," she said, "seven, I think."

She's such a good liar, he thought. What else could she have lied about without his knowledge? "Was the friend a dragon rider as well?"

Elarie looked out the window. There was no glass, only curtains that had been tied off to the side. A breeze came from the ocean, cooling them in the sun. "I don't want to talk about it," she said faintly. Elarie closed her eyes. She put her elbows on the table and covered her face. "I don't like thinking about my past."

How much of a past? Calix considered her in front of him. "What's your last name? Mine is Lathin."

"Crosha," she said into her hands.

"Elarie Crosha," he said. "Any middle names?"

She pushed her hands off her face and to the back of her neck. "Grace," she answered. Elarie smiled faintly. "And you?"

Calix leaned back in his chair, "I am Calix Orin Ezra Lathin the second, Prince of Ceptari, Heir to the Throne and all the titles."

Humming, she set one arm down and put the other against her cheek. "Orin Ezra," she said, "how nice."

"Don't you dare make fun of my name, Elarie Grace Crosha," he pointed at her, "it's not nice."

"I am not a nice person," she replied, "and friends tease, don't they?"

He smiled. Calix tapped on the table between them. She'd softened a bit since seeing Ave. He could see she was reliving the past she had no desire to speak of in the dark part of her mind. Calix had no desire to let her get trapped there. And now... he'd been tasked by a person from that past to ensure she didn't run. This made it two warnings he'd received about Elarie. The first from Terisa—accept her. And now Ave. Don't let her run.

So Elarie was a misunderstood murderer who ran from her problems and he was supposed to be the person who stopped her. Easy enough.

CHAPTER SEVENTEEN

ELARIE

He was trying to figure her out without asking questions she didn't want to answer. She resented him for it. Elarie watched him watch her, her head in her hand. A Pekgul Dragon landed on the sill of the window on her left. It crooned for her attention, yet it was still on Calix.

"Teach me something else in the dragon language?" He asked.

She blinked in shock, looking at the dragon. It relaxed and hummed, tucking in to watch. "Anything specific?" She asked, deciding to perk up. This would take her mind off Ave. Elarie had shared a few things with her, but not her favorite language. No language at all.

"Friend," he said with some strange *I know better* smile that sent a chill down her spine. She ignored it. Elarie folded her arms on the table. She didn't know what to do with them. All her nervous energy had decided to show itself at once and left her wanting to move. She was seated and couldn't get up until they were finished eating whatever food they ordered.

Elarie said, "*paentre*," and he nodded, considering the word in his mind. "Pa-ent-re," she sounded out.

"You are my paentre," Calix said.

"Téni al rinaet," she replied. Elarie watched the smile grow on his face for a moment before turning her head to the room around them. Being on the edge, she had a view of everyone. All the people eating seafood and drinking at a bar. There were two servers, both wearing aprons with stains on them.

One was making her way over. She smiled nicely, her lips painted a nice red color. She moved around the chairs and tables with the ease of experience. "Well hello," she said with a sigh, her voice deeper than expected. Elarie smiled. "My name is Lione, I'm in charge around here. Can I get you two something to drink?"

"Water, please," Elarie put her hands together on the table, twisting her fingers around while Calix asked for the same. He sat casually, as if he was at perfect ease with everything around him. She wondered how he felt about being served. If he thought this was comforting or different when compared to his normal life, one where a prince was waited on. She imagined he liked this much better. Not being known was better than the consequences of awareness.

"Perfect, now on the menu today you can get the shellfish platter, feeds two, and there's also a seafood boil chef's been perfecting," she said. "If you ask me it tastes the same as it did a few years ago, but everyone loves it. We also have a nice conch ceviche or some roasted eggplant. I'll give you two time to think on it while I get your drinks."

And she left. Elarie watched her go, seeing her move through swinging doors into the kitchen. Noise clanged around behind the doors and through a window she could see someone pushing plates through. "What do you think?" She asked Calix, watching the second server carry out a platter piled with different steaming shellfish.

"That looks delicious," Calix said, looking at the same thing she was. Elarie laughed faintly, facing him again. She brought one of her legs up on the seat and watched another little Pekgul land on the sill to her left. It sat the same way the other had. "They're adorable," he whispered.

"They can bite your eyes out of your skull," she replied, making him cringe. "Can't you?" Elarie cooed at them, clicking her tongue. They responded with a similar noise, one flapping his wings. "You are so strong, aren't you?"

Calix laughed at her. "Do you prefer the small ones or the big ones?" He asked, moving forward. He put his elbows on the table, looking at the dragons.

"I am not allowed to have a preference," she answered. Elarie said, "they all love me and I love all of them, that is just how it's supposed to be. And you?"

Loine returned, setting two brown cups down. "Pesky little things," she muttered about the dragons. "I'll need to remind you not to feed the wildlife." She straightened, shaking her head at the two dragons. "I have to keep my garden covered, they keep eating my snakes," she said as she rubbed her hands on her hips. "I keep thinking they're going to pick up my cat and carry her off, but that hasn't happened yet." Lione clicked her tongue and began to walk away. "Right, I forgot—food."

"We're going to share the platter," Calix smiled.

Lione eyed Elarie, raising a brow. Elarie looked from her to Calix. "What? Is that not all right?" Lione chuckled softly and walked away, calling out to the kitchen. Elarie's brow furrowed.

"I think she just wanted to confirm with you," Calix said gently.

Right. Elarie sighed and picked at a bit of dirt under her nail. She flicked it off to the floor, glancing up to find him staring at her. He said nothing and she was sure that he was still trying to work her out. Did he have a list of things to consider? Strength, smarts, death-defiance. He'd put them all in one place and try to pick through them to see what she was. Elarie decided to change the subject. She breathed in and asked, "when do you come of age?"

He blinked a few times. Calix cleared his throat and took a sip of water, sucking a bit of ice into his mouth. "This year," he answered with it tucked into his cheek. His dark brows had a tightness to them. It was a touchy subject, something to completely take his mind off her. "It's not that far away, actually."

"You turn twenty two, yes? And then there is a year of study?"

Again, Calix took a drink. He chewed on the ice, his Lathin eyes aimed out the window. "It's an honorary king sort of thing," he said. Calix said, "I come of age and spend a year working directly with my father and his council. I can work to build my own if I wish as well depending on how well I get along with them."

"Or don't get along," she suggested, "because isn't having a bit of an opposition to your own opinion beneficial?"

He nodded. "I hate thinking about this stuff."

"Does the prince not want to be king?" Elarie teased, raising a brow, "how stereotypical of you."

Calix rolled his eyes, "it's not that. I'd love to be king, I love my people, I love learning. It's just..."

"Greilor?" She tilted her head. He looked at her. "You know he'll burn down the roof of whatever tower your council meetings are in to get you out."

"I don't doubt that, actually," he admitted, "but I feel like after spending years doing this—" Calix motioned around vaguely. "Flying around the world, helping people. Going from this to sitting in a cramped room full of people who will constantly be telling me what I'm doing wrong is a big change. I don't know if I'm ready for that."

She nodded. "I'm sorry I don't know how to help with that, especially if it is inevitable."

"Shame, I thought you'd suggest something," he sighed, putting his arm on the back of the chair next to him. "Perhaps something extravagant. Impossible but fun to think about."

"Something to keep you out of a cramped room?" She asked. He nodded. Elarie looked at the small dragons watching them. "Build a nest and have all your meetings there. That way the council members you may or may not choose will have to be accepted by dragons—the best judges of character—and with the demands of dragons, the meetings will have to be short."

"I only have one dragon," he told her.

Elarie shrugged. "Where there's one..." Calix laughed again, shaking his head. "And you know you can help people from a cramped room," she said. His laughter softened. "Maybe you aren't fighting pirates on the open sea, maybe your sword gets turned to a quill, but," she pulled her water toward her, "there are still things that you have the power to do. You'll have more power than anyone, won't you?"

"I suppose," he sighed.

"I can see you being the king that gets it all done," she said. "Nest or no nest."

Calix said, "no, I'm seriously considering a nest for one dragon."

"If you want more than one dragon in a nest you just have to ask," Elarie said, quieting herself slightly. She shrunk in her chair and sipped her water.

He was staring at her as the platter was put down. It did not disrupt his eye contact, nor did Lione, who seemed to catch the seriousness of his expression and decide to set the platter on the table and leave. Elarie rolled up her sleeves innocently.

"Please tell me how you do it," he said as she picked up a crab leg.

"Do what?" She asked, snapping it.

He widened his eyes at her, leaning forward and hissing, "the dragons, don't mess with me about this!" He cleared his throat, "sorry. You just implied that you can bring dragons to my hypothetical nest, care to explain how you'd do that?"

"You're adorable, Calix," she smiled. He glared at her. Elarie chewed on the crab while he began picking through the platter. "There are far too many locals around to speak of dragons that way," she said, picking up a mussel. Elarie smelled it and put it back down, trading it for another crab leg. Calix took her mussel and sucked it down.

"Do the locals not like dragons? The island is full of them," he nodded to the small ones now begging Elarie for the food she did not want to eat. They wouldn't tell anyone if she shared.

"They don't like riders," she answered, dipping a shrimp into a sauce. "They believe that dragons should not be ruled or ridden. Having someone like me go around saying even something as small as," she lowered her voice to a whisper, "'I can speak to dragons,' is enough to get me thrown off the island. Once," she raised her voice slightly, though she was still quiet enough for him to have to lean over the table, "I had a few Pekguls following me around and I was accused of some sort of spellcraft."

His brow furrowed. Calix took a drink and swished the water around in his mouth. "Why?" He asked after swallowing. He ate another mussel.

"This matealn said I spelled my blood to attract them to me so I could control them," she ripped a chunk of lobster, again using the sauce.

"Bleeding?"

She shrugged, "insulting for a woman even if I don't have a monthly bleed." Calix stopped chewing. She raised her eyes to him, slowly turning them to a squint, "I hope you aren't about to say something sexist."

"You don't have a monthly bleeding?" He whispered.

"You do not mention such things at a table," she pointed an accusing finger at him. Sauce dripped onto the worn wooden table.

His mouth opened, then shut because it was full of food. "Sorry," he mumbled, looking away as he thought.

It was her mistake, really. She *should* bleed. She shouldn't have said that she didn't. Of course, Elarie could claim that it was because she was so malnourished, but that seemed like more work. A bigger lie to keep up with. So it became another one of the things he'd store in the back of his mind.

"Never mind," Calix said. "It's not my place."

Elarie sucked on her fingers and continued eating.

CHAPTER EIGHTEEN

KAELUM

"We have to find Elarie!" Kaelum shouted, his voice cracking as he gripped his left wrist. Terry, bless Terry, was trying to hold him still while he wrapped Kaelum's hand in a shirt.

"I know that," he said in the calmest voice he could manage. "I know, I know, but we can't go out there if your hand is glowing."

"I don't care—" he started to stand.

Terry shoved him back onto the bed and went for his bag, grabbing yet another shirt. The shining white light was bleeding through the fabric. "You heard what she said on the beach, you could die if someone sees this shit so you are going to sit there and let me wrap it."

He cursed. And cursed. Kaelum felt tears in his eyes. He had sweat on his brow. It had gotten to the point where he just wanted to scream at the top of his lungs when a knock sounded at the door. Terry got up. Kaelum stared at his hand. "Is everything all right?" Jamison's kind voice came through.

"Have you seen Elarie?" Terry asked rather than answer the question. The answer was no. Nothing was all right. Everything was terrible. His hand was glowing. Kaelum was far from all right.

Jamison said, "last I saw she was headed toward the beach with Calix. Look, I can hear you down the hall, what's happening?"

"We just need to get to Elarie," Terry said tightly. Kaelum stood, stuffing his wrapped-up hand under his arm. He gasped in pain, his entire left side reacting with a violent wave as he walked to the door. He fell against Terry before shoving it open.

"I can't wait anymore," he managed. Kaelum's throat was raw. He had to be dying. Perhaps his hand glowing meant he was dying. He stumbled down the hall until Terry put his arm around him. "Nice walk on the beach," he gasped, "in the moonlight. How romantic, huh?"

Terry managed to chuckle, but he was too worried. They got down the stairs and Jamison jogged to Kaelum's other side. "Can I help?" He asked.

"You can lead us to Elarie," Terry told him. Jamison pushed the door open and held it for them. The street wasn't too busy, but people still looked over at the three of them. Elarie had been right, they were judgmental locals. They stared. Kaelum tried to tuck his arm in further and felt Terry pull his jacket over it. He was going crosseyed. "It'll be all right, she'll fix whatever it is," Terry mumbled, probably to himself. "She'll fix it."

"Is this the magic she was talking about?" Jamison asked in a quiet voice.

"Seems that way," Terry said. He grunted, now dragging Kaelum because his legs weren't working. Were they there at all?

He said, "it's like the thorn, like a thousand thousand thorns... I can't feel anything else."

"I have no idea what you just said," Terry told him. Kaelum whined, seeing the blurred sand of the beach.

"It's not far," Jamison said. He was a little ways ahead, leading with the bouncing nerves of a kid given too much responsibility.

The walk was endless. Terry was speaking to him, but Kaelum couldn't hear it. He must've been in and out of consciousness, otherwise the pain was turning his vision black. It wasn't until he was slapped in the face with a warm hand that it returned. Elarie was looking at him like he was a sick dog. And yet she hit him? How wrong was that?

"You need to concentrate," she told him plainly, "are you listening?"

"That hurt," he mumbled.

"Excellent," was her reply. "Now come here." Elarie bent and wrapped her arm around his legs. She lifted him into the air and began to walk. "The first time is always the hardest," she said.

How was she doing this?

She set him on the firm, wet sand. Elarie lowered the both of them to their knees. "Kaelum, look at me," she placed her hand on his face, the other on his upper arm. He met her eyes. The moon allowed a bit of light to brighten the area. Or it might've been his hand. "Do you know what Metar means?"

"No, just make this stop," he breathed.

"It means 'Maker of Stars,'" she said. Elarie's warm hand brushed over his cheek. Despite his sweating, it was comforting. "You are making a star."

His eyes widened. "A *what*?"

"A star, I thought you were listening," Elarie shook her head at him. "You need to focus otherwise this will continue. So listen to me." He swallowed and nodded. Kaelum took a deep breath, seeing a glow behind her eyes. What was she doing to him? "Good, now I am going to unwrap your hand. It will be very bright, it will be frightening, but you need to stay focused."

"What do I do?" He asked, looking from her to his hand.

"Relax your hand completely. You were probably stressed when you made it, stress or agitation was probably the cause, so you need to relax. I can explain everything clearly when this is over, I promise."

He nodded, "relax. Relax, right sure." Kaelum watched her pull the first shirt off. The white light got significantly brighter. Calling it a star seemed to be a proper name for it.

"It's all right," Elarie whispered. She flattened his hand, holding it with both of hers. Red shined in circles around it. It was a calming sight, almost. It moved like paint through water. Its heat brushed his skin, but concentrated around the light. "Relax."

Kaelum grunted, shaking. He focused on one body part at a time, releasing the tension from one place after the other. His legs. His stomach. He forced the tight knots of nerves to begin to unravel. At his chest, he breathed in. His shoulders. His upper arms. Slowly, he worked on his mind, focusing on what Elarie said—it's all right. She'd explain everything after.

And finally, his hands. One after the other.

The excruciating pain began to fade. It was slow. Kaelum watched the bright light ebb until it was only Elarie's magic that was around his hand. She lifted it, revealing a rock in his palm.

"A rock," he said.

Elarie picked it up delicately. It steamed at her touch. "It's magic, Kaelum," she said, "you created raw, pure magic."

"Great," he breathed, "now how do I never do that again?"

She looked at him with such disappointment in her gaze he almost felt guilty for not wanting to be in pain.

CHAPTER NINETEEN

KAELUM

The star was like any other black rock. Black. Rough. Boring. Kaelum turned it over in his right hand, the left stuck in a bowl of ice that balanced on the arm of the chair he was sitting in. This had come out of his hand. His *hand*. Kaelum compared it to the size of his palm. If he closed his fist he could barely see it. The rock fit perfectly in his hand, as if it were built for him. Kaelum tossed it up and caught it, feeling the absence of it the moment it was in the air.

Terry walked over with a brown cup. "Rum," he said.

"Don't drink too much," Elarie mumbled from the opposite wall. She was picking off bites of the bread neither he nor Terry had eaten with their dinner. Kaelum took the cup, swallowing half of it, and watched Calix take a piece of the bread she was holding. He sat in the chair she had her foot propped up on while she leaned. "What happened to stress you enough to create the star?"

The door opened. Jamison and Lester. The only people Kaelum trusted, all in one room to hear a great tale of magical explanation.

"Is the answer to that question necessary for this discussion?" Kaelum asked, taking another swallow. He pursed his lips against the burn of shit alcohol.

"Knowing what caused it is beneficial for the further prevention of creation," she said as she got off the wall. She put the rest of the bread in Calix's hand and walked toward Kaelum. "However, if it makes you that uncomfortable to share with your closest friends, then you don't have to say anything." Elarie lifted his freezing hand out of the ice.

Kaelum said bluntly, "you feel like a fever."

"So many people have said that I'm beginning to take it as a compliment," she muttered, inspecting the black mark on his palm. It stung as she touched it.

"Do people call you a lot of names, then?" He inquired.

Elarie took the bowl away and flicked water in his face. "Plenty," she said. Calix took the ice from her and set it on the table. He gave a piece of bread to her. Kaelum cringed and looked up at Terry, who stood on his right side with a similar look on his face. "Your hand will be fine if it isn't already."

"Just numb," he mumbled, swinging it around and flinging water to the floor. "So..." he put the cup between his legs and held up the rock. "This is magic?"

She took it from him. Elarie held the rock in two fingers and turned it slowly. "Anyone could do anything with this. Jamison," she handed it to him. Jamison blushed as he took it. "Where is Greilor?"

The rock began to shine. "He's on the other side of the island," Jamison said. He stared at the rock, "digging a hole in the sand. It would take a day to get there, maybe two depending on which path you take."

"Digging a hole," Elarie repeated quietly. She took the rock back, "why would he be digging a hole?"

Terry suggested, "maybe he's burying something. Continue talking about the magic, the dragon is fine."

"Wait, is he not fine?" Calix asked. Elarie moved around both him and Lester to get to the window. She pushed the shutters open, then the window, and stuck her hand out. "Elarie could there be something wrong with him?" She began to mutter to herself in another language. Elarie pulled her hand back into the small room and put it to her cheek. "*Elarie*," Calix urged.

She shook her head in thought, touching the back of her hand to her other cheek, and looked toward the beach in the far distance. Kaelum and Terry's room faced the trees and a mountain. Wherever Grey was she wouldn't be able to see him from where they were.

"Can you at least mumble in Ceptareei?" Calix asked, exasperated. Kaelum glanced up at Terry. Complete displeasure covered his face. Terry obviously didn't like Elarie and seeing Calix get so close to her so quickly upset him.

"Can we get back to the main topic of discussion?" Terry countered. "Elarie, you're supposed to be helping Kaelum."

Elarie didn't acknowledge Terry. Instead, she mumbled, "he has to be practicing. Has he done this before?" Her lips hardly moved. She walked away from the window. "Obviously we aren't supposed to know. No one can tell him we know."

"Elarie," Calix deadpanned. She tossed the rock back to Kaelum, still lost in thought. Calix said her name again, standing this time. "Elarie I know you can hear me. If something is wrong with Grey I should know."

"Nothing is wrong with him," she said, her eyes distant. She put her hands on her hips. Kaelum again looked at Terry, who was even more displeased than before. "I can't remember... and if I can't remember the answer is no, gods know I'd remember..."

Calix breathed in deeply. He closed his eyes, counting in his head. He did it when he was annoyed with his siblings—and Kaelum. "Elarie, please."

"It's not time yet, so he's practicing. He knows what to do, no doubt about that. He must be nervous."

"Oh my gods," Calix pinched the bridge of his nose. Kaelum snorted. If he wasn't going to get answers, at least he'd be entertained. An annoyed Calix was always a sight to see. He was usually patient. He was trying to be now. "*Elarie.*"

She turned to Calix and said, "he is practicing nesting."

"Nesting," the prince repeated.

Elarie nodded.

"Nesting?"

She placed her hands on the sides of his confused, annoyed face. "Calix, your dragon is going to lay eggs soon."

Calix said, "he's a male."

"He's a Great Dragon, matealn, do you know nothing about them?" She asked. Calix reached up and took hold of her wrists, slowly pulling them away. "We have much to discuss," Elarie shook her head as if his shock was shameful. She pulled her arms away from him and turned around. Calix was staring at the back of her head, his eyes wide and his mouth open.

"Are you going to talk about what we're all here for now?" Terry asked.

She looked at him. "Kaelum has been given the power of a god. If he does not learn to properly control the magic within him people will die, which is why I am going to help him. He'll have to make another star before he can harness the magic. Ideally, this would be done in a safe space so try not to stress him out any more than usual."

"What do we do with this?" Kaelum asked, holding up the star.

"Don't lose it," she suggested, "and don't let anyone else use it."

He looked at the rock, at Jamison, at Lester, then at Calix. Kaelum made eye contact with Elarie as he held it out for Terry. Terry took it silently, sliding it into his pocket.

"I don't give a shit which one of you has it, but what a lovely display of trust," Elarie rolled her eyes. "Goodnight," she finalized by grabbing the neck of Calix's shirt and dragging him to the door. Kaelum caught Calix looking back and mouthing a quick *what?* as they left the room.

"That wasn't very enlightening," Lester said as he followed them, "I'm going to bed."

"Same," Jamison mumbled.

Terry waited for the door to shut, then a few moments longer, before asking, "are you going to say yes?"

"Of course I'm going to say yes," Kaelum replied. He got up and wrapped his right arm around Terry's neck. "Did you think I'd say no?"

"I think that when I told you I wanted to marry you you freaked on me and created a magic star," he said. Terry slid his hand over Kaelum's hip, "so maybe that stress was you thinking 'how am I going to tell him no?' and not what I want you to say."

Kaelum kissed him slowly and put his head against Terry's. "I want to marry you, too, Terry. Eventually."

Chuckling, Terry hugged him. He buried his face in Kaelum's neck. "Did you see them interacting?" He asked. How very 'Terry' of Terry, to get the answer he wanted and switch to the next subject he wished to discuss. "It's been less than a week and they're sharing food."

"I don't think we can stop them from that," Kaelum said. "Can we make it a tomorrow problem?"

He hummed, "I suppose."

"Great," Kaelum kissed his head and pulled away. He took a few steps before he dropped onto the bed and closed his eyes. "Tell me about all the things we need to get before we ship out so I can fall asleep."

He heard Terry laugh.

CHAPTER TWENTY

There was something wrong with her.

Very wrong.

Calix listened to the sound of her soft breaths coming from the chair in the corner of his room thinking that there must've been something wrong with her. More than the usual. She'd pulled him out of Kaelum's room after a strange conversation and while he thought she was going to explain everything to him, Elarie sat in the chair and started trying not to cry. She'd fallen asleep after he asked her to stay.

Mixed with her breathing, he could hear birds beginning to wake. Maybe the little dragons as well. Calix turned his head and lifted it, seeing Elarie with her legs folded and her face pressed against her arm. Her mouth was open. She might've been drooling. The blanket he'd put over her had fallen to her knees.

He sat up and rubbed his face, making the bed creak. Elarie didn't stir. Calix inhaled deeply and grabbed his prosthetic off the ground, throwing his legs over. He rolled his pant leg up, plans to build a nest moving through his mind as he did. How did one go about *building* a nest? He'd studied them, of course. When Grey first found him Calix had done research on common places dragons of his size spent their time living in. His conclusion had been caves, mountains, and the sides of cliffs. Of course, Grey slept on the side of a cliff, just not in a covered, enclosed area.

So would Calix have to build or dig? He looked at Elarie as he buckled the prosthetic to his leg. She'd know, he had no doubt about that. And he believed she'd share the information she had, she wouldn't keep it over him, it would probably just take time. Time, which she had plenty of.

As he stood, Calix made a point of trying not to wake her. He stepped quietly around her and went to relieve himself. Upon re-turning, she was in the same position. Calix watched her while walking to the basin of lukewarm water sitting on the long table. A mirror was next to it, rusted on the edges. He rubbed his jaw, scratching the forming scruff.

How was he going to convince his father to let him build a nest? Where would they put it? In Grey's field? Under it? Over it? Calix brought water to his face and ran it into his hair, then looked at Elarie.

"Wake up," he whispered. "I want to talk to you, wake up."

She did not.

Calix walked toward her, bending over. Light from the window touched her hairline. The curtains had been drawn shut, but just the sliver had peeked through. It covered her hair like a crown. From the way she was lying, sitting up with her knees against the arm of the chair, her hand was bathed in it as well. Calix looked at her fingertips, counting small scars from anything from knives to teeth. The marks were on her wrists as well, and some were on her face.

"Elarie," he whispered again. She opened her eyes wide and shoved him. Calix stumbled back a step, catching himself on the footboard of his bed. "Sorry," he rubbed his chest. "I'll never do that again."

She put her feet on the floor, breathing a little heavily, "stand over me while I'm sleeping or wake me up while being that close to me?"

"Both?" Calix sighed, rolling his shoulders. "Gods, you are so strong."

Elarie rubbed her eyes, "you deserve it. You can't just do something like that. What did you think I was going to do, smile?"

He sat down. "Not shove me with your inhuman strength," he suggested. Elarie sneered as she stood, walking away. "I was hoping you would tell me about Grey now," he called as she went to the other room. He played with where his pants rested on his leg. "You know... because you didn't last night."

It took a moment for her to respond. Elarie came out and went to the basin of water as he had, not looking at him as she rinsed her hands. "You know that Great Dragons were the first to be created, yes?" She asked, running her fingers through her hair. He nodded, though wasn't sure if she saw it. Still, she continued, "well they were created with the ability to reproduce without the need for another partner. A male dragon can lay eggs same as a female and they can fertilize them on their own."

"If they can do that why are they going extinct?" He asked. Calix watched her walk without speaking back to her chair. She moved her hair over her shoulder and began braiding.

"Because their eggs are difficult to care for and humans are evil," she answered. He nodded. Elarie smiled just a bit before saying, "a Great Dragon's egg clutch is usually three or four and it's not uncommon for only one or two to actually hatch. Their parents have to take care of them in ways that most other dragons don't have to."

Calix adjusted to face her, "what, can they not leave their nest?"

"They have to be laid on their parents fire and that fire cannot go out," she told him. Elarie leaned forward, putting her elbows on her knees, "this means that the parent dragon—Greilor, for example—would have to find a safe place to lay, light his nest on fire, sit on it for however long it may take him to lay his clutch, and ensure that his fire is always lit."

"So he can't leave," he repeated.

"He can, but only for short periods of time and it's difficult to know how long that may be. Great Dragons that aren't prepared to be parents can either die of starvation or dehydration or kill their eggs if they are out for too long."

Calix asked, "do you think Grey can do it?"

"Of course I do and you need to as well," she said, "we have to have full confidence in him."

"Why would he be nesting now?"

Elarie's eyes moved. She had her theories. She laced her fingers together and began scratching her skin. "I don't know," she said. Elarie shrugged one shoulder, "maybe he's finally ready to be a parent."

He squinted at her. Elarie pulled her lips into her mouth then popped them. She stood. "Come on, we need to check on Kaelum."

Calix rolled his eyes at her evasion, but stood. "Will you go into more detail about the magic with him?"

"Not now, my head is splitting," she replied. "When are we leaving?" Elarie walked across the creaking floor while Calix grabbed the bag he'd brought. He pulled it over his shoulder, holding his jacket in his hand.

"We'll have to ask Kaelum and Terry," he said as he walked through the door she held open for him. It shut behind her. "I'm only here for the adventure."

Elarie smirked, watching him lock the door. "Some adventure, hmm?"

"Oh yes," they made their way down the wide hall. Each of the doors was occupied by one or more members of the crew. Most would sleep in because Kaelum didn't give a set time they'd be sailing off, so they'd wait until the last minute. "The dragon girl telling me all the things I'm doing wrong has been such an adventure. The best part, I'd say."

Her brow furrowed, "I'm not telling you everything you're doing wrong."

Calix hummed, knocking on Kaelum's door. A curse came from inside, then the sound of someone falling out of bed. Elarie leaned on the doorframe opposite Calix while they waited for whoever it was to lumber to the door. Terry appeared, his dark hair a mess, shirt off and pants loose around his waist. "Oh it's you," he said, his breath a little heavy. He scratched his stomach and yawned. Terry looked at Elarie, "What do you want?"

"I'm here to check on Kaelum," she said, crossing her arms.

"He's fine," Terry said, "is that all?"

She asked, "where's the star?"

"I ate it," he lied, "is that all?"

Elarie smiled, "sure." She straightened and grabbed Calix's hand. "Goodbye."

Calix pulled her back before she could drag him down the hall again. She stumbled a bit, squeezing his hand tight. He asked, "when are we setting sail?"

Terry's mouth opened. His dark eyes moved from Calix to Elarie. They rested on their hands, which were still locked together. Calix had the sudden urge to pull away from Elarie, like holding hands was too much too soon. Like some childish part of his mind was arguing that they just met, boys and girls that just met shouldn't hold hands so soon. Terry seemed to share that feeling.

"This afternoon," they heard Kaelum say. He padded over and opened the door, the sheet of his bed around his waist. "And I feel much better than last night, thank you for asking."

Elarie let go of Calix to grab Kaelum's left hand. She ran her thumb over the black line on his palm. "You should be fine," she said.

"Then why show up so early to check?" Terry asked.

"I had a nightmare," she answered, dropping Kaelum's hand.

He asked, "and your nightmares lead you to investigate things that don't need investigating?" Kaelum looked at his hand. He squeezed it into a fist.

"One can never be sure if it's a message from the gods or a false worry," she took a step back from the door. "My dragon dreams mean something, why shouldn't you getting your hand cut off mean something?"

His eyes widened, "who cut off my hand?"

Elarie shrugged. She said, "it was just a nightmare, no need to investigate."

Calix said, "and on that happy note," which brought Kaelum out of the shock he was burrowing himself into. Terry, on the other hand, just looked pissed. Calix used to think that was just his rested face. That he constantly looked pissed because that was when he was relaxed. "Have a nice morning," Calix squeezed Elarie's hand and pulled her down the hall. She laughed softly as they turned the corner to the stairs. "Did you really have a nightmare about Kaelum getting his hand cut off?"

She said, "no. Although, I did have a dream about you being overwhelmed by three dragon hatchlings."

"How so?" They walked down the stairs, releasing each other's hands when they got to the door. The sound of crowing dragons echoed down the relatively empty streets.

Elarie said, "well your hair was singed on one side, you weren't wearing a shirt, and you had ash all over you. One was asleep in your arms and another was trying to sit on your head while the third was chewing on your wooden leg."

"How kind of them," Calix said, following Elarie. She walked down the street, turned around to face him, and pointed in the direction of a cart vendor setting up for the morning market. "Sure," he nodded. Elarie grinned, bouncing once before speeding up to get to the cart. Calix dug through his bag to get out his coin pouch. He heard her ask what coin they took.

"Any and all," the man said, "just give me one moment." He was old, his hair grey and his light skin weathered. The man bent slowly to pick up a crate, though he lifted it with ease. Elarie had her hands behind her back, inspecting what was on the short table and in the cart. "All the baked goods are fresh," he said. In the crate were glass bottles of something clear. They were small and hand-sized. "And these," he pat the crate, "are said to bring eternal youth. Beauty like you might like to purchase some."

Elarie laughed, picking up a small loaf of crispy bread. "Do you take your product?" She asked.

The old man set dried meat in the shade. Elarie took a few pieces of that as well. She found cheese next. "No, no," he said, "I want to die. To be eternally young sounds horrible."

She looked at Calix. "Right, how much would that be?"

"Ceptari? Six of the small ones. I collect 'em in a jar." He smiled. The old man looked at Elarie, "you two on the ship with the dragon flag?" She nodded, having a mouthful of cheese to chew on. Calix set six of his smallest coins into the man's open hands. "Staying over at Hallo's?" Again, she nodded.

Calix looked from the man to Elarie. He stepped closer to her and took some of the bread off the loaf. The man did not look away from Elarie.

"How long you staying for?" He questioned.

Calix answered, "we leave today."

"So soon? You only just got here," he said. Calix recalled Elarie saying the locals were judgmental, but this one was beginning to be far too friendly. At least for Calix's taste. "Tell you what, before you go why don't you come down to my shop, just down this road," he pointed to his right. It was the direction Calix and Elarie had been headed. Down to the beach. "I got bread, flowers, you name it. Maybe you'd like to find a souvenir, eh?"

"That would be lovely," Calix said. He put his arm around Elarie's waist and pushed her just a little, "we'll see if we can stop by before we cast off."

"Have a nice day," Elarie said with food in her mouth. The old man bowed his head with a smile, though he didn't give one to Calix. Calix pushed Elarie some more, getting her to walk. Once they were out of earshot she said, "I think he was just being friendly."

"Maybe so," Calix said. He transferred his arm from her waist to her shoulders, still keeping her close to him. She sighed. "I'm sure you can handle overly friendly old men," he said.

Elarie smiled, "I can, thanks for noticing." She ripped the cheese in two and handed one half to Calix. He smelled it. It was soft cheese, covered in a layer of wax. Elarie was biting the cheese, bread, and piece of meat in order. He decided to do the same. "What do you think about being a parent?" Elarie asked him.

"What, now? At the young age of twenty one?" He asked, laughing a little. "I suppose I'll have to have at least one child within the next two years to start a line of heirs. Still, right now the thought only brings dread."

"Part of your year of study is a year of courting, isn't it?"

He nodded. They moved out of the way of a horse-drawn carriage, the driver giving them a dirty look. Calix said, "I have options. Ladies of my court. A princess of Duness will be eighteen and eligible next year."

"You're going to court an eighteen year old?" She cringed.

"No, she's just one of my options," he said. The buildings thinned and sand began to fill the street. Calix listened to the sound of crashing waves. "Why? What brings up parenting?"

Elarie said, "I was leading in to talk about dragons."

"Being a parent to dragons?"

"Absolutely," she said, stopping once they were on the beach. Elarie slipped out from under his arm and took his jacket from his hand. "Greilor will expect his rider to be there for his children."

He said, "I don't doubt that, but *parent* dragons?"

Elarie laughed. She spread the jacket onto the sand and put their food down, sitting next to it. Elarie moved her braid off her shoulder and he lowered himself to the ground. "Think of it like being an uncle."

"My siblings are both children, I've never been an uncle," he said.

She gave him an incredulous look, "you've never read a book with an uncle in it? Imagined what sort of uncle you'd be?" He shrugged. Had he? "I thought you were more creative than that."

"Excuse me," he pointed a finger, "I do not have to be creative. I only have to purchase and consume other people's creativity."

Elarie laughed and nodded, "fine, you've got me there." She bit off a piece of the dried meat. "Then can you imagine being a babysitter?"

"Oh, that I can do," he took a piece of bread, speaking again with it in his mouth, "I do have children for siblings."

"I remember that," she smiled, her eyes drifting to the sea. "I used to hate it, now I wish I hadn't complained about it so much."

"You had two younger siblings, yes?" He asked. Elarie nodded slowly.

She said, "Ashter and Danien. I resented both of them when I was younger for the love my mother gave them. Especially Danien because he was the youngest. My mother's joy. And I loved him, truly," she glanced at Calix and continued, "but it was like they could do no wrong. It changed when I got older, you know... I came to realize that they did nothing to me, that it was all my mother and to place blame on them wasn't what I should've been doing."

"So you babysat more after that?" He asked, trying to lighten her mood.

"Well, Ashter found his wings and Danien was far more interested in dragons than he had been before, so of course," she smiled teasingly, swaying toward him. Elarie took another bite and looked away again.

Calix asked, "do you think they know it?"

"What?" Her eyes moved, her head didn't. Calix couldn't tell if she was looking at him or not.

"In the afterlife, do you think they know?" He elaborated. Calix leaned forward to get a better look at her. "Do you think they're watching over you?"

Elarie flinched. "I hope not," she said quietly, "I can't imagine what they'd think of me now."

"Maybe they'd see a survivor," he suggested.

She said, "or a murderer," and looked at him, "like you."

"Maybe," he mumbled. Calix placed his attention on the food, taking one of the pieces of dried meat to rip off a bite. He popped it in his mouth. "But maybe they understand you the way you haven't let me yet. And that means their perspective of what you do is different from mine."

"Your perspective," Elarie leaned back on an elbow, "is that when I was kidnapped and murdered three times," she held up three fingers just for emphasis, "I should have just walked away. And when I didn't, when I demanded justice for what happened to me, I became the one at fault."

His eyes moved. When she put it that way he sounded like an asshole. "I just don't think you should've killed them."

"Then what should I have done, Calix?" She faced him. Elarie turned to her side, her expression one of pleading. "You can't just walk away from something like that. Had you been in my position you wouldn't have either."

"You don't know that," he said.

She sat up, "and you don't know what it feels like to die. You don't know what it feels like to be stabbed over and over, you don't know what it feels like to have a male chant for your death and slice your throat open. You have no idea." Her brows pinched together, "Calix." He braved a look at her. "Why would you judge me for my actions when you have no knowledge of my experience?"

"Explain it to me then," he said. "All of it."

CHAPTER TWENTY-ONE

ELARIE

Was it supposed to be simple? Was it supposed to be easy? Elarie had said much to many people in her life. She'd shared her identity with few, her background with even less, but had she shared this? No. It was her trauma, it was what she wanted buried. But Calix had asked for answers like they'd known each other long enough for her to be comfortable sharing.

If Greilor were sitting next to them her mind would be full of his voice. He knew how trustworthy Calix was. He knew that even in the week they'd known each other Calix was prepared to keep her secrets. Greilor knew that Calix was the right person to tell. Dragons were the best judge of character. He wouldn't have chosen this human had he not been the best type of person.

Did the best type of person judge others so quickly? Did the best type of person do that? Or was he trying to find a way to *not* judge her? Was he only looking for an explanation?

"When you go through the things that I do you have to change," she said, "you can't be the person you were before. I can't." Elarie breathed in slowly. His gaze was directly on her. His Lathin eyes were heavy, searching. "I didn't use to be like this."

"I figured," he said softly.

Elarie said, "the first time I killed someone I threw up. It had been an accident, too, and I still sort of regret it even if it was technically justified."

"How?"

Right, he wanted reasons. Elarie paused, her breathing stopping for a moment. "She went too far. She didn't stop when I asked her to and I reacted defensively." Elarie watched him wince. "Do you think that was justified?"

"Self defense," he said weakly.

Elarie asked, "and with the Fae, that wasn't?"

"That was revenge, it's different." Calix shook his head. He seemed to be trying to justify it to himself now, though she wasn't sure in what way.

She wiped sand off her arm slowly. Nervously. Elarie said, "when magic is taken from you it hurts. It hurt more than the knife. Hurt the way Kaelum hurt. It feels like the most important parts of your body—the things you need to survive—are being ripped out of you and you can only watch it happen."

Calix was only staring. Waiting for that *one thing* he could have to say it was fine. She was fine, it wasn't murder. Or maybe he was waiting for her to finish so he could say that it still was.

"It's happened before and each time is the same," she said. "I am killed and stuck with a thorn that digs into my body trying to plant roots in my bones and I wake up in a new place with people waiting for me to bleed on their land. They taunt me and laugh at me and whisper in languages they think I don't know that I'm an ugly thing disguised by a beautiful face and I deserve to die." She felt tears build in her eyes. "They drag me out to be presented to their people. They touch me and they push me and they look so excited waiting for me to die."

Her breath caught. Elarie wiped a tear off her cheek. Calix no longer looked impassive. His brows were together, a slight frown on his lips.

"And they put me on an alter. They chant, they praise the gods for such a blessing," she sniffed, swiping at her cheeks. "They force me to eat *dirt*, Calix." He winced as she repeated, "dirt. Dirt and ash and they pour water down my throat until I swallow and choke. Then they slice my throat open. My magic is ripped from my body, it spills with my blood into the ground they live on and I die for them. I've been buried alive and forced to wait until nature has bugs eat the thorns out of my body. I've spent years underground."

Calix looked down.

"Knowing this," she said, leaning forward, "did you expect me to go quietly? Would you have?"

"No," he answered in a whisper. "No, I don't think I would have just left."

Elarie breathed out shakily and straightened. She hadn't expected it. She'd expected him to do what he had before—said it was fine and moved on. She didn't think he'd admit that she was right. "Really?"

He looked at her. "My morals are different than yours, but I think..." he sighed shortly, shaking his head, "I don't think I'd be able to let something like that go. Maybe I'd become an angry person."

Her eyes burned. Calix got up, avoiding the food they'd stopped eating. He sat next to her. Elarie put her head on his shoulder. "I've never told anyone that before," she said.

Calix said, "you can tell me anything."

"You know," she sniffed, "I actually believe that." He chuckled softly, making his shoulders bounce. "How did we get from talking about being uncles to dragons to here?"

"Siblings?" He guessed, "I think it was our siblings."

"How evil of them," she said, "always turning something fun into something overly emotional and difficult to talk about."

Calix said, "my siblings don't do that."

She hit her forehead against his shoulder a few times, groaning. He laughed at her. "So you have good relationships with all of your family, then," she concluded.

"My father and I have a strained relationship, but we get along," Calix brought his knee up, resting his arm on it. "It's civil." Elarie hummed, digging her head into his shoulder. "That hurts," he informed. She let up, mumbling an apology as she did. Elarie sighed. "Elarie?" She grunted, not wanting to lift her head. "I trust you."

She froze, her eyes open and wide.

"Maybe it's stupid of me to," he said, "but I trust you."

Elarie straightened. "It is stupid of you."

"Oh, so I shouldn't?"

"No, you should, it's just stupid of you," she said. Elarie smiled, "not to mention we've known each other for just a week."

Calix leaned back on one hand, "I take it back, then."

"It's probably for the best," she nodded. Calix laughed.

Chapter Twenty-Two

Kaelum

"Where would you get married if you had to do it right now?" Kaelum asked, looking over at Terry. He was squinting in the wind, his hair waving around so much that Kaelum wanted to grab it and tie it back. Terry hated that. He, apparently, liked the feeling of his hair whipping around his face.

"Right on this ship," Terry answered.

Kaelum smiled. "Sounds perfect." He looked away, surveying the deck. A few of those they rescued would be staying on Moro, braving the judgmentals. Most of the others were moseying around the deck with nothing to do. But perhaps that was the best sort of thing for them. Elarie was one of them. She wasn't moseying, exactly, but she looked comfortable. She and the old woman were on the starboard railing talking quietly. Elarie was sitting eating an orange. She had another one in her pocket.

"Where's Calix?" Terry asked.

"Last I saw he was below," Kaelum answered, though he began looking around for him. The prince couldn't disappear for long, even if this was a big ship. "Imagine if we left him," he laughed.

Terry snorted. "Two days in and we just realize we lost the Crown Prince of Ceptari."

He said, "we'd be dead men."

"We'd never return. Be lost at sea."

They laughed together, watching the subject of their conversation come out from below with a book he tossed to Elarie. She caught it, then had to catch herself on the rail. Terry said, "run species with me."

"Got it."

"Human, Fae, golden blooded monster," he said, "and the Fae are part of the faerie and there are a bunch of different subspecies right?"

Kaelum watched Calix sit next to her, their heads close as they read from the book. Terisa took the orange from Elarie, who used her now empty hand to shift closer to Calix. "We don't know all the subspecies," Kaelum said. "How long until we get to Ceptari?"

"Three weeks after the Reefs," Terry said, "gods, now I want an orange." Kaelum laughed. "All right, but what do we know? We know she's not human, she's got too much fire magic, and if she dies she comes back."

"She knows what the Metars are," Kaelum added, "and according to her there aren't very many of us left."

He nodded. Terry said, "I don't like that she's the only one that knows about them. That she's got that hanging over your head."

"At least she's sort of sharing. I am a descendant of Fae that have magic. I make stars out of a line in my hand and those stars are magic," Kaelum smiled as he recited his information. "These magic rocks can be turned into anything and make people powerful."

"And can get you killed," Terry added in his deadpanned tone. Kaelum leaned into him. They went quiet and this meant Terry was about to change conversation topics. He had too much on his mind, Kaelum felt it was like trying to navigate a ship in the fog, in the dark, without instruments. Still, Terry always gave him a light. "You know why Lester isn't up here?"

He answered, "he's sleeping. Told me he had a rough night."

"He's mapping."

"Mapping? Or napping?"

Terry chuckled. "No, did you notice how that island wasn't on any maps? Say we were here," he held up a hand, using a forearm to keep them steady. Terry touched the edge of his palm. "And that's mapped out, we know where that is, been there before, it's been measured before."

"And the Fae island wasn't," Kaelum concluded.

"Yes, but get this," he held up a finger, "the distance we traveled from where we were before the monster attack to where the island was—in uncharted territory—was like a month of sailing, if not more, and we made it there in, what? Ten, fifteen minutes?"

Kaelum asked, "wasn't that the magic the things were using? The storm was carrying us to where the other Jiiver things were."

"True, *but*," Terry faced him, excited now, "we made it to Moro Island in a week. How?"

His eyes moved. "The whole area is magic? Meant to confuse you?"

"How close to the Barrier were we?" Terry countered, his voice quieting. "More than anyone has gone in a while, I'll bet. In one of the areas no one went at all, no one charted because they knew it wasn't for sailing. You saw Elarie looking up when we were on that island. Why?"

"The stars?"

"They were in different positions that night," Terry said, his dark eyes alight. "Isn't that insane?" Kaelum smiled at his genuine excitement. "So Lester has been trying to map it, you know, but he can't because the time doesn't add up."

"The 'month' to get there and the week to travel to Moro," Kaelum looked away from him. "You're right, I'm sure that would keep him up. You know we can boil this down to one thing, right?"

Terry sighed, "magic. Everything can be so easily explained if you just say 'magic.'" He shook his head, "it's like cheating."

Laughing, Kaelum said, "gods, I love you."

"It is! Just ask Calix with his reading, he talked about it for hours once, remember?"

"No, I don't—"

"You were drunk, weren't you? You know what? Calix!" Terry shouted down to him. "Calix!" The prince looked up, using a hand to block the sun. "Is using magic as an excuse to justify something cheating?"

Calix looked at Elarie. She said something to him that made him smile. Calix turned back, shouting, "yes!"

"See?" Terry motioned. "It's been decided. Magic is cheating."

"Uh, no, using magic as a justification for any unexplainable thing is cheating. Just to be clear," Kaelum said.

He leaned against the helm laughing. Terry sighed heavily, holding on like he'd fall over otherwise. "You'd know, wouldn't you? Because you're magic so you now have an excuse for anything that happens around you."

"You know my hand hasn't bothered me as much since I made the star," Kaelum said. Terry reached into his pocket and held it out. Kaelum took it. "This thing came *out* of me, that shouldn't be possible." The rock began to shine like a star in the daytime.

Kaelum breathed in slowly, closing his eyes. He turned it over and let it rest over the mark. "Holy gods—"

It was ripped out of his hand. When he looked, it was Elarie. "Let's not use magic for the first time on the open water," she said, giving the rock back to Terry. "Leave the magic with the normal people until you're on the ground."

"But..." he found himself saying, looking at the rock, "but I could feel it."

"I'm sure you could, but Kaelum," she put her hands together imploringly, "you could kill people if you aren't careful."

His chest ached. He found himself wanting to curse Elarie, grab the magic, and play with it. See how bright he could get it to glow. "Like you?"

"No, when I kill people I want to kill them," she said, "if you go around lighting stars and your magic gets out of control you could rip this ship in half. People will die if that happens."

Terry said, "she has a point there." He put the star in his pocket. "So no star until we're on land."

"I thought you'd be happy I want to mess with it," Kaelum argued, looking at Elarie. What was he doing challenging her about this? She was right. "You seemed so disappointed when I said I wanted to get rid of it."

"Do you want to be the reason the love of your life dies?" She asked plainly.

Kaelum glanced at Terry. "No," he said.

"Then don't mess with magic until I can teach you what to do. Got it?" She stepped away, running into Calix. He put his hand on her back to steady her, the book in his other hand. Kaelum saw words in a language he couldn't read. Of course they both could.

"Has that ever happened to you?" Kaelum asked her. "Have you ever been at fault for the loss of the love of your life?"

Her eyes flashed. "It was *not* my fault," she said firmly. "I am not to blame for any of their deaths and you do not get to use the people I loved as some sort of counterargument or a jab to get back at me. I'm trying to help you, Kaelum, do not make me regret it."

She walked away, headed down the stairs in a rush. Kaelum looked at Calix, who seemed relatively impassive, though a bit defensive. Of her, not of him. Of a girl he'd known for a week. "Any idea what she is?" Kaelum asked.

Calix shook his head, "no. Not human is the farthest I've gotten. I think I'll have to consult the books on faerie species or..." his eyes moved as he shrugged, "I don't know. It's really confusing."

"How?" Terry asked.

"Looks like a human, acts like a human, hates Fae," he listed off, "but that doesn't mean she's not a humanoid faerie."

"Or using someone's skin," he suggested. Terry cringed at his own words. "That one can't be true, can it?"

Calix shook his head, "I doubt it." He was cringing also. "Imagine? Gods, that's vomit worthy. Look, I'll get it," he assured, "it'll just take some studying."

Before he could walk away to follow after her, Kaelum asked, "she has more than one love of her life? I thought you could only have one."

Again, he saw that Calix knew something they didn't. Calix, Kaelum's best friend of nearly his entire life, was hiding something. The prince said, "maybe you can, maybe you can't. Maybe it depends on the person."

"Or the love," Terry suggested.

"Calix," Kaelum said as he went for the stairs. Kaelum turned and faced him completely. "You know I can tell when you're lying, right? Keeping things from me?"

Calix nodded.

"And you don't care that you're lying to your best friend for her?"

"I am going to figure out what she is," Calix said, "but that doesn't mean I have to tell you everything I know right now. And besides," he took the first step down the stairs, "Elarie is my friend now, too. I'm not going to break her trust."

Terry said, "yet."

He looked at Terry. Calix nodded shortly. "Yet." He went down the stairs to find Elarie without another word.

Kaelum turned to Terry. "What do you think?" He asked.

"I think Calix is attached, but it's not dangerous yet. She's not going to hurt him," he said, looking out to sea, "but I also think he's not going to tell us what he knows until the last second. He's going to protect her from us and everyone else around her."

"He doesn't even know her," Kaelum scoffed, facing the ship. They weren't on deck, they were below somewhere. Terisa was still in the same place. She had the other orange Elarie had in her pocket before and was tossing the peel over the side of the ship one piece at a time.

"Maybe he knows everything about her that he needs to know right now," Terry suggested, "or maybe he's playing us and her. We should be watching both of them now. Maybe put Red on it."

They both looked down at Red, who was sharpening his cutlass while sitting on a tied-down barrel. He was tall and broad, the kind of man you wanted defending you from other people, maybe not from magic. His hair was red, but not like Lester's. Lester had naturally red hair, Red dyed it the way Jamison colored the tips of his black hair. It was the color of blood from this distance.

"What do we tell him?" Kaelum asked, watching the pirate. Red and the two of them regularly went drinking, they were friends, but not the trust-with-magic type the way Lester was. Kaelum wasn't sure if he was truly trustworthy at all.

"The basics," Terry said, "we need to know what she is, so maybe more than that. He can spy on their conversations."

Kaelum said, "right, until they're in the air."

"Grey's not here right now."

Right. "Red!" Kaelum called. The pirate looked up. "Get up here!"

CHAPTER TWENTY-THREE

CALIX

"I know what you are," he said over the table. Elarie looked at him over the rim of her cup.

She set it down carefully, though didn't look all that worried, "do tell."

"A sore loser," he said. Calix watched her roll her eyes. "You are, aren't you? You can't stand that I beat you." He set the cards down, adjusting his leg. Elarie shook her head. They were sitting on the floor across from each other at the table that had his knitting bag under it. Calix had brought her to the captain's quarters for the privacy it provided—being spelled helped in that area. After Kaelum's comment about losing a loved one the day before, it seemed that she needed to be somewhere no one was.

Kaelum and Terry had been gracious enough to allow them to have the room for a few hours. It had been two, they'd played four rounds of cards.

"I am not a sore loser," she said. Elarie took the cards off the table and began shuffling them. "In fact, I am a great loser. I just hardly ever do it."

He laughed, "you've lost four times."

"And I've lost gracefully," Elarie continued shuffling. She was terrible at it, but seemed to enjoy it. Even if she lost a few cards in the process.

"How does one lose gracefully?"

"She doesn't knock the table over screaming," she answered with a raised brow. Elarie put the stacked cards on the table between them and nodded to them. "And she will win this time."

Calix laughed, taking the cards up again. "So how are you?"

"Fine," she said in a short tone. Elarie sighed, "I wish to release some energy, but it's not a huge thing."

"It happens when you're stressed, right? The way the star thing happened with Kaelum because something set him off." Calix gave her three cards, then the same for himself. He set the stack back where she had.

Elarie inspected what he'd given her, frowning at them. "Magic like mine feeds off emotion. When I feel too much it becomes agitated," she explained, "like... like a volcano." Then she smiled, "I love those."

He hummed. Calix picked up his cards, trading one out and getting a fresh one. "How do you release it?"

"Lots of different ways," she did the same with her cards, only she traded two. Elarie then smiled and placed them face down on the table. "Expelling energy, so using my magic to an extreme level. I could do something like the sculpture on the beach to get rid of it, I could kill someone using my magic. That's always satisfying, especially when they deserve it."

Calix frowned at her. "Let's not kill."

"Whatever," she said, "anyway, I could also find release sexually."

He swallowed, raising his brows, and put his focus on his cards.

"It's all about finding a way to get all of the bottled-up energy out of my body," she continued, "whether it's through using magic or using someone else."

"Someone else. So you use people?" His brow furrowed, "how does that work?"

She picked up her cards again, leaning toward him, "you find someone that wants to have sex with you without attachments. Have sex with them. Say goodbye, then go about your day."

"Men and women?"

She nodded then said, "I prefer women."

He smiled, "look at that, we have something else in common." Elarie laughed a little. "Ready?" He held up his cards. She nodded happily, probably thinking she'd win. They both slapped down one card and she made a gleeful sound, taking both of them back to her hand.

"You haven't won yet," he told her. She organized her cards. It was a child's game, one she shockingly had never played. Calix and Kaelum used to all the time, betting candy or trinkets. Calix had lost a rather expensive ring to Kaelum once. He never wore it.

"Maybe," she said. Her knees were bouncing. They slapped down another card. The object of the game was to gain nine cards starting with three. Only three cards could be traded out for each turn. Afterward, the player with the nine cards had to make them add up to nine. It was silly. Easy. And yet Elarie was terrible at it. At least she was graceful when she lost.

Calix took the cards so she was back at three. "Do you think Grey will come back with something we have to eat as well?"

"Most likely," she said. Elarie took the cards that round. And the next.

"When will he lay the eggs?"

She moved her cards around and drank some more of her water. He was amazed she still had some in the cup with how much she was drinking. "He'll wait until he's home, so whenever we go back to Ceptari." Calix nodded. "And even then he might wait until we build a nest for him."

"And how would we do that? Go to the mountains? Create one ourselves?" He tried to picture himself lugging stones to build a hut big enough for a dragon and its babies. It was a difficult sight to imagine.

"I'll end up doing most of it," she said, "but we can see what Greilor wants. The last nest he was in was underground, he might not like that." Elarie now had eight cards. She waved them around. She'd gotten to this point before. Never lasted on it, though.

"Then what?"

She shrugged. "We'll figure it out, won't we? If he's practicing laying it's almost guaranteed he's going to have them, even if it's in the field you have him sleeping on now."

"Wait," Calix put his hand up before they could go another short round. She looked at him. "Is the field a bad thing? Because it's not like I *told* him to sleep there, he just started doing it."

"It isn't necessarily a bad thing. Plenty of dragons sleep in the open air, like the Grater Dragon, but those dragons tend to have some kind of shielding," Elarie explained almost dismissively. "And—"

The door opened, bringing in Kaelum and Terry. Kaelum was humming a tune when he turned his head. "Nines?" He pointed to the table. There was a bottle in his hand, half empty. "Who's winning? What's the bet?"

Kaelum sat on Calix's right side and looked at his cards. Calix put them to his chest. "We're betting secrets," he said with a smirk in Elarie's direction. Terry looked over her shoulder at her cards and shook his head. He sat on Kaelum's right side.

"No we aren't," Elarie straightened. "Since when?"

"Since they walked in and asked," Calix answered. He reached for Kaelum's bottle and smelled what was inside only to cringe and give it back. "Now there are stakes. Please continue explaining the dragons."

She scoffed and they slapped down cards. "And Greilor doesn't have that shielding," she continued, losing a card. Quickly, Calix was in the lead. "Dragons get sunburnt and while yes, spending all that time lying around in the sun has affected his skin, you don't have to worry about it."

"Why not?"

"Because he's happy," she said. Elarie lost yet another card. "I think your friends are bad luck," she told him, sipping her never-ending cup of water. She shook her head and clicked her tongue. "But we are going to have to do something with the eggs, they can't be open to the sky."

Kaelum asked, "why not? Is Grey really laying eggs?"

"Probably, and because other dragons like to eat dragon eggs," she said. "And poachers like to steal them."

"He sleeps right next to the castle, no poacher is going to come near them," Terry said, waving it away while he watched Calix take another of Elarie's cards.

Elarie looked at Terry. "Maybe not, but Great Dragons were the first dragons ever created and now happen to be the rarest because of poachers and scared humans. I do not care how close he sleeps to the castle, I will protect his eggs from anything and anyone that tries to touch them."

"Sounds like it's happened before," Kaelum said before drinking from his rum, doing that overconfident thing he did sometimes where he threw out a statement hoping for a reaction. Like fishing.

"Maybe that's the secret I'll win from you," Calix smiled at her. Elarie looked at the nine cards in his hand as if seeing them for the first time. "I just won," he laid them out. All nine cards in number order. Her lips pointed down and he said, "remember to lose gracefully, Elarie."

She said, "you are such an ass," and put her cards back on the pile. "It has happened before. This woman had disguised herself and was working around the nest to familiarize her scent with the dragons. I believe she probably went into the nest a few times. One day she managed to steal three eggs and hid them in laundry baskets full of clothes."

Calix watched her begin to mess with the cards. She used her thumbnail to flip through them.

"I wanted to help so I took a basket and followed her. When I set it down and looked inside I found one of the eggs. She stopped me from screaming and poked me with faerthorne, then she hit me. I woke up in a bag far away from home," she said, glancing at Calix. Elarie sighed, "I suppose she and her partner thought that the dragons wouldn't harm them if I was with them, I remember they claimed that fire burned me with the faerthorne in my arm but that wasn't true."

"Hold old were you?" Calix asked her.

"Six, I think," Elarie thought back. "I lost an egg that day. It cracked open before it was ready and the hatchling died. Another egg, however, hatched right in front of me," she smiled, "and I took care of it all by myself." Elarie grabbed her cup off the table, finally saying, "that dragon turned out to be the one that chose Ashter to be his rider."

Kaelum asked, "were they Great Dragon eggs?"

"No, Greilor was the only Great Dragon in the nest and he's never laid before," she said. Elarie drank from her water.

"How many times have you died?" Terry asked suddenly, making Elarie choke. She coughed and set her cup down. Calix sighed and began shuffling the cards again to give himself something to do, hating himself for resenting Terry for the question. She was in such a good mood, this would ruin it.

"Many," she answered. Elarie looked at Calix, then at the table. She adjusted the way she was sitting.

He asked, "you die often?"

She put her arms on the table and held her cup again. "I suppose," she said. Elarie breathed out slowly, her mood slowly dissipating. "In many different ways to answer your next question."

"Stabbing and ritual sacrificing," he nodded. Elarie scowled. "What about other things? Choking?"

"Sure," she drank again. "Food, water, hands..."

Kaelum's brow furrowed, "you've died choking on food?"

"It's not that hard," she mumbled almost shamefully. Calix pushed down a smile. She hit his leg, evidently seeing it.

"Beheading," Terry said. Was he trying to find the wildest ways for a person to die and see if she'd done it? What did that prove? Not what she was, which was the goal from the beginning. They'd established that she couldn't die, implying that she'd died many ways, so what did it matter now?

Elarie looked at Calix. He shook his head slightly, setting the cards on the table. "No," she said. It was a lie, he could see it.

"Though I imagine it would be painful, so I hope it never happens. And on that note," she stood with her cup in hand, "this conversation is finished."

They watched her leave. Calix leaned over Kaelum and smacked Terry's arm, "what are you doing?" He asked hotly, also standing. "I'm figuring out what she is, don't mess this up."

"You aren't getting very far," he deadpanned.

Calix walked around the table, "it's been a week you impatient asshole." He left, slamming the door shut behind him.

CHAPTER TWENTY-FOUR

ELARIE

He found her, though it wasn't difficult. Elarie sat with her feet hanging off the side of the ship close to the bowsprit looking out at the dark sea. Night had covered them, only pushed back by the lanterns lit close to the middle of the ship. They were at her back and were soon to be at Calix's if he could get his leg over the side.

"Beheading, huh?" He asked with a breathy, casual tone. She looked at him. He thought he had her figured out. Was she that transparent? Did she *want* to be transparent? "You don't have to talk about it."

"Then I won't," she turned her head front. Calix sighed. "Feel free to find another conversation topic, though. Maybe I'll talk about something else."

He laughed, "you know what, you find one." He got his leg over and sat at her side. "Woah," he said before steadying himself. Calix looked at her, "got any ideas?"

Elarie said, "how about why your friends are such asses to me."

"Right, that," Calix looked away from her. "Well to start, you're also an ass to them sometimes even if it's in defense of yourself. But they don't know what you are and that scares them. I think they think being hostile will get them answers."

"But you're supposed to do the figuring out," she said, "isn't that right? You get close to me using the dragon as middle ground and learn what I am safely."

He nodded.

Elarie looked at him, meeting his eyes even in the dim light. "Figure it out?"

His head shook back and forth. "Not a clue."

"Liar," she countered.

"Maybe some clue," Calix shrugged, "but I'm not going to share my theories right now. It's too soon and there's still evidence for me to gather."

Elarie smiled, "fine. As long as you aren't afraid of what you find, hmm?"

"Come on, you know I won't be."

No, I don't. Elarie nodded, though, and looked at the water below them. It was black, rushing by as they made their way to the Reefs. She imagined what the Calix she knew now, at that moment, would do if he learned what she really was. In her mind, he'd run. He'd decide it was too much, he wouldn't accept her. The dragon being middle ground would not be enough. In her heart, though, he'd say, *'right. Sure, uh, would you like to come in for tea and cake?'* And take her into his home knowing her differently than anyone had before.

"Do you think they'd lose us in it?" Calix asked. She saw him looking at the water the way she was, though his hands were tight on the railing.

"Sure, if I didn't have magic," she said, "I could just..." Elarie showed him her hand, where a sparking flame crackled around on her palm. She tossed it up and it popped in a shower of sparks. He smiled, holding his hand out. A spark landed on his finger and he hissed. "Did you forget that it's fire?" She laughed as he sucked on the burned part.

"You know, I did," he waved his hand around. "Can you make it not burn?"

She said, "I could, but I don't want to."

Calix looked at her, putting a hand on his chest. "Ouch. I thought we were closer than that."

"We can be close, but I'm not sharing my fire with you," Elarie shook her head, looking away from him, "it's like," she thought for a moment, "as intimate as seeing someone you love naked for the first time."

He adjusted, his knee pointed at her. "To clarify," he put a hand up between them, "making it so that I don't burn when your magic touches me is the equivalent of intimacy?"

"Exactly," she smiled at him, taking his hand with one of hers. "I can show you something. Ever gotten frostbite?"

"No," he said. Elarie focused on his hand, slowly taking the heat from it. "Oh gods, shit," he yanked his hand away and cradled it in the other, blowing hotly on his fingers.

She laughed, "give it back." Elarie reached for his hand and he gave it over, his breathing heavy. "I can take off a body part that way," she told him, holding his hand between the two of hers. A soft glow came to them, making him sigh. "I can make your hand so cold your blood freezes and snaps off."

"That is a lovely thought," he said with a heavy amount of sarcasm. Elarie held the tips of his fingers. "And that feels amazing," he nodded to their hands. "But this isn't your fire?"

"No, it's only warmth," she said, looking at him. He was looking at her. Calix seemed to go soft. They were close enough that she could see his eyes clearly. His Lathin eyes. His family was an ancient one, they'd ruled Ceptari justly since the revolutions against Duness. Calix was the heir to a great kingdom. A great family. "Yours mostly," she said quietly, trying to learn what he was thinking. How long could he just stare at her? "Is this better?" Elarie asked, letting go of him.

He cleared his throat and squeezed his hand into a fist, straightening. "What else can you do? To a person?"

"To kill them? Or otherwise?" She leaned away, resting on her hand.

Calix said, "kill. Or can you heal with fire?"

"'Heal with fire,'" she repeated, chuckling. Calix blushed. "I can clean a wound, cauterize it. When someone is cold I can do what I did to you. Dry someone off quickly. I've heard that even just being around me can keep a person warm, so I suppose there isn't such thing as hypothermia with me."

"And... killing," he glanced at her.

Elarie said, "lots of things. Things you don't want to hear about." She put both of her hands in her lap. Elarie looked at them as she said, "when I was in the Rings I had a name. They called me Firefeeder because of the signature move that they loved so much."

"What was that?" He sounded a little scared now. Scared enough that she wasn't sure if she wanted to continue. Still, this was part of trust. The bad parts people had to know to trust.

"It was usually at the end of a fight. I'd get them on their knees, force their mouths open, and 'feed' them fire," she said. Elarie hesitated before continuing, "and it killed them."

Calix reached out and took her hand, squeezing once. "You aren't there anymore. And I know that even if you *like* killing people," he said and she looked at him, "everything that happened there wasn't your choice. It wasn't you."

She felt tears well up in her eyes, hating them completely. "I went from that to Rol," she said softly. Elarie swallowed thickly, "I went from that to him in two months." She looked away from him. "You know I used to say that every horrible thing imaginable has happened to me while every good thing runs away."

"Not to demean your experience," he said in a joking way, "but you've never been kicked in the balls before." Elarie laughed loudly, her shoulders shaking. "I'm serious, it's a terrible thing you'll never experience."

"And I shall thank the gods every day for that," she laughed. Elarie wiped her eyes. "You're very good at making me feel better."

He smiled, "thank you."

Elarie breathed in and out to calm herself. Much had been said. She anticipated him sorting through it all later to see what he thought was worth being placed in the pile he might entitle 'what is Elarie.'

"Every horrible thing?" He asked as if just hearing it.

"Other than the average male's most painful experience," she mumbled.

Calix breathed a laugh. "All right. What hasn't happened to you?"

She sighed. Elarie searched the black water below them. "I have never given birth," she said, "I've heard that is a painful experience."

"I imagine so," he agreed. "I witnessed my mother giving birth to Ryd, I watched my father hold her as she screamed. I don't think

I could ever do something like what she did. I developed a new appreciation for my mother that day."

"Were there any complications? Was she safe?"

He nodded, "she was. It was Ryd we were worried about. He wasn't breathing at first, but everything got sorted. Now Ryd is a healthy boy and mother dotes on him."

Elarie said, "I'm glad everyone is all right now."

"Would you ever have children?" Calix asked, looking over at her. His head turned quickly she thought she heard it crack.

"I would if I could," she answered. He looked confused. "I just can't. Physically, I can't have children yet."

He repeated, "'yet.' What does 'yet' mean?"

"I haven't found the right man, I suppose," she said, swaying slightly.

"And when you do?"

Elarie decided, "I don't want to talk about it." He caved and began searching for something else to converse about while she began to spiral. Elarie would act like having children wasn't the biggest of deals, as if for years she hadn't considered it. Her options, what the gods wanted. What she wanted. All of their conditions, but also what it meant for her. It meant a child. A baby, a future adult. She was ready for that years ago, not now. She'd convinced herself it wasn't for her in order to stop all the wishing and wanting. In fact, she hadn't thought about it in years until Calix brought it up.

He said, "favorite color."

"Grey," she answered.

"That isn't a color, but I'll take it," he said.

She replied, "I could be colorblind. Then you've just been extremely insensitive to my feelings and deficiencies."

Calix looked at her, his eyes again searching her face for something. "Are you?" He asked. She shook her head and watched a smile grow, crinkling around his mouth and eyes. "Mine is yellow."

"Why?" She asked.

"I don't want to talk about it," he looked away.

She laughed, "oh, is that how that feels?" Elarie looked over her shoulder and nodded to the sky, "Greilor is back." They watched the dragon begin his descent around the masts. Elarie looked at Calix, who was following the dragon with his eyes trying to guess what was in his claws. "Don't mention the eggs," she warned quietly.

"I wasn't going to," he looked at her, mouth open as if she'd accused him of something. "I am not an amateur, I can keep secrets. Just look at what I'm doing with you. I'm keeping secrets from my best friend for you."

Elarie turned around and put her feet down on the deck, looking back at him to say, "I know. And thank you."

This seemed to satisfy him. Elarie left him there and walked over to Greilor. The dragon was wrestling with a live giant squid and enjoying it while he did it. He bit off an arm that wrapped around his face, gleefully tearing at its smooth flesh as it screamed. "That's disgusting," she heard Calix whisper. He was a step behind her, their shoulders touching. "We have to eat some, don't we?" Greilor tossed the arm at them. It writhed at their feet. "Nasty."

"You've never eaten squid before?" She asked, cooking it. The arm went limp. "How interesting, given you live by the sea."

"I've eaten squid," he rolled his eyes, "this is just..." Calix motioned to the whole scene of his dragon munching on the sea creature. "Something else," he finished with a cringe.

Elarie bent and ripped off part of the arm. She stood with it, waving it around for him to look like he might be sick. Laughing, Elarie took a bite, then handed it over to the prince side-eying her. "We don't have to eat the whole thing," she told him as he bit off a decent mouthful. Calix shivered as he chewed.

Everything felt fine. Elarie hadn't felt that way in a long time. Eating squid with him and with Greilor, she felt *fine*. Even after the short interrogation on his friend's part, this was almost nice. But when that began to set in, she pushed it down. Elarie looked away from Calix and put her eyes on Greilor. The dragon met her eyes with a squid arm suctioned to his jaw. He knew. Of course he knew, he knew everything. Every part of her life before, he was there for. He knew her, he knew her moods and could guess what decisions she would make, so he knew about this.

He was calling her a matealn. Inwardly, so was she.

CHAPTER TWENTY-FIVE

ELARIE

She was good at avoiding. She let Calix believe their conversation had gone too far and even enlisted the help of Terisa, who told him that the effects of the sea were getting to Elarie and she wished to be on land. These excuses and more had lasted enough for the two of them to only have short conversations, ones that had little meaning, for nearly two weeks. Greilor was spending time on the ship with them, so they couldn't talk about eggs or nests or baby dragons, and that left little else to discuss so she was safe otherwise.

Now there were Reefs. It was an unnatural island in the sense that it made little sense to her. The workings of it. The Reefs were truly reefs, the island itself was Gerton. It was a thin stretch of land with minimal trees and buildings stacked up on each other. The docks were large and long, the water deep enough for even the Greyscale to fit.

Elarie stared at it. She mumbled a goodbye to Greilor, who wouldn't be joining them for this. She'd overheard Kaelum saying they wanted to keep this quiet, get as many people off the ships without a battle. There would inevitably be one, especially if they were stealing slaves from each of the three pirate ships docked together.

"Elarie," Calix walked up to her. He'd changed. Same pants and boots, but his shirt was brown now and his coat was leather. "We—"

"Will you braid my hair?" She asked without looking away from the island and reefs. She could make out the ship names and the symbols on their flying flags. Elarie looked at two in particular. "That's the symbol on Terry's finger, isn't it?" She asked as Calix gathered her hair behind her head.

He said, "it is. Listen, we decided that you shouldn't get involved. You should stay on the ship away from everything. We don't need it to get too violent."

"The Verlori, right?" She continued. The snake symbol was the same. "And its sister company next to it?"

Calix slipped the tie off her wrist. "Weralori, yes." He began to tie the braid off. She stared at the flag. Velori's symbol was a sea snake. Weralori's was a bird holding the same snake. Both were meant to be giant, though one was richer than the other. It all depended on what they trafficked. Weralori was founded first, Verlori branched from it. They soon became male and female slave operations, sharing profit by trading bounties over time. Here is where one of the trades would be. Men and women would be marched from one side of the dock to another only to end up in just another cage.

The braid hung down her back and Calix moved to her side.

"You heard me, didn't you?" He asked. "We can do this without you, we've done it before, and you could hurt more people than necessary."

"I can hurt the right people, Calix, I'm old enough to know the difference," she argued. "I know how to avoid casualties."

He pulled on her arms and made her face him, taking her eyes off the island and the reefs. "Elarie, you do not need to get involved."

"Maybe I don't," she said softly, "but unless you plan in using the faerthorne one of you pulled off my dead body," Elarie pulled her arms away from him, "you can do nothing to stop me."

He whispered, "Elarie."

"Calix," she replied in the same tone. She took a step back from him and looked at how close they were now. There weren't many people on the docks. A dock master was waiting for the Greyscale to dock under a different flag than the familiar dragon usually flying through the air. It looked like there was a child as well. Everyone else would be in the little town either sleeping or getting ready for the morning. Calix took a step back from her. He didn't seem all that surprised when she climbed onto the railing, and he said nothing when she dove into the sea.

Elarie swam much faster than a human even without magic. The ship seemed to melt behind her as she moved through the clear water. Fish and other marine life darted out of her warm path and hid deep below. She climbed up a ladder, breathing in her first breath since her dive. Elarie looked back at the ship, squinting in the morning light to find Calix still standing there. She couldn't read his face, nor could he read hers.

"Where did you come from?" Asked the dock master. He walked forward like a duck, waddling from one side to the other. He didn't look pleased. "What—" Elarie punched him in the face and he dropped. She grabbed the list from his hands and flipped a few pages as she walked.

"Kid," she called to the one running. He stopped and turned. "Don't tell anyone, understand?"

He nodded, "I'm going to my bucket," he pointed to a barrel. Elarie saw the bell hanging right by it and melted it. "They tell me to hide when people's coming so I hide."

"Go ahead," Elarie waved him off, tossing the list to the ground before climbing onto the Weralori's ship. It looked different from the Greyscale. On the one hand, it wasn't as large. There were no nail marks in the deck and permanent scarring. This ship's wood was darker, making her wonder if the captain had an aesthetic for it.

"Oi!" A pirate shouted, moving toward her.

"Do you have slaves on this ship?" She asked impatiently.

He countered, "would you like to join 'em?" and made a grab for her. Elarie snapped his arm, then his neck. She looked around, smelling the stale air, musty with rotting wood and some sort of alcohol. It only got worse as Elarie went below. Memories floated to the front of her mind as she descended the stairs and entered the brig. She killed the next pirate snoring in his seat when he should've been standing guard.

Elarie looked around. There were women, a few that presented as female, and even a few Fae. "I won't hurt you," she said faintly, breathing through her mouth, though that left a taste on her tongue. She broke the locks on each of the four cages. "There's a ship called the *Greyscale*, the men rescue slaves," she said as she opened the doors, "they won't hurt you either."

She saw a child hiding in the mix.

"Come on," she walked away. It took a few brave ones before the rest followed, whispering about her as they went up to the deck. A whole crew was waiting, a female for a captain. She was inspecting the body Elarie had left.

The women behind Elarie trembled, backing up. They stayed on the stairs and held each other in fear as the captain beheld Elarie. "You did this?" She asked, almost impressed. "One of my worst fighters." She had an accent as she spoke in Polinae's tongue. Perhaps she wasn't truly from there, but most were. The pirates all had their pale dirty faces and sloped noses. "Would you like my best?"

"I'd like you," Elarie replied. Without a single wave of her hand, the crew around her turned to ash floating away in the wind. "You should be ashamed of yourself," she said. The captain stared with an open mouth, fear dancing in her black eyes. "As a woman, I hope all you feel in your afterlife is pain. I hear the gods do not take kindly to your kind."

"How..." she whispered.

Elarie was such a liar. The gods loved terrible people. Elarie, it seemed, they did not like, but this woman might as well have been given a one-way ticket to a true paradise.

"Say your prayers," Elarie told her as she walked across the deck, "this will be painful." When she reached the captain, she faced a frozen woman. Her name was called. Screamed, even, from the other ship. Elarie turned her head, distracted, and found Calix. What had he said about not needing her help? Now he was calling for it, cornered.

She waved her hand and the two of his enemies melted into the floor.

Then there was a knife in her gut. Elarie grunted, looking down at the gleaming hilt. Pain struck her slowly. The captain began to laugh. Elarie looked at her, flames burning in her eyes. She grabbed the woman's face with one hand, pulling her wrist off the handle with the other. She crushed it. First her arm, then her jaw. The pirate whined and cried, pathetic tears in her eyes. Elarie brought her ear to her mouth and whispered, "I do not pray. But just this once," her grip tightened, "I beseech the gods to give you the justice these women believe you may deserve upon your death."

Elarie snapped her neck and dropped her.

Her head turned. "Get to the *Greyscale*," she ordered and pulled the knife free. The women rushed to the exit, their fear of her now just as great. Elarie looked at the red blood coming from her fresh wound and closed her eyes. She listened to the sound of fighting coming from the ship on her right side. The one Calix was on.

She held her hand over her wound and walked to the captain's quarters. Just in case. She opened the door, leaning heavily on the wall as she made her way into the small room. Elarie took in a perfumed scent and an empty made bed. She scanned the room.

A small cage was in the corner on a desk, most of it covered. Elarie swallowed and went toward it, throwing the blanket off. "Frei," she said as she looked at them. The tiny faerie creatures squealed and screeched, running into each other in their cramped space. There were too many of them, it looked like they were trampling each other. "I'm going to get you out," she told them, "let me get you outside."

They shut up for a moment, judging her character. Elarie picked up the cage while they decided whether she was a good person or not. Not, in her opinion, but it was up to them. She used the wall for support, bleeding heavily. Elarie limped past two bodies and flakes of ash.

"Would you like to stay on this island or come with me to Ceptari?" She asked them. A chorus of their clicking language rang in her ears. She squinted, grunting as she walked across the dock. Elarie burned anyone that came near as she knelt. She broke the lock. "Feel free," she opened the door. Many of them spilled out, though a few remained. They were adorable little things that were often made into a snack by many Fae. "All right," Elarie grunted, "I'll just shut this again, I won't lock it."

They nodded their big heads and she got up with them. "Elarie," she heard.

"Oh hello," she said to Calix. He had blood on his shirt and a tear at his side. Elarie looked at the gash he'd sustained at some point. "You need medical attention," she mumbled, "that could get infected."

"I need—no, it's nothing... Elarie, were you stabbed?" He held her side. Her front was slick with blood, running down to her pants.

She said, "only a little bit. Help me?"

Calix put her arm over his shoulder and began walking back to the ship. "We got the men out, I saw you did the same for the women," he said as they limped to the edge of the dock, "and Kaelum has people looking on the other ship."

"Can I please light them on fire when you're done?" She asked, though wasn't sure why. She didn't need permission.

"Why not?" He shrugged, which felt strange, and they walked up the ramp. "Oh great," Calix said when they stopped. Lester was unconscious, as were a few others. Elarie counted twenty pirates that were not part of Kaelum's crew.

"Want to see a fun trick?" Elarie asked him.

"No, I do not," he shook his head. She frowned, almost pouting in her deranged, tired, and dying state. "Could you just..." he didn't want to say it.

The pirates surrounded the men and women. A few were walking toward them. "Hand over the sword and the cage," a gruff sounding one demanded.

"All at once, like blowing out candles," Elarie told Calix, then actually blew out a breath through pinched lips. The pirates turned to ash as well. She laughed a little. "I'd like to die now, I'm in so much pain."

"The fact that you say that so casually is terrifying," he dragged her onto the deck, looking behind them.

Elarie took a deep breath and died in his arms.

CHAPTER TWENTY-SIX

"Do you have any idea how horrifying that was?" Calix asked as soon as she opened her eyes.

"Oh you poor thing," she patted his cheek, "I'm so sorry you had to witness me dying, it must've been terrible—" he scoffed and hit her hand away, sitting back while she brought herself up to her elbows. Calix shook his head, watching her lift her wet shirt to her ribs. She wiped blood away. "Sometimes the scars are bigger," she told him.

Calix touched her bare skin, running his finger over one. "Like this?" He asked, indicating one large, knotted one. Elarie stared up at him. He couldn't read her expression, but she didn't blink. "Sorry," he said, taking his hand away. She shook her head slightly, saying nothing. He cleared his throat and looked at the cage, "what are those?"

She looked at them. Many shoes walked up the ramp and Kaelum shouted, "someone get Lester, Will, John, and Johnson below, Terry sail us out of here." He then looked at Elarie. "That's a lot of blood," he said to point out the obvious. There was a small puddle below her.

Elarie looked to Calix. "Help me up, you said I could burn the ships."

"You said what?" Kaelum turned to him. Calix lifted Elarie to her feet, grasping her hand. It warmed against his palm, the heat beating like a heart. She ripped her hand from his when it happened, waving it through the air. "Calix—"

"You don't want anyone following you, do you?" Elarie threw over her shoulder. The Greyscale began to move on a strong wind that gushed through quickly opened sails. The crew moved with expert efficiency. They'd never been followed before, but her warning seemed to stop Kaelum.

Elarie smiled at Calix and the water under the ships began to boil. His mouth opened. He walked toward her, staring ahead as sparks came from the water. "How are you doing that?" He asked as if he hadn't seen amazing feats of magic from her. Sparks in the water? This shouldn't have surprised him. Still, watching fire lick the tight boards of pirate ships while they danced on the shining sea was somehow different. The water didn't steam the way it had when she made the dragon sculpture. The flames grew. "Elarie..." he found himself breathing in. The ships caught fire just when some of the crews came from in the town.

"What?" She looked at him. Elarie had such a satisfied expression on her face, he knew saying what he was thinking would only boost her ego.

"Find the release you were looking for?" He nudged her, wanting to tell her it was amazing. It was beautiful. Worthy of paint, worthy of art. He kept it to himself. He had two excuses—her ego, yes, but also Kaelum. He'd hate to say that in front of Kaelum.

The captain walked away. Even then Calix didn't say it. As the flames roared higher Kaelum stood on the steps to the quarterdeck. "Can I have your attention!" He shouted, pressing his thumb into his hand. He let go once people were looking at him. Still, his hand was in a fist. "You are safe on this ship, I know that may be difficult to believe. No one here will harm you. Elarie will not harm you."

They looked at her. Elarie smirked, leaning back while her fire lit her silhouette even in the morning light. She crossed her arms.

"When we are further out to sea we will have clothes provided to you should you want them. Water will be available, as will soap. We are low on shoes, I'm sorry about that, but every option presented to you is clean and new. It will be your own," he said. "Cots and hammocks will be made for you below."

A short murmur moved through them, most likely at the prospect of being below again. It went that way for many.

"You in no way will be forced to go down there, but I have to warn you there is a rather large dragon that sleeps on the deck. His name is Grey, his rider is Calix," Kaelum nodded to Calix, who smiled warmly at everyone, "and though it may not seem like it, the dragon will not harm you either."

"So it's either sleep down there or with a dragon?" A man with dark hair asked, protesting the two options.

Elarie said, "would you rather be stripped naked and branded?"

Calix elbowed her. The man turned to face her angrily and Calix realized he was a Fae. His ears were pointed and curled, his dark cheekbones pronounced. It looked like tattoos had been inked in brown swirls around his eyes. "What would you know of it?"

"Please stay calm," Calix whispered, "Kaelum just promised you wouldn't hurt them, remember?"

She glanced at Kaelum.

"Nothing," the Fae snarled, "keep your words to yourself, undying *E—*"

Elarie stood quicker than Calix thought possible and threw a ball of flames at him. People screamed and ducked away, horrified by her. The fire exploded over the Fae's chest and burned a hole in his shirt, though it did nothing for his skin. It was a warning. Far behind them, the slave ships exploded. Upon looking back Calix could see the docks went with them.

"Elarie," Calix said softly, "please calm down."

The Fae laughed. Why did they all have to be so antagonistic? Calix had never had any trouble with Fae before this. Before her. Was it her? Was she making this happen? No. No, all she was doing was standing there. He started it. "I would listen to the little rider," the Fae said, "you cannot prove you are better than what you are by attacking me."

"Stop provoking her," Kaelum said in the commanding tone of a captain. The Fae's ear twitched, but he didn't look away from Elarie. He was challenging her. Everyone knew it, including the former slaves that had backed to opposite sides of the ship. And the other few Fae, watching their friend goad her on. They were smiling. They thought they were right.

"Lose control," he taunted, leaning toward her with his hands at his sides. "Come on, you want to kill me. I know what you are, you cannot risk the humans knowing as well. Can you?"

Calix moved to her side. "Elarie," he said, "look at me."

"No," she said tightly. "You'll tell me not to."

"I'll tell you not to kill him," he whispered, "you know that." Calix stepped close to her, as close as he could get. He put his head against hers, his lips to her ear, "but if you really don't want me to know right now. If that's what you want... then you don't have to kill someone to get them to stay silent."

She twitched, tense when he took a small step back. Elarie let out a slow breath. "People can be afraid of me if they want to be," she decided. The Fae began to scream. All of them. All four males and each of the three females grabbed at their throats, dropping to their knees as they choked on flames. Horror rose around them as their hands turned blue. Like frostbite. Elarie faced Calix. When he looked at her she was the one that looked afraid.

Their fingers fell off and their tongues had somehow burned to nothing. Calix felt horror creep up his throat the way that demanded a scream. It was what he'd told her to do, though. Rather than kill them. He couldn't fault her for doing what he'd said.

"I could really use a dragon ride right now," he found himself saying, his voice breathy.

"I can't run from this," she said softly. Elarie inhaled shakily, "I have to stay."

Calix nodded, "then we'll stay. Go up," he nodded to the quarterdeck. Elarie turned around, but before she walked she bent for the cage and opened the door. Whatever was inside scurried out and disappeared. She then moved the small crowd as she went to the stairs without a word. Calix followed her, though when she went all the way up Kaelum caught his arm. Calix looked at him.

"What did you say to her?" He asked. His grip was tight. Afraid.

"I told her not to kill them," he answered. Calix shrugged him off and walked up the rest of the way, finding her seated against the door to Kaelum's quarters. She had her face in her hands and her elbows on her propped knees. Terry was staring at her the same as he always did.

Calix sat next to her. "I'm so angry," she said, "and I don't know what to do."

"Breathe," he suggested.

She laughed. Elarie uncovered her face and looked at him. "You know there were years that I wore faerthorne on a bracelet? One thorn." She pointed to a spot on her wrist. Under a bit of dried blood was a round white scar. "So I didn't have a choice but to breathe."

"What happened that made you take it out?"

"I died," she said, "I was murdered and thrown in a ditch then buried with a few other bodies of girls that I'm sure looked like me at one point." Elarie put her head back against the door. "I woke up and three years had passed. If I had this," the tip of her thumb lit to bright flames, "It wouldn't have happened."

The flames went out. Calix asked, "why did you stop using it in the first place?"

She smiled, "it was my first time pretending I was a human."

"Really?" He adjusted, his knee now pointed at her. She nodded. "Why would you pretend to be human?" He no longer cared that Kaelum and Terry were there—neither did she, apparently. It was obvious now that she wasn't human. The Fae made that happen.

"It was a really low point in my life," Elarie told him. "I'd... gone too far when it came to drinking. Alcohol poisoning killed me more times than I care to admit, so I decided to challenge myself and stop drinking. At first it was really just me threatening myself with a long death, then a little while went by and I was feeling better. A lot better actually."

When she looked at him he smiled.

"I could've taken it out, but I didn't. It turned into me pretending I was normal and could only die one time, then it was me learning how to be human," she swayed in his direction before rocking back to the wall. Elarie said, "cooking was difficult, I never had to wait for a pot to boil before then."

He laughed, which gave her room to join him.

"I'm serious. And baths? Gods, how do you do that," she laughed some more. He could see her anger dissipate. "I started liking it. Doing everything the way you do. And suddenly no one saw me as an elemental at all and it was so freeing. So I pretended I was a human."

"And you stopped when you died," he concluded.

"I had to get my revenge," she said with a shrug, "and I lost the faerthorne."

He asked, "what did you do to him?"

"Burned off a few layers of his skin, beat him, and buried him alive where he put me," she answered easily. "That was so satisfying."

Calix nodded slowly. "I get you now. Only took me a couple weeks."

"I'm hungry," she muttered, looking around like food would just appear out of thin air. "What do you get about me?"

"I think I get a lot," he said. Calix smiled at her confusion. She was a runner, a murderer, and probably enjoyed torturing people, but she was many other things too. He'd figured her out. "And I am also hungry," Calix got up, "so I'm going to go steal food and you are going to go in there," he pointed to the door.

Elarie had an open mouthed smile on her face. Calix passed Kaelum and Terry, going back down the stairs.

On the last step, something exploded off the port side.

Chapter Twenty-Seven

Elarie

"Calix?" Elarie stood. She'd rolled across the quarterdeck with Terry and Kaelum, who were still knotted together. "Calix!" She shouted, walking at an angle as the ship righted itself. People were screaming. Her ears rang as another explosion boomed close to the bowsprit. Already Elarie could see bodies. Former slaves, dead before they felt free.

She gasped for breath, stumbling down the stairs. People were boarding the ship from another that had appeared as if from thin air. This one was just as large as the *Greyscale*, though its sails were black and its crew looked far more deadly than the one Kaelum commanded. Where had it come from? It had just *appeared*, how was that possible?

They were cutting people down. It didn't matter who.

"Calix!" Elarie screamed. The ship lurched and she tripped, nearly running into a jagged knife. Its owner laughed at her before he burst into flames. "Terisa!" She saw the old woman holding onto the starboard side with Jamison in front of her. She was concerned, but she also didn't look shocked by this.

Why did she never tell Elarie about the prophecies and visions that mattered?

She shoved through the crowd, her skin burning and the clanging echoing in her ears. Elarie continued to look around for Calix as she reached Jamison and Terisa. The old woman said, "I am so sorry," in a voice loud enough to be heard over the noise, but sincere enough to show she was about to experience a great amount of pain.

"What?" She asked anyway, burning the next person that came close to them. Elarie looked at Jamison, "are you all right?" She grabbed his arm as another explosion hit, this time somewhere at the back of the ship. Everything lurched and she fell against Terisa. "Where is Calix?"

"Over there," Terisa pointed her wrinkled finger. Elarie turned her head and spotted him with a cut on his head and a sword that wasn't his in his hand. "Better hurry," she said.

Elarie backed up, looking at Jamison, "stay here, do you understand me?" He nodded tightly, his eyes wide and bulging with tears. He held his cutlass tight. Elarie shoved through and tripped over a few dead people, killing as she went along.

"Drop your weapons!" She heard Kaelum shout and she killed the man trying to kill Calix. "Drop them!"

"Are you all—" Elarie started, then she was thrown forward by a heavy force. She screamed in pain, her voice mixed in with the rest of them. Calix grabbed onto her, his sword out of his hands. His eyes were wide. Elarie sobbed as she looked down at the thick arrow protruding from her shoulder. The faerthorne wrapped around it sunk into her body, digging into her bone.

"Elarie," Calix squeezed her arm urgently. Still gasping for air, she turned her head. Kaelum had told everyone to surrender, which meant every member of his crew left was unarmed. She looked at the ship, not recognizing the flag. "They traffic magic users, use them for everything. It's probably why we didn't see the ship until it was too late," Calix whispered. Elarie's knees began to give before he lifted her up again. "It's Captain Finnal," he said. His voice trembled. "He'll kill everyone that doesn't have a hint of magic."

The captain in question was a skinny man with black hair. He smiled with thin lips. "Begin," he commanded in Ceptareei. Two of his men, twins by the look of them, began moving through the group that was still alive. They grabbed arms and sliced cuts in them, then licked the blood. Once they made some decision, they either left them or killed them.

Lester was one they killed. He knew he didn't have magic and chose to put up a fight, but he was too weak, too tired, and too confused. He didn't last long. He bled out choking.

"I know you," Finnal said, his sly smile pointed at Elarie. She met his beady blue eyes and he laughed, half of his mouth quirked up. "Ah-ha, I do know you." He stepped over a body.

Out of the corner of her eye, she could see both Terisa and Jamison had passed whatever test the twins were doing. Elarie turned slightly, gripping Calix's shirt. The smell of blood and desecration filled her nostrils. Finnal seemed to like the smell. He breathed it in.

"You escaped, didn't you," he said, again stepping over a body, "you got out." The Rings. He must've sold to them. "Ready to go back?"

Elarie couldn't think of her options. Death, though it was likely they wouldn't remove the faerthorne. She'd sink to the ocean floor and wait the gods knew how long for the thorns to be eaten out. By then Calix could be dead. Surrender and go back to the Rings? No, she couldn't do that.

A small fight broke out. Kaelum. The knife was aimed at Terry, who had no magical properties in his blood. Kaelum kicked the twins and they fell down the stairs. He was pulled off by another pirate and started screaming for them not to touch him.

Finnal looked. "I'll keep that one," he said simply. They backed away and Kaelum grabbed Terry. "What wonderful leverage loved ones make," he said as he turned. His eyes were on Calix. "Good to meet you."

Oh gods. Elarie looked around to distract herself for just a moment, as if there was much that would distract from this. There were so many dead people.

"Firefeeder," Finnal taunted. Her head snapped to face his. "Would you like to see one of those arrows in his chest?" He asked, nodding to the one wrapped in faerthorne and to the person behind her. Calix squeezed her arm tight enough to draw blood even with his short nails. She tightened her jaw, shaking her head. "Then come here," he waved his hand casually. People were being chained around them and he was casual. People were dead around them and he was casual.

Elarie had to pull her arm away from Calix, who swayed without her. She stepped over the legs of a woman who looked to have been her age.

He held her jaw gently, his fingers small. They turned her head from side to side, brushing up her cheeks. His beady eyes were hungry. He smiled, "you're mine now. Say it." She didn't. Finnal grabbed the arrow and pushed, twisting as she sunk to her knees, her face turning red. "Say it."

She would not. She would not. Elarie would not.

Finnal laughed. "Put her in my monster cage, make sure he's right across," he said, pointing to Calix. He turned the arrow in a circle and Elarie's vision went fuzzy. "And with everyone..."

His voice faded as she was dragged away. Elarie could hardly lift her head, sure that with her eyes closed the trip was much faster. So much faster. Fast enough that at one moment she was looking at water and the next her body was being dumped onto a damp hardwood floor. She did not try to get up from it.

"Elarie," Calix's voice said. "Elarie!" He shouted and she jumped, not moving otherwise. "Good, you're alive," he breathed. Such a strange thing.

"Get up," Kaelum grunted. She turned her head, seeing him at an odd angle. He was across from her with Calix and Jamison. Terry was in the cell next to them and a few others were shoved into the cell by Elarie. "You need to get us out of this."

She laughed, turning her forehead to the deck. "When I figure out how to pull an arrow wrapped in faerthorne out of my shoulder, I'll get right on that."

They were moving. Elarie could feel the water beneath and around them shifting to be carried by the winds. Where? To the Rings. She blinked slowly, again trying to find the right scenario to escape it. The arrow *could* kill her, but it most likely wouldn't. Finnal would have to pull it out eventually. Bleeding steadily from the faerthorne she could feel digging into her bone might work. But again... she had to stay alive for Calix. And everyone else.

Elarie pushed herself to a kneeling position, staring ahead at the dark brig. Small candles dripped wax down the walls but did little to light the room. There were four cells, none well packed. Finnal only collected those with magic, and that left very little. Her eyes stung and she looked away. Down. Elarie scratched at a shining dot on the wood beneath her.

"My new monster," Captain Finnal banged on the bars. *It's just another cage,* she told herself, but was only contradicted by him. "Do you know what I kept in here? Eh, Firefeeder?"

"When are you going to take the arrow out?" She asked dully, struggling to stand. She didn't look at Calix as she turned around to face the skinny pirate.

He smiled. "You can't fight with one hand?"

"Two is more entertaining," Elarie replied, walking toward him.

Finnal laughed. "I've seen such horrifying things from you," he said. "I was disappointed to hear you escaped. The Rings lost quite a bit of money while you were gone."

"So you're selling me back," she concluded.

"Of course not!" He laughed again. "Why would I do that when I can take you to every different fighting pit in the world? I'll never have to pirate again with how rich you'll make me."

Elarie wrapped her hands around the bars. "Take the arrow out," she said. She watched him run his tongue across yellowing teeth. "Promise I'll keep the faerthorne in," she put her head against the cool metal. When he said nothing Elarie ground her teeth.

"I always thought you were so pretty," he told her. Elarie adjusted her head. "Too bad the Rings didn't sell that sort of thing, no?"

She tightened her grip with her right hand, the left beginning to go numb. She'd have to take the arrow out herself. "They tried," she whispered to him, lying through her teeth and a fierce smile. "I killed too many patrons."

"Hands can be tied, magic can be taken..." he mused, looking over her body.

"You should see what I can do with my legs," she moved closer, "I'd have to wash your blood out from between your toes."

Finnal chuckled. "You spit fire as well as you feed it," he said. He took a step back. "Enjoy the monster cage, we'll be at the Rings before you know it." He began to walk away, though he stopped and said, "and if you attempt to remove the faerthorne before it's time... well, the seer in my quarters will pay for that mistake painfully."

He said nothing of the arrow. Elarie watched him go up the stairs quietly. Her arms shook.

"Golden blood," Kaelum said. Elarie looked at him, then the wall his eyes were pointed toward. A monster had been painted in golden blood, this one resembling some twisted sort of salamander. Its body was long, the tail coiled like a snake. Scales were painted in some places. The head was large, as were its front arms. There were four fangs and five claws. Its hands were almost humanoid. "A golden blooded monster."

"I've never seen one like that before," Terry said, "do you think it's real?"

Elarie grunted, "who gives a shit," and looked at Calix. "Your name is Ezra," she told him, then put her back against the bars. Her vision blurred before she jerked quickly to the side, snapping the feathered end of the arrow. She groaned, peeling herself off the bars once again. Elarie reached back, wrapping her hand around the prickly shaft, and snapped it the rest of the way. "Terry, say something nice to me."

He asked, "why?" In a disgusted tone.

She put her back against the wall this time, closing her eyes. Now the wall could be stained with red as well. "It'll shock me, give me something to think about," she answered. Elarie breathed slowly and wiped her hands on her pants.

It took him a moment. In some way, Elarie appreciated the short pause. "I really appreciate the way you sort of helped Kaelum," he said. It wasn't as shocking as she'd hoped for. Elarie wrapped her hands loosely around the thick arrow, thorns pricking her palms. "You have pretty eyes?" He suggested, though sounded confused. Elarie yanked the arrow out, dragging vines with her. A few broke off, others latched on. They dug deeper into the wooden shaft until she had to drop it.

"Ow," Elarie breathed. She sunk down the wall and put her bleeding hands on her knees, facing them to the sky. "Thank you. I want to die," she mumbled, ignoring the footsteps on the stairs.

"Oh, dear," a new voice said. She didn't look at him. Elarie wished to go to sleep. "We would've done that for you." Again, she didn't look. She either wished to die or to kill something. Killing seemed like so much fun. It felt so good, how she wished to kill. "Which one is hers?" Asked the voice, the question directed at someone else. "Good, fetch him." There was a pause and the sound of a key turning in a rusted lock. Elarie opened her eyes when she heard Calix grunt. He was being dragged out of the cell.

Great, she thought, *leverage.*

CHAPTER TWENTY-EIGHT

CALIX

"Firefeeder," the man said. She turned her head. This was another skinny man like Captain Finnal, though he was short and had rather red cheeks. He motioned for her to stand. She looked at Calix, who decided to pretend he wasn't scared shitless even with the knife pressed against his stomach.

Elarie stood and walked back to the bars. She didn't look amused, surprised, or even all that angry. She just looked tired. Calix guessed she'd be glad for this bout of pain to be over quickly, even if it was for a moment of relief.

"Arm out," said the thin man. She rolled her eyes and stuck out her left arm. It shook with the effort to lift it. The man simply grabbed her wrist and ripped off her sleeve. Calix began to think of different things he could do. He wouldn't stand a chance against a knife in his gut and doubted he'd catch the large man by surprise. He could risk another good slice to the side by jumping the skinny one. Then what? Elarie wouldn't do anything, would she?

She seemed to choke on air, her eyes flashing with pain as the man wrapped another vine of the thorns around her entire arm. Calix watched the thorns begin to bury themself into her skin.

"Now," he said, satisfied with his work. He reached into his pocket and produced thick looking gloves. "I do love this part. I enjoy guessing how high pitched the screams will be. However, my favorite screams come from the ones who say they will not scream. Music to my ears."

He arched his finger toward himself. She took a step.

"You look like you won't scream until the very end," he said pleasantly. She just stared at him, her lips slightly parted and her eyes hard. She wanted to kill him. Calix thought she would if it weren't for him. Hopefully, anyway. "So exciting," the man whispered before grabbing the thorns protruding from her shoulder and collarbone. She grunted, hitting the bars when he pulled them forward.

Elarie didn't look away. She didn't blink. And the man was so disappointed. He dragged the long vines out of her body, spraying blood from the wound in the process, and once they were all gone and it was just a shrinking plant in his hand, she smiled. Elarie lifted her hand up and dug her fingers into the gaping hole, knuckle by knuckle. She moved them around, searching, and when her hand left her body she was holding a single thorn.

She flicked it at him.

The thorn flew through the air and sliced across the man's ear. "Ah," she deadpanned, giving him a scream. He was too stunned at first. The thin man stared at her with his mouth open.

"Not impervious to pain," he muttered, looking her over, "but stubborn. Perhaps too stubborn to feel it."

"I'll feel it if you ask nicely," Elarie said sweetly, tilting her head. Calix recognized this gesture in many ladies after his attention. She was practically flirting with him. He wondered what it would be like if Elarie looked at Calix that way. Without the blood and the torture, if she tilted her head and smiled.

Horrid thoughts flashed through his mind, wiped away by the thin man saying, "I think I am going to enjoy you very much."

"Up until the point that I wrap that vine around your neck and pull until your head pops off," she smiled as if she'd said something pleasant. "But then *I'll* be the one enjoying you." The man stepped back in surprise, waving at Calix. He was shoved, stumbling, then was shoved again. He nearly fell on top of Kaelum and the door was slammed shut behind him.

He turned, watching them walk up the stairs. "Am I going to be dragged out and threatened every time they want something from you?" He asked, looking at Elarie. She had one hand around the bar, her forehead against it. "Elarie?" He asked, softening his voice. Calix glanced behind him at Kaelum, who looked just as concerned as he felt. Even Terry was showing some emotion other than anger or indifference toward her. Jamison, though, had silent tears of horror and sorrow streaming down his face. He faced Elarie again. "Elarie, look at me."

She shook her head, slowly sliding down until she was on her knees. Elarie breathed in deeply and out shortly, then inhaled sharply again. She was stopping herself from crying. Calix could only see the side of her face, screwed up and in pain. "You are so lucky I like you," she whispered.

"Can you call Grey?" Terry asked, looking at the both of them. "If he comes then maybe—"

"He'll be killed," Elarie said. "If I call him and we're stuck down here when he comes he'll be killed. This ship," she swallowed, "they've killed dragons on it before, which means they are equipped for a dragon to attack."

Calix asked, "so what do we do?" She was quiet. "Elarie, you won't survive the Rings if you do it again, we have to figure something out."

"If I take the faerthorne off and even try to go up there they'll kill Terisa. If I attack anyone down here they'll kill you," Elarie said, "and Finnal collects magic users, who's to say he doesn't have one that will be able to sense my magic after the thorns are gone? I won't lose Terisa and I won't lose you so I have to figure something else out."

"We can figure it out together, Elarie, it's not just you on this ship," Jamison told her. He wiped his face. "We can help you."

She rocked backward and sat, then fell onto her back. Elarie seemed to fall asleep after that. Or she was unconscious, at least. Calix turned around and sat. "Kaelum," he said, "how are you feeling?"

"Like my hand is going to fall off, why?" He grunted.

"Because if there is someone up there that can sense Elarie's magic then they'll be able to sense yours," he said, looking around. He counted twenty people. Twenty people, fifteen being part of the crew. How did that happen? He knew magic was relatively rare, but this? They started with maybe sixty former slaves and a crew of twenty five and now only twenty of them were left.

Kaelum whispered, "Lester's gone." He breathed in sharply through his mouth and Terry reached over, clasping his hand. There were tears in Terry's eyes. They'd been friends the longest.

It was Terry who introduced Lester to everyone years ago. "Shit," he sniffed and swiped at his eye.

"We'll get out of this," Terry assured him, "and we won't lose anyone else. Got it?" He squeezed Kaelum's hand, then looked at Calix. "Got it?"

Calix nodded, swallowing the knot in his throat. "Jamison?"

The kid was pulling at his hair, something he did when he was nervous. Calix had heard once he'd developed a bald spot because of it. "We could leave Elarie out of it," he suggested, "next time someone comes in here for you we can fight him off. Maybe sneak up and find Terisa, then some weapons."

"And Elarie stays put," Terry nodded.

"If something goes wrong?" Kaelum asked. He looked from one person to the other, then let his gaze wander. "Who dies if that happens?"

Terry said, "I don't see you suggesting anything."

The captain looked at Elarie. "She'll get us out of it. She started all of this," he motioned around with his left hand, the right clasped tightly with Terry, "as soon as she stepped onto the *Greyscale* everything went to shit. Very same day, in fact, so she's dealing with it."

Calix wanted to argue on her behalf, but it seemed that everyone agreed. Red, even. He was in the cage across from them to the right of Elarie. He nodded. Everyone looked angry with her, but Calix felt it was misplaced. The Jiivers showing up—Elarie's first offense according to Kaelum—was a fluke. That could've happened at any time. And the island? That was *her* being tortured. The Reefs? Elarie had saved just as many people as they had. And now this... the Rings. She wasn't at fault for people dying, Kaelum couldn't blame her for that. Now they were on their way to a fighting ring, one Elarie had escaped by killing.

He looked back at her, still unconscious, and wondered how long they'd leave her like that.

CHAPTER TWENTY-NINE

KAELUM

His stomach churned. Whatever magic was inside him was agitated. As night grew nearer he could feel it coursing through his veins. Kaelum shifted uncomfortably. He had his arm around Jamison, who'd just stopped crying. They were all watching Elarie, waiting to see if she'd wake up. There was a pirate in her cell, after all. The same one that put the thorns around her arm. He was squatting on her right side, smiling at Calix.

"You ever seen the Rings, boy?" He asked to torment him. Kaelum looked at Elarie's chest to see if it was still moving. How she wasn't awake he didn't know. Calix shook his head, making Kaelum recall a rant about them from years ago. "I have. I've seen your little Firefeeder. You know what this is?" He produced an opaque glass tube.

"Cosmetics," Terry guessed, loud enough in the hopes it startled Elarie.

But it didn't. And the pirate chuckled. "This is what the Fae many years ago for one of their petty wars. They gave it to their soldiers. Care to guess what it does?" He waved it slowly through the air. There was something in it. Some sort of drug. "Strips away the personality. Muffles memories. The Fae wanted to ensure their soldiers thought of one thing—not family, not what's waiting at home, not even their own wellbeing—just the fight. Win the fight."

Kaelum looked at Calix. The rant had said something about forcing the fighters into it, he couldn't recall anything about any magic drug. Calix shifted, turning toward them just a bit more.

"I've seen fighters only need two to get through as many rings as they can, but your Firefeeder," a sick smile spread over his stained teeth, "she *burns* right through them. A dose every ring. Imagine what that does to a person. Get stripped away, start to come back, get stripped away, start to come back. Confusing, I imagine. Lucky me," he laughed softly, "I was there for one show. She killed two Fae, got beat bloody just for show, and stumbled out of that ring like a completely different person. A scared little girl."

Calix tensed more than he had been before. The part of his face that Kaelum could see was a mask for the pirate, but Kaelum knew him better. He was scared for her. Beyond belief. The way he'd be scared for Kaelum. Was that how close they'd gotten? In a few short weeks they'd developed a friendship that rivaled the one he had with Kaelum—one that went back years.

"Started speaking in a language no one knew," he whispered, "asking for people. Names. Greilor, Matian, Saying En—"

Elarie opened her eyes and lashed out, grabbing the pirate's throat and throwing him over her body like he was a mere rag doll. She didn't have to fight him over the tube, she simply grabbed his hand and squeezed. Nothing was broken yet. She was holding back, only ensuring he couldn't use it on her. All she was doing now was putting a decent amount of weight on his throat so the pirate choked and grew even more red in the face.

"Anything," he gagged, "you do—" she pushed down harder, baring her teeth like a Fae. "To me happens," a gargling sound came from the back of his throat. A laugh. "To him."

It took her a moment to let go even after he said it. Elarie removed her hand and breathed heavily, twisting his grip on the vial to take it from him. She stood with it, taking a step back to distance herself from the pirate. It didn't seem that she trusted herself if she remained close.

The pirate coughed.

"You tell your captain," she said, her eyes moving with the pirate as he stood, "that he can bet everything he has on me. I only lose the small rings when I'm told to and I won't this time. I'll win, I'll make a show of it, but if he has anyone else harmed," she tossed the tube back to him and he threw his arms out to catch the valuable substance, "if anyone touches any of them—"

He laughed slowly.

"I'll let the Messenger kill me," Elarie finished, "I won't make a show of that."

His small hand waved the tube through the air as he backed away. "The Firefeeder can negotiate," he chuckled, "but how will she remember her orders if all is muffled?"

"I don't need to remember this conversation to know how much I want him to kill me," she told him. Elarie watched him lock her inside, saying, "Finnal wants to make money, not lose it. If anyone else is harmed I'll lose on purpose."

He hummed, slowly clinking the tube against the dirty iron bars. The pirate walked around the cage without looking away from her, his head turned in her direction even as he walked up the stairs. Elarie took a step back, her head moving to a corner of the brig no one was in. It was dark, the small candles not bringing enough light to the area.

"How are you supposed to die if you can't die?" Terry asked the important question.

She kept her eyes on the corner. "He's killed me before, I just have to stay dead for long enough."

"I thought you didn't have control over that," Calix said.

Elarie squatted, using her right hand to balance. Something in the corner made a clicking sound. "I can feel it, too," she said, "we'll have to figure out a way to get him to calm down before the sun sets, won't we?" The sound of clicking continued. "Why yes, you can help." Kaelum was about to ask what she was talking to when a small blue thing ran out of the shadows. It made a gleeful sort of clicking noise and jumped up high. When it landed it continued running until it was in front of Elarie. "Hello, Gee."

"Holy gods, is that a Frei?" Calix turned, grabbing the bars. The blue thing turned. Kaelum tried to recall what a Frei was. The name was familiar, sounding like something Calix would go on a rant over. Kaelum was beginning to think he didn't pay enough attention to his best friend's interests.

"Yes, this is a Waterdweller," Elarie said, "his name is Gee."

'Waterdweller' made sense considering how blue its skin was. The thing was small, small enough to fit in an open hand. Its skin churned like deep ocean water. Its eyes were black and took up most of its face, making it look wide-eyed and childlike.

"Gee, this is Calix," she whispered, "but we're calling him Ezra to keep him safe." The thing nodded, whistling as he motioned to the eager looking prince. "Yes, he is my loved one. And everyone else is his loved one." Again, it spoke and she listened intently to it. "No, none of them are my loved ones. We aren't even really friends.

Ezra is the one that brings us all together. His friend Kaelum is the star maker."

"That's me," Kaelum waved, the title only bringing the reminder of pain. "This is my loved one, Terry," he pointed to the other cell. Terry smiled just a bit, probably thinking the Frei was adorable. He'd never say it, of course. "And on this side is Jamison."

Jamison waved to the Frei, who chirped while looking at him. Elarie translated, "he says you have a good soul."

"Thanks," Jamison blushed, his mood picking up. At least that was a good thing to come out of the Frei showing up.

Elarie sat down, giving the Frei her full attention while it chirped to her. She crossed her legs and it hopped onto her knee, sitting with its small legs also crossed. The Frei spoke with its hands, animated like a child. Elarie nodded to the story, smiling or laughing every so often. It took a while and Kaelum could see a change in her as it went on. Her shoulders seemed to relax, even the one with a hole in it. Elarie grew calmer. "Thank you," she said to Gee, touching her finger to his blue stomach. A little hiss came from it, showing that she was still unbelievably warm compared to the water thing. "Yes, please do," she nodded.

The Frei got up. He ran across the little walkway and into their cell. First he pat Calix's knee and whistled something, then went to Kaelum.

"Put your left hand out for him," Elarie said. He did, letting the little thing jump into his palm. "He's going to tell you a story now. You don't have to know what he's saying, just sit and listen to him."

Kaelum looked at her, finding her eyes on Calix. She wasn't paying attention to anything else, even as the Frei began to tell his story. Calix was looking at it as well, he didn't see her or feel her stare. Kaelum adjusted on the wall. He focused on the little thing in his hand, lulling to the chirping sound. It wasn't like crickets, though it had sounded that way before. Kaelum couldn't quite place the sound. He found himself relaxing. His pain began to fade. The story the Frei was telling was a long one, long enough to make Kaelum want to fall asleep, and when it ended the Frei cheered.

Kaelum cleared his throat, hearing Elarie ask, "how are you feeling?"

"It doesn't hurt as bad," he managed to say, swallowing thickly. Kaelum looked at Terry.

"You started falling asleep," he whispered gently, then watched the Frei jump off. Gee stood in front of Calix, hands on his hips, and whistled something else, then motioned to Elarie with one arm. Terry laughed, as did a few others. They were all watching the Frei—those that were awake, anyway. A few had taken to sleeping to pass the time. But looking at an adorable little blue creature? It brought a little laughter to the dark brig.

"What'd he say?" Calix looked at Elarie.

She pulled her lips into her mouth. Elarie breathed in and answered, "he asked if I am your loved one. Gee is attaching himself to me and is sort of choosing his allies in a way. Who to trust when it comes to me."

"Oh, then you can trust me," Calix said to the Frei. He tapped his foot. "Uh, yes..." he cleared his throat and glanced around, "yes, she is my loved one."

Gee nodded his big head and ran back to Elarie. Kaelum looked at Terry and his afterlife whispered, "you're my loved one, too." Kaelum scoffed and laughed, pushing on his shoulder. Terry chuckled, closing his eyes.

CHAPTER THIRTY

CALIX

The Frei was the only thing that made anyone happy. No conversations lasted. The only reprieve from pain and anguish hollowing them out as the days went on was Gee. According to Elarie, he was working on speeches and tricks to impress the Earthfoot hiding with the food. Freis had little mating rituals. Dances like birds. And in order for Gee to impress his hopeful mate, he had to dance and jump for him.

He was quite good at jumping. He could jump taller than Kaelum and as tall as Terry. It was the dancing and the words he was having trouble with. Elarie was on her back, her eyes closed, and Gee was on her forehead. He was pacing the short distance.

"Are you in love with him?" Elarie asked him, tapping on the floor with her left hand to keep her blood flowing. Calix watched her hand move up and down, his body twisted uncomfortably and his shoulder aching from the bars he was leaning on. Gee paused. "If you aren't, why are you trying to mate with him?"

Gee replied. Calix longed to ask how someone went about learning the chirping language. Did it involve more than one tutor? Could she chirp the way Gee could or only hear what he was saying?

"But you can fall in love if you aren't mated," she argued, "what if you mate with him and you never fall in love? What if you're just rushing the whole thing because you're afraid?"

Gee tapped his blue foot on her head, whistling.

"No," she shook her head to make him stumble, "it's different for Fae." Elarie stopped shaking her head when Gee chirped something else. "Well Fae have mates to begin with, they don't get to choose. Nature chooses a pair and designates them mates and leaves them to find one another."

"Is it just Fae with Fae?" Terry asked. She opened her eyes and turned her head. "Or can a Fae and a human be mates?"

Gee was standing on her temple now. Elarie said, "I think so." And looked at Kaelum. The closest thing to a Fae in the brig. Gee ran across her forehead as she straightened.

"And you?" Terry questioned. "Because you aren't human."

"Why don't humans have mates?" Jamison asked.

Calix asked, "how do you know if you have one in the first place?"

Elarie groaned, going crosseyed to watch Gee walk down the crooked bridge of her nose. He did a spin on the tip, showing off his balancing skills. Gee tiptoed back up to her forehead and she said, "I don't know; because the gods made you to be like them and they don't have mates; and your senses."

"What about your senses?" Calix asked.

Jamison asked, "why are we more like the gods?"

"What are you?" Was Terry's question.

She sighed, closing her eyes once again. "Some of your senses change when you're around them, which ones depend on the person. Uh, Jamison, you're more like gods because the gods wanted it to be that way. Same reason you have more magic than Fae."

"What about my question?" Terry grunted.

"I have no idea," she threw her arms up and set them back down. Gee chirped. "I am perfectly calm," Elarie told him, "mostly annoyed."

Kaelum said, "this is what happens when people get bored."

Calix pulled on the strap around his thigh, scratching under it. It had been on for days and was beginning to hurt, but he was afraid to take it off. What if he had to get up again? What if they took his leg and he had to hop around? "What do you mean your senses change?" Calix pressed, turning his head to look at her. Elarie was in the same position, head up and eyes closed with her fingers tapping on the wood.

"Smells, tastes, sounds," she mumbled, "they're all a little different."

He looked at Kaelum, his mouth open. Calix searched around, asking, "like they smell differently?"

"Maybe," she said faintly. He turned and looked at her. "Maybe," she repeated. Elarie sighed, something paining her. *Matian*, he thought. The man she was in love with, the one from her past, the one she talked about.

Calix thought he had her figured out, but this was new. This was fresh. *Mates*. He'd never liked the term or the magic. It was too animalistic. Calix had read a few books—written by humans, so he had to take it with a grain of salt—where the Fae were mates. Often it turned into something that made him uncomfortable. It was usually the male that knew it first and they became possessive of their female mate, which on its own he viewed as wrong. He especially didn't like it when the female did not want anything to do with the male and he took to pressuring her into reciprocating the bond. Then, like any good story, they have sex and all is well. The male becomes overly dominant, but it's *fine* because they're *mates* and they're in *love*.

But now... in his reality, without the books and the concepts, mates became very serious. Because there was something wrong with his sense of smell when it came to her. When Kaelum and Terry said she smelled disgusting and that she needed to bathe, all Calix smelled was a warm hearth. That wasn't right. And when they slept together on the beach, when somehow they'd gotten close and he'd opened himself up to her, she didn't have any morning breath.

Did he?

Calix recalled her initial reaction to him telling her she smelled like fire. She'd been uncomfortable. She distanced herself. She got a far-off look like she'd heard it before, long ago, and thinking of it then brought something back.

He leaned forward and smacked Kaelum's leg, mouthing, *ask her more.* Kaelum's brow furrowed, his lip curling on one side, but he looked at Elarie. "So if I'm sort of Fae," he began, shrugging at Calix. Calix nodded him on. "Could my potential mate have a completely different scent?" His eyes widened at Calix and he asked without speaking, *do you think—* Calix shrugged, but he was a little desperate for answers. "Elarie, are you asleep?"

She sort of whined, "I am in so much pain, Kaelum why do you want to know about this?"

"Uh," he looked to his right. "Terry."

Elarie huffed, "it's possible. I tend not to speak to Fae about this sort of thing, so maybe I'm completely wrong about all of it."

Calix waved his hand at Kaelum.

He rolled his eyes, "well what do you know? This has suddenly become extremely important."

She paused. Calix looked back at her, trying to keep his desperate curiosity at bay. Her green eyes were pointed at him. Gee slid off her forehead. Elarie looked at Kaelum. "To my knowledge, it's not as rare as everyone thinks it is. Nature loves the Fae and treats them to love all the time, but even if Terry is not your mate it doesn't mean your love for him isn't just as powerful."

Terry said, "so if I don't smell or look different to him then I'm not his mate."

"I seriously recommend talking to an actual Fae about it," she mumbled, pulling her hair out from under her. Gee began to play with it.

As Elarie turned her head once again to face the ceiling of creaking wood above them, Kaelum asked, "do you think you have one out there?"

"I had one," she said faintly, what Calix could see of her face taking on the distant look. "He died."

"What happens if your mate dies?" Calix asked. At the sound of his voice, he could see her twitch. Her ears moved and her lips tightened.

Elarie said, "I still love, I still feel for others. It's just... like a part of me is forever different. Like when he died I stopped being the person I was when he was with me." She moved her hair again, running her fingers through it and fanning it out around her head.

"How different are you?" Terry asked. He'd get to the bottom of the *what is Elarie* question if it was the last thing he did. Perhaps knowing what sort of person she was before she lost her mate would give him some clue. Calix was close to figuring it out himself. He had his theories, and knowing how she used to be would be helpful, but he doubted it would lead anywhere. Not if she began to do her avoidance thing.

"The sort of different that makes a person question whether they'd still love you if they found out who you were now," she answered.

Calix said, "he would." Elarie turned her head, a fearful look in her eyes. "He'd still love you, Elarie. People don't stop loving someone because they adapt to survive and change because they need to."

"I don't like it when you say things like that," she told him. His brow furrowed. "They make too much sense and then I have to rethink my whole look on life. How do you manage that?"

A smile grew on his face, "an otherworldly knowledge and a loving mother."

She hummed and straightened her head once again. "So that's what I'm missing," she mumbled lazily. Calix didn't say that he was sure her mother loved her. He knew that wasn't what she wanted. She wanted the finality of the conversation—wanted it to be over. One last remark not to be digested further.

Calix looked back into his cell. Terry was massaging the inside of Kaelum's left hand and Jamison's eyes were on the star Terry must've given him. He turned around and it glowed faintly, making Elarie breathe in sharply and sat up. The glow stopped.

"Put it away right now," she hissed and Jamison handed it to Kaelum, who gave it back to Terry. Terry then shoved it in his pants, glaring at her. "Are you out of your minds?" She asked each of them.

Jamison said, "we're six days from the Rings and the *Greyscale* is on its way south. It would take over a week to sail to it." He took a deep breath, "and Grey is about the same. He's probably tracking the ship, maybe he doesn't know we aren't on it."

"What'll happen when he figures that out?" Kaelum asked. They looked at Elarie, but it seemed that she didn't hear the question. Or maybe anything about the *Greyscale* at all. Her mouth was open partially, her green eyes moving slowly. "Elarie? Is Grey going to find us here when he finds out we aren't on the *Greyscale*?" She didn't say anything. "Elarie?"

Calix shook his head at him. Even Terry patted his hand and grabbed Kaelum's attention. "She's six days away from the Rings, Kaelum, it has to sink in."

Kaelum's head moved to Red, who'd been silently taking everything in. He wasn't speaking to anyone at all, Calix hadn't heard his voice once. Even to the three others in his cell. Red just sat there. He didn't look particularly worried or distressed, he was just sitting there watching them. Red nodded to Kaelum.

Shit, Calix thought. He looked away from them. Kaelum was having Red spy on them. That's what he was doing. *Shit. Bastard.* Calix sighed, never having expected to feel betrayed by his best friend. Did Kaelum really not think Calix would be honest with him? Was he so desperate for answers that he'd enlist *Red* to get them? How long had this been happening?

Calix shifted and stretched his leg, wincing as he pulled on it. He pressed between the wood and his leg. "What if I tell them who I am?" Calix asked suddenly, looking at Kaelum. It was a solution. Perhaps not a good one, but one all the same. "I could buy our freedom," he said.

"Or he could make you a hostage and demand money from the crown for you," Terry said.

"I am the crown," Calix argued, "I could buy our freedom with the crown's money because it's mine."

Terry sighed, "all right, let's say you can and it doesn't end badly for everyone, yes?" He straightened and motioned with his hand, "how much is she worth?" They looked at Elarie. She'd laid back down, her hair once again fanned out for Gee to play with. "How much are you willing to pay for her? Because she's the most expensive thing on this ship and Finnal knows it."

"Elarie," Kaelum said, "how much do you think you're worth?"

"I'm the second most expensive in all the Rings," she said quietly. "There's never been fire like mine."

He asked, "but how much? Do you have any idea?"

Calix found himself saying, "I'll pay whatever it is. You know that, right?"

"You'll pay for me, how sweet," she deadpanned.

"Elarie, please I'm trying to help you."

Her head slowly turned. Gee chirped at her, probably annoyed that she moved again. "How much do you think I'm worth, Calix?" She asked, her eyes set on his for answers.

This felt like far heavier of a question than a simple number. She wanted something from him, maybe to know how much he valued her in a monetary sense. Calix asked, "how much does Grey weigh?"

Her brow furrowed, "a lot."

"You want a number, so do I," he countered.

Elarie pushed a smile down. She said, "maybe two hundred tons."

"Two times his weight in gold," Calix said.

Jamison leaned toward Kaelum and whispered, "how much is a ton?" Making them laugh quietly. Elarie was blushing. Must've been the right answer.

CHAPTER THIRTY-ONE

ELARIE

If only the faerthorne took more than just her magic. Her keen sense of smell, for instance. Aside from constantly being able to smell the ever growing stench of sweat and other bodily functions, she could smell the saltwater being carried down in a sloshing bucket. Water spilled on every step, though the carrier didn't seem to mind.

It was the first time Captain Finnal had graced them with his presence since the beginning of the trip. Elarie thought it was good of him. He'd taken to heart what she said about loss and they hadn't been visited by anyone beyond the one giving them food and switching out the buckets they were sharing to use to relieve themselves. No one had gotten hurt, Terisa was still above them.

But now the captain stood watching her. Elarie did not stand, she saw no point. She'd been on the floor for days, that wouldn't change simply because he was there. "We'll be at the Rings soon," he said with a stained-tooth grin. Another pirate walked down. It wasn't the same as either time. This one was broad with a large stomach. "How is my Firefeeder?"

"Fine," she grunted.

"Your name's Elarie, isn't it?" He handed the bucket to the big man, who walked around to the door. He was carrying clothes as well. "Not very intimidating, is it?"

She said, "more personable."

"Old name, Elarie," Finnal said. "Sounds like something my great-grandmother would be called." It made him laugh, though no one but the big pirate joined. "El-la-ree," he mused, the name rolling through his mouth. He chuckled. "Ela for a nickname, no?"

Elarie sat up. Gee, thankfully, was with Kaelum attempting to calm his pain. He'd had a minor panic attack the hour before, so he'd been holding the Frei ever since. The door opened. "To some people," Elarie answered, watching the bucket be carried inside. A small bar of soap was dropped inside followed by the clothes being thrown next to it.

"Like who?" Finnal asked, "lover boy?"

"We aren't that close yet," she mumbled, inspecting the shirt. It was black, tight, and old with frayed pieces in some places. There were no sleeves, only straps of fabric. Like a corset without all the ribbing and lace. She inspected the dark brown pants, finding them to be perfectly suitable. Nothing inappropriate about them, at least.

"Not that close," repeated the captain. "Well I'm sure you're going to get much closer now. You have to bathe before the Rings, don't you?"

Elarie looked down at herself. She was covered in blood and general grime. It made sense for her to bathe, not only because she looked disgusting, but because being covered in blood but also being alive might hint to a few betters that she was more than she seemed.

Part of her wondered, if that was the case, if Finnal wished she were short. Short and malnourished.

"I don't suppose you'll let me dress my wound," she said, looking at the captain. She'd ignore the comment about Calix watching her bathe. They'd all watch her bathe. She couldn't get around some part of her being seen by at least one person in the brig. No doubt some of them would take the opportunity to gawk at a naked girl.

"We'll see," Finnal smiled.

Elarie gathered the clothes and the bucket before she stood, finding a ladle inside with the soap. She got against the wall with her back to the rest of them. Still, there was her right side to contend with now. A few of Kaelum's crew and a rescued slave were looking at her. It was Red that made her nervous. Elarie had never spoken to him, but Calix had pointed each of the crew out to her once and the way he looked at her then hadn't sat right with her. Now? She wanted to curl up and face away from him.

She took off her boots and set them aside before she knelt and picked up the ladle. Elarie let the cold water fall over her head, soaking into her hair and the nasty shirt. Salt soaked into her wound, making her grit her teeth against the shock of pain. Finnal said from behind her, "you don't call her Ela?"

He must've been talking to Calix. Elarie dunked the rest of her hair into the bucket and squeezed the water out. She used the bar of soap to scrub her wet face, neck, and some of her chest and shoulders using only her right hand. She wouldn't even try with the left.

"No," she heard Calix say.

"Ever thought to? I'm a man for nicknames myself," Finnal told him, "even some of my crew call me Finn."

Calix replied, "that's nice. And no, I've never thought to call her Ela."

She smiled a bit, wetting her stomach and scrubbing there. She struggled with her sides a bit with the faerthorne trying to reach for her hand as she got her left side. Elarie then worried about her back. All the reaching and the stretching would hurt both her arm and her shoulder.

Instead she unbuttoned the pants and worked on her waist and the thigh that had received the largest amount of her blood when it had spilled from her stab wound. After that there was really nothing left for her to do other than take her shirt off.

"Ah, the best part," Finnal whispered as she got her good arm through the wet shirt. Elarie winced, struggling to get the shirt over her head. She heard Calix snap for Red to stop looking at her and became even more grateful to him than she had been thus far. Elarie got her hair stuck in the thorns around her arm. Finnal gasped, "she has a tattoo, what an interesting development."

She glanced back. It wasn't *that* interesting. Except maybe to Calix, who she saw had his mouth open and his eyes wide. Elarie ripped the shirt the rest of the way, now topless in front of everyone. And yet the thing that bothered her the most in that moment was that Calix could see her tattoo. Her wings. Elarie had gotten the tattoo years ago. She'd decided she wanted something permanent after all the years without any lasting connections. A tattoo seemed like a good, permanent thing, and what better tattoo than her very own wings?

Elarie had sworn off tattoos of dragons, leaving her with the wings she found when she was a child. The ones that meant she could fly. The butterfly was large, each wing pointed up or down. They were green and lined with black. The subtle hints of red and orange were close to the body of the butterfly. She called them her sparks. Her wings, her magic, her everything.

"Did you get the butterfly to cover some scars?" Finnal asked, sounding like he was teasing her about what was on the body he wanted to see so badly. "There are so many, your butterfly couldn't possibly cover them all."

"I don't need to hide my scars," Elarie said, getting the new shirt over her left arm. "There's nothing wrong with them."

He laughed, "so you're one of those. The 'every scar has a story' type."

"I can't remember all of them, so no," Elarie pulled the shirt down her back and situated it over her body. It was tighter than she expected. She dragged her hair out of her new shirt.

"Ah! Another one!" Finnal shouted gleefully. "Let's see it then."

She looked over her shoulder. "That's the Ring brand. They tattooed mine." Elarie began washing her scalp, ringing her hair out into the bucket. She ignored everyone, moving the bucket behind her before she took off her pants.

"Red if you don't stop looking at her I'm going to kill you," Calix practically growled. She turned her head. No one else was looking at her, only Red. His eyes were on her legs. "Red!" He shouted. Red looked away, rolling his eyes as he did. Elarie decided against washing everything. She just put the new pants on and slid her boots over them.

"I'd like to see you kill someone over her," Finnal said. Elarie stood. She placed everything in the bucket and carried it to the door. "Have you killed for him?" He asked.

She said, "a few times but he doesn't like it so I try not to." Elarie motioned to her shoulder and the wound now dripping with salty blood. "Can I bandage this?" She asked.

He looked at it, shrugging with a curled lip. "No," he decided, "it makes you look weak this way."

Elarie scoffed and walked back to the end of her cell, sitting against the wall by the wet spot. It wasn't a gaping wound and she could live with it. She put her head back, not listening to Finnal's little rant about how much money he'd make because she looked weak and tired. She didn't hear Calix offer any money. Perhaps he was saving it.

He said she was worth two times Greilor's weight in gold. She couldn't wait to tell the dragon that. He'd be ecstatic. Elarie was. The idea that Calix didn't truly hesitate. He looked at her, saw what she wanted from him, and gave it. That conversation had been days ago. She'd been avoiding any other deep conversation since that one and the one about mates, but in her mind she was replaying it. *You want a number, so do I,* he had said. *Two times his weight in gold.*

Ceptari had plenty of gold as it was, but it was so specific. Elarie didn't know how much Finnal would want if Calix decided to give up his identity to him, whether it be less or more, but she'd never forget it.

Finnal left telling the big man about gold and diamonds for some reason. Elarie continued staring at nothing. *You want a number, so do I,* her mind repeated. Again. Again. Elarie looked at Calix, who was pulling at the strap that held his leg to his body. She couldn't imagine it was comfortable. She stared at it, moving her head and her wet hair. He needed to be able to bend his leg without the wood bothering him. Magic helped, but it only went so far. He needed some sort of durable mechanism he could use to rest his weight.

"Calix," she said. He looked over, eyebrows raised to indicate he was listening. "How much of your leg is missing above your knee?"

This wasn't what he expected. Calix blinked quickly a few times, finally saying, "maybe two inches," and held up the distance with his fingers. "Why?"

"Thinking about your leg is distracting," she answered. Elarie looked at her own, holding her fingers at about the same distance as he had. She placed her fingers above her knee. "I'm working on your prosthetic."

He said, "I cannot wait to see what you come up with." Elarie smiled, still staring at her leg and her measurement.

"Maybe you need some sort of wheel," she muttered, watching her knee bend. "Or two pieces instead of one."

Calix was looking at her leg as well. She felt his eyes on her the same way she'd feel a dragon. It was warm and heightened everything. It gave her a sense of spatial awareness. She knew what was around her, she knew how much danger she was in. Elarie lowered her leg, looking at him to find his Lathin eyes trailing up her body. When they met her own he seemed taken aback. The feeling she'd gotten settled. The warmth faded slightly.

"You never told me about the butterfly," he said, resting his temple against the bar he was leaning on.

"We've only known each other for a few weeks," she replied.

Calix argued, "it's been over a month."

"And that makes all the difference," she rolled her eyes. Elarie smiled, though. She looked around, again finding Red staring at her. "What?" She asked him finally, "what do you want?"

He frowned and shook his head, sighing as he faced away from her. He leaned against the wall and crossed his arms, closing his eyes to sleep. "He's reading you," Calix said. Elarie didn't move. "It's what he does. His magical talent. Makes for a good spy."

Gee ran into her cell, chirping about the Earthfoot once again. Elarie looked at Calix as Gee spoke, then at Kaelum. It was Terry who gave it away. For once he wasn't passive or angry. He looked guilty in the sense that he knew he was wrong for something but also didn't care. And in the context of Red... he and most likely Kaelum were using him to spy on Elarie. Calix wasn't giving them answers about what Elarie was quick enough. They were willing to betray their friend because they were impatient.

Chapter Thirty-Two

CALIX

He liked the top. It was horrible of him, but he liked it. Calix knew Elarie was malnourished. He knew that once she was eating regularly she'd return to her normal weight, whatever that was, and found himself wishing to know what she'd look like in a shirt like that when she looked more like herself. He also questioned whether it was wrong of him to request that seamstresses make her dresses with the top in a similar fashion.

Was that wrong? To deliberately dress her in the way he'd like to see her?

The question fogged his mind so much that he nearly missed the fact that everyone was getting up. Kaelum helped him to his feet saying, "we're docking."

"So it's actually happening," he muttered, turning his head to look at Elarie. "I'm going to do it," he said to Kaelum, keeping his eyes on her. She was still seated, waiting. Her eyes were distant, probably reliving everything that had happened to her the last time she was at the Rings. The closer they got the quieter she became, only speaking when she had to and mostly to Gee. Yesterday she hadn't spoken at all, she just stayed curled up against the wall not facing anyone. Gee sat with her, also silent.

Now the Frei was with Jamison, who seemed far too scared.

"Give yourself up?" Kaelum asked, whispering as someone came down the stairs. The big one and Finnal again, followed by the short one that had the vial of whatever poison stole a person's memories and turned them into shells of violence. "Now?"

"No, just wait," he replied. The cage at the back of the brig was opened, followed by the others. When theirs was open the big pirate grabbed Calix's arm and dragged him out himself.

"Go," the skinny one commanded, waving his hand to the stairs. People moved in a line going up to see the sky for the first time in weeks. They were all weary. Depressed. Kaelum nodded to Calix as he went up with Terry. Calix vaguely wondered if he was glad the attention wasn't on him. Would he be able to stay calm the way Elarie was?

Then again—was this calm?

She stood when it was just the two of them and he found her shaking. The big man opened the door for her and she walked through. Finnal made a gleeful sort of noise when she stopped in front of him. He flattened her hair and placed his hands on the sides of her neck. "You are going to win me so much money," he said. "Aren't you, Firefeeder?"

"What are you going to do with everyone else?" She asked.

He grinned at her, then pushed her toward the stairs. Elarie went to them but looked back at Calix. She was waiting for him. She wasn't going to move until he did. Calix tried not to smile when he was shoved. There was a person between them, but she was going up the stairs. He followed, squinting in the bright daylight.

Calix blinked hard, moving only with the push on his back because otherwise, he could hardly see.

"Everyone is for sale," Finnal said happily. "Well, everyone but you my dear," he touched Elarie's cheek and she jerked away.

Calix looked around. They were close to the shores of both Ceptari and the Faerie Lands. The Rings rested on the crest of a hill its buyers and sellers and fighters had to walk up while their carriages were left below. If he squinted he could see them, but he had no trouble seeing the giant building. It was round and made of white stone, clean like it was kept up with constantly. The dome roof was lined with gold and shined so brightly against the sun that he couldn't look at it for too long.

"If Elarie was for sale," Terry asked, "how much would she be worth?"

Finnal laughed. They were in a line shoulder to shoulder and Calix was standing at the end. Elarie, Finnal, and the skinny man were in front of him. "Do you plan on bartering a price?"

"I will," Calix said. "I'll make you an offer right now."

Again, he laughed. Finnal tossed his head back to exaggerate it, his hair flying behind him. Once he'd calmed he asked, "and what money do you plan on paying for her with? Pocket change, perhaps?"

"Her, Terisa, and all of us," he nodded to his left where everyone else was. "I'll be using what gold is mine by right as the Crown Prince of Ceptari."

"The Crown Prince," he snorted, "the Dragon Prince is what he's called, yes?" Finnal looked around. A few of the crew that had gathered in a short amount of time began nodding. "And yet I don't see any dragon. Nor do I see a prince."

Elarie said, "he takes pride in looking like his people," and Calix felt a warmth in his heart similar to the one he felt when she held his hand.

Finnal flicked her on the mouth and took a step toward Calix saying, "prove it. Call your dragon here to prove you are who you say you are."

He glanced at Elarie, who shook her head slightly. "I can't call him to me," he admitted, which was basically true. He was in the process of learning. "His name is Grey. The ship we were on was named after him. The *Greyscale*?"

"Call your dragon," Finnal insisted. "I hear it's a big one."

"No," Calix shook his head. "Do you still want my offer?"

It seemed to bring joy to Finnal that Calix was refusing to do as he asked. Calix expected someone to get hurt because of it, but Finnal only laughed. His grin seemed to grow as he did. "Wow me," he decided.

"Whatever price they're worth is paid," Calix said about the people hoping they didn't get sold to anyone else. "As for Elarie," he looked at her, "the Rings is going to offer you money to buy her back. I'll double it and however much you make betting on her when she fights."

He said, "quite a hefty price even for a prince." Finnal pulled Elarie closer, his grip firmly in her hair. "Tell me, do you think you're worth it?"

"Not particularly, but who am I to stop someone from saving my life?" She answered.

"But how do I know this is the real Prince Calix of blah blah blah?" He asked, humming as he pushed her closer to him. Calix touched her waist, feeling the fabric of the shirt he liked so much. It was soft and worn, probably ages old.

Elarie said, "you could always look at his eyes. Only members of the royal bloodline have the ring of blue."

Finnal pulled on her hair so her head tipped back at a painful angle while he peered at Calix. One of his pirates cleared his throat. He was a skittish looking thing wearing thin glasses that reminded Calix of his tutor. "That's correct. They're called Lathin eyes. Not a single person that isn't of Lathin blood has them. In fact, that's how they find bastards so easily."

Calix said, "I don't have bastard siblings."

"Yes, well," the skittish man said, "that's all. It's proof."

"You can let go of her hair now," Calix said. Finnal looked at Elarie, who was only looking at the sky. He threw her to the deck and she landed on her rear, a look on her face he'd seen before. Recently, even. Finnal kicked her temple and she fell back, her head smacking down hard.

Finnal grunted, "thick damn skull," and kicked her for a second time. Then a third for good measure. He sighed and turned back to Calix. "If she loses just once," he said, holding up a finger, "I'm keeping her. You can have everyone else if you're good for the money," he waved a dismissive hand in their direction, "but you don't get her."

"Fine," he agreed, holding his hand out, "she'll win and you'll be rich."

He shook Calix's hand.

CHAPTER THIRTY-THREE

ELARIE

The rocking was making her nauseous. Or was it bouncing? Elarie groaned. Up, down. Up, down. That was bouncing. She opened her eyes, slowly growing more aware of her surroundings. She was on the big man's shoulder, he was walking on gravel. Her hair was waving. Chains were clinking around her wrists. The left one kept brushing against the thorns.

Where was Calix?

Had knocking her unconscious truly been necessary?

Elarie lifted her head when they were in the shade of the giant building. Her hair blocked most of her vision, but it consisted of the hills and ocean. Ships were docked and people were walking up the path the same way they must've.

"Elarie," Calix gasped and she was dropped. She groaned from the ground and he knelt in front of her, one knee bent and the other at an odd straight angle. He pushed her hair out of her face and winced at what must've been a cut on her head. "You have to win, all right?"

"What?" She cringed, dizzy when he pulled her to her feet. "What happened?" She asked, trying to look around but he held onto her.

Calix put his hands on her cheeks, "Elarie, you have to win every fight or he'll never let me buy you, do you understand?"

"What about everyone else?"

"Everyone else is fine, I need to focus on you right now," he moved his hands down to her neck, though his thumbs remained on her jaw. Calix looked over her shoulder, again not letting her look. "It's going to be all right, Elarie," he said. "Just... be good at killing people."

She laughed. It was short and sharp, but she laughed. Elarie was pulled away, tripping on the gravel as she was dragged to the line people were making. It wasn't long, but it was significant. People who wanted to pay to watch or bet and people who wanted to fight or had fighters. They'd be placed on a list and pay an entry fee.

Elarie looked up at the fountain covered in shade. The statues were not gold or lined with gold. They were black. Rumor said it was the first thing built after the first finished concept of the monstrous building. Elarie thought it was as hideous as the white stone and gold roof—seven female Ring Leaders to represent the seven rings, all naked, all thin, all with their arms facing up to the sky with a large ring in their hands. It was hideous and dysfunctional as a fountain on its own.

She'd passed it once when escaping the burning building and never needed to see it again. Now she stared at the featureless faces until Calix distracted her. "Are you all right?" He asked with a nervous twinge in his voice. He stood in front of her blocking most of the fountain.

"It's just killing people, Calix," she assured, "and we both know I'm very good at that. You have nothing to worry about."

"But with the drug—" He started.

As Finnal began to laugh at him Elarie said, "it doesn't affect my ability to fight for my life." Even with the assurance, he didn't seem to feel any better. Perhaps he was feeling for the both of them, or he thought he had to. "Are you all right?" She asked as they grew even closer to the entrance. Elarie ignored the thumping of her heart to hear Calix.

"I feel guilty," he told her quietly. Her brow furrowed and she began to shake her head, but Calix stopped her with a look. "I should've fought my father harder and destroyed this place," he told her, "but I didn't and I hate to say that I feel even more guilty because I forgot about all of it until you brought it up."

"You aren't king, Calix, there's nothing you could've done and nothing you can do now," Elarie said, moving her head to look at how close they were. They were three people away and yet the person writing names down was looking at her. His eyes moved over her and the people around her—Finnal, who he probably recognized as well, and perhaps even the two of his men, and Calix—before he grabbed another man by the collar and whispered something to them, then shoved him away. "Say it again," Elarie found herself whispering. She reached forward and gripped his old, dirty shirt. She pulled him closer to her, "say it's going to be all right again."

Calix put his head against hers, his hand finding her right arm. It moved down, tracing over her warm skin until he reached her fist and squeezed it. He pressed his fingers into her hand and opened it. "It's going to be all right," he said only to her. "It's just this once. One more time and you're free of it."

Someone broke through the crowd to exit, someone in charge. Elarie looked over and inhaled sharply, gripping Calix's hand to the point where she was sure she might break something. The man, Retch as he named himself, grinned at her. His gold tooth shined at her. "Look what you've brought us," he said to Finnal and yanked Elarie away from Calix. He wrapped his large hand around her throat and lifted her into the air to sniff her hair and neck. "Smoke and fire, eh Firefeeder?" He squeezed and she gagged. "Oh, Finnal, the Rings are very grateful for this gift."

"She is not a gift," Finnal said. Elarie kicked one of her legs, her face turning red. "I own her."

Retch clicked his tongue to the roof of his mouth, "unlucky little Firefeeder. Aren't you?" He then laughed and dropped her. "Right this way, sir," he motioned with his hand, "I'm sure we have much to discuss."

"She'll be fighting first," he said, watching Elarie cough at their feet. "I want to see what she's worth before you give me an offer to buy her back."

"We shall start her at ring one," said the male. He had to be something, Elarie was never sure. He wasn't Fae so he had to be faerie. Maybe a giant. While those were rare, it wasn't like they were on their way to becoming extinct. Most were just ugly due to inbreeding and kept to the mountains of Trec. Who's to say one didn't corrupt the clean giant line and sleep with a human? Maybe more than one over a few generations.

She was dragged around the people in line and down the iron stairs. Elarie had never been up, she'd never been sure what was in the building part of the Rings, only what was below it. It was round like what could be seen from the ships, but wider to account for the size of the rings and the crowds. Tapestries and signs were hung in crooked ways along the walls. The ceiling was lit with circles of flames on short chandeliers.

As Elarie walked down the curved stairs she was able to see all seven rings, six smaller and one large one in the middle. At each was a Leader. They were all women, all bald, and in charge of presenting the fights and keeping track of the bets for each one. Elarie knew all of them. They never changed. Didn't seem to age, either, which Elarie wasn't comfortable with. She wanted to kill one of them just to see if they came back the way she did.

"This way," Retch said as if they didn't all know where they were going. Ring one, where minor fights began. If Elarie was right she'd make the rounds until they put her against the Messenger. He was inevitable.

"Welcome back," the Ring Leader said. Elarie's head snapped to her, her fear beginning to take over. She held up a tube and Elarie stepped back.

Final pulled on her hair and turned her to face Calix. "Here, Highness," he said and Calix looked at Elarie. She breathed heavily, practically on the verge of tears. *I don't want to do this again, please don't make me do this again,* she thought like a whining child. "Watch this," he said. Elarie didn't look away from him as the tube was cracked, trying to find some comfort in his frightened face as it was stabbed into her neck.

Her eyes closed and her knees buckled. Someone was laughing, though it was muffled. Elarie was being held by someone, her head back against their shoulder while the chains around her wrists were removed.

The tube was taken out of her neck and Elarie swayed, practically unable to feel the pain of the faerthorne being removed from her arm. She blinked slowly and was forced to face someone with dark hair and ugly teeth. "Don't show your fire until the last moment," the man told her. Why was he telling her things? Elarie tried to pull away but he yanked her back, "do you understand?"

She grunted and pushed him, beginning to panic as she blindly crawled through the opening to a smooth floor. Her hands landed in blood, which she stared at as she stood. The opening closed behind her. Elarie squinted, backing into cold bars. Someone was in front of her. She was bald and a golden ring glowed on her head as she announced. Elarie wiped her hands on her pants.

"First dose?" Someone asked from her right side. She looked at him. A Fae. "This is, isn't it? First of many, I assume." People were screaming for him to hit her as he gave her a pitiful frown. "Shall I make it your last?"

Elarie got off the bars and moved away from the male, but the ring was small and he was large. She watched his fists get bigger, which only made him larger. *What is happening?* Elarie asked herself as he swung one of the large fists. She dodged, a bright, hot feeling in her chest convincing her this male was trying to kill her and she had to fight him to prevent that. Elarie did not want to die.

When he laughed and tried to punch her again Elarie grabbed his wrist and pulled, throwing him into the bars behind her. They dented with the weight and force, magically snapping back to normal as soon as he stood again. "You're a strong thing, aren't you?" He asked, wiping blood off his face.

Kill him, kill him, kill him. Elarie took a step back. How would she kill him was the question. Elarie could kill him—she would kill him—but how would she do it? Her head spun with options so dizzily she was nearly hit by the next swing.

How unentertaining it was to watch someone be beaten to death.

What was better than fists?

Elarie dodged a few more times until people were screaming at her. She wasn't entertaining enough. Perhaps they'd leave her be if she wasn't entertaining enough. Elarie let the next punch hit her in the chest. It sent her backward.

"Come on, I'm not getting paid to dance with a little girl," grunted the Fae.

"You're getting paid?" Elarie blurted, looking away from him. Was she getting paid? Why was she in the ring in the first place? The male laughed at her. People were cursing at her. "I'd like to leave," she breathed, looking around for an exit. The male punched her in the side of her head. Elarie hit the ground and her ears rang, but she was looking at someone. The only person that wasn't screaming at her or cursing things.

"Kill him," he said and Elarie felt a hand in her hair. She cried out, reaching up to grab it while the Fae lifted her to her toes and forced her to face him.

He said, "people like watching little girls get beat, didn't you know that? That's what you're here for. To get beat."

No, that was wrong. Through the pain in her scalp, she knew that was wrong. "I'm here to win," Elarie said faintly. People wanted her to die. They wanted the Fae to land a killing blow. "I have to win," she said and he bared his teeth. Elarie punched him in the mouth and he dropped her, stumbling back. She landed on her feet, breathing evenly. She was there to win. She had to kill him. The man with the pretty eyes told her to kill him.

The Fae spit out one of his fangs, blood dripping from his mouth now. He growled at her, making a sort of bubbling noise because of the blood. When he ran at her she kicked him in the chest and ran her hands through her hair. Elarie moved it over one shoulder and began to braid it, waiting for the male to stand. His hand was on his chest. He was coughing.

"You're dead," he told her, pointing a big finger at her.

She tossed her braid back over her shoulder. "Get it over with, then," she said bluntly. He ran at her. *Kill him, kill him, kill him.* She grabbed his wrist and snapped it, making him howl in pain. Even more so when she cracked his knee to the side. Elarie climbed onto his shoulders and used her legs to hold his arms down. The male thrashed and began to scream. Elarie's fingers pressed into his hairline, heat burning over his skin. She grit her teeth. *Kill him, kill him,* she insisted and pressed harder. The Fae was only screaming now, his hair aflame. He thrashed, throwing her against the bars.

Elarie laughed, feeling something melt over her hands as they lit to wild flames. *Kill him, kill him, kill him.* The male dropped to his knees and scratched at her arms, begging her to stop.

So she did. Elarie let go and looked up, finding the man with the pretty eyes. He looked concerned. She didn't know why, she was doing what he told her to do. Elarie got off and walked toward him to ask him what it was, but the Fae grabbed her leg and yanked her down. Elarie landed on her chest, the wind knocked from her lungs. She was forced onto her back.

"Fire elemental bitch," he grunted. His hair was gone and his skin had taken on some sort of melted looking texture. He climbed on top of her. "I'm going to kill you, fire bitch—"

He burst into flames. Elarie crawled backward as the Fae screamed and thrashed. He tried rolling over the floor and running around flailing his arms. When he ran out of energy he fell to his knees, then onto his face. People cheered. For her, not for him.

The woman with the gold ring on her head came into the ring and shouted something about fire. Elarie was being pulled out. She looked at the man with the pretty eyes. He was much closer, now looking nervous and queasy. He took another step and opened his mouth to speak, but didn't.

"Firefeeder," said another man.

"Dragon," Elarie mumbled, unsure where she was going with it. "You smell like a—" Another tube was stabbed into the same place on her neck and the thought went away. As she struggled to remain standing, she could hear the man asking her something. Something about a dragon, something that sounded important, but Elarie was pulled to the next ring and away from him.

CHAPTER THIRTY-FOUR

CALIX

Finnal had thanked him for making him so rich. Because he owned the fighter he wasn't allowed to bet, so the skinny man had done it for him. He bet everything he had on Elarie, banking on her being underestimated because she was confused, weak looking, and a woman. And it had worked. Sexism won.

Calix didn't want to think that for the first ring, she was so confused that she might've actually lost if it wasn't for him telling her to kill the Fae. He wished to pretend that didn't happen. That Elarie, in her personality-less state, had listened to him. He said *kill him* and she did.

On ring two she didn't need to be told. By ring three she was getting better at understanding what was happening. That they wanted a show. So she made a show of it. Calix knew she could kill any of them without blinking, this was purely for their benefit. She was getting back into a familiar routine. Feeding people her fire, making good on her name.

But after the fifth ring, there was something wrong with her. She was sparking when she shouldn't have been. She was overwhelmed. Elarie was desperate to see someone familiar but she couldn't. She didn't know anyone there, she looked right through Calix. When they stuck the sixth tube into her neck she fainted. They broke her smallest finger on her left hand to wake her up then proceeded to give her another dose, smaller this time, and force her into the ring.

Elarie killed two people in that ring. A Fae and a human that had a handful of marbles he let fly through the air. One of them went through part of Elarie's arm. Calix had seen fear, especially when it came to her, but the look on the human's face when Elarie shattered every one of the marbles at once was something that would haunt him. He began to spiral, wondering who was forced and who wasn't. How many of them were like Elarie? How many of them were bleeding and frightened, how many of them didn't know who they were?

She got out of the ring to the same onslaught of shouting. Someone spat on her as she was led by. People were throwing things, screaming because she lost them money. Why people were betting on anyone but her, Calix didn't know, but when someone pushed her she fell against him and all thoughts of anything else faded from his mind in an instant.

"I don't want to do this," she told him as if he had anything to say about it. Tears welled up in her eyes, "please, I don't want to see him again, please don't make me do this."

"What?" Calix held onto her, looking back to see the tube being walked over for her. "Elarie, what are you talking about?"

She sobbed, "he killed Damilla and he said if he ever saw me again he'd kill me too but if I die—" The tube was stabbed into her neck, whatever drug it was entering her bloodstream. Elarie's grip on Calix's arms went slack and she fell against him. People began to quiet, a slow humming cheer growing around them. Calix looked around fearfully, then at Finnal.

"Last chance," said the captain, "do you think she'll win now?"

Elarie lifted her head, her green eyes seeming to have lost their color. "Why do you smell like that?" She asked.

"Like what?" Calix asked. They were all waiting for something. Every ring had stopped, and the fighting paused. Was it the Messenger person? Was he so powerful he deserved his own silent entrance?

"Dragons, my dragons," she looked him up and down weakly.

Calix said, "I ride one of them. Greilor, I ride him."

"No..." she was pulled away from him, "not Greilor, not..." Elarie was shoved into the largest of the seven rings and Calix walked next to Finnal. They looked up at her and she looked back at them. Elarie got on her hands and knees, "you can't smell like him, he's dead. He died centuries ago—"

"Can I get another tube over here?" Asked the Ring Leader in a passive, unamused tone. Calix glanced at her, looking for the tube for only a moment before putting his attention back on Elarie.

He repeated, "centuries?" Then felt a hint of guilt creep up his spine. He shouldn't ask her things like that. He shouldn't get his answers when she was in no state to choose what to say.

"He was with the hatchlings, he must've gotten crushed when the Keep went down like everyone else. You can't smell like him because he's dead," she shook her head, "you shouldn't smell like dragons, what are you?"

"What?" Calix felt his eyes go a little wide. "I'm a human, I didn't do anything to change the way I smell."

Next to him, Finnal chuckled. The Ring Leader came from behind Elarie, moving her head to the side to stab the tube into her neck. Calix could see welts had formed on some of them, each of them pink or red and angry looking. When she removed the tube Elarie fell onto her side. The Ring Leader walked away with a scoff, avoiding stepping on her.

Heat began to waft off of her. Elarie rolled onto her back, her breathing deep and heavy. One of her arms was crossed over her stomach and the other was extended toward him. Elarie was covered in ash and blood. Bruises were forming on her body and her left arm was practically unrecognizable. Her hair was coming out of its braid and was somewhat knotted at the top of her head.

Calix couldn't stop staring at her. He hated her situation, he hated that she was afraid, confused, and uncomfortable, but the way her hand moved up her chest and covered her face was doing something to him nothing had ever done before. Gods, did he want that feeling to stop? What would he do if it didn't?

Elarie sat up with a grimace and touched her neck. When everyone went silent, she looked to her right at the other side of the ring. The Messenger was a dark man, perfectly built. For some reason he reminded Calix of his father, though he was younger and had no facial hair. The Messenger was clean, unmarred by the bloody fight of the rings Elarie had gone through. He was their last contender, the one winners faced and lost to.

Like Elarie.

She stood slowly. The Messenger smiled at her, "our little Firefly," he said, "back to the fold?"

"No," Elarie shook her head.

"No," he repeated calmly, practically in a taunting whisper. "Came to die, then?" The Messenger stepped further into the ring. Calix looked around at the silent watchers. Even people in other rings had paused to see what the two of them would do. They now stood next to each other, watching as if they hadn't been trying to kill one another moments before. Elarie backed up, hitting the bars. "Answer me, Firefly," he ordered, making Calix wonder why he had a separate name for her. Firefeeder and Firefly? She looked down and at Calix, someone she didn't know yet placed her attention on. "Oh," the Messenger chuckled, "replaced Damilla, have you?"

Elarie snapped her head to the Messenger. "I didn't," she shook her head and breathed in, "I didn't do anything."

"She'd be so upset that you moved on so quickly," he said.

"I didn't do anything!" Elarie shouted.

"No, you don't even remember her," he moved toward her, ignoring the shout for them to fight already. Taunting was fine for a while, but they paid for violence not to watch a girl lose herself over her lack of memory. "The stone that separated you, the touches you shared, you don't know any of it. How *pathetic* you are, Firefly."

He was in front of her. The Messenger held his hands on the bars by her head.

"Look at you trying to remember who I am," he said just for her, but it was loud enough for Calix to hear. "Who you are? I know, do you? What you are, who you are, isn't that what you are so afraid of? Does he know you?"

That was what it was. It was Elarie, not wanting anyone to know what she was, being threatened by it. Like the Fae. Even if she wasn't sure who or where she was, her instinct told her to protect her secrets. She snapped like she had with the Fae. Elarie head-butted him, her forehead connecting with his nose. When he stumbled back a step she kicked him in the chest and sent him flying backward. He landed on his back and began to laugh as people cheered.

Sparks flew around her defensively. She took a step away from the bars as the Messenger stood. Calix looked at Finnal and asked, "why do they call him the Messenger?"

Finnal grinned. "The Messenger of Death. It's said he knows when someone is going to die, that he knows when he'll win or lose."

"What's his power? Why is he a fighter?"

He said, "darkness snuffs out light, does it not?"

Calix looked back to the ring as the fires above them flickered. The candles dotting the walls did as well. Elarie didn't seem all that affected by it, but she was still nervous. So was the Messenger her equal? Her opposite? Water was the opposite of fire, darkness only fed it. What better place for fire to be than in darkness?

The shouting for blood grew louder, distracting Elarie. She looked at the few who sounded the loudest and a tendril of that darkness shot out at her like a punch to the chest. Her head hit one of the bars and she slid down it.

"Just kill him," Calix found himself saying. What was wrong with him? Morally—well, who gave a damn about morals in a place like this? He breathed in deeply, watching fire climb up Elarie's arms. It sparked through her braid, tracing like lines and strands of hair. As she stood the flames coated her, flickering like wind blowing through her clothes.

People cheered for her. The betting was even. Her or him, counterparts. He wondered how many people had seen them together before. How many times he'd won over her. The Messenger didn't seem to be affected by the tubes, so perhaps he was doing it willingly. Getting paid, even. Which meant that Elarie was at a disadvantage already. And she only lost when she was told to. Every fight was rigged.

But this one.

She was thrown back again and again and again, taking a beating with no marks. People laughed and cheered, numbers were thrown around and the Ring Leader kept track of them all. Was it some sort of magic? Every time Elarie got hit the bets on the Messenger grew higher. She looked weak. Tired.

The next time she stood she was swaying.

"Doses and more doses," said the Messenger, clicking his tongue as he circled her. The crowd laughed and cheered. Even Finnal got a laugh out of her struggling. "Firefly," he taunted, "look at you trying to get it all back. What will the first thing be? Your brother?" He kicked her to the floor and her fires went out. "Your kingdom?" The Messenger kicked her in the face and blood bloomed under her nose. "Your dragon castle or your pathetic little family?" When she reached up with her hand blazing he grabbed her wrist and twisted her body, "or will it be Damilla and all her stories?"

"Elarie!" Calix shouted, "kill him!"

She yanked him down, nearly breaking her arm in the process, and as he fell toward her she put her feet on his shoulders and got her wrist free to catch his head in her hands.

The room went silent. All of Elarie was on fire, a burning inferno that melted the floor. The Messenger was screaming, thrashing with his magic and body as she pulled and pushed at the same time.

And ripped his head off of his body.

CHAPTER THIRTY-FIVE

ELARIE

She threw the head away and crawled out from under the body. Elarie was no longer on fire, it was just her. She felt naked without it. Not like herself. Too much was happening. People were shouting at her, they were screaming. Her vision was blurring. Blood was pooling at her feet. Someone was grabbing her.

Why did the man know so much about her? The Messenger... she knew him, but she didn't.

Elarie was being dragged out of the ring. Blood dragged off the bottom of her shoes. She breathed quickly, finding herself panicking. That was bad. She shouldn't be panicking, panicking was bad in the Rings. Someone was saying her name, but everything was fuzzing over. She was being pulled one way, but her cheeks were being held by someone else. They smeared the splatter of blood on her face. So many people were touching her. Someone with an angry look spit in her direction, the wad of saliva landing in her hair.

Elarie sobbed, still hearing her name but she didn't know who was saying it or where it was coming from. She did know what the flash of opaque glass meant. It meant all of what she was feeling would stop. And she welcomed that. She let the painful stab into her neck seep liquid into her system and flood her mind until there was nothing left of her.

There were still hands on her face, only now she was able to register it was a man with a face filled with worry and eyes that made her think they were something important, but she didn't know what.

"Elarie?" He asked like she might've known him. But he was forced away from her and she was dragged up a set of curved stairs. Elarie's mind fogged as they turned again. Were there hallways? Something was cold. There was a big room with a window facing the sea. It reminded Elarie of something. It spread a sad feeling through her, though the feeling didn't last.

"You understand how much money I am going to lose now that she killed my favorite fighter?" A harsh female voice asked. Elarie was pushed into a soft, plush chair. "People come to see the Messenger kill, now what am I supposed to do?"

The man with the pretty eyes knelt in front of her but didn't say anything. He just looked at her while an argument began. Money. Elarie knew she was worth money. Her name was written on the wall next to the window that faced the sea. It was a total of some kind, like how much she'd earned within a certain period.

"Make me an offer, then," said a scratchy, happy voice. The owner of it leaned against the desk in Elarie's field of vision. The female voice moved as well, choosing to sit in a large chair opposite them. The man looked behind him at her. "He already has," said the man leaning on the desk, motioning to the man kneeling in front of her. So the man with the pretty eyes wanted to *buy* her.

The woman considered something. "How much?"

"Double whatever number you offer and double whatever we earned betting on her," said the man on the desk. "Seems like you aren't going to buy back the Firefeeder."

"How do you know he's good for it?" The woman asked, "you know I am."

A large chest was placed on the desk and something clinked inside it. The man on the desk said, "he's the Crown Prince of Ceptari. I'm sure he's good for it. And if not I have people to kill to punish him and I'll come right back here."

"I doubt that," grunted the woman. Elarie blinked slowly. She swooned backward, hitting the chair. The man with the pretty eyes put his hands on her knees. Again, there was something familiar. It went away in an instant.

"You're out of luck, then," said the man. The one in front of her stood, looking at the two of them.

He said, "so she's mine, yes?"

"When I have your gold on my ship, she's all yours," agreed the man. He had a ship. What about a ship? "And when the Rings make me an offer."

They both looked at the woman so Elarie did as well. The woman stared back at her, then turned her head to the total on the wall. "Double that is my offer," she pointed. The man with the pretty eyes tensed. It was a lot of money, after all. Five years? Yes, five years amounted to quite a lot of money. The Rings was offering double the large number to buy Elarie, money she didn't think they actually had, and that meant that the man with the pretty eyes had to double that number. Did princes have that much money?

"Are you good for it, Your Highness?" Asked the man.

He nodded.

"Doesn't seem like you're very sure," the woman said with a smirk. Perhaps she had some idea of how much gold Ceptari had when no one else did. "And what could you possibly do with the Firefeeder? What do you want with her?"

He said, "that is my business."

She chuckled and leaned forward, lacing her fingers in front of her, "you know, it's quite easy to get her to talk when she can't say no," she nodded to her, "and want to know something I've learned?"

"Not particularly," replied the man with the pretty eyes.

"Everyone that comes near her has a way of ending up dead," she said, "friends and lovers alike." Elarie winced, unable to remember any of them. Did she want to? This was much easier. Sad, but easier. "Most recently? Damilla."

Damilla, Damilla, who was Damilla? The name sparked much within her. Many emotions, though Elarie couldn't place a face or a reason for any of them.

The man said, "I don't care. My dragon likes her so I'll spend whatever I need to keep her from people like both of you. Now," he slid his hands into his pockets as if he was attempting to hide a nervous twitch, "are we finished?" Elarie looked at his face. He had a dragon. What kind of dragon? He seemed like he'd ride something small with a back like a horse he could easily mount. Perhaps with a saddle. But that was wrong. Something was wrong with that.

"What dragon?" She asked to alleviate the annoyance of not knowing the answer to the question. This bothered her more than anything else. Dragons were important, after all—even if she didn't know why.

"Greilor," he answered easily, like it was no problem she asked. Perhaps he wanted her to. Still, she shook her head. That was wrong as well. "He didn't die with the hatchlings, Elarie. You know that—"

Her arm was grabbed, stopping him from continuing, and sharp thorns began to wrap around her. Elarie screamed, pulling away. Her other arm was grabbed roughly and twisted behind her back, then her neck was placed in a chokehold.

"I knew you'd scream eventually," said an unfamiliar, skinny man. He laughed at her, turning something she didn't understand into a joke for everyone else while her breath was cut off. Elarie could've fought back. She realized that these men were not as strong as she was. Elarie could've beaten them, then perhaps the man with the pretty eyes would take the faerthorne vine off so she'd have access to her magic. But she didn't. She let them choke her, she let them laugh at her, and decided she could use the rest even if the sleep was forced.

CHAPTER THIRTY-SIX

CALIX

They dropped her in the cell and left her body in the position she fell in. Calix could do nothing to help alleviate the twisted form she'd been forced into. He only watched them shut the cell door on her and then on him and waited for the pirates to leave before he turned around and looked at Kaelum.

"Come here," he said after a moment and Calix took a few steps, putting his arms around him. "How bad was it?"

He didn't tell Kaelum that Elarie ripped someone's head off their body. He never would. That was something Kaelum and Terry would abuse. He didn't even tell them about the fights themselves. Instead he said, "she's worth forty million gold pieces."

Kaelum cursed.

"Double that twice and add double what he won betting on her fights," Calix said in a low, self-pity-filled tone. "That's how much I'm paying for her. The rest of you? No idea yet."

Terry asked, "what about the ship?"

He shook his head and shrugged, "I don't know, I didn't ask." What did it matter? Why was he asking questions like that right after Calix agreed to pay for *people*? People! And he was worried about a damn pirate ship? One that was easily replaceable. Calix's army was mainly one that fought on the sea, he had plenty of ships for them to choose from.

Calix turned around and looked at Elarie.

"What happened to her?" Jamison asked quietly, though everyone in the brig heard him and wanted the answer all the same.

"She seemed so scared," Calix said. "Even when she was fighting, she didn't know what she was doing. Everyone laughed and cheered and the whole time she was so confused."

Terry asked, "she killed people?"

"She had to," he looked at him.

"Because she's good at it," he said.

Calix faced him, "why are you acting like she had a choice? Do you really think she wanted to be drugged, lose every memory of the life she had, and be told to be beaten and kill for entertainment?"

"I'm just saying I'm sure she'll be fine when she wakes up," he said in his stupid uncaring tone, "she's got to be used to it by now."

He stared in complete disbelief. Even Kaelum hid a cringe from next to Terry. Calix said, "you know what, she was right. The only way you'd come close to understanding is if it was Kaelum in her position."

"Of course it would be different if it was Kaelum, Kaelum's never killed people for the fun of it," Terry threw his arm up, "and you can't deny that! Elarie is a murderer, she enjoys killing people and gets satisfaction from it. The Rings was just her killing whether she wanted to or not and she'll be fine when she wakes up. It's that simple."

"But you weren't there," Calix pointed at him, then at her, "you didn't have to watch her beg them to stop, you sat on your ass and complained while she fought for her life—"

"Evidently she has more than one of those, so that wouldn't make all that much of a difference either," he shook his head, "gods, how blind are you? She promises to teach you how to ride a dragon and suddenly nothing she does is wrong in your eyes?"

Calix scoffed and took a step back. "I never said what she did wasn't wrong. I agree that she kills people and that's wrong, I just happen to know why—"

"And you won't share that!" He shouted. Terry stepped toward him, "you won't share anything you know about her! I wouldn't be surprised if you knew what she is and refused to tell us for some bullshit reason you justify in your thick head!"

"Why would I share anything with a person so set on her being some kind of monster you'd let someone spy on your best friend?" Calix spat. "Why would I trust you? Either of you," he looked at Kaelum, "if you won't trust me?"

He supposed neither of them expected him to know. Kaelum had paled, his eyes shocked and scared. "Calix," he began, but Calix shook his head.

"I hope you learn something from Red," he took yet another step back, "because from this point on *she* decides what either of you know. When she trusts you so will I. Right now you don't mean shit to me."

Calix turned away and rubbed his face with both hands. Terry said, "way to choose her over your friends. It's only been a month, hasn't it?"

He grit his teeth and faced Terry once again. The pirate waited for some sort of reply. A snarky remark or a quip. Instead, Calix channeled Elarie's energy and punched him in the face. Terry fell back into the bars of the cell holding his nose and a few people in the brig gasped. One made a loud '*ohhh*,' sound. "Stop," Calix said simply, and sat down.

They waited hours, completely silent. Terry's nose had bled for some time and Kaelum fussed over it for longer, though his first mate wanted none of his care. He wanted to sit there and bleed as if that would make Calix feel bad. He didn't think he ever would.

"Calix," Jamison whispered, sitting up. He turned around.

Elarie was pulling her right arm out from under her and rolling onto her back. Her eyes were shut tight and her body tensed up. No one said anything as she sat up slowly, her legs falling to either side. She looked at her left arm. Her right hand shook as she hovered it over the vine. Elarie touched it and a thorn grew out of it, latching onto her finger. She ripped it away and shook her hand through the air, then stared at her finger.

"Elarie?" Calix asked as she rubbed her thumb over her blood. Her head turned. "Do you know me?" She breathed in slowly and looked around. "Elarie," he said and again, she looked at him, "do you know me?"

"I don't," she said, "I don't know." There was an accent that wasn't there before. Something pretty and light. Elarie stood and he did as well.

He asked, "what do you know?"

"This hurts," she lifted her arm, "can you take it off?"

Terry whispered, "what accent is that?" To Kaelum.

"It's complicated Elarie, I need you to listen to me," Calix said, ignoring the two of them. She walked over to the cell door and looked at the lock. It was part of the door, not something she could break off. "Are you listening, Elarie?" He held the bars. Elarie was not. She shoved the door open, cracking and breaking it, then stood in front of him.

"Take it off," she held her arm up, "please."

"Can you open the door?" He jerked his head toward it. Elarie stared at him. "Please," he added. "I want to help you but it would be easier if we weren't speaking through the bars of a cage."

She surveyed him, then everyone else. Elarie walked to the door and yanked it open. "Are you going to explain?" She asked, backing up as he stepped forward. He searched her eyes, finding them blank when she looked at him. She didn't know him.

"Elarie," he said, "I will take this off I promise, but you need to listen to me." She managed a nod. "When I take it off someone up there may sense your magic. If that happens people will die, are you prepared for that?"

"*Prepared*?" She repeated with a furrowed brow, "why would I be prepared for people to die?"

Terry said, "you do it a lot."

"Do what a lot?" She looked at him.

"Kill people," he said simply. Elarie stared at him, her lips slowly parting. "You're good at it, it's what you do best."

She seemed to want to contradict him like she had something else that she was the best at, but Elarie started to go numb instead. Calix wondered what part of her past she was stuck in. She closed her eyes and went back to Calix, opening them for him to find they were swimming with tears.

"Is Ceptareei not your first language?" Kaelum asked, diverting her attention, "where are you from otherwise?"

Elarie opened her mouth and Calix put his hand over it. Her eyes went wide and she pulled back but he only pressed further. "When you are the Elarie I know you'll thank me," he said with a nod. Because he didn't know where in her past her head was, he couldn't risk her saying anything. Whether it be six years ago or when she was still with Matian, he didn't know. So he'd protect it.

She lifted her hand and held his wrist, pulling it away from her mouth. Elarie looked at his fingers, more specifically his nail beds. They were stuck with dirt and blood. He needed to clean them—clean all of him—but that obviously had to wait. Still, Elarie held onto his hand. She looked at him, "this is Greilor's ash," she said and showed him his own hand, "how did you get this?"

"I ride Greilor," he said, "I call him Grey. Remember?"

"No," she shook her head, "I ride Greilor, his name is Greilor, and you are a Ceptarian, how could you possibly know him?"

He winced, "Elarie—"

"If he's been going to Ceptari he would've told me," she argued, "he knows how much I want to go. Where is he? Take this off right now I need to call him."

Elarie held her left arm up for him. Calix took it, but said, "you can't call him or the people on this ship will kill him. They do it to dragons, you know this."

"They kill dragons on this ship?" She asked and he nodded. Elarie's eyes flashed before she held her arm up again. This was a much different Elarie than the one he knew, that was quick to understand. Both Elaries were determined and fiery, but the one in front of him had a drive the other did not. She had something to live for, she had people she loved. Dragons. Gods, she had her dragons.

The ones Elarie was raised with, who she'd probably defend to her last breath. They were still alive in her mind.

"What are you going to do?" Kaelum asked when Calix got the first thorn out.

Elarie winced but looked over. She looked younger somehow. Worried and worn, yet younger. The tension in her body eased off her face and allowed room for other things. She said, "break things."

"Break—Elarie, they're threatening the lives of our friends. Of your friends," he said, "and you plan on going out there and breaking things?"

Quite a serious look crossed her face. Calix pulled the thorns off down to her elbow. "Dragons are as sacred to me as your stars are to you, Metar, I would expect you to at least somewhat understand."

"That doesn't answer the question," he said.

"I will do what I have to do to protect the things I care about more than myself," she nearly snapped, "even if that means killing for them."

Calix asked, "have you done it before?" It was wrong of him, but he wanted to know this Elarie as much as the other, even if he somehow preferred the meaner, more broken one.

"Once," she said, "but I was justified in my actions, even Matian thought so and he's always been so very against violence."

"Does he know you're an angry person?" Calix asked. *Stop,* his mind told him. She wasn't in the right state to answer questions.

Elarie looked him up and down. "He likes it. That doesn't mean he likes violence. What do you know of it?"

"Last thorn," he nodded to it. Elarie took a deep breath.

She bounced from one foot to the other, then smiled just a little bit at him. Calix pulled it out and watched her go up the stairs like this was a game. He followed, leading a line of pirates behind him. Calix found Elarie standing on the deck spinning in a circle, confused.

He went toward her. Elarie looked at him, sighing like the sight of him brought some sort of comfort, and he said, "try not to break everything, we need the ship."

"How did you get out?" Asked Finnal, more amazed than offended.

"Excuse me?" Elarie turned to him, "I woke up in *your* cage?"

Calix moved in front of her quickly, holding a hand up, "there's something wrong with her memory, she's stuck in the past—"

"Get back downstairs, both of you," he said, though he eyed her curiously. Same as everyone else.

"No," Elarie snapped. Something on the side of the ship lit on fire. "No, I will not stand for people hunting dragons and I will have justice for those you killed."

He ground his teeth. "Put that fire out right now."

"No," she insisted.

"Get me the old hag!" Finnal turned partially, looking up at the quarterdeck while yet another thing caught fire. The heat of the flames carried to them. They were different from her usual ones, Calix could see it. Her normal fire—what he'd seen—was nowhere near as dark or as red. The flames in front of him flickered with other colors, so hot they ranged down to a white-blue. *This* was her fire, not anything he'd seen before. This was magic. Pure, hot, and dangerous. It was her magic.

Amazing.

Terisa was led down the stairs and Elarie asked, "should this affect me somehow? I don't know this woman."

"Elarie," Calix faced her, his hand on her arm, "you do care about her, you know her."

"No, I don't, get off," she pulled and a spark zapped between them, forcing him to rip his hand away. Elarie again faced Finnal, "I will not go back down there. You will deliver every dragon-killing weapon you have on this ship to be destroyed before you regret not listening to me."

Calix looked at Terisa. She looked at Elarie with a sense of sorrow, a look he'd seen before. "You don't want to listen to me? Fine, there are other people I can kill to get through to your thick head," Finnal decided. He quickly pulled a knife out of his belt and gripped Terisa's grey and white hair. He slid the blade across her throat and held Terisa still while she gagged and writhed, though her eyes remained on Elarie. She knew she'd die. She knew this would happen.

Jamison screamed from his place across the deck, his hands covering his mouth. Finnal dropped Terisa and her body landed with a thunk on the wood, still squirting blood.

The two fires went out and Elarie staggered back a step. Finnal said, "shall I start killing the members of the crew you so desperately wanted to protect?" He motioned to the few of them still left and a pirate began walking toward them. Not one they knew, but one that looked pleased to kill. "The kid, perhaps?"

Calix looked at Elarie. "Do something," he whispered. Like in the Rings, she listened to him. Her skin heated, coiling with flames like dying coals. The pirate beginning to stalk forward screamed.

And then the killing began.

CHAPTER THIRTY-SEVEN

ELARIE

Finnal was not a very smart man, Elarie understood that the moment he chose to kill Terisa rather than knock Elarie unconscious or shoot her with faerthorne. What smart man would allow her, the famed Firefeeder, to walk on the deck without a single thorn blocking her magic? And now people were burning up. They took steps and their insides warmed. Their blood boiled.

Elarie didn't move as she did it. She didn't look at Calix either despite him seeming to want her attention. She couldn't yet. She wasn't finished.

Someone tried jumping into the ocean to put out the fires on his body. Another burst to nothing but ash. There was no audience aside from Finnal, so she did not have to make a show of it. Only what she enjoyed. Elarie stepped over Terisa's body. "Tell me you're afraid," she said.

"Excuse me?" He spat, retrieving the cutlass from his belt. Finnal held it in front of him and the metal drooped, melting. "Damn Firefeeder bitch—you belong to me until your lover pays for you!"

"I belong to no one," she told him, keeping up with him as he began to back away, "and insisting such a disgusting thing as you *owning me* is enough alone for me to kill you but you know what? I will kill your crew for that." He stopped, a captain keen on protecting his men. "Do you want to know why you are going to die?"

As his pirates ran from their various positions to defend their evil captain they turned to dust in front of them. The fear on Finnal's face set in when the big, fat pirate dropped to the deck as nothing but char.

"For Terisa," she said, kicking him to his knees. The smell of rotting, burning flesh now filled their nostrils. It wasn't the same as the smell that coated the ship when Finnal first arrived. That had involved people's body parts still being intact and able to perform their final functions. In this case, it was only fire they could smell. Fire and people worthy of death. "And for dragons," she whispered, "their creators demand it."

He spit on the deck between them.

"Elarie watch out!" Jamison cried and she stepped to the side, watching a faerthorne arrow fly into Finnal's head. It sunk into his eye and knocked him backward. The skinny pirate that wanted her to scream was screaming himself, having just killed his captain because he had no situational awareness. He was crouched like a bird on the crosstrees above them with no other arrows and a large bow in his hand.

Hot flames knocked him over and he fell dangerously down to the main deck. "How disappointing," Elarie mumbled when he landed on his head. She wouldn't get to torture him if he was dead.

All of her flames went out at once. Elarie stood there in the leftover smoke, ash churning around her feet as the wind pushed it, and wondered what other disappointment she'd find in the silence. There was no more crew to fight, they were all dead. The ship drifted lazily on the water with no one to steer it. Yet she felt warmth shift behind her. A distinct one she was beginning to recognize. She was growing a sense of how much warmth was in his human body. She turned around.

"It's all right," Calix whispered with a slight nod.

"All of it?" She asked, feeling tears brim her eyes. It wasn't what she needed to hear, she could live with him still hating and fearing her willingness to kill to get things done, yet she also knew herself enough to understand that what she wanted was to hear him say it was fine. That he was fine with it. The Calix she met over a month ago would not.

But this one nodded once again, stronger this time, and repeated, "all of it."

Elarie inhaled sharply. She walked toward him, practically throwing herself at him to wrap him in a tight hug. Calix groaned a bit but put his arms around her. She buried her face in his neck, sobbing for the first time, and felt his grip tighten like the pressure of his embrace would fit pieces back together and she'd be as all right as everything else.

They did not, but Elarie pretended they did.

"I'm so sorry," he whispered, "Elarie, I'm so sorry about all of it."

She pulled away from him quickly and dragged her hands up to his face. Elarie was on her toes in the nervous way children often did when they were about to ask important questions. Calix still had his arms around her, looser now, and kept a wary look on his face. "Fly with me?" Elarie asked, her throat tight. "On purpose without Greilor making us or him just taking us from one place to another—*fly* with me?"

"What about my leg?" He asked.

"We don't have to fly the proper way to fly the right way," she told him.

Calix nodded. "Maybe you can still teach me a thing or two," he suggested, somehow both nervous and confident. Elarie wondered how many times he had to ask to be taught something this way. He was a prince, after all, one with access to any sort of education he desired, and yet he had to ask her to teach him things he wouldn't get from a book or any other tutor.

"Greilor is going to be so happy," she said faintly. Elarie put her arms back around him, her eyes open. She looked at Kaelum and Terry. Terry was speaking to Red, though it didn't seem to be about her. The little crew that was left began to see what they could do with the ship and how many hands they had left. Elarie met Kaelum's eyes for a moment, seeing a darkness she hadn't before. Her brow furrowed and he looked away, headed up to the quarterdeck. Elarie breathed in deeply and put her lips against Calix's ear. "Thank you," she whispered, "for not letting a younger version of myself give away all my precious secrets."

He chuckled and she let go of him. Both of their arms fell to their sides, though now Elarie felt cold, a feeling both rare and unwanted.

"Did you like her?" Elarie asked, "what you saw of her."

"She seemed like she'd be more open to conversation," he put his hands in his pockets, "but I kind of like my little mystery."

She said, "I'm still surprised you didn't take advantage of it. The tubes, my memories being mixed up..."

"I want you to be the one to tell me," Calix said. "The Elarie in front of me, I want her to share her precious little secrets. It's not as fun the other way—and besides," he added, "I prefer not to take advantage of a woman in a state of mind she has no control over."

"As opposed to taking advantage in other states of mind?" She furrowed her brow.

"Only the consensual state of mine," he decided after a moment of frowning at how she posed the question.

Elarie nodded, "that's fair."

"I do adore consent—"

"Try to call your dragon," she laughed, waving him off. Calix chuckled and looked around. She did as well, at both the skies and the ship. Elarie waved a hand and cleaned up the bodies left over, seeing that Jamison was at the head of the helm, tears in his eyes because he had to be. It didn't look like he wanted to be. He was talking to Kaelum and Terry, moving their heading in the opposite direction. Against the wind. They must've been looking for the ship, which was now south. Calix was looking for his dragon. Elarie focused on him, watching him concentrate and adjust his breathing. He was thinking too much, but she didn't say anything. She just watched him bring his lips together in a sharp, long, and clean whistle.

"How was that?" Calix asked.

She looked away from his lips. "Good," Elarie nodded, "we won't know if it works unless he shows up. Then again, if he was too far to hear you he won't come at all."

"So we wait?" He seemed disappointed.

"And whistle a few more times—"

Jamison shouted, "he's coming closer!" He pointed southwest, "that way!"

"Whistle again," Elarie urged excitedly, watching Calix do it. He was grinning, sharing it with her. Elarie knew Greilor would fly fast to get to them. After weeks without? He'd be steaming with joy that they found each other again. Elarie couldn't imagine what it would feel like—lose Elarie, find Calix centuries later, and lose both at the same time. He must've been so worried, and with the lack of Elarie's magic, he wouldn't even know what direction they took.

A gust of wind filled the ship's sails as they made their heading toward the *Greyscale*, wherever that was, and Elarie grabbed Calix's hand.

"Come on," she pulled him up to the quarterdeck and faced Terry and Kaelum, two people happy to abuse her state of mind for answers they thought they deserved. "We'll see you in a few days."

"What?" Kaelum's eyes went wide.

"It's only a few days," she said with a smile, "unless you'd like to tell Greilor otherwise, he's going to want us to himself for some time. If that is the case, we will most likely find you after you get your ship back. Or Jamison will find us," Elarie looked at him. "I am sorry about Terisa, I know you cared for each other."

He gave her a grim, heartbroken look. "You did, too, right?"

Elarie nodded. "I cared about her. I'm sorry I couldn't save her."

Jamison then stepped toward her and wrapped his thin arms around Elarie's chest. Her eyes widened and he squeezed. "You have to save everyone else, all right?" He asked, sniffling. Elarie put her arms around his shoulders. "Even Terry. No one else can die. Promise."

"I can't make promises like that," Elarie said regretfully and Jamison got off her as if that bit of honesty was the greatest betrayal. "But I can promise I'll try to protect them. Even Terry."

Terry asked, "wouldn't the best way for you to protect us be for you to leave us alone? People weren't dying until you showed up."

"Don't ask stupid questions, Terry," Calix put his hand on her waist, "she's not going anywhere."

Her heart fluttered as Calix pushed her toward the side to wait for Greilor to show himself as a dot on the horizon.

CHAPTER THIRTY-EIGHT

CALIX

Elarie was out of her mind. He'd seen a lot from her, but this was it. This was where he drew the line on her madness. "You want me to—" he started.

"Jump, yes! How many times do I have to say that?"

"A few more, I think," Kaelum grunted from behind them.

She ignored him expertly, so Calix forced himself to as well. "He's going to come at us slow," she explained, "when he tucks his wing and starts to turn—" Elarie moved her hand flat, showing him what Grey would be doing. He'd come at an angle and they were supposed to just... jump onto his back. "We jump. He's going to push up quickly and spread his wings to catch the wind again, then we're off."

"But what if we slide off?" Calix asked.

"I won't let that happen," she rolled her eyes, "and this is your problem, by the way."

His brow furrowed, "I don't have a problem." She gave him an incredulous look, calling him an idiot without words. Calix scoffed and looked away from her. She climbed onto the railing and held her hand out for him. "If my leg comes off because of this you're fishing it out of the ocean," he said, which made her laugh as she lifted him up. Calix looked down at the water rushing below, then at the dragon banking to turn around for them. Grey was at level with the ship, a great beat of his wings bringing him close. "Shit," Calix breathed when Grey turned to the angle Elarie said he would.

"Jump!" Elarie shouted and he actually did. He did it! They fell only a few feet before landing heavily on Grey's back. Grey pushed up as Elarie had said he would, easily moving up to the clouds. Calix did slide, but not off the dragon and his leg remained intact. "Yes!" Elarie threw her arms up, high on her knees. She laughed, tossing her head back and closing her eyes. The wind tossed her hair from the braid and sent it flying. Calix watched her come undone. Relax, free herself. She heaved a sigh that rolled through her body as she spread her legs and laid down, knees bent and arms out.

"That looks comfortable," Calix said and flicked her knee. She laughed and held her arm out. He took it, pulling her against the wind so she was sitting up. "How do you do that?"

"Do what?"

He looked her over. Here was a mix of both the younger Elarie and the one he knew. Here was her, free. "Move the way you do."

"Move?" She put her brows up, "well for one thing I have both of my knees," Elarie bit her lip, waiting for him to laugh. Calix did and she grinned wide. "Or do you mean things like this?" She stood, covering her eyes with one hand. Elarie walked down Grey's back still facing him, a smile on her face. When she was at the point where his tail began, she jumped. Calix yelped thinking she'd fall, but she landed back on her feet, did a twirl, and walked back to him.

She was much closer than before. Calix stared with his mouth open, "*how*?"

"I'll tell you your problem," she said matter-of-factly. He waited. "You fear falling."

Calix said, "I'm not afraid of heights."

"No, you aren't afraid of heights," she agreed, "you're afraid of falling. Of the fall, of hitting the ground or the water. See," Elarie straightened, kneeling between his spread legs. Calix hadn't moved from the position they fell in, so Grey's head was on his left and she was close to his right wing, "your dragon makes a connection to you when you ride with them, it brings you closer, it lets you read each other and communicate together, but by you being afraid of falling you're expressing that you do not trust him completely."

"Anyone can be afraid of falling," he shook his head, "there's nothing wrong with that. And besides, I haven't fallen yet so who's to say—"

"But Calix, you will fall!" She clasped his hands with her own causing heat to spread over his chilled fingers. "You will fall over and over again but it's not about falling, it's about trusting someone to be there to catch you when you do. Your dragon feels your joy when you ride him, he feels your worry for him, but he also feels your apprehension. You need to trust him."

He said, "I do trust him."

Again, she gave him a look. "Calix," she implored, putting his hands against her chest, "when we ride together we make a connection as well. This is the first time we've both accepted it. *I* can feel your fear. You questioned whether or not we'd fall off Greilor before he was even close."

His face heated.

"It's perfectly reasonable to fear it."

"Did you ever?" He asked painfully.

But Elarie shook her head. "Calix, I was raised with dragons. Some of my earliest memories are ones of them and I have an understanding of them that you do not. But I can help you. Greilor is your wings, he will catch you. He'd lose a wing before he let you hit the ground."

Calix looked away from her at the open ocean, then the head of the dragon most definitely listening to them. "Where do we start?"

"We stand," she said instantly. Elarie got to her feet, gripping his hands. Calix took a deep breath and she helped him up. He moved his hands to grip her arms. "See? Simple and easy."

"So simple," he mumbled breathlessly and Elarie moved, pulling him to face the direction they were flying in. "So simple," he repeated when she swung his arms back and forth.

She said, "breathe, Calix," and turned around. It forced his arms to twist around her, pulling her into his chest. "Close your eyes," she insisted, tilting her head to look at him just to check if he was doing it. He was not. "Come on, trust me," she nudged him, "take my hands."

Calix breathed slowly, sliding his hands down her arms. "Don't fault me for being terrified," he warned.

"I'm faulting you for never trying this, not for being afraid," she replied.

"For your information," he said carefully. Elarie moved his arms from around her and began extending them like a bird. His stomach did a flip. "I have tried standing on him before, but then I had a saddle to fall back on. If I fall right now, I fall into the ocean and at this height, I would—"

"Don't you dare say it," she snapped. Elarie had their arms out completely, her own eyes closed, "just feel this."

Calix looked at the calmness on her face, then at their hands. Her arms were slightly shorter, so his elbows bent, but their hands were connected. Her hold on him was firm. Calix focused on feeling as she wanted him to. Not inwardly. Physically, he had cold wind rushing over his face and arms. He had Elarie's warm body against his chest. Every once and a while a strand of her hair would brush his cheek.

"Are you flying?" Elarie asked.

"I mean..." he glanced around, "yes?"

She then said, "you think like a human," and turned back around while twisting one of his arms over her head. She started to cross her arms but realized their hands were still interlocked, meaning she couldn't, but she did put them on her hips. Calix looked at them, his arms now scrunched uncomfortably. They were extremely close now, chest to chest and locked together. He moved his eyes up the top he hated that he liked, and found her with a quirked brow. "Do you like the shirt I was forced to wear?" She asked him.

His cheeks heated more than they ever had before.

"You can say you like it," she said easily, taking a step back, "but I will let go of your hands."

"All right, I like the *style*," he squeezed her hands, "the style. I think it looks nice." She began pulling, "Elarie, come on, I know you aren't comfortable—" she pulled again and Calix decided not to risk it. He got down on his knee, the other stretched awkwardly to avoid the pain of bending the prosthetic. "I like the shirt," he said from below her, his hands still on her hips.

Elarie smiled. "I have a prince on his knee for me, who would've thought?"

"Just so you don't throw me off," he told her. Calix went so far as to pull on her waist so her knees buckled. Elarie landed in front of him, their chests and heads bumping together. He groaned at the pain throbbing in his skull and Elarie began laughing. She pushed back from him, touching his head. "It's not going to swell, is it?"

She laughed again, biting her lip as she ran her warm thumb over the spot, "no, I doubt it. You have a thick skull, I'm sure you'll be fine."

Calix pushed her and rubbed his head. Elarie fell back comfortably, still laughing, and rolled onto her side as Grey flew lower. The wind rushed in his ears and Elarie sat up sharply, grabbing his arms again.

"Lay down, come here," she pulled, which had him falling onto his stomach half on top of her. "Lay here," she commanded. Calix did as he was told, laying on his stomach with the wind blowing over his face. Elarie put his hands in certain places on the edge of Grey's shoulder, "are you holding on tight?"

"For what? What are you about to do—"

"Dive!" Elarie shouted and Grey tucked in his wings, aiming straight for the water. The slowly setting sun glinted blindingly off it. The wind pushed and pushed, Calix was sure Elarie's tight grip was the only reason he wasn't flying off, but she loosened up. Calix, wide-eyed and terrified, looked to his right at her. She was holding on with one hand and the other on Calix's shoulder. "Fly, Calix!" She shouted over the roaring wind.

Oh great gods and fantastic books, Calix thought, turning his head back to face the sea. It was lit up orange and yellow like great flames they were growing closer and closer to. Tears flew by on his frozen face. Calix let out a yell, hollering so much that his voice was hoarse. Elarie laughed, shouting out as well. She kicked off Grey's back and her legs floated through the wind. Calix inhaled sharply, grinding his teeth. Sharper. Faster. Until Calix kicked his leg up and was flying.

Flying. Like he had his own wings, he was flying. His fingers dug into Grey's scales and his stomach churned with fear, but this was nothing like anything he'd ever experienced. He'd dreamed of flying nearly his whole life, now he was in the air with his dragon and with Elarie.

When Grey threw his wings back out and straightened to keep them from diving straight into the ocean, they dropped down heavily onto his back. Calix coughed, the wind knocked out of him, and Elarie rolled onto her back. She sighed with her eyes closed. "I've never done that with someone else you know," she said quietly, the only sound around them being the slow-moving ocean and the rise and fall of Grey's wings.

"That was amazing," he breathed and rolled over as well. Thin clouds colored pink filled the sky, all of them slowly darkening.

"I wish I was a dragon," Elarie whispered as if it was something scandalous.

He said, "maybe you are one," and turned his head. She did as well, looking at him carefully. "Your fire, your hardness, the way you snap and the way you do whatever you want. You have your own wings, don't you?"

"My butterfly," she said. "But what if I don't want to look like Elarie with her skin and her hair and her fingers, what if I want to..." she moved onto her side and rested her head on a propped hand. Once again Calix was below her. "Have scales and a tail and breathe fire from my mouth?"

"What, you can't do that now?" He blinked in shock.

"I can but it tastes bad after," she sighed, disappointed in herself. "If I was a dragon it wouldn't. Do you wish to be a dragon, Calix?"

He hummed, thinking. "I suppose it would be nice. I'd have my own cave and no responsibilities. But I like my life now, so I'm not sure."

Elarie adjusted her head and pushed hair away from her face. "Maybe if I liked my life I would want to be Elarie."

"If you were a dragon we wouldn't be friends," he told her.

She gasped, "you'd stop being my friend if I turned into a dragon?"

"If you turned into a dragon right now, no, we'd be friends until I died and you found something better to do with your long life—"

"Shit, that's the same as my life now," Elarie laid back down and put her hands on her stomach. He reached over and grabbed one, holding it between them. "I'm glad you'll stay my friend, though."

CHAPTER THIRTY-NINE

KAELUM

"This man was disgusting," Terry said as he wiped down the chair he was planning on sitting on. "Everything everywhere," he muttered and wiped off the part of the bolted down table that was in front of him. "Kaelum?"

"Hmm?" He turned his head, sitting on the very table Terry found disgusting. Kaelum had one foot propped on the arm of a chair with a thick rip and too many stains on it. "Yeah, disgusting."

Terry sighed and went toward him. He stood between his legs and wrapped his arms around his waist. "He'll get over it," Terry said, "just say that it was my idea and you went along with it because you love me."

He put his forehead on Terry's shoulder. Kaelum reached around his pants until he found the star, faintly hearing Terry call him a tease. "Maybe he was right," he said, watching the star begin to shine. He breathed deeply, enjoying the feeling of it sitting in his left hand again. "Maybe we acted too soon."

"Just say it was me," he said again, kissing the side of Kaelum's head. "I'll take the heat—figuratively and literally." He chuckled, which made Kaelum chuckle as well.

He lifted his head. Kaelum pulled him in and kissed him slowly, feeling Terry's hum and groan against his lips. "I love you," Kaelum said, brushing their noses together, "but I don't think I can lie about this. He's my best friend."

"I thought I was your best friend," Terry frowned.

"You're my afterlife," Kaelum said, "the love of my life, my future husband," he pecked Terry's lips after each name. "Also my best friend, I suppose," again, they kissed. His star brightened, reflecting his lifting mood. He said, "but Calix has been my friend since we were children. I don't want to have my relationship with him be ruined because of this."

"Because of Elarie," he replied and went in for another kiss.

Kaelum held the star up before he could. "What am I supposed to do with this?" He asked. "How can I use this? Can I use this? What *is* it, really?"

"I don't know."

"Elarie does," he put his arm down, "she does. Maybe the mistake in rushing things was also risking her not explaining this shit to me before she stopped trying to get us to trust her. And now with Calix? Calix tells her what we did, Calix tells her that it's up to her to be honest, then it means she's not going to try to be our friend for him anymore."

"That's what she's been doing?"

Kaelum groaned, "I love you," and got up. He dropped the rock into his pocket. He walked a few paces into the room. It was disgusting, Terry had been right about that. Everything was everywhere and the place smelled like something foul. But through the garbage stacked against walls, Kaelum saw it. The glass sculpture Elarie had done was leaning against the far wall, black and shining in the faint candlelight. It made his chest ache. Lester had been so happy he got it on the ship before they left the Fae island. And that meant *Lester*.

"Kaelum?"

He took a deep breath. "We should wait until they get back to hold a vigil for everyone," he said. Kaelum grimaced, his hand aching. "We'll be on the ship, which is better. And Terisa's body," he swallowed, feeling Terry come to his side, "we should give her a burial at sea when Elarie is there."

"Good idea," Terry said, probably because he couldn't think of anything else to say. He wasn't good at those sorts of things.

"How are you?" Kaelum asked. His throat was tight, now given the opportunity to tear at him because now, in front of Terry, he could cry over his losses. Lester, John, Gerero, Ivan, Polo... "Terry?"

He looked at the sculpture Lester loved. "I'm not good at this," he said thickly. Kaelum nodded, putting a hand on Terry's back. "So I don't know... How I'm going to tell his aunt? How am I supposed to do that? What do I say? She's an old lady, what if it kills her?"

"You say that we..." Kaelum looked around, "we got into trouble." His brow twitched, "we got into trouble and Lester didn't make it. We gave him a burial at sea, we couldn't bring his body back. Something like that."

"Something like that," he repeated numbly, moving on to the emotionless yet still emotional side of himself. "Will you come with me?"

"Of course," Kaelum kissed his cheek, keeping his lips against his skin, "we can go to each house together. Tell the families ourselves, yeah?"

Terry nodded. "Maybe she's a dragon," he said.

Brow furrowed, Kaelum opened his eyes. "What?"

"Elarie," he said. Right, a conversation change. Kaelum pulled his head away so Terry could explain, "the fire, the evilness. Maybe she's a dragon that did something horrible so the gods turned her into a woman."

"That's an interesting theory," he muttered, "if it's true it would explain the killing thing, wouldn't it? Dragons don't have human morals."

"And they're monsters," Terry continued. "How would we prove that?"

He shook his head, "I don't think we can. Unless we can turn her back into a dragon," Kaelum laughed a little, catching a smile on Terry's face. "Maybe that's what my magic will do, huh?" He pulled the star back out and made it shine, something that was bringing far more joy to him than he thought possible.

"Would she want to be a dragon again? Or do you think she likes being a human?" Terry touched the rock and it hummed.

Kaelum said, "would you like being trapped in a body that wasn't yours?"

"No," he said, frowning though. "So we play nice and get her to teach you magic so you can turn her back into a dragon. She leaves us alone, problem solved." He seemed pleased with the plan.

"What about Calix?"

"If she's a dragon he won't be able to be her friend," he argued, "she'll eat him or something."

He nodded, "good point." Kaelum looked at the sculpture again and finally thought, *this is not going to work.*

CHAPTER FORTY

ELARIE

Elarie ripped her boots off, hopping on one foot as she got out of her right one. "This is where you were? I thought you were looking for us," she looked at Greilor, having already taken in the vast natural scenery that Calix was slowly admiring. Greilor had found an island, saying he wanted to relax and force them to spend time with each other without him there. It was lovely and far better than the Fae island. Even the smells were better. In the twilight, the greens and browns were dark and the fireflies lit the area for them. Something glowed in the water before them, full of life and thriving by itself. "He wants us to be friends so badly," Elarie nudged Calix.

"We are friends," he smiled. Elarie nodded, her heart beating quickly. She stayed still so he could use her to balance while he removed his one shoe, touching his foot to the warm black rock Greilor had led them to. It was part of a short waterfall, one that splashed down from a tall mountain. "Close friends?"

"Close friends," she repeated jokingly, then ran. Elarie jumped into the water with Greilor cheering at her, chuffing happily as he found a place to bask in the night, one foot dipped in the cool water. Elarie laughed, pushing hair out of her face. "Come on, jump."

He said, "I don't want to get the leg wet."

"Then take it off, I can help you balance," Elarie swam to the edge, finding herself to be the perfect height. The water went to her collar and she stood easily in the soft current. "Unless you don't want to..."

Calix shrugged, "not right now."

She said, "maybe later, then," and pulled her shirt off. Elarie dragged it off her body and twisted it out of her hair, setting it flat on the rocks in front of her. Calix's jaw dropped when she began taking off her pants. "What?" She asked him, "I feel dirty."

When she was naked he looked as if he might faint. Calix sat down where he was and seemed to calm down after that, though the level of heat she felt rising and falling on his skin kept changing.

"Are you all right?" She asked, folding her arms on the rock. He couldn't see anything but her shoulders, perhaps a little lower than her collarbone. Of course, he was also a squinting human, even in the well-lit area. *He* was the one scandalizing the situation. Did Elarie have to take her clothes off? No, but this was far more comfortable than the restricting feeling of the shirt soaked in water. "Calix?" He raised his brow. "You have seen a naked woman before, haven't you?" She tilted her head.

"Of course," he nodded tightly, looking to avoid. "Tell me something."

"What would you like to be told?" She asked, going along with the distraction. Elarie backed up, keeping low to the clear water. She tipped her head back and ran her fingers through her hair, waiting and waiting. "Calix?" She asked again, looking over at him.

He said, "your tattoo."

"What about it?" She questioned, enjoying his nervousness far too much. This was new. He was blushing, warm all over.

"Shit, just…" he got up, "stay." Calix put his hand out to motion to her as if she were a dog that needed to obey its owner. And he walked away. Elarie lifted her head, watching until she couldn't see him anymore.

She looked at Greilor, whispering, "what do you think?"

I think you broke him.

Elarie laughed. She lowered herself into the water blowing bubbles as she swam to the falls. The sharp pelting of the drops sparked differently over her head and face. Elarie knelt on stones in front of it sure to keep her back to the direction Calix had gone in. Half of her body was still under, but she was exposed from the waist up. How would he react? What would his face be? If it was only her back now, how would he react if he saw her front?

She ran a hand through her hair and opened her mouth to taste the cool water, her hands in front of her to catch it. Elarie spit out some of it, bending her head forward. She rubbed her face and neck and shoulders, letting the fresh water wash away the blood and muck and the layer of disgust she felt.

Calix was there when she turned her head. He was seated, his leg removed, and had his shirt off. It revealed the same light brown skin as his face, only softly toned with muscle. His eyes were on her. His stupid Lathin eyes. "Can I see it?" He asked, putting his leg in the water. It swished around the cold current. He'd calmed down somehow, as if he'd gone off to argue with himself about her and came to the conclusion that everything was fine.

He averted his eyes as she got down from the falls, looking at Greilor. The dragon chuffed on about him being sweet and con-

siderate and *see, isn't he the best sort of friend?* and Elarie wasn't sure
if she liked hearing him say it. She stopped below him, her arms
in the same position as they had been when she was teasing him
before. "Calix," she poked his thigh and he looked at her, "maybe
you should get in the water."

"Yeah, maybe," he mumbled, staring. Calix took a deep breath,
"good idea," he said and slid down the rock into the pool. He gasped
and cursed, "shit that's cold, you didn't say it was cold."

"I feel temperature differently than you do," she looked at him,
watching his eyes widen and his torso shake. "Are you too cold?"
Elarie couldn't recall the temperatures that would kill humans, she
didn't want to be responsible for killing the Crown Prince of her
favorite kingdom.

He both nodded and shook his head. "Just takes getting used to,"
he swallowed and splashed water onto his face and over his hair.
Calix sighed slowly and let out a big shiver. "Better."

"Are you sure?" She asked. What if he *did* die? What if he froze?
No, no human froze in water like this... Elarie knew freezing temperatures, he would be perfectly fine. He'd be cold, maybe, but he
wouldn't freeze.

Calix turned to her, his shoulder pressed against the rock. Of
course, his eyes moved. They flicked back to hers a few times and he
held his hand up. Elarie nodded slightly, keeping her eyes on him
as he moved closer and touched her back. Calix brushed her long
hair to the sides, his fingers gentle and purposeful. He still glanced
from the tattoo to her face, but as he got closer his focus was on the
mark. Elarie breathed in slowly as he traced over the thick and thin
lines, creating the shape of it.

"What kind of butterfly is it?" Calix asked faintly. The tattoo was no bigger than his palm, and yet it felt like he was touching all of her.

"One that lives only in my imagination," she answered, moving down partially so part of the tattoo was in the water, her chest pressed firmly to the rock. He didn't believe her. Of course he didn't, she doubted she could call him Calix if he believed her right away. Elarie asked, "do you have any tattoos?" While he moved his hand through her hair, again pulling it off her back.

His hand dragged over her bare shoulder, pushing her hair down. Suddenly Elarie thought being naked wasn't the best idea. Not when he was touching her. "I am afraid of needles," he admitted, "the idea of something poking ink into my body is just... not the best idea. Why'd you get it?"

"Permanence," she answered. "It's me and my pathetic need to have something last while I run away from everything that could."

Calix said, "well you don't get to run from me." His eyes met hers, nervous like that might've been the wrong way to say something like that. The wrong wording or maybe the wrong time. But Elarie was only wondering how a prince didn't know the language spoken by his closest neighboring kingdom—or if he lied to hide the fact that he knew what Ave was saying on Moro Island. The part about running.

"I don't think I will yet," Elarie replied faintly. Calix's hand moved up her back once again.

"'Yet,'" he repeated, "how about 'at all?' You won't run at all."

She sunk lower into the water, finding herself closer. Had she moved or had he? Elarie felt herself warm, unsure what she should do to fix it. She knew that he could feel it, of course, but did he know what it meant? Did she? Did it bother him? Calix didn't seem bothered, he seemed like something else. "Not at all?" Elarie asked as his hand brushed over the back of her neck. He was warmer, too.

"Not at all," he said. She saw him swallow. Saw his eyes move. Her heart thumped loudly in her head, almost as loud as his level of speaking, making her almost not catch the standing offer to live in his home and his desire to have her meet his mother.

Elarie hardly ever felt this sort of tightness in her chest. Matian did it, had their whole lives. Damilla did it just with a brush of their hands. Why was he doing it? She didn't know Calix well enough to have her chest be tightening and her breathing wavering. "Meet your mother, that's... a big thing to tell someone you met a month ago."

"It's been more than a month now, hasn't it?" His thumb brushed her jaw.

"Maybe," Elarie moved her arm down. She dug her fingertips into the rock for some sort of purchase. Otherwise she'd fall forward. And if she fell forward, then many things could happen. "Do you think?"

"Come home with me," Calix finalized. "I want you to come home with me. Live with me."

She breathed in shakily, her eyes darting to his lips before quickly moving to his eyes again. "Live with you?" He nodded. "That's a big offer."

"It's a room and a kitchen and a dragon," he leaned forward, "and a me."

"And a you?" Elarie began trying everything to fix her breathing when he moved his hand gracefully down the curve of her neck. "What does that mean?"

He countered, "what do you want it to mean?"

She stared at his mouth and began cursing inwardly. All the words she knew, all the languages she knew, and in each one with each word she was telling herself to look away. "I asked you first," she said, very sure that if either of them moved any closer they'd stop being friends.

"Well maybe—" he began and Greilor lifted his head. Elarie looked away from Calix for the first time, staring out into the night sky. "What's going on?" He asked with a tight voice, evidently upset he was interrupted.

She peered through the sky with Greilor, who was insisting something was coming, then saw it. A shadow darting through the darkness. Elarie turned quickly and shouted, "get down!" She threw herself on top of Calix, pushing him unprepared into the cold water as a dragon's fire roared down on them. Elarie felt it burn over her back and the dragon flew back up. She pulled Calix back to the surface and he gasped, looking wildly around. "Go, go now," Elarie grabbed her clothes.

"What's going on?" Calix climbed out of the water and she touched him to dry his body quickly while he reattached his leg.

"The dragon is claiming the area," Elarie answered as she got up. She tugged at the shirt, looking at Greilor. "What do you want to do?"

He looked at the sky, then at her. *Run*, he said.

"Run, I'm good at that," she nodded and grabbed Calix's hand, dragging him back the way they walked so peacefully only minutes ago. "We get to the beach," she called back to Calix, "and Greilor will fly us away."

"How did he not know this area was already claimed?" Calix asked loudly, pushing leaves and sticks out of the way. He tripped, forcing them to slow momentarily. Elarie almost considered carrying him.

"That's not what happened," she told him, "it's more like—" Elarie pushed him to the ground and landed on top of him, getting his knee pointedly pressed against her ribcage. The dragon came down for another torrent of fire and Greilor stood on his hind legs to return. Elarie looked down at Calix. "The dragon saw Greilor and decided to challenge him."

His brow furrowed, "that sounds like a stupid thing to do."

"It is, but it puts both of us in danger of getting caught," she looked over her shoulder, seeing the dragon had flown off again, "in the crossfire." Elarie pulled Calix back up and started running again. They were headed down, navigating rocks they'd climbed to get to Greilor's chosen spot.

He must live in the nest on the next island, she heard Greilor say.

Elarie stopped short and turned back to the dragon following them. "There is a *nest* on the island next to us?" He nodded. "W—" Elarie stopped herself. She looked at Calix, who did not share the same outrage as her, and decided to drop it for the moment. She continued pulling him along until they were nearly there.

"So," Calix said, jumping off a rock. He held her hips to pull her down. "Live with me?" He asked.

"You know, it's perfect you're asking this now," she said as she pushed him against a tree.

He said, "I thought you'd like it, actually," and the dragon blew more fire. He wanted Greilor to be in the air, which complicated things further. He wanted a fight and of course Greilor could give him one without an issue—but what about the two riders? "Your answer?"

"Yes, I suppose that would be nice," Elarie pulled him back into a run, "you'll get tired of me, you know," she told him. Calix laughed. He just laughed. Elarie smiled to herself and her bare feet hit the sand of the beach they'd first landed on. Greilor bent for them to climb on faster.

"Where are we going?" Calix asked, his voice directly in her ear. He held on tight to her, his arms around her waist while she knelt between his legs. Greilor beat his great wings and took a bounding step, sending them into the dark sky. Elarie looked around trying to spot the dragon.

Greilor told her he was just going to circle wide a few times. Elarie said, "we're going to fly for a while, it'll be fine."

"Has this ever happened to you before?" He asked.

Elarie turned her head to look at him. He needed assurance. He was nervous on the dragon without his saddle as it was, but now they were running from something so the part of his human mind that said *danger* was probably screaming. "Only once," she explained, "it's rare for other dragons to want to attack a Great Dragon. Most likely this one will back off after some time." Elarie then bent closer to Calix, holding his jaw to turn his head to the side and whisper in his ear, "it could probably also be the nesting. Some dragons can tell when another is going to nest and see it as an opening for attack."

"Why?" He asked quietly.

Elarie said, "some dragons see the reproduction of other species in their territory or area as hostile. Even if the dragon didn't claim the land it lives around here. It could feel threatened by Greilor."

He nodded. "I can't wait to know more about this stuff," Calix said when she sat back. Elarie let go of his jaw, finding herself to be smiling brightly at him. And he was smiling back at her. Afraid, yes, but he was sure of her.

He was sure of her.

How sure of her?

Elarie looked at the skies again, twisting her damp hair over her shoulder. She'd dried herself off for the most part so it was beginning to fly everywhere, holding it was only giving her something to do other than focus on how close she was to Calix and how his arms were around her and how he was cold and warm and he smiled at her like he already knew her. Elarie looked at him again. As if he could sense it he turned to her as well, squinting in the dark. "Will you accept me?" Elarie asked.

"I already do," he said.

But she shook her head, "no, I mean... I mean what if I'm not what you think I am? What if everyone hates me? Would you accept me even then?"

"Elarie," he placed his hands on her face, his grip firm as he brought her close. Calix still had to speak loudly over the wind, but every word was certain, "I already know."

"What?"

"I *know*," he repeated strongly. She shook her head. No, he had some idea. He couldn't possibly know. "And I accept you."

He couldn't possibly. "What do you think I am?" She asked him.

Greilor screeched and shot straight upward. Calix grabbed Elarie hard around the waist as the dragon rammed into them from below. Calix screamed, his grip only tightening as they flew up into the air. He cursed. And cursed.

"It's going to be fine!" She shouted in his ear and Greilor screamed for them. The other dragon breathed fire over Greilor's scales and dug clawed feet into his body. Calix and Elarie flipped backward, turning around and whirling through the air. The entire time they went down to the black sea Calix screamed.

CHAPTER FORTY-ONE

CALIX

In the span of twenty minutes he knew three things with certainty—one, he was going to kiss Elarie Crosha while she was naked in a lake; two, she might've wanted to kiss him back; and three, Calix was doing absolutely nothing to keep them afloat on the choppy ocean waves. He'd stopped kicking to rest for a moment and remained in place. Calix couldn't think of a reason fire would keep them from drowning, and that meant one thing.

She could control more than one element. It wasn't possible. It wasn't *allowed*. The gods never gave one person that much fire magic, let alone two elements. Elemental magic was the most powerful magic as it was. It was both closest to nature and closest to the gods. The ability ranged from needing to carry a bit of the element around with the wielder—a vial of water, dirt, something to create a breeze, or charcoal to start a fire—and grew to summoning magic. It came from within, sort of like what Elarie was doing but her magic went beyond that as well. She was *creating* fire.

And now water?

Calix recalled the ritual. She told him they were taking her magic, that she was a sacrifice, but at the time it had just been fire he thought they were taking. If it was water as well, what if there was more?

"I'm cold," Elarie whispered faintly. She'd been crying, her eyes peeled on the dark sky. They'd been trying to follow the fight, but the screaming had stopped only to double a few minutes later when a second dragon went in for the attack. Elarie had practically lost her mind when it happened. "I'm cold..." she repeated, shocked by the statement.

"Mhmm," he nodded while attempting to keep his teeth from chattering. He was freezing, certain the only reason he wasn't dead yet was because he was right next to her.

She looked at him. "Oh, you're human I'm sorry," Elarie pulled him closer, her body flush against his, and heat spread through him. He put his head against hers, sighing slightly. "Sorry, I forgot."

"How could you forget?" He lifted his head, then took her hand and pressed her warm fingers against his face.

"Because when I'm with you I don't think about it. It all goes away," she said, "and I'm almost peaceful."

Calix stared at her, watching through the dark as she looked around again. He felt the same. Was that... bad? Was the wrong? Kaelum and Terry would yell at him for admitting he no longer truly cared about finding out what she was—aside from his natural curiosity. But he felt no danger when he was with her. She wasn't going to hurt him. She wasn't a monster, as Terry was so insistent on her being. She was Elarie when she was with him and Calix couldn't find a reason to think that was so terrible.

"Do you hear that?" Elarie asked, now searching the surface of the ocean. Calix looked around with his human eyes, blinking in shock as fire lit in a circle around them. It was the same dark and powerful red color as before.

"Is that your real magic?" He asked.

She looked at him, then the fire, "oh, no. It's Dragonflame, I have both. Greilor will tell you it's because I was meant to be a dragon, but because I don't have the classic scales and wings, it's for something else."

Calix wanted to touch it. Damn. "What else?" He moved her hand to his ear, which felt numb, and she wrapped her fingers around it. It hummed as she cupped it, like putting a shell over his ear to hear the ocean.

"Nothing," she said while still searching around them. "Are you sure you don't hear that?"

"No," he removed her hand from over his ear, "I don't—"

"Calix!"

He froze. Calix's eyes went wide and Elarie looked to her right, his left.

"Calix, I found you!" Marcella shouted. His jaw dropped when he saw her, standing on a rowboat without any oars. He looked around for a ship, but saw nothing. "We can go home now!" She said gleefully, getting on her knees to hold her hand out for him, "come on."

"Don't," Elarie shook her head. "Is that what she actually looks like?"

He nodded. Marcella had skin darker than his, taking after their father. She often had her hair styled in rows of braids she liked to have shapes made out of. Her hairdresser used some sort of magic to make things like antlers and flower shapes. Now, though, they were only falling around her shoulders. She was waving her hand through the air for him, urging him forward.

"It's not actually her, it's—" But someone was saying her name. Coming from the other side, his right, was a deep, sure, and strong voice calling her Ela. "Pa," she said fearfully.

Calix looked at the big man. Elarie didn't look like him at all except for the eyes, which were both the bright green he found to be far more mesmerizing than he'd ever admit. Elarie's Pa had broad shoulders and a wide stomach with shoulder length brown hair. He was kneeling as well, only on what looked like a strip of land and not a boat.

"Elarie," Calix said.

She shook her head and her Pa said, "you must be tired."

"I am tired," she agreed, tears rising to her eyes, "you told me my life would be easy and peaceful."

"We cannot always be correct, darling Ela, you used to love it when I was wrong," he said.

Her voice rose slightly, "when I could tease you for it not when I die over and over again."

"The gods—"

"They did this to me!" Elarie shook. Calix looked at his little sister. Marcella was still waving her hand around, grinning.

Her Pa turned solemn. "You long for a final death more than you long for your happiness, I know that. Take my hand and it will be over, I promise." He extended his hand to her the same as Marcella to Calix. He seemed gentle yet firm, telling her that the death she faced if she took his hand would be the real one. But he didn't have control over that, the gods did.

"Elarie," Calix said, "it's not him, he can't kill you."

"I just want him to hold me," she whispered. Marcella whispered his name, but his focus was on her. If she died, so did he. He'd freeze to death in the time it took her to come back, even if it was just a few seconds. Elarie sobbed and put her hand up. "I just want him to hold me," she repeated painfully. Before Calix could object flames fanned out from her hand and something screamed. The fire engulfed everything, blasting out in a circle from the surface to what was below.

Calix looked at her hand, which was still raised. "Elarie?" He asked.

"He'd never offer to kill me," she said. "My Pa, he'd never," she shook her head and sobbed, inhaling sharply. The Dragonflame around them flickered, "he'd hate me."

"No, that can't be true—"

"He—he'd hate me for even wanting," Elarie sniffed, trembling, "to die, he'd hate me, they'd all hate me."

Calix took her hand, removing it from the air. "No, they wouldn't. They're your family, they wouldn't hate you."

"My family," she sobbed, looking at him, "what kind of family wouldn't hate their daughter for wanting to die, let alone mine? Mine—mine and their traditions and their duties and *my* duty, I'm doing everything wrong and they'd hate me because of it."

"Elarie," he cradled her face, wiping away tears with his wet hands, "Elarie," he whispered. She kept crying. "Surviving isn't wrong," he told her, "you are doing nothing wrong by surviving. And wanting to die?" He wasn't sure what to say to that. Calix had never met anyone who no longer wanted to live, let alone someone who couldn't seem to die. "Elarie," he wiped at her face again, "how do I help you? What do you need?"

At first she didn't have an answer. She just stared at him, tears falling to his fingertips as she tried to come to some sort of decision. Her voice cracked as she weakly shook her head and said, "just hold me."

Calix wrapped his arms around her, holding her head on his shoulder. Elarie sobbed, her grip on him tight, and Calix stared at the flames. His mind wasn't on the information he'd been given, it was on ways to keep someone who didn't want to live alive. Or convince her that life was worth living. But how could he do that when Elarie had surely lived more than one life? She'd seen everything, probably been everywhere. She was wise and in pain. She knew when there was nothing left. How terrible could her life have been? Or was it just too long?

She needed to stop running. She didn't *have* a life if she was always running like Ave had suggested. She told Calix to keep her from running from him. Perhaps Elarie just needed someone to be there. Without questions or expectations, just to sit with her or hold her. He was giving her a place to stay, giving her a dragon they'd share, giving her a friend. Was that enough?

How would he know what was enough at all?

Chapter Forty-Two

Calix

The crying was close to stopping. He couldn't think of anything to say to make her feel better. Or if there was anything he could say. She'd probably heard it all before. Nothing Calix could tell her would be anything new or any better than the advice of others.

Elarie pressed her face into his neck, her body heating further. "Do you get warmer or colder depending on your emotions?" Calix asked to pass the time. They hadn't heard from or seen a single dragon for the past half hour. Calix was a prune, starting to feel like he needed to piss, and his back was colder than his front. They both needed a distraction and he would gladly be the one to provide it.

She hummed and breathed in slowly. "Yes. I don't get that much colder than usual, but the warmth usually pulls in. When I'm flustered I blush warm," she said, and where her cheek was on his collar heated nicely. It went away, though. "And angry..."

"I've seen angry," he nodded, "you glow."

"Fire in the flesh, huh?" She seemed to tease.

Calix asked, "when you have sex with someone do you burn them?"

It made her laugh, which was good. Elarie moved, lifting her head to look at him. "Sort of. I can lose control if it feels good enough."

"Say you're with a man..." he mused, "and you do lose control..."

"While I haven't had sex with a man in years, I've never burned anyone's cock before, Calix. I don't lose *that* much control," she rolled her eyes, "it tends to be more of burning the bed, sometimes the surface skin. No parts to be harmed."

Calix chuckled and put her hand on the back of his neck. The water had calmed some, there was no sign of a storm—not that Calix could really see. "I'm actually surprised you haven't burned anyone's groin before."

"Not sexually."

"I wonder if anyone would like that."

"Ew," Elarie cringed.

He continued, "some people like that sort of thing. Kaelum has this wax lotion he and Terry use."

"That's different than a man asking me to light his—"

"Is that Grey?" Calix squinted behind her. Elarie turned her head, looking for the shadow flapping against the dark clouds in the distance.

Elarie turned partially, putting out the fire around them. "No," she said warily, "I don't think so."

"It's coming for us," he told her as if she were blind.

She pushed on his shoulder, "dive, down," she turned and shoved him. Calix took a deep breath and dove, feeling her against him. Fire shot out from her hand, a little ball of flame that hovered around them as they began swimming down. Blood pumped in his ears and something splashed above them.

Elarie's scream vibrated against his ear as something wrapped around them. They thrashed, being shaken under the waves while the dragon attempted to fly back into the sky. Calix grabbed Elarie's arm as they were jerked upward. He coughed when they surfaced, the water moving further away. "Elarie?" He shook her. Calix felt something warm against his stomach—warm differently than her skin was. He looked down. "Elarie, are you bleeding?"

She didn't respond.

"Elarie!"

She coughed up water and gasped. Wind blew her wet hair around. Every movement sent pain over her face. "It's fine," she assured him with a nod, "I think I just lost part of my side."

"What?" His eyes widened, "how is that fine?"

"I'll just die and it'll be normal," she said.

Calix shook his head, "you can't die—you aren't allowed to die on me."

"It's the easiest way to avoid pain and heal the injury," she said, "dying is so useful, why would I stop now?"

He said, "because I asked you to."

Elarie's head fell forward and hit his. "Not dead," she said loud enough for him to hear. "Promise." Calix allowed himself to feel at least some of the relief that should've come with convincing her to live so he didn't have to watch her die. Was that selfish? "It's not talking to me," Elarie breathed in shakily, "it won't tell me anything."

"What do you think is going to happen?" Calix squinted as he tried to see what was behind her. Her head was still against his face and all that moved in front of him was her hair and a dust of freezing clouds. The dragon was smaller than Grey, carrying them wasn't smooth. They were being held in both front paws and it seemed that Elarie was being stabbed by one of its claws. "Elarie?"

She forced her head to straighten. He could hardly see her at all. Elarie looked around as they banked to the right somewhere behind Calix. "Hopefully you don't get eaten," she said.

"Why just me?" His eyes widened. Calix never thought he'd be outraged that he'd be the *only one* getting eaten by dragons.

"Dragons love me, you're a human," she told him, "you'll get eaten and I'll scold them after."

He gasped, "after?"

"Maybe I'll stop them," she said, bringing a playful lift to her tone, "I can't be responsible for the death of a royal."

"Or your *friend*," he insisted. Calix would've crossed his arms had they not been pinned. The flapping of the wings quickened. When Calix craned his neck he saw they were in the shadow of an island, one he recognized. "Are we going to the nest you were talking about?" Calix asked as the ride got bouncier, jarring him as the dragon landed on the flat side of the mountain. Elarie whined, sniffling with her eyes shut tight.

"Dying sounds lovely," Elarie muttered. They were set in a cave of sorts. While Calix remained standing, Elarie buckled. "So lovely."

He knelt next to her, "a little light please," he said and she reached up, flicking the side of his head. "Ow," he rubbed the spot, "was that really necessary?"

"Absolutely," she replied and produced the same small balls of light around the area. The dragon sat waiting at the opening of the cave. They were surrounded by jagged rocks and some sort of crystal. "It's like my obsidian," Elarie told him faintly, "Dragonflame creates it, many nests have some around."

"Does it do anything or is it just for decoration?" Calix asked, trying to keep up the light conversation as he looked at her newest injury. The blood shined in the firelight, heavy around her. It pooled below quickly, already wetting his pants. She'd been right—part of her side was gone. It wasn't just a few layers of skin, which would have been the most ideal situation. The claw had taken a chunk from her.

"Bad, then?" Elarie asked. He looked at her face. "Your mouth is open," she motioned. "How are you going to fix me, Calix? If dying is still off the table." The dragon made a chuffing sound and Elarie's head lifted, finding it. "Greilor's here. They took him here, we have to find him," she grunted, ignoring the blood that gushed from her body as she sat up on her elbow. "Get me up."

"You shouldn't move," he said faintly.

Elarie grit her teeth and rolled over, gasping in pain as she did. "Look, I moved," she said in a painful, joking tone. Calix stood, grabbing her arms to lift her to her feet. "We have to find Greilor." She looked behind her at the dragon. In the light, Calix could see it was colored a dusty green, something useful for blending into foliage. It had long claws and spikes above its eyes like eyebrows. "Take me to him right now," she ordered.

The dragon hung its head and began walking further into the cave, which turned out to be a passageway. "This would be utterly amazing if you weren't bleeding so much," Calix told her, then took off his shirt. Elarie said nothing as he folded it, but she did curse colorfully when he put his arm around her and pressed it to her wound. "You're ruining my dragon experience."

"I could give you a dragon experience," she muttered and limped weakly.

"Oh yeah? What would it be like?"

"Fire," she said, "so much fire."

He frowned, "doesn't sound that fun."

"Singe your eyebrows and your arm hair," she continued. Was she messing with him? "Burn everything."

Calix said, "come on, Elarie, give me something."

Her knees gave out. Elarie gasped, sort of crying out as he lifted her up. Calix put his arms under her knees and shoulders. Elarie transferred a hand to hold his bloodied shirt and Calix began carrying her. "He's not mine you know."

"Who's not?" Calix adjusted his arm, following the dragon. The small balls of fire lit the area. It was some sort of tunnel that led in a curve down the mountain.

She said, "Greilor. He was never really mine." She put her head on his shoulder, "I used to hate it."

"Used to?" He repeated. Calix had the back of his mind working on how he was supposed to fix her side that didn't involve letting her bleed to death. Could he stitch something like that?

"I rode him more than anyone. He was my wings and my best friend. I had a connection to him that no one else did, not even my brother," she told him. The turns became tighter. "Ritker. He was Ritker's birthright, he was never mine, and it made me so upset because I felt like our connection was more important than a birthright to a dragon he hardly rode, but now it's like Greilor is all I have left of them. My brother and my father."

Calix looked at the dragon ahead of him. For the life of him he couldn't picture losing his family. His *entire* family all at once, and only having a dragon be what was left of them. "You have memories, don't you?" He asked.

"So many," she mumbled faintly. Calix shook her. "Ass," she whined and hit her forehead against his shoulder, "you are such an ass."

"You like me, though," he argued. "Don't you?"

"I don't like you being an ass," she told him.

Calix smiled, "I bet you do."

"Ass," she replied. Elarie grunted as she moved her shoulders. "You are such an ass and you are," she breathed in slowly, "kind to me when no one else is and you seem reliable and... other nice words."

"This isn't a final speech, right? You aren't dying, remember?"

She said, "I think I trust you, Calix," and his steps faltered to a stop. He looked down at her, but her eyes were closed. He kept walking, slowly and carefully, and the dragon looked back impatiently. They were headed to a big opening. Everything was bright inside, full of fire and noise. "Keep being nice to me, Calix," Elarie told him.

"Holy gods," Calix said from the opening, his jaw dropped and his eyes as wide as they ever had been. He let out a breathy laugh, "I might faint."

Elarie threw herself out of his arms, landing hard on the stone ground. "Where is he?" She asked in a commanding voice she hadn't had before. It didn't waver. She stood with a straight back, though he could see her shaking with effort. Blood crawled down her side, still shining with the flames.

It was a cavern, a giant hole in the mountain. Towering over them were what looked like thousands of different dragons. The nest. They crawled over walls and into alcoves, they ate from a giant pile of food in the center of the room. A waterfall fell over what looked like another entrance. "Elarie," he said, putting his arm around her. Dragons moved out of their way as he pulled her to Grey, who was lying there bloodied up on the ground. There were small dragons the size of cats with long tails that were crawling over him, but he didn't seem bothered by it.

"Greilor!" Elarie shouted and he lifted his head. She began speaking the dragon language, her desperation sparking around her. Calix let go of her so she could fall onto Grey and grip the horn on his nose. He moved next to her and laid on Grey's snout like she was, feeling him hum happily.

CHAPTER FORTY-THREE

ELARIE

She was on fire lying on the hard ground. Greilor insisted. Her body was shutting down, so he lit her to flames, and it was times like these that Elarie wondered what it would be like to die on fire. She wanted to know what it would feel like to turn to ash and be reborn like a fairytale animal. It hadn't happened and it never would. Fire would never kill her.

Calix sat next to her, leaning on his one bent knee. "Do you hear all of them talk like you're in a crowded room?" She nodded. "Is it annoying?" She shook her head. Elarie put out her fire and he came even closer, sort of hovering over her. "Please tell me everything."

"Have some patience," she patted his arm and looked behind her. Jitter Dragons were dragging leaves onto a flat rock making a mat for them fit with leaf pillows. "Get me up there." She held her arm out and he took it, standing and dragging her with him. His arms were around her, practically carrying her as she attempted to stop the blur from covering her whole eye. "You don't want me to die?"

"Ever again," he said as he helped her lie down. Elarie groaned and looked at the wound. It shined. *Shit*. "Fine... all right, rip the shirt."

He looked at it, then at her. "How?"

"I need," she swallowed, looking around, "Jitter Dragons. You three," Elarie pointed. Jitter Dragons, one of the only species of dragons that were not born with the knowledge of languages. Dragons like Greilor or even the one that snatched them from the ocean were already adept in every language known to the world, but Jitter Dragons had to learn. Elarie switched to the dragon language, telling them of a large flower she needed, then a leaf that was often found on plants near the flower. She needed plenty of both and she also needed fresh water. The dragons flew off with a few friends to complete their tasks. "And you," she said to another watching with an interested eye, "are going to light my wound on fire."

The dragon then dipped her head to make herself smaller.

"Come here," Elarie motioned. She took Calix's hand and held it out saying, "this is Calix. He is my friend, he's going to help me but he can't do that without you." The dragon, Masha, came forward and sniffed, ashy steam snorting from her nostrils. "Will you help?"

She walked closer and climbed onto the rock bed nervously.

"Calix," she said in Ceptareei, "this is Masha. She's going to light the wound on fire. It's going to burn me."

"How is that possible?" He asked, watching Masha sniff their linked hands.

Elarie pressed the soaked shirt into the wound. "I have to focus and I won't be able to for long so you need to do everything I say." He nodded. "Rip the shirt so Masha has more access to the wound."

Calix let go of her hand, which was somehow wrong of him though it was what she instructed. She removed his shirt and Calix took a deep breath as he looked at the wound he insisted she not die from. He hooked his fingers under the initial rip and Elarie closed her eyes, focused on Masha purring like a cat while rubbing her head on Elarie's arm. Her scales scratched against her skin, nearly enough to distract from Calix ripping the side of the shirt open. He pulled the sides apart, tucking one under her and folding the other over her stomach, leaving her breasts covered. "Next?" Calix asked.

"Wait," she mumbled. "When the dragons come back you need to grind three of the healthiest looking flowers with one leaf and mix it with water so it makes a paste. Spit in it. Masha is going to burn my wound and you need to rub the paste on every burned part even if it looks like char, then take the stems off the rest of the leaves and lay them on the paste without pressing them down."

He nodded, scooting closer to her. He put the back of his hand on her cheek. "How hot are you usually?" He asked. "Elarie?"

She hummed, "hot, warm, lukewarm," and laughed a little. Calix began pressing the shirt back against her side as numbness set in around her mind. "Your kingdom is my favorite, did you know that?"

"It's everyone's favorite," he said, moving his cold fingers over her face. "Ceptari is the best kingdom and it has been since the revolution."

"Didn't you almost lose that revolution?"

He clicked his tongue, "your wound is making you delusional. We won our freedom in a landslide."

"So like a ruler to lie to his subjects," she replied weakly.

"You aren't one of my subjects so it's perfectly fine," Calix said. She pressed her face into his hand. "Unless you'd like to become a citizen of the greatest kingdom on the continent? I can lie all about the war we won our freedom over."

She opened her eyes, feeling Greilor lumber over. He was limping and his pride was bruised, having lost the fight between the two dragons. No one else faulted him for it, of course, but Greilor would shame himself like a human would. He liked that about himself.

"'Elarie Crosha of Ceptari' doesn't sound as grand as what it actually is," she said, giving him a half smile.

"Elarie of what, then?" He asked, returning the same gesture.

Greilor, for once, was silent. This was for her to answer. He wasn't going to urge her into it this time. Elarie had to choose, and her heart was going both ways. She told Calix she trusted him, but the disgusting, damned part of her mind kept asking, louder and louder, whether it was the smart thing. He did start their relationship intending to discover what she was to share with his friends. Yet he covered her mouth when she almost said it.

"What are you going to do if I tell you?" She asked. This was it. It had to be it. She trusted him almost the way she trusted Matian, something that hadn't happened since Matian died. She'd never felt it for anyone. Not a single one of her loves. Ave, Damilla, Carmen, Franine—none of them. She'd never trusted them with it. And now there was Calix. What about Calix?

"Nothing, Elarie," he whispered, even closer now. His cold hands moved again, this time to her jaw, holding on to get his point across. "I don't want to do anything. And at this point I don't even think I need to know." But he wanted to. He wanted her to say it.

Calix was smart, he claimed he already figured it out, and all he wanted was to hear it. Be right.

Elarie felt her chest tighten, only adding to the pain rolling through her body. She opened her mouth and a dragon screeched. A Jitter Dragon. She turned her head, watching them come flying through the waterfall carrying her supplies. Elarie said, "there's a shell for you to use."

He didn't seem disappointed in her lack of answers. He was used to her avoiding. Calix just took the shell from the mouth of a dragon gently and crushed flowers and a leaf then went to the waterfall. Elarie looked at Greilor. The dragon blinked slowly, only saying *I'm proud of you either way.* Her eyes watered. She held her hand out and he came forward, still limping, but he put his head against her hand and began to purr.

Calix was by the waterfall looking unsure for some time. When he came back his knuckles were a greenish color. He sat once again and took a deep breath. "Ready?" He looked from Elarie to Masha. "Masha?"

"She doesn't speak Ceptareei," Elarie told him, "say *tryonae.* T-rey-ona-e. It means prepared, it's the same as ready."

He nodded and looked at Masha, doing a perfectly fine job at the pronunciation. Masha purred for a few seconds, then looked at Elarie. Elarie just nodded. She watched the small dragon turn around and back up so far that her back legs fell off the rock. Calix snorted, disguising it quickly with a cough. Angry smoke drifted up from between her lips. Masha looked at Elarie. She focused on allowing the burn, letting the Dragonflame break through her defenses and her fireproof body. Elarie nodded again, grinding her teeth.

Masha breathed her small fire, the hot orange flames lighting over the bloody wound, and Elarie choked, gagging on air as she struggled not to scream. She pulled her legs in, dragging her heels against the rock.

"Elarie?" Calix asked tentatively when it stopped.

"Just do it please," she cried softly, covering her eyes. Masha moved up her body and curled over Elarie's neck while Calix touched her side. Elarie whimpered at the first contact, breathing in sharply through her nose. She wanted to scream at Calix when he apologized. She could spit fire at him, but instead she sobbed until her body forced her to sleep through the pain.

CHAPTER FORTY-FOUR

CALIX

Part of him wanted to gripe at Elarie for not telling him the stems of the leaves were spiked. His fingers were still tingling. He couldn't find it in his heart to forgive her, either, even though she was weak and dying and it was one little thing. He'd woken up before her, finding himself much closer than where he started. Elarie hadn't moved at all—other than her arm, which was crossed over his. She had fingers curled against his, her head pointed in his direction. Calix feared moving.

The little dragon, Masha, did not share that fear. She yawned and stretched like a cat, pawing at the air as each of her limbs moved. Masha then huffed, snorting fire out of her small nostrils before walking onto Elarie's chest. Her small claws pressed against the shirt and Elarie grunted, muttering something in the dragon language.

Masha moved closer, claws now against her collarbone. Calix smiled at her, then at Elarie, who again said something in the dragon tongue. It didn't seem to satisfy Masha, however, because the Jitter Dragon decided to stand on Elarie's face next. Elarie reached up with her free hand and lifted Masha off, setting her gently back onto the rock.

Calix chuckled, which made Elarie open her eyes slowly. Her eyelids were heavy but she had no trouble seeing him. "How are you?" Calix asked as Masha climbed back onto her chest.

"I am not dead," she informed him and he nodded. Masha crawled over their arms and to his chest, where she curled into a ball and laid down purring. Elarie smiled gently, "she likes you."

The child inside him jumped for joy. Calix, in all his life, hadn't ever truly expected a dragon to ever show up for him. He dreamed, but never thought he'd get it. And now he was in a cavern surrounded by them. "I like you too, Masha," he said. Elarie lifted his hand and moved his fingers. She put them under Masha's nose.

"Stay still," she said, "don't pull away." Masha sniffed his hand, her hot steam blowing against his skin. Calix winced, his eyes widening as Masha opened her mouth and bit him. Elarie's grip on his wrist tightened slightly as Masha gnawed on him, her teeth not sharp. "Jitter Dragons are special little things," she said, petting Masha's face, "they primarily eat plant life when they're young. Their teeth are small and easily breakable, but they grow back like a shark." Elarie whispered something and Masha opened her mouth wide, making the same 'ahh' sound a kid would. "You can tell approximately how old a Jitter Dragon is this way because they grow back sharp."

Calix looked into her mouth, chuckling. "They're so amazing."

"That dragon up there," Elarie pointed above their heads, "at the very top is a Windryd."

He laughed, sitting up. Masha fell into his lap. "Oh my gods," he laughed again as he watched the Windryd's white tail disappear, "oh my gods."

"Never seen one of those before, huh?" Elarie teased.

"Elarie I've only ever seen one dragon in my lifetime outside of pictures in books—this," he stood, holding Masha like a baby. The dragon remained still, purring warmly against his torso. Her long tail wrapped around his waist. "I mean... I mean I *never* would've thought this was—we've only theorized! And there are so many!"

She said, "there should be more hiding in the walls."

Calix spun in a circle trying to catch sight of what was hiding from them. From him, more likely. He expected they'd all be out and about if it was only Elarie in their nest. He could see more Jitter Dragons flying around, a Skeep or two, and one of the fat Dindaruo Dragons Ryd liked so much. That plush was his favorite, he slept with it. "So why wouldn't the gods make these?" He asked.

"Come back down here," Elarie waved her hand. Calix sat, crossing one leg under him and extending the other. "Masha," she said, then transferred to the dragon language. It warmed Calix, making him think of his comfort places. His mother's study, his brother's art room, his garden. Even Grey's field. "Here, look at this," Elarie touched his knee. Masha was on her chest, sitting very much like a judgmental cat would. Only cats did not have glowing chests. Masha sat proudly with her back straight and her chest out. It glowed red. "What's this?" Elarie touched the spot.

"Fire, I assume?" Calix shifted to lay on his side, inspecting the hot spot.

Elarie nodded, "fire, but not the kind you know."

Masha sneezed and fire shot out of her nose just barely missing Calix's head. She purred sheepishly and walked away embarrassed.

"I'll show you," Elarie grunted.

"You shouldn't be sitting up," he put his hands out. She was doing it anyway.

She said, "too late, just look." Elarie groaned, looking down at the leaves on her side. Calix decided against telling her of his tingling fingers when he saw she was shaking. Elarie took in a deep breath and held up her hands. "Fire." Her right hand burst into flames, lighting the area like a torch. "Dragonflame," her left hand also lit up. "See the difference?"

Calix studied both as if he was being tested on it. "The Dragonflame is a different color. It's darker, probably hotter."

"Definitely hotter," she corrected. Masha returned and rubbed against her Dragonflame hand. A few other Jitter Dragons did as well. "This is not natural, is it? You won't find this anywhere else but in my body and in the bodies of these great beasts, right?"

"Right," Calix nodded. He looked from one to the other.

She said, "it's an altered element," and the regular fire went out. Elarie held it between them, "but if the gods didn't make it, who did?"

Calix put his hands against the hot air around her hand. It stung his skin, making him sweat. The tingling began to fade. The fire itself was beautiful. It twisted and curled, somehow wilder than what he used to light his room when he was reading or writing. This did not want to be contained. "Can you glow the way they do?" He asked, holding his hand out for Masha to bite him again. She gnawed on his knuckles.

"Are you looking for an excuse to stare at my chest?" She asked, the fire going out. A smirk was on her face when he looked at her.

His cheeks burned, "no, not like that."

"But you like this shirt so much and it offers a nice view—"

"Stop, you know that's not what I meant," he rolled his eyes. Calix still fought not looking at the shirt. It was ruined, but the neckline was still there.

Elarie smiled. "Answer my question and I'll answer yours."

"Who could have altered an element?" He asked and she nodded. "Well I would assume it was an elemental."

"Any elemental?"

"A powerful one," he shrugged, thinking on it. "But I've never known any elemental to be powerful enough to alter an element and create a whole new species. And it would have had to have been done ages ago because dragons have been depicted for ages..." he hummed, watching the *come on, you're almost there* look grow on Elarie's tired face. "You're that powerful, could *you* create a dragon?"

She shook her head.

Maybe she could. She had the fire, she had the language, she had the power. Not to mention the water magic she was hiding. Elarie smiled and said, "I really want you to come to this conclusion on your own." He scoffed. "I thought you were smarter than this."

"I *am* smarter than this," he countered and laid down. Elarie hovered above him, her green eyes pleased. Calix sighed, "maybe it was whatever is across the Barrier." She gave nothing away. "We know there either is or was a civilization over there. Our ocean excavation has been quite fruitful around the frozen edge."

"I've seen the museums," she nodded. Elarie had such a knowing look on her face that forced Calix to question what he knew. "Come on, Calix," she bent over, nearly expertly hiding her cringe of pain. Elarie hovered over him and rested on one hand. "Think about it."

"Elementals," he said and she nodded. "Elementals."

"How did they come to be?"

Calix said, "the gods and nature made magic—" but she shook her head, again forcing him to question his thinking. And now his education. Calix tilted his head. "The gods and nature—" she shook her head again.

"After the creation of the Fae, everything was made out of spite. Did you know that?" She asked and Calix shook his head. "The monsters, the humans, and..."

"The elementals were people?" Calix sat up, taking her with him accidentally. Their heads smacked together and he held her arms to steady her. While Elarie grimaced, taking the impact of the blow, he asked, "are you sure the elementals were people?"

She reached up to rub her head, "yes, I'm sure."

"So maybe that's who's on the other side of the Barrier!" He exclaimed, which made her jump. "Oh my gods, Elarie if that's true it would not only change the way we understand how magic is given, but it also paves the way for the discovery of an entirely different species!"

"That really hurt, how thick is your head?"

Calix glared at her, but she wasn't looking. "Elarie," he implored, holding her face so she had to look at him. He'd startled her, though he hoped not too much. "You have to tell me everything you know about them."

"I really don't know that much," she put her hand down impatiently, "I thought we were talking about dragons."

He relaxed his shoulders. "You're right, we shouldn't talk about the elemental species until I can write things down." Elarie rolled her eyes. Calix looked at her head, reaching with his thumb to brush over the forming bump. "So the gods created elementals and put them across the Barrier," he said, finding her eyes to be dead set on him. They were soft, perhaps appreciating the move back into dragons more than he anticipated. "And those elementals created dragons. Why?"

"Spite," she said with a smile.

"Spite," he repeated and she nodded. "I take it you like spite?"

She nodded again. Elarie said, "it's fun to see how the world is made when you take into consideration *why* it was made." She laid her hands over his, leaning forward, "and dragons are the best part."

Calix moved his hands off her face onto her neck. "Elarie," he said.

"Yes, Calix?" She replied innocently.

"I believe you are about to disprove my entire education," he told her.

Elarie's eyes lit up brightly, "oh, absolutely."

Calix stared at her for some time. She was waiting for him to say something, but the only thing that had come to mind at that very moment was something he couldn't say aloud. "Prove me wrong, then," he said, swallowing thickly. "Humans were created first." She shook her head. "You cannot be serious," he said. The idea that his own creation was wrong was not enough to distract himself from the now warm, buzzing feeling rising in his chest. The same one he felt when he almost kissed her. They'd gotten so close. As close as they nearly were sitting together. Calix looked at her lips, wondering how warm they'd be.

"Fae first," she said quietly. "Nature made the faeries, the gods wanted to experiment." It had to be getting hotter in the cavern. It had to be. His hands were still on Elarie's neck, there was no way it was her. He'd feel it, he'd have to let go. But Calix was sweating.

"Then the gods wanted something that looked like them so..." she breathed in.

"Humans," he nodded.

"No," Elarie leaned forward slightly, shaking with the effort. This would've been the perfect time to pull away from her, but Calix couldn't. It was like when they pulled together while sleeping. The way she grew closer or he grew closer. Her head ended up on his arm or their hands were together. "Golden blooded monsters," her hand moved down his arm to his elbow. "But nature hated them and Fae hunted them," she was trailing off, breathing heavily.

Calix stopped breathing altogether. "Elarie," he said. She hummed, her eyes darting up to his and down to his lips. "Can I kiss you?"

She paused long enough for him to have to breathe in. He was losing his momentum and she was biting her lip. Elarie was warmer now, he could feel it. Like dipping his hand in hot water for the first time. She whispered, "yes," and Calix leaned forward so she didn't have to strain her injury further.

This is such a terrible idea, Calix thought as he put his nose against hers. He could feel Elarie's warm breath, feel her trying to pull in the heat at the surface of her skin. It beat like a heart, flickering like blowing on a flame. *I cannot believe—*

Calix kissed her. Like a fool that had never kissed a woman. He moved closer, shifting his leg to bend the knee he didn't have. Elarie's hand switched to his jaw, then the back of his neck. He could feel how much she wanted it as well as how much she was shaking from the pain.

She pulled back, pressing her head against his. Elarie breathed in raggedly, "I have so many voices telling me to stop."

"Dragons don't like kissing?" He brushed his lips against hers.

"The only dragon rooting for us right now is Greilor," Elarie told him. Calix lifted his head to look at the dragon while Elarie laid back down, groaning as she grasped her side. Grey nodded his head. If he was a human Calix imagined he'd be smirking.

He shifted so the prosthetic wasn't digging into his skin and looked at Elarie. She had a hand on her side and the other on her forehead. "Are you all right?" Calix asked carefully, unsure of her expression. Her eyes were open, as was her mouth. Elarie's lips were pink, her cheeks were red. "Elarie?"

"I haven't kissed a man in years," she told him.

"We don't have to do it again if you don't want to," he found himself saying as he looked away painfully, though something tore in him when the words left his mouth. He couldn't tell if it was a bad thing or a good thing that she hadn't kissed a man in years. The thought occurred to him that by *years* she meant since Matian. Her mate, who happened to be a man. "Elarie?" He placed his eyes back on her. Her eyes were closed. Her arm had fallen above her head and Masha had curled up next to her face.

Calix looked at Grey again.

"She is going to ruin my whole life, isn't she?" He asked the dragon. Grey did nothing. He gave no indication of a yes or a no. He didn't even blink.

Elarie's hand touched his and his eyes widened. "Come here," she pulled on his small finger. *Gods, she heard me.* Calix obeyed her, laying on his side. Her eyes were still closed, her body relaxed. "I think I make your life more interesting," she said, "but I did ruin one thing."

He brushed his thumb over her cheek and her eyelashes fluttered involuntarily, "what's that?"

She said, "you're never going to want to kiss anyone else."

"Oh, you're just that good?" He leaned down, his elbow aching against the rock. Leaves only went so far as to protect them. He had no idea how she was comfortably lying on them.

Elarie put her hand back on his neck and pulled down, kissing him again. Perhaps she was right. He might not ever want to be kissed by anyone else if it didn't feel the way she was making him feel. Did that ruin something? He imagined it did, but he couldn't think of it. "I won't want to either," she whispered against his mouth. Masha growled, annoyed, and Calix felt her laugh.

"You should rest," Calix whispered back.

"Sleep with me," she said. He just nodded, again thinking she was going to ruin his whole life.

CHAPTER FORTY-FIVE

KAELUM

The star in his hand was much bigger than the first one. It must've been why it hurt so badly, even with the attempt at relaxing breathing exercises Elarie had told him to do. Kaelum watched it shine.

"Do you think the Jiivers will come for that?" Terry asked as he poured an expensive rum into a goblet. He handed it over.

"Not if they still think Elarie is here," he said. Kaelum took a sip and leaned back in his chair. He was still sweating, weak from the pressure of getting the rock out. Luckily there hadn't been any screaming this time. He knew what it was and what to do.

Terry sat next to him, "can't they sense her magic?"

Kaelum again looked around at everything in Captain Finnal's quarters. The nasty bed that wreaked of sweat and the chandelier above it. They'd only lit the seven candles on the bottom, not wanting to get on the bed to light the others. Other candles were shining in the room. Small ones, ones on candelabras, ones he put in dishes. Finnal was strange about them.

Looking at them, though, all Kaelum could think about was Elarie. "The dragon figure," he said faintly, his attention again on the star, "it's radiating some kind of energy. I can feel it when I'm doing this," he held up the star.

Terry reached out and Kaelum dropped the rock into his hand. The light went out. "I wonder what a regular human could do with this," he said, "if a Fae can manipulate it to use the magic, can I?"

"We'll have to ask Elarie," Kaelum leaned the seat back further, balancing on the back two legs. "Can I have it back?"

He chuckled before handing it over. "Are they addicting or something?" He asked, watching Kaelum use his knee to steady himself. The star began to glow once again.

Kaelum squeezed it and something hummed strongly in his chest. He'd felt it before, with the other star nights ago. "They can't be addictive if they're mine," he argued, squeezing to make the feeling more intense. It traveled through his body, boiling in his stomach and spreading like fire through his veins. It must've been what Elarie felt. "Can they?" He looked at Terry, who was smiling at him like he knew everything. Kaelum asked, "what?"

"Your eyes are sort of glowing," he said with the same smile.

Kaelum fell out of the chair. He hit Finnal's smelly carpet and got up quickly, searching for one of the four mirrors in the room.

"We'll be at the ship within the hour, right?" Terry asked, moving on in conversation with ease. This time he had to have been doing it on purpose. Kaelum looked through a mirror. "Are they still glowing?"

"Shit," Kaelum breathed, leaning closer. It was the same white as the star, only faint and centered around his pupil. He reached up and pulled the skin under his eye down. "Shit," he repeated and squeezed the star even harder, concentrating on making it brighter. "I'm magic," he said.

"We knew that already," Terry informed him as he stood. He picked the goblet up and set it on the table, walking to Kaelum. "It's sexy, by the way," he said as he wrapped his arms around Kaelum's waist.

Kaelum smirked at him through the mirror.

"Maybe this is what Elarie was talking about before when she said she'd help with it once you had a second star," he put his chin on Kaelum's shoulder. Terry said, "she'll teach you all about how to use the magic."

"Then we can turn her back into a dragon, right?" Kaelum turned around, leaning back against the wall and the mirror. He slid the star into his pocket.

Terry nodded confidently.

Kaelum recalled going to one of Calix's houses in the south as he stood at the helm watching Finnal's home grow closer. Queen Vienn called them holiday houses as some sort of joke. They were old and often in need of renovation, once belonging to great lords that had sided with Duness during the revolutions. Many of them were converted into things like orphanages or shelters, but a few remained in possession of the crown. Calix had taken Kaelum to one the year before they got the *Greyscale*. It had been an excursion he needed.

Seeing that house for the first time was a great reminder of how much money his best friend had. Because it was not a house. It was a castle.

Finnal's home didn't look like Calix's holiday house had, but Kaelum was reminded of it all the same—even if they were in Polinae's waters. The mansion in front of them was styled after their architecture. It looked newer, obviously bought through terrible means. Most things that were tended to have a horrible air to them. Finnal's house was tall. Three stories. There were many windows all framed in white that stuck out against the red stone blocks. A great door led down to the docks, where three ships were on standby.

One of them was his.

"Shouldn't be too hard," Terry muttered to him, rubbing his back. They were lucky there weren't any spotters, otherwise the rowboat holding Red, Tran, and two others would be spotted. They were pulling next to the *Greyscale* as Kaelum and Terry spoke.

Jamison walked up to the quarterdeck, snapping his fingers nervously as they docked on the other side of the *Greyscale*. They watched, covered by the dark of the night, as four people came walking down the dock with empty bags, a large box, and a handful of chains that clinked together loudly.

"Good so far," the kid mumbled. "Everything is ready to be moved."

They had to be quick about it. Gods knew how many men Finnal had just hanging around his house. Kaelum doubted very many, but they didn't want to make too much noise. The four men stopped and Kaelum's men slid the gangway down. They drew their weapons.

Killing the four was easy. The scurrying began. It made Terry laugh a little as they watched their men run low to the docks back and forth, avoiding the shining lights coming from inside the house. He grew quiet when they moved Terisa's body. Jamison was with her, guarding her body dutifully. Behind them was the sculpture. It was stupid of them to keep it, really, but it reminded Kaelum of Lester so it was bound to come along.

Gold was passed down. Jewels were passed down.

Kaelum sighed as he lovingly touched the wheel of his ship. They raised anchor quietly.

As soon as the sails dropped and they peeled away from the dock a siren wailed. It was sharp like a bird, practically deafening. Pirates shouted and magic boomed toward them. They ran down from the house, at least sixty of them crying for murder and throwing magic-like bombs to get the *Greyscale* to sink in their port.

"Defenses!" Terry shouted, throwing orders around. There were two left on Kaelum's crew with any sort of defensive magic, and neither had very much. One was good for shields, the other was good for a spell that had the strength to make an earthquake. Their magic rose to the challenge, though, fending off the magic that was actually pushing them further out to sea. An earthquake cracked the dock apart, sending many magic users to the depths. Terry came back up the steps and smiled at Kaelum. "Easy, right?"

He nodded despite the ship trailing after them. The *Greyscale* caught a good burst of wind. "Jamison?" He called down the kid ran up the steps, also smiling. He lived for a fight they were guaranteed to get out of. They had a head start and the *Greyscale* was a speedy ship when there wasn't a dragon on the deck. Kaelum tossed a star to him.

Jamison held it delicately, watching it shine for a moment. "They're in a sort of cave system or a cavern on an island with a waterfall. It'll take a week or two to get there depending on the seas." He gave the star back, sighing.

"You all right?" Kaelum slid the star back into his pocket as Jamison charted their course regretfully. He nodded tightly. "Right," Kaelum nodded, "swab the deck when you're done."

This made Jamison grin. He much preferred being in his little bubble on the deck than at the helm. Jamison fixed their position and handed the helm off to Terry, who started writing things in his sketchbook while holding the wheel with his elbow. Once the kid had run off he said, "we should drop spikes once we're in deep enough water."

"I was thinking the same thing," Kaelum observed his ship. Everything seemed to be in order. It didn't look like they'd stripped the thing to bones. "I'll take over here, will you get an inventory started? And have Tran go through our food stores, we'll probably need to ration."

"You got it," Terry closed his book and kissed him before he went off to carry out the orders. Kaelum sighed and leaned against the helm, squinting out at the black water, then up at the stars. They blinked brightly, almost welcomingly. His eyes drifted behind him. Toward where the other ship was. Kaelum had no desire to use the spikes. There was a reason Terry waited to say anything until Jamison was gone. The spikes were monstrous.

Below him was a crate of dead sea creatures. They were like sea urchins only with fewer spikes and were shaped more like conch shells. Once dropped into the deep sea they would grow at an alarming rate—seconds if you have the right one. They were used to stab enemy ships a pirate couldn't escape. Once the spike latched on it would shrink again and drag the ship down to the depths. No one survived them. It was illegal to have them in Ceptari.

If anyone inspected the *Greyscale* and found those... Kaelum and Terry would both never see the water again.

Kaelum held onto his ship. They wouldn't use one, they never had to. The *Greyscale* was too quick for it, so the spikes even being on the ship wasn't necessary. Still, it made Terry feel better for some reason.

By the morning they'd have lost the enemy ship and would be on their way to Calix and Elarie, then their only worry would be her again.

CHAPTER FORTY-SIX

ELARIE

The injury on her side was getting to her far more than she was letting on, though despite her secrecy she was sure Calix imagined the worst and treated it as such. He spent weeks babying her. Coddling her. When she was hungry he dutifully braved the dragons guarding their food hoard to select something for her, even offering to cook it so she didn't strain herself. When she needed to relieve herself he practically carried her from one spot to another. *Coddled.* She was being *coddled.*

And she utterly enjoyed it. All the days with the kisses and the carrying and the talking about small things like he thought she was too weak to talk about the big ones. Days of pain, sure, but days of calm and peace, too.

He was standing in front of her, hands on her elbows waiting for her to fall over. "Let go, Calix," she said, "I can walk."

"Maybe I like taking care of you," he said, though he put his arms down. He didn't step away. Calix was tense, ready to grab her if she so much as swayed wrong. "Is that so bad?"

"I think you like me being all weak and injured," she said and took a step with her left leg. Her knee gave out and Calix caught her against him. "Every man likes to be the hero, right?" She asked breathlessly. Elarie wrapped her right arm over his shoulder.

Calix said, "seeing as I've been the damsel in this relationship for the most part, it's a nice change of pace."

"For the most part?" Elarie asked jokingly, letting Calix do most of the walking. They went across the cavern to the opening shrouded in water. "I think it's been mostly even, don't you? Jiivers were me, I can give you credit for the faerthorne, and I saved your ass twice on the Reefs. The Rings, however," they stopped next to the water. Elarie faced him, "you saved me."

He smiled. "I'll keep doing it if you keep doing it," Calix offered, "we can be those friends that save each other."

Her brows creased slightly and she shook her head, "we aren't friends, Calix." He frowned, about to ask the brave *well then, what are we?* question, but she just said, "friends don't do this," and pulled him into her. She was glad they were the same height, sure that if he was taller she wouldn't have been able to get on her toes to reach his mouth. Calix grunted when she did, though he opened himself up for her instantly. Elarie gripped his shirt, pushing him into the heavy waterfall so he gasped and groaned at how cold it must've been for his human skin.

Calix dragged her with him and the water beat heavily onto her head and shoulders. He pressed her against the damp wall, being more gentle than she wanted, and said over the roar of the falls, "this is freezing!" With a clear laugh that sent chills dancing over Elarie's skin. She looked at him, watched him squint at her with a smile on his face.

Shit, she thought when looking at that smile. It was Greilor's voice next, faint like he didn't want her to hear it. She couldn't see him through the white and blue water, but she could feel his warmth among the other dragons. *He's perfect for you,* Greilor told her, like he never told her for Matian.

Elarie pushed Calix off, using the wall for support as she moved to the side. Elarie stepped out of the falls onto the ledge. She faced the island, full of life in a familiar, distant sense. The light from the rising sun made the leaves of tall trees shine like gold. They shook with the wind and the weight of animals. Dragons flew through them hunting or playing.

"Elarie?" Calix asked hesitantly. "Can you tell me if I did something wrong?"

She closed her eyes and bit her tongue. Gods, maybe he was perfect. Elarie shook her head.

"Would you like to be left alone?"

Again, Elarie shook her head. Calix was quiet, not asking anything else. He stood a step behind her, probably wary of the drop off the mountain that would most definitely kill either of them. "Can I ask you a stupid question?" She turned, putting her back on a warm rock. Calix nodded. He moved closer, his shoulder resting by hers. "Have you ever been in love?"

His eyes shined with something she couldn't identify. It wasn't pity, it wasn't hurt or joy. "No," he admitted, "I don't think I've ever come close."

She slid down the rock needing to sit. Her legs were shaking so much she worried he wouldn't have been able to catch her before she went over the ledge. Someone would, but she wanted it to be Calix. He sat next to her silently. "You know something my parents used to say..." she swallowed thickly. Elarie glanced at him, "it was something that was sort of just for them but we all heard it and it was like this big example of love and dedication and everything your parents are supposed to show you when you're young."

He nodded.

"I remember the first time I heard it was as a kid. I had been talking about my wings, telling my nursemaid all about them for the hundredth time like she truly cared about them at all and I heard my mother say she wished she had wings," she said. Elarie found a dragon crawling over a rock. One of the smallest ones that Greilor called gnats. "I couldn't imagine not having them. Everyone knew that I would find them, there was no way I wouldn't. It was like I was destined to fly... but she wasn't. My mother married into the dragon family and I think she was always a little jealous of the flying thing."

"My sister is, too," Calix said, "she gets upset when Grey won't fly when she's on his back. She likes to pretend."

Elarie smiled, "Greilor's good with kids."

"Are you?"

"Of course, kids love sparks and magic. It's easy to please them," she laughed, grateful for him when he joined. Elarie sniffed, wiping water off her forehead. "My mother," she continued, "wished for wings, wanting to feel that connection to something. My father told her that he was her wings."

Calix gave away a bit of shock. Wings were sacred, after all, and to just say that so casually? Of course it gave him pause.

She said, "I told him people can't be wings but he didn't listen to me. He just took my mother's hands like he'd done it a thousand times, said the words a thousand times but meant it each one of them. He told her that he would be her wings. That he would be there to catch her when she fell and provide hope when she thought all was lost. It did not matter if she could not fly because he would do it for her."

"That's sweet," Calix smiled gently, though he might've been hung up on the wings as Elarie had been.

"I never said it to Matian," Elarie said. "My father treated my mother like one of the gods humans worship, he would've given up flying for her. He would've given up anything for her. He amounted his love to something sacred and showed me what it meant to love someone like that, but I never said it to Matian."

He tilted his head, "Elarie, I don't think you had to."

"Greilor never liked him," she shook her head, feeling tears in her eyes, "they had an understanding. They both knew that they were the two most important things in my life and that I needed them both, but Greilor never really liked him." A tear fell down her cheek, "but he loves you."

Calix didn't say anything. Did she want him to? He couldn't deny the fact that Greilor loved him, but saying it was true would undoubtedly upset her.

"Everything in my head since the beginning is *Calix is kind, Calix loves deeply,*" she waved her hand around, "*Calix would never leave you sad, Calix would understand you,* and on and on. He never talked about Matian like that."

"Did you want him to?" Calix asked.

"I didn't know that I wanted him to until now," she admitted. Elarie looked at Calix. He still didn't pity her. "Is that bad?"

He shook his head. "Elarie, you lost your mate. Anyone would feel badly about being with someone else, especially another man, and being here is probably bringing a lot of that up. I understand."

Elarie looked away. Another small dragon crawled over the rock, this time into the waterfall. "Are you perfect, Calix?" She asked him.

"No," he said instantly.

"What about for me?" She amended, "Greilor thinks you're perfect for me, do you think you could be perfect for me?"

Calix went quiet, considering. Out of the corner of her eye, she could see it on his face. Not his answer, but his wariness. Like he had an answer, but wasn't sure if he could say it. She wondered then what he knew. About her, about the world, and about them. He knew she was a good liar, but how good? Did he figure she lied to herself as much as she lied to everyone else? Or did he just see good things—or try to see them?

"Do you want me to be?" Calix countered. He sat up partially. Calix reached up to her chin, turning her head so she had to look at him.

"I don't know what I want," she whispered.

Calix's Lathin eyes considered her. "Yes, you do. What do you want, Elarie?"

Her throat seemed to be closing up. She didn't look away from him, though her ears told her that a dragon was shushing another dragon, obviously trying to hear them through the falls. She wondered if Greilor was among them, bouncing on sore, bruised, and cut up legs waiting for her to say it. Whatever it was. "I want peace," she told him, "and quiet. I want to die of old age so badly."

"And?" He pressed.

"A home I don't have to run from in seven years when it's too obvious I'm not aging," she continued, "and for people to not be afraid of me when they find out what I am and what I've done."

His hand moved up to her cheek, swiping over a tear. "Do you think I can give you that?"

"A peaceful home where people aren't afraid of me? Maybe. Old age? No."

"Why not?" He asked. Elarie looked over his face, from his eyes to his chin and his ears. "There's a way, isn't there?"

She said, "not a good one."

"What is it? Maybe I can help you," he shifted, ready to save her like it was some back-and-forth game for them. Elarie just smiled weakly and shook her head. "Elarie," he implored, "you can tell me."

"I can," she agreed, "but I won't. Because if I do then this will stop."

His brow furrowed, "what will stop?"

"You'll stop looking at me like this," Elarie told him, "because if I tell you whatever we have right now, no matter how screwed or happy or sad it may be, will be ruined by it. And I don't want this to be ruined."

Calix was probably going to argue. He'd make a good argument, Elarie was sure, but she was saved by a dragon and a ship that was lowering anchor near the beach. Calix squinted out at it. "It's the *Greyscale*. They got here quickly."

"We've been here for weeks," she told him when she followed his eyes, "and there isn't a heavy dragon onboard."

He held her face, bringing her back to him. "You are going to tell me," he insisted, "you're going to tell me everything, Elarie, because I'm probably perfect for you and you're probably perfect for me. Do you understand?"

She nodded despite knowing she'd probably never tell him.

"And Matian was perfect for you, too," he said strongly. Elarie winced. "He was. I don't need a dragon to tell me that and neither do you. Wings, no wings, mates, no mates, it doesn't matter. He was yours and you were his. You were perfect together."

Shit, she thought once again before she kissed him. It hurt to do so, the angle of her back with his and the words he said both sending two different kinds of pain through her. She kissed him hard anyway. He was *probably* perfect for her and she was *probably* perfect for him.

Another dragon roared at the top of their lungs and she pulled away, looking at the beach. "They can't set foot on this beach," she told Calix, "get me up, you have to tell them." Calix lifted her to her feet and she gasped in pain, ripping his stained shirt with the effort to not accidentally hurt him by squeezing his arm too hard. Calix was instantly apologetic as he pulled her back under the waterfall, but she just said, "you can't take Greilor he's too weak to fly."

Greilor growled at her, denying it.

"You have a hole in one of your wings, you stupid lumbering dragon," she snapped, "no flying until it isn't at risk of a tear. Calix, take the dragon that snatched us out of the water."

Calix looked at the green Gurin Dragon.

CHAPTER FORTY-SEVEN

"You're kidding, right?" Calix asked faintly. He set Elarie on the bed and she instantly laid down, groaning as she held her side. "Elarie, I can't just ride a different dragon."

"Yes, you can, or Kaelum is going to die," she mumbled, her eyes shut tight. "The dragon won't let you fall."

He began, "but Grey—"

"Will be upset with me and not you," she said, then took his hand. Elarie looked at him with the same weak look she thought she was good at hiding. "If they touch this island the dragons will kill them."

Calix asked, "can't you do something to stop that from happening?"

"Yes, but it's a last resort sort of thing, I need you to try to get everyone to stay on the ship first," she squeezed his hand, "just call me if you need saving." Calix looked down at her, watching her eyes slowly close.

He bent over and kissed her forehead, the urge to do it more than once taking over. Her forehead, her temple, her cheeks, and her lips. Oh, to kiss every part of her. It was coming on too quickly, he knew, but he didn't want it to stop. When he looked at the smile brushing her lips, he thought she might feel the same. Calix took a step back from her and glanced over at Grey, who stared knowingly.

So Grey had never truly liked Matian, whom Elarie loved. The two of them shared a mutual love for her and her alone, which meant they were only cordial with each other. But with Calix it was different. Grey loved them both and—if it wasn't evident before, it was now—he wanted them together.

Did Grey know what Elarie wasn't sharing? That what Calix felt, how he felt it so quickly, meant something? More than just the fact that he thought she was lovely and beautiful and he wanted to kiss her often. Quite often. It was a feeling that had developed greatly over the past few weeks they'd been together. Elarie was *very* good at kissing and it was on his mind like he was a teenager again. But did Grey know something he couldn't communicate? About her—about them, about them being together.

Calix passed the Great Dragon. He wouldn't look at his rider. He went to the other dragon, this one slender and green. It was large, with big enough claws to take a chunk out of Elarie's side, but as Calix wondered how he would mount it he found it looked to be far more similar to a horse than expected.

He looked back at Elarie, who was asleep with her left arm hanging over the side of the rock. Calix almost went back to fix it so she was more comfortable seeing as everything seemed to happen to that arm, but a dragon roared loud and angrily from outside. She stirred, not waking, and put her arm on the rock.

"All right," Calix said, watching a few dragons crawl or fly out of the cavern. A few growled at Calix. He was an intruder in their home, after all, only tolerated because of Elarie and Grey. Grey, a king among dragons, and Elarie a... queen among them. Just in humanoid form. "I can do this, right?" He looked at the dragon in front of him. It nodded surely. Calix took a deep breath, glancing at Grey. "Do you think I can?" He asked his dragon.

Grey slowly turned his big head. He was jealous. An ancient, powerful dragon was jealous. The powerful dragon blew smoke through his nose and nudged him toward the green one, lumbering over to be closer to Elarie. He laid down and began licking the hole in his wing.

Calix breathed deeply and followed the green dragon to the opening, climbing up carefully. "We can do this," he told the dragon before it bounded out and dove through the waterfall. Calix screamed, grabbing onto the dragon's thick neck. Greenie, he decided. His name was Greenie. Greenie made no indication he was upset by the name Calix had thought up. He just flew down the mountain happily. Calix began to wonder if Greenie considered this his retribution for what he did to Elarie.

Elarie, who had a piece of her side missing and was lying about how much it hurt. Had it been a mistake to not let her heal by dying? Would she be fine? He was sure that she would, Elarie was quick to heal her wounds. The ones on her wrists from the Fae had healed quickly and the trail of marks on her arms she'd received from the faerthorne Finnal's men put on her were all scabbed over and nearly healed.

She was still lying on a rock bed with some paste and leaves slapped onto her body, a healing practice Calix was unaware of. Was it a dragon healing practice—

Pay attention, Greenie seemed to snap.

"Sorry," Calix adjusted upward, looking at the beach Greenie was speeding to. The dragon had tucked his wings into a dive, growling and snapping at the air the closer they got. There were two rowboats in the water being pushed onshore. "Shit," Calix said. Greenie landed on the beach but Calix didn't put his feet down. "Get off the beach!" He shouted.

"Calix?" Kaelum stepped forward, "where's Grey? What happened—"

"Get off the beach!" He shouted again while Greenie fidgeted, "this is a dragon island, you can't stay here—they'll kill you! Get back to the ship!"

A dragon roared overhead, soaring with the might of its translucent wings as it made its way to the ship. Its wings spanned wide and pointed with sharp spiked ends. Its neck was long and seemed to be dangling with necklaces. It flew over the sea faster than Grey or Greenie ever could and breathed hot, magic fire. Kaelum let out a scream and they all started pushing the boats back into the water.

Greenie took off into the air on powerful legs. He followed the white dragon, screeching at it. The dragon roared in response, turning in the skies to face Greenie. Its mouth was open, fire crackling at the back of its skinny throat, but it stopped when it saw Calix. Its mouth snapped shut and hot, angry steam blew from its nostrils. The dragon flew away and Greenie landed on the deck, tilting his head at the flames crawling down the mizzen.

Calix climbed down and began shouting orders. "Raise the anchor *now*, be prepared to set sail as soon as they get back to the ship," he turned to the dragon, "Greenie—" he bounded off the side of the ship and flew away. "Shit," Calix looked around, moving to help pull the anchor out of the water. The remaining crew members went about their tasks without hesitation. They were ready to sail as soon as a cloud of dragons covered the dot of the rising sun. Calix froze upon seeing it. Many did. He'd thought seeing all of the dragons in the cavern was one thing—*this?* This was what authors meant when they wrote about dragons being the sight of death. A cloud of them flew forward like bats out of a cave, clustered together to make them look large and horrifying.

As if one dragon on its own wasn't horrifying enough.

"Fire's out, Captain," someone said to Kaelum, who just climbed over the ship rail. Two pirates went to pull the rowboats up.

"Terry get to the helm and catch any wind there is, leave the boats," he ordered, then grabbed the ripped sleeve of Calix's shirt. "Tell me what in the name of every sea god is going on."

Calix said, "dragons are some of the most territorial creatures alive and humans just stepped foot on their island. Elarie said they'd kill you for it, I didn't stop you in time."

The captain turned his head to the dragons almost upon them. "All right, battle positions! If you are not here to fight get in the captain's chambers—Terry!" Terry was there instantly to catch the key to unlock the door. The few rescued ran inside. Kaelum walked further onto the ship, "Jamison I want water at the ready, put out as many of those fires as you can." Jamison nodded tightly, handing the spears off to Red. Red took them and began distributing them. "Calix—"

"I'll get a spear," he nodded.

"No, what happened to Grey?" He pulled the prince back. Calix looked at the dragons. They didn't have time for this.

He said, "we were attacked and he was injured, so was Elarie. She's on the island now."

"Why didn't you two set off the dragons?"

Again, Calix looked at the dragons. He could see small ones that looked like Masha flying amongst the big ones. They were preparing for a dive. The *Greyscale* was no match for it. "Because of Grey, he's like a king and we're his riders."

"But he's an injured dragon and you're a human—"

"Kaelum!" Calix shouted, "that doesn't matter right now, people are going to die if we don't do something—"

Elarie fell out of the sky. It didn't look like she'd intended to do it, either, with the way she smacked against the rail Kaelum had just climbed over. Calix got across the deck quickly as dragons began diving one by one, breathing bright fire over the sails and masts. Yet nothing burned.

Calix grabbed Elarie's arms and pulled her over. "I can fix it," she mumbled faintly, falling against him. Calix tried to straighten her as her knees buckled. "And I'll do it without dying, I promise." She pushed off him and grasped the rail, her breathing uneven and heavy.

He looked at her back. Her side. The leaves had ripped, revealing the injury to the air and everyone else.

Fire grew from where she was standing, but Calix wasn't looking at that. His mouth was open, staring down at the blood on his shirt. People were screaming, the fire chasing them off before they realized it wasn't burning them.

"Calix," Kaelum said.

He looked at Elarie. She was swaying, standing only by sheer will and the hand digging holes in the wood railing so she didn't fall over. The fall... the fall must've ripped something open, something more than the dragon had. Blood poured down her side once again, shining in the air.

She raised her right hand, stumbling on shaking legs. Elarie brought fire to it, a ball of thin flames like the ones she used to calm Kaelum when he was creating the star. It beat like a heart, thrumming with a noise he'd never heard before. Sharp like a string on a violin played to the highest note, but just as powerful and booming as a dragon's roar.

The dragons above them balked at the sound. A few flew away outright. One, the white one with its translucent wings, flew down to meet Elarie at eye level. She didn't look small in front of it. She stood her ground as it brought in a great breath.

Elarie pointed her flaming hand at the dragon and a blast of fire so hot it was white shot from her, barreling through the air. The flames shot through the dragon's mouth and out the back of its head.

Killing the dragon.

Everyone fled when she did it. The fire coating the ship, coating Calix's feet though he hadn't realized, drew back into her body. Elarie's flames winked from existence and she fell backward the way the dragon had.

She hit the deck and no one moved.

Chapter Forty-Eight

ELARIE

The throbbing feeling had no central point. It was inside her, everywhere. Elarie's chest was different. Her chest was on fire, burning for the dragon she killed using the power she'd taught herself without knowing what it meant. She'd known one of them would challenge her, she just didn't want it to be one that had children to protect. They'd die without their mother now.

Elarie now had a burn behind her eyes that she tried to blink away. She sniffed, turning her head to the familiar warmth of Calix. His head was in his hands, elbows on the mattress like he was praying for her. "Calix," she said, her voice strained. Elarie found herself in the med room, a place she'd never been despite her many injuries. It was small, with two beds chained to the wall so they'd fold when they weren't being used. A cart of medical supplies was bolted to the wall as well. Elarie touched him, her pinky brushing over his elbow. "I didn't die, see?" She motioned weakly to herself.

He breathed in deeply, sliding his hands over his face. His eyes were red and puffy like he'd been crying. "Elarie," he strained to say.

"What happened? Is everyone all right, I thought—"

Calix shook his head, his lips forming a thin line. "Elarie," he said again, his voice shaking. He pulled himself away from her, forcing her to think the worst. It wasn't Greilor who was gone, he was safe in the cavern. Was it Kaelum, his best friend? Or Jamison, the kid he loved? "Elarie, what color is your blood?"

A thrum echoed in the back of her mind, followed by the ringing of a bell—some god telling her time was up. "What?" She asked quietly.

"I thought it was red," he said painfully, a tear dropping from his eye, "it has been this whole time, but when you fell," his face constricted. Elarie began sitting up no matter how painful it was. "When you fell it was golden."

She shook her head, "it doesn't mean anything."

"Yes it does," he said, "it meant a lot." Calix sat straight. "What kind of monster are you, Elarie? I need you to tell me before they make you tell them."

"I'm not a monster," Elarie shook her head again, getting up to her elbows. She looked at her left side, which had been bandaged but was still bleeding. Gold, not red. Gold. Her spell had run out in the caves, where she was happy and at peace with him. "Calix, you have to believe me, I'm not a monster—"

"Only monsters have golden—"

"Please don't finish that, please," she breathed. Elarie turned painfully, "I am not a monster, I never had been and I won't ever be, you have to believe me."

Another tear dropped down his face. She wanted to wipe it away. She wanted him to give her the chance, the breath, to explain, but humans were human. He was human. And humans reacted a specific way to the sight of golden blood. It was a wonder Terry hadn't removed her head.

"Tell me what you are," he said, not like an order. Like a plea. He wanted honesty, he needed it more than he ever had. She focused her senses enough to know that more than one person was listening behind the door, but it was just Calix and her to him. *He* was asking, not them.

She pushed herself up further, trying to level with him. "I'm an elemental—"

"Elementals aren't monsters," Calix contradicted as if he'd know better than her. "Don't lie to me."

"I'm not," Elarie shook her head and got her leg over the bed, struggling to straighten any further. Did Calix care anymore? Hours ago he'd hiss at her for moving too quickly or tell her she'd strain herself too much. What about now? How did he feel seeing a golden blooded in pain? "The elementals are golden blooded, but we aren't monsters, I promise."

"Liar," he whispered.

Elarie paled, feeling her blood turn cold. "I'm a person, I'm not a monster. I was born this way, I was made this way, we were created this way. I told you about spite—"

"I don't want to hear any stories, I want to hear you tell me what you are."

She stared at him. Calix had hardened his features. He put up a mask against his feelings. Not even his Lathin eyes gave him away. "I am Elarie Crosha, the fire elemental. I'm your friend. You... you are my," she swallowed thickly, now the one driven to tears, "you're my friend, you're supposed to accept me for who I am—"

"I don't," he said sharply. Elarie could hear the pain in the two words, but it wasn't enough to make a difference. "Tell me what you are."

Elarie saw his mask. She saw it, took it in, and put up one of her own. Her breath was labored, but it was strong. She got to her feet and swayed, pain shocking down and up her body. "I was going to tell you today," she said, "I had this story to tell and I'd tell you exactly what I am at the end."

"What are you," he said, this time with a quiver. He was losing it. And losing her.

"Angry," she whispered and walked around him, careful to keep her distance because she didn't want to see him flinch away from her. Elarie pulled the door open, finding three people standing there listening. Terry, Kaelum, and Jamison. The latter looked the most scared, the former looking almost satisfied. Kaelum... "I hope you leave Terry before you become too addicted to your magic and kill him," she said. Kaelum gaped at her, suddenly terrified. "It won't be my fault when you do."

Elarie limped a few steps before the warmth at her back changed, indicating that Calix had stood and was in the hallway. "Elarie," he said. She turned around, her hand pressed firmly to the wall. "Will you let Grey come back?"

"I'd never keep him from you," her brow furrowed, "ever. I won't make him choose between either of us. Just whistle."

He didn't say or do anything else. Elarie didn't either. She said her piece, he finalized it. What did it matter? It wasn't like she'd spent weeks kissing him. It wasn't like much of that was with him partially on top of her. It wasn't like she did think that he was perfect for her and she was perfect for him. There was no probably other than the probability of her being in denial.

But it didn't matter. He wasn't it. He wasn't perfect.

And of course she didn't believe it.

Elarie climbed the stairs and stumbled across the deck in the dark. The ship swayed, pushed on a mild wind that wasn't carrying them quickly. She passed the stain of her golden blood and stopped on the railing.

Golden blood.

Golden blood.

Golden blood.

It never should've mattered. The fact that Elarie was a *person* with a heart and a mind meant that it shouldn't have mattered to anyone. Not a prince, not a pirate, not a villager or a king or a lord. Elarie should have only ever been Elarie to anyone, as it had been for the entirety of her first life. *For people to not be afraid of me when they find out what I am,* that was what she had told Calix she wanted. He implied that he could give it to her, but never said it. They'd moved on in conversation before she could hear it.

She ran her fingers over the indent she'd made. The wood she'd broken while trying to save them. *Save them,* why did she even try? Why did she ever try? Ever in all her life after the first, why did she try? What good was saving people when all they did was stab her in the back afterward?

Elarie sent a burst of light down to the black water, resting her elbows on the railing. She could feel herself being watched on more than one front. The four she'd woken up to, someone on the other side of the ship, and someone at the helm. What did it matter? None of it mattered.

A dragon broke the surface, breaching like a whale. Water slid off its fish-like scales, shining in the moonlight. Elarie straightened and whistled halfheartedly. The dragon, a Fyndall—one of the first water-dwelling dragons—swam right over. She was happy to help, waving an arm that had webbed toes. She rose up, both swimming and flying.

"Can you get me back to the dragon nest?" She asked.

The dragon, another like Masha to only speak her dragon language, said *of course, my lady*, in an annoyingly formal way. Elarie just smiled. She winced as she brought herself over the railing. The Fyndall had gone back to the water waiting for her to jump. She swam along the ship as it moved lazily.

Elarie took a deep breath and pressed her hand to the wrap covering the gaping wound she could've died from. Could still, if she wasn't so stubborn.

Without looking back Elarie dropped over the side of the ship and mounted the water dwelling dragon.

PART TWO

THE LAND

CHAPTER FORTY-NINE

KAELUM

It was just the two of them like it was when they were kids. Just the two of them on the floor of a ship, both crying. Calix had yet to calm down in the hour since Elarie jumped off the ship. He was still bent over with his hands digging into his hair, sobbing. Kaelum had no idea what to do. With Calix, with Elarie, or with himself. He'd managed to keep himself from making a star this time around, but her words were still in his head. Kaelum could become addicted to his own magic and kill Terry.

Terry had all the stars, but Kaelum could feel them like they were a part of him. At night he could feel where they were on the ship—below, in the room Jamison had run to after Elarie left. Terry would be trying to calm him down from whatever panic attack might overtake the kid.

"What did I do?" Calix sniffled. Kaelum handed him a handkerchief and Calix stuffed his face into it, wiping everything. "What did I do? What did I do?"

"What did *we* do," Kaelum corrected faintly. "How badly did we mess up or is it the opposite?"

"No, I messed up. I messed up so badly," he shook his head. Kaelum put a hand on his back and ran it up to his shoulder, squeezing.

He said gently, "tell me what happened?"

Calix began hyperventilating. His best friend was falling to pieces. Kaelum shifted to face him, pulling him close. He kept one hand on his back, the other wrapped around to his chest. "The things I said in that cavern," he breathed, "and the things I did."

Kaelum couldn't imagine Calix having sex with Elarie while she was injured so badly, so it didn't leave a lot of other options, but the things he said? Calix had always had a way with words, he was good at talking and sounding like he meant what he said. And when he did mean it, truly meant it, it was something else entirely. Kaelum recalled the first time Calix had told him he loved him like a brother. There had been lots of '*I love you, man*'s said between them before that, but the first time Calix had said it without being prompted Kaelum could feel it.

So what had he said to Elarie?

"I want her," Calix said, "and I didn't tell her that, but I do. I want her in so many ways—I messed up so badly."

"Calix, she has golden blood and she can't die," Kaelum said, "you can't want her in so many ways." Calix began shaking his head but Kaelum continued, "she doesn't grow old, right? So you can't be with her the way it counts. She can't have children so you can't marry her. And both of those things aside, she's a golden blooded monster. Only monsters have golden blood."

Calix wiped his eyes again, rocking slightly in Kaelum's arms. "And you can't have a golden blooded monster teaching you how to control your magic?"

"I guess not," Kaelum replied. He sighed, "I'll figure it out on my own."

He didn't believe it. Not for a second, he didn't believe he'd get a handle on whatever it was inside him. Not with how much, at that moment, he wanted to see what he could do. He wanted to take a star and play with it. The magic was active at night, as was he, and he wanted to watch it curl in his eyes.

"She told me there's a way to make her begin aging again," Calix said, "she didn't say what it was, I guess it was something bad."

"You can't be with someone who has golden blood."

"What if I was her mate?"

Kaelum froze. His body tensed up, he couldn't find a way to stop it. He pulled back from Calix, removing his hand from his chest. "You think..."

"The way she talked about it," he said, "and it makes sense."

"But she has one," Kaelum argued quickly, "she told us she did and he died, she described what it felt like to lose him."

Calix shook his head, "I think she either just says Matian was her mate because it felt right to her or maybe because she's not a Fae it's different and she can have more than one."

"What kind of monster gets a mate?"

"Nature hated them," he said faintly. Calix's eyes moved, "nature hated the golden blooded monsters and the Fae hunted them, that was what she told me."

Kaelum said, "the Fae hunt her, we've seen evidence of that."

Calix leaned back until he was flat on the ground and his head was angled against the chair behind him. He was in the same place he'd been in when he played cards with Elarie and it looked like he realized that as soon as he looked across from himself. "It's different for her, it has to be. They just kill golden blooded monsters, they don't ritually sacrifice them for their magic."

"Nature would never give a golden blooded monster a mate," Kaelum told him shortly. "There's no way. She has golden blood, she hid it from everyone—"

"Why do you think she did?" He pushed further down so his head rested against the floor Kaelum never cleaned. Still, Kaelum sighed and laid down next to him. They stared blankly up at the dark wood ceiling. A few of the beams were different, caused by repairs needed after battles with slavers. Never battles with dragons, though. The ship was in pieces after that, even with Elarie's help. Calix said, "I would've."

Kaelum shook his head, calculating the cost of damages to his ship while Calix calculated the damages to his relationship. "Why do you think that?" He asked. He'd need a whole new mizzen and fresh sails... Would Kaelum have to pay for that or would Calix? Calix had been generous enough to do it thus far, but they also had what they took from Finnal that they could use.

"If I had been alive for as long as I think she has been—"

"Are you going to tell me what you thought she was now? Now that we know she's not whatever you thought," Kaelum turned his head to his friend. He could feel Terry walking up the steps to the quarterdeck. He'd be at the door...

Now. Terry knocked before opening it, though he didn't wait for either of them to say he could or could not come in. "Jamison's asleep," he said, going across the room to get a nearly empty bottle of rum. Kaelum would take it, he doubted Calix would. He wasn't one for drinking while upset. "And the rest of the crew has been informed that Elarie left but she could come back."

"Why do you think she'll come back?" Kaelum asked, lifting his head slightly. Terry was drinking slowly, tipping the bottle back until it was finished.

He sighed and wiped his mouth. "You."

"Why me?"

Terry set the bottle down and grabbed another. "I think she'll blow off some steam and come back. She's been trying to protect you this whole time and she wants to teach you about your magic."

"She said it wouldn't be her fault if I killed you," Kaelum contradicted, "that sounds a lot like 'you're on your own.'"

He sat next to Kaelum and popped the cork of the bottle, also nearly empty. "I'll bet my best art supplies that she's killed someone accidentally and that is why she'll come back to help make sure you don't kill me. What she said was said in anger. Right Calix?"

They both looked toward their prince. "The first time she killed someone after losing control was because someone tried to force herself onto her."

"But do you think she'll come back?" Terry asked, not caring about the sob first-time-I-killed-someone-it-was-justified story.

Calix sighed slowly. His chest rose and fell, his eyes never leaving the ceiling. "For Kaelum, yes," he muttered before he got up, "eventually."

"Not for you?"

"Fuck you, Terry," Calix replied, snatching the bottle from him before he left. They watched the door shut behind him, both quiet for some time.

Terry said, "I think she ruined my relationship with him."

Kaelum sat up. "Terry, honey, I love you. I am so in love with you, right?" Terry nodded. "*You* ruined your relationship with him. *I* ruined my relationship with him. It wasn't Elarie telling us to make the choices we did and it wasn't Elarie telling you to say the things you said." Terry just frowned. "I'm going to go take the bottle from him."

"Why? He should be allowed to get drunk because of this," Terry shook his head, motioning around. "All of it, not just her."

"Calix hates drinking when he's upset, it only upsets him more," Kaelum kissed his cheek and stood, "I'll see you after I get him to bed."

His afterlife said nothing. Kaelum gave him a chance to mull over placed blame while he walked to find Calix. His prince was where Elarie had been. Kaelum could see him putting his fingers in the same place Elarie had, digging them into the railing of his ship with the same hold. Kaelum walked slowly, careful to be heard, and Calix pulled his fingers out. "Here," Calix said, holding the bottle out on his right side. Kaelum went to it. "I hate drinking anyway."

"Liar," Kaelum said, but he took the bottle away. "I distinctly remember a game we play right over..." he turned, pointing to the wall with a red dot painted on it, "there and it required us to be drunk."

Calix turned and leaned against the railing. "I knew I was wrong as soon as she left, Kaelum," he said, ignoring the chance to settle down and think about happier things. He was still thinking about Elarie. "I know I'm wrong."

"About her blood?" Kaelum leaned next to him, taking a swig of the drink only to spit most of it back out. He looked at the bottle, squinting. "This is nasty," he whispered, setting it down. Kaelum observed his breaking ship.

"What monster would save our lives? What monster would care about dragons—what dragon would let a monster ride it?" He countered himself, motioning to the scars in the deck in front of them.

Kaelum considered taking another drink. "Ask him," he suggested. "Can you call him?"

Calix sighed slowly. "I'm afraid I'll accidentally call her."

"She can ignore it," he shrugged.

"I don't think that's how it works," he said, "remember with the Fae, how I whistled to her then?" Kaelum nodded and Calix continued, "how she lurched forward?" Again, he nodded. "I think it's this need for them to go to the whistle. Her and the dragons."

Kaelum laughed a little, "you know Terry and I thought she was a dragon the gods cursed to be human?" A smile crossed Calix's face. "We were thinking she could teach me how to turn her back or something."

"Funny, we talked about her wanting to be a dragon. She doesn't like herself so she wants to be a dragon but she wants to still be friends," Calix toed the deck, "and I said that of course I'd be friends with her if she were a dragon. We'd..." he sighed, "we'd be friends until I died and she flew off somewhere else. Gods, she was so happy when I said it, too." Calix pinched the bridge of his nose and breathed deeply.

Kaelum stared at the golden stain no one had mopped up yet. It was Jamison's job, but he hadn't done it in days.

"She was going to tell me," he whispered as if just realizing what Elarie had said. "She was going to tell me of her own volition, she was going to tell me. She was going to explain and I didn't let her."

"This is the most interesting trip we've ever taken," Kaelum said plainly. "Come on, you should try to get some sleep." Calix whistled instead. Loud and airily, the way Elarie whistled for Grey. "Are you going to risk her showing up?"

"I want my dragon," he said and whistled again.

Kaelum looked to the skies, his head dipped back. He leaned further, squinting with the help of the moonlight.

It took a long time. An hour, maybe more, but Calix didn't stop whistling and Kaelum didn't leave his side. He wouldn't. Whether the dragon showed up or not, whether Elarie was on his back or not, he'd stay.

CHAPTER FIFTY

CALIX

Grey landed roughly, making Calix realize he'd just forced his dragon to fly when Elarie, a dragon expert, advised against it. He'd ridden Greenie because he couldn't ride Grey. And yet the dragon made the trip because he had to. The dragon huffed steam and turned his head to Calix. Elarie wasn't on his back, which meant calling him worked—*worked*—but he didn't find it as satisfying knowing that Elarie wasn't there to cheer the way she had the first day.

"Grey," Calix said.

The dragon growled deeply, snaking low as he crossed the short distance to halt in front of him. His wings shuddered painfully and his head bowed. He sniffed the blood spot, eyes flicking to Calix.

"I know," he said. The dragon growled as if to ask *do you? Do you know?* Calix's chest tightened. "How badly did I mess up, then?" Gods, did he wish he could speak to dragons. Or have a translator...

Grey scratched one long nail across the blood and it flaked into the air, disappearing on the wind. Grey took a deep breath and roared, his hot breath aimed at Calix. His jaw opened wide, the sound of his outrage with his rider echoing over the water and vibrating in the air. Calix's ears rang painfully.

"A lot, I think," Kaelum whispered when Grey was finished. Calix winced. Had it been a whisper? Grey snapped at Kaelum, his teeth clanging together so Kaelum slid a step to the side.

Elarie had said she wouldn't make him choose.

But Grey was choosing. In that moment, he had to have been choosing. Calix, his rider of three years who had failed at so many things, or Elarie. Elarie, his family, his home, his reminder of who they both lost.

He hummed mournfully. The dragon put his head against Calix, engulfing him in the smell of flames and blood. It was goodbye, wasn't it? He'd pick Elarie and Calix would never see him again?

Calix wrapped his arms around him, wondering what a lifetime of being able to do this was like. What her lifetime was like. He'd probably get to ask if only he'd given Elarie a chance. He imagined she'd start with a small thing, revealing one thing or the other. Would it happen after she decided he was perfect for her? After they mutually decided it? She'd say *fine, you are perfect and if you promise to accept me for who I am then I'll tell you everything.*

They should've stayed in the cavern.

Grey suddenly turned his head and a *crack* echoed in his mind. Calix's eyes widened. It sounded like bone, but it wasn't. Calix didn't have a bone in his left leg, not the bottom half.

The dragon pulled and Calix went with, shaking and jerking until his leg popped off. "Shit," Kaelum stumbled back as Grey waved it around like a dog with a toy. He tossed it into the air and blew fire at the magic prosthetic.

"What was that for?" Calix asked painfully. He'd torn half his pants off as well, exposing the stump to the air. The once whole prosthetic fell into the sea, making no noise as it met the ocean waves. Grey's judgmental eyes pointed down at him. He'd been crippled by his dragon. Now he was on the ground against the rail, staring up at the beast like he might be the next kill. "Grey?" Calix asked.

He just snorted, satisfied with whatever he'd done, and turned around to go to sleep in his spot. Calix stared, dumbfounded, as Kaelum got him to his foot. "Why did he do that?" Kaelum asked softly. He helped Calix hop back to the captain's quarters, where Terry was drawing a rather large portrait of Elarie. He was humming, drinking, and standing while he drew, which meant he was drunk enough to dance while he worked. "Terry," Kaelum said, "can you get the crutches from the bin?"

Terry looked back and a pencil fell out of his mouth. "Did Grey rip off your leg?" He asked. Calix nodded, sitting down. He put his leg up on the table he played cards on. "Why?"

"No idea," he answered, looking at the trashed pants. "Give me whatever you're drinking, please." Of course, Terry looked at Kaelum, but Kaelum just nodded. Terry corked the bottle and tossed it over. Calix caught it, opened it, and drank without taking a breath for the entire time it took Terry to find his crutches and bring them to Kaelum, who requested them. "Her eyes are closer together than that," he said, pointing at the drawing.

"There will be no pointing at my work unless one wishes to never see my work again," Terry waved a finger through the air. Calix groaned and pressed his head back against the chair.

"She's got all these scars on her face and a crooked nose," he said with his eyes closed, picturing her. Calix had spent days with his knee between her legs and his arms on either side of her, hovering over her to look at her while she tried to steal small kisses. There had been no touching, though she implied that she wanted it, and Calix had found that he liked to look at her. He imagined, in that moment, what Elarie would look like if he was the one that was under her. The control he'd see compared to the softness when she was below him.

Terry and Kaelum were whispering to each other. A door opened and shut. When he opened his eyes they were gone. Calix took another long drink and looked at the drawing, then began imagining what would've happened in the pool weeks ago if a dragon hadn't shown up to challenge Grey.

Something more than kissing, a part of his mind said.

Calix groaned and closed his eyes.

CHAPTER FIFTY-ONE

ELARIE

Greilor was gone when Elarie woke up, off to please his prince. Elarie groaned and rolled onto her front. Masha was in front of her, taking the spot Elarie had usually laid in. She'd fallen asleep in that place and woken up where Calix had been. "Good morning, Masha," she said in the dragon language.

Teach, she replied.

"Teach what?" She asked, blinking slowly.

Calix talk, Masha answered. Elarie sighed. It would have happened eventually. But Masha was not alone in this. She and five other Jitter Dragons wanted to learn. They were joined by dragons who could speak the language but simply wanted to hear Elarie translate words because it was funny sounding.

She nodded slowly, reaching up to rub the side of her nose. "Food first," she said in Ceptareei. Only a few knew what she said. In the dragon language she asked, "did Greilor tell anyone how long he would be gone for?"

Elarie crawled to the edge of the rock bed and received a few 'no's. Masha said that Greilor had heard a whistle and left to follow it. At that word, *whistle*, her heart ached. She recalled Calix's jealousy at not being able to, then his willingness to learn. And now? He'd done it. He'd done it! But she was not there to celebrate with him the way she had expected they would once he was successful.

Once she pushed herself onto her feet she fell, catching herself on the dragon now calling herself Greenie. It was Greenie who delivered Calix to the ship, then upon returning, she had roared for Elarie to wake, saying the humans needed her and there were many dragons. Elarie had fallen off of Greenie's back, slipping off her smooth scales and landing painfully on the railing.

And then...

Greenie helped her walk to the pile of food, indicating the freshest selections of it. Elarie began to desperately crave the slow-cooked pork and orange juice sauce popular in southern Ceptari. Or the coffee she discovered in a small mountain town when hiking. The family of sixteen had their own coffee farm going back generations. They made it themselves and were happy to let Elarie try it. With added sugar, it was delicious. Elarie had bought a bag of beans and used them sparingly to make her coffee as she went along.

In central Ceptari, even up to Lyburn despite it being on the coast, there were too many foods from too many places to keep track of. Ceptari was known as the kingdom of art. It cultivated many of the talents known throughout the world. Art was its currency and, in Elarie's opinion, food was art.

It had begun as a rebellion. Ages ago they were simply people on continents, but as the world turned one a man decided he should rule. He was joined by other men and after a long struggle of killing those who did not bow to them and destroying native land, they created Duness. Duness ruled on one continent for a few hundred years, establishing itself as a world power, its advancements something to be feared. Until Ceptari revolted.

They nearly lost their revolution, but with the aid of the People of the Muntaiins, they held off Duness until a treaty could be forged. Two, because the People of the Muntaiins had decided they would not be ruled by anyone anymore. After that, people flocked to Ceptari for the freedom it provided. It was on the coast, their cities could face the sea. Its valley was plentiful, its mountains strong enough to hold off Duness.

That had been fifteen thousand years ago. Somewhere in between, Trec rebelled, then the Faerie Lands solidified itself as its own stretch of land, one rarely entered by things that weren't faeries. One continent of one kingdom became three kingdoms, a territory, and a mountain civilization that remained untouched.

Elarie's favorite kingdom was Ceptari. She'd wanted to go when she was young. It was the first place she went following the death of her family. She'd loved the art and the people and she loved watching them cultivate their history and story.

The food was to die for as well, and as Elarie peeled the skin off a fish and fed it to Jitter dragons, she thought of seasonings and spices and wondered if it would be so bad if she took Greilor and went to Ceptari as they had planned before. She could brave Lyburn, brave seeing Calix. They could share the dragon like separated parents share their children.

CHAPTER FIFTY-TWO

#

He'd been standing in front of Grey, who was pretending to be asleep, for most of the morning. The crew was out trying to patch the ship up enough so nothing fell apart. There were so few of them left that the jobs were stretched between them. Calix had a few of his own, which he'd completed when it was only Red on the deck. He'd stood at the helm steering them toward Lyburn all night, hadn't moved. Red was asleep now. He took the night shift. It was Terry keeping track of their heading as the day moved.

"Calix," Jamison said. Finally. *Finally,* because the kid had spent two days working up the courage to say something to his prince. Two days since Elarie bled gold. Two days since she left. Two days since a hole had dug into Calix's heart. "Your Highness," the kid swallowed nervously.

Calix turned, Grey now at his side. The dragon was no longer pretending to be sleeping, he had one shiny black eye pointed at them. Oh, the drama. "You don't have to say that," he said, shifting the crutch under his arm. He hated using these ones. The padding was tearing and there were splintered pieces where his hand usually went. These crutches were a last resort. He'd forgotten they were on the ship at all.

"I would like permission from my prince to not be charged for whatever I'm about to do."

Oh, he's going to punch Calix. "Sure," Calix said anyway. He could benefit from being punched. By Elarie. A few times. Then kissed. By Elarie. A few times.

"You remember Terisa, right?" Jamison asked, his voice strained at her name. They'd sent her to the depths only yesterday. Jamison hadn't held in his pain watching the wrapped body float away. Calix nodded. "You remember how she was a seer?" Again, he nodded. "And you remember what she said about Elarie? What I told you specifically—what she said about you two specifically?"

Gods. "I have to accept her," Calix said softly. "I thought she meant the Fae island, that I had to accept her killing people."

"Evidently she was talking about the fact that her blood is golden," Jamison said, "you were supposed to accept her for who she was—what she is—and you didn't do that. You failed to do that and now everything is ruined."

"What's ruined?" He asked. His relationship. His life.

"Everything!"

Calix slowly squinted at him. "Jamison, what else did Terisa tell you?"

He took a deep breath. "She said," he began, breathing nervously, "that Elarie is the only person who can keep us alive. You. Keep you alive. So you have to fix whatever you broke, she has to stay with you."

"Terisa told you I'm going to die?" Calix straightened, "and you're just saying this now? Jamison—"

"You aren't *listening*," Jamison snapped. He stepped closer, "Terisa told you to accept her and you didn't, then you let her leave."

"We all let her leave, I wasn't the only person there. And you were terrified of her, you were shaking—"

He said, "I was in shock, when was the last time you saw a golden blooded thing? *I* wasn't the one that was supposed to tell her it was all right, I wasn't the one that was supposed to let her explain." Jamison stopped in an attempt to calm himself. Calix said nothing because he was right, he should have at least let her explain. She tried but he didn't let her. "Terisa said that Elarie was meant to be known by you. I don't know if that means in general or because of her blood, but you were supposed to *know* her. She keeps you alive, she keeps all of us alive, and all she needs in return is for you to accept her."

"And I failed to do that," Calix concluded. He mulled over what Jamison said. All Elarie needed in return was for Calix to accept her. How had he messed up that badly? "So I should..." He looked at Grey, "I should go back?" The dragon lifted his head. "And apologize?"

Grey shook his head. He stood and stretched, flapping his wings as if to check them. He looked from one to the other and snorted, shivering.

"Where are you going?" Calix asked, taking a step back so Grey could have more room. Grey nudged him, breathing steam through his nostrils. "Elarie," he said, holding his hand over it the way she did. She found it comforting. It stung his skin, reminding him of how human he was. "You're going to go get her?"

The dragon did nothing but jump into the air and flap his wings strongly. Calix opened his mouth and watched the struggle it took to climb the skies. He'd forced him to do that. Calix had whistled over and over and made him do that.

"You can apologize when she gets back," Jamison said pleasantly, smiling like he'd won and knew better. "Also, Terisa told me to do this," Calix looked at him and Jamison punched him weakly in the jaw. Still, his head was knocked to the side and he struggled to keep his balance. He hopped once, instantly seeing the apologetic look on Jamison's face.

"Thanks," he said though, rubbing where the mark would be under the stubble on his face. Now he just needed Elarie to do it. He imagined what that would feel like. How much strength would she have to pull away? And if she used all of her strength, what would happen to him? He imagined he'd die.

Calix walked away from Jamison and climbed the steps to the quarterdeck slowly. He went to Terry. Terry had his eyes on a map, squinting as he drew on it. The maps were his own, most looking nothing like the charts Calix usually saw. Only he understood them. "Grey left to get Elarie," Calix told him.

Terry looked up. He searched the skies for Grey. "We'll reach Ceptari's coastline in seven days, Lyburn in six after that." He wasn't speaking his mind. Terry, who usually loved speaking his mind, was silent. He went back to his sketches.

"Kaelum told you not to say anything, didn't he?" Calix picked at a splinter on his crutch.

"He said I could say it all to him later," Terry said without looking at him.

Calix nodded. He didn't want to hear it. He imagined he'd hear it from Elarie as soon as she came back.

CHAPTER FIFTY-THREE

KAELUM

No one knew when Grey would come back with Elarie, which meant everyone was tense. Even as they ate the food that would normally calm them to a lull that made everyone happy, people still looked to the skies and anticipated her showing up. If she did at all.

It had been three days. Terry had given Kaelum an earful about Calix and Elarie for each of those days. Now, he sat next to Kaelum on the steps to the quarterdeck stuffing his face with Tran's excellent cooking. It was pickled fish stew, not everyone's favorite, but that was Tran's magic—able to make something out of nothing and ensure that the nothing was always delicious. The stew, however, was one of Terry's favorites no matter who made it. He said it reminded him of home, though he could hardly remember where and what that was beyond the flashes of parents and a smell like the stew.

Kaelum wiped his mouth, watching Calix go in for seconds. It always made Tran happy, especially when Calix did it. Something about the prince of all the kingdom liking his cooking enough to want another helping? Not to mention the fact that he accidentally cooked for the crew they had before, not the few they had now.

"I'm going to get more," Terry said, "want me to take your bowl?"

"Sure," Kaelum handed it over. He'd finished anyway. Kaelum laid back on the stairs, the step digging into his neck, and looked at the stars. *Star maker, magic creator, stars are magic...* what god up there made that possible? Kaelum's thumb reached for his pocket, brushing over the empty place. Terry still had them. He'd always have them if Kaelum didn't learn control.

Golden blood or not, Kaelum needed Elarie. He needed her to come back so he didn't kill the love of his life. His *mate*, no matter what signs he was missing. Smells and tastes and all those things.

Mates. Calix and Elarie, at least Calix thought, were mates. He was her mate.

How messed up was that?

Terry returned, smacking his thigh lightly. He squeezed his knee, "how are you?" Terry shifted to rest on a hip, leaning toward him.

"Nervous," Kaelum answered softly, still tracing the stars. He imagined holding them. Being able to reach up and take one, wield the power in his hand.

"Kaelum," Terry said and he snapped out of it. Kaelum looked at Terry, finding peace in his dark eyes. He smiled gently, "just breathe."

He said, "I love you," like there would be nothing left of him if he didn't. He sat up slowly. "I'd never hurt you, not like she thinks I will."

"It's the only reason I want her to come back," Terry said, "not for Calix or Jamison's silly seer nonsense, but for you. So you stay you."

Kaelum knew that otherwise, if they didn't need her, Terry would be on a mission to figure out a way to kill her. Terry hated doing research, but he would for this. He had trouble reading and he hated knowing that he still had to sound out some words, but he'd hit the books to find a way to kill a monster. When Kaelum found out Terry couldn't read very well, it was devastating. Yet another reminder of how young he was when he was taken from his family, and also the conditions he was forced to live in.

Terry hardly ever spoke of it, but when he did it was heartbreaking. He'd been taken at seven. He lived in a communal area in Trec and knew all his neighbors like he knew his family. He'd been chasing a fox in the thin woods, hadn't been wearing a shirt or shoes, when he was snatched up. That was what he said—snatched up. Kaelum held him close when he did. Once he said it, Terry seemed to want to get everything out no matter how much it hurt. He told Kaelum of the first time he remembered being touched. He remembered the silk bedding, he remembered the toys. He told Kaelum of the first time he was paid—as a child, apparently, he hadn't been. And at thirteen he developed a plan of escape. Right after the coins touched his hand he knew how he'd get out.

Terry's hair was too dark for dye, he could exaggerate his worth. He built it up, hid his money in places no one ever found it, and paid his way out.

Calix was the one who taught him to read. He was a damn good tutor, even Terry admitted it. He was patient and understanding.

Terry was the person who gave Kaelum his first tattoo. A fish on his elbow done when they were both drunk and he couldn't feel it.

Days after that, before they developed a real relationship beyond Kaelum not understanding why his chest burned so much when Terry looked at him, Terry showed him the tattoo he was most proud of. The misspelled saying of Ceptari. On his ass.

This way, he said, *my value goes down.*

And Kaelum had said, *you're the most valuable thing to me.*

"What are you thinking about?" Terry leaned back. He spooned a bit of stew into his mouth, resting his elbow on the step behind him.

"Your ass," Kaelum answered. "I have a distinct desire to bite your tattoo."

Terry chuckled, "you don't want any other flesh in your mouth?"

"I could put other flesh in my mouth after I bite the tattoo," he mused, wiping a bit of stew off Terry's mouth.

"As long as you don't bite down," his first mate replied. Kaelum grinned as it began to rain. It pelted down on the two of them, flattening Terry's hair down and making him squint. Kaelum brushed his thumb over the bag under his eye. "Later, though, and I want to go first," Terry brought toward him for a kiss, "I have work to do."

Kaelum accepted the kiss, but asked, "you're leaving me?"

"Wait for me in our room," he kissed him again, slowly standing, "be naked."

"And if I'm not?" Kaelum put his elbows on his knees, raising a brow.

Terry leaned down and whispered in his ear, "I'm not going to put you in my mouth for the rest of this trip."

"The rest of it?" He mock gasped, "that's so long."

"And I'm not going to put myself inside you for even longer," he threatened.

Kaelum grinned, "I'll be naked, then. No question."

"I love you," he kissed his cheek and turned around, shouting orders. Kaelum sat and admired him until Terry turned and pointed up the stairs, giving his captain his own set of orders. He laughed as he walked up, catching Calix sitting by himself in the spot Elarie and he jumped onto Grey's back from, next to the stairs no one ever really walked up.

"I'm risking sex to talk to you," Kaelum informed him, "but you look far too depressed for me to leave you alone."

He swiped rain off his cheek. "I'm pretty pathetic, aren't I?"

"No," Kaelum leaned on the railing next to his best friend, "I mean... not *now*, but sometimes." He gained a smile. "It'll turn out fine between you two, you know." He pat Calix's arm, "you do know, don't you?"

"No, how do you know?" Calix looked at him. He had rain sliding down his face once again, but did nothing to stop it. It almost covered the apprehension in his expression. Did he feel wrong for asking his friend for advice about a woman? Or was it because it was Elarie? Did he think Kaelum wouldn't approve of a relationship with her? He wouldn't, of course. Not to a golden blooded thing. Still, Kaelum felt it necessary to assure his friend.

"Because, my friend," he put his hand on Calix's shoulder and squeezed, "you are far too pathetic for her to not feel bad and be your friend again."

Calix laughed a little, pushing his arm off. "Thanks," he said, laughing a little harder, "as long as I look like a prince doing it, right?"

"Pining for a girl? I don't think anyone looks like a prince doing that," he shook his head.

The prince in front of him straightened, "I shall be the first."

"I look forward to seeing it, then."

"Go have sex, I need to think of ways to make her pity me into friendship," Calix pushed him away, but headed in the same direction. They parted ways at the stairs Kaelum had been sitting at before, where Calix looked at Terry. Terry, who was pointing to their quarters. Calix laughed, helping clean everything up before the rain hit too hard.

Kaelum turned around and went into his chambers. He dumped his boots by the bed and took off his shirt. He laid back and groaned, untying his pants with his left hand as it ached for starlight. He rubbed his wet face, breathing hotly into his palm. Kaelum held the left one above him and shimmied out of his pants. He was naked, as he was ordered to be, and he stared at the black line in his palm. It glowed faintly, but no pain came. Kaelum watched the line brighten and begin to shine around his hand as it did for Elarie when she killed the white dragon.

The shining light hovered just over his skin, white and a light blue. Kaelum waved his hand around, watching wisps of it remain. It made him smile. He didn't want more the way he wanted more stars, he just wanted to look at it, to know what it did.

"Hands above your head," Terry pushed them down. He removed his shirt, already kicking off his boots as he jumped onto the bed beside him. "Making pretty lights?" He kissed his jaw. Terry nuzzled closer, his hand traveling up and down Kaelum's chest, "is that new?"

"Mhmm," Kaelum hummed, closing his eyes. "I was waiting for you," he told Terry, "got bored, made pretty lights."

They kissed for some time, neither of them daring to touch anything just yet. Kaelum kept his hands above his head. Out of sight, out of mind. And eventually Terry... Terry knew where to put his hands. He knew how to slowly move them, how to make it feel like they were already as close as they could get. "Tell me you'll marry me," Terry said, his hand now sliding into the curls between Kaelum's legs. He brushed his fingers over Kaelum's length, glad to watch the lack of concentration on his captain's face.

"I will most definitely marry you," Kaelum told him with all the assurance he could muster. "I will marry you so hard."

Terry laughed and took hold, cutting off Kaelum's groan with a deep, unending kiss. Their tongues clashed together and his hand moved up and down the way it always did. They'd been together for years, learned every part of one another, and still every time Terry touched him he felt like an idiot in love.

"Where and when?" Terry asked, moving down his body.

"You want to talk about this now?" Kaelum asked, watching Terry kiss his stomach. Down, down, down until Terry had his mouth around him, his tongue flat and determined. Kaelum's head fell back. "Spring," he breathed while Terry worked, spreading his legs and kissing and sucking. Terry would stop if Kaelum didn't continue. "When it's still cold but the sun makes it warm."

Terry hummed, which made Kaelum go cross-eyed. His body tensed for release, but he held it back.

"Have it on the ship under the mizzen," he gripped the sheets above his head, feeling something warm. Kaelum didn't look. Terry was all the way down, his gag reflex forcing him back up.

Then back down.

Then back up.

Then back down.

"Oh my gods," Kaelum squeezed his eyes shut. He couldn't con-centrate on marrying him when both of Terry's hands were on him, one in the back and one in the front. Terry would be the one to push inside, but he'd wait until Kaelum finished even while preparing for it.

There was no speaking. Minutes upon minutes went by.

Everything was hot, flushing through him until Kaelum couldn't stop himself.

"We talked about warning each other before we finished," Terry said from between his legs.

"I can't breathe," was Kaelum's response.

Terry licked everything up before getting up to kiss Kaelum. "I want to not be able to breathe," he informed him, saying it as easily as he said Kaelum's name. They moved up on the bed, righting themselves against the pillows they piled together. "Do you ever feel guilty?"

Kaelum moved his body for Terry. "For what?"

"Having sex with the whole crew knowing we're doing it," Terry said, hovering over Kaelum.

"No," Kaelum replied easily. "Sometimes I hope they hear it so they know we're getting some when they aren't even with that privacy spell on the door."

"Oh, is *that* why you're so loud?"

He said, "no, I'm loud because you are the best thing I've ever had and I've never felt as good as when I'm with you."

Terry smiled like that was the right answer. He pressed forward. They both let out equally long groans and sighs, their body twinned perfectly together. Terry moved in.

Then out.

Then in more.

And out again.

It always felt like forever until they were skin to skin. Terry always sat there for a moment, eyes closed like he was waiting for something. Once—and only once—Kaelum had asked if that moment was him trying to stop the memories. He knew that Terry had to do things he didn't want to, whether that meant being the one on top or on the bottom, and the pause used to worry Kaelum.

It had been after weeks of seeing that face over his shoulder, above, or beneath him, of feeling the hesitation the way he was now. Before Terry would begin drawing back and rocking forward. They'd laid together, flesh on flesh and sweating so much it was nasty but they couldn't pull off each other. Kaelum had been kissing Terry so much that his lips hurt before they settled and he asked. *It has nothing to do with my past,* Terry had told him, *it's because it feels so good when I'm first inside you that I have to force myself not to finish right then and there.*

Terry moved with ease, assuring Kaelum that he never once thought about his past experiences when they were together. In fact, Terry's words rang like music in his ears, it always felt like the first time. Kaelum had never had more of a mutual feeling.

CHAPTER FIFTY-FOUR

ELARIE

Dragons were excellent when it came to learning language, which was how she knew Masha and the other Jitter Dragons were pretending to be confused. Elarie had gone through the alphabet, she'd sang songs for them, she'd gone through the words she thought they'd hear most often—dragon, fly, hello, goodbye, yes, no, thank you—and yet they were acting like they knew nothing.

Elarie was ignoring them as they sang the songs wrong. She used the plants the Jitters had gathered for her and crafted a sad version of soap, cleaning off her clothes as much as possible and getting the remaining blood off her body. The leaves she'd replaced the human wrap with were not waterproof, so she had to be careful not to get water inside.

The shirt was no longer ripped in two pieces. She'd taken off the bottom half completely. It was tight enough to not be a problem when it came to potentially flashing dragons, and now she didn't need to tuck anything into it. It was almost freeing, having her stomach so exposed.

She was drying off when Greilor returned. He flew through the waterfall, his landing less than graceful. "You were gone for days," Elarie told him as she limped back to her bed. Far more leaves and even some moss had been added to make her more comfortable. She sat and a Jitter named Dina crawled into her lap. She was small, a baby, so Elarie pet her like a cat and waited for Greilor to defend himself.

He stared.

Elarie shifted uncomfortably, "what?" The dragon said nothing. He snorted and lifted a wing, inspecting. The tear wasn't horrible and was already healing. "Come here, let me help you," she held her hand out. He looked at her. "I'm strong enough to help you, Greilor, please let me."

The dragon knew what it meant to her. Elarie, though no one knew it—not even her own family, she never told anyone—possessed a 'new' ability. It was never recorded by anyone except the dragons. In her own way, she could heal them. It wasn't like Kaelum's magic, where he'd give some of it to help another, it was more like the way a long hug makes a person feel better.

It meant a great deal to Elarie and Greilor didn't want to take that from her. So he walked over, grumbling to himself, and laid down in front of her. Elarie lifted his heavy wing into her lap, forcing the baby Jitter to move. She apologized softly. "How is he?" Elarie finally asked. There was only so much she could do to avoid the question haunting her heart. "Calix."

Greilor was satisfied with her, told her he'd expected her to hold out a little longer. Elarie just ran her hand over his wing. She wasn't near the tear, but she didn't need to be. Sometimes her just sitting against a dragon could help them heal faster.

"Well?" She raised a brow, finding Greilor smiling naughtily. "Greilor, how is he? Please tell me."

He misses you, the old dragon told her. Elarie rolled her eyes. *He regrets what he said, you know.* She again rolled her eyes.

"He shouldn't have said it at all," Elarie began picking at dead skin, something Greilor didn't like so she forced herself to stop. "You told me he'd accept me, you told me he wanted to... to *be* with me, and yet he said he doesn't trust me. He threw me out!"

Greilor said, *he was scared.*

"Don't defend him," Elarie snapped. She pushed his wing off her lap and stood, her face in her hands as she paced pathetically. "You need to be on my side right now, not his."

Fine, he's a terrible friend and an even more terrible potential lover.

She sighed, "thank you."

But he knew he was wrong the moment you left.

Elarie looked at her big, loving dragon. Greilor had been with her family for, according to him, as long as he'd been alive. She once tried to imagine what Greilor would look like small, having never seen a baby Great Dragon, but Elarie could never see him as anything but her protector. Her best friend. "You want me to go back," she crossed her arms, "but why should I? I could spend an eternity here in this nest—"

Greilor said, *it's not my nest.*

"You don't have one, Calix said you sleep on a grassy cliff," she contradicted, but her heart wasn't in it. She didn't want to argue with him, she wanted him to understand. Understand that her heart was broken and she had no desire to ever see the person who broke it again.

I would like your help building my own, the dragon said, shifting so he was right in front of her, head raised and eyes set, *I would like to nest, Elarie, with my two riders helping me.*

Her heart throbbed. Elarie brought her hands up to cover her mouth. "You're nesting?" She asked. Of course, she knew it. She hadn't expected him to tell her so soon. Elarie beamed and jumped toward him, squealing as she wrapped her arms around his face. His warm steam blew over her. "I'm so happy for you, Greilor," she sniffed, tears blurring her vision. "Why did you decide to nest? You never have before," Elarie stood straight, wrapping her hand around the horn on his nose.

You are my home, he said softly. Elarie felt a whine build in her throat, something tight and painful. *When I lost you I had no home. I found Calix and had part of a home, but it is my Elarie that makes me complete.* Elarie sobbed, tears pouring down her face. *I would like to settle down again, with my two halves of a home, and nest.*

She sobbed again, her body burning up. Steam floated around her. She hadn't caught on fire because of her emotions in years, and now Elarie struggled to contain it. "I'm your home?"

Come back with me.

"I really thought it took more to convince me to do something," she wiped her eyes but the tears kept coming. Elarie's chest ached, sending shooting pains down her side. She'd gone lifetimes thinking something similar. She'd lost everything, had nowhere to go that she could truly call home. When Greilor landed on that ship and she saw him again, her only goal was to stay with him. Her home. And now he was telling her he wanted to lay eggs. Nest. And by doing that he wanted Elarie to be directly involved in the care of his future children.

Are you ready? Greilor asked happily. Elarie looked around. Even
if she wanted to she had no right to stay in the nest for as long as
she wanted. This was not her nest. Yes, she was welcome, and they
would allow her to stay for as long as she wished, but they would
not want it. She had no right to overstay her welcome and force
them to continue allowing her to live with them. Even if the Jitter
Dragons say they want to keep her forever.

She walked to her bed and sat down. The baby Jitter Dragon
came back over, though she curled against Elarie's side rather than
sit on her lap. "How many eggs would you like?" She asked to avoid
his question. She was not ready. Of course she wasn't ready.

Still, Greilor obliged her, *five.*

"Oh, five? That's quite a few."

There were five of you. Ritker, Cammie, Elarie, Ashter, and Danien,
Greilor said and Elarie smiled softly. He shifted forward and placed
his head on the rock bed to her left. Elarie put her hand on his face.
Do you believe Calix will be happy?

She nodded, wiping under her nose. Elarie's eyes watered further. "So happy," she said, "Calix will love the idea of having more
dragons." *You know him so well,* Greilor praised and she said, "I've
known him for what, three months? Four? I can't know him that
well."

Well enough, his voice said in her mind, *to know how he feels about
dragons. You made your connection to him, I was there.* She stared
ahead of her, almost hating Greilor for reminding her. Reminding
her of that day, up in the clouds, where she watched him fly. She
hadn't thought he would do it, kick his legs up and let himself dive
with Greilor, but he did. And that was the moment she tied her
connection to him.

Elarie wanted to live up there with him. Before the injury, before the blood.

"I made my connection and he broke my heart," Elarie said, her eyes moving to the dragon curled against her.

Let him mend it, the little Jitter Dragon said. Elarie smiled, laughing lightly as she ran her fingers over the dragon's neck.

"Do you think that's a good idea?" She asked the sweet thing. Dina purred and nodded. "And if he breaks my heart again?"

She said, still in the sweet, little voice, *then cut his heart out and eat it.* Elarie blinked in shock and Greilor chuckled. The little dragon went on purring.

"I don't eat people's hearts," Elarie told her, "and I have no desire to kill him. Although, I expect I may hurt him."

He may let you, Greilor told her, *he was quite distressed.*

Her heart ached. Elarie groaned and laid back slowly, her muscles tightening and her side protesting. She would go back. She had to. For Greilor, she had to. Elarie would not make him choose between the two of them—she knew it would be her. Greilor, no matter how much it would hurt him, would choose Elarie over Calix. She was too important to him. With all the love he had for Calix, it would not be enough to make the decision difficult.

"Can we eat first?" She asked, her voice lacking emotion. Greilor was up in an instant, headed to select something for her to eat. He'd cook it, too, and Elarie would eat slowly as he nagged her to finish so he could take her to Calix. The ride would take days.

CHAPTER FIFTY-FIVE

CALIX

It had taken days for the rain to finally stop. It had felt never ending and hot, with fat drops that dropped and dropped painfully onto his face and shoulders. But finally, Calix could see the sun. It broke through the clouds to say hello.

They were on the coast of his kingdom now, keeping it within sight. Calix couldn't wait to be home. He needed a hug from his mother desperately, he needed to sit down for tea and knit while he told her of all his problems. And of Elarie. How he wished he could speak to his mother about Elarie. Not even considering the golden blood, he wanted to tell her of Elarie's goodness. Of her strength. Of how much he wanted to hear her say *mates*.

Calix had begun obsessing over the possibility. He didn't want to think of it so much that he convinced himself it was true, but it wouldn't stop spinning in his mind. Every turn he asked *what if*. What would it mean? What did he want it to mean? Was it a terrible thing?

He walked across the deck headed below. The fishing line had torn sometime in the night, he needed to know if Tran was going to need them to fish again before they reached Lyburn. Calix could mend it, but he didn't exactly want to. If Tran said they could hold out it would make his life easier. Or, mildly better.

But the familiar scream of a dragon came from above them. A roar only one kind of dragon could make. It had Calix stumbling out of the entrance to what lay below the deck and looking toward the sky. To the southwest, a beast of magic and power flew perfectly toward the ship. Grey roared for their attention, seeking all of it.

He gained it. What was left of the crew and the rescued came out from below and from their posts to watch the Great Dragon land. It was less graceful than the flight, his wings still bringing him issue.

"She's back," Kaelum said, appearing next to him. Calix's breath caught, stuck somewhere in his throat as Elarie slid off. She managed to look amazing while injured. In the days she was gone the leaves around her side had gone from green to red, the color spreading to the tips. She'd been eating as well, continuing to gain back the weight she'd lost. Elarie had told Calix she usually had much more of a 'pillow' about her stomach than she did because of the time she'd spent as a slave. He thought she was saying it to test him. Calix didn't tell her he preferred it when the women he made love to had more to hold.

Calix's gaze snagged on her shirt. Or lack of it. How did he manage to like this more?

"Elarie," Jamison walked toward her. He wrapped his thin arms around her, shocking her enough to have her arms remain at her side. "I missed you," he said, not only shocking Elarie but shocking everyone around them as well.

"You did?" She asked faintly.

Jamison nodded. He stepped back, "I'm sorry about my reaction. I was scared, but I'm not anymore."

Her brow slowly furrowed. Elarie's eyes darted over his face, then around. She looked at Terry, who stood with a hand on his sword, to Kaelum. Her gaze lingered as if she could sense what he'd been doing. If he'd been doing anything.

No one else knew what to say. No one moved other than the dragon. Grey had laid down to watch them as if this was a show. Steam blew through his nose, which Elarie's hand drifted to. She looked away from Kaelum, her fingers dancing in the steam, and looked at Calix. It was for a moment. Only a moment, and when she looked away from his face Calix nearly fell over.

The Frei marched in a group toward her. Her features softened as she looked at them. They'd been hiding around the ship so well Calix forgot they were there. Gee was at the head of the group, his skin a deep, angry blue like the color of a sea Calix didn't want to dive into. He stopped with his hands on his hips, tapping his little foot.

"I brought you something," Elarie told them before Gee could begin what seemed like a planned rant about her. He perked up, watching her dig into her pocket. Elarie lowered herself down to her knees with a wince that made Calix step forward to help her.

She did not look at him.

"I am sorry I left without a goodbye," she said, dumping a handful of teeth, scales of both fish and dragons, and seeds onto the deck. The Frei gathered in a circle to look at her offering. "I won't do it again," she told them.

Part of Calix hoped she might've been telling that to him as well.

"Elarie," Terry said. Her attention went to him, her tired hand reaching out for aid. Grey provided it, allowing her to stand by holding onto him. How badly was her side hurting? Was there any-thing Calix could do? What happened to the wrap he put around it? "Would you like to explain a few things? Like what you are?" Terry's grip on the pommel of his sword was tight. He was prepared to hurt her even though he desperately needed her.

She breathed deeply. "I am golden blooded," she said, causing a stir, "and I hide it. I hid it. It's a spell I put on my body that makes me more human," her eyes darted to Calix when she said it, "and changes my blood color. It's for my own protection, not to disguise myself to hurt people."

Terry scoffed, "why would you need protection?"

"Use your imagination," she deadpanned, then again looked at the chirping Freis. She nodded about something, easily giving them her attention.

Look at me, Calix urged silently. *Please look at me.* She didn't. Elarie's attention left the faerie creatures and turned southwest. She groaned slightly and Grey joined her. His was far more exas-perated than hers. Elarie faced the southwest and opened her arms for a small dragon to fly right into her chest. She stumbled back and fell against Grey, who only seemed to grow more annoyed.

Elarie said a few things in the dragon language, cradling the dragon.

"Masha?" Calix asked and she perked her head up. The adorable Jitter Dragon looked exhausted, her breathing labored and her body slouched against Elarie, but at the sight of him she perked up and made a strange squeaking sound. It made Grey growl. "You flew all that way?" Calix asked, ignoring his dragon for a moment. There was an approving look on Elarie's face and Calix's focus was currently on her.

She walked toward him, though didn't seem particularly happy about it, and finally looked at him. From the corner of his eye Calix could see Kaelum waving his hands at other people, probably telling them to disperse. "She's learning Ceptareei for you," Elarie told him, "she says so that when you tell her you love her she'll know what it means."

Masha purred and crawled over, wrapping her small body around Calix's neck. She was still breathing heavily, her rough scales scratching at his skin, but she seemed to relax. Her long tail curled around his waist. "Can't I say it in the dragon language?" Calix asked.

"I'm not teaching you how to say that," Elarie shook her head instantly, her eyes full of the hurt that he caused. She reached into her pocket, "these are from the dragon you rode, she said you named her Greenie?" He nodded, though was now cursing himself for assuming the gender of a dragon. Elarie held out scales and teeth twisted into the strings of the tie he'd made for her hair. She'd taken it apart and turned it into some sort of necklace. "She told me to tell you that when she visits she'll take you for a real dragon ride."

Grey huffed.

Elarie glanced at their dragon before saying, "she's faster. And Masha," she nodded to the Jitter Dragon asleep on his shoulder, "wants to claim you."

This time Grey growled low.

"I suppose that's a bad thing?" Calix looked from the big dragon to Elarie, taking the string of scales and teeth.

"Only if you say no," she wrapped her arms around her middle gently. Calix waited, tilting his head. Elarie sighed and said, "when a dragon attaches itself to you it's not like what Greilor did, you aren't dragon and rider. It's a relationship. You would be her human."

Calix asked, "what if I say no?"

Her eyes flashed painfully, but she said, "you are well within your right to. Masha is young, she may recover from your rejection." She whistled gently and the dragon on his shoulders stirred. She unwrapped herself from Calix and crawled over their arms. Elarie picked her up and cradled her like a baby, hushing her sweetly. She said, "not many dragons find a reason to continue once their hearts are broken like that."

"Dragons can't take rejection well?" He asked, trying to joke but she didn't take it that way. Her body stiffened, her shoulders squaring like she might have to fight for the dragon in question. Or for herself. Elarie, somehow a dragon in her own right.

"It's not that they don't take it well, they aren't human," she snapped, "they don't feel the way you do, their hearts are different from yours."

Terry, who Calix had forgotten was there, asked, "what about yours? Is it golden?" In a manner indicating he wanted a challenge. He wanted to test her.

"It's like you rip something from them," Elarie continued without so much as a glance at Terry. It didn't please him, but Kaelum smiled a little. She said, "they give you something, they choose you, and when you don't accept that it's like part of them is gone."

Calix stepped toward Elarie, reaching out for Masha. She shifted, moving her arms so Calix could take the dragon. "How much Ceptareei has she learned?" He asked. Masha was asleep, or at least pretending to be, so he held her the way Elarie had been. Like a baby.

"She pretends she knows less so I'll keep singing the silly songs we used to learn the languages," Elarie told him, "but she'll understand your answer, whether it's a yes or a no."

"Songs to learn languages?" Calix asked teasingly. Only a ghost of a smile flashed over her face. He moved on, asking, "so what do I say?" She looked him up and down like she expected him to refuse and break a little dragon's heart. "To seal the deal officially?"

She breathed in slowly through parted lips. Calix couldn't help but stare at them. They formed the words of her first language, a language he now desperately wanted to learn. Elarie touched Masha, heat radiating off her hand. "Masha," she said gently, like waking a baby. "Masha, Calix." At his name, Masha yawned and shivered. She crawled up Calix's shoulder, purring against the back of his neck and around to his cheek. "Tell her you accept her."

It really was all Elarie needed. Calix only had to look at her and tell her he accepted her. How did this feel now? Watching him so easily say *yes, I will be your human, I accept you* to a dragon when he couldn't say it to her? He took his eyes off of her, suddenly immensely guilty, and tried to see Masha on his shoulder. Her head peeked out. "I accept you," Calix said softly.

Masha did not react softly.

She screeched loudly, causing his ear to ring and Elarie to laugh. Masha jumped on his shoulders and onto his head, prancing over him. Calix bent, pulling his shoulders up to his ears as the little dragon celebrated. She bounded onto Elarie, doing the same only she did not balk and avoid Masha's small claws. She stood there, a small smile on her face, and let Masha rough up her hair and tangle herself into it. When she made the jump to go back to Calix, Elarie caught Masha and tossed her in the direction of Grey.

The Great Dragon growled as Masha landed on his head.

"Dragons are territorial," Elarie said to Calix, "and he hasn't had to share you all these years. It will take some getting used to. Having children will make him much nicer."

"Chil..." Calix started, turning his head to her. His eyes widened. Elarie nodded with a smile, jerking her head in Grey's direction. "He... I can..." she looked at him like he'd gone mad, but nodded once again. "Grey!" Calix walked toward him, grabbing his horn the way Elarie did. "Children?"

He hummed and closed his eyes, sinking to the deck. Masha purred on his head, lying down and rubbing their scales together.

"He just needs a nest," Elarie walked next to him. "I can do that, you just need to tell me where I can dig."

"Dig?" He looked at her.

She said, "Greilor wants a nest like the one we had. It should be easy to build, I just need to know where."

"Under Grey's field, maybe? It's a pretty open space by the cliff," Calix looked over at her, "and we can build it together, right?"

"For Greilor, yes," she said and walked away from him.

CHAPTER FIFTY-SIX

ELARIE

Together, he said as if everything could be fixed so easily. Together, as if this would heal whatever was between them. Elarie walked away from him cursing the word. It wasn't like he'd be able to do much when it came to building—and it hardly counted as building. Elarie was going to have to destroy a cliffside. Calix could what? Watch?

She ignored the staring, again wrapping her arms around herself as she stopped in front of Kaelum and Terry. Terry was refreshing. He still hated her, he still thought her to be a monster. The only difference was that he now knew what kind of monster. Everyone else stared warily and stole glances to see what she was doing, where she was going. Calix... Calix was another story.

"I can sleep in the brig," Elarie said, "I'm sure it'll make everyone feel safer."

"You can break out of the brig," Terry told her.

She said, "then put faerthorne around it, I know you still have some. And because everyone that's alive is a magic user of some kind, only you and Calix will be able to let me out. For safety or whatever you may deem it."

The two of them looked at each other, silently conversing about her while she considered her new position. Golden blooded, her secret was out. One of them, anyway. She expected Calix and possibly the two in front of her would go to great lengths to learn what *kind* of golden blooded. They'd seen what monsters looked like, but Elarie did not look like a monster. Elarie would have to deal with question after question and deal with Calix badgering her for so long...

"Terry will lock you in," Kaelum decided.

"Oh, good," Elarie rolled her eyes.

He then asked, "do I need the stars to make magic?"

She looked at his hands, then his eyes. "Did you?"

"It was," he glanced at Terry, "like a mist, sort of light. Like the thing you did when you killed that dragon."

Her expression darkened. Elarie looked at the place where it happened. "What a horrible thing," she said to it, then sighed. She looked back to the two pirates. "You need the stars during the day, you can't use magic without them. At night it's different. Your magic is with the stars. When the stars are out as is your power."

"So what was that thing you did," Kaelum pointed to the spot, again bringing her attention to it, but she couldn't hold it for long. Her eyes shifted, as did the amount of warmth behind her. Elarie shifted to the side as Calix approached, his familiar heat bringing back many things, brushing over her like a breeze on her bare skin.

"I doubt what you did was anything like what I did," Elarie said, attempting to avoid Calix's stare. He was so good at looking at her it was revolting.

Kaelum pressed, "but what was it?"

Did they think that now that they knew about her blood she would be open to answering every question they had? As if that was the only secret she was keeping? Or were they hoping for honesty? Perhaps they thought that if she shared, she wasn't so terrible. "Ancient magic," she answered, "like yours, that may be why they looked similar."

"But yours is fire and mine is what?" Kaelum asked, "starlight?"

"Yes, actually," she nodded, "if I'm correct in assuming what it looks like, it was merely starlight. You have complex magic, Kaelum, magic with many layers. Stars, magic creation, starlight."

He looked at his hand as if it would light up before them. "And yours?" Kaelum nodded to her hand. "It looked different from the usual fire."

"Because it's ancient," she said vaguely. Elarie rocked on her foot and allowed a glance at Calix. He had a smile on her face like he knew her so well. Did he know her so well? She didn't think so. He knew she was avoiding the question, but that meant nothing of knowing *her*.

Terry scoffed and gritted out, "will you just answer a question honestly for once? No more avoiding or only partially answering. Just be honest."

"I don't have to be honest with you—"

"How is anyone supposed to trust you if you aren't honest?" He countered.

She hissed, "I should not need to regain your trust." Elarie stepped toward him only because she knew he'd hold his ground. "I have done everything possible to keep all of you alive—"

"You missed a few people."

"I am not responsible for the lives of everyone on this ship!" Elarie shouted, her voice cracking. Masha and Greilor both lifted their heads, one to defend and the other to watch the drama un-fold. "I am responsible for the lives of two people and by extension you and I have done nothing but keep a promise to an age-long vow and to a dragon."

"And along the way you have misled each of us," he said.

"By not telling you about my blood or by choosing not to tell every person every single thing about me and my past?"

"Both," he said through grit teeth.

Elarie smiled painfully. Both. Why was it always both? "Maybe you should be nice to me, Terry. My blood shines and I am the only person that can keep Kaelum from killing everyone he loves."

"You wouldn't let Kaelum kill me, it would be too similar to what happened to you and Matian," he said calmly, not showing the fear she could smell on him.

"I am not the reason Matian died," Elarie steamed. She could feel Calix's hand on her arm, pulling her back. "Don't ever suggest that again, do you understand me? Never again."

He scoffed, "or what?"

"Or Calix will be teaching you how to walk with a crutch be-cause I'll start ripping off pieces of you," she spat, allowing Calix to drag her away from the two of them. Terry had gone pale, his eyes wide, and Kaelum was ushering him away. They spoke softly. Elarie turned to Calix and asked, "why are you using the crutch, I thought you'd wait until you were home to stop using the leg."

"Grey ripped my leg off," he answered quickly, "now why would you say something like that?"

She ignored him and looked at Greilor, "why did you rip his leg off?" He met her eyes, telling her his reason in a monotoned voice. Elarie laughed, stifling it when she saw Calix's face. "Another reason for me to come back," she explained. "Apparently I really do have to give you a new leg now."

He cracked a smile. Elarie wasn't sure if she wanted to be this close to him if he was going to look at her like that. His Lathin eyes were full of apology, he was bent toward her as if they weren't the same height. "Elarie," he whispered, "I'm so sorry." Her pulse quickened. She was still steaming, Elarie could see it wafting between them slowly. "I was scared and confused and maybe betrayed," his hand dragged up her arm, sending chills over her warm skin, "and stupid."

"And?" She found herself asking, "is that it?"

"No," he said. Calix touched her neck, his thumb on her jaw. Butterflies flew through Elarie's stomach. "I'm asking again if you'd stay with me."

Elarie removed his hand, pushing it to the side. "What if you change your mind again?" She asked, "I don't think I'd be able to handle it."

"Don't run away," he breathed in, "please don't run away again."

Masha told her she wanted both of them to be with her. Greilor told her she had to say yes. Elarie tilted her head, trying to block the two of them out. "What will you give me?" She asked, now forcing her eyes back to Calix.

"Anything," he answered.

"I don't want 'anything' I want you to tell me what you think I want," she said, watching him shift uncertainly. Good, he should remain uncertain when around her.

Calix swallowed, again placing his hands on her arms. "I don't want to speak on what you want, Elarie," he said, "but I will tell you what I want to give to you." She said nothing, he seemed to take this as an opportunity to continue. "A bedroom to call your own with a window close to the sea. If you open it you'll see Grey's field and what will eventually be his nest. I want to give you clothes no one will force you to wear—"

"That look like this?" Elarie interrupted, motioning to what was left of her top. His eyes drifted and his breathing slowed. "You can say you like it."

"What are you going to do to me if I say I do?"

She smiled. "Nothing, but only because I like it. It's far more freeing than I expected, I didn't realize I could wear shirts this way."

He gnawed on the edge of his lip, his eyes on the shirt. Calix moved one hand, touching the right side of it. He pulled on a string and it began to come undone, which forced him to stop. He looked at her eyes once again. "I like it," Calix told her almost as if he still expected her to do something to him. When she did not, he breathed in slowly and continued, "I can give you many shirts like it. I'm sure the whole kingdom will be scandalized."

"You'd like that, wouldn't you?"

His cheeks warmed, "I might."

"And your father?"

"Gods, please never wear something like this in front of him," he breathed quickly, "I want him to like you, this would be too much."

She raised a brow, "why do you want him to like me?"

"I want my father to like you, I want my siblings to adore you," he transferred his hands to her neck once again, partially cradling her face. There wasn't any sort of joking in his eyes as he said, "and I want my mother to love you."

"Are you going to change me for each of them?" Elarie asked, "perhaps my clothes for one parent, you may tell me to act differently to your father than I do to your mother or siblings. More like a lady for one, more fun for the other? Do you want me to pretend for each of them?"

She couldn't believe he let her finish. Calix seemed to want to stop her, but he let her speak and he listened to what she had to say. His fingers pressed into her skin firmly. Calix had a distant look in his eyes, like he wished for her to stay forever and be loved by them—and him—forever. He knew it wasn't possible, but he wanted to ask anyway. "I don't want you to change for anyone," he told her, "I just want you to be there. Here, with me, always."

"Always?"

Elarie could see the twitch of pain marked in the corners of his eyes. He brushed his hands upward, holding her like suddenly there weren't people and dragons staring at him. He looked at her like the deck was empty. He looked at her like he wanted to kiss her but wouldn't because he knew that wasn't what she wanted. At least not then. "I know," he breathed, "I know you can't grow old. Even if there's a way and you won't tell me what it is—"

She began to shake her head.

Calix held her still, taking in a determined breath, "I know that forever isn't possible for us, I know that like I know you're a damn good liar but gods," he cringed, as if bringing them into the conversation wasn't the right thing, "I want so desperately for you to tell me how I can keep you with me for the rest of *both* of our lives."

"I can't," she told him. "It's not fair to you, but I can't."

His jaw flexed, but not in anger. Here he was, admitting how he felt, and all she was telling him was that it wasn't fair. "I think you're underestimating how desperately I want to be with you," he said.

"Maybe I am," she pulled his hands away from her face and stepped back, "and yet."

"And yet," he repeated. He watched her walk away from him, but wouldn't stay watching for long. The gods knew he'd never stop following her. Perhaps he was afraid that if he didn't, she'd run.

CHAPTER FIFTY-SEVEN

ELARIE

"Do I have to be some kind of mother to Masha?" Calix was asking. Elarie watched Gee unlace her boot with much difficulty. She absently pulled on the skin around her stomach, her side aching from her position.

They were both across from each other, not close enough for anything but their boots to touch, and both of their backs were pressed against the bars of the brig. Elarie stared at Gee, her eyes empty, and tried to imagine everything Calix was going to say before she interrupted. That he wanted her to be with him always, that he knew she wouldn't tell him her 'cure' for immortality.

"Elarie?" Calix asked.

She looked at him, "no, no mothering is necessary."

Someone came down the stairs. Elarie recognized him as Tran, the cook. Calix told her he liked to collect spices. Apparently he had a room full of them in his home where he grew his herbs and things. He gave her an apprehensive look before he walked into the open cell. He handed her a bowl filled with cut fish and carrots. "Leftover day," he told her, "carrots were going bad... you might find a potato in there, too, I had a few left." He cleared his throat and gave a bowl to Calix. Tran backed up with his eyes on her, looking over his shoulder as he left.

Elarie spooned through the leftovers. She did not have any potatoes.

"So what's it like?" Calix asked, nudging Masha's head away when she sniffed into the bowl. He ate some, caving and giving her some carrots. Elarie smiled softly at him, watching Masha chew happily and allow him to pet her while she did. His hand moved gently over her, fingers poised the way she'd shown him days and days ago.

She said, "a friendship, really."

"Did you ever have one like this?" He looked at her, "or is this what you have with Grey?"

Elarie took a large bite and ignored him while she chewed. The mix of leftovers burned her nostrils, causing her to straighten and cough. She swallowed, seeing half a smirk on his face. "It is not too spicy, don't you dare say anything," she pointed at him and set the bowl down. "No," Elarie sniffed and coughed again. She cleared her throat, "this is what I have with every dragon."

"Really?" Calix looked at Masha again. She was begging for more carrots.

"They are all like family to me if they wish it," she said, smashing a carrot with her spoon. Elarie crossed her legs and moved her hair over one shoulder. His eyes flicked to hers, following her action and a frown grew over his face. "I repurposed your gift," she told him, guessing what he was thinking. She was right, of course, because he nodded dismissively. Elarie couldn't find it in herself to apologize, so she just took another—smaller—bite.

Calix decided, "I'll just have to make you something else." He gave his new dragon another carrot. Masha crawled into his lap and purred.

Her chest began to ache. Elarie took a deep breath and her brows creased. "Calix," she said. Instantly his eyes found hers. Her words were lost in her throat, burning with the leftovers. "I'm really tired," she said, which was true. She was exhausted and somehow he was making it worse. He was taking all her energy and turning it into something else she didn't want to deal with.

"All right," he said regretfully, but lifted Masha off his lap. She crawled up and draped herself over his shoulders as he stood, easily balancing without the crutch. Calix's lips pulled into a thin line, paired with a creased brow. He took the small steps to the door saying, "Terry said he wanted to be the one to lock you in." She didn't reply. He turned around. "Elarie," he began.

She shook her head, "please don't say anything important right now."

The breath left his chest, escaping through a shocked exhale. His eyes darted around before he nodded grimly, leaving her alone.

Elarie covered her face when she was sure he wouldn't hear her and sobbed into her hands. Finally, she was free of dragons and men, alone as she wanted to be, and found no relief in it. Her tears wet her cheeks, smearing over her skin. Elarie cringed, dizzy, and wiped at her face.

It wouldn't have felt real if he said it. If he said he accepted her it would've felt like he pitied himself into telling her what he thought she wanted to hear. Calix, perfect-for-her Calix, with his eyes and his hands and his heart, probably wanted nothing more than to fix what he ruined. It wasn't bad of Elarie to want it too, but how could she give in so easily? And Calix, how could he say it so quickly? Did it take him a few days to realize he was wrong? How did he *know* he was wrong? Because suddenly he was lonely without her? Or was it because she had his dragon's love and he knew he needed Elarie to keep Greilor?

Elarie shifted onto her back, moving the leftovers away from her.

The presence of someone else in the cell had not woken Elarie. The pain had. She grunted, her fingers twitching. The muscles in her arms protested the movement, in enough pain already. Elarie winced and blinked a few times, fighting the blur that somehow developed in the night.

"Got it off the door," a voice said. *It* being a vine of thorns. Elarie stared at them, her head throbbing. They were wrapped around her wrists, but a few thorns had decided to grow through her skin and up her arms. "Decided to use it myself..." boots stopped in her peripheral. "I had to use gloves, of course, because they tried to sink into me like this," he picked up a part of the vine and Elarie hissed, unable to pull away from him.

Red.

"Looks painful, I don't know how you aren't screaming," he chuckled and let go. Elarie's hands dropped, the thorns scraping down one of the bars of her cell they were wrapped around. "Now," he lifted her hair, turning her head to face him. Red had a sick smile on his face. The sight of it brought her back to how much he stared at her. "You are going to tell me two things."

He had a short knife in his other gloved hand. Red dragged it over her cheek.

"What kind of monster you are," he sliced into her cheek, wetting the blade with her blood. She hadn't spelled it, so it shined before the both of them, "and how I can kill you."

"What makes you think I'll answer either question?" She asked hoarsely. It was a struggle to move even her mouth. It was as if she'd lost control of every function.

Red said, "you don't have to answer the second," and let go of her hair. Elarie's head dropped onto her arm and her eyes found a beautiful little blue thing. A Frei, with a scale in hand. Gee had probably come down to show her something or to tell her a story. Instead his black eyes went wide and he backed into shadow. Red dragged the blade into her half-cut shirt and over the spot where her tattoo was. "But you will answer the first. Someone has to know. It's only right."

He sliced down, cutting it in half. Elarie screamed as the cut continued. Down to the center of her back. Down to her lower back.

"Scream all you want, monster," he taunted, "no one's waking up."

Elarie jerked her arms, her eyes drifting to the food she hadn't finished. Calix had thought it was because of the spices that it hurt, Elarie had assumed the same despite the pain being in her throat and not her mouth. "Did you drug everyone?" Elarie asked faintly.

"That I did," Red brushed her hair back so she looked at him. "So tell me what you are," he nodded, "and I'll kill you."

"How do you expect to do that if I don't tell you what to do?" She countered. Elarie felt him rip the leaves off her side.

He showed her a single thorn that he must've cut off of the vine and simultaneously cut open the wound in her side. Elarie's breathing quickened. What ways were there to get herself out of this? Die, sure. Dying was always an option and usually ended up being the best. However, like Finnal, Red would most likely throw her body overboard. It would take ages for the faerthorne on her arms to be eaten away, let alone if he put one inside her.

Everyone was asleep.

Including, possibly, Masha, who'd eaten a few carrots.

She could hardly move.

"Tell me what kind of monster you are," Red waved the thorn in front of her, "it's an easy request. I'll be kind and kill you quickly."

Elarie shook her head, shaking. Tears welled up in her eyes when Red sighed as if she was only making things harder for herself.

"Now I'm sure just doing this," he settled at her side, "will kill you, so you need to answer my question quickly. Are you ready?"

She faced her head front trying to see if Gee was still in the shadows. Candles flickered around her. Elarie let out a soft, shaking whistle that was overtaken by a scream that ripped through her. Red had his hand in her body.

His hand was in her body.

His hand was in her body.

His hand was in her body.

Red released the thorn, laughing as he did. Elarie gagged painfully, acutely aware of the thorn growing inside her, searching for a bone to sink into. Her ribs. Her spine. Her hips. Whatever was closest. A dragon roared above her, his voice cracking in fear. He'd never heard Elarie scream like that. The ship shook and swayed and all the while Red laughed.

He held her jaw, tilting her head up. "What kind of monster are you?" He smiled, squeezing her face like that pain would ever amount to the feeling of a thorn twisting around her rib cage. Elarie was bleeding internally, sure to die, and he was smiling with his face so close to hers.

She lunged forward, biting down on his nose. Red cried out and shoved her off, but she had his flesh in her mouth and he was bleeding down the bottom half of his face. Red punched her and grabbed another thorn, thrusting it into the gash he'd created in her side.

Elarie's head fell. She spit out the piece of Red's nose. A flash of small magic erupted in front of her, but Elarie couldn't keep her eyes open to see which Frei had created it.

CHAPTER FIFTY-EIGHT

Everyone was waking at once to the screams of a dragon. Two, because Masha was on top of Calix roaring in his face and stomping on his chest. A chorus of questions floated through the room, people falling out of hammocks to inspect what was happening that had Grey so scared.

Calix grabbed his crutch and stood, watching Masha run hurriedly through the doorway screeching for him to move, too. The distinct feeling of needing to get to Elarie ached within him, similar to the physical pain he'd gotten from Masha's stomping. He couldn't even check on Grey first, he had to get to her.

Masha was at the base of the brig's stairs, anxiously hopping from foot to foot. Gee ran next to her and chirped madly only to run back in the direction of Elarie's cell. Calix nearly fell trying to get down the stairs.

Two people were in the cell where there should've been one, and one of them was dead. "Elarie," Calix breathed, throwing the cell door open. He hardly looked at Red, dropping next to Elarie. "Shit, what happened?" Steps thundered on the stairs as Calix lifted Elarie's head. Blood rubbed onto his thumb from a cut on her cheek.

"Red?" Terry asked suddenly. The pirate was in the corner covered in different elements. They held him down and surrounded him. Frei stood determined and angry all around him. There was one fire Frei next to Gee that had its little arms crossed, an inferno blazing where hair usually was.

Calix turned. "What did you do to her?"

Red was silent, though he did smile. Calix would have his head for this. Or Elarie would. She'd rip his head off and feed it to a dragon and Calix would smile as she did it.

Terry knelt in the other cell and started pulling on the thorns the way he had when they found her with the Fae. "It'll be fine, Calix, she'll come back," he said, yanking one thorn out. At his touch, they began to shrink, following the command of someone with no magic.

"Right, but what is she going to do when she comes back?" Calix snapped. He didn't need to, it wasn't right, but for all he knew Terry was involved. It was his thorn and Red was his friend. Not to mention Tran, who might've been the one to do something to their food. "Shit," Calix looked at her side. Gold had pooled under her, sticky and drying. Red had cut open the wound. The leaves were discarded off to the side, a slice had been made, but it looked like it had ripped further.

Calix moved her hip and Kaelum hovered above him. "Oh gods, I'm going to vomit," Kaelum gagged, a hand flying to his mouth as he backed away.

"Go tell Grey we're taking care of her," Calix dismissed, though he also felt ready to vomit. Kaelum rushed up the stairs at his command and Terry stood. Calix looked over. Terry took a deep breath, stretching his back. He'd gotten the vines off her wrists, now he wrapped his hands around what he could without cutting himself, and pulled. Calix grabbed her shoulders to prevent her from sliding forward.

The vines dragged out of her arms slowly, each of them shining as they left. There were holes in her body from them. Calix could see two large ones and more when he turned her over partially.

"Elarie?" Calix touched her face. Any second now. It was quick last time, wasn't it? Just one moment she was gone, the next her green eyes were bright and annoyed with him. "Come on," he whispered, lifting her limp head up, "wake up, Elarie."

Gee tapped on Calix's leg, his skin a pale, worried blue. Calix watched the little thing point with a shaking arm, one finger extended toward Elarie's side. Terry walked into their cell and whispered, "holy gods," like any one of them would care.

Calix shifted down Elarie's body, practically sitting in blood. He moved her body so the gaping hole in her side was in front of him. His hands shook as he pulled her skin apart. "The thorn," he swallowed thickly, now pushing down bile. "He put it..."

Kaelum rushed back down the steps, "Grey's shaking like crazy, you can feel it when you walk. I told him you're with her, but I don't think it helped." He was breathing heavily, "and I have Tran being watched now. Why isn't she awake yet?" He put his hands on his hips and squeezed them.

"Because Red put faerthorne inside her body," Terry said painfully. There was no disdain or annoyance like usual when he spoke of Elarie. This time it was something close to empathy. Calix doubted Elarie would ever hear it and he also doubted she'd believe Calix if he told her about it.

Calix grit his teeth and rolled up his sleeve, cursing and cursing and cursing in his mind. Terrible words danced around, flashing in front of his eyes as he stuck his fingers into Elarie's side. Kaelum made a gagging noise that nearly caused Calix to vomit, but he just pushed his hand further in.

"It's going to be fine," Calix breathed, "everything is going to be fine." He felt around past blood and parts of the body people were not supposed to touch until he found something hard. "Shit, how am I supposed to tell if it's a bone or a thorn?" He glanced back at Kaelum and Terry. Red chuckled.

"Pull and see what happens," Terry suggested without the usual layer of sarcasm. He was pale, his arms crossed tightly over his body like he might be the next one to have a hand fish around for something in it.

Calix gagged and wrapped his hand around the hard thing. It wasn't her spine, he knew that much, and it didn't feel like a rib, so he pulled. Elarie's body jerked with his movement. The thing his hand was around quivered. "Hold her down," Calix said, finding Kaelum instantly at his side despite the need to vomit. Terry held her legs down and Calix pulled again, fighting against the vines that did not want to leave her body. His hand was partially out, each of them could see a piece of the thorn. It began to shrink, but didn't want to detach from what felt like Elarie's ribs.

"Just yank, she'll heal," Terry said.

"She only heals the injury that kills her," Calix grunted, his hand free. "If I break something doing this it—" Calix fell onto his back when the vine sprang free. It shrank and shrank until it was nothing but a single thorn in his bloody hand. Calix looked behind him at Red, who only smirked. Masha growled, chewing on his boot.

They looked back to Elarie. She was still dead. Kaelum felt for a pulse, but nothing came of it. He said, "there's another one in there."

Calix trembled with rage. He wasn't a violent person, he wasn't an angry person. He was calm and Elarie was violent, he'd told her she could be angry for him and he could be calm for her when they were on the beach together. They were opposites and Calix liked that about the two of them, but suddenly he was angry and did not want Elarie to be the one to feel the emotion. He had rage boiling inside, something he wanted to use against another person. Red.

Red was Elarie's kill, it wouldn't be right of Calix to take that from her, but he desperately wanted to do it.

Calix pressed his hand back into Elarie's side, much less afraid of vomiting this time, and looked at her blank, bloody face while he felt around for the thorn. Calix recalled watching her root for one in her shoulder on Finnal's ship, flicking it casually like it hadn't hurt. Then, when they were gone, she'd crumpled down the bar of her cell and fallen unconscious only minutes later.

"I found it," Calix grit his teeth and pulled. Her hip tried to follow.

"Do you think that if it was in her spine," Kaelum asked, "and you pulled the wrong way she could wake up and not be able to walk?"

Calix stopped. He looked at Kaelum. "Why would you say that right now?"

They stared at each other, Kaelum's mouth slowly opening. "That probably wasn't the best thing..."

"No, it was not the best thing to say right now."

He continued pulling while the two pirates fell into a tense silence, watching the thorn drag out of her body, clinging on as if its life depended on it. Calix grunted, slicing his thumb on one sharp piece, and watched his red blood mix with the gold in her body.

"Do you think all her organs are gold?" Terry asked faintly.

The thorn snapped and Calix fell again, watching it shrink. "Did I get all of it?" He asked faintly. Calix pushed Kaelum out of the way, looking from her face to her side. "Please don't make me do that again—"

Her eyes opened. Calix could've cried. "You heard my whistle?" She asked, her voice broken and quiet.

He winced, "not soon enough." Calix again looked at her side. She was bleeding rapidly, the gold spilling anew. "Elarie," he began, but when he looked at her she had her eyes closed. Not quite dead, but he doubted she'd wake for him. Calix said, "I need to get her to Grey," and put an arm around her shoulders.

"Calix, you can't carry her and walk at the same time," Kaelum reminded him, "I'll carry her. Get up there."

Calix nodded, but he didn't want to leave her. Still, he moved out of Kaelum's way and grabbed his crutch, dragging himself to his foot. Blood had stained his pants and his hands. It had gotten onto his shirt as well as inside his boot. He was covered in it. Calix walked to the cell opening and watched as Kaelum carefully lifted Elarie into his arms. He walked to the stairs, looking back every so often to see her. Calix couldn't tell if she was dead, but if she wasn't she wouldn't be alive for long.

Grey was shaking, as Kaelum had said, and it only worsened when he saw Calix. "It's all right," Calix put his hand up, "she's safe, she's right here."

Kaelum stopped next to Calix and looked at him, "should I put her down or take her somewhere else? She'll want to be clean."

"Is she still alive?" Calix asked as Grey nudged her limp hand. Grey's scales had turned ashen, he was shivering despite the warm morning. Calix looked at Kaelum, who shook his head slowly. "But she'll come back," Calix put his hand on Grey's face, "it may just take time."

Grey didn't want to wait. Steam floated shakily from his nostrils, drifting to Elarie's hand. He whined. Calix tried to think back—had the dragon ever actually seen her die? She came close in the cavern, but had it happened in front of Grey before?

"How long until we reach Lyburn?" Kaelum whispered to Terry, adjusting his hold on Elarie. The answer wasn't heard over Grey's roar. He sought Elarie's attention and he would get it if he had to yell at her to get her to wake up.

She jumped, her arm flailing out. Her nails scraped against Grey's head and she threw herself to the side, gagging. Calix grabbed her arms and Elarie vomited. Her knees buckled, golden blood spilling from her mouth. Elarie sobbed and Calix fell over. "It's all right," he was saying, "it'll pass, it'll pass." Elarie gripped his shirt and coughed.

"Raise anchor," Terry was saying while Calix cradled Elarie. Red must've lowered it. "Hoist sails, let's go!"

She was dead again, thankfully for not as long as the time before. The crew rushed around them, avoiding the agitated, humming dragon that curled around Elarie and Calix. Grey chuffed low and Elarie breathed in deeply. "I'm going," she mumbled weakly.

"To kill him, I know," Calix nodded, pulling her close. He rubbed her upper back, noting the long cut down her spine. "Just rest for now."

Elarie shook her head, pressing her face into his chest. It was hot and if he didn't know any better he'd say she was so feverish it would kill her. She groaned and said, "stay with you." Calix's heart fluttered like the wings of his butterfly were brushing through it. She said, "I'm going to stay with you."

He loosed a sigh, wrapping his arms tightly around her. "You're going to rest, all right?" He whispered, "we'll clean you up and get you some bandages, then you and me are going to fly to Lyburn together. I'll get you a room and a proper space to call your own."

She hummed, "close to yours?" Elarie was rubbing her face against him like a cat or a dragon. He wondered if she could purr like one.

"In the same wing," he agreed.

"I'm still upset with you," she said.

He nodded, "I'm perfectly all right with that and I completely understand. Just stay with me and I'll make it all up to you." Elarie just nodded.

CHAPTER FIFTY-NINE

ELARIE

She'd seen the castle before, but never from the sky. The windows shined in the sun, many of them stained glass. Spires upon spires made up the large building. Its stone walls were high and covered in bright green vines, some dotted with winter flowers. "It was fashioned in the Trec building style," Calix was telling her, his chin on her shoulder so he didn't have to shout so much. She knew this, but let him continue, "some great great grandfather of mine married a Trec Princess to establish a long lasting treaty and he had that castle built as a wedding gift. The old one has been converted into a historical preservation."

"A museum?" Elarie asked. No, it was not a museum.

"No, but it does have artifacts inside. I use it to study," he said.

The Trec-styled castle was further inland. A stone path had been fit to it, the rocks traveling with smooth turns down the hill to the city of Lyburn below. Its buildings, like the two castles, were fashioned in the old and new styles. At its center were Ceptari's tan stone and dirt structures. As time went on and more migrated to the beautiful capital, the city expanded. It stretched down the cliff as far as to touch the ocean and weaved around the forest meant to never be cut down. The buildings began growing taller and pointed.

Elarie looked down at what once was the kingdom's castle, now turned into some sort of historical preservation. It was a pyramid, one with many layers and stairs leading up the sides. Guards were posted in front of it, all looking up at the dragon slowly landing on a stomped down patch of earth.

Greilor's field.

It was a large space in the shadow of the tall castle. The ground had been molded the way Greilor liked it, with bumps he could roll over and dips he could sleep in. He landed on one of the bumps and lowered himself down to help Calix off just as the prince's family came through a curved door. It was part of a tunnel built mostly of glass.

"Calix!" A little girl shouted, her arms up and welcoming. Marcella, Princess of Ceptari. She was a beautiful little girl with a bright smile and a joyous laugh. A dress of pale pink covered her dark skin. She must've been cold in the growing winter. Her hair was braided thickly on top of her head and small jewels had been placed into it. Elarie slid off Greilor's back before Calix and Marcella screamed, "Mama he brought a *girl* home!"

Elarie took the crutch and his bag from Calix and helped him down. He used her to support himself for a moment, his weight bearing down on her to no effect. She looked at him carefully and handed the crutch back, putting the bag over his shoulder despite him being able to do it himself.

"Ready to meet my mother?" He whispered playfully.

A blush colored her cheeks and Elarie looked away quickly, settling her eyes on the queen. Calix's mother, Vienn, was pale, her hair the color of chestnuts and straight down her back. A soft smile was on her face, her hands clasped tightly in front of her, holding the hand of Ryd, Calix's little brother.

Ryd was tall for a child with hair the same color and texture as Calix's, though his skin was much lighter. He stood angled toward his mother, nervous.

"Ryd is very shy," Calix told her, tugging on her hand. Masha arrived, flying lazily above their heads much to the delight of the two siblings. Ryd flashed a bright smile and Marcella squealed. "Marcella is not," Calix whispered when they were nearly to them. Elarie looked back at Greilor. The dragon only nodded, urging her to keep going. "And my mother is gentle, don't worry."

Elarie was quite worried. She worried that Calix would turn on her. That Terry or Kaelum might. That someone else would find out and it would turn out to be like all those years ago with an angry, fearful village and a lord with a broad sword.

"Mama," Calix said happily, kissing her cheek, "how are you?"

"Well," she said in a soft voice, "and yourself? You're back late and without your leg, did your trip treat you kindly?"

Calix said, "quite kindly," and glanced at Elarie. His mother gave a coy, knowing smile that made Elarie's gut twist. "My, my Marcella are you finally getting taller?" He bent over to look at her.

"I am!" She jumped and wrapped her arms around his neck. He groaned as he lifted her up with one arm. "I measured myself last week and grew a whole finger taller," she told him.

"Cause for a celebration," he said and kissed the side of her head. She let go and bounced from foot to foot giddily. "Ryd?" Calix held his hand out.

Ryd smacked it.

"That's my boy," he chuckled and straightened while he adjusted the bag. "Family," he addressed in a confident voice, "this is Elarie. We sort of rescued her and I've offered to give her a place to stay."

"How strange given that the rescued have lodging in the city already established," his mother said with a soft smirk. Calix had been correct about her being gentle. Everything about her seemed to be warm and soft. It was no wonder Calix's father fell in love with her, Elarie could see it after only minutes of knowing her.

Calix touched Elarie's back, careful to avoid the cut he'd cleaned and bandaged himself before selecting a shirt for her. This one Elarie was sure belonged to a man. Its sleeves billowed down to her wrists, but she'd rolled them to her elbows because they chafed against the bandages on her forearms. It buttoned down her front and tucked into her pants.

"This is a special occasion," he said.

Elarie motioned behind her. "Grey knows me," she said, "we spent some time together before he found Calix so he offered to let me stay here so we could be close again."

"Oh is that all?" Vienn raised a brow.

"Are you in love?" Marcella asked and wrapped her arms around Elarie's waist. A twinge of pain rolled up her back. "I saw you looking at each other and I know what that means."

Elarie smiled, "do you?"

"Mhmm," she nodded, digging her chin into Elarie's stomach, "Mama looks at Papa like that."

"And how could you tell from over here when we were all the way over there?" Elarie jerked her head to where Greilor was.

Marcella said, "I have very good eyes, I see so many things—"

"All right, bird eyes," Calix peeled her off Elarie. "We are not in love." She heard him add, "not yet," in a low whisper. When Calix straightened he looked at her and shrugged, perfectly aware that she'd heard him. Marcella giggled.

The little princess said, "she can be your pick at the ball for your birthday and then you can court her and then you can marry her!"

"I don't think," Elarie glanced at Calix and bit her lip. He gave her a pleading look. "Well, we can see." Elarie wasn't sure if the look was for himself or his sister. Was he saving his own pain or the disappointment brought on by her refusal?

"I bet you she'll dance with him and they'll be married before the end of next year," Marcella turned to her younger brother.

Their mother said, "dear, we shouldn't bet on those things, come along." She ushered them toward the curved double doors and looked at the two behind her, then only at Calix, "King Ritan would like to see you in his study."

Masha landed on Calix's shoulders and the first thing Elarie heard come from Ryd's mouth came with a disappointed tone, "Mama I didn't see the dragon."

"I'm sure Calix will introduce you to it personally, darling," she said sweetly, "for now he has things to do."

"But dragon," he pointed behind them as they walked away. Marcella began to run, singing some song about falling in love as she skipped down the glass hallway. "Dragon," Ryd sort of whined.

Vienn said, "why don't we go to your art room so you can draw the dragon as a gift to it, hmm?" She pulled Ryd along. The child huffed, looking to be on the verge of tears.

"This way," Calix nudged Elarie. "That hall goes toward the throne room, we need the west stairs."

Elarie walked with him, her gaze on the pyramid. It was ancient now, far older than the 'great great grandfather' Calix had been talking about. Magic had preserved it over the centuries, and yet it still looked as if it was wearing away. She'd never been allowed inside and now, with Calix, she'd get to explore it.

"'Not yet,'" Elarie turned her eyes to Calix. His face warmed, she could practically see it. "Very presumptuous of you given our most recent conversations."

"I have a plan," he told her lightly. She raised a brow when he glanced at her. "I do. Step one, get you to come home with me."

Elarie chuckled softly, watching Masha for a moment. Greilor called her to speak with him and she flew begrudgingly over. They walked around the castle to a large set of smooth stone steps, guarded by two guards at the bottom and two at the large doors above them. Calix addressed the guard they passed by name, asking how her children were in passing. They had a brief conversation that lasted the walk up the steps and ended with a loud farewell at the doors that were opened for them.

The entry hall was taller than Elarie expected, with arching ribs and architecture she'd seen many times, yet it never ceased to amaze. It reminded her of trees, each thin stone limb climbing to reach the other at a curve that led to a great chandelier.

"Have you ever seen anyone clean one of those?" Elarie asked, gazing at the crystals mined somewhere in Ceptari.

He didn't answer. Instead, he pushed on her hip and urged her to the side, "let's go this way."

"What?" Elarie looked at the two ladies in lovely dresses walking with a pompous-looking man with a golden embroidered belt. Calix pushed her through a door in the wall despite the fact that they'd been spotted. It was well-lit, a servants' corridor where soft sounds floated through to indicate it was busy. Calix pushed her to a junction in the halls before she stopped. "Are you trying to *sneak* me into you—"

Calix covered her mouth, listening for something. Outrage boiled in her eyes and suddenly Calix was ripping his hand away hissing. "Why did you do that?" He blew gently on his hand.

"Are you serious?" She snapped.

A grin spread over his face and he touched her lips, again burning his skin on them. "It's part of the plan, Elarie," he whispered. Her gut twisted. This wasn't good. If he really had a *plan* and was looking at her like that, she'd cave quickly. Even if it wasn't for forgiveness, it would be for something. Especially when Calix asked, "if I kiss you right now would you let me burn?"

Her breathing snagged somewhere in her chest. "If you kiss me right now I'll knee you so hard you'll taste your own—"

"I'm going to fall so greatly in love with you," he said, forcing her to stop.

"I just threatened you, why would you say that?" Her eyes widened. Elarie looked him up and down. What was wrong with him? Calix began laughing softly, pulling her close. "Calix," she breathed.

He put his head against hers. "I'm not kissing you," he said, though she considered kneeing him despite that. Elarie remained still, her eyes closed. "It's part of the plan."

"Do you really have a plan or are you just saying that?"

Calix brushed his hand over her cheek. She could feel her burn on his hand. Had she left a mark? "I know I have to do more than say nice words and give you things to get you to forgive me for not accepting you," he said. Elarie squeezed her eyes tight. "I know that I can tell you how stupid I am hundreds of times and it won't mean anything to you because I broke something that won't be fixed with an apology. And I know better than to ask you what you want me to do to make up for it so I won't. But I will—I *will*—get you to believe me when I tell you I accept you."

She stared at the blankness behind her eyes. "And how would hiding me in a servant's corridor help you get to your final goal?"

"It's mostly for my benefit," he shrugged, "but all part of the greater whole."

"Do tell me how this fits," she pulled her head back but didn't step away. Calix would give her time to forgive him, she doubted he'd expect it from her, and Elarie wouldn't have any trouble not forgiving him for some time, but she would have trouble not letting him kiss her given the way his voice sounded when he whispered. It would take much to distract her from it.

He shrugged one shoulder, "I've got to get people talking about you." Her brow furrowed.

"People are going to talk about me, I don't understand what difference sneaking me into the castle will make," she shook her head.

"Ah, well," his hand slid down to hers, "for one, servants are how gossip spreads. And for another," he laced his fingers in hers, "I'm sneaking you to my bedroom. How scandalous."

Elarie had to force herself to roll her eyes to stop herself from smiling.

CHAPTER SIXTY

He did not have a plan until she asked about it. Calix had planned on sneaking her into his bedroom, but only for his purposes. He managed to fit it into a greater vision only at that moment. Servants would talk, yes, and people of the court staying in the castle would hear their whispers. They'd wonder about Elarie, they'd wonder about Calix, and his life would be better for it. Ladies would see Elarie has a threat, no lord would try a go at Elarie if Calix was showing interest, and given the approaching ball, it was all beneficial to him.

How did it fit into his plan?

It showed... devotion. Sure, he'd go with that.

Calix watched Elarie walk into the center of his bedroom like she was the first woman he'd ever brought in it. He was aware that he didn't clean his room before he left months ago and since no one was allowed to clean his personal space a layer of dust had collected on everything.

Elarie turned in a circle. "This is as expected, actually," she said. Calix wasn't sure if that was bad or good, she gave no indication of either. He found himself looking around the room for flaws. It was smaller than other rooms, smaller than both Marcella's and Ryd's bedrooms. He liked it that way. His four-poster bed was pressed into the corner of the right wall, a window latched closed above it. Calix had pinned fabric and things to the posts that had once had drapes on them. He'd ripped them off ages ago.

A chest was at its base, full and disorganized. On the wall across from the bed, he had a table with a mirror. A smile flashed on Elarie's face when she looked at it, on her way to his bed. Calix watched her sit and sink into his soft mattress.

"I thought you'd have a mannequin," she said, her hands stretched on either side of her.

Calix went to the closet and pulled the doors open, wheeling one out for her. The mannequin had nothing on it, he hadn't been working on any clothes before leaving. A smile flashed over her face and Calix managed to heave a sigh that had grown heavy in his chest. He usually hid the mannequin from people. "Will you stay here until I'm finished with my father?" Calix asked, walking into the full closet to grab a leg from a drawer. He held it under his arm and heard her shoes click lightly as she walked toward him.

"You're sneaking and hiding me now?" She asked, touching the fabric of a velvet shirt he never wore because Ryd didn't like the texture. It seemed that Elarie didn't either. She wiped her hands on her pants and took the leg from him. He watched her inspect it for a moment before he went to collect dark pants and a much nicer shirt.

"Actually," he said, throwing the clothes over his shoulder, "I am going to ask for a room to be prepared for you, have seamstresses come to take your measurements while you wait, and feed you here in the meantime."

She squinted, "still sounds like hiding. You're tucking the dragon girl away until she is ready to be presented to society."

Calix smiled and walked past, taking the leg with him. He changed in his bathing room, washing his face, neck, and hands before rubbing his jaw. He needed to shave. He looked far too much like his father. Calix itched his stump through the pants before opening the door again. Elarie smiled, holding a tape measure up. "What are you going to do with that?" He asked accusingly.

"I have my own plan," she shrugged. Elarie stood in front of him, "at the request of a dragon that tore your latest leg apart."

"Ah, right. Measure away," he said. Of course, Elarie could just look at the other legs he had in his closet, but she purposefully got onto her knees. "The leg cuts off right here," he bent to touch the space. "Have you ever done this before?" Calix watched her decide which part of the tape went where.

She said, "no and I will probably get it wrong."

He chucked, trying not to think about Elarie being on her knees in front of him. Instead, he anticipated the scolding he'd get for whatever or whatever. By Calix's calculations, they'd been on the sea for longer than promised but not by very long. If his father heard about Elarie, which was likely, Calix would be questioned about her as well.

It brought his concentration back to her and her hands around his thigh. "Calix," she said as she stood. He looked at her. Elarie held up the measuring tape, "I need to speak to someone about buying iron."

"Iron?"

She nodded, then amended, "iron ore."

"For the whole thing?" He had a few legs that were built with iron. The one he'd been wearing before had been fitted with an iron support lining. It was what Terry had stamped into.

Elarie said, "don't you trust me?"

"I do, I'm merely curious about using only iron," he said, "it can be heavy, you know." Elarie rolled her eyes and walked away from him. She removed her shoes and climbed onto his bed to push the window open. "How much iron ore?" He asked. Calix moved toward her, "and why ore?"

"Calix," she sighed. Elarie folded her legs under her and faced him. "I am a magical being with the ability to bend fire to my will. Why doubt me?"

He said, "curiosity. I thought you knew me enough to know I like understanding things." She raised an accusing brow. "I was just a little slow when it came to you."

Elarie groaned a little, looking away from him. Her head faced the sea. "Go speak to your father and find a way to get me ore and *then*," she looked at him, "come back. Not before."

"Fine," he sighed, "stay in my bed until then."

"No," Elarie snapped, but she laid down, wincing when she landed on her back. "I have things to do. Measurements to be taken, gossip to spread."

Calix backed away, looking at her on his bed, wondering if he could lie and say no rooms were ready for her so she'd sleep there. Next to him. He suddenly wanted his pillows to smell like her, the warm hearth and flames he'd gotten used to in the dragon cavern. That had been on a hard rock that put a crick in his back, this was his *bed*. And Elarie was laying there with her hair fanned out over her shoulder and her eyes trained on the book Calix had left on his bedside table.

"Lialan Cos," she said, waving it around for him to see.

"It's a good read," Calix said, "you might enjoy it." She smiled and opened to the title page, her finger running over the deckled edges. "I'll see you soon," he went to the door.

She replied, "don't get in trouble."

Calix laughed lightly and left, rushing now. He would get into trouble for being as late as he was. Even if they'd taken the servant's corridors, Calix had made a game of sneaking around. Elarie had only partially enjoyed it, but it was a thrill for him. That coupled with Calix changing and speaking to Elarie, he knew he pissed off his father already.

The study was large, something Calix would be glad to inherit when he became king. Two tables had been pressed together in the center of the windowless room, the middle holding a tower of candles that nearly reached the small chandelier. Papers were strewn about in an order only his father knew. Touching one would ruin the order, and Calix had learned to leave his hands off the center tables at a young age.

He walked around to the large cushioned chair his father sat at. The king was writing quickly, drafting a law or something. "Calix, how was your trip?" He asked without stopping.

"Eventful," Calix pulled up a chair. "We rescued over two hundred on the way around to Trec and coming back."

"I'm glad, truly," he smiled at his son. Calix was reminded of their argument about the slaves fighting in the Rings. "And this girl someone came in to whisper about?" He raised a brow, "a rescued you didn't want to lose?"

Calix found himself trying not to embarrass himself. "In a sense. Her name is Elarie, she was the more interesting part of the trip." Ritan sat back, tossing the quill onto the parchment dedicated to the action. Small ink stains dotted the page. Calix laughed nervously, "she knows Grey. Elarie used to ride him, Grey was like part of her family before she thought he died. We came upon her on Captain Rol's ship, they knew each other instantly, and now she's with me."

"For Grey?"

"And for me," Calix said. He rubbed the back of his neck, "she's amazing. I wanted her to stay here, I even begged for it."

His father said, "I see. I'd like to meet her." He stood with a groan and walked to a bookshelf, selecting two crystal glasses and a wine bottle. "You worried your mother, you know," he said before handing a glass to Calix. "And I worried."

"It won't happen again," Calix held the glass out for the wine to be poured. It wouldn't happen again, a realization that hit him in the chest. He doubted they'd go back out to sea before his birthday and after that... he'd have no time. "Is that what you wanted to discuss?"

Ritan fell back into his chair with a sigh this time. He sipped his wine. "There is something we need to discuss concerning your kingdom." Calix nodded. His father dragged a map of Ceptari forward, one marked with red along the border to Duness and in the north. Calix pulled it closer and leaned over it. "Each of those markings is farmland where a disease has spread. Tell me what action you would take as king."

Ah, so it was a test. Calix inspected the map, asking his first question, "has there been any report of crops dying in Duness?"

"None," his father answered.

"And have we informed Duness?"

A nod came from his father. Duness would most likely have some magic invented to ensure the disease didn't spread. They would most likely cut off buying grain or otherwise from Ceptari as well, which would hurt both kingdoms on its own. "But what about our people, Calix?" Ritan took a drink of wine.

Calix said, "well we should have people sent to discover what sort of disease this is and see to protecting what farmland is left." There was a good amount. Enough to feed a kingdom for a single winter. "I hear Trec is having a good year, we could request food from them... it's interesting the way it's moving. Arcing like this," he motioned with his finger. The border had been affected and the disease spread north, but nothing had been hurt to the south. "I wonder why that is. It's not the wind and I can't think of what it would be carried over with."

"Animal migration, perhaps?" His father suggested.

"It's possible of course, but most animals flock south, definitely not to the mountains," he tapped the range of Knowles Mountains and the Twin Peaks. "Have we heard from the Twin Peaks?"

Ritan said, "not a word. They'll keep to themselves until it's too late, I'm afraid." He sipped again. "You'll be going to North Reidle to investigate yourself and you won't be taking that dragon."

"What?" Calix's head turned quick enough to crack his neck.

"You'll take the Yaerlings," he continued. Yaerling horses, bred for speed and only speed, would get him from the castle to North Reidle in two days. The average horse would take a week, perhaps more. "Investigate, I thought you'd enjoy the leg work. Better than being stuck in the castle, eh?"

He said, "well, yes, it's just that I *just* got back from a difficult trip—"

"I'll give you three days to rest," he decided and clinked his glass against Calix's with a smile. "It'll be fun. No dragon."

Calix looked at North Reidle. It had a marking but South Reidle did not. "When was their disease reported?"

"Two days ago, but you know North Reidle and how stubborn they can be," his father said, "so it could've been weeks ago and we're only hearing of it now. Three days and two for riding? You'll get your answers."

Sighing, Calix took a drink.

CHAPTER SIXTY-ONE

CALIX

He opened the door gently, chilling in the breeze coming through the window. Elarie was still lying on his bed, asleep on her stomach this time, with her hand between the pages of the book and a dragon curled up on her upper back. Calix stepped in and shut the door as quietly as he could manage, but the dragon still opened one eye. Masha purred and stretched happily, sliding off Elarie's back and under her arm.

Elarie grunted sleepily, her hand slipping out from between the book pages to curl around Masha. The little dragon hummed and Elarie chuckled, replying in her soft dragon language.

"Two people asked if I was a whore while you were gone," Elarie told Calix as he walked into the room. He wondered if he'd ever be able to sneak in on her or if the fright he gave her on Moro Island was the closest he'd get.

"And what did you answer?" He asked in return. Calix sat on the edge of the bed, picking up the book she'd lost her page on. He set it aside and pulled a slip of paper out of his pocket.

Elarie said, "I told one I wasn't and I told the other only you call me a whore but that's because I'm so excellent in bed, not because you pay me." She began laughing softly before she turned onto her side and stretched the way Masha had. She opened her eyes.

"Are you excellent in bed?" He raised a brow. She squinted playfully and he said, "here," holding the paper out, "the order for your iron ore to be delivered tomorrow afternoon."

She snatched it from him and read through his scrawled, rushed writing. "Excellent. One of two tasks is on its way to completion."

"I have to tell you something else, don't get too excited," he said and picked up the sleepy Masha. Calix pulled her to him as if she were one of his plush toys and sighed, falling onto the bed beside Elarie. Masha only purred and adjusted slightly. "I have been given a task of my own by my father."

"What did he think of me?" Elarie propped herself onto her elbow, her fingers sliding up and down the slip of paper.

Calix answered, "he wants to meet you." She nodded, probably expecting more. He could tell her of the way his father chuckled as they were leaving the study when Calix told him how he made her angry and now had to make up for it somehow. His father had told him it reminded him of him and his mother, which only made Calix think of the book written about their love story and how Vienn had sent him on a journey to complete a task. "And," Calix said, "he's sending me away."

Any hint of a smile she'd been wearing dropped. "Why?"

"A disease is being spread through the crops in my kingdom," he answered, "it's affecting many. I've been sent to North Reidle, it's one of our largest farmlands that supplies for much of the kingdom, to investigate the disease with a few others and try to find a way to prevent it from spreading elsewhere."

Elarie looked away from him. "It's spread to the whole king-dom?"

"Not all of it. The border and to the north are what we know is being hit by whatever disease it is," he said, "it's strange because most diseases are spread by wind or rain, but whatever this is it taking hold of farmland that's miles apart."

"How many places have reported diseased crops?"

"Twelve," Calix said, "six on the border and six in the north. No word from the People of the Muntaiins yet, but we doubt we'll hear anything at all until it's too late unfortunately."

Elarie nodded. "Reidle... that's over a week's ride isn't it?"

"We're taking the Yaerlings," he said. She nodded again. "Elar-ie," he reached up and brushed his knuckle over her jaw. Elarie turned her head, smiling softly despite the guard she was putting up against him. "It'll be fine. Just a few days."

"Sorry," she tried shrugging off whatever was bothering her, "it's not the time that's bothering me."

"You can tell me anything," he said quietly.

She swallowed, glancing away from him. She looked at the room, then at Masha. The dragon's eyes were closed, she was sleeping on his chest. "It's," she began. Calix moved his thumb over her chin. "It's the sort of thing I would get sacrificed for. Dying crops and disease."

"It'll never happen again, not with me around."

Elarie smiled at him, though she still had a bit of uncertainty in her eyes. Grey roared from outside, the sound coming right up to his bedroom. She said, "your brother is outside."

"Again?" Calix sat up sharply and crawled to the window. There little Ryd was, sitting in front of Grey with his drawing things spread out. "He's not supposed to be out there without a chaper-one."

"Does he do this often?" Elarie asked and Calix nodded before climbing out of the bed with Masha in his arms. "Is he as fascinated with dragons as you are?"

Calix said, "it's not the dragon that's the problem, it's the cliff." Elarie got up to follow him, trailing at his side. Calix broke into a run, which made her laugh, and he said, "he lost a paper down it once and tried jumping to get it. Grey stopped him, but ever since then my mother hasn't allowed him to be out there without someone watching him."

"Somehow he manages to slip away?" She asked, following him down stairs and through the throne room to get to the glass hall-way. Some tour of the castle that was. "Sounds like me when I was a child."

He pushed the door open for her, spotting Ryd in the same place. "Really?" He asked Elarie. Calix walked across the grass with her. Grey was lying down, feet crossed and head low, watching what-ever Ryd was doing.

Elarie said, "I used to sneak away all the time to see the dragons. And I regularly jumped off cliffs just to scare them. One of my biggest punishments as a child was my parents saying I wasn't allowed in the nest. They'd shut the door and tell all the dragons that Elarie was in trouble and she wasn't allowed to speak to any of them."

"Did they listen?"

She laughed, "of course not, I was the one they listened to."

Calix sat down next to Ryd wondering why dragons would rather listen to a child than to the ones disciplining the child, but he didn't ask. Elarie sat down on Ryd's other side not as close to him, and Ryd continued drawing.

"Oh, that's amazing," Elarie turned her head and looked at what Ryd was drawing, "Masha, look at this." Masha crawled out of Calix's arms much to the delight of the child and began inspecting the drawing before them.

It was of Masha, yes, and Ryd was talented, yes, but it was just as any four year old would draw. Calix was very proud of his brother's ability, many commented on it. His art was how he communicated, but it was still at the level of a child. Despite this, it didn't sound like Elarie was faking amazement for Ryd.

Masha was still pleased with it. She strutted confidently, her long tail sliding behind her, wings flapping slowly. Ryd had his big brown eyes open wide, the same wonder in the Lathin blue that Calix had. It was something only they shared, the love for dragons. Marcella adored them, but no one else looked at them the way Ryd did.

"The scale pattern is incredible," Elarie mumbled. "Can I see your book, Ryd?" She pointed to it. Ryd blinked quickly, tearing his eyes off the dragon to look at Elarie. Calix smiled. He hardly ever looked at anyone, not really. It used to upset their mother. But Ryd looked at Elarie and slid the book toward her.

It was one of many full of his dragon drawings or paintings. Elarie flipped to a random page and grinned, "Calix, do you realize how talented your brother is?" She showed him the drawing of Grey. There were many in the book, this one was one of the first drawn into it. In the drawing Grey was sitting as he was now, paws crossed and head down. It was his whole body.

"I know he's talented," Calix said. Ryd began looking from the dragons to Elarie as if he were attempting to pay attention to both.

"Look at this," she flipped back to the drawing of Masha and put it on the grass in front of all of them, "Ryd saw Masha for only a moment, remember, and not up close, yet everything is exactly as it is on Masha. Even the proportions are correct." She pointed to the legs and neck.

Calix nodded, "he's got a good eye."

"Calix, the *scale pattern* is the same," she touched the place where Ryd had begun drawing the scales. He often switched from lining to coloring. In this case, Masha was green, yellow, and had hints of light brown. The shape of the scales in the drawing was the same—perfect, even—but so were the colors he was using.

"That's amazing," he looked from Masha to the drawing. "Ryd, I didn't know you were that talented. Is it just you that knows it?"

Ryd smiled.

Elarie flipped through the drawing book again. "You are a wonder, Ryd," she said before setting it back where it had been. She leaned forward, "you know I can speak to dragons? I know what they're saying like I know what your brother is saying, isn't that wonderful?" Ryd nodded. "And you know what Masha says about your drawing?" He shook his head. "She says that no one in the whole world has ever drawn her and she loves that you did. She says that she would be happy to pose for more drawings as long as you put one in Calix's room so she can look at it before she goes to sleep at night."

Ryd's smile turned to a grin.

"And you know what Grey says?" She asked. Ryd shook his head. "He says that he is proud to be drawn by you."

After bouncing apprehensively a few times Ryd jumped up and threw his arms around Elarie, squeezing tight for only a few seconds before it became too much physical contact for him. Calix stared at her. Ryd never hugged strangers. He hardly ever hugged their mother. He went right back to his drawings like it was nothing, but Calix was quite sure something had just happened.

Elarie got up slowly and walked to Grey. She whispered something to him and Calix stood, walking toward her. He was drawn toward her. Elarie looked at him, the same protective arms wrapping around her freshly healed middle. Before he could ask, she said, "he's drawing things other than dragons, isn't he?"

"Sure," he slid his hands into his pockets.

"Like..." she rocked on her feet once, "bugs? Birds? Bats?"

He must've been struck with something. Calix stumbled back a step and looked at his brother. Ryd was switching his pencils, showing each of them to Masha. The dragon would sniff them and continue watching. Calix turned back to Elarie. "Do you think he found wings?" He asked.

"I know he did," Elarie corrected.

Calix stepped toward her, placing his hands on her face. He liked doing this far too much. "You are the most beautiful, amazing person, thank you so much for being alive."

She looked at him apprehensively, her eyes darting over to Grey before again settling on him. "You're welcome?"

He very much wanted to risk getting kneed in the balls to kiss her, but instead of violating her consent he let go and watched the apprehensive look settle to something just short of fondness. Elarie walked around him and sat back down with Ryd, watching him perfect his childlike drawing of Masha. Calix looked at Grey and the knowing look that came off his otherwise blank face. "How are you supposed to fall in love with an immortal?" He whispered. And with just a blink, Calix thought he was saying *patiently* as if Calix could fall as quickly as he wanted to, but he was to be patient for her. An immortal with trust issues who would rather run than face her problems. He'd have to be patient for her.

CHAPTER SIXTY-TWO

KAELUM

The morning was cold enough to make him sniffle, but Kaelum was on a mission and wouldn't let the coming winter stop him. He'd made it halfway up the path that led to the castle before Terry caught up to him, cursing for leaving him in bed, but he didn't regret doing it. Kaelum needed to speak to Elarie and it was better if Terry simply wasn't there. Still, he apologized and kept climbing. Guards nodded to him. Kaelum knew plenty of them and was friendly with most because of his relationship with the prince. Many did not like Terry, however.

They walked between the old castle and the new one to Grey's field, where he often found Calix even as early as just after sunrise. The Great Dragon was there as well as the little one. It—she—was flying circles around Grey's large body. Kaelum saw Elarie walking around Grey. She had a ball of yarn in her hand as well as a great many sharp sticks she was stabbing into the ground and wrapping the yarn around. It was turning into a large semicircle.

Elarie looked better this morning than she had in days, finally wearing clothes that actually fit with her hair braided in a crown on her head. Something golden—a pin, maybe—glinted in it. *Golden, golden, golden beware those of golden*—

"Kaelum, I was wondering when you'd show up," Calix said. He walked out of the open glass doors holding a bundle of rope. "We're building a nest."

"How?" Terry asked, looking around for stone or wood.

Elarie walked past them while counting, her number at fifteen. She put a stick in the ground when she reached thirty, then turned toward the cliff and walked to the end of it. They watched her stop and look to her right at where another stick of yarn was, then behind her. She backed up a few large steps and put the stick in the ground, wrapping the yarn around it.

"Elarie is going to blow a hole in the cliffside," Calix said with a proud smile as she walked back. She tucked a strand of hair behind her ear and he looked at her like she was his whole world. The way Kaelum looked at Terry.

"Are you well?" Elarie asked Kaelum, ignoring Terry completely. She didn't even look at him.

Kaelum said, "I was hoping you would begin teaching me how to control my magic. I had a difficult day yesterday—"

"Talking to the families of the people that died because of you," Terry interrupted sharply.

Elarie merely glanced at him before continuing her conversation, "did you make a star last night?"

"I did. This one was more painful than the last and it was smaller," he took it out of his pocket. Terry had the others. He always had them. Kaelum could feel each one in his pockets.

She put her other supplies down and took it, making it shine faintly. "Interesting," was all she mumbled. "Well I can teach you how to break the stars if you'd like to be rid of this one. It's not very powerful because it was created out of sorrow."

"How useful is breaking the stars?"

"If you have too many it draws attention. At some point anyone with magic will be able to feel it and may demand to see it or know what sort of magic it is. Fae especially," she waved it a little, "would kill for them. Breaking them will get rid of the magic and also ensures that the wrong people don't get the magic."

Kaelum thought of his father suddenly. The black powder on his hands he hadn't understood. He'd been murdered when Kaelum was thirteen, found dead after a late night working on the docks. He had a wooden ship toy in his bag for Kaelum, something a thirteen year old kid would think was silly, but a twenty three year old Kaelum now treasured.

"All right, how do I do it?" He breathed deeply, hating the idea of getting rid of the stars suddenly.

"First you need to learn to make a burst," she held the star up. "Use a different one and hold it in your left hand." Elarie demonstrated while Terry gave Kaelum a rock and Calix moved closer. She looked at him while saying, "tie it around my waist please," and ignored the smirk on his face. "You call the magic to you, make it shine. Right now I suspect you feel the magic everywhere, yes?"

He nodded, then said, "well at night it's just in my hand."

"You need to direct it to your right hand. The magic should flow through you from one place to another," she motioned as Calix wrapped the rope around her waist. She didn't pay any attention to it or him.

"Elarie, what are you doing?" Kaelum put his hand down.

"I'm jumping off a cliff without a dragon, pay attention," she said, "you can find some way to picture it—" Calix tightened the rope and she inhaled sharply, but continued without acknowledging his apology. "Like you do at night with the swirling light you want to focus it into a ball above your hand."

He watched her do the same with the red light above her palm. It swirled and twisted, raw power that was there one moment and gone a second later. Calix stared at it from over her shoulder then walked away to go to his dragon. He began tying the rope around Grey's front leg.

"This is something that will be difficult for you to learn during the day but I think it will be beneficial to practice it when it's difficult," she said, "just concentrate on bringing out the light in your hand, then forming it into something else."

She gave the star back and walked away. Kaelum stared at it, then at her, and finally looked at Terry. "Do you think I'll be able to concentrate right now?" He shook his head with a frown. Kaelum watched Elarie twist the knot around to her front, again pushing the stray hair behind her ear. His eyes went to another piece on her head. The cut part that flapped in the wind.

Terry began walking and Kaelum followed, stepping over the yarn. The nest would be underneath them, what were the measurements for when she wouldn't be able to see them from down there? The center of the marked off space was to the right of the doors, not directly in front of it. It made room for the field to still be used. Calix's mother enjoyed having tea parties by the pyramid, so her still having space must've been a necessity for Calix.

"Then I'll die and come back, it's no big deal," Elarie was shrugging much to the annoyance of Calix. He was holding the rope connected to his knot, tugging it. "It'll be fun, maybe I'll get you to jump with me someday."

"Hanging off a cliff?" He asked, though he didn't seem scared by it. He didn't sound scared, anyway.

She rolled her eyes and pushed his hand away, "no without a rope. Greilor will catch us." Elarie looked at Kaelum and Terry. "No practicing?"

"There is no way I'll be able to concentrate with you about to jump off a cliff," Kaelum replied and she flicked her brows up and down before walking away. To the yarn. Elarie stood next to it. "Don't die, I still need you," Kaelum said.

Elarie laughed and looked back at Grey, who sat and waited. He was her anchor and the rope seemed tight enough, so Elarie ran. Kaelum saw Calix tense greatly next to Grey, far too concerned for the golden blooded monster. There was nothing Kaelum could say that would stop him from caring for her. Calix left all logic behind in the dragon cavern, it was obvious. She disappeared over the side and they ran to it, stopping to watch her jerk to a stop some ways down.

She stood against the cliff, measuring with her eyes, and shouted a word he didn't know. Grey walked forward a few steps and she began to lower on the rope until she shouted something else and Grey sat back down.

Elarie jumped, swinging back and hitting the cliff again. She jumped again, gaining momentum. On the third swing, she straightened and a white hot flame caught on her feet. When she hit the cliff a hole blew into it.

And Elarie climbed out unscathed but covered in dirt and rubble. She shouted in another language and Grey walked backward. Elarie climbed up the rope and over the cliff hardly breaking a sweat.

"Easy," she told Calix and walked to the other end of the yarn with Grey, doing the same to the other side.

Calix said, "I find her terrifying."

"I do, too, but I doubt for the same reasons as you," Terry watched her jump like he wished the rope would snap.

Kaelum was about to reply, but Calix beat him to it. He grabbed Terry by the collar and pushed him toward the edge of the cliff. Terry grabbed his wrist, eyes wide despite knowing that Calix would never let him fall. "The only thing Elarie has done wrong is lie and we both know it's completely understandable that she did. You and I both know that she could be so much worse than she is now but she is trying and you aren't. You want someone to blame? Blame yourself. Blame Kaelum. Blame me for all I care but Elarie is not at fault for the deaths on that ship. Do you understand?"

Terry ground his teeth.

"She doesn't deserve your hate or your blame," Calix spat, "you don't get to come to my home and call her a monster. Do it again and you won't be coming back." He stepped to the side and threw Terry to the ground. Elarie was standing a few steps away, her expression unreadable.

She watched Terry get up and walk away, then looked at Kaelum. He shoved the star deep in his pocket and said goodbye to the two of them, going after Terry to hear all the shit he was about to say about his best friend. He wasn't sure if Terry deserved to be held over a cliff, but what Calix said made sense. Terry wouldn't hear it. Now Kaelum would have to deal with the aftermath and decide whether or not he wanted to defend Calix or side with Terry.

CHAPTER SIXTY-THREE

KAELUM

Terry was tearing apart pages in his journal when Kaelum finally got to their home. He'd run, so he was sitting on his bed with his face red and his eyes watery. Kaelum sat next to him and instantly he was speaking, ripping up a picture of Calix. "He picked a golden blooded monster over us."

Over you, Kaelum thought, because Kaelum wasn't the one being rude or blaming Elarie for everything. Not even when they found out about the blood—he even encouraged Calix. "Maybe—" he began but Terry wasn't finished.

"Does he not realize that Elarie could be lying?" He asked hotly, crumpling up pieces of paper. "That the fact that she knew who he was right away might be suspicious? How do we know she's not in disguise to worm her way into the royal family and kill all of them?"

"That doesn't explain Grey," Kaelum said.

Terry countered, "she spelled him."

"Then how does she know the language?"

"Are you on my side or not?" Terry snapped loudly, making Kaelum flinch. Terry didn't apologize, he just groaned and went back to destroying his drawings of the prince.

Kaelum took a deep breath. *No,* he wanted to say. Instead, he said, "I'm just trying to find a good argument, that's all."

"I don't want a better argument," he grunted, tearing another page out of his book. This one was Kaelum. In his rage, perhaps he didn't see that it was, but Kaelum didn't try to stop him. He got up and went to their alcohol cabinet, just grabbing a bottle and no cups. Terry snatched it from him angrily before Kaelum could sit back down.

He asked, "what do you want?" Terry drank and drank and drank. If it burned his throat or his nose he didn't care. He was going to drown himself in it. Kaelum sighed dejectedly and got up as Terry continued drinking. He wasn't going to be stuck with a drunk, angry man. "I'm going to visit my mother," he said before leaving and locking the door behind him. Terry didn't even look up.

Kaelum's mother was the most wonderful woman in the world. He'd meant to visit her yesterday, but after speaking to family after family he couldn't bring himself to go. Why put out his mother's light with his dark mood? He told himself he'd wait until he was better, which he had been until Terry.

She lived across the street, her window facing an alley. The entrance to her place was in that alley, which always smelled of shit and something dead no matter how many times it was cleaned up. Kaelum believed it was coming from someone's home. He climbed the step and knocked three times, his eyes moving to every window like he'd be able to guess which one.

The door opened and his mother smiled, "I heard you came in yesterday."

"We did," Kaelum followed her inside, shutting the door for her. He walked down the short hall to the only room other than the two bedrooms and bathing room between them. It held the dinner table full of all the marks from Kaelum's many tantrum-filled meals. Next to it was the wall the kitchen was placed on, every bit of it in a line. Kaelum's mother often complained of having to walk from one side to the other because the brazier was on one end and the counter was on the other. She did not, however, want any solution to the problem.

"And why didn't you come to see me?" She asked, kneeling to open the cooling box in the floor. She pulled out a pitcher of tea with lemon slices floating through it.

As glasses were filled Kaelum crossed to the couch against the wall. It was set under the window closest to the door, giving the perfect view of everything in the room. "I had a hard day, I was resting," he sat.

"You were gone longer than expected," she walked over, her smile trapping him with the *I'm your mother, I know you better than you think* frame of mind. Her thin frame shook with age as she sat on his right, using her forearm to brush tightly curled hair from her eyes.

"We ran into trouble on the way back," Kaelum took a cold glass from her. He sipped the tea and put his head on his mother's shoulder so they both settled. "I need to speak with you about something," he sighed, reaching into his pocket. His mother hummed, taking a large swallow. The tea was her favorite, she grew the herbs on the roof of the building and distributed them dried to everyone around her. For as long as Kaelum could remember they both drank it with plenty of sugar and lemon. "Have you ever seen one of these before?" He held the star out.

There was a dreadful silence between them as his mother stared at the black rock. "I thought it wouldn't happen," she said in a soft, fearful voice. "When you never said anything about the pain, I thought..."

Kaelum looked at her. Sorrow had etched itself into her face. The wrinkles on her eyebrows and around her mouth stretched thin as she took the star from his hand. She trembled and her lips shook, nostrils flaring on her flat nose. "So my father really did have magic?" He asked.

She nodded and sniffed, covering her mouth. "He wanted to tell you when the pain started. That was when his father told him and his father's father and so on." His mother turned the star over, her brows creased. "When he died he left something to you that I was instructed not to give you until you told me about the pain. Or I suppose," she waved the star, "showed me this."

"He left me something?" Kaelum's throat tightened. His father had left him many things. The apartment was one, which he instantly gave to his mother. His clothes, though none of them fit. Nicknacks Kaelum had in a box under his and Terry's bed.

His mother stood, setting her tea on the floor like she always did. A ring of water had stained the wood. She went to her bedroom and rooted around there for some time. Kaelum was having trouble breathing. He picked up the star left on the couch and squeezed it in his right hand as his mother returned. "He showed this to me once," she said, sitting and placing the wrapped object in his lap. "Told me it was a book ages old."

Kaelum unwrapped it, running his fingers over the dusty cover of an old book. He didn't recognize it—though his father liked to read as much as Calix, so he doubted he would've paid attention to what was in his hands. A star had been stamped into the brown leather.

"He told me, he said, 'darling Rosette, if there is anything in this little place worth a damn it's this.' And I asked what he meant and he told me it had to be as old as time and was in a language only the Star Makers and those sworn to protect them can read. Had to be worth something," she chuckled sadly. "It's been in his family for more generations than we know."

Kaelum looked at her, "did he know what it said?"

"He was going to teach you, I promise," she ran her hand over his hair and rested it on the back of his neck. Tears shined brightly in her eyes, "he would've answered any question—" a large bang sounded from up the street. All the way to the castle. "What are they doing to make all that noise? It's been happening all morning, is Calix up to something?"

"Elarie," he realized, "she can read it! Oh, Mama," Kaelum faced her quickly and put his glass on the arm of the couch. There was yet another ring stain, this time from him. "I love you so much, thank you for giving this to me."

Her brow furrowed, "I don't know an Elarie, who's that?"

"She's..." he hesitated, looking away. What was Elarie? "Calix's friend," he decided to say, "and she knows every language that can be known so she knows this one." He kissed her cheek and went for the door quickly. "I'll tell you all about it—"

"I want to meet her!" She called before Kaelum could shut the door. He cringed for a moment, standing there with the shit smell as he tried to find a way that Elarie meeting his mother could go right but came up empty.

He held the book close to him, the worn leather rubbing against his shirt, and jogged down the alley. Kaelum looked at his building and thought of who was inside. He should be telling Terry about the book first. He should go home and show it to him, tell him that he thought Elarie could read whatever was inside so they could take the book to her together.

But what would Terry say? That he shouldn't trust her with anything? That they were better off just guessing and leaving her out of it?

No. No, Kaelum couldn't do that. Not with this. He ran down the busy street toward the castle, his heart beating so fast he feared it bursting from his chest. Kaelum had never once suspected his father of having some sort of magic. His father had been a boring man with a fish-smelling job and Kaelum had adored him, but magic? There were no shining lights in his memory, no stones or stars. And yet there was a book in another language that only one person in the whole damn world would know.

His legs burned, practically numb by the time he was in the field. Calix and Elarie were together again, this time trying to get the rope off and not on. Elarie had her hips out and her arms partially raised at her sides while Calix sawed stubbornly at the rope. His head turned, though, and he straightened.

"Kaelum," he said.

Elarie took the knife from Calix and cut through the rope in one short jerk. He gave her a rather annoyed look, discovering that she'd been humoring his attempt at helping her. Elarie was covered in dust and dirt. It coated her clothes and skin, turning her fair hair into an ashy grey color.

"My father was like me," Kaelum said nervously. Everything was going to spill over. Perhaps he'd cry. Elarie just grabbed the loose sleeve of Calix's shirt and wiped her face on it followed by her hands. "Right?"

"I'm sure he was," Elarie tucked the same stubborn hair over her ear and gave the knife back to Calix.

Kaelum took a few brave steps forward, his nostrils filled with the smell of stone and soil. There was a hole in the ground by their feet, deep and dug out to walk into. "Did you finish..."

"No, I was just hollowing out the cliff, it's not safe for a human to walk in yet," she picked dirt off her tongue. "Did you need me to confirm what your father was because I can't do that without a body—"

"No!" Kaelum gasped, his eyes wide. He clung to the book, "why would I want that, what's wrong with you? He's been dead ten years I'm not digging him out of the ground!"

She winced and said, "sorry that was insensitive." Elarie cleared her throat, "what do you want instead of that?"

"Can you read this?" Kaelum flipped the cover and showed her the stamp. Her eyes lit up, which answered his question.

"You have a star book!" She reached for it but yanked her hands back quickly. "Wait, wait," she backed up staring at the old leather book, then turned and walked to Grey. The dragon lit her on fire. Kaelum looked at Calix, whose fond eyes were trained on Elarie, but turned to his friend quickly.

He asked, "what's a star book?"

"My father left it to me," he answered as Elarie returned. Much of the dirt on her was gone though she didn't really look clean. "He told my mother that she couldn't give it to me until I told her about the pain in my hand. When I never did she assumed that I didn't inherit whatever magic this is."

Elarie gingerly took the book from him. "Some say these books were the only artifacts to be truly held by gods." Calix, with all his studying, looked prepared to contradict her with some fact or other, but she opened the book and he decided against it. Elarie held the book in one arm, keeping it propped against her chest. She picked up a slip of old parchment.

"My mother said the only people that could read it were Star Makers and those sworn to protect them," Kaelum said.

"This is for you," she showed the page to him. Kaelum didn't recognize the handwriting or the language. "From your father," she told him and his breathing stopped altogether. He felt as if all the life had been drained from him. Elarie put the page back and he thought *what are you doing you mad thing, read it!* But she shut the book. Elarie held it on her hip and touched his arm, her warm fingers shocking him into breathing again. "Let's go inside and sit."

Calix quickly took up the order. He said, "we can use the west parlor, it's right down the hall." Kaelum never liked the west parlor, it smelled musty no matter how many times it was cleaned, but he simply followed, not knowing what to do otherwise. He followed his prince and the only person that could read the book.

CHAPTER SIXTY-FOUR

KAELUM

The musty smell was still there in the west parlor, sticking to every old thing. Elarie seemed to smell it as well because she cringed when she entered and walked to a leather couch in the center of the room. There were two of the same kind that faced one another and a third chair that matched between them. They surrounded a low table with a few books and candles on it. Light shined through a large window that took up the expanse of the wall. They could see Grey sniffing the hole in the ground.

Kaelum walked around the couch. The room was smaller than he used to think a fancy prince's parlor would be, but it wasn't even the smallest room. There was a piano and a harp poised on a stand in the corner by the door. Art hung on each of the walls. He recognized one to be the work of Terry, the only new thing in the room.

"I called for tea," Calix said as he sat on the couch across from Elarie. Kaelum finally moved next to her. It was a musty room, but at least it was comfortable no matter how much the leather creaked.

Elarie set the book on the table and opened it carefully to the title page. She picked up the letter that was apparently in his father's handwriting in a language Kaelum never knew about. "He didn't date it so I can't be sure how old it is," Elarie told him, "but this is your name." She pointed to the first word. "I can teach you the language, it's not very complicated. I can also translate the book for you, but something like this wasn't meant to be translated—"

"Just read the note," Kaelum said tightly.

She took a deep, somehow sympathetic breath, and did as he asked. "'Kaelum,'" she read before the door opened and a servant pushed in a cart for tea. Kaelum had a rage boiling around his ears, making his hand ache. The servant, a young girl with red hair and a scarred hand, set the trays down quickly and curtseyed silently. She looked at Elarie for a moment but said nothing. When the servant left Elarie told him, "they all think I'm Calix's whore."

It made him laugh, clearing a bit of the tension he seemed to be collecting.

Elarie smiled at Calix, who was dutifully manning the tea with a smile on his face that told Kaelum he was trying not to blush.

"'Kaelum,'" she read again, "'my father did this and I was confused. He called it a just-in-case letter. Just in case he died before he could answer my questions. I'd hate to say I'm plagiarizing him,'" she paused. "He spelled that wrong," Elarie muttered and Calix chuckled softly. Kaelum swatted her knee. She turned, crossing her leg under her and facing him. "'However his rules always made sense to me so I'm sure they'll make sense to you. One, don't tell anyone you wouldn't let kill you if it gets too bad. I know that sounds morbid, but it needs to be said. Two, tell your husband or wife. Do not keep this from them, especially because it is always passed down.'"

Elarie leaned forward and picked up a delicate tea cup, setting it in Kaelum's hands. They'd been shaking before, this gave him something to hold. The hot tea burned his fingers.

"'Three, assume every Fae wants to kill you,'" her brows flicked up and down at that, as if it were obvious, "'and four only because my father wrote it so I should as well, if you ever come across one of these 'sworn protectors' of ours—' that's me," she whispered, motioning to herself with a soft smile, "'understand that they swore to protect you for a reason. Even if we're more powerful than they are we'd be dead without them.'"

She turned the page over. "Is that true?" Kaelum asked.

"That you need me? Yes. That you're more powerful than I am? Not anymore, but a long time ago. Well," she put the page in her lap and looked at him. Elarie assessed him. "Maybe. We'll have to mess with your magic to figure that out."

He nodded and swallowed. "Is that it?"

Elarie lifted the letter, "'if you're reading this and I'm next to you I hope we both get a laugh out of how morbid your grandfather was. I wish you'd met him, but he passed before you were born. Destroyed all his stars and swore that he'd haunt me if I never told your mother. But if you're reading this because I'm not there to share this book with you,'" she paused, a breath escaping her sharply. Elarie said, "'right now I am looking at you in your bassinet and all I can think of is how proud I already am of you.'"

Kaelum's eyes watered.

"'You are going to do great things if you remember that you are only as powerful as the control you have over yourself. I love you and if I go before you read this know it wasn't my choice. Don't tell your mother I said that,'" Elarie cracked a smile. "'But if I am gone tell her that the afterlife is nothing short of horrible without her but I'll wait as long as I have to if it means seeing her again. I love her more than every star in the sky. And you, my son,'" she reached out and held his wrist because his hands were occupied, "'you are my greatest creation. No star would ever amount to you.'"

She set the page down and Kaelum asked hoarsely, "so what's it like?" She looked at him, confused. "The afterlife, what's it like?"

Elarie shook her head slowly. "I've never been. When I die I see it and it's beautiful and bright and everything any person might want it to be, but," again, she shook her head, "I've never been. I'm pulled back into my body before I reach it."

"Even with the Fae? You were dead all day, how can you not reach it?"

She slowly removed her hand from his wrist and pulled it into her lap. With a look at Calix, he knew that his prince had already asked this question. He knew that answer like he knew all the other ones. Elarie said, "it's different."

"How?" He pressed.

"Normally," Elarie shifted uncomfortably, "I surface in water and see the afterlife. Sometimes it feels like I'm in the ocean, sometimes a lake, sometimes a hot spring, but it's always water. I see where I'm supposed to go but the gods pull me back into my body—"

Kaelum asked, "why?"

She just said, "because I'm not allowed to die," and moved on. "With the Fae it's different. It's a punishment for something I did a long time ago so when they kill me I go to the hill I was on when my family was killed. I stand there and I can't move," she swallowed painfully, "and I watch them die over and over until the faerthorne comes out."

Staring probably wasn't the best thing. He knew it wasn't. And yet he just stared and said, "but you were dead for hours."

"It would've been longer," Elarie said.

"What was the longest?"

Calix didn't seem to like these questions, he seemed just as uncomfortable as Elarie, but he remained silent. He didn't need to defend her and he knew it. If she didn't want to answer then she wouldn't.

"It's been years before," she said vaguely, then quickly turned away from him. Elarie cleared her throat and gently placed the letter back. "The book," she flipped to the first page, "is almost like a guide and a history book put together. There are a lot of these—or there were—and some of them will have entries from other Metars. Things they learned and warning and things of that nature."

Kaelum shifted forward on the couch and set the tea down. He looked at Calix. His lips were pressed into a thin line and he seemed to be trying to urge Kaelum into going back to the subject of his magic, not of Elarie's deaths. "So," he pushed the tea further onto the table. Kaelum looked at the book, "what does it say about you?"

She sighed and stood, going to the door. Masha trotted in and flung herself onto Calix's shoulders. Elarie shut the door again. "The people sworn to protect you, myself included," she faced him, "all have golden blood."

Kaelum swallowed nervously, glancing at the look on Calix's face. A curiosity that he wore so well, but also ease. He was at ease with her.

Elarie sat down. "It's not in your book because it's my history, not yours," she told him. Elarie's attention was on Kaelum, not Calix. She was speaking directly to him. It was comforting, yet somehow managed to be intimidating. "A long time ago my people and yours were peaceful. We were friends. My blood color didn't matter to the Metars and oftentimes Metars were in relationships with golden blooded people so you might have some in you as well."

He blinked a few times. She'd rushed the last part and probably regretted saying it. Kaelum looked at his veins like they'd spout gold.

"But we were hunted because of our blood the way you were hunted because of your magic only there was no ceremony, no stars to steal or magic to draw out, we were just killed," Elarie began pulling on her fingers nervously as if she was trying to find the right thing to say. Something that was honest but wouldn't implicate her or tell them what exactly she was.

Had they reverted back to before she trusted Calix? Hadn't she said she would've told him everything? And now she was thinking everything over and giving them half truths.

"Everyone was killed," she said.

Kaelum wanted to laugh suddenly. "What, and you're all that's left of them?"

"It's not funny," she snapped.

"No, it's not funny, it's ironic," he said. Her brow furrowed. "The only person that knows anything about me is also the only person alive that swore to protect Metars. It's ironic."

Elarie glanced at Calix.

"And not only that, but she doesn't trust any of us," he said.

Again, she glanced at Calix. Elarie returned to the book, flipping through pages absently. Kaelum couldn't tell if she was actually reading.

CHAPTER SIXTY-FIVE

She was doing her avoiding thing again. Elarie was leaning over the book and reading, her attention on the worn pages. "I already knew all of this, how uninteresting," she muttered eventually. Kaelum grew more annoyed by the second. She flipped to a random page and straightened slightly.

"What?" Kaelum scooted forward. Calix pulled Masha off his shoulders and set her in his lap, leaning forward. Masha purred when he scratched her chin. "What is it, is it something important?"

"My native language. I don't know why it's in here," she mumbled, her voice strained and faint. Elarie touched the page. "'Bon is dead. I fear Inaji is next. She did not heed my warning to stay clear of,'" her voice faded further, her eyes moving silently over the page. They shined with tears. Her breathing quickened and the room warmed. Kaelum shifted back a small amount, though he looked more concerned than frightened.

The tea in their untouched cups began to boil. The humidity in the room felt heavy, increasing as if it were summer. "Elarie?" Calix asked. Masha got off his lap and walked across the table toward her. She put one foot on the book and Elarie snatched it away, standing quickly. She backed away from everyone and turned the page, sobbing and flipping back to the side with her language. "Elarie, what's wrong?"

She ripped the page out of the book. Surprisingly, Kaelum didn't say anything. Elarie pressed the book into his chest and went for the door, yanking it open so hard it broke off. She didn't stop. She just ran.

"Go, Calix," Kaelum said, looking out the window. Calix ran after her, only steps behind. She could go faster than that, did she want to be caught?

"Elarie, Elarie," he grabbed her arm when they were outside. His skin burned but he refused to let go. "Talk to me, please tell me what happened." He stood in front of her. Tears poured down her face and steamed against her skin, simmering like splashed water on a pan. Calix reached up and wiped it away. His palms burned red. "What did it say? Tell me what it said Elarie, please."

Elarie choked back her tears, shaking more than a leaf about to fall from a tree. "He did it, he—" she sobbed. Both Masha and Grey came forward with the same soft, tentative step. "He's older than—he did it, Calix, he's been doing it."

"The man that killed the people in the letter," he began.

She gasped, "he killed my family, it's the same," Elarie coughed, her whole body hot. Calix nodded, pulling her toward him, and wrapped his arms around her. She crashed against his chest, the page crinkling between them. "It was the same person," she said in a much sharper voice. Elarie pulled back when Kaelum came out. "They thought he wanted the Metars but he wanted us the whole time, he only killed the Metars when they got in the way."

"Why would anyone hunt you?" Kaelum asked without any of Terry's fire. He was concerned. When did he get concerned for her? When she became useful to him? Or in the few days they'd been together on the ship up until this moment?

"Kill us and nature—" she stopped suddenly, golden blood dripping from her nose. Elarie touched it, but did nothing to stop the flow down to her lip. Her watery eyes turned to Calix. "It'll be fine, I promise," she told him.

Her knees buckled and her entire body went limp. Kaelum came forward, "did she just die?"

Calix lifted her into his arms just as Grey roared angrily, blowing fire into the air and onto the grass. He stomped it down and Calix imagined he was cursing as he did. Cursing something. Calix looked at Elarie, "what killed her?" He asked and watched blood roll down the side of her face. "Shit I need to get her inside," he looked around as if a tissue would just appear in front of him.

It was Kaelum who tucked the book under his arm and pulled his other sleeve down over his hand. He wiped the gold off Elarie's face and pushed her head to face Calix's chest. "You know I don't agree with Terry," he said when he stepped back. "I told him I did, but I don't think Elarie was the reason everyone died. I think a lot more of us would probably be dead without her. Maybe all of us."

Calix let the words settle in his chest. "You should tell Elarie that," he said.

But Kaelum shook his head with a frown. "I better see if Terry vomited all over himself," he took a step back, then forward quickly to snatch the page off the ground. He looked at it, first at the language Elarie knew as her own, then the back. He put it in Elarie's lap looking completely lost for a moment. "I'll come back tomorrow."

"Come back tonight," Calix suggested, "maybe she can teach you about stars without getting distracted if they're above you."

He laughed, "she does get distracted a lot, doesn't she?" Kaelum looked to the sky. "Sure, I'll be back tonight."

Calix turned to Grey. "I'm going to take her to her bedroom up there," he jerked his head to the room right next to Calix's bedroom, "and I'll open the window so you can see inside, all right?" Grey sort of nodded, so he backed up, "all right. Come on, Masha."

He started inside, going down the hall. He jogged to the second set of doors and pushed them open, immediately met with people. Ladies were walking down the second hall speaking softly to each other. There were three of them, each Calix recognized as ones that lived in the castle. They knew him. They would say hello to him. He needed to get past them.

"Masha," he hissed and the dragon bounded forward happily as if she knew exactly what Calix wanted. He rushed forward while Masha made loud noises to either scare or enthrall the ladies.

It only partially worked. Calix had gotten past them, but Enid, daughter of one of the richest lords in the kingdom that was one of Calix's most 'valuable' options for marriage according to his father, turned around. "Your Highness," she said in a sharp, shocked voice. "Who are you carrying?"

"This is Elarie," he turned slightly hoping Elarie didn't look dead from the distance they were at. "She hit her head."

"Elarie… your whore?" Enid almost sounded hopeful. She should. Calix only having a whore meant he was still open for marriage. His mother once said that ladies' claws were sharper than Grey's when they wanted something and nothing was a greater want than a crown. Elarie blocked their opportunity for it.

Calix said, "Elarie, the love of my life. Good day!" He jogged slightly and Masha ran to his side, her long tail wagging.

Chapter Sixty-Six

Elarie

The house of the gods was made of river stones and mud that would never dry. It resembled a grey pyramid. Six windows on the bottom level, then five and four and so on until the very top. A bright light shined to a blinding degree. Any time Elarie tried to ask what it was the words died on her tongue and she never dared walk the steps to find out herself.

Twice she'd refused to walk into the house. A god never met her outside, they were just as stubborn as she was—if not more. Instead, they brought her back to her life with some form of punishment. Once it had been the removal of all of her hair, the other time had been starvation. She'd woken up skin and bone, aching everywhere for every step.

Elarie did not look into the mist hiding other houses on either side of her. She did not look up at the grey sky. She did not wish to see what was truly hidden around her. She just walked up the uneven river stone path, stepping carefully up the two hollow stairs. The deck was mud with nothing decorating it. It squelched under her shoes. She reached for the brass door handle. The round handle was smooth as if it had been touched by many hands. How many people did the gods call to their house?

She pushed the heavy door open. The hall in front of her was made of wood boards. A constant breeze brushed her cheeks and the smell of a dead thing wafted with it. Elarie shut herself in the house and went to the first door. Locked. Second door, locked. She went from one to the other looking for the god that called on her. Each of the doors represented one of them, though nothing in them was ever pleasant. Elarie had known no god was kind early on. Her people never worshiped them and for a long time, she didn't think they were real.

Now each door held something horrible and the more stairs she climbed the worse it got.

Elarie reached the second floor, the stairs twisting and the smell growing worse. The floor creaked under her and echoed in the empty house. She stepped onto a faded carpet that ran from one side of the path to the other, sinking into it, and walked to the first door. Then the second. Then the third.

Everything was a maze and she hated it. Elarie could go one direction and think it was the right one only to turn around and find herself in a completely different place. She knew better than to call out. Too many things answered back.

Elarie twisted a golden door handle and the door clicked open. A slick black rope wrapped around her middle and jerked her into complete darkness, slamming the door shut.

"No magic here," a twisted, strained voice said.

"Parind," Elarie breathed slowly as she tried to pull the rope off, "what do you want?" Parind was one of the younger gods, he thought he had a sense of humor. Each god added to the creation of the things roaming the land, whether it be to the monsters or otherwise. Parind provided little more than cunning and deceit to the humans when he could've given more. He was hardly worshiped.

His hands brushed over her back and up to her shoulders. Thick black oil dripped over her. "Someone wished to speak to you," he said, chuckling madly, "you opened the wrong door."

"What?" She twisted, "why would you—" Elarie gagged, her hand flying to her mouth. Parind giggled as oil spilled from her lips. None of it was real and Elarie knew that, but she felt everything like it was. She fell to her knees and vomited. Blackness dripped from her mouth as Elarie crawled back to the door. All the while Parind laughed. She fumbled for the handle and yanked the door open, gasping and coughing against the red carpet.

The door was closed behind her.

Elarie wiped her hands on her pants and spit a few times, gagging at the taste. She got to her knees and slowed her breathing. Why were there so many doors?

I hate the gods, Elarie thought and the house shuddered as it did every time the words graced the forefront of her mind. She stood and walked along the wall trying doorknob after doorknob. When this failed, she went to the third floor. The one that would have four windows, and yet there were eight doors and not a single one opened.

She groaned and went up again.

The first door she tried swung open before she could get her hand around it. Elarie looked into the bright room. The window behind the desk of the god that resided in the room showed a winter forest beyond it. A blizzard blew through the woods and a tree cracked with the force of the wind. "I called for you," said the god. He had his back to her, the high seat covering all of him. Elarie took a step. He was a god of many faces, Elarie did not know what was the true one, nor did she know his name the way she did many others.

Once he showed himself in the form of Cammie. Another time her mother. The voice was always the same, however, because gods could not mimic them.

Elarie shut the door. It was a long room and seemed perfectly symmetrical, though it wasn't and that drove Elarie mad each time she came to the god. Everything was the same along the walls on both sides. Bookshelves, tables with mirrors over them. Only if there was an object on the tables the one on the other side of the room would be turned around or on its side. Books weren't in the same place when they were front facing.

And everything—everything—was just slightly off on both sides. Elarie could always see it through the mirrors.

She sat in a tall backed chair careful not to touch the arms of it. The chair liked Elarie. It wanted to keep Elarie. It dug its claws into Elarie's arms and pulled her back like it could have her forever.

"What is it?" Elarie asked, still squeamish.

The chair turned around and the face of Calix smiled at her. It wasn't exactly him just as the room wasn't exactly symmetrical. There was always something different. Here, this Calix had no Lathin eyes. "You've been busy," the deep, unnerving voice said. It itched down her spine. "Making friends with a Metar and a prince," he set a book on the desk, "finding a dragon."

"I—"

"Would you kill him?"

Elarie swallowed. "Kill who?"

"The prince," he motioned to his face and sat back. One leg crossed over the other under the desk. "Would you kill him?"

She hesitated. This wasn't something she should've been speaking to a god about. While they couldn't influence what was happening in the world, it didn't mean this god would not attempt to shift her feelings or opinions to what he wished to see out of his window. "I don't know," Elarie admitted. Tea appeared on the desk in black cups and a black pot. "Is that why I'm here?"

"Do you love him?" He asked, pouring the tea. Again, she hesitated. The room grew colder and she shifted, forcing her skin to warm. "Because he does. Look," he moved the chair and the window changed from the winter setting to a hallway. Calix was holding Elarie's body, which meant it was recent. He was stepping back nervously, attempting to keep a calm smile on his face.

"Elarie... your whore?" Asked a female voice. Elarie couldn't see who it came from. She very clearly heard and saw Calix say, "Elarie, the love of my life," in response before the window returned to the cold winter blizzard.

Elarie's mouth fell open. He must've been exaggerating. Wasn't it just days ago he was telling her was *going* to fall in love with her? They hardly knew each other. And with her blood he should have no desire— "He thinks you are mates," the god said plainly, spooning sugar into tea. "Isn't that adorable?"

"W..." she breathed. He set the cup in front of her. "Why am I here?"

"Are you going to kill him?" The god repeated. "Your 'mate' as he thinks himself to be. Are you going to kill him?"

"I would like to wake up now," she said faintly and started to stand. An invisible force knocked her back and a golden cord wrapped around her torso, tying her back against the chair that hummed pleasantly against her spine. "Why am I here?" Elarie gasped, "drama? Is that all?"

He sipped his tea. "The direction your life is headed is quite interesting. Our little princess could become queen at the rate you're getting this boy to fall in love with you."

"I am not doing—" he gagged her, evidently preparing for a monologue. Elarie groaned.

"But this *monster* you've invented in your head," he leaned forward, lacing his hands together and resting them on the table. Calix's face twisted into a smile, "your little element family's killer. Do nothing about him. He is mine, do you understand?" She glared at him. "You will not go looking."

Of course she wouldn't. Why would she? Elarie had spent lifetimes running from him, hearing about his connection to the Metars was not going to change her mind about it.

"Do you understand?" He stood, his body much thinner than the one she knew to be Calix. Taller as well. He leaned over the table, waiting for her to nod. Such an easy instruction from a god that was usually so much more cruel. Elarie nodded. "Now, princess," he said, "are you going to kill your prince?"

He wanted a yes or a no answer. Elarie had neither to give to him.

"Do you need more time to choose?" He pouted. Still, she nodded. "And tell me," he said with the same faux sadness and the same pout, "is he your mate?" Elarie shook her head. The gag and the cords disappeared at once. Elarie stood quickly and avoided the chair before running to the door. "Do not forget what I have told you, Elarie, or there will be consequences."

She left the god wearing Calix's face and ran down the hall and stairs, leaving the house that seemed to want to cave in and crush her.

As soon as the door snapped shut behind her Elarie tripped on the mud stars and found herself in crystal clear water before she could fall. She swam up and gasped, the afterlife glistening perfectly for her, calling her to finally rest and singing a peaceful song, but a cruel grip pulled her back into the ocean and back into her body.

CHAPTER SIXTY-SEVEN

ELARIE

"Elarie," Calix gasped and she opened her eyes. He was smiling, so happy she woke up like he thought it would never happen. It was dark in the room, so Elarie could see why he might've thought that. "What happened? Why did you die? Are you all r—"

"Are you in love with me?" Elarie asked and his eyes widened. She sat up slowly, looking at her front like the oil would be there. Elarie was in her own bed, one covered in lilac sheets and surrounded by sheer curtains that Elarie had pinned back almost immediately. Flowers had been carved into the bedposts and headboard, turning the room into something Elarie had found to be fit for both a princess and a prince's *guest*, as she had been called in a judgmental tone.

Calix said, "I can... I can not be. If you don't want me to be I'll stop."

That couldn't be possible. Elarie shook her head. She shifted over and pushed the blanket down. "Lay with me," Elarie pulled on his hand. Calix seemed far more apprehensive than he usually was, but he got onto the bed. The leg and his shoe was already off, as were hers, so he slid next to her.

"I told Kaelum you'd tell him about stars tonight," he said as she folded herself against him. Elarie was partially on his chest and his hand was on her back. It wasn't like at the cavern, which had been stiff and well-lit and full of dragons. In her bedroom, there was only one dragon and she was asleep. "I said you wouldn't be distracted."

Elarie closed her eyes. "Do you believe there are good gods, Calix?" She asked, dragging her finger over the fabric of his shirt.

"Sure," he nodded. Calix rubbed her back, "there has to be, right?"

"If I told you there weren't any would you believe me?" She turned her head and shifted upward. Elarie leaned on him, searching his face for his answer.

He said, "I'd probably believe anything you tell me."

She looked at his lips. "There are no good gods anymore," she said softly, "they're all dead. The last good god gave her magic to the Metars and ever since the world has been watched over by cruel and malicious beings that fashioned both golden blooded monsters and humans to be just like them."

Calix breathed in deeply, making her rise and fall on his chest. "I believe you," he said with a nod. "Humans can be monsters, that makes sense."

"I see one more than I see the others. He has no name, he wears the faces of people I know to taunt me. Even you," she reached forward and touched his cheek. "The only influence gods have on this world is creation. They can do nothing unless they create something and they can only create something once. It's why I'm so important and it's why this god told me I'm not allowed to look for the man that killed my family."

"Because he created him and he won't be able to create him again?" Calix asked. Elarie nodded and he asked, "why would you go after him? Do you want to?" His hand slowed, the lovely Lathin eyes brimming with concern.

She said, "I don't ever want to be anywhere near him again," and they settled into silence. Elarie didn't like it. She didn't want Calix to be silent. "They watch the world through the windows of an ugly house," Elarie told him to fill it and await his response, "and they can see the past, present, and depending on the god even the future. I was shown you telling ladies I am the love of your life."

Calix seemed a little afraid again. "Maybe just a little bit," he whispered.

"Does it bother you that I don't feel that way?"

He swallowed, making a nervous groaning noise in the back of his throat. Calix reached up and tucked her stray hair behind her ear. Elarie had considered cutting it off her head a few times throughout the day, having no desire to take down the braid and make him do it all over again just to add in one small bit, but to have him tuck it away like that seemed worth the trouble. "No, it doesn't," he said, "it's all part of the plan."

Elarie laughed softly. She came to the conclusion that he most definitely did not have a plan, but it was adorable when he said he did. Calix had been making things up as he went along from the very beginning. This only proved it. "I'm going to kiss you now," she whispered. He nodded. "This doesn't change the way I feel," she added.

"I'm not the kind of person that assumes all is forgiven after one kiss," he told her. Calix ran his thumb over the shell of her ear and down to her jaw, "and I am never going to demand you forgive me or assume you forgive me or any of that until you tell me explicitly."

Yes, Elarie thought, *he is perfect for me.*

She hated it about him because it made it difficult *not* to forgive. The part of her mind that longed for his attention and love was doing everything possible to convince her whole body that he was just afraid. That scared humans do and say things they don't mean and Elarie should forgive him because he took it back and regretted it instantly. The damaged side of herself would say that if he did care he would've let her speak. He would've let her explain. No matter how afraid he was, if Calix loved her he would have allowed a moment for an actual conversation. He would not have snapped that she was a liar and looked at her like she was a monster.

Calix lifted his head from the pillows and Elarie shut the arguing parts of her mind off to focus on one thing. His lips were soft. He'd bathed while she was dead. His skin felt smooth. He'd shaved as well. Elarie kissed him slowly, now able to settle a curious thought in her mind.

What would a prince, future king and ruler of millions, do if a girl was on top of him telling him what to do? The thought had graced her mind in the cavern when Elarie wasn't strong enough to hold herself up and take control so Calix was the one over her. He'd been good at leading, which only made her wonder if he was good at following as well.

She lifted her leg over his waist and he groaned breathily. Elarie smiled and pulled him up to a seated position, shifting back and making him groan again. She asked, "if I have sex with you right now what will you do?"

"Die," was his immediate answer, though he seemed confused by it, as if that word was not supposed to leave his lips. "Not die," he said. "Have you ever done that?"

"Died while having sex with someone or have I ever killed someone while having sex?" She asked. His mouth opened. "Neither," Elarie said and pulled his head toward hers. Calix grasped her hips, his fingers pinching into her body. They would leave marks on her skin as he dragged them up into her shirt. "So what would you do?" She breathed in deeply, eyes closed as his lips caressed her neck, "if I had sex with you right now?"

His mouth stayed on her throat. Calix said, "whatever you told me to."

Too bad, Elarie thought. She might've gone through with it just to see what that really meant. Calix presented himself as a confident prince, his people called him the Prince with a Dragon. He held the room's attention like he knew how to keep it and was smart enough to do just that. What would that sort of person do if he wasn't in control? If she told him to put his hands above his head and not touch her? If she told him to only touch once and to make it count? If she told him to be silent?

His hands were on her bare waist itching to go higher, but he was waiting for her permission. Calix pressed his fingers into her, shaking slightly as Elarie stared at the wall behind her bed. She sighed and said, "Kaelum is in your bedroom."

"What?" Calix turned his head, one hand leaving her to be used for balance as if he'd be able to see through the wall, "how do you know?"

"I am magic," she said with a smile, kissing him again and again as she climbed off his lap and padded over the stone floor to the rug in front of the fireplace, then walked onto stone again once she entered the bathing room. Elarie shut the door and placed her hand on the wall, the other over her heart.

CHAPTER SIXTY-EIGHT

KAELUM

Elarie opened her bedroom door and Gee, who had ridden on Kaelum's shoulder because they were both looking for Elarie, jumped onto her head and started chirping. Kaelum couldn't tell if he was upset with her, but he watched Elarie raise her brows and look up as if she'd be able to see him stomping around and ranting.

Kaelum looked at Calix, leaning in the doorway as Elarie walked away. He crossed his arms. The prince was snapping his leg back on, leaning against the rumpled sheets. "Terry is outside," Kaelum told both of them. Calix was the one that tensed. "He isn't going to apologize."

"Does he think I will?" Calix asked as he stood and let his pant leg fall over the prosthetic.

"He wants it," he replied, then looked at Elarie. A tray had been placed on the desk under one of the two windows in the room. On it was one of their dinners, mostly eaten. Elarie was finishing off the chicken. "Why did you die?" He asked her.

She popped what looked like a brussel sprout into her mouth. "A god wanted to tell me what to do," she answered with her food in her cheek. "It wasn't fun and I will not be telling you about it, move on in your questioning."

Kaelum smiled. He was glad Terry wasn't with him to hear that. "All right," he said, "will you come outside and help me with my magic?"

"I am so hungry," she muttered.

"Does dying do that?"

Elarie said, "sometimes, it really just depends. Like when I was gutted this one time," she moved her finger over her stomach to show where the cut must've been, "and all my insides came out. When I died I had to regrow everything and I woke up famished."

"You weren't gutted this time," Kaelum informed her.

She looked at him. "No, but is a woman not allowed to be hungry without an explicit reason for it?" A brow raised up on her head. Gee, still standing there, crossed his arms and looked at him. Calix just had a smile on his face as he messed with his sleeves and pulled on his jacket.

Kaelum cleared his throat, "no she doesn't need a reason—I was just curious, that's all. By all means, eat."

That seemed to satisfy her, though she didn't continue eating. She wiped her fingers on the napkin Calix must have used and whistled softly. Masha seemed to have been waiting for it. She jumped into her arms and slinked around Elarie's neck like a scarf. The long, thin tail wrapped around her waist and pressed her shirt tightly against her body.

"Elarie, can I ask you something?" Kaelum straightened. Gee jumped off before she left the room, forcing both Kaelum and Calix to follow her. "About your blood—"

She stopped so quickly that he almost ran into her. Elarie turned around slowly. The hall was lit by sconces on the wall, but otherwise it was full of dark edges. There weren't any around her. Elarie was bright and easy to see, as if she was a star and he just carried the name. "Never ask me about that when people can hear you," she warned.

Kaelum nodded and she kept moving, faster than before. He looked at Calix. "There's always someone listening," the prince said, "and when one person hears it, everyone hears it." They began to walk again and he added, "how do you think my father found out about the raccoon we snuck into my bedroom?"

"Didn't it scream?"

"No, that was me, remember?"

Kaelum snorted, transferring his hand to his pocket. He ran his fingers over the star as they passed people in the halls and on the stairs that Elarie might've been afraid of, but Calix was friendly with. He knew a few of their names and recognized them even in the dark. Calix had a lightness to him as they walked down the glass hallway, something Kaelum didn't think had to do with his servants. Something in his walk.

They stepped out into the cold night. Terry stood with a torch in one hand, the book propped in the crook of his elbow while Elarie was speaking to Grey in the dragon language only she could understand.

"Did she tell you what that page said?" Kaelum asked Calix, watching her lay against Grey. Small sparks traveled over his scales.

"No," Calix shook his head, "and I don't feel comfortable sharing with you what she shared with me. Please understand that."

Kaelum sighed and rubbed his temple. They reached Terry, whose demeanor remained guarded around both Elarie and Calix. He stood at the mouth of the hole Elarie had dug, his grip tight on the torch and his protective arm firm around the book. Kaelum wasn't sure if even *he* wanted to take it from him. Kaelum touched his elbow and smiled, the flames warm against his face. Terry only partially returned it and as small as it was, the smile faded when Elarie walked over to them.

"What was your question?" She rubbed her hands together and caused the fire to flicker with her nerves.

"You'll answer it?" Kaelum asked.

Elarie said, "I'm trying to be nice."

He glanced at Calix. His prince was curious, but he wouldn't ask Elarie anything. He believed in her answers coming in due time. Terry did not. Terry wanted to demand answers from Elarie. What did Kaelum want? Not to wait for them to come out over tea, but he didn't want to make an enemy of her the way Terry slowly was.

"Is your blood really gold?" He asked, "as in... liquid gold?"

"Would you like to sell it?" Elarie asked tightly.

He shook his head, "no, I'd just like to know how it works. How you work."

"How I work," she repeated softly. "The same way you do. I am a person, I have the same bodily functions as you and my insides look like your insides. I just come back after I die and you don't."

"Why do you look the same as us?" Terry asked, "even the Fae look different."

He was right, of course. Most of them had at least somewhat pointed ears and sharpened teeth. They all had a more animalistic look to them, each of them strong and powerful even without the magic they so coveted. Elarie looked like a human, she hardly passed for a Fae if not because of the way she held herself. Even now, with her nervous tick of pulling on her fingers, she still stood the way a Fae would. Confident and sure. Strong. Elarie was each of those things. Her otherworldly wisdom and the bright look in her eyes only added to it.

"My species was created to look like humans so that nature would mistake us for them and stop killing you," she answered with a hint of trepidation. Elarie's eyes darted between the three of them. They remained on Calix specifically. This was what she wanted to tell him when he refused to let her speak.

Terry asked, "what? Nature never wanted to kill us."

"What do you think natural disasters were created for?" Elarie countered as if that had any merit. Natural disasters were *natural*, they weren't created for anything. "Why would nature destroy itself if not for a purpose?" They stared at her, even Calix, and she grew impatient. "Shall I map it out for you?" She rolled her eyes and a map did in fact appear before them. It glowed a foot above the ground like the coals under the fire. There was the continent with its four countries. The mountains and rivers were drawn out and circles hovered over the major cities. Lyburn included. "When was the last time you heard of a natural disaster striking the Faerie Lands?"

"We don't record that," Calix said.

"You should, that's quite stupid of you not to," she told him, then answered her own question, "never. Nature never attacks the Faerie Lands because that is where its creations live. And the Fae? Fae territories only ever see the edges of things like hurricanes. Strong winds, heavy rain, but no one ever dies. And then you have Polinae."

The large island was drawn in front of Terry. Terry stepped to the side like it would burn, but he tilted his head and watched, paying as much attention as anyone. "The volcanoes?" He asked.

"They regularly erupt, don't they? And how often does a tornado hit Duness' valley?" She pointed to the space very few people lived. Duness was a large country, the biggest of the four, and yet people steered clear of the valley. Hardly anything grew in its center and anything that might would get ripped up by a tornado. "Trec gets hurricanes and Ceptari gets earthquakes, yes?"

"But it's all natural," Calix argued, "we can calculate a pattern between the attacks, it's science—"

"Darling, what does 'natural' mean?" She asked. His mouth closed abruptly, Kaelum couldn't tell if it was because of her sound contradiction or the *darling*. Both, if he knew Calix. "Now look at all of that and picture it far, far worse. The story of humans is not kind to nature."

"The gods created us and gave us the tools to build our societies and our temples," Calix said as if reciting it from his studies. Perhaps Elarie would test him like a tutor. "We were their last creation."

The little fire map disappeared and she said, "I forget how biased history is."

"So enlighten me," Calix said playfully, "prove my bias wrong."

They were flirting over history. How strange. Kaelum cleared his throat and took the book gently from Terry. He seemed to struggle to hand it over. Perhaps he felt his only purpose was holding it. "Does it say anything in here about *my* creation?" Kaelum asked, holding it out.

"You were created after humans," Elarie took it, "but before me. Nature saw humans and how the gods had given them so much magic only for them to abuse it and abuse what was around them that it beseeched the gods. One in particular." She flipped through the book, the old pages crinkling under her fingers. "The gods are evil, don't let yourself believe otherwise. The last good god was Metarina." She flipped the book around to a drawing they squinted at. Elarie then clicked her tongue and Terry's torch went out. Terry was about to say something, but stopped short when the lines of the drawing began to shine like the stars above them.

"I've never heard of Metarina," Calix said faintly, the soft white light washing out his features.

"She was killed," Elarie told him. She said, "nature didn't want the Fae to have magic, it liked the feeling of being molded, of worn hands using its resources and thanking it properly. The humans didn't do that, the gods ensured that they only worship them. Nature was left out. The humans abused nature and thanked the gods for their bounties."

Kaelum said, "so nature asked Metarina for magic?" He gazed at the drawing. It was of her profile. The eye was open and full, as if the god had no iris or pupil, only light. She had a large nose and full lips. Her chin was soft and her neck large. Beautiful hair flowed like water around her.

"Metarina did not participate in the creation of the golden blooded monsters or the humans. They were too cruel, they did not deserve her magic. She grew tired as time went on, so when nature asked for more she willingly gave it. Metarina poured all of her power into the creation of a new species of Fae, one unlike anything ever seen before. She gave everything. When the gods found out, they killed her. Her body is what created the Barrier that separates us from the Forgotten Lands."

"Why didn't the gods kill the Metars?" Terry asked, "wouldn't they find them offensive in some way?"

"The gods can only influence our world by creating something. They created a rumor," she turned the book back to her, "that the

Metars hold magic. They gave the Fae specifically the secrets to taking it."

Kaelum asked, "a ritual like yours?"

"No, mine is different," she said faintly, closing the book. "Mine is a punishment for something I did, yours is a punishment for what a god did."

Calix asked, "what kind of magic does Kaelum have, then? What exactly did Metarina give him?"

"Kaelum was gifted the power of creation," she said just a little proudly, looking at Kaelum as she said it. "Given time and practice he could create nearly anything and nature would be pleased with whatever it is."

"Like dragons?" Calix asked. He was trying to make connections to things Kaelum didn't quite understand yet.

Still, he asked, "can I make a dragon?" And pulled out his star.

"No," she shook her head.

"Can you?" Terry asked.

Grey growled behind her. The dragon stretched his wings, flapping them once and creating a strong wind that blew Elarie's little strand of hair over her face, though no other part of her moved even when Calix had to fix his steps before stumbling. "No," Elarie said.

"So the answer is yes, Grey just doesn't want you to tell us that," Terry concluded as the dragon walked away. He crawled down the cliffside, his long tail snaking after him, flicking impatiently.

"He's just going to see what part of the nest he'd like to lay his eggs in and tell me what he needs done before that," Elarie said. "Dragons don't like the gods, that's why he's agitated. It has nothing to do with my ability to create."

"Why can't I make a dragon?" Kaelum asked, "shouldn't I be able to create anything?"

A small smile brushed her lips they could see in the dark. Kaelum's eyes had adjusted easily. He could see Elarie's smile and the way she moved her foot, rocking it from side to side. "Because you cannot create elements."

"Why not?"

"Elements are nature," she said, "you need elements to make a dragon."

He nodded and looked at the star. Kaelum turned it over. "How do you know all this?" He asked next, "did you have some kind of book like that one?"

"I had to study you growing up," she said with a shrug, "and I knew a Metar years ago." She ran her fingers over the spine of the book before handing it to Kaelum. "She was a good friend."

Kaelum looked at the book, finding a shine over the stamped cover. "Did she die?" His mind went to his father. A Metar that died, that left him a book he didn't understand. Maybe it was the same for the girl Elarie was talking about.

"She found out what I was and killed me," Elarie held her wrist, her arms hanging in front of her. "Blew a hole in my chest with the magic I taught her how to use."

That would be why she didn't trust any of them fully. But she was *trying* for Calix because she cared about him. Even after he didn't accept her on the ship, she was trying for him. Kaelum looked between the two of them. They weren't standing close, but they still seemed like they should fit together. The only thing missing was the trust Calix lost when he didn't say what she wanted.

"How old are you?" Terry asked in an impatient tone. He was still holding the torch despite the lack of light or even warmth coming off it.

"Twenty," she said shortly, then looked at Kaelum, "shall we get started?"

Kaelum didn't want to look at Terry as he nodded.

CHAPTER SIXTY-NINE

He forgot to invite her. He told his mother he would, and yet he forgot. What kind of idiot was he? Calix knocked on Elarie's door harder than necessary, bouncing slightly. He was already late and of course he *forgot to invite Elarie to family breakfast*. It was the last breakfast he'd eat in Lyburn because he'd be leaving that afternoon. Everything was already packed, he'd remembered everything but asking Elarie to eat breakfast with his family.

She opened the door, her hair disheveled and her shoulders slumped. Elarie perked slightly at the sight of Calix and said, "good morning."

"Will you have breakfast with me?"

Elarie opened the door wider showing her bedroom. Light spilled inside, the smell of the ocean floating from the open windows. "I've already started, but you're welcome to join—"

"Damnit," he breathed as he entered. Elarie had eaten half of her plate already. He turned toward her, "I was supposed to invite you to have breakfast with my family this morning."

She rubbed her eye with a frown as the door closed behind her. Elarie walked toward him gracelessly, the picture of fatigue, and pressed her face to his shoulder. "How could you forget that?" She asked into his jacket, heating a circle of skin and cloth. Elarie groaned and faced him. Calix was desperate and trying not to beg, he was sure she could see it given the smile growing on her face. "All right, I'll eat with your family," she said.

Calix beamed and went to the closet. It was in the same spot as his and was easy to navigate before he stopped short. Calix looked out at Elarie, who was drinking water and swishing it around her mouth. Elarie walked into the bathing chamber completely indifferent. "Is it all right if I select a dress?" Calix asked through the wall.

"I will not wear red," she called back.

His brow furrowed. She had a few red dresses hanging. In the last two days, the seamstresses had made six dresses for her, all of nearly the same style. They'd filled a drawer with pants and shirts as well. Two different boots had been found and shoes to match the dresses were lined up in their respective places. "Why don't you want to wear red?" Calix asked as he pulled down a dusty blue dress. The color reminded him of a time when he and Ryd were looking for colors. It had been an activity Ryd created where he wished to go outside and match the colors of the world with his pencils. It had been quite fun when he gave Calix a page to draw as well. They'd played until dusk, which had turned the world to the shade of blue on the dress. Some grey, some blue. The soft spoken Ryd that couldn't spell really anything had told him the color was 'goodbye sunset.'

Elarie appeared with her face clean and damp like she'd washed it. Her hair had been brushed and she'd braided a few pieces to pin in the back. "Your seamstresses are looking to spark drama," she told him, "apparently red is a whore color. Every woman," Elarie took the dress, "in this building wants me to be your whore."

"Perhaps we should spread different rumors, then," he suggested as she turned to the wall of shoes. Elarie took off the loose night shirt and tossed it into a bin, gathering the skirt of the dress to fit it over her head. Calix touched her tattoo with his thumb saying, "this is healing nicely." The cut Red had made was little more than a scab now. "I thought it would scar more."

"I am not human," she replied and slipped the dress over her head. "Shit," she then said, "will you undo the buttons?"

Calix chuckled and unclipped the back of the dress. They were late and he should be rushing, yet he found this far too enjoyable to move quickly. Calix helped her get into the dress, buttoning the last clasps for her and adjusting the skirt, and began to think that this was the sort of thing he wouldn't mind doing forever.

Elarie took the satin sleep pants off and added them to the bin, then picked a heel that matched before leaving. She got the shoes on and looked in the mirror with a frown.

"What is it?" Calix walked toward her. *Please don't let it be the dress,* he thought as he gazed at her. Calix leaned against the wall by the large ovular mirror and crossed his arms. The color looked amazing on her, the fit was excellent. The dress went to her ankles, showing off the shoes. It wasn't a layered skirt so it fell smoothly down her long legs with little in the way of design or any sort of pattern. Marcella would call the skirt plain, if anything else. The bodice was similar, though he could see the lightest brush of swirls on her sides. The neckline covered her shoulders and cut down in a sharp 'V' shape. It wasn't scandalous in any way, but it plunged more than something he'd see a lady wear.

"I am too thin," Elarie decided. She smoothed down the long sleeves, then the front of the dress.

Calix said, "eat at your leisure," and got off the wall. He held his arm out for her and she chuckled, lacing her arm through his. "What did Gee want last night?" He asked as they exited her room. Calix led her down the wide, bright hall and to the staircase he once slid down on a knight's shield. He'd lost a tooth and broken his nose when he slammed into the wall.

"To tell me of his newest conquest," she said.

"What happened to the earth one?"

She sighed, "it wasn't meant to be." Elarie laughed a little and continued, "Gee has set his sights on a Firelight Frei, apparently this one has 'steamed him up' a few times, he's curious to know if it will go farther."

Calix paused so they both stood awkwardly on a step. "What does 'steamed him up' mean?"

"What does fire do to water when they get close?" Elarie countered.

"Steams," he answered.

She nodded, "and what is one reason for two Freis of their respective elements to get that close?"

He shook his head with a mystified frown, "no idea. Perhaps an example?" Elarie laughed and shook her head, pulling on his hand to get him to continue down the stairs. Calix groaned jokingly and followed her. They headed to where his mother enjoyed hosting her tea parties when it was warm. Only now the wind cut with a chill, so a four postered tent had been pitched. Three sides of the white fabric had been closed, the last one remaining open so Calix and Elarie could enter. It was a table meant to seat six. On it were many different plates of breakfast items, the favorites for either member of the family. Calix could see plantain arepas already stacked like a tower on Marcella's plate, a bowl of syrup for dipping directly to its left. His father, with his standard twelve eggs scrambled with pork fat and a cup of the rich, expensive coffee he loved so much. Mother, halfway through fried eggs over charred tomatoes.

And of course, little Ryd. Shrimp for breakfast, lunch, and dinner if he had a choice. He liked to spear through them with a two pronged fork he called his trident. Now though, he was climbing off his chair with a drawing in his hand and running around the table to Elarie.

"Hello, Ryd," she said with a smile, squatting to move to the same level as him, "what have you drawn now?" He showed her proudly. It was a water dragon of some kind, though Calix could only tell because of the blue wave lines above it. Elarie, though, grew increasingly interested in it. "How did you do this?" She asked him, "no human has ever documented this dragon, did you dream it?"

Ryd nodded.

"This is absolutely wonderful," she told him sweetly. Calix caught the looks on both of his parents' faces. Ryd never took well to strangers. It took a year before he showed Terry a single drawing, which meant a great deal. Now there was Elarie, speaking to him like she understood him. Queen Veinn had a hand over her heart and King Ritan smiled fondly. No one other than family ever received a *fond* smile. "When you dreamed it were you riding it?" He shook his head. "Watching?" He nodded.

Calix touched her shoulder and leaned toward her, "we should sit down."

Their mother called Ryd back and Elarie stood, showing Calix the drawing she was now holding, "this species of dragon went extinct two hundred years ago. The most you'll find of them is skeletons," he pushed on her lower back and she began walking where he intended. "I wonder if he's just seeing them," she said as she sat down in the chair next to Marcella. The princess was cutting an arepa in lines, hardly paying them any attention at all. Calix pushed Elarie's chair in.

"I see why you like her," his father chuckled. Elarie looked up and blushed brightly. Calix sat at the second head of the table, using tongs to grab two arepas before his sister could take them all. "An affinity for dragons, eh?" He addressed Elarie, who set the drawing on the warm table.

"Yes, I adore them," she nodded. Calix set arepas on her plate and she reached for the green avocado and jalapeño sauce, spooning only a bit next to the food. Calix took it from her next. "Dragons are a gift to the world."

He chuckled, "certainly a gift to my sons."

"Absolutely," Calix stood and grabbed the coffee, pouring it into two cups with heaps of sugar. He spooned eggs and sausage onto their plates, then a plain fried plantain. Elarie said nothing about him piling her plate even when he caught a smile on her lips. "Elarie is the reason I have Masha," he said.

Ryd laughed at Masha's name, discarding his trident-speared shrimp to flip through his pages. He'd discarded the book, now the table was piled with drawings held down by rocks.

"I still haven't met Masha," Marcella frowned, dunking her arepa in the syrup. She stuffed the slice into her mouth, still frowning.

"Darling, I'm sure Masha will introduce herself in her own time," Vienn said gently. She then added, "oh, Calix you should find a way to add her to your museum the way you feature Grey! Wouldn't that be lovely?"

Elarie looked at him as she raised her fork and mouthed the word *museum?* while Calix swallowed a great deal of coffee. He cleared his throat, setting the cup down, "it's a project of mine for when I am king. I bought land and had a building constructed to create a dragon museum."

Her shoulders relaxed as she let out a breath. Thankfully a smile was on her face, "that's amazing, why didn't you tell me?"

"I was hoping to show you," he said, "I'd like your opinion."

"Are you sure?" She spooned more of the avocado sauce onto her plate, "what if I tell you everything is wrong?"

He said, "then I'll fix everything and make it correct."

Ryd found his picture and held it up. Another of Masha, though closer to her face. Elarie's eyes went wide, "look at that, you even got her spotting correct!" Calix looked at it. There were spots, yes. "Ryd, you are going to be a wonder to the dragon world, you know that?"

He giggled pleasantly and went back to eating his breakfast shrimp. Their mother placed a fried plantain on his plate and he sort of growled at it. She ignored him and said, "do tell us about yourself, Elarie. Calix has only said so much, I'd love to hear all about you."

"What did Calix share?" She glanced at him before stabbing an egg or two. She ate awkwardly, as if she was trying to be more ladylike in the way she brought her fork to her mouth, no matter how quickly she was eating. Calix watched her hands, recalling how messy of an eater he'd seen her be, but they were clean now.

"Just that you met under unfortunate circumstances and he cares for you dearly," Vienn answered. "I'd be happy to hear you say you feel the same."

Elarie sipped her coffee and said, "I do care for Calix very much." It didn't pain Calix to hear her say it so vaguely, though it seemed to upset his mother. Elarie put food in her mouth to avoid having to speak again. She alternated between each thing he'd put on her plate. A forkful of fried plantain was poised for the next bite. Calix never thought he'd like watching someone eat, and yet here he was.

"Right," his father broke whatever awkward tension his mother was creating. "Where are you from, Elarie?" He reached onto Vienn's plate and scooped some of her tomatoes onto his own, mixing it with half of his eggs.

She said, "north of here," while looking at Ryd. He had his trident in one hand and a pencil in the other. "But I've never stayed in the same place very long," she said.

"You can stay here forever," Marcella suggested casually. Ritan laughed. Marcella continued, "and marry Calix and have babies and wear the crown Mama never lets me wear."

Elarie smiled, "oh, and which one is that?"

"The coronation one, *duh*," the little princess rolled her eyes. She looked at Elarie, "it's the traditional one that's put in a box to be preserved when it's not being used and I don't get to wear it. If you marry Calix and have his babies then you will!"

"All in good time, dear," Ritan pat her arm. The traditional crown, right. Calix hated the thing. There were two meant for a king and a queen, though the king's was much larger. They were made of feathers and quite itchy. Calix's father had let him put on the king's headdress once as a boy and all Calix could think about was that he understood why the past Ceptari rulers decided to forgo tradition and adopt the Trec and Duness way of dressing.

Still, he'd be crowned in the feathery thing and would also be forced to wear the traditional garb that went with it. As would Elarie if she was his queen.

Vienn said, "don't worry, dear," and waved her hand at Elarie, "he's not expected to ask for your hand for another year."

Elarie eyed Calix over the rim of her cup. She sipped coffee, setting it down slowly. "Calix doesn't want to marry me," she said in the same casual tone Marcella had used, though hers was laced with the tension Vienn created when she wanted something.

"I very much do, Elarie," Calix told her, "no need to put words in my mouth."

"That's what a wife is for," Marcella said, "Mama told me that."

Elarie's face creeped with blush and she pulled her hand away from her cup as it began to steam with her nerves. Elarie placed both hands in her lap and stared at Calix. He couldn't read the look on her face, but he liked it very much. Calix decided it was a mix between 'I'm going to kill you' and 'I'm going to bed you' and the idea made him grin at her.

Ryd said something Calix didn't understand, but Elarie's head snapped to him. He was chewing on his shrimp with his mouth open, trident still tight in his hand, and the pencil was poised over the dragon drawing.

"It's his gibberish," Vienn told Elarie. She touched Ryd's back in a mothering way, rubbing in a circle Ryd didn't like. "We're told it will fade as he gets older."

Fascination grew on Elarie's face. "He does this often?"

"It's how he speaks to himself," she nodded.

She folded her arms on the table in an unladylike fashion, pushing her nearly empty plate away from her in the process. Elarie looked at Ryd and spoke in the language Calix was growing more familiar with. It was a short sentence, three or four words, and formed as a question. Ryd looked up from his drawing. The tent silenced. Even Marcella was paying attention, her syrup covered arepa poised in her hand. Syrup dripped onto the table.

"What is this? Are you toying with him?" Vienn grew defensive. "I will not take you teasing my son—"

"Mama, she's speaking another language," Calix told her. "Elarie?"

She said something again, her tone gentle this time, and Ryd dropped both the trident and the pencil to flip through his drawings. Calix moved food over so he'd have room to place the discarded pages, holding them down for him. Ryd found what he was looking for and thrust it out for Elarie to take. She held it delicately in her hand, sitting back slowly.

"What is it?" Calix pressed.

"He's not fluent, he's catching words in dreams," she said faintly.

Vienn asked, "he's dreaming a language? How is that possible?"

"It's common, actually, and is mistaken for gibberish if the family doesn't recognize it," Elarie said, "and it does fade as you said if it isn't repeated. Ryd has a dream and he hears the people in the dream speaking the language so he repeats it the way he did now."

Marcella leaned over Elarie's arm and looked at the drawing. She sneered at it and said, "it's bad still. When is he going to get better?"

"I thought he just dreamed of dragons," Calix put a rock over the other drawings to hold them down, "what's he dreaming of now?"

"Dragons," she shrugged and showed him the drawing, "when they were created, specifically."

CHAPTER SEVENTY

ELARIE

It was perfect. His drawing was perfect no matter how much Marcella didn't like it and even though Calix squinted at it. It was perfect. The hands of creators sparked the life of dragons and Ryd had drawn just that. He'd depicted the swirling light and the bright colors to a perfect degree.

Calix turned to his brother and said, "why were you hiding this talent, hmm?" He poked Ryd's arm. Elarie wanted to say that he wasn't hiding anything. He expressed himself through his drawings, he was showing them what was happening and even speaking to them, but they weren't listening. Elarie didn't think she'd be wrong in assuming this was the first time anyone had heard Ryd and thought it wasn't gibberish.

Ryd pointed to the drawing as if to express exactly what Elarie thought.

King Ritan shifted in his chair. "The creation of dragons?" He repeated, "my son witnessed the gods creating dragons?"

Little Ryd snorted to himself. Elarie said, "the gods didn't create dragons. The elementals did."

Again, he shifted. It reminded her of her father, who shifted and cleared his throat when he needed to control himself. In the case of the king, he probably thought she was trying to fool them. People's beliefs were strong, after all, what was some girl doing claiming their holy gods didn't create dragons?

"The elementals," he repeated, running a hand over his jaw. "Fire, water, air, earth, those elementals? They created dragons?"

"The first elementals did, yes," Elarie nodded. "Elemental creators."

He looked at his wife, then his children, and his eyes settled on Calix. Ritan cleared his throat, "I will tolerate my son marrying someone without a drop of noble blood," he said and shifted his eyes to her, "but I will not tolerate such..." he waved his hands toward her as if searching for the best word to describe her as, and went with, "blasphemy."

"Father, it's a cultural difference," Calix argued gently, "not everyone agrees on the same thing as all others, that's how religion has always been."

"That may be true of practices and beings of worship, however," his lip curled, "claiming someone else created the beasts is some form of blasphemy and I will not stand for it."

Elarie didn't realize it was that easy to get on the bad side of the king. She looked at Calix, then Ryd. Ryd was taking in everything possible. Elarie had, after all, just proven he wasn't just speaking gibberish and was the first person to believe him. This discussion about dragons was sure to be important to him. "Your Majesty," Elarie said as she turned in her seat to face him. "I believe that the gods did not create dragons because it was passed down through my family that a race of people long extinct had been the ones to do it."

He scoffed.

"And is religion not what is passed down through family? Calix has learned from you and his mother, Marcella and Ryd are learning as they grow just the same as you learned from your parents when you were young."

"To claim that *people* created dragons—"

"I didn't say they were people, sir, I said 'elemental creators.' Those were not human, they were something else," she interrupted, much to the distaste of the king. "You can always ask Grey," she argued, "he will understand you."

The shadow of the Great Dragon loomed over the side of the tent. The fabric waved with his breath and the might of his body as he made his way to the opening. Steam floated from his nostrils as they first appeared and a low hum traveled from within him. The two guards that had been posted at the entrance to the tent tensed and trembled.

"I will not stand for this," Ritan grunted and put his hands on the arms of his chairs to help himself to his feet.

"Father, sit down," Calix said in the firm voice of a future king. Elarie let the commanding tone tingle over her shoulders and down her back, enjoying it far more when Ritan listened. "You and I both know that Grey understands us. Ask him if the gods created him and his species."

Greilor moved his head into the tent, the flaps sticking to his scales. His black eyes looked around at each of them, inspecting and listening. Ryd bounced in his chair and showed him yet another drawing while both Marcella and Queen Vienn sat still and fascinated.

"Go on," Calix urged.

Ritan looked at the fearsome beast and asked, "did the gods create you?"

Grey shook his head. Calix smiled at the look on his father's face, then turned to Elarie. "Are you finished?" She nodded. Calix stood, wiping his mouth with the napkin under the knife he hadn't used. Greilor's head drew away from the tent as Calix said, "that's settled, yes? And to settle another thing," he held his hand out for Elarie, "father, if she consents I will be more than happy to marry someone who does not share the same beliefs about the gods as you or me—and who knows? Perhaps she will convert me."

Elarie took his hand and stood, smiling silently at the king while his youngest daughter did a gleeful little dance in her seat. Calix pulled her from the tent and she said, "very impressive."

"Did you appreciate that?" He asked with a smile. Elarie simply nodded. "Shall we go riding?"

"No, we're going into the nest," she pointed. Greilor's tail disappeared down the side of the cliff. "I'll keep you safe, I promise."

Calix said, "I believe you," as easily as he said please and thank you. He laced his fingers with hers as they approached her entrance. It wasn't perfect and most definitely needed some work, but it would do the job. "Where did the sticks come from?" Calix asked, indicating the great many of them dotting the ground.

"Dragons are similar to both birds and reptiles, didn't you know that?" She waved his arm pleasantly, "Greilor's got to build his nest from something and there are plenty of trees around."

Elarie pulled him into the hole in the ground, kicking aside rocks and pebbles he might trip on. "I am amazed you were able to do this so quickly," Calix said from behind her. When she glanced back he was squinting, an open mouthed smile on his wonder-filled face. Elarie nearly tripped because she wanted to keep looking at it.

"It's not like the nest he used to live in," she said. They reached the level ground, "but he says he likes it and there's room for other dragons. See, this," she pulled Calix to a dip in the ground toward the middle of the nest, "is where the food could go. Each of these large alcoves along the wall," Elarie motioned to the imperfect yet spacious rooms she'd made, "a dragon can nest. Greilor's is over here, his is the biggest because he's the king." Again, she pulled him along. Away from the light of the giant hole in the cliff, Greilor had his own space. It was three times the size of him and perfect to house both him, his nest, and however many eggs he laid. The dragon was there, blowing great fire over the far wall to create shining glass.

"Why's he doing that?" Calix asked, his lips close to her ear so as not to disturb their working dragon.

Elarie said, "it's a way to see the fire from the opening, look," she turned. They could see the entrance to the nest from where they stood. "With the glass on the wall he'll be able to see it still shining from anywhere he is in the nest, it helps ensure the flames never go out."

"You're proud of him," Calix said softly, wrapping his arms around her. She leaned into his back.

"Aren't you?" Elarie turned her head and looked at him.

A perfect smile was on his face. Yes, he was proud. Calix said, "maybe I don't quite understand everything about my dragon or your dragon world, but I am so very proud of him."

"I can't wait to be a dragon babysitter again," she whispered as the fire went out and the glass wall shined with the reflection of the bright morning light spilling into the nest. Elarie said, "I used to do it all the time. They wouldn't even rope me into it or wait for me to show so I'd be forced to watch them..." she shook her head and sighed, "it was always the greatest feeling, taking care of them and watching them grow."

"I imagine they grow quite fast," he said. He pressed his lips to her cheekbone. Calix breathed in against her skin as if he was smelling something delicious but attempting to be casual about it. Elarie said nothing. The attention seeking part of her longed for the exploration. For his curiosity. She allowed it to control the front of her mind while he inhaled and exhaled against her hairline. Elarie knew how she had gotten to this moment in so few days. She knew how the half of her that longed for the completion he could provide was winning. It had been two things. Hearing him say that she was the love of his life when he thought she'd never know and this very morning when he asked if he could pick out clothes for her. Somehow those two things were burrowing in, pushing past the distrusting, hateful ball of leave-me-to-rot-alone that often surrounded her heart.

She said, "they do," and watched Greilor move his collection of sticks around. He was pretending he couldn't see them despite his eyes wandering. He was more than pleased. Elarie held Calix's arms, sending warmth through him. "After only a few months they're impossible to carry. Great Dragons get too big to carry at around four months, I'm told. We'll have to see."

"Yes we will," Calix confirmed. He then asked, "how is he supposed to light the eggs on fire and keep them in a nest if the nest is made of flammable material?"

She chuckled. "He urinates on the flammable material."

The prince paused for a few moments, digesting what she'd said. "Urinates," he repeated, "that... well," he clicked his tongue, "right. Sure. Show me everything else?" He began turning both of them to the side.

Elarie laughed and turned around. His arms remained around her shoulders and she'd moved hers to his chest. "How would I convert you?" She asked pleasantly.

Calix hummed, "let's see." He began to sway them like a dance, "you tell me of your grand adventures. You answer my questions, you..." he pretended to think. Elarie grinned as she watched his mouth. She wondered if there was music in his head, if he had a tune they were dancing to. He put his head against hers. Their noses pressed together, the large bridge of hers fitting against the slope of his. Then, like it was the greatest thing she could ever do, he whispered, "tell me how to make you stay with me until we're both old and grey."

There was nothing stopping her from saying it. The god that wore Calix's face came to mind. He had asked *would you kill him* and Elarie hadn't been able to answer. What would Calix say if she told him the whole thing? If she explained the gods' perfect plan to keep her alive forever. To keep her from ever wanting to settle down and begin again.

"Calix," she whispered.

"Then tell me something else," he said. Calix's hand rose to her neck. He moved it under her hair, his thumb creating a slow circle by her ear. "Tell me I can kiss you."

She bit her lip, relishing in his asking. Maybe one day she'd tell him to stop asking and simply do it—surprise her—but for now she allowed his anticipation to soak pleasantly into her bones. "You may kiss me," she said.

Calix's mouth was upon her instantly, tasting of rich royal coffee and the hot ash she associated with pleasure. Elarie moved her hands from around his torso. She dragged them up his chest and gripped his jacket. Calix pulled her against him, breathing her name as if he were praying to a god. It danced over her face and into her mouth, the coffee and ash spinning and coating her.

Far, far away someone was calling his name. Someone Elarie did not know, so she hardly cared. But Calix cursed and looked above them. "Shit," he breathed heavily. He didn't physically pull away from her, but she knew their kissing had ended before it could get any more interesting. "I have to go," he wiped his mouth, "I'll be gone for a week. Just a week and then..."

Calix's eyes were on hers. He wanted something desperately, but he didn't want to say it out of fear. "And then what?" Elarie pressed.

"Then you're going to give me a new leg," he swallowed thickly. "And teach me how to walk on wings and fly and all of that."

It wasn't what he wanted to say. Of course, Elarie could guess what he wanted to say. She could argue with him now to tell her the truth, but she liked this goodbye, she did not want to ruin it by denying him what he wanted. So she nodded. Calix smiled and stepped back from her, but she held onto his shirt. "Calix," she said and he raised his brows with just the slightest quiver of fear. "Never wipe your mouth after you kiss me."

He chuckled, "yes, ma'am," and kissed her again, walking backward and pulling her along. Calix poured himself into her and swallowed her breaths as he made his way to the exit. Elarie didn't want to say goodbye to his attention. The curve of his mouth, the heat of his breath. Not then, when everything was growing far sweeter than it had been in a long time. "Better?" Calix asked when they broke apart.

Elarie sighed, "I suppose."

"I will see you in one week," he pecked her lips, "and we will be dragon riders together," he pecked her lips again, "goodbye."

"Goodbye," Elarie said and watched him walk away. He looked back quite a few times. Elarie breathed in deeply, dragging her hands through her hair. Her head turned left to the dragon poking his head around the corner. "Shut up," Elarie rolled her eyes and started to another part of the nest.

CHAPTER SEVENTY-ONE

KAELUM

Kaelum stepped carefully into the nest. Calix had said this was the last place he left Elarie, so this was where he was headed after Calix's goodbye in the see-you-in-a-week-don't-kill-anyone-while-I'm-gone sort of way he'd been doing their whole lives. Still, now it was far more real given the magic. And Elarie. Had he given the same message to Elarie?

"Elarie?" Kaelum asked, kicking a rock the size of a child's fist. It fell down the uneven slope she'd created and rolled across the flat ground and into a giant bowl shaped dip. Elarie had her hand in a small hole in the wall. "Are you busy?" He asked.

She looked at him, "sort of. Did you need something?" When she released her hand fire remained. It traveled in lines and swirls over the tall ceiling above them. Kaelum watched the flames crawl to the other side of the nest and settle into holes in the walls.

"This is impressive," Kaelum muttered. It was like he was in a giant entryway surrounded by alcoves and tunnels to explore. Nothing looked neat and finished, but even in its raw form, it was amazing she could do it in a matter of days.

"Thank you," she smiled warmly as if she hadn't been expecting a compliment. She rubbed her hands together as she walked toward a heavy crate Calix had delivered the day she died. "It's not finished, obviously, and isn't nearly as impressive as the one from home, but..." Elarie sat on the crate and said, "it feels really good to be able to do this myself. Like it's sad but rewarding."

He nodded. Kaelum heard a noise coming from a large tunnel and craned his neck to catch sight of Grey's tail. "Does he like his spot?"

"He does," she smiled proudly, "and he'll be finished preparing either today or tomorrow. Calix will come back to a clutch of eggs."

Kaelum looked around again, inching toward the sheer, windy drop off the side of a cliff. "Damn," he muttered when he looked over. A pile of rock from the explosions was below, jagged and broken with whitewater crashing over them.

"Why are you here?" Elarie had stood when his back was turned. Now she was standing over the crate and pulling the top off with her hands. Kaelum would've needed a wrench for it.

"I wanted to show you," he walked toward her and dug into his pocket, "I dunno, maybe get some praise if you're feeling nice today."

He dropped a shattered star into her hand and she dropped the lid to the crate. "You did this after you left? How?" Her eyes were wide with shock.

"You aren't going to be nice?"

She rolled her eyes and moved around the crate to face him completely. "Ready?" She asked.

Kaelum's brow furrowed warily. "For what?"

"I am so proud of you!" She said, "this is amazing, you did so well!"

"Right, stop doing that," Kaelum waved her away. Elarie laughed and stepped back. "I was experimenting with the bursts and I put the star in my right hand instead of my left. It worked, the burst formed around the star, and I got so excited to show Terry that it exploded."

She gave him a sincere smile, something a genuine friend would give, and said, "well this is really good. I mean it, it's impressive you managed to break a star so quickly."

He beamed. His father would be proud, he knew it. "So what now?"

"Well the pieces are useless, but I doubt you want to be seen with them," she shook them around in her hand. "You can bury them or try to continue a burst, maybe you'll turn them to dust."

"During the day?"

Elarie smirked and gave the pieces back, "you can do it. It's just more difficult."

"I wish I didn't have any drawbacks," he muttered as he looked at the shards of what once was magic. "Do you?"

"Everyone does," she returned to her crate, "but being given the power of a god simply comes with more. You cannot use your power during the day unless you have a star in your hand. You have to protect yourself from many beings that want your magic. The magic can become addictive."

"What are your drawbacks?" He asked.

Elarie lifted metal out of the box. A great heavy deal of it. She set it on the ground. "I am a very emotional person. It isn't always the best thing to be when your power is fire."

Kaelum said, "I bet that was difficult when you were a child."

She chuckled and nodded. Elarie's hands glowed a dangerously hot red. Kaelum could feel the heat pouring off of her, causing a sweat to build on his skin. "I was the problem in my family."

"Did you all have magic?"

Her hands were on the raw metal. They melted into it. Elarie began to dig a chunk out. "Yes, we all did," she answered. "My eldest brother was a water elemental, wind for Cammie, I had fire. My second youngest," she pulled the metal off and started molding it. Kaelum watched her push and pull as it if was dough she was forming for baking. "Had water as well and the youngest had earth."

"What are you doing?" He asked, distracted by the stick thing she was making. She stretched it out, compared it to her leg, and stretched it out just the slightest bit more.

"Building Calix's leg," she answered and set it down. It began to steam and hiss. Elarie grabbed another chunk, apparently for the foot.

He nodded. Kaelum put his hands in his pockets and watched for another few minutes before Grey lumbered out and grumbled something off to her. Elarie nodded and said goodbye. "Where's he going?" Kaelum asked as the Great Dragon dove off the cliff, his powerful wings outstretched.

"I need a wyvern so he's going hunting before he settles into his nest," she told him, kneeling to attach the foot piece to the leg piece. "This way he'll have something to eat in the days he'll rest in here."

Kaelum squatted in front of her. Her eyes lifted to him, the foot and leg attached. They both hissed and steamed between Kaelum and Elarie, only partially blocking his view. "I need to know something," he said. She straightened slightly as if she was preparing for the worst. "If your blood is golden why aren't you a monster? Just tell me right now, I need to have a real answer. Please."

Elarie breathed a sigh and sat down. She crossed her legs, setting the metal creation aside. Kaelum sat as well, watching to see if she'd lie. Perhaps she was a monster in disguise like Terry said and it was a terrible mistake to be alone with her. Perhaps she was using him. And yet Elarie said, "I am a person, Kaelum. You know that, right? I am a living, breathing person with a heart and a mind."

"I want to know that," he said, "but I don't know how to be sure."

Her nostrils flared and she looked at her hands in her lap. She lifted one between them, palm facing the fiery ceiling, and used her nail to cut a small hole into her skin. Golden blood bloomed before him. "The golden blooded monsters were the second creation of the gods. They are the most like who you worship."

His brow furrowed, but he let her continue. He couldn't have her going off on a tangent. Kaelum needed to hear all of it.

"They wanted something made in their image so they made the monsters. They used to be called something else, I'm sure, but no one knows it now," she breathed in deeply and took Kaelum's hand. Her fingers trembled with nerves. Elarie said, "they only know violence, death, and bloodshed. They cannot take any form but the ones they were given. Not very many have a thought process at all. The Jiivers are an exception, for example."

Shit, the Jiivers were golden blooded?

"The humans were created after. Red blood like the Fae, bodies like the Fae, thought processes and minds and hearts just like the Fae," she said, "just with some of the same tendencies as the gods. The violence stayed. The destruction stayed. Nature took its revenge with the natural disasters. To prevent the deaths of their precious humans, they created elementals."

Kaelum nodded slowly.

"But everything is created from spite. Humans were created out of spite, natural disasters are from spite, Metars were created through spite, and the elemental species had one thing that the humans did not because of spite."

She put her palm against his, rubbing her blood onto the black mark his stars came from. Kaelum attempted not to cringe. Even without the golden blood, wiping it onto him was still nasty.

Elarie removed her hand, leaving the shining substance behind. "We were created to protect the humans but the gods are cruel. They placed us somewhere we couldn't leave and no one else could enter. The Barrier created by Metarina's body kept us apart. But on the off chance one or two of us got through the Barrier our golden blood would terrify you enough for us to be hunted and killed."

"I'm confused."

She tilted her head. "What are you confused about?"

"Well firstly," he looked at the blood, having nowhere to wipe it. "Have you told Calix all of this?"

Elarie said, "no, I can't right now."

"Because of the nonacceptance thing?" Kaelum asked. She said nothing, though her eyes gave him the answer. "You know, I'm probably not supposed to say this, but after you left and he was finished bawling his eyes out for a few hours talking about how much he messed up he told me he thinks he's your mate."

She just said, "I know."

"Did he tell you?" Kaelum's eyes went wide. This was something Calix would've told his best friend, why hadn't he?

"No, a god did," Elarie answered almost shamefully.

He relaxed his features and his shoulders. "Well... is he? Is he your mate?"

She winced, "no."

"But the smells... you talked about those and he told me—"

"It's not the same," Elarie shook her head, "I..." she let out a short breath, looking away from him. "What I have," she hesitated, "what we feel or smell, it's not the same thing. I don't get mates, elementals don't. Only Fae."

His brow furrowed. "What about Matian?"

Her lips formed a thin line and her eyes watered as she brought them to him again. "If you lost the love of your life tragically wouldn't you say the same? Wouldn't you call it something magical?"

Kaelum nodded. He called Terry his afterlife, after all. "But if you don't have mates then why does he feel so intensely and why do you smell different to him than you do to everyone else?"

"A connection between us began when we were on Greilor the very first time," she explained, "it's rare that it happens so quickly, but it's the type of connection that shows we were meant to be together. We were meant to ride together. Greilor knew it from the very moment he met Calix—and no, that was not the reason he chose to allow Calix to ride him, it was simply something he recognized because I was his favorite."

Kaelum just wanted her to go on. He didn't speak.

"We are a perfect match," Elarie smiled just slightly. "Not romantically, though that happens often and it *did* happen, but it's not mates."

He nodded. "Are you going to tell him that?"

"I sort of have to," she began to play with her heel.

"Try not to crush him," Kaelum said.

Elarie looked at him carefully. "It's bound to happen eventual-ly."

"Not if you tell him how to get you to start aging again," he countered with a sly smile. Kaelum waited for her to lash out, but she only rolled her eyes. They stared at each other. Elarie sat like she had all the time in the world and she knew he wanted many things from her, she was simply waiting to see what it was. "Can I practice making bursts during the day while you work on Calix's leg?" He reached for it only to have her pull it back.

"It's still hot and it's too heavy," she said before standing with it.

He asked, "how are you going to make it not heavy?"

"Magic," Elarie replied and turned her back on him to work. Kaelum pulled his one star from his pocket, longing for the others.

 CALIX

The wind cut like a sword against his face. Not even Masha liked moving this quickly. She'd chosen to bundle up in his saddle bag. They'd stopped to rest for the last time, having been pausing riding every few hours to warm up, and the girl that had been looking at him for days finally approached. She was beautiful, with pale skin and rosy cheeks. They flushed bright in the cold as well as the tip of her small nose. Her hair was the same sleek black as Terry's, though hers was cut under her ears and not her shoulders. Even their eyes were similar, indicating they were both from Trec. Beautiful, but nothing next to Elarie.

She bowed her head on approach, breathing as heavily as he was. "Your Highness," she said, "I am Macri. Macri Fengge."

"It's good to meet you," Calix smiled warmly, "and Calix is fine, the formality isn't necessary."

"Of course," she blushed. "I just wanted to introduce myself."

He continued smiling, patting the neck of his horse. He'd never liked blushing. When ladies blushed at him he couldn't take them seriously. Calix assumed they were either doing it on purpose as some sort of flirtation tactic, or they were unable to contain themselves around him. Either way, he didn't like it. Except for when Elarie did it. The way her cheeks flushed red and it rose up her neck... he'd never get enough of that. Of making her do that.

"Is that all?" He teased Macri. Many people introduced themselves, but it wasn't uncommon for them to have an ulterior motive.

She cleared her throat. "I was wondering if you knew of my father, Titani Fengge. He served your father and was killed six years ago."

Calix thought back. "The attack in the market, yes?" Macri nodded, swallowing her nerves. "I am aware of him and am sorry for your loss."

"Thank you, Your Highness," she smiled, "I was hoping to follow in his footsteps."

He looked behind her. Calix was going to North Reidle with five guards, two botanists, and a cart of food. A few of them were speaking amongst themselves, two guards were listening to what Macri was saying. One chuckled at her wording. Follow in his footsteps by serving the king, hopefully by dying. Calix said, "my father isn't taking on any more guards."

"I was hoping to be one of yours, sir," she nodded her head in a short bow. Her fingers flexed at her side. "I have experience and references if you like."

He chuckled, "with you?"

Her red cheeks seemed to burn more brightly, "no, back home. Sorry, nerves have me messing up. My Gran helped me with this whole speech, she pretended to be you and everything. You should have seen her—drew her hair on top of her head and stood straighter than I'd ever seen her—sorry. Sorry, I shouldn't have rambled."

"Not to worry," he waved it off. Calix said, "I'd love to see your application. I can hear of your references now, have you been in the service of the king for long?"

"No, sir," Macri said, "just two years. I guarded Count Recin from age sixteen to eighteen, so two years with that."

Calix nodded. "Count Recin is dead."

"Yes, his wife poisoned him."

His brow furrowed. "Do you know why? I always wondered."

"She discovered he raped three of their servants," Macri answered knowingly, "it wasn't on my watch."

"Huh," he looked away at a tree with bark peeled off, most likely from a deer. "Is that your only reference?"

"No, I was also a personal guard to Duke Lagoo," she said proudly, "he wrote me a glowing letter of recommendation."

Duke Lagoo, that was impressive. He had many enemies and was attacked by them a few times every year. And to be as young as Macri was and serving as his personal guard was even more impressive, especially considering how paranoid the man was. "I'd be happy to read it," Calix said, "and everything else, of course. And I'll take your superior's report firsthand when we return."

"Really?" She grinned.

"Yes, really," he smiled, again patting the neck of his horse. "If all is well there I'll have a test for you."

Her smile faded. "I hope you mean physical," she said faintly.

"I do. If I like what I see on paper I'll have to also see you fight," he said. The steed snorted, wanting to keep moving. "If you can hold your own against Elarie you'll be accepted into my future kings guard on sight."

She asked, "Elarie? The woman you came home with?"

Calix smiled, "the very woman. She's the best fighter I know, you just have to hold your own against her."

Macri didn't seem to have an issue with this. The two eaves-dropping soldiers behind her, however, chuckled and rolled their eyes. No doubt because of the rumor surrounding Elarie. How could a whore be a good fighter? Macri merely said, "I look forward to it." Calix was relieved, then. He wouldn't have taken Macri on if she made any sort of comment about her being a whore. "I've seen her on the field with your dragon."

"They're close," he said and breathed into his cold hands before putting his gloves back on. They needed them, otherwise a finger or two might come right off.

"She's not a Fae, is she?" Macri asked.

Calix said, "no," and drank from his waterskin. He could see everyone preparing to move on from their break.

Her eyes moved curiously. Did she not believe him? Macri hummed and pulled her lips into her mouth. "And," she cleared her throat and sort of squeaked out nervously, "*is* she your whore?" Calix shook his head. "Is she just your friend? Are you two together or is she free and open to other relationships?"

Calix grinned. It spread wide over his face, which only made Macri more nervous, but he couldn't help himself. He chuckled, "we are together, I'm sorry. And I'm not laughing at you, please don't take it that way. I just like that you asked for her. She'll like it as well if you'll let me tell her."

Bobo, the oldest of all of them, walked forward with his horse moving silently behind him. The Yaerling matched the general in stature and strength as well as silence. Bobo was tall and broad. He towered over everyone, the muscles on his body unhidden by his layers of warm clothes. He had a strong, intimidating face. Dark skin common with citizens of central Ceptari and the coast was marred with a scar that ran from his right cheek, over his mouth, and directly down his jaw to his throat. It was the reason Bobo didn't speak, though Calix never learned the story behind the injury.

He signed a simple wave and a few letters, nodding to the horse by Calix. Macri straightened and bowed her head to her superior and walked off. She flashed a smile to Calix before mounting her anxious Yaerling. The rest of the guards followed suit.

Bobo smiled fondly and signed that he heard whispers about a girl and if any of it was true. Calix laughed airily, wondering how long he'd have to defend the rumor before everyone got the message. "She's not my whore, if that's what you're wondering." He turned and mounted his Yaerling. "I am going to get her to marry me." Bobo made a snorting noise. Calix said, "it's just going to take some time."

Lots of time, I'll bet, Bobo signed off before beginning the last leg of their ride.

North Reidle was a conservative farming town. They tended to have a rather backward way of thinking—the kind of thinking like they would 'not allow' Marcella to become queen if Calix were to die. Given this, Calix knew instantly they were in the wrong place.

A band played a lively tune that they followed. He dismounted and adjusted his leg, tracing his eyes over the cut out banners hung over the dirt, stone, and stacked buildings. They'd arrived in a square, though apparently not a main one, and each of them led their horses to a water trough. Calix continued to look around. Windows were open, clothing lines hung between small alleys.

"Are we in the wrong place?" Calix asked Bobo.

His general frowned. The scar on his face crinkled as he did. He signed for them to follow the music and walked partially in front of Calix as he did.

Perhaps they were in South Reidle.

Oh, they were *most definitely* in South Reidle.

In front of them was a celebration that would be found nowhere near the north. Calix laughed as he watched the band strike their lively tune and the crowd of what seemed to be the entire town cheered for the dancers on a rickety old stage. A child was sitting in a chair in a pretty dress with an unmistakably joyous smile on her tan face. Around her were dancers. Each man matched a specific color palate. Pink. They sang and danced and mimed things Calix was sure he'd understand if he had the context for the celebration.

Calix clapped when it was over. He was joined by his guards and soldiers. Even Bobo put his hands together a few times. It was the general that caught the attention of the people on stage. As they were helping the child off a few noticed, pointing and straightening. The band's music stopped and one dancer jumped off the stage. He was thin with long limbs and pale skin. Freckles covered his bare arms and chest, not hidden by the pink frills of the shirt he had on. Tight thin pants hugged his legs and he wore heels to match.

The dancer walked over with his back straight, though his glance behind him indicated he was nervous. He stopped in front of Bobo and cleared his throat. "Can we help you soldiers?"

"I think we mistook you for North Reidle," Calix chuckled, "that was a wonderful performance."

"Oh," he blushed, "well you won't find anything like it up north." The dancer looked behind him again, "we were just finishing up a last birthday song. We had five children born the same day so every year," he motioned around with a smile. "All in good fun."

He said, "it looks wonderful."

Bobo nudged him with his strong elbow.

"Right," Calix said, "have you heard from North Reidle at all? Perhaps they requested aid from you?"

"No, sir, not for weeks," he said as a woman approached. She wore streaks of pink fabric in her hair that was braided into a thick pile on her head. "Although they're usually silent."

He nodded, "and have you had any trouble with your crops of any kind?"

The woman said, "no. Is the North having problems?"

"It would seem they are," Calix listened to the sound of wings and Masha flew high above them, warming her cold scales in the sun. A few from the village gasped and screamed at her, which she enjoyed far too much as she circled. Masha began to descend into a landing, amazing everyone around her. Calix smiled and whistled so she shot right down from the sky and into his arms.

"You have a dragon!" A child screeched. She was being held back by an adult. "Mummy, he has a dragon!"

"I see that, darling," said the woman in front of them. She smiled in a sort of apologetic way, her nervous eye on the small thing. "Her and her brother are always talking about going to see the Dragon Prince. Heard he's got one of the big ones sleeping on his lawn."

Calix chuckled, "well he's got a nest now," and Masha crawled up to his shoulders. She purred in his ear. The woman's eyes widened slightly, unsure, while the man had turned red under his cosmetics. "And they're welcome to visit, Grey loves children. He's having some of his own soon."

Bobo nudged him yet again, telling him they needed to get a move on. Calix rolled his eyes as the little girl began shrieking that he was a prince. Her mother said, "my apologies. We weren't expecting..." she looked behind her. A few people had bowed improperly. Masha seemed to enjoy it. "I thought you'd look older, truthfully. I imagined," she motioned to her jaw.

"I don't like facial hair, sorry to disappoint," he said. And neither did Elarie, so he would forever have a clean face just to please her. "Thank you for humoring us, we should be traveling up to North Reidle now."

The little girl was moaning about how the dragon was having babies. Or, as she put it, "*baaaaaaaabieeessss.*" Calix smiled. Children were wonderful.

"Feel free to visit again, Your Highness," squeaked the red faced dancer.

"If you take the main road up this way," the woman moved and pointed, "you'll get there in maybe a half day just by walking."

He said, "thank you. Great show," Calix motioned to the stage as he backed up. He waved to the child and followed Bobo back to the horses. "Could you ever imagine yourself doing that, Bobo? Dressing up and dancing for a kid's birthday celebration?"

Bobo looked at him head on, his face free of any emotion, and simply signed *yes* before mounting his horse and moving the group along.

CHAPTER SEVENTY-THREE

The smell of death wafted from the cold northern winds. North Reidle was right ahead, the arch above the dirt road now decorated with a body. Calix shifted nervously and looked at the seven around him. They had to be all thinking the same thing. They had gone to learn of a disease and feed starving people—what was a body doing hanging off an archway like he'd been thrown up there?

Bobo moved first, urging his Yaerling forward slowly. His hand was tight around his sword as he passed over the dried blood and intestines that must've slid out of the man at some point. Flies flew around them, buzzing and hungry.

Calix urged himself next to Bobo. The general put a finger to his lips, his sharp eyes moving over the scene as they walked into town. When he dismounted and drew his sword as did everyone else. Calix tied his Yaerling to a post. He hadn't been prepared for a fight, but judging by the next body they passed he doubted there would be one. The woman must've died weeks ago.

He pushed down bile, his feet quiet. North Reidle was like its southern counterpart in a few ways. Its people were the same mix of types, it was a farming town, and its buildings stacked on top of each other. Stairs and ladders were strewn about. They were always building more. Now there were smelly bodies on the stairs and the ladders were snapped to prevent escape.

"Oh my gods," someone whispered as they found the main square. Red stained the ground. Bodies were strewn everywhere, weapons or no weapons. "Is that..." the same voice choked on the words.

Calix did not. "Golden blood," he said. All the warmth drained from his body as he stared at the mess of it. Something had attacked them. Some monster had attacked and while the villages fought it off and gained a few good cuts to it, the monster slaughtered them.

Hurried footsteps echoed over the silent town and they prepared for a fight. A man slid into view brandishing a knife. His eyes were wild and fearful. He breathed through his teeth like he was snarling. "Show me your blood!" He shouted, his tired voice cracking, "show it to me!"

"We aren't here to hurt you," Macri began to say, but he shouted at her, the cry carrying. "Sir—"

"Show it to me!"

"All right," Calix put his hand up, "it's all right." He slid the edge of his center finger over the sharp blade of his sword. Red burst from the wound. "See? I'm human." He took a few steps forward and sheathed his sword, "my name is Calix. I was sent here by the king because you asked for aid. A disease spread over your crops—"

He shook his head, "we asked for no such aid." Calix looked back at his men. Each of them had followed his lead and was now showing the frightened man that they were all red blooded. He lowered the knife. "They can look like us," he said, "the monsters can look like us. They've... *evolved* to look like us."

"Can you tell us what happened?" Calix asked.

"There are only twelve of us left," he whispered. "That thing killed all but twelve. And it meant to... it meant to leave twelve of us. It counted."

Calix took another step, "where are your people? We have food and medical supplies to give to you."

The man nodded with his mouth open. He seemed relieved. At least somewhat. With the knife still tight in his hand he walked away. Calix's boots crunched over yellow sand as he followed. Through the gaps in the towering buildings he could see where their farms had been, now piled with the same yellow sand. His eyes found gold everywhere. "With this much blood," Rint said behind him, "surely they would've killed it."

"It kept coming back," the hopeless voice of the man said from ahead of them. "No matter how many times we killed it—and we killed it lots—it came back. There was nothing we could do. Couldn't even get the children to safety."

"It killed all the children?" Macri asked.

He nodded. He led them in silence to the temple at the edge of town. It was old and meant to be separate from everything else, receiving the light of the north, east, and south with its doors facing west. They were open. Soft voices spilled from inside. "Polly," croaked the man, "they're soldiers. I checked their blood, they're all good and red."

A woman about the same age as Calix's mother stepped out. She had kind, tired eyes. "You're a bit too late," she said, looking at each of them. "We weren't expecting anyone... we don't have enough food, the thing destroyed all we had."

"We've come with food and medical supplies," Macri stepped toward her. She took her hand gently, "we'll take care of you."

"Not many are injured. Just hungry," she moved over so they could see inside. Calix couldn't tell who the temple was made for, but it was filled with ten people older than he was.

Calix turned, "bring the cart. We should get them comfortable before talking about getting them out of here."

"You want us to leave?" Asked the man.

"Will you be able to survive if you stay?" He countered. It wasn't kind, but what else could be said? Every one of them would die if they didn't pack up and leave. "We can take you to South Reidle and have this town cleaned up. Depending on the state of your fields you might have to sew new land—if there's anything left. And there aren't enough of you."

He trembled.

Calix nodded to Bobo and walked away, weaving through the buildings and bodies to get to their fields. *Golden blood,* he thought, *a real golden blooded monster.* How was that possible? Calix thought Elarie was the only humanoid golden blooded, so how did one exist now? Had she lied when she told him she was an elemental? Was she really a golden blooded monster that just *happened* to have fire magic? Fire was monstrous. Fire was dangerous. A monster could have that type of magic, couldn't it?

In front of him was a wasteland. He doubted anything would ever be harvested from the plot of land again. Calix bent, picking up some of the yellow sand and letting it fall between his fingers. It was coarse and stung. He wiped it away and tried to find any sign of life around him. He walked into the field, unable to tell what had grown there before. Calix kicked the sand around and took a vial from deep in his pocket. He collected some for his father and left the two fearful looking botanists to do the real investigation.

Masha growled in an aggravated way and Calix straightened, reaching up to scratch her cheek. "Don't like this stuff?" He asked her and she snorted, huffing another growl. "What about it? Can you help me with this?" Calix walked out of the field and found his way to a river. There were fishing poles leaning up against a nearby tree. The river and its occupants must've been the only source of nourishment for the villagers. Calix sat on a smooth rock and stretched his leg out. Masha crawled over his knee. "What about this is bad?" He asked her, turning the sand in the vial over. He pressed down on the cork with his thumb.

The dragon sniffed it and then swatted at it.

The crunch of boots brought Calix's attention to Macri. She smiled gently. "I wasn't expecting anything like this either," she said.

Calix held up the vial and shook the sand inside. "It can't be a natural disease, can it? Not with everything turning to sand."

"Perhaps the golden blooded monster had some sort of magic as well," she took it from him carefully and held it up to the sun. "If they're evolving it's possible they developed some."

"What sort would this be?" He began petting Masha to calm himself down. Elarie was not a monster. She wasn't. Calix knew her and she was *not* a monster. "I've never heard of any kind of magic that can do something like this."

She handed the vial back and said, "neither have I. I thought the things were going extinct not turning into people-looking monsters."

Elarie is not a monster. "With some sort of destructive magic," he added.

"My Gran used to say the golden blooded monsters were what humans could've been," she squatted and tilted her head at Masha. The dragon paid no mind to her, but Macri still looked at her with an innocently curious face. "She says a lot of things," she added softly.

"What else?" Calix asked. Masha began to steam, her body humming with warmth. She had some sort of smile on her face, the edges of her wide mouth stretching and lifting.

Macri sat on the ground. "About the monsters?" She sighed, not giving him a chance to answer. "Well she's one of those nuts that thinks the golden blooded monsters were the sort of..." she waved her hands, "'test run' before they made the humans." Calix nodded, having heard something similar from Elarie. She continued, "maybe that's why they're evolving."

"Because they were meant to be human?" Calix looked at her.

"I suppose," Macri shrugged as if she was trying not to take credit for a sound theory. "They spent all this time becoming like us and developing thoughts and magic and personalities."

His eyes moved over to the water. Sunlight danced off the steady stream, shining brightly. "Any kind of magic?" He asked, "even elements?"

"I don't see why not, it's a gods-given magic," she said.

Calix ran his fingers over Masha's wing, extending it outward. The leathery wing trembled, though she didn't seem bothered by his touch. Calix pressed his finger against the spiked end of the bone before folding it back against her body. "I don't know what to think," Calix admitted softly.

Despite not knowing what he was talking about, Macri's words were still comforting. Or, her Gran's words. "My Gran used to say that the moment you don't know what to think is the moment all the best things happen."

He smiled. Calix looked at Masha. The Jitter Dragon placed her chin in his hand. "Your Gran sounds like a wise woman," he said, "I'll take her word for it."

Chapter Seventy-Four

Elarie

Elarie's back was turned when a ball of starlight came flying at her from Kaelum's hand. He let out a gleeful laugh, doubling over to hold his stomach when she ducked and yelped. Elarie straightened, "really?" She tried to look outraged at the throw she wasn't expecting, but couldn't wipe the smile off her face. Elarie had never had any fun with Kaelum before. He was turning out to be a great person to mess around with.

"Yes, really," he walked toward her, his hands glowing. Kaelum was grinning, just getting used to the feel of magic coursing through his veins. In the darkness he had no need for stars, so he was free to let the magic float around his fingers and up his wrists. "That was great, what's the problem?"

"They may be weak bursts but it could still kill me," she told him without any real seriousness in her tone. Elarie held his wrist and inspected the glow under his skin.

He shrugged, "and you'll come back." She said nothing. Her warm, orange magic sparked around his. "That's insensitive, isn't it?" Kaelum pulled his hand away. The glow went out around both, which forced her to look at him. "The constant 'you'll just die and come back' thing."

Elarie said, "it hurts sometimes." He was silent, waiting for her to elaborate. Maybe this was the moment Elarie really, truly made a friend besides Calix and things that weren't human. She said, "even if I joke about it, you know, it's mine to tease because only I feel it."

He nodded, his eyes moving away from her.

"It's torture," she admitted quietly, "I see where I am supposed to be. I swim as fast as I can thinking that maybe *this time* I'll get to stop fighting. And I'm ripped away from the peace I should have the right to." Tears swam in her eyes that she stubbornly forced down. "So I find humor in it because otherwise I might go mad—I have gone mad—but when other people say it sometimes it's a reminder that no matter what I'll be this age forever."

"Not no matter what," Kaelum said. "There is a way to stop being this age forever. You and I both know that. Plus someone else that would probably do anything to make you grow old with him."

Elarie said, "probably."

"So how bad is it?" He asked, "the way to restart your aging, how bad is it?"

She clicked her tongue to the roof of her mouth and turned away from him. Elarie tilted her head back to the stars. "Do you think the gods are above or below?" She asked.

"Above, now answer my question."

Elarie stared at the bright stars. They danced for Kaelum. They wanted to watch his magic move. She straightened, now looking out to the distant horizon. The invisible line where the darkness of night met the black sea. Wind brushed her cheeks and chilled her to a pleasant temperature she would have to regulate on her own.

Elarie said, "bad, I suppose." Her heart ached. *Would you kill him?* The god had asked and Elarie had been unable to answer.

"You can tell me," Kaelum said, "I'm good at keeping secrets."

A smile brushed her lips. "Terry's coming," she said as she ran the soft fabric of her dress through her fingers. Kaelum turned around. The field was empty aside from the two of them. Greilor was below sitting on his nest. He was trying to find a comfortable position, grumbling about nothing feeling right. It reminded Elarie of her mother. When she was pregnant both times she was always complaining about not finding the right position to rest in.

Terry ran across the field, gasping and sort of coughing. He skidded to a stop in front of them and said, "Red escaped," with such dread that Elarie couldn't tell who he pitied—Red or her. Did he feel for his friend or the woman he tortured and killed? Was he glad Red escaped or was he worried about what would happen next?

"Elarie," Kaelum said warily.

The ghosts of magic thorns wrapped around her heart, digging into it for the sole purpose of spilling her blood inside her. The golden blood would fill her up like a cup of water and turn to tears that spilled from her eyes or vomit that fell from her mouth. "I won't break anything," she whispered.

"They're already looking for him," Terry said, "his description is out and the palace guards know to arrest him if he tries to get in."

She still couldn't tell who he was concerned for. Elarie stepped back. Both of their bodies pivoted to follow her, but she moved quickly enough to get away. Elarie should have killed Red when she had the chance. She should have gone to the brig as soon as she could stand on her own, yet she'd allowed herself to get caught up in Calix. She got lost. Even when she was angry and unforgiving, she let herself be pulled into him and his kindness and his smile.

She opened the door to his bedroom and sobbed.

"Are you all right?" A small voice asked. Elarie jumped and every candle in the room lit to life. Marcella was on Calix's bed. She gasped as she sat straight up, her innocent eyes wide at the display of magic around her.

Elarie swallowed, "what are you doing here?"

The little princess crossed her legs and adjusted the silk bonnet on her head. She cleared her throat, "I missed Calix. What are *you* doing in here?"

She stepped away from the door, "I missed him, too."

"You have fire magic," she said.

"I do."

Marcella said, "no wonder Calix loves you."

Elarie smiled gently and walked toward her. Marcella was twisted in his blankets. The window above her head was shut, ensuring the room was nice and warm. Elarie sat on the bed, "he likes fire, hmm?"

"And dragons. Dragons have fire," she nodded, "and you have fire. And you're very pretty so that helps, too."

"Thank you, Marcella," Elarie reached out and took her hand. Marcella squeezed it. "Do you miss your brother a lot?"

Marcella shrugged. "He was gone for months and Papa made him go again. And I know it's part of the," she straightened her back and put on a pompous expression, "'he's the future king and he's got duties!' but," her face returned to its former sad expression, "going off somewhere to look at dead plants is not what a future king should do. That's servant work."

"What should he be doing instead?"

"Other future king things," she said.

Elarie waited, but it didn't seem that Marcella had any examples. She smiled and moved closer to her. "Like?" Elarie urged.

Marcella shrugged, warming. "Like teaching you the dances you'll do when you dance together at his birthday ball," she nudged her with her shoulder and clasped both hands around Elarie's as she said, "make you a dress!"

"That doesn't sound very kingly," Elarie teased. "Shouldn't he be writing laws and things of that nature?"

"I don't know, Calix doesn't do those things around me," she laid back, throwing her legs out. Only her ankles and below hung off the bed. "He reads with me, though. Boring stuff and fun stuff sometimes. And he makes me dresses for balls and parties and things, that's kingly if I have anything to say about it."

Elarie laid next to her with a sigh, folding her hands on her stomach. "It does sound kingly," she agreed.

"Good, so he can make you one," Marcella grinned. "I think green would suit you nicely."

She laughed. "I prefer blue, is that all right?"

"Fine."

"Good."

Elarie had grown up with brothers on both sides of her. Like any young girl, she'd wanted a sister, especially given her distant relationship with her mother. If she stayed with Calix... if she told him how he could make her age again... and they...

She closed her eyes. And they what? Married? Could she do that? Elarie had all but sworn off men after she lost Matian and had violated that unspoken promise with Calix already, but to marry him? When she had been so close to marrying Matian? "Why do you want me to marry Calix?" Elarie asked, somehow seeking the advice of a child even if the little girl didn't know it. Elarie had the image of it in her mind. Ceptari's marriage traditions involved marrying in the sea fully clothed. They would both wear the thick topaz necklaces that were passed down through the family. Calix would stand with the sea behind him and she would stand with the land at her back. He would be smiling. Grinning, even. He loved her. He wanted to be with her until they grew old. He wanted to marry her next year. Calix wanted to spend the rest of his life with her.

Marcella took up the question with the excitement of a baby dragon about to be fed fresh meat. "Oh because he has my Grandmama's ring!"

Her eyes snapped open. "He what?" Elarie turned her head to Marcella.

"I wasn't supposed to tell you that," she had such a sneaky look in her eye, like she wasn't planning on keeping it a secret at all. "Somewhere in this room is my Grandmama's red diamond ring. He got it from Mama the day you came to Lyburn. Calix told me it came from a volcano in the ground that hasn't been active for a thousand years and it's been in the family for forever." Marcella turned onto her side and propped herself on her elbow, continuing, "he said that Grandmama used to wear it all the time. It didn't used to be a wedding ring, but I bet he's going to propose with it."

"A red diamond ring that came from a volcano," Elarie stated. "And he told you he was going to propose with it?"

The little princess shook her head, "no he just told me about it. It's very pretty you know. The band is black like obsidian."

"That does sound pretty," Elarie looked away from her. Holy gods. Wasn't it too soon for that? They'd only known each other a few months, Calix couldn't *possibly* want to propose. And yet he believed they were mates. They got along so well already. He seemed to know her already. The ring came from a *volcano*. How Elarie loved volcanoes. It fit her so well. Red like the fire that churned under her skin on the beach. Red like her magic. Red like the molten lava she could create.

"I think he should propose before the ball so that everyone sees the ring," Marcella said.

Elarie stared at the ceiling. "When is the ball?"

It upset the girl to say, "oh, next month."

She loosed a breath. "Next month, oh gods," Elarie sat up and put her hand to her forehead. "Next month."

Marcella grunted as she got to her knees, "love does not know time, Elarie, all the best poets and writers and songs say so."

"But I do not love him," Elarie argued.

After a very obnoxious eye roll, Marcella said, "you are a liar."

"I am not."

"Yes you are!"

Elarie would not get into an argument with a seven year old about love. She simply would not.

Marcella touched her shoulder. "I like big words like my brother and I have one for you," she said, "it's called 'denial' and it means you don't want something to be true so you pretend it isn't."

She turned her head, lowering her hand. Elarie just looked at her.

"You think on that. Now," she removed her hand, "I hope you aren't planning on sleeping in here."

"No, I just wanted," she started. But no, Elarie didn't know what she wanted. Why she chose to open this door and not her own. "I'll go. Goodnight, princess," she stood. Elarie's eyes darted around for hiding places. Where would he put a ring? In a drawer? Hidden in a ball of yarn?

She left the bedroom and went to her own. Elarie took off her dress and pulled the pins from her hair, flopping down onto the bed. Gee waved from the bed Calix had made for him. It was a pillow, really, with two smaller pillows sewn to it. Gee loved it. Tonight there was a snoring Firelight Frei next to him. They steamed together.

Elarie pulled her blanket over her and thought about the wedding Marcella was sure would happen. Elarie would have half of his family's topaz necklaces. She imagined it would be heavy. Below them would be one she made herself. Elarie and Calix would remove each other's necklaces one after the other until it was the two that they created. It represented a new family. A new lineage. The necklaces would be placed in a basket held by a person on both sides of their choosing. Family was most often the holder.

There would be vows. They would touch heads and cross their hands over the basket and be considered one.

Elarie turned onto her stomach and stuffed her face into her pillow.

CHAPTER SEVENTY-FIVE

ELARIE

The knock at her door was Kaelum. The feel of his magic was so distinct it was a wonder it hadn't been noticed yet. That no Fae in Lyburn had felt it as she did. Elarie grunted when he knocked again, reaching down and groping for the robe she'd left on the floor the day before. She slipped forward, landing on both of her hands.

"Elarie?" Kaelum asked.

Blood rushed to her head. She chose to simply fall the rest of the way. "Hold on," Elarie said, slipping into the smooth fabric. While she rubbed her eyes he continued knocking. Elarie was forced to stand, squinting out at the bright sky outside her window. She wrapped the robe around her and synched it.

"I haven't seen you all day, come on," he knocked again, "I know you're probably upset—"

She opened the door. Kaelum stumbled a step, having been leaning on it, and flashed a comforting smile at her. "I was asleep," she said, "I had a hard time falling asleep and the window..." she moved to the side. He entered her space.

"Was it Red keeping you up?" He asked.

Elarie shut the door and yawned. "No, Marcella told me that Calix has a ring. She thinks he's going to propose."

He looked at her for some time. Kaelum had two very distinct things about him written in the way he stood in front of her. His still present wariness of her telling him golden blood should not infect the royal line, and his love for his best friend. Kaelum had torn his relationship with Calix at one point, he couldn't voice that he didn't want him to be with her without damaging it further. But he loved his best friend. He knew being with her would make him happy. "Does that upset you?" Kaelum asked.

She searched the room for her breakfast and went there. How she managed to sleep through its delivery amazed her. And she'd been nearly naked while it happened. How embarrassing. "I'm just worried," Elarie warmed her eggs as she bit into an arepa.

"About?" He walked toward her.

"What happens depending on my answer," she said, then whispered, "why am I even thinking about this right now?" Elarie looked at him as he stood awkwardly waiting for her to do something, "what do you want?"

He said, "well I knew you were probably in a bad mood," as he stepped closer once. Elarie ate a few bites of eggs before she realized they'd probably been sitting out for hours and put the fork down. "And I came by earlier looking for you, left, came back again and asked Grey but he shook his head when I asked if he had seen you, so this time I knocked."

She swished water around her mouth before spitting it back into the cup. "Why?" She asked. It was more curious than rude, but given their history Elarie wasn't sure how he'd take it.

"I wanted to distract you."

Her eyes moved over the room, settling back on him. "Do you want to practice the bursts, because I'd prefer it if we weren't inside for that."

"No," he shook his head. She waited. Kaelum said, "my mother wants to meet you. She's wanted to for a few days but I kept pushing it off and I figured... you're upset about Red and could use a distraction before you blow up a—"

"I'm not going to blow up anything, Kaelum," she rolled her eyes and went to the bathing room, shutting the door. Elarie had control. She had *perfect* control. Even when it might've been reasonable to have some sort of magical reaction to finding out someone who had stuffed painful thorns inside her body had escaped, she had control.

Elarie relieved herself and washed her face and hands. She surveyed her face in the mirror, poking her cheek and pulling the skin under her eye down just to give herself something to do. A door hadn't shut, which meant Kaelum hadn't left yet. Elarie sighed. Stupid men. She exited the bathing room finding him sitting in the soft chair where her desk was. Elarie hadn't used it yet, she wasn't sure how comfortable it was.

"I'm sorry," he said when she came out. He stood once again.

"Why does your mother want to meet me?" She asked, crossing her arms.

Kaelum answered, "the star book. I told her about you when she showed the book to me—well, sort of." His brow furrowed, "sort of, I said your name in passing and that you'd be able to read the book. Then I said I'd explain it later and she said she wanted to meet you."

With a falsely annoyed sigh, Elarie went to her closet. She didn't have much else to do, really. Work on the nest, sure, but she didn't want to bother Greilor while he was nesting. He was so close to laying his eggs, she didn't want any loud noises to disturb him. Elarie had four more days until Calix got back, so she couldn't be with him. Either of his younger siblings was an option—she had yet to visit Ryd in his art room.

Other than that Kaelum was her only option. And... perhaps he was trying to be her friend.

Elarie dressed in high-waisted pants. It was awkward given the gash on her side. Dresses usually flowed and covered it, but the pants synched over the linen shirt she'd tucked in and made a strange dip on one side. Elarie grabbed a pair of boots and socks, then walked out with her arm extended, "will you tie this?" She held it out for Kaelum.

He chuckled, "I do this for Calix sometimes," and helped lace the tie around her wrist. "He hates using his teeth." Kaelum switched to her other hand while she dropped her boots to the floor. "So what would happen if you said yes?" He asked after a moment, finishing the knot. Elarie moved to the chair he'd been in. The plush wasn't as comfortable as she'd thought it would be. Elarie ended up sinking into the wood. She put on her socks and boots.

"Nothing," she replied.

"How about if you said no?"

She repeated, "nothing."

Kaelum sighed. Elarie ignored him. She laced the boots quickly, her fingers flying through them, and felt herself warming as she did. A deep, controlled breath rolled through her. Elarie went back into the bathing room and brushed her hair. "Is your mother just curious?" She asked as she braided her hair from the center backward. Elarie pulled it over her shoulder and looked through the open door at Kaelum.

He said, "she likes knowing the people I know."

Elarie nodded and looked at herself through the mirror once again. Her braid was tied off. She could practically feel Kaelum growing impatient as she brushed her teeth. It might've been her imagination, however, as if her mind was betraying her. He didn't seem upset with her at all. Elarie wiped her face, glancing at herself again. The cut piece of hair at the top of her head stuck out of her braid and wouldn't stay down.

"You look fine, Elarie," Kaelum said.

She tried tucking it under one last time before giving up. "I hate it," she told him as she walked forward. Kaelum led her to the door.

"It's not obvious unless you're really looking," he told her, "I promise."

A smile brushed her lips, her cheeks warming. Elarie didn't thank him aloud, but when he shut the door he flashed a knowing smile. Kaelum walked next to her after that, his eyes moving around and settling on each of the people who stared at Elarie as they went the way he intended for them to. It wasn't the same as to the glass hallway, where they could've gone through the big domed throne room to get to, this time he was moving the way of the entry hall that Calix had pushed her through a servant's corridor in. "Why are we going this way?" Elarie finally asked. The glass hallway, despite Calix implying otherwise, was faster.

"I wanted to look at people looking at you," he answered, watching a courtier size her up. Elarie surveyed Kaelum instead. "Do you think Calix likes this?"

"He is one for the dramatics, isn't he?" Elarie smiled. Kaelum, who had known Calix much longer, simply nodded with an exasperated sigh. "I can have fun with it, too. For instance," they began to pass the familiar voice of the woman that asked Calix if Elarie was his whore before he said he loved her, "I'll tell you that before he left," the passing began, "Calix told me he loved me in thirteen different languages. And he only knows four, can you believe it? He's such a romantic."

Kaelum chuckled. The ladies stared as they went by. "That was fun?"

"What a scandal, the prince being in love with his whore," she whispered just for him. Kaelum snorted.

"Why do they think you're a whore?" He asked as they walked across the great entry hall. Elarie again looked at the chandelier wondering if it was dangerous to clean. It was so high up.

She said, "everyone would rather think the worst of the competition. Calix is a prince that does not have to marry for station. There are no treaties to be negotiated, no wars or skirmishes that need kingdoms united, and he has a father that wants to see him simply marry one of his own people."

"You're not one of—"

"Shush," Elarie waved her hand, "I'm from the north. *Anyway*," they stepped outside into the cool air. "What does it mean when a prince doesn't have to marry a princess?"

Kaelum said, "he can marry anyone from his kingdom."

"And what, dear friend, does it mean when not only does that same prince bring home a slave girl while there are loggings for her already," she looped her arm through his, "but he clears out a room for her that is right next to his own, visits her, smiles at her, rides dragons with her—"

"I think I get it," he laughed.

"—has pretty dresses made for her, tells people he loves her," she continued while Kaelum started grinning, "and not to mention invites her to family breakfast in that special royal tent."

He added, "and the prince's best friend takes her for a walk to meet *his* mother. I couldn't tell you, what does it mean?"

"It means I am competition. Every lady here that had any chance at marrying Calix months ago is starting to think she has none now," Elarie sighed. "Poor things. They will say anything to make me look lesser than."

Kaelum hummed and they walked for a while. The land flattened, leaving the castles behind. Elarie observed the town. She'd been many times, so right away she was able to tell what changed and what hadn't. The hat shop, for instance, was now a dress emporium. Further down the butcher had been replaced with a tanner. New buildings spread around them, though it was all the same mixture of sweet and rotten smells.

"You know none of what you just said matters if you don't say yes to Calix's proposal," Kaelum said.

"I'm hungry," she muttered in response and he suddenly steered her to the right. "Does your mother live here?" She stared at the open bakery door.

He said, "no, but she doesn't cook so I'll feed you before you get grouchy."

"Grouchy," Elarie repeated with a sneer. "You haven't seen me grouchy," but she went into the bakery before him.

CHAPTER SEVENTY-SIX

KAELUM

Kaelum didn't have many female friends, so he wasn't sure if the bouncing while eating cake was normal. Perhaps it was a sugar rush. The bakery was new, the building bought by someone from Polinae. No one really trusted the place until Calix went in. The bakery was mostly cake and the like, no bread or anything, and Calix had been craving something with chocolate in it. He saw the new place and probably didn't even hear Polinae before he went in. Now business was booming and the baker was making Calix's birthday cake.

Elarie bounced silently while she ate half of the small round frosted cake. Kaelum stared at her. He'd had two bites of it, found it delicious, but he wasn't sure if he should eat any more.

"I haven't had cake for breakfast in a long time," Elarie sighed halfway through the cake. She licked her lips and looked across the street, her elbows on the table. "Who is that? The bald man with the pointed mustache."

Kaelum turned in the metal chair. Usually they were hot, but given the covered sky and the season, they were cool. Kaelum and

Elarie had sat at one of the street tables outside the bistro next to the bakery. They tended to share tables because they shared customers. If someone bought cake and wanted to eat it right away like Elarie, they'd go into the bistro for a drink, and a drunk might like to wander into the bakery to get something sweet. There was a gate that separated them from the street, and across from that was a pirate with a bald head and a pointed mustache.

"Shit," Kaelum whispered. They made eye contact. Kaelum turned around and addressed Elarie, "he says I owe him money."

"Well do you?" She raised a brow, a fresh bite on the way to her mouth.

He said, "no, Terry did once but we paid him off plus interest."

"So why is he on his way over here?" Elarie asked, swiping her thumb over her lip. Kaelum decided not to look. "Do you want me to get rid of him for you?"

"I don't want him dead—"

"*I am not a monster*," she hissed with a light smack to the table. The pirate walked through the gate and pulled a chair from another table. He sighed as he sat, turning it so the back was facing the table and he was straddling it.

He said, "Captain Kaelum," with a smile Kaelum didn't think was meant to be friendly. His eyes dragged to Elarie, who he was closest to. "Moved on from men, I see. Hello, miss," the smile he gave her was different. "I am Tahra. Kaelum and I go back years."

Elarie didn't look pleased with either of the men sitting at the table with her.

"You are lovely," he continued. "But you know you're in with the wrong kind," he jerked his head to Kaelum. "He's a rat that'll cheat you for your money."

She said, "I don't have any."

"Oh," Tahra chuckled and his eyes traced her, "didn't think Kaelum could afford such nice things."

"I can't," Kaelum tapped the edge of his fork against the slowly warming table, "she's Prince Calix's future wife. And I didn't cheat you for your money, we played cards, you won, and we paid you what we owed."

He was still looking at Elarie as he said, "I am not satisfied."

"That doesn't matter. You were paid, stop bothering us," Kaelum sat up. His hands began to ache. There was a star in his pocket, perhaps he could create a burst around Tahra's head—a sharp kick cut off his thinking and Elarie shook her head slightly. Kaelum gritted his teeth. "Tahra," he said as calmly as he could manage, "we paid you what you were owed and then some."

But Tahra, it seemed, was no longer paying attention to Kaelum. "Does our Little Prince treat you well?"

"He does," Elarie smoothed her hands over her pants as she stood, "excuse us, we have somewhere to be." She looked at Kaelum, who nodded and stood. Why not let her lead? He had just considered using dangerous magic on someone. She'd have more control about it. He grabbed the cake as he got to his feet, folding the little container's lid overtop.

"That'll have to wait," Tahra said and decided to reach over and jerk on Kaelum's arm. He tripped to the side to maintain his balance and the cake fell back onto the table, slid out and hit the stone ground with a disgusting splat. "You've been away for months, don't be a stranger."

Kaelum sat back down because he had to avoid ripping his shirt. As soon as he was sat, Tahra turned to Elarie. She was looking at the cake. *Shit,* Kaelum thought as he watched the anger flash over her face from the loss of her dessert breakfast. A hint of steam floated off the top of her head and her eyes flashed.

"Future princess," Tahra sighed, "I am sorry about this."

"Do not touch me," she snapped when he raised his hand. Tahra was a head taller than her, yet somehow even if she was looking up at him she was glaring down her crooked nose.

He motioned to her chair, "please sit." She looked at the chair and he chuckled, grabbing the cut piece on top of her head. Kaelum closed his eyes for a moment and loosed a slow, exasperated sigh. When he opened them it was to Tahra twisting his finger around it, "what happened here, princess? Did you let your baby brother play with scissors?"

A fire burned in her eyes as they found Kaelum. His lips formed a thin line and he nodded merely begging inwardly that she didn't kill him. Elarie reached up faster than he'd seen any Fae move in his whole lifetime. She grabbed his wrist and twisted so he cried out sharply. The bustling area around them silenced to watch as she slammed his head into the metal table and let him slide off. His face landed in the chocolate cake and he groaned, shifting painfully.

Elarie grabbed him by the back of the neck and lifted him easily. Tahra could hardly swat at her. "I told you not to touch me," she said. Cake slid off his face and splat against the ground. "To apologize," she said sharply, "you are going to go buy me another chocolate cake. If you do not I am going to rip your eyes out of your head and make you swallow them. Understand?"

He croaked, "yes ma'am," and was dropped again. Elarie sighed and sat back down, watching with a smile as Tahra crawled away from the bistro and toward the bakery entrance.

Kaelum sat back. "I'm surprised you didn't light anything on fire."

"Sometimes it's nice to get physical," she shrugged, "and be-sides—I can take all of my magic frustrations out with you tonight."

"Ahh," he leaned back, "I can't. I have plans with Terry."

She frowned, "then I should've lit his groin on fire."

Kaelum surveyed her. She seemed to be in a fine mood despite the intrusion of her personal space and the loss of her cake. He said, "you seem to threaten to rip off body parts a lot." His mind was on the threat to Terry. She'd rip his leg off if he said it was her fault that Matian died. It would've been the second time, he believed, that someone had said something like that, and Kaelum had been the first to suggest it. Elarie had taken it personally. "How did Matian die?" He asked.

Her decent mood disappeared. Elarie shook her head, "I won't talk about that with you. With anyone. Don't bring it up again."

"Or what?"

"Or nothing, Kaelum, please don't ask about him again. I'm having a hard enough time as it is, I don't need you asking about him," she looked away.

Shit, he thought. "Elarie," Kaelum shifted in his seat. She winced and looked at him, seeming ready to apologize. It wasn't like she snapped, her words were justified. Still, he said, "you don't have to feel guilty because you're with Calix and not Matian."

"I didn't say..." She started. She didn't finish.

"How long has it been since he died?" Kaelum tilted his head, trying to be sympathetic. He had lost people, after all. Friends and family. The wounds regarding the former were still fresh. He had a few funerals to attend over the next month. Still, he hadn't lost the love of his life. In fact, he was now working toward ensuring they were together forever.

She winced, "long."

Kaelum said, "and he loved you?" Elarie's lips drew into a thin line. She definitely didn't want to hear what he was saying. She was struggling with it alone, she probably knew what he was going to tell her. Perhaps she'd just been too heartbroken to say it to herself. "Don't you think that after all this time—" she began to shake her head, so he sat up and poured a bit more urgency into his voice, "don't you think that after all this time he'd want you to be happy?"

"I can't," she said, swallowing thickly. "I can't be happy for long periods of time, I can't do that."

"Why not?" His chest was pressed into the table now, as close to her as he could get without standing.

Her eyes watered. She kept shaking her head. "I can't," she repeated.

"Elarie, tell me why," he urged.

Her shoulders sagged. A tear fell down her cheek, dripping over her skin and falling off her jaw. Elarie looked behind her to the bakery's door. She was stalling, waiting for an interruption like there always seemed to be. But Tahra was still in the shop, there was a line going out the door that he was mixed into somewhere. Kaelum whispered her name. When she turned back she looked smaller than she ever had. In their months together, nothing had seemed to affect her the way this was. "I have to kill him," she whispered, her voice cracking. Elarie breathed in shakily, her body trembling as she said, "if I marry him I have to kill him. So I can't be happy, I won't do that to him."

He straightened slightly. "That doesn't make any sense. How are you supposed to be happy if he's dead? And have children... that doesn't make sense."

"He has to be deemed worthy in the eyes of the gods," tears streamed down her face that she didn't wipe away. "But I am more valuable immortal so why would they bring him back?"

"Calix would come back from the dead?"

"That's not the point, Kaelum," her chest heaved with a building sob. "Why would they let him live?"

He stared at her. "Because you're perfect together," he decided even when she sniffed and shook her head. "No, Elarie, look." Kaelum stood and walked around to the chair Tahra stole from another table. He pulled it close to her and took her hands in his. They were hot, unnaturally so, but it didn't burn. "I don't approve. I don't think you're blood should mix with his, I think you're a dangerous risk and if it was up to me you wouldn't be anywhere near as close to him as you are now, but *listen* to me." He squeezed her hands. *That* burned. "You two are perfect together."

"Every god is evil—"

"Damn the gods right now," he snapped, making her blink quickly in shock. "There is a dragon up that hill giving birth for the first time because of you two. There is a connection unlike anything else in this world between you two. Maybe it's not mates but it might as well be because you are perfect together. You fit the way Terry and I do."

She said, "you won't risk him dying because of me."

"But he would risk it."

Elarie shook her head. "I won't."

"Then you're being selfish," he said. She didn't deny it. Kaelum asked, "have you ever stopped to think that maybe the gods are just scaring you?"

"No, I know that this is real," she said, "I have rules to follow and this is the one that matters the most."

Tahra returned with a red bloody mark on his face and a cake for Elarie. "Here," he grunted as he set it on the table gently. He bared yellow teeth at Kaelum as he straightened. Elarie wasn't even looking at him.

"If you come anywhere near Kaelum or Terry again you'll never see or walk again," she said in such an emotionless voice it sent chills over Kaelum. He looked at her empty face, the tears shining on her cheeks. "Now go away," she said. Tahra listened. He nearly fled.

"Elarie," Kaelum said as she breathed in and wiped her face.

She said, "please don't tell him, I'm not ready."

"You're going to tell him," he said, "as soon as he gets back."

"No, I'm not," Elarie stood with her cake in hand.

Kaelum looked up at her. They wouldn't be visiting his mother, then. "You spent a lot of time being upset with him for not accepting you. You still haven't explicitly forgiven him for not believing in you. And now you've become a hypocrite because you aren't believing in him. You aren't trusting him."

A dragon roared up the hill. It was a sharp cry that hung in the air. "Don't lose my cake," Elarie said when she dropped it in his lap and took off toward the castle. Kaelum stood, watching her weave expertly around people either going about their business or listening to another cry of pain travel over the water.

CHAPTER SEVENTY-SEVEN

ELARIE

Her ankle twisted on the way down and Elarie tumbled to the flattened ground. Greilor growled and breathed heavily, unable to see her but knowing she was there. Elarie rubbed her lower back and dusted off her pants as she went to his spot. "I'm here," she breathed, filling a trough she'd carried into the nest with water. Elarie grabbed the large sponge floating in it, squeezing the water out.

Greilor grunted weakly, a whine building in the back of his throat.

"You're so strong, Greilor," she whispered gently, wiping the scales around his nostrils. Water dripped into his open mouth. "Talk to me, what can I do?" She soaked the sponge again as he told her nothing, which meant he had something he wanted but wouldn't ask. Elarie knelt and he laid his head partially in her lap, mouth open. "So stubborn," she said.

Where do you think you get it from?

Elarie chuckled and squeezed water into his mouth. "You'll get a long massage when this is through. Remember those?" He hummed, eyes closed. "I'm so proud of you, Greilor," Elarie whispered as Kaelum's footsteps came down into the nest. He was breathing heavily and holding her cake.

"Did he lay the eggs?" Kaelum asked quietly.

Elarie looked at the nest, then at Greilor. "He's taking a break for just a moment," she said, wetting the sponge again.

"Right. Uh, there's a little crowd out there. A few royals and curious servants. A noble or two."

She looked back at him, "will you tell them that he shouldn't be disturbed right now but I will let them know when he's all right."

"Of course," Kaelum set the cake down, "I'll leave this here for you. You're doing great, Grey."

He chuffed a thank you as Kaelum left. Elarie turned back to her dragon. She'd helped many through births like this. None as important as Greilor, however. She recalled how proud he sounded when each of the dragons laid their eggs. None were ever his, but he became a sort of uncle to them as they grew older. Greilor was their king, sure, but he was like family to them more than anything else. Elarie was the queen if she had any sense of herself.

"You're doing so well," she cooed gently while he cried and pushed. A dragon egg birth could happen slowly or quickly, and it seemed Greilor was headed toward the latter. "Good job, you're doing wonderfully. You're so strong, look at that!" Elarie felt tears in her eyes as she counted four sticky, gleaming black eggs. "I'm so proud of you, look at them."

He huffed a heavy, sparking breath and pushed again, this cry partially deafening her for a moment. She blinked hard and shook her head around. Greilor nuzzled against her face before sliding around his great nest and breathing his beautiful flames over the eggs. The nest and its occupants lit to the same bright fires.

"Six?" Elarie stood. She walked over slowly as he nuzzled and she counted again. Greilor had wanted five, yet she'd expected less from him. Still, six! Six was so exciting. Elarie sat on the edge of the nest and watched, not touching Greilor or his eggs. "Look at that," she whispered. "You're a Papa," Elarie's eyes watered again. "Papa Greilor? Or Pa? Which would you prefer? Not *father* that's far too impersonal."

Greilor chuffed and began to purr.

"You know who is going to be so happy?" Elarie leaned in. If dragons could blush this one would be. Elarie grinned, "Calix is going to be so happy for you. He is going to be so proud."

He continued purring.

She bit her lip and pride swelled in her chest. "I'll leave you with them. Call me when I can come meet them, all right?" Her dragon said nothing, but Elarie didn't need him to. She stood, staring back at them as she left with her cake and without the sponge. She swayed when she was back in the open, lightheaded and giddy. Kaelum jogged forward. She couldn't see anyone else. Perhaps they'd been ushered inside quickly after the cries continued.

"Is he—"

Elarie dropped the cake and threw her arms around Kaelum. She sobbed and inhaled sharply. Her entire body pulled close to him, closer when his arms slid around her as well. Her tears burned somehow, soaking into the coat that was rough against her face. Elarie choked and coughed, shaking as he began to whisper it would be all right. He didn't know what, of course. Elarie wasn't sure if she wanted to tell him. But he was her friend, wasn't he? Maybe he'd go and spill her secrets to Terry, but he'd keep some of them safe, wouldn't he? And Calix wasn't here to talk to. Why not Kaelum?

"He's fine, right?" Kaelum asked, "Grey's fine?"

She nodded.

"Are you fine?"

She shook her head. Kaelum held her a little tighter, but it was clear he didn't know what he was doing. Or why. "I miss them," she said, "I keep missing them and it won't stop."

She felt him sigh. This was something he understood, after all, he could offer his input. "It's not going to stop, Elarie," he told her gently. "It's always going to follow you. The pain fades with time."

"No it doesn't," she said, "it can't. I've had time, I've had all this time but it won't stop."

He pulled away from her, seemingly intent on looking at her face. "Have you actually allowed yourself the chance to grieve?"

"My memories from my life before are perfectly preserved in my mind. They won't fade, they won't leave," she said, "everyone says that you need time and you need to accept that they're gone, they tell you that the pain only lasts a little while," Elarie shook her head over and over, trembling, "but what if you can't grieve? What if the pain won't leave?"

"There isn't a required amount of time to grieve, Elarie," he said in a gentle, pained tone. "It could take years and maybe... maybe sometimes you don't move on the way everyone expects you to. My mother writes my father letters still. She keeps them in a box on her dresser and there's seventeen more under her bed. She's never going to be with anyone else and in that sense she'll never move on, but she's healing. She's *still* healing. Sleeping in his shirts, carrying their rings around her neck, keeping trinkets. Every year he's gone it's like an open wound and that's all right."

"I don't have anything left of them," she said.

He touched her forehead. "You said you have memories that won't go away. Pick out the good ones." Elarie sobbed again and he put his arms around her. He said there wasn't a required amount of time. But how many years could go by before it was pathetic? "I'll tell you what," he rubbed her back, "you are going to eat some cake and take a nap and tonight I'm going to show you what I do when I miss my Pa, all right?"

"What about your thing with Terry?" She mumbled.

"I'm talking about after. It'll be late, but I'll come and get you."

She could refuse. She could wallow in her own self pity for a bit longer. But maybe she could learn something from him. Maybe Kaelum had the right idea. Elarie had spent years pushing her pain aside enough to be able to talk about them like she did with Calix. She could think of them and not sob uncontrollably, but maybe she'd been pathetic for too long. "All right," she whispered.

Chapter Seventy-Eight

Elarie

She paced the length of her room and turned back around. "I shouldn't do this," Elarie said to the two Frei watching her walk back and forth. Gee and the new love of his life named Renci. The Firelight was far too amused by her plight, making Gee the more sympathetic of the two. "Why should I? I'm fine. Denial is a fine thing to have and I have it, why change that?"

Gee chirped something about health when Elarie was on the other end of the room. Elarie groaned and went to the bathing room while Renci went about telling his mate that what was healthy for a Frei may not be healthy for someone like her. Elarie washed her hands, the candle by the basin sending flickering shadows over her sour expression. She rubbed the cold water over her face and walked out just as Kaelum came in. He didn't knock, which was somehow rude, and he was smiling.

"Sorry it took so long," he said.

Elarie surveyed him. "Are you?" She tried for a light tone. Kaelum sort of shook his head with a suppressed smile. "Where are we going?"

"On a long walk," he waved to Gee and Renci. The two waved back. "Bring a jacket—well," he looked at her, "have you ever needed a jacket before?"

"I have actually," she went to her closet to grab one. "I do get cold, you know. Snow affects even the hot blooded."

He repeated, "hot blooded, that's interesting." Elarie pulled a warm jacket on and took her braid out. She shut the closet door. "Are you wearing one of Calix's shirts?" Kaelum faced her. He had a star in his hand, twisting it around absently. He tossed it up and down a little. When he found Elarie looking at it he slid it away, though his hand lingered in his pocket for a time.

"It is," Elarie said, "he has quite comfortable shirts."

Kaelum hummed with a nod. "I've never worn one. But anyway, here," he reached into a bag over his shoulder and produced a wrapped slab of meat. She looked at it, then at him. "I didn't know how you'd like to eat your steak so I brought you an uncooked one. For your dinner or breakfast."

"Oh," she wiped the confused frown off her face. "Thank you. That was thoughtful." It was considering how late he had her up. It was well past midnight, every star was out and bright. She'd been pacing for an hour, sleeping through the day. Elarie took the cold meat and he led her out through her bedroom door like he had before. Kaelum was silent, contemplative. Elarie opened the packaged meat. It had been seasoned already. The spices stuck to the wrapping. Elarie breathed in the smell of rosemary and pepper.

"My father died when I was thirteen," Kaelum said when they were out in the cold air. His breath fogged before him. Elarie looked over, cooking her food while they walked down the stairs. "So I have good memories, but sometimes I think that I made them up, you know? Because a few are so detailed it's like it happened yesterday, but some are foggy and in pieces."

Elarie bit into the steak. She'd cooked it perfectly and he'd chosen a perfect cut of it. She wiped her mouth, deciding listening was the best choice.

He said, "he knew I wanted to be a pirate. My Ma thought it was silly, thought I could just be a sailor or a fisherman like Pa, but ever since Calix showed me a book with pirates in it I wanted to be one." They began walking down to the beach, both of them quieting to admire the expanse and beauty around them. Clouds still dotted the sky, but the crescent moon broke through as if it was peeking out to see them. Elarie breathed in the smell of the ocean as her boots hit the sand. It crunched beneath her, soft and cold.

"Sounds like Calix," Elarie mumbled before she took another bite. Kaelum handed her a handkerchief to wipe the juice off her chin. "He hasn't shown me his library yet."

"Probably afraid you'll scare off his favorite tutor," Kaelum told her as he kicked up sand.

Elarie replied, "with my knowledge, yes."

He laughed, "tell me something, then. With your extensive knowledge, inform me of something I've never heard before."

She eyed him as they walked. Elarie could tell him anything, really. Something about Trec, about Duness, about any of the other places she'd gone in her years of bouncing and running from one place to the other. "There was a pirate that collected the hands of star makers," she said much to his dislike, "he'd lace them on rope like garland."

"I was hoping for something fun," he told her. "Like did you know that on this very beach Calix stepped on a dead jellyfish and screamed so loud his mother swears she heard him from her study? That is a fun fact."

"Fun fact," she sighed, "what fun facts do I know?"

He laughed again, something as clear and bright as a cloudless sky. "Come on, I don't know how long you've been alive, but in all that time you have to have a fact that is funny and fun."

"Age is such an annoying thing," she said while she thought. Kaelum waited silently. "Fine, did you know that there is a light festival in Trec?"

"Everyone knows that," he said, "just like everyone knows we have a knockoff version here. Terry celebrates it to keep close to his culture."

Elarie continued, "right, but did you know that the very first one was on accident?"

"Liar," he scoffed with another laugh.

"I am not lying," she said, "the light festival you know today is specifically for the celebration of the summer season, it's been that way for thousands of years but this—" Elarie stopped and held up her hand. He watched as a burst of colorful light flew from her palm and exploded with a loud pop just above their heads, "was an accident. A fire elemental in Trec was running from the authorities on the day of the festival in the capital and they ran into the tent where they kept the powder that used to be used. 'Light' as in color."

He started walking again, "huh." Kaelum asked, "so they used to, what, throw color around?"

"Sort of. They painted their streets and bodies on the day of the first summer rain. It was believed that the powder would soak into the ground and help the crops grow and prosper in the fall. What they didn't know was that the powder was flammable," Elarie explained, "and when the fire elemental ran into the powder tent it caught fire and exploded. Boom, color and light everywhere. First light festival."

"And they just haven't stopped doing that," Kaelum concluded. "But the festival isn't for the first rain anymore, or for crops at all, what happened?"

"Time," she answered. "Time changes everything. What was once a festival to praise the rain and help the earth is now a festival for life in general."

He looked over at her as their steps turned rocky. Elarie took a bite of her steak and climbed along with him. "Time changes everything but you won't let it wear down your grief?" He asked in an accusing manner she didn't appreciate. Elarie ignored the question. She followed him over the rocks, watching the water flow below them. It moved through the cracks in the stone, slowly wearing them down. The rocks were part of a cliffside that seemed ready to cave in on itself. Waves crashed against it. Time made it look like it was bowing to the ocean.

"Where are we going?" Elarie finally asked. They'd been walking for an hour, the rocks keeping them both distracted, especially in the dark. Kaelum had tripped twice, causing her to make a ball of warm light at their feet.

"My special place," he dropped into a gap in the rocks. "My father made it, I guess with his magic, but it never clicked until now. Come on," he held his hand out and she clasped it to drop onto the wet sand. The water rose to her shins and she sank slightly. Elarie wrapped her leftover food back up and put it in Kaelum's bag.

She looked around. The rocks had grown long and flat. They were in a pile of them right by the bowing cliff. "He made what?"

"How long can you hold your breath for?" He asked as he put the bag over one shoulder so it crossed securely over his chest. "Better follow or you'll get lost," he called back while he walked further into the water. Elarie stared at him. He said *walk*. They were going on a long *walk* and now he was regulating his breathing like a diver in front of a watery hole in the rocks.

Elarie sighed and wiped her hands on her pants before she followed.

"It's pretty far," Kaelum told her, taking large breaths and short breaths in some strange way to expand his lungs.

"How did you get there as a child, then?" Her brow furrowed.

He pointed to his chest, "you can do this as a child. Do you need me to show you how?"

"No, I'm fine," she waved him off.

"Seriously?"

"I'm not human, I can hold my breath for longer than you."

He stopped and squinted at her. "How long?"

Elarie shrugged. "I haven't counted in a while," she said, "maybe an hour? Maybe more."

Kaelum just shook his head and turned away, finishing his 'expanding' and crawled into the hole. He slid forward and disappeared like he'd gone down a tube. Elarie sighed and got onto her knees, looking into the hole in the ground. It was, in fact, a tube. She took a deep breath and crawled in, her eyes adjusting as her body floated forward. She crawled further, squinting. Elarie could feel Kaelum, of course, she wouldn't lose him, but amazingly enough, there were bright spots on the inside of the tube. Elarie followed the star-like pattern and left the opening behind.

The tube grew in width, now three times her body size and still growing. She stayed close to the bottom where vegetation had grown probably using the magic the tube gave off. It wasn't enough to attract attention, but it hummed in her ears the further she went.

Elarie saw the kick of Kaelum's boot and swam forward. He was headed into another tube opening. There was more than one, probably to throw off intruders. That must've been why he thought she'd get lost.

He swam with a purpose, of course, and a human need for air. Elarie moved lazily behind him, touching the white lights on the walls. His father had made all of this? Or had he come across the structure and used it for himself? The white dots were warm and magical, seemingly embedded in the walls. Elarie heard a thump come from ahead and swam after Kaelum. He was above her now. They were in a large pool. Kaelum must've kicked off the ground below them.

Elarie did the same, surfacing in a brightly lit room. She thought they'd left the stars, but they were above her again. Star-made, of course, but shining like they were real. Elarie breathed in the cold air, a chill covering her cheeks.

"Ta-da," Kaelum said as she swam to the spot of land he was sitting on. "I don't know how I never caught on," he looked around with a smile. "You would think I'd know something magic was up when we came here."

She climbed up and shivered, steaming to dry off. "It does have a taste of magic," she said, "not enough for a star maker that isn't of age to pick up on." Elarie looked around while Kaelum steamed off. He groaned a little while it happened, sighing when he was warm. The room itself was more of a giant air pocket Kaelum's father had converted into a space he could stay in. She and Kaelum were on a rounded bit of rock with water on three sides. "It's impressive," she said and pointed to the dots of stars above them, "that especially. You'll be able to do that one day."

"What is it?"

"Just light," Elarie walked over and sat next to him, "your father just created it in one place, he made it part of the rock."

He asked, "when am I going to learn that?"

"The moment you can hold a burst of magic, move it around, make one from a distance, and create a shape from one is when we'll talk about real creation."

Kaelum sighed, "that's a lot."

"It'll be easy, you're powerful enough," she nudged him. He smiled softly and Elarie sighed, laying back. She stuck her legs out and stared at the stars above her. She said, "your magic is some of the most beautiful magic in the world."

He replied, "yours is pretty nice too."

Elarie laughed and closed her eyes. The air in the room was thick and moist but breathable. There must've either been some connection to the air above them or Kaelum's father's magic went further than she expected.

"Shall I show you why we're here?" He asked after a few minutes. Elarie could've laid on the rock for hours, but she had a purpose for being there so late at night or early in the morning. She turned her head and looked at him. Kaelum stood and walked to the wall behind her. Elarie turned over. "This is my shrine to him," he said.

Elarie sat up and looked at the space carved out of the wall. Inside were candles and coins, letters, and trinkets. Kaelum was telling her that he tried the letter thing the way his mother had, but it hadn't felt like enough for him. He knew this place, this place was just theirs, so he made this place where he sat and spoke to his father. He gave him a shrine the way people gave them to gods.

"Terry has one for his parents over there," Kaelum pointed to one of the two corners in the room. There was one single tall candle, unlit, and a ring box. "So I thought you could make one, too," he said and removed the bag from his body, setting it between them. He pushed it open. "You can make one or not, this is optional, and you know... you can just make one and never come back here if that's what you want, but I thought it would be nice for you to give them a place to rest. A place that's theirs."

Elarie pulled the bag toward herself weakly. Inside were candles and paper. Tools for digging into rock. She found string, cloth, and beads as well mixed in with the carving wood and tools. "Thought of everything, didn't you?" She breathed shallowly.

"I know you don't have anything but memories," he said gently, "so I thought you might want to make something for them."

Her heart ached. She picked up the bag and held it close to her. "I don't have anything of theirs," she whispered, running her thumb over the dry canvas. Kaelum said nothing. Even if she had something that belonged to them she would've lost it over the years. She looked around. "Anywhere?" Elarie asked, her voice painful.

"Anywhere you want," he nodded.

Elarie looked at the genuine sympathy on his face. He was sharing his space with her. He was letting her in and hoping the door opened the other way, too. It looked like he had tears in his eyes as well. He'd been in her position, after all. Finding a place, making a place, saying goodbye.

This is just another reason for you to stay, she thought as she crawled across the stone and went to the edge. Water lapped lazily below as Elarie's hand warmed. She touched a part of the wall that was right above the water, not the land. Her handprint melted into the rock wall, sinking in and causing the melted rock to drip. Elarie put pressure into it until there was a deep enough space. She smoothed the bottom out slightly.

Elarie stared at the hole in the wall she'd created, melted permanently into place. It was another reason to stay, her doing this. She was putting down roots in some depressing way. If here was where she placed her family, why would she ever leave?

She looked into the bag and took out one of the small candles. It hadn't ever been lit, the wick was still covered in wax. Elarie put it against the rock where her palm print was. She melted it into place, wick still unlit. It remained floating against the wall, some parts dripping down.

Her family was that of elementals. The god without a name had called them her element family. They were the holders and creators, now left to nothing but a handprint in a wall with an unlit candle pressed into place. Elarie put her head against the wall and squeezed her eyes shut. She had funeral traditions she could be doing. She could be burying gold in stone, she could be placing elements inside, but suddenly her entire body wasn't working. Suddenly she was frozen, trapped in an uncomfortable bent position with her shoulders shaking.

"Here," Kaelum whispered. He sat next to her and she opened her eyes. In his open hand was a red bit of paper folded into the shape of a butterfly. "Calix told me they're important to him and you have one tattooed on your back, so maybe they're important to you, too."

Elarie's throat was closing up. A knot in it wanted her to choke. She was going to die. Her head ached, it was going to burst. Elarie took it and sobbed sharply, trembling. She slid toward him and his arms moved to hold her. It took an unimaginable amount of strength to keep from tensing and clenching her first around the paper.

"It's all right, Elarie," he whispered as he rubbed a soothing line into her back, "it's all right."

She inhaled sharply, her skin burning. The ground cracked under her, a red crevice traveling up the wall. It glowed like dying embers and cut into the handprint she'd created. "I don't want this," she sobbed, "it wasn't supposed to happen like this."

"I know," he began rocking slightly, "I know, but it did. It's so hard and it's so unfair and hurts so bad. You shouldn't have been alone for so long, Elarie."

Maybe not. Maybe not, but moving kept her safe. It kept her heart sheltered no matter how many times she loved someone. No matter how many connections she had, running broke them so she didn't have to deal with goodbyes.

"You're going to be all right," he told her, "I know it. Just take your time. There's no limit on how long we can be here and there's no limit on how long you can grieve for. We don't have to do anything but this for as long as you need."

Elarie did not want to stay like this. She wanted to run. Not away, she couldn't in that moment. With this air pocket bit of land she now shared space with both Kaelum and Terry, how was she supposed to? With Calix, how was she supposed to? With Greilor and his eggs, how was she supposed to? No, she wanted to run east to North Reidle and to where Calix was. She wanted to take him somewhere with enough privacy and tell him every possible thing about her. She wanted to spill it before him and see if he says *I accept you.*

Would that feeling change before he came back? Would she close herself off again? She didn't for Kaelum. He reacted just fine to her confession.

"Thank you, Kaelum," she managed to say, but did not speak again after that.

CHAPTER SEVENTY-NINE

CALIX

The first thing he did when he got home after speaking with his father was hug his mother. Calix had his arms draped over her like he was a child again for more minutes than he could count. Vienn soothed him, spoke softly about small things. She'd be planning a party for the day after tomorrow. He would be required to come and was welcome to bring Elarie. The only condition was that they weren't late. Elarie, according to his mother, had important news for him. She gave no hint as to what it was.

He went to his bedroom after to wash up and change out of his riding clothes. Elarie was next door. *Golden blood, golden blood, golden blood*—his mind ached, the reminder jarring as he washed his face. He ran his hands over his hair. He'd have to tell her. He needed to, didn't he?

Of course he did.

But what if—

Calix groaned to himself and walked next door. He knocked and opened it slowly. It was afternoon, but there was a chance Elarie was still in her bedroom. Calix stepped in and looked around. It looked much more like a bedroom than it did a week ago. There were clothes thrown over chairs and shoes on the floor. A robe was at the base of her bed in a bundle. Calix smiled to himself before shutting the door.

Gods, he was tired. The week had been spent exhaustingly. Collecting people's things, helping twelve survivors travel down to South Reidle, and asking them for aid. They were a full village, he'd been helping build temporary homes for them. He was drained thinking about everything. It swirled in his mind, always finding its way back at the forefront.

"Calix!" Kaelum's familiar voice shouted. Calix managed to straighten, brightening slightly at the sight of him. "I was on my way to see Elarie, I didn't know you were back!"

Calix embraced him with a sigh.

"How'd it go?" He asked even though he never cared for plants and princely things. Still, Kaelum knew Calix and he could probably tell something was weighing on him.

"Horribly," Calix let go and leaned against the wall. They were in the hall by a stained glass window, the work in the shape of a flower in bloom. "It wasn't..." he looked away from the flower and his friend, "gods, it was horrible." He reached up and rubbed his face. Kaelum waited patiently for him to say, "it wasn't a disease that did it. I don't think it's a disease doing any of it."

"Any of what?" He leaned on the wall next to him.

He said, "we thought some disease was destroying the crops in some farmlands to the east and north. I thought that the spots were strange because a crop disease wouldn't travel the way it was. It turns out that a person is doing it. He went to these places specifically, twelve places, and is using magic to destroy the crops, the homes, and kill nearly everyone in the village."

"Do you know why?" Kaelum crossed his arms and turned. He was still leaning against the wall, but just his shoulder touched it.

"No," Calix shook his head. "Twelve locations and he left twelve people alive at this one. No children, no way for the people left to start over. Kaelum," he said desperately, lowering his voice to a whisper, "he had golden blood."

He was off of the wall completely.

"They fought him off," he continued, "the people. They said he wouldn't stop coming back, no matter what they did he wouldn't die and stay dead. One of my guards had a theory that the golden blooded monsters are evolving to look and act like people."

"Like Elarie," Kaelum whispered, "shit. Does she know?"

He said, "no, I was going to tell her—"

"Don't tell her," he shook his head fiercely, "don't tell anyone."

Calix stood straight, "why, what do you know?"

"I know that this was Terry's theory," he hissed, his nerves getting the better of him. Kaelum's eyes were wide. He began to pace in short steps. "He told me he thought she was in disguise, what if *this* is what she is?"

"But golden blooded monsters can't have elemental magic," Calix argued.

"If they're evolving who says they can't develop it? Or mimic it?" His breathing quickened.

Calix shook his head, "no, Elarie isn't a monster. Kaelum," he grabbed his friend's arms, "she isn't a monster. We have to trust her. We have to accept her. Think about Terisa! Terisa told Jamison that Elarie is who keeps us alive. She keeps *me* alive. She implied that I'm going to die without her."

"That doesn't mean she isn't a monster, it just means she's going to save your life or something," he said, though he wasn't as tense anymore. "If there is a humanoid golden blooded monster out there right now who's to say she isn't one too? They're evolving, you said that, so how do we know she didn't just evolve feelings?"

Calix let go. He breathed deeply.

"Don't tell her," Kaelum urged, "not until she explicitly says what she is. Says all of it, the whole thing."

An ache formed in his chest. He'd be lying to her. *How do we know she didn't just evolve feelings?* Calix thought about it. If Macri suggested they were evolving and becoming humanoid to blend in, could they also develop feelings the way they could develop magic? "This could end so badly, Kaelum," Calix said. He wondered if it was the right thing to trust him over Elarie. After all, Calix's heart had cracked when he found out Kaelum and Terry were using Red to spy on them. Could he trust Kaelum with this? Was it time to accept *him* the way he needed to accept her—and this was just the first step? He missed his friend. His *best friend*.

"I'll take the blame for it," he said instantly. "If anything happens just tell her it was all my idea. That I didn't trust her and begged you to keep this quiet."

"Shit," Calix breathed, "shit, this is shit." His father had gone silent when Calix told him what he saw and what he knew. He didn't touch the vial with the yellow sand. He stared at it like it would poison him if he lifted it. There wasn't a way to combat this, no one knew what to do in this situation. How were they supposed to stop a golden blooded monster that looked like a human? He had the power to destroy entire crop fields—and that was only what he was doing now. What was next? Forests? Ecosystems?

"Look, she wants to see you. She's been waiting all week for you to come back," Kaelum said, "and she has things to tell you, I know she does. But I don't think you can tell her this."

Calix took a deep breath. This was a mistake. This was going to be a huge mistake. "I won't tell her on the condition that you won't tell Terry."

"Deal," he held up his hand. Calix clasped it with his own. "We should go drinking. Play the toss?" Calix nodded. "Also, Red escaped. And Elarie told me that Marcella told her about the ring." Calix's eyes went wide. "A lot has happened in a week."

"Where's Elarie?"

He dropped his hand, "she told me she was going to spend time with your siblings today, I just came by to see if she was free."

"Why?"

Kaelum shrugged, "we're friends now. My Ma wants to meet her."

Calix nodded. His mother enjoyed meeting the people who made a difference in her son's life. Calix could easily recall the first time he met her he'd been so nervous. He'd never wanted to impress a woman before meeting Kaelum's Ma. He'd brought flowers from his little garden and had Kaelum help him choose what to wear. It had been the most nerve-racking experience of his life. "That'll be fun to watch when it happens," he said and Kaelum grinned. "I'm going to find Elarie, sorry to ruin the meeting."

"No, you find her," he said, "she has something *very* important to tell you."

He squinted at his friend, searching for the answer to his unspoken question as he continued down the hall. Kaelum chuckled, waving before Calix turned a corner. He made his way to the east wing of the castle, thinking hard. There were a few things Calix wanted to know, things only Elarie could tell him. Maybe that was the important thing.

But why would Kaelum know about them? Were they that close?

Calix peeked into Marcella's playroom, all pink and frilly, then walked further down the hall. Having both of his siblings play-rooms in the same place was so helpful. They were even connect-ed by a bathing room. Calix turned the corner and looked inside. Ryd's art room was covered in his dragon drawings. There was a giant window in front of him with a table below it. Papers and paint covered it. There were counters pressed on the other two walls, drawers filled to the brim with different things. They were color-coded for Ryd. The blue pencils, paint, paper, and otherwise were in blue drawers, red for red, yellow for yellow. It was quite organized for a four year old's playroom.

And Ryd was drawing, sitting on the floor. Two couches faced each other and a low sat table between them like in the west parlor room, and both Elarie and Ryd were leaning against one. Ryd had Elarie's finger in his hand and he was drawing with it on a smooth slab of oak wood. Everywhere her nail trailed a mark would be.

Elarie grinned at Calix, but she had to wait for Ryd to be finished to greet him. She looked beautiful. Her cheeks were fuller and pink with blush. Her hair was down. She wore a lilac colored dress that scooped over her neckline and was patterned with flowers and trimmed in white. *Come here,* she mouthed and he stared at her lips as he moved into the warm room. It heated with her feelings and Calix chose all the good ones. He lowered himself down next to her and Elarie fisted the front of his shirt, pulling him in for a kiss.

It was light, soft. Calix touched her face for the first time in days. "I missed you," he said against her. Elarie's hand traveled up his neck. It beat with heat, as if she couldn't decide what temperature she wanted to be.

"I missed you, too," she whispered. Ryd must've let go of her hand because she grasped his face with both of them, squeezing harder than necessary, but an excited, joyous look in her eye seemed to wipe away all the pain. "Greilor laid his eggs while you were gone!"

Calix's glee burst like a cry from his chest. He pumped fists with Ryd in greeting and told him his burned drawing was amazing, then lifted Elarie up. "How many did he lay?"

"Six!" She ran out of the room, looking back and waiting for him to follow. Calix had to say goodbye to his brother, of course, but jogged to catch up with her. "He hasn't let me near them yet, we have to respect that boundary if it's the same today," she reached for his hand and pulled him to move faster. "Dragons are territorial, we both know that, but dragons that give birth need time with their eggs. Even if Greilor knows both of us and loves both of us, there's a chance he won't let us near them."

"Is he all right? Did everything go well?" Calix could skip he was so happy for him. Grey, a father? This was the greatest day of his life.

She nodded, "he's perfect. I'm so proud of him."

"I am too," he agreed, "can't wait to tell him."

Elarie jogged down the steps and pulled him along, forcing him to hop on the last few and adjust for the quick change in level from stairs to floor. They were on their way to the glass hallway in a rush when she asked, "was the trip fine? Did you identify the disease in the crops?"

Calix's gut twisted as much as his heart did. He tried not to look at her, focusing on opening the door instead. "No," he lied, "we still aren't sure."

"Can I help in any way?"

She probably could. Really, it was probably her insight that would hold all the answers. But he listened to his friend. Calix lied again, "no, I don't think so. Thank you for offering."

"All right," she smiled warmly, heating him from the inside. Calix squeezed her hand as he was dragged down the glass hallway. Clouds now dotted the sky and a cold wind blew from the sea outside, but it didn't seem to affect him when they were touching. "Oh, and I finished the first prototype for your leg yesterday," she straightened with such confidence that he couldn't help but lean in and kiss her again.

She laughed and pulled him into the dragon's nest.

CHAPTER EIGHTY

#

Elarie descended first, her voice light and sweet as she went around the corner. "Greilor," she sort of sang, "guess who came back." A great purr came from the grey and black dragon, though he looked more ashen from where Calix stood. "He missed you."

"Damn right I did," Calix smiled, "I missed the birth, huh?"

Grey steamed pleasantly. Elarie reached into a trough and produced a sponge, which she handed to Calix. "Can you believe he came to see me first?" She asked with a second sponge in her hand. Elarie pulled him to where Grey's head was and sat. He followed her lead, now partially behind her. "What a surprise it would've been if he came here first."

The dragon opened his mouth and she squeezed water onto his tongue, nudging Calix to do the same. "I'm so proud of you, Grey," he told the dragon. Grey shut his mouth and swallowed, sighing. Calix looked at the large nest. It was holding up with the red and orange flames dancing over it. The whole room was hot because of it, like a bubble of warmth while the entrance to the nest was trying to push back at them. The eggs were large and beautiful, the detail of their scales slightly different for each of them. "Look at that," Calix whispered with a smile, "that's amazing."

"Isn't it?" Elarie leaned against him. She put her head on his shoulder. "Your dragon is going to have little versions of himself, isn't that exciting?"

He wrapped an arm around her waist. "You know? So is your dragon. And it's so very exciting I could cry."

She chuckled and settled down with him. Calix kissed her head. "Like an uncle, yes?" He asked with the same laugh. Elarie turned her head and kissed the edge of his mouth, saying nothing.

"He says we can touch them, are you ready?" Elarie pulled on him, almost like she wanted his arm to stay around her but knew they both had to move. They slid over the rough ground to the nest. "I'll make sure you don't burn, all right?" She said gently. Grey moved his head to watch attentively. "We're both going to touch the same egg at first, just one hand," she shifted and he moved closer, folding one leg, "go slow."

"I'll follow your lead," he said. Elarie took his hand and pulled it into the fire. It kissed his skin, tingling like a hot bath. Calix breathed out slowly and she looked at him, somehow making the temperature ease. She placed his hand flat on the egg and tears instantly bloomed in his eyes. "Oh my gods," he whispered. Elarie's hand slid over his and touched the egg. "What is that?"

Her smallest finger remained over his. Elarie breathed deeply. "That is a dragon egg," she said and swallowed, "it feels Greilor's love for you because it was once part of him and it's now welcoming you."

"I want to give it a hug, why do I want to give it a hug?" He felt a tear fall, seeing one fall on her face as well. The dragon egg hummed powerfully beneath his hand. It churned and curled with magic and heat.

She said, "it knows you'll protect it."

"So," he looked from the egg to her, "the egg is a sentient thing?"

"In a way," she shrugged, her small finger brushing over his. "It's like a baby. You know when they're born and tiny and only want their mother? There is an instinct telling them to do that, same with the dragon eggs. Dragons are the most intelligent creatures alive, so much care was taken into their creations that even the eggs have a kind of knowledge we do not possess."

He rubbed his finger over the scales. "That's amazing. I always thought they were like any other reptilian egg."

"Not quite. Come on, Greilor wants to steam them," she pulled his hand away. "We should get him something to eat, I have a wyvern in another alcove. Just remember to move slow."

Elarie crawled back a few steps before she stood and whispered kind, loving words to Grey. Calix watched her with a smile, following her lead. He looked back at the eggs and told Grey how proud he was and how happy he was for him. Grey hummed and curled around his eggs with thick steam coming from his nostrils.

"This is amazing," Calix said, feeling like *amazing* was the only word he knew how to say. He walked out of Grey's hot space and found Elarie ripping a leg off of a wyvern. There were already bites in it and pieces of the wings looked to be cut out. "He's not going to hunt for a while, is he?"

"We need to take care of him, keep him hydrated," she said as she passed him with the leg. Elarie set it gently at the entrance before coming back. "The most important thing is to make sure he has water. I've been coming in here a few times a day for it. He drinks from the trough but likes the sponges, apparently it feels nice." Elarie took his hand and pulled him to the cliff opening. "When it comes to food he'll eat the wyvern until it's nothing but bone, then he'll be forced to go hunting. We'll stay with the eggs when that happens."

Calix sat down and hung his legs off the side. "He's lucky to have you."

"And you," Elarie sat facing him. One of her legs was folded under her and the other hung off. Calix watched a sense of dread and calm cause her shoulders to slump. She pulled her lower lip into her mouth. "I need to tell you something," Elarie decided. She scooted closer and pressed her leg against his.

It wasn't about Grey, he could tell that already. Elarie sighed and put her head on his shoulder, taking his hand. Calix squeezed it and waited. He ran through the options. Bad news, good news, in between? She's leaving? She's staying? She'll disappear in the middle of the night and never return? Maybe she was teaching him about the eggs so she could leave and he could care for them.

Elarie straightened. "Calix," she held his hand with both of hers. Her thumb ran over his skin. "I don't get a mate." He winced and she pushed on, "I was created to blend in among you, I was supposed to be mistaken for a human by nature so it doesn't destroy humankind, that means I don't get a mate."

He stared ahead at the water. "I guess I blew it out of proportion, then," he said faintly. "I let it get to my head."

"What you feel is real," she said, "so is what I feel."

Calix was an idiot, he knew he was. He became obsessed with the possibility that he allowed species to stop mattering. If humans didn't get mates, why would Elarie? "As long as you don't think I'm stupid," he said, still looking at the water. It was darker than he liked, the clouds that dotted the sky covering the sun and making the ocean seem far more menacing than it was.

Elarie said, "I don't think you're stupid. And I can explain something if you'll let me." He just nodded. Calix shouldn't be upset by this. He shouldn't be upset with her. "We're a perfect match," she said, flustered like she wasn't sure exactly where to start. "When riders ride a dragon together they have to make a connection. It helps with their communication and with the communication to the dragon and it's normal. It's what's expected, riders need that connection to properly function, but what we have," she pulled his hand closer to her, "is a connection that started before we even rode together. The moment we got on Greilor together it was like we were meant to be."

"I think he'd agree with you on that," Calix said.

"You do as well," she put his hand against her chest. "The reason I don't smell to you and you don't smell to me is because dragon riders are in close proximity to each other at all times. Not being able to smell body odor is a blessing."

He managed to laugh. Still, he was disappointed.

Elarie moved even closer to him, shifting a leg over his. "It doesn't always lead to love," she told him, "but I like that it did."

Calix put his head against hers. "Then," he breathed a slow sigh, "is it all right that the hopeless romantic in me focuses specifically on two things you said?" She hummed questioningly, already moving to kiss him. Calix said, "that we're a perfect match," she brushed her lips against his, "and that we were meant to be."

"That sounds perfect," Elarie replied faintly. "You keep being a romantic, all right?" Calix just nodded and waited for her to kiss him again. There was magic behind being mates, some sort of nature-created thing that says two Fae were supposed to fall in love and be equal and forever be happy. It was fine not being mates. Calix never found them realistic anyway. A *perfect match* felt different. They may not be equal—Elarie was Elarie, after all—but they were perfect together anyway. She was angry and he was calm. That was perfect.

Elarie pulled her head away before she actually kissed him. "What happened?" Calix asked stupidly.

"Can I show you your leg first?"

It was a struggle not to laugh at how nervous she seemed suddenly. "Of course, please show me the prototype," Calix scooted back so he wasn't hanging over the edge while she walked into yet another alcove. The nest had gotten bigger while he was gone. Bigger and brighter. "Has Ryd been down here yet?" Calix asked, moving further from the edge. How would they prevent him from going off the side?

"No, he wants to wait until it's all finished," she came back holding the leg she'd made him. It looked more like a metal stick with some sort of bowl attached to it. "Where's Masha?"

"She's upset with me because I didn't let her stay in my saddle bag for the whole ride back," he said, "as soon as we arrived back she flew away."

"Oh, and she won't come near here yet," Elarie knelt and looked at the pants. "How much do you like these?" Calix shrugged plainly and she ripped them open halfway up his thigh. Calix gaped at the tear. "What?"

He gasped, "I didn't think you were going to rip them!"

"Don't pretend you don't dream about me ripping your clothes off, Calix," she warned teasingly and took off his leg. That and the pant fabric were put off to the side. Calix now had the image of her ripping his clothes off stuck in his head while she situated herself and the leg. "So I don't know how to do the spells that keep the leg on and I don't have the leather straps or anything," she said, "but because this is just to see how it fits I figured I didn't need them right now."

"No, that can come later," he dismissed, watching her press his leg into the bowl. It was soft, he'd expected metal. The fabric was breathable and holes had been put into the metal to help with it as well as the weight.

She smiled at it. "And I made it so you can bend it," Elarie showed him, lifting his whole leg and bending it. It squeaked as she she did. "That will be fixed as well," she told him. "Come on, stand up," Elarie bounced to her feet. She held her hands out and he let her pull him to his feet. "What do you think? Comfortable?"

"Yes, what kind of fabric did you use?"

"Wyvern wing," she answered and he shivered in response. Elarie backed away, inspecting. "Is it heavy?"

Calix took a step with it. The wing skin stuck to his leg, though it did start to slip down. "A little," he answered, holding onto the edge of the bowl, "it's definitely lighter than I expected when you asked for iron ore, but it feels taller. My hip is cramping."

She nodded. "I can shave off the footpiece. I have to account for shoes as well, I forgot about that," Elarie began to mumble for a moment, tilting her head at her creation. Calix bent his knee and the contraption bent as well. He grinned, now squatting.

He straightened again and limped toward her. Calix wrapped his arms around her waist and lifted her into the air. His back bent. Elarie laughed, moving her arms around his neck. "I have two knees, Elarie," he whispered against her throat. Calix buried his face in her skin, grinning like a child. Even if it squeaked and it was a first try, it worked. He didn't know how she did it, but it worked.

"Thank you, Elarie." His whole life not one of his prosthetics could bend like a knee. He'd had one or two that tried, but they never lasted. *This* would last. And she did that.

"Are you ready for the real test?" She asked as he set her back on her feet. Calix squeezed her tight. "Get on your knees, Calix," she pushed him playfully. "Come on, you've done it before, do it again."

"If it's not too bold to say," he pulled away and watched her brow raise. "If this works I'd be happy to get on my knees whenever you ask."

Elarie's face turned red and she pushed him again. Calix looked at the prosthetic, nervously bending that one first. Pressure built around his leg, the wyvern wing constricting around him. Calix got the other leg down and looked up at her. "Talk to me, Calix, I need to know what to fix."

"It's still a bit tall, that's going to hurt my hip, but the wyvern wing is soft and that's taking a lot of pressure off that was there before," he said. Calix flattened her dress around her thighs and dragged his hands down. He swayed from side to side. "I'd like to see how well it holds up on a dragon," Calix finalized before pulling on her knees. Elarie yelped, dropping into his arms. She slid down, her dress rising up as his arms moved over her body. "Still the same height," he whispered when he was looking into her eyes.

"Not if I get on top of you," she said. Calix started to lean in but was cut off. "I was thinking that maybe it should be like a peg base instead of a foot. You would have to stuff your boots, but do you think it would make kneeling easier or—" Calix pressed his mouth against hers and she sighed, apparently getting the message. No more talking just yet.

Chapter Eighty-One

Elarie

While she did want to have sex with Calix, she did not want to do it in front of Greilor and his six babies. Still, Elarie was on top of him and she couldn't bear to break away. Calix had started that. He'd pulled on her knees, he'd pulled on her hips. The metal leg had scraped over the rock beneath him as he twisted it around to sit. It was his fault she was in his lap.

"You want to know," Elarie swallowed. Calix nipped at her lower lip, his breath hot against her face, "a fun trick I can do?" He hummed, his mouth trailing a line of kisses down her throat. "I can make you finish without touching you," she said with a smile, pulling on the edges of his jacket.

"Please touch me," he dragged her head down and kissed her. Calix's mouth fumbled like this was his first time, but he tasted sweet and warm. His fingers dragged down her back where the ties and buttons held her dress together. He put his finger between, pressing against her spine. His hands splayed over her while she pulled on the belt he was wearing and Greilor growled that they needed their own space because they would *not* be doing that sort of thing in front of his children.

Elarie stopped moving, her breath quick. "Greilor says we need to leave," she told him. Their noses brushed together. Elarie did not want to stop kissing him. Perhaps it was the way it seemed that things were finally coming together. That she felt his acceptance the way she felt his love, even if he'd only really said one of those things. Everything was rushing together, pressing like two bodies far too attached, and she had no desire to stop it.

There were only a few more things to tell him.

She could tell him a few more things.

"Your bedroom," she demanded softly. Elarie reached blindly for the leg he was comfortable with and lifted her hips to detach the one she made. Calix gazed at her longingly. *He better not say it now,* she thought as she put the leg back, straightening it. Elarie tore her eyes away to strap it on. "Is that good?" She asked.

"I'm not keeping it on for long," he replied and turned them over, groaning as he stood while attempting to keep her in his arms. Elarie smiled and pulled him to the entrance. Her magic beat like a heart into his hand. It had been a silly, uncontrollable thing that happened too often. When she was flustered, when she was elated, when she wanted him. *Denial*, Marcella had called it. Perhaps that's what the beat was telling Elarie now—she's in denial.

"Calix," the very person Elarie was thinking of stood with her fists on her hips in front of the entrance. She tapped her foot. "You forgot to say hello to someone," she said.

He said, "no I didn't," tightly. Calix stood behind Elarie, clearing his throat, "I was going to see you just now."

"Liar," she squinted accusingly. "You forgot me."

"I did not," Calix said. He was trying to calm down. Elarie could feel it against her.

She said, "it was my fault. I was with Ryd when he was on his way to see the both of you and I told him Grey laid his eggs. We came down here right away."

Marcella surveyed Elarie with the same accusatory expression. "Well did he propose at least?" She asked.

Elarie's hand flew to her mouth and she turned to the side in an attempt to hide the steaming embarrassment she now felt. Her face burned and sparks danced across the fingers wrapped around Calix's hand. "Marcella," Calix choked out, "why would you say something like that?"

"Because I want a sister and pressuring you into proposing is the best way to get one," she raised a brow, now crossing her arms. "It's working, I think."

The sparks got worse and she breathed sharply, beginning to laugh. "Oh my gods, I love this child," she whispered as she turned again, this time to put her face against Calix's shoulder.

"You shouldn't have done that, Marcella," Calix halfheartedly scolded. His hand flattened over her back. "And I wasn't going to... well," he stuttered, "you sort of ruined things, don't you think?"

"No, I think this just showed that Elarie would say yes," Marcella said. Elarie laughed again. "So you better propose before the ball on your birthday so every lady is jealous and you can be married next summer."

He ground out, "Marcella," but her footsteps were receding. Elarie looked back to find her leaving, the swish of her yellow dress somehow reflecting how confident and sassy she was. "I am," Calix breathed, "so sorry."

Elarie snorted. She shook her head, "you know I would say no if you proposed before your birthday, right?"

"I know, that's why I wasn't going to," he muttered. Calix shook his head, "I shouldn't have shown her the ring in the first place."

She transferred her arms to around his neck. "When would you have proposed?" She asked.

Calix held her waist. He closed his eyes with an exasperated sigh, placing his forehead against hers. Elarie was just slightly taller than him in her heels, though it seemed he liked it. "I don't know," he said, "probably as soon as you tell me how I'm going to get you to grow old with me."

Yet another thing she needed to tell him. She told Kaelum. She could tell Calix. Elarie touched his face, frowning. "Let's go somewhere not in the castle," she said, "or the town or the grounds or anywhere near here..." Elarie said, "got any streams with lots of river rocks? I can teach you how to walk on wings."

"Plenty of streams with plenty of rocks," he hugged her close. "It's almost disappointing."

"Don't worry, matealn," she kissed him, "I am not going to end the day without having sex with you."

He chuckled, "I'll try not to hold you to it. You do get distracted quite a lot."

Elarie shoved him playfully and walked toward the woods by the castle grounds, sure to find a stream and plenty of rocks.

"I don't care that you only have one leg, you need to keep up with me," Elarie said from five stones ahead of him. She put her hands on her hips and turned around, breathing heavily and not sweating half as much as he was, only he was human. Calix had stopped again, barefoot just like her and whining. "You can't walk on wings if you have to pause on every stone," she told him.

"Come here," he breathed, waving his finger. Calix held his side, "right now, come here please."

Elarie sighed and hopped over. She was a rock ahead of him, waiting. Calix pulled her onto his rock so they were pressed together once again. "Please for the love of dragons," he shook her for a second, "can we please take a break? I am begging you, Elarie, think of my human lungs. They'll break if we keep going."

"Your poor human lungs," she pouted and he rolled his eyes. Elarie sighed and looked around. "The stream connects to a river, we can walk to it and talk there," she pointed to the edge of the stream.

"Thank you," he heaved a sigh. Elarie began stepping away but he pulled her back, "matealn," he said in a low tone that made the hair on her arms rise and tingle. "And you should care about my one leg."

She raised her brows, "oh, I should?"

"Mhmm," he nodded, "I think it's brought us much closer, don't you agree? Without it where would we be?"

"In the bedroom most likely," Elarie replied dryly, then waited for him to grin before she kissed him and hopped over to the edge. Elarie pulled on her hair, twisting it behind her head while he took his time moving from rock to rock. Calix pinched the front of his shirt and waved it through the air, creating a breeze beneath it. Around them, the wind picked up. It rushed through what was left of the leaves after autumn and spun along the bushes and tall grasses underfoot. Elarie smiled at the sigh rolling through Calix.

He tipped his head back and put his arms out while the breeze cooled him.

She looked away as it faded, beginning to walk along the bank of the stream. Calix caught up to her, taking her hand as if it were the most natural thing. "So walking on wings takes an immense amount of balance, yes?"

"Balance and the ability to be light on your feet, hence the skipping from rock to rock," she motioned with both of their hands to the bubbling stream. The water rushed a bit faster the closer they got to the river. "You're fighting the wind when you walk on a wing, you need to trust yourself and your dragon."

"Does he think I still have a problem with that?"

Elarie nodded. "I'll help you get over it. We'll jump off a cliff and everything."

He didn't say anything, though she doubted he was upset by it. "Tell me about your wings, Elarie," he looked at her. Elarie blushed, the idea of sharing something so sacred instantly making her nervous.

"They," she sighed shortly, "they were green and black with this perfect orange and yellow center. Like sparks of fire, they were so beautiful." Elarie stepped over a log. She contemplated leaving it at that. "My wings came to me young. In my culture, before we can ride a dragon alone we must find our wings. I'd spent years looking at different birds and bugs trying to find that spark, trying to settle into my magic."

"And when did you?"

"When I was four," Elarie waved their hands around, "I had thrown a tantrum and burned part of our garden, gotten in trouble like usual—I was quite good at doing that if you hadn't guessed." Calix laughed. She continued, "my brother had gone off before it happened and returned two weeks later. I wanted to show him that I planted bulbs for his favorite flower. He teased me, I told him to leave me alone and laid in the grass. And there it was."

Calix smiled, "your butterfly."

"My magic is so chaotic, any small fit could damage things or people. Everyone was counting on the day I found them just as much as I was," she said, "I remember there was this moment that I couldn't breathe. As everything came into place I thought I was going to die. I was like a snuffed out candle, sitting up begging this butterfly to land on my finger."

"That happened to me," Calix told her softly. "They were just the most beautiful things I'd ever seen I thought I was going to die. I couldn't breathe, you know, and had been leaning so far out of the window in my mother's study I thought I would fall."

She let go of his hand and wrapped her arm around his. "I'll catch you if it happens again," she said.

"If I'm hanging out of a window?" He laughed a little, the soft rumble in his chest making her smile far more than it should.

"Anytime you're about to fall, I'll catch you," she put her chin against his shoulder, faintly thinking of her parents. Wouldn't her father use those words regarding her mother?

Calix stopped. There was a smooth, large tan rock in front of them and a river sliding lazily next to it, but he stopped in the dirt. "And I'd trust you," he said, turning them both. Elarie stared at him, her heart lodged in her throat. "I'd trust you to catch me every time. And I hope you feel the same for me even if it's been difficult lately and you keep holding yourself a step away from me. Because I accept you, Elarie Crosha, *wholeheartedly*."

Elarie cursed herself in every language she knew. In any way possible, she was calling herself an idiot. Chanting it in her mind.

"I'll tell you how to make me age again," she whispered, practically unable to hear herself over the lapping of the water she knew was cold. She wondered where it ran to. If it went down a hill or cascaded over the cliff into the ocean. Elarie licked her lips and brought them into her mouth. "And I trust you," she said, "to catch me."

Because she was falling in love with him. Or perhaps she was already in love but the idea of admitting that the love was already there made her want to vomit, so being in the act was far easier to handle. But it was there. In the back of her mind.

CHAPTER EIGHTY-TWO

CALIX

Elarie was shaking. She was facing him, the sun that peeked out from behind clouds making her eyes bright and shiny. The river moved downstream toward the cliff and fell off it. It was higher now, warm rains in the mountains had caused it to flow more and rush in some places. Elarie was staring at it. Calix made no move to get her to look at him or to force her to speak, he just watched her try to calm down. To slow her heartbeat and even her breathing.

She closed her eyes. "I am the most important being in the world," she said, "my survival means the survival of humans because if I die and I don't come back all elemental magic with cease to exist. It will stop and if it stops the gods lose their favorite creation."

When she opened her eyes again she was looking at him. Calix tried to mull over every word she said. This was the most important thing she could possibly ever say to him, and to begin she told him the survival of the human species *depended* on her being alive. All elemental magic *depended* on her being alive. If she died nature would destroy humanity. The gods would not let her die because of it.

"The only way for me to age again is to have children. A daughter specifically," she said next.

"But you can't have children," Calix said, "you told me you couldn't."

"I lied," she shrugged painfully, the shaking getting worse. She wrung her hands together. "I have to get married and have children and only then will I be able to age."

It couldn't have been that simple. She would've done it already if it was.

Elarie sniffed and wiped her cheek, though she hadn't begun crying yet. "If you proposed and I said yes and we married," she breathed in as deeply as she could manage, practically unable to meet his eyes. Dread twisted and twisted in his gut and she said, "before we consummated the marriage I would have to kill you." He straightened slightly. She pushed on, "you would go to the house of the gods and be forced to navigate its many floors and doors. You would have to be deemed worthy. I don't know if that means you have to plead your case or if it just means you have to survive the house, but they would decide if you come back to me."

"And you don't think they would?"

"Not because I don't think you're worthy of me, I think you're the best person for me and you would complete me and I would be so happy," her lip shook, small tears falling down her cheeks, "but because it's easier for me to remain immortal and keep the humans alive this way, not by furthering my line."

Calix said, "but you're worried I'll recklessly tell you to kill me."

"I don't want to lose you," she whispered.

His brow furrowed. "Wouldn't you lose me anyway? I have to get married to someone next year, I have to become king and have a wife and begin to have children. I can't do that with you if you don't marry me. I doubt you'd want to be my actual whore, either."

Elarie's eyes raced over the scene before them. The warm rocks, the trees shading half of them, the water and the things inside it.

"I don't want to be with anyone else. I don't want to live with anyone else, I'll never love anyone else, I don't want to share my bed with anyone else," he said, "and I don't want to make another woman miserable." Calix paused, waiting for a response, but she didn't give one. He asked, "how do you think it would've worked between us if we didn't get married? We'd have sex and ride dragons and I'd go home to a wife and children while you sleep in the west wing and we both remain in love but alone?"

She met his eyes. No, Elarie would run.

"Will you marry me?" He asked. She didn't move. "I told you I'd ask after you gave me this answer, so marry me."

"Calix," she breathed.

He said, "the ring is in my bedroom, but you just have to say yes."

"But what if you don't come back?"

"Then you'll be executed for murder, you'll come back after and take Grey and his children and live on a farm in the north," Calix answered with a sure nod. "But I'm perfect for you, remember?"

Elarie wiped her face.

He said, "so why wouldn't they find me worthy if I'm perfect for you already? We're already compatible on a dragon, we're compatible as a team, who's to say the gods won't find us compatible when it comes to having children?"

"Calix," she said again.

"You can't age because you are needed to keep elemental magic alive, which keeps humans alive," Calix took her hands so she couldn't continue swiping at her face. They were hot, nearly painful, and beating faster than his heart was. A hint of steam floated between them. "In order to age you have to have children to further your line and keep the magic going, right?" She nodded. "So who better to give you children than a prince that will be king in a year?"

A cloud covered the sun, dulling her features. Still, her eyes gleamed.

"Our children would be protected better than any child in the whole kingdom," he argued, "your line would be safe, my line would continue, and you would age with me."

"Calix—"

"Would you marry me?" Calix asked, "if this wasn't a problem—if you didn't have to kill me or any of it. Would you marry me?"

Elarie trembled but nodded. "Not right now, but I think I would."

"Why?"

She looked at their hands, tearing hers away to again wipe her face. She sniffed and a great quake ran through her. An agitated look flashed in her eyes before they settled on him again. "Because you said you would be calm for me and I could be angry for you. Because I need you and you really are perfect for me and I know that, but Calix—"

"Say yes because of that," he urged, "not because of any gods or rules or bloodlines." She didn't say anything. "Elarie, you have the potential to lose me either way. To a knife or another woman. Only one of those two has the option to end happily. Pick that one."

"We've known each other for maybe six months, Calix," she started to say.

He tried for a laugh, though it came out strained and painful, "so if I ask you in six more you'll say yes then?"

Elarie climbed over his leg and kissed him. It was wet and painful. She pressed into him desperately. "I want to," she said.

He held her face, moving it back. "Please, Elarie, give me an answer."

She groaned weakly. Her eyes moved over his face. She knew what she wanted. She knew exactly what she wanted, she was just in pain. Elarie had spent years running, trying not to feel and hiding herself from people. Now she was faced with someone who knew her—nearly all of her—and was scared beyond belief because she knew what it meant. She knew he loved her and didn't mind if the feeling wasn't returned right away. Elarie also knew he wanted to marry her. And she wanted to marry him. People that were perfect for each other weren't meant to be apart.

"Gods," she whispered and pulled back, looking around her. Elarie stood, forcing Calix to turn and watch whatever she was doing. She picked a yellow flower. Then another, this one a blue weed. When she returned she straddled him. "This is you."

She gave him the yellow flower, just three petals surrounding a white dot with a thin light green stem.

"This is me," she showed him the blue one. It was a spiky looking thing that was actually quite soft, something that perfectly represented her.

Calix smiled at it. "What are we doing, Elarie?" He asked. She held hers against the heel of her hand and he did the same. Elarie then put their hands together. She laced her fingers with his and began to press hard. It crushed the flowers together.

Her hand relaxed and she slowly pulled her hand away from his. Elarie took the two flowers that were now crushed together, then looked at her palm. "We did this with different flowers. It's one of those little kid things," she explained with a soft voice, "a complimentary test. My brother did it with all the girls." Elarie rolled her eyes. "You would take two different flowers and hold hands and crush them. If the flowers stay together after you blow on them then you're meant to be."

"Both of us blow on them?" Calix had his eyes on the weak, wilting flowers wondering if this would mean the beginning or the end of their relationship. When Elarie nodded he took her hand, waiting for her lead, and gently blew on flowers. He could see why this was a game for children.

Still, the flowers stayed stuck together.

Elarie smiled and lowered their hands. Her cheeks were flush, her nose red and stuffed. "You realize you're asking me to murder you, right?" He nodded. "And you don't think that maybe that's not the smartest thing to do?"

"Asking you to kill me is the smartest thing I've ever done," Calix confirmed.

She put her forehead against his the way they would if they were in the middle of a ceremony. "Calix?" She asked and he hummed. "Can you ask me tonight?"

"Why?" He asked, but of course he would.

"Because I want you to," she said, "and because I have something to show you that should only be seen in the dark."

Calix chuckled, elated. "As long as you say yes. Don't break my heart, Elarie, it's quite fragile."

"That's because you're a romantic," she replied.

CHAPTER EIGHTY-THREE

KAELUM

Chucking the cork at the target on the wall of his ship, Kaelum's body went with it. He stumbled and Calix laughed from his place high above. He was swaying in his seat, probably going to fall. "You missed, asshole!" He shouted, his voice carrying over the dock. They were surrounded by ships of the same size, thankfully without onlookers.

"You do it, then!" Kaelum shouted. He didn't care if people could hear them or that it was the middle of the night, Kaelum was drunk and happy. They hadn't played toss in ages.

Calix grunted and came down, falling on his ass in the process. "I'm going to marry her," he said when he stood, swaying like a drunken prince with only one thing on his mind.

"I know, congratulations, go toss go," he went to get the cork he threw while Calix lined up his shot. "How'd you get her to say yes?"

"I have no idea," the prince threw his cork at the painted dot. "Ha!" He pointed to it. "Got it!"

Kaelum picked up his cork as well as his own. "I've been with Terry for four years," he said as he squinted at them, "and we've just now discussed marriage. How did you—*you*—get a woman to say yes to you in *five-or-six* months." He began slurring, taking another drink to numb his lips further.

"I am a romantic," Calix took one of the two corks. "That's what she told me."

"I'm romantic," Kaelum paused, frowning. "I am. Shit, do I have to ask him to marry me? Or is he going to ask?"

Calix answered, "both of you ask at the same time."

"Now my hand hurts," he muttered, tossing the cork as he took a drink. The cork hit the deck and rolled to the wall. "How'd you do it?"

"I begged and she put a flower on my hand," he answered. Kaelum stood there, mouth open, and stared at the prince in front of him. Calix threw his cork and groaned. Begged and she put a flower on his hand? That wasn't helpful. Kaelum couldn't do that for Terry. What did flowers have to do with proposing? Well... plenty.

"Help me out, Calix," he sort of whined.

Calix came back with two corks. "You already spoke about marriage, yes? So now just ask him."

"But *how*," Kaelum groaned, head pointed up to the stars as if he was beseeching them for answers.

"Well do you have a ring?" Calix put his fists on his hips, alcohol dripping down the neck of his bottle.

Kaelum muttered, "no, I should get on that." He looked out to sea, suddenly dying to be back on it. They had nowhere to go at present—couldn't because so many repairs were still needed to be done on the *Greyscale*. But Kaelum desperately wanted to be on the rocking waves with Terry. He imagined proposing out there. Perhaps he'd rent a small boat like one his father worked with and ferry them out and ask the most important question of his life. "It's not fair you're getting married before me."

"I'm not getting married before you, I'm proposing before you," he grunted as he bent for his cork.

"That's a familiar ship," Kaelum said.

Calix stood next to him, squinting out to spot what he was looking at. "All of these ships are familiar," he said, "what are you looking at?"

"The one with the candles in the windows," Kaelum pointed with the hand occupied with his drink. "Doesn't look like one of your fathers, does it?"

The prince, who would soon be in charge of the fleet of ships around them, opened his mouth. His jaw slowly dropped. "No, that's not one of mine. It's docking now," he pointed. Yes, the ship was being pulled into the dock in a spot three ships over. It was slowly disappearing. Calix moved to the right, "why would a ship be docking over here, this is for the military fleet. And your ship," he waved at Kaelum. Of course, Kaelum didn't like it being referred to as part of the fleet. It was a pirate ship. They'd painted it and everything.

Kaelum walked to his side. "Maybe there's no more room at the public dock so they needed to come over here. I don't see a flag, though."

"Only one way to find out who it is," the prince shrugged. He went to the side, holding the railing to look down the dock. His guard would be posted there. It was a requirement when Calix went beyond the village, especially when he didn't have a dragon with him. It was Kaelum's understanding that he was meant to have more than one, but Calix had argued his father to madness before they agreed on only one. "Moy?" Calix called down. He set his bottle on the railing and bent further. "Moy!"

"He's tied to an anchor below the dock," a familiar voice said.

Kaelum turned, straightening. "Red?" He asked, "what are you doing?"

Red was wrapping a thin rope around his fist. "A job," he answered, "I lost my last one for defending my prince and crew, remember?" He began tying a knot, making the rope into a noose.

"Attempted murder tends to make someone lose their job," Calix said dryly. Kaelum could see he was attempting to sober up. Kaelum had stopped feeling the joyous numbness after Calix called for Moy the second time. He wrapped his hand around the bottle, his grip changing.

"It's a monster," Red replied. "That's not murder."

Suddenly Calix gagged. His hand flew to his throat. Kaelum threw his bottle at Red, but the pirate wasn't the one holding the rope. Calix disappeared off the side and a splash indicated he'd hit the dark water below. "Red, what the—"

He had no idea he'd hear a *clunk* in his own skull when something hard connected with the back of it.

It smelled like fish. Dead fish.

Kaelum blinked slowly, able to taste it as well as he could smell it. A hand was in his hair forcefully massaging his head. Nails scratched over his scalp. "Is he waking up?" Kaelum heard Red ask. "Is this working? I see Terry do this sometimes, you know." Kaelum grunted and his hand left, smacking the back of his neck.

The stinging made him straighten, hatefully glaring at what was in front of him.

Only it was Calix. The glaring stopped. His prince was tied to a chair. It was a rickety old brown one that looked like it would creak if he moved. His wrists were tied to the arms and his legs were as well. Or, leg, because the prosthetic had been taken off. A gag was in his mouth and upon further inspection Kaelum felt he was mirroring his friend.

"To get past the confusion," Red moved behind Calix, placing his hands firmly on his shoulders. He squeezed and Calix winced. When he flexed uncomfortably Kaelum could see a red mark on his neck from the rope. "The ship you saw belongs to the Great Captain Rol."

Rol? Seriously?

"I've been working with him for a few years," Red said.

Kaelum felt that specific betrayal like a blow.

"At first it was looking in on our lovely prince here, but then... guess who?" He chuckled. "She bought her freedom using dragon teeth that she pulled right from the source, that's what really got to his curiosity. But the messages I've been sending are what's kept me rich. Coins stack up when you're spying on a golden blooded monster, right?" This time he laughed.

Movement caught Kaelum's eye. He'd guessed they were in the fisherman's village by the smell. This looked like one of the big shacks his father worked at. It was a few rooms put together, some—like this one—even had a balcony. Two windows on his right faced the sea. In the shadows, though, were other people. Pirates most likely.

"And a Metar," Red added. Kaelum looked at him. Red sighed and rested his forearms on Calix's shoulders, placing his chin on his head. "And you know what he wants from you?" He whispered with a mock pout. "We got the one that was in your pocket already, but we've got to have more than one. So," he flicked Calix's cheekbone. "Channel that pain and give us a few stars."

Kaelum tried to speak, which made a few in the dark laugh. He glared and Red got up. He pulled the cloth from Kaelum's mouth. "You realize this is your last day alive, right?" He asked.

"Because Elarie is going to come kill me when Terry tells her you're late for your midnight dinner you promised you wouldn't miss after you play toss with Calix," Red nodded. "At first she'll brush it off, but Terry will tell her you're never more than twenty minutes late even when you're plastered and it's been however long. She'll find you because she's attracted to your stars, she'll bust down the door and we'll shoot ourselves a golden blooded. Rol gets her and your stars, both of you live because he loves a good chase."

Kaelum looked at Calix. Calix shrugged.

"I'm not making any stars," he said.

Red straightened, sighed, and turned. A clean punch sent Calix rocking backward. The chair creaked and fell, smacking his head against the smooth stone floor. The laughter drew closer as Calix was lifted back up, receiving another punch in the face. And another.

"Stop it!" Kaelum shouted. His hand throbbed.

They were Fae. The ones that were laughing were Fae. There was a mix of humans in them, even one faerie with blue skin, but the damn Fae were the ones that were laughing.

Red turned. "Are you making a star?"

"No," Kaelum said.

So Red punched Calix again.

CHAPTER EIGHTY-FOUR

ELARIE

What did one wear when being proposed to? Gee was being no help—he was naked, technically, and would propose to his Firelight Frei while naked. So Elarie walked into her closet, looked around desperately, and walked out again. Nothing was to be done. She was panicking.

Elarie was actually going to say yes. She would say *yes*. Her heart thudded as loud as the banging on the door. It wasn't Calix. She was not ready for it to be Calix. It could not be Calix—

Terry simply burst into her bedroom. "Kaelum is missing," he slammed the door shut, looked at her standing in her robe with her hair pinned back, and went into her closet. "He was supposed to have dinner with me after he got drunk with Calix," he was saying as he threw out a pair of pants and a shirt. The socks landed at Elarie's feet. "And he was late."

"Maybe he got lost," Elarie sat on her bed.

"No, do not dismiss me like that," he came out with his finger pointed at her and a pair of brown knee high boots in the other hand. "I would not be here if this wasn't important, you know that. Now get dressed and find him."

She sighed and held her hand out. He gave her the boots.

"And Calix," Terry added for incentive.

Elarie gathered her clothes and went to the bathing room. "So how late was he?" She asked as she shut the door.

"Twenty five minutes," he answered, "and that means Calix was late for whatever you two were going to do. I saw him before, he was nervous and jumpy. You didn't break him, did you?"

She pulled the pins from her hair and tied it back. "Not yet," she told her reflection. Elarie walked out and waved at Gee. He told her that Calix would love what she was wearing. Elarie beamed at him before turning to Terry, "didn't he have a guard with him?"

"Anyone can kill a guard," he rolled his eyes before pulling on her arm and pushing her toward the door.

"I would argue that there are some people who might not be able to do that," she said as she walked. Terry grunted and pushed her again. "I'm walking, you don't have to push," she moved away from him. He was agitated, sure, but that didn't constitute hitting her because he was frustrated. Elarie walked faster than he did in the first place, pushing wasn't necessary.

"We should bring Masha," Terry said when they exited through the large entry hall doors. "A dragon would be good."

Elarie said, "you can't, she's braving the nest."

"What?"

"Masha is going to sleep in the nest with Greilor to get him used to her scent again," she explained, "he won't let her go anywhere near his eggs, but this way she'll be able to come and go as we do without having him try to kill her for entering."

Terry was silent for a moment, skipping down the last of the hill and forcing her to do the same. "Do you think that Grey would kill Masha if she got too close?" He finally asked.

"I think Greilor could accidentally, yes," she answered. Elarie looked at the town at night. Nearly everyone was asleep, though the stragglers that drank the taverns dry were still out, as were a few guards who seemed to be off duty. They drank and sang in groups. Terry and Elarie passed unnoticed.

"So where is he?"

Elarie thought of food for a moment. A tavern was selling something sweet and something savory. Perhaps if she found Calix and he was unconscious on a ship somewhere she could have him buy her something to eat before he proposed.

"This way," Elarie sighed as they passed the food. Kaelum's magic was like a pull to her, as it was to anyone with the sense to pay attention. It was strong tonight, like he'd been making stars. What stressed him enough to make a star? Or was he doing it purposely as she explicitly told him not to do?

"What did you do to Calix?" Terry asked. They moved closer to the smelly fisherman's village. Terry pinched his nose at one point, cringing as he looked around. There was no one over here—no one but Kaelum, it seemed. And Calix. Hopefully. How could they have wandered this way in their drunken states?

Elarie looked at Terry incredulously. "I did nothing to Calix. Anything wrong with Calix he did to himself." Terry didn't seem to believe her, but he didn't speak again. He just urged her on while also trying not to push her. Elarie struggled not to snap at him when she saw his hands motioning her on. *As if I'm not worried now.* They were deep in the fisherman's village. It was set apart from everything, distinctly smelling of dead things, and too dark for any prince and his pirate friend to walk around in.

Elarie stopped, looking at a building two doors down.

"Where are they?" Terry grabbed her elbow.

"In the only building with a light going," she replied. There was only one entrance as well, which was inconvenient for all.

Terry straightened as he stared at the building, "why there?"

She heaved a great sigh and rolled her shoulders, "so I can kill some people." Elarie pulled her arm away and began walking toward the building. Silly little traps and their silly little trappers. "Just stay behind me," Elarie ordered. She reached the old door and waited for Terry. He didn't look pleased, but only a fool wouldn't listen to her. "There's always something funny to say about you humans," she told him. He sneered, but let her finish, "you always think you're the first to do something."

Elarie touched the door and it blew off its hinges, flying into the building. There was a distinct yelp coming from inside, as well as the singing of many arrows. A few embedded themselves in the ground at Elarie's feet, the rest burned.

"No one has been the first in years," Elarie said plainly before stepping over the arrows and walking into the smelly building. Calix and Kaelum were at the end of the room by two windows. Both of them were gagged. Kaelum was sweating, obviously in pain, and the entire left side of Calix's face was a swollen bruise. Terry rushed forward while the ash of dead people rained from the balcony. Elarie walked carefully, a boiling rage in her gut. She'd kill plenty of people as the night stretched on, but she'd torture whoever did *that* to him.

Calix had yet to look away. He breathed laboredly in and out. He was missing a leg. Where was his leg?

"It's Rol," she heard Kaelum say. Terry was struggling to untie him, but he'd taken his gag out. Rol. How surprising. "He wanted stars, I couldn't stop."

"You did nothing wrong," Terry told him.

Elarie stopped in front of Calix. She found herself shaking as she pulled the cloth from his mouth. The thin rope around his wrists and ankle burned away along with it. Terry hissed in pain when she did the same to Kaelum's bindings. She did not care. Elarie was focused. Trying to decide what best way there was to kill someone. Anyone.

"Red is here," Kaelum said from behind her, "he's been working with Rol this whole time." Terry cursed. "Elarie, we need to get my stars back."

She touched Calix's cheek. "Who did it?" She asked quietly. He reached up and held her hand. "Tell me who did this," she demanded. *Tell me I haven't already killed them.* Elarie would hate to have given them a swift, ashy death.

A Fae skipped into view, grinning with a curved blade in his hand. "The great elemental, I've been reading up on you," he mocked a bow. Humans and Fae were coming from the shadows to surround them. A few were holding faerthorne, but none had a long enough vine of it. "How do the words go?" He asked. He was pale, like the last Fae that held that sort of blade. Did this one know what to do with it? He kept spinning it around. "If it is given? So it is given?" Elarie said nothing. "Can't I just slit your throat and be done with it? Spill the blood and get the goods?" He laughed. Many joined him. Elarie then counted. Seven Fae, six humans. No Red yet.

"Give me a moment, love," Elarie said to Calix, brushing her hand over his cheek. Calix said nothing. He just turned to watch. Elarie walked to the Fae with the blade. "Where are Kaelum's stars?" She asked. He laughed, spewing the overconfidence of his species. "Fine," Elarie sighed.

The Fae next to him coughed.

"I can find them myself, but cooperation tends to mean a swifter death," she said. Another Fae coughed a few times. They all shifted nervously. "Calix?" Elarie asked. Weapons were dropped. A few Fae doubled over. Blood and smoke spilled from their mouths.

Calix said, "Red did it. He wanted Kaelum to make stars while we drew you out so Rol could take you back."

"Red did it," Elarie repeated, hardly hearing anything else. *Good*, she thought as the Fae burst into flames. The humans scrambled for the exit, which caught fire. The Fae writhed on the floor, their deaths prolonged and painful. "Anyone else?" Elarie asked. Calix said no.

"Wonderful display, Elarie," Red said. She turned to where he was and a bolt of faerthorne launched toward her. She sidestepped and it flew into a human. Elarie burned the bow Red was holding.

"You made a mistake," she told him. The confidence Red carried with him dissipated. "You should've run when I showed up." Suddenly everyone was dead but the people who mattered. They crumbled up on the ground, wind churning them into a pile. Silence followed her flames putting themselves out. "This was quite a poor plan. Did you think of it or did Rol?"

He hissed, baring his teeth.

"That's pathetic," she rolled her eyes. "Now try to run, I beg you." Elarie stepped to the side, giving him the opening. Red didn't seem to know what to do. He was just now realizing that yes, the prince was bait and so was the star creator, but *Red*. Gods, Red was the perfect thing to draw her out. He was meant to die. It was just hitting him.

"She's spent quite some time imagining ways to kill you, Red," Kaelum said, which was not true, "I'd run. Maybe she'll let you hide. Maybe you'll get to town where she won't be able to kill you."

Red loosed a short, worried breath. He did not want to die. He was a fool who did not want to die.

And this was all planned. Rol was watching no doubt to see what she'd do. Red shifted to the side, worry making his knees shake. It was as if he was trying to sneak away. Elarie's brow furrowed as she watched the strange reaction, then she turned to Calix. "Want to see a fun trick?" She asked him like she had before. Calix, still seated, gave her a smile and a wave at the exact moment Red started running. "Molten," she whispered and Red's left foot sunk into a pool of bright orange, thick lava. Calix straightened, his eyes wide.

"You made that look difficult before," he said over Red's screams.

Elarie shrugged. The lava cooled in an instant and Elarie walked toward Red. He was screaming and crying, holding his leg where it snapped off. Elarie kicked him in the back and he toppled forward, his foot staying where it had been. He screamed himself hoarse, looking at his leg.

"Do you know what happens," Elarie said in a low voice, speaking just for him. She squatted at his side, "when you piss off a monster, Red?" The pirate growled, attempting to stay strong while his body temperature rose to that of illness. "Any other monster would simply eat you and be done but I am a special kind of monster, do you know why?" Sweat dripped down his face and soaked into his clothes. Piss, too. Elarie whispered, "because I know all the best ways to tear a man apart while he's still conscious. And you know what else?"

He tried to hit her.

Elarie snatched his arm from the air and leaned down, squeezing until she felt the bone crack and split. "Not a single one of these men is going to stop me." Blood spilled from between her fingers and Red began to cry. The smell of burned flesh was beginning to sting. His nostrils flared.

"I'm sorry," he gasped.

She laughed and his arm gave one last snap before it was falling limp and broken, held on by nothing more than sinew and skin. "*Sorry,*" she chuckled, "sorry, that's so funny. Why are men always so apologetic only after they commit their horrible acts?" He grunted and whimpered. "Well, I am not sorry. I won't be sorry after you're dead and I won't be sorry when the humans look at me with horror and disgust because gods," she sighed, "this feels amazing."

Elarie stood and walked where one human had died. They'd turned to a pile of nothing but left behind a perfectly good arrow tipped in faerthorne. She surveyed it on her walk back, burning away the clothes on her victim. He lay naked and sobbing, holding his forearm.

"Please," he begged.

"Where did you put Calix's leg?" Elarie asked, kicking him onto his back.

He swallowed thickly, "the office, it's in the office, please! Please—"

Elarie stepped on his leg and he writhed, screaming when she simply touched the faerthorne end to the thing he was struggling to cover between his thighs. The thorn, sensing his power, began to burrow into his flesh in search of a bone. The closest was his pelvis. Elarie let go of the arrow and the other thorns attacked. They lunged for his bones. She stepped back with a smile as he reached down and grabbed at the thorns. They tried to attach themselves to his one good arm, so he ripped it away and screamed.

"Your Highness! Your Highness, *please*," his voice cracked. Elarie looked behind her at Calix. He was walking toward her, his leg having been retrieved by one of his friends. "I beg you, help me. Help me, please!"

He stopped behind her, wrapped an arm around her shoulder, and simply said, "I can't wait to see what she does to you next."

CHAPTER EIGHTY-FIVE

#

He couldn't say he found the writhing, burning man attractive, but Calix could argue that the look on Elarie's face as she watched him die was something close to it. *Attractive.* What had become of him? Once he'd been a man with morals. Now he was wondering if she'd make the same face while on top of him. The same satisfied, pleasured expression.

"What now?" Calix asked when Red had stopped squirming.

She whispered, "he's still alive," and kicked him. Red choked out a faint cry.

"This isn't as fun, though, is it?" He asked, glad his two friends were gone. Once the torture had begun Kaelum and Terry opted to go home. The stars had been stolen, sent off while everyone waited for Elarie to show up. They'd most likely wait until the morning to bother her about getting them back, if that was possible. Until then, it was just Calix and Elarie. And Red. "He's given up, where's the joy in torturing him now?"

"You may be right," Elarie sighed, "but I don't want to just put him out of his mystery, his death has to be painful."

"He's a crisp, darling, he can't feel anything."

She blew a breath out from between her lips, leaning back against him. Calix had watched her torture him from the same angle she could see him. He was practically in her shoes witnessing someone that used to be his friend be burned and scarred until he was nothing but a husk of the man he once was. "Is there anything else that can be done?"

She'd taken his manhood, she'd made him swallow his eyes, she'd ripped off fingers, she'd taken an ear... "I can't think of anything." She seemed disappointed by this. "He still has a tongue."

Elarie just clicked her own and turned around. "I think I'll melt him from the inside. Shall we go?"

"That sounds like a plan," he agreed and moved his arm. She hooked hers through his while Red gasped. "So this was just for Rol to see what you can do?" He asked as he opened the door.

"Sure," she shrugged. "Well, if the arrows had worked then I'm sure he'd love to have me back now, but I think this was more of a way to make him known to me. He has Kaelum's stars, got a glimpse of what he'll have to leverage to get more—that's you and Terry—and he saw what I do to my enemies. And knows what to leverage to get to me—that's you, by the way," Elarie smiled.

"What a simple plan," Calix said.

She said, "Rol is a smart man. He's calculated."

"Did you..." he tried to think of the best way to ask. They moved through the fishing district, leaving Red behind. "Did you know him well?"

"Terisa knew him better than I did," Elarie sent warmth through him as a cold wind blew between buildings. "He spoke with her often. I think she told him something about me and with what Red probably told him he's got some reason to want me back."

Calix didn't look back, though he almost wanted to. Like Red would pop out of the shadows with a knife. "Does that happen to you often?"

"Only when I'm weak and have something to lose."

"Are you both of those or just one?"

She smiled faintly. "I just have you to lose, Calix."

"How wonderful," he put a skip in his step to make her laugh. They walked with him skipping his step every so often so she had to do the same to catch up. Calix was elated. Nervous. Glad the only pockets they checked were Kaelum's and no one thought to look in his own. Then he might have lost the ring. "Come on, I have a very important question to ask you and I don't want to have any more interruptions." Calix brought her into the nearly empty center of town. The last around were the stragglers who didn't want to go to bed hovering in the doors of the only two places that stayed open late. A tavern and an inn across the street that doubled as a good drinking spot.

"Your Highness, what happened to you?" Asked a straggler Calix knew. Styd. He was mixed among a group of guards still in their uniforms. It wasn't allowed, actually, and if Bobo caught them they'd be in serious trouble.

"Oh gods, were you in a fight?" Macri asked. She was the only one among them that only had the colors on, not her uniform.

Calix reminded himself that not only were they his subjects, but were charged with protecting him. Their concern was important. "We handled it," he answered. "Ah, this is Elarie," Calix shifted to place the attention on her.

Macri grinned at her, "Elarie. It's good to meet you."

She smiled good-naturedly. "And you as well, I—"

"I look forward to our fight, I hope it's soon," she said too quickly.

Elarie looked at Calix, then back at Macri. "I wasn't aware that we were fighting, um," she looked at Calix again, "what fight?"

Macri answered, "oh, I've applied to be one of Prince Calix's guards," she straightened her back, "his condition was my recommendation letters and that I hold my own against you in a fight. Apparently he doesn't think I'll be able to best you."

"He would be right about that," Elarie again looked at Calix. Her green eyes pierced into him. "I'll see you—"

"Tomorrow on the training grounds, excellent."

Her brow furrowed but she said nothing. Perhaps Elarie could tell Macri was just excited. Perhaps a little drunk. A few of her friends were asking to join since Calix was putting so much faith in Elarie even before seeing some of their one-on-one combat abilities. "Goodbye," Elarie said shortly. She pulled Calix away and squeezed his arm. "You realize," she said, "that I am neither a trainee nor a trainer?"

"I do realize that, yes," he nodded.

"And do you understand that in order for your little decision-making fight to happen I would have had to *consent* to it, yes?" She asked.

Calix found his cheeks warming as he said, "it was stupid of me to volunteer you without your consent. In truth, I couldn't stop thinking about you so it just came out." He heard her satisfied breath before continuing, "it doesn't hurt that you are the best fighter I've ever met and if people can't at least hold their own against you I don't think they should be defending me."

She hummed, tipping her head back with her eyes closed.

Calix pulled her up the hill while she walked lazily next to him. "So would you like to be proposed to outside or inside?" He asked as casually as he could manage. His tone still rang with nerves.

"Well," she huffed, "outside is better, but then we have to go all the way up the stairs and risk having to *speak* to other people before I can ravish you."

"So inside, then?"

She said, "but inside is so confined."

"We could be right by the window," he suggested.

Elarie frowned.

Calix laughed and kept pulling her while she contemplated the benefits of proposing outside versus inside. "Let's go inside," he decided for the both of them, looking down slightly in a poor attempt to hide the bruising on his face. The whole left side throbbed. It would swell horribly in the night, he knew it, but for now he just needed to get past the people paid to be concerned for him.

He got up the main stairs and made a break for the west wing. Elarie laughed as she was pulled behind him. Calix found himself thanking all the good books in his library that they didn't run into anyone on the way up. Then, of course, distracted himself by wondering if it offended Elarie to thank the gods. If he should thank the gods. *She* thanked gods, but perhaps there was an alternative? Books, dragons, what else? Calix would have to question her on it. They'd have to come up with an alternative if all the gods were evil.

"Calix," Elarie said when he opened the door to his bedroom. He hummed happily and looked at her, tracing her with his eyes as she entered his bedroom. He was like a child. A boy with a girl in his room for the first time. "Before you do anything else, I need you to brush your teeth."

"Of course, sure," he straightened. Calix shut his door and locked it. Elarie lit a few of his candles as he was on his way to brush his teeth. It wasn't the smell, so it must've been the alcohol and blood mixture. Calix grabbed his toothbrush and the paste he'd added his own oil scents to so it was to his liking, then began to scrub his teeth, tongue, and the roof of his mouth.

Elarie leaned in the doorway. "Greilor is going to be so excited," she told him before taking the paste. She smelled it and muttered that his smelled better than hers did and walked away. Calix spit and winced, watching her pull her hair down and run her fingers through it. She paced the length of his bedroom slowly, as if she was moving merely for him to watch her do it. He watched her turn and pace back casually. "You're making me nervous," Elarie told him.

"Oh really?" He crossed his arms, "this is you nervous?"

She rolled her eyes and sat on his bed. Elarie crossed her legs and somehow the wind picked up around them, blowing through the windows she'd opened. It settled as if it was merely taking a deep breath. Calix ignored it the way he ignored how they floated when stranded in the ocean the night of the dragon fight. The night he saw her naked. The night they almost kissed. "Come here please," she whispered. He smiled and uncrossed his arms, doing as she asked. "You know in today's society this is supposed to be one of the most important days for me," she said.

Calix sat next to her, sinking into his mattress. "Me too."

"Right, you're a prince about to complete an age-old require-ment," she teased and leaned into him. "Making your whore your princess?"

"I'll make you my queen, actually," he countered, "that hierarchy nonsense is only a thing in Trec. You would be queen, no need for the princess title."

She hummed, "so if we married tonight I would be queen and you would still be a prince?"

Calix groaned, "that's not what I meant," and touched her chin. He pulled her in, his heart beating quickly. "But I am going to be king before we marry, so technically I am correct."

"I'll give that one to you," she breathed before she kissed him. His face throbbed when the pressure increased. Elarie moved back, "now you give me something, all right?" He just nodded. "I don't want to be presented like some trophy at your ball."

His brow furrowed, "you wouldn't be—"

"The way Marcella was saying it," she argued, "how she wants me to wear the ring and show it off and have everyone look at me, I don't want that."

Calix nodded slowly and asked, "what do you want?"

"I don't know," she said.

"We don't have to tell anyone but my parents," he brushed his thumb over her cheek, "and I can ask them not to mention it to Marcella. When it comes to the ring," he quickly shifted to pull the round box from his pocket, "it's not a wedding ring. You don't have to wear it on the correct finger."

Elarie stared at the box. "Will it hurt you if I don't?"

"Of course not," he laughed gently, "although I hope you let me put it on the finger it's supposed to go on tonight." Calix eyed her while she eyed the box. "Elarie?" He ran his thumb over her cheek, "will you tell me what's going on?"

A small smile broke the tension gathering between them. "I have this thing," she said, keeping her tone light. She was attempting to convince herself everything was fine, that nothing terrible would happen if he opened the round box between them. "Where I dream of dragons."

"Really? Who knew we had this much in common," he laughed.

Elarie covered his mouth, "shh." She grinned, though, and continued, "sometimes they're golden." He nodded. Calix never dreamed of golden dragons, though he could picture one now. Long and twisting and shining. "And whenever I dream this dragon important things happen."

When she uncovered his mouth he asked, "did you dream one last night?"

"Before you came back from your trip," she nodded. "I dreamed of one the day you attacked Rol's ship and I used Greilor's teeth to buy my freedom, too. Throughout my life it's been showing up and every time something big happens."

He thought of her birthday, however many years ago that was, and of her family dying. Of Matian. Had she dreamed of a golden dragon then as well?

"You're my something big, aren't you?"

Calix said, "I know you're mine."

A grin marked her features. The small flames in the room brightened and his fireplace lit to life, burning without a spark. Elarie leaned forward, her nose brushing his, "you can ask your question now." Calix was suddenly flush was nerves, his body shivering and the hair on his arms rising. She brushed her lips against his, wanting.

"Elarie," he said between her soft kiss and a breath of warm air. "Will you grow old with me?"

She paused, moving her head back. Her brows pinched together and her warmth became intense. Elarie must not have expected him to word it that way. Grow old, not just marry. But she nodded and said the single word.

CHAPTER EIGHTY-SIX

CALIX

She did a giddy little bounce when she looked at the ring. "You know me so well," Elarie told him. He did. He had her all figured out.

"Feel free to ravish me now," was his idiotic reply. Elarie laughed, though, and the red diamond glowed with her feeling. Calix watched her look at it shine on her middle finger before she shifted so she was settled in his lap rather than his bed.

"Want to see a fun trick?" She whispered. Calix truly wasn't sure. She'd already shown him plenty and had told him of one he'd already said no to. Still, she held up her hand and waved her fingers around. Elarie touched the backs of her fingers to the growing, swelling bruises on his face. "I can't get rid of it," she said. She was cold somehow, or she might've been drawing the feverish heat from the wound. "But I can make the swelling go down."

Calix saw her clearer. She was brighter, somehow, her concentration on her task. Calix dragged his hands up her waist.

"Wait, Calix, I have plans," she said. He stopped moving. "There is an order," Elarie told him as she wrapped her arms over his shoulders, "a method. Are you going to let me do what I want?"

"Elarie, I'll do whatever you tell me to do and say please and thank you while doing it if it means you never leave me," he said. She grinned and nodded, leaning down to kiss him slowly. Her chest pressed against his and her mouth was firm in its control.

Elarie breathed against him, "I really hope you don't care about your bedspread," and pulled his jacket off. It was tossed somewhere in his bedroom and suddenly every light went out at once. Calix blinked quickly, watching sparks like stars flash around his room. They flickered and swayed. He laughed. "Do you trust me, Calix?" She whispered in the dark.

"More than anyone," he said. "I trust you and I accept you in all your forms; murderous, golden, on fire, all of it."

The sparks blinked slowly, disappearing one by one, and there was a shifting in front of him. The sound of fabric being moved and tossed away. Calix breathed deeply, his heart racing. Elarie's hands moved his. He pressed his fingers into the bare skin of her waist. Her body hummed with energy, sending hot shivers like static up his arms.

A glow appeared before his eyes. Soft at first and bright white like the strike of flint over steel. Calix watched it warm and turn orange. It twisted beneath her skin. It continued to morph, different shades of flame catching as it spread like a fire. The magic started between Elarie's breasts, but quickly moved over the top half of her torso. He could see her collarbones like a dark silhouette. Her ribs followed. Calix could see all of her. Like she was the flame around her bones and her skin was merely a container.

"This is what I feel all the time," she said. Calix could see her face now. The magic within her spread up to her neck. It swirled in her cheeks.

"It's your magic?"

She smiled, "no," and took his right hand. Elarie pressed it to the center of her chest. "If I tried to show you what my magic really looks like you'd go blind and burn up. Think of it like trying to hold the sun, I can't show you that. I can show you what it feels like."

He watched the magic draw inward. His palm heated strangely. Calix knew it was supposed to be hot, he knew he should feel as if he was on fire, but the beat of her heart—of her magic—beneath his palm was somehow the most comforting thing he'd ever felt. Quickly agitated, flickering and waiting for something he couldn't name. Calix looked at Elarie.

He gazed up at her beautiful face. The light still beneath his hand shined over her soft features, highlighting her bright eyes and the apprehensive part of her lips. Her fingers were light as she moved his hand. Calix swallowed as she pressed it against her breast. The magic followed somehow, trailing his touch and spreading to a slow spiral around her chest. Elarie breathed slowly, shaking. He hadn't expected her to be nervous and wasn't sure of the reason. The magic or him? Both were raw in their moments, both meant a great deal.

The last time she had sex with a man it was Matian, he reminded himself. Elarie held his gaze with forced confidence, her stance as if she was in control but otherwise she was unsure.

Calix moved his hands and cradled her face. "Tell me if this is all right," he insisted, "we can stop if it's not, we can just sleep."

"I want to," she nodded, "do you?"

"I do," Calix said. He moved forward, getting to his feet. Her eyes darted over his as he set her down in front of him, evenly looking into her eyes. "Can I take the rest of your clothes off?" Elarie nodded silently. She was used to being in control, he anticipated her regaining her confidence soon, but she was still a girl that lost the love of her life and shut off intimate relationships with men as soon as it happened, now with another man.

Calix untied her pants and kissed her as he did.

"You're amazing," he told her.

Elarie smiled. Calix sat and lifted her leg, untying and removing one boot, the sock, then the other boot and sock. Elarie's toes curled against the stone floor. He pulled her closer, his chin against her diaphragm. "All right?" He asked, looking up at her while hooking his thumbs into her pants. Again, she nodded silently. Calix pushed them down, pressing a soft kiss over a particularly gnarled scar. She held his head, breathing slowly. Elarie stepped out of her pants and he continued trailing his mouth over her skin.

She tugged on his shirt so he removed it. Elarie pushed him and he laid back. The blanket hugged his form, his body sinking partially onto the soft bed. Calix watched a few of the candles help light the room, but the magic traveling around her body brought the brightest glow. Elarie stood in front of him completely naked. Firelight reflected on the skin of her arms and her round thighs. It flickered over her stomach and full breasts.

The Elarie in front of him looked nothing like the one he met months ago. Elarie was full now. She was strong and sure. *I am so in love with her*, he thought while she reached down and unbuckled his belt. Elarie was slow in her movements, gaining her confidence once they were equal. "Can I take this off?" She asked, touching the leather strap holding his leg up. Calix nodded, watching her unbuckle and set it on the ground.

"What's the next part of your plan?" He asked gently.

She crawled onto the bed and captured his mouth with her own. Elarie settled on top of him, holding his face while he traced his hands up her hips. "I have to tell you," she said, "that I get quite hot."

"I know," he kissed her again.

Elarie pushed him down, "and you need to let me know if it's too much."

Shit, how hot is too hot? Calix nodded and pulled her further onto the bed, his back propped against his pile of pillows. He brushed his nose against hers. The intense beat of her magic warmed his skin, but he doubted this was what she was referring to when she said *quite hot*. Calix ran his hand down her back, placing it firmly on her hip. She took his other hand and moved it between her thighs in a silent indication of what she wanted. He obliged, not expecting her to spit in her hand, reach back, and return the touch.

Calix groaned, perfectly aware of every callous on her hand, every pad of her fingers. He breathed hotly against her face with the curious thought of whether he smelled like his paste or if it was the same as what he smelled on her breath.

She pressed her head against his. "You realize," she said. Something sparked over her shoulders, "that when I say you're perfect for me or that I'm perfect for you..."

"*Please*," he shifted his hand, moving his fingers downward and making her stall as he dipped into what she was most likely indicating was the *quite hot* part of her. Elarie gripped the pillow by his head and pushed up so she hovered over him. He looked up at her, a smile spreading over his face. Her eyes were closed, her skin beginning to shine as heat poured off of her in waves. Calix was already sweating. Just being near her was doing that. But Elarie, gods *Elarie*, was practically gleaming.

Sparks traveled over her shoulders and down her arms. Her mouth opened, brow furrowing. Calix added a finger just to watch her twitch and spark. Her hair fell over her shoulders, spilling and hanging over him. Fire danced down the strands as if she'd put some kind of shining tinsel into it.

Her eyes opened as if sensing he was staring. Her green eyes burned and the heat around his hand grew. She bent and kissed him again. "Please say it," Calix whispered against her.

"Say what," Elarie groaned, moaning as he deepened his fingers.

"You never finished."

"I'm about to," she replied. Elarie covered his mouth with her own and he worked harder. He moved his free hand off her hip and began using both. She lost her concentration and ability to hold him, now pressing a blazing hot hand onto his chest. She'd undoubtedly leave a handprint and he knew he should be telling her it was too hot, but that would interrupt the bliss and pleasure growing on her face. It spread like a blush. It was perfect.

The hand that gripped his pillow caught fire and her eyes fluttered. Elarie managed to contain it, but he felt the singe as the hair by his ear burned. She shook, near collapsing.

This is what it means to be perfect for another person.

And Elarie says we aren't mates.

She collapsed against him, fires going out, and her head smacked against his. "Sorry," she breathed.

"Please never apologize for that," he said and her lips pressed against his cheek. They made an obnoxious smacking sound and she laughed, snuggling against him. Calix removed his hands and she trembled. He rubbed her back in smooth strokes. Above him, sparks were dancing. He watched them move, watched as it looked like they found partners to spin and dip with.

Elarie kissed his cheek again. Then again. Then the edge of his mouth. Calix smiled, turning his head to capture the full thing. "To finish my sentence," she said, rising and sliding back, "when I say I am perfect for you or you are perfect for me it can mean we are a perfect fit."

"Fit," he repeated, watching as she lowered herself onto him. Yet another flash of bliss crossed her. Calix breathed out slowly, reaching for her hips. The room brightened. The magic churning under her skin swirled. With Elarie's first movement, he squeezed her hips hard enough that he was sure it hurt, but she just smiled and moved again.

She rocked.

And rocked.

And rocked.

And Calix was sure nothing in the world would ever feel as amazing.

CHAPTER EIGHTY-SEVEN

ELARIE

Calix pressed a kiss to her shoulder, already knowing she was awake. He sighed and kissed her again. "You're my future wife, aren't you?" He asked, his voice sounding like a smile. "And I'm your future husband."

She turned over and touched his cheek. Her fingers danced down his skin to the collar of his leather jacket. "Why are you dressed, I want to have sex again," she stated plainly, her voice hoarse and tired. It had been, though she wouldn't ever admit it aloud, the best sex of her life. And that was just their first time, she couldn't imagine what they'd do when they knew each other.

"We have plans," he said, though he looked longingly at her body. She heaved a great, long sign to accentuate her breasts, which he stared at. He groaned, "please, Elarie, this will actually benefit our future. I picked something out for you, please."

Elarie looked around him at the dress he laid out on a chair for her. It was one she'd worn before that seemed to send him into a frenzy when he saw her in it. "The training fight?"

"Yes," he said.

Her brow furrowed, "why would I wear a dress to that?" She sat up, "and you realize you won't need a guard around me, don't you?"

"I do, this is just a formality. Come on," he held his hands out. Elarie took them and he pulled her out of bed. She ran her fingers through her hair, looking back at him as she went to relieve herself. "Your toothbrush and things are in there as well," he added, his eyes where they should-not-but-should be. Elarie simply walked away.

She returned to him with her hair back and her face fresh saying, "the dress is for your benefit, isn't it?" She went for the food brought to them, stuffing her face with Calix's egg white omelet. "Why do you get better food than I do?" She asked as she pulled a string of cheese out of her mouth, twisted it around her finger, then put it in her mouth.

Calix came up behind her. Elarie's tray was there as well, looking far less appetizing next to his. Her eggs were scrambled, her arepas were not toasted, and her coffee was plain. He, on the other hand, had a delicious omelet, a dish of salt, toasted arepas with a small jar of jam on the side, fruit, *and* he had breakfast sausage. Not to mention that his coffee came with milk and sugar on the side.

"I am the future king," he said, "I get a hearty breakfast." She grunted and ate one of his sausages. Calix reached for her hand, turning it from one side to the other to admire the ring still placed on the proper finger. "I'm sure you'll get the same meal when you are the future queen."

Elarie stuffed a sausage in his mouth and wiped her hands. She went to the dress. "So do you want Macri to be part of your guard?" She asked as she slipped it on. Calix helped with the buttons, his hands dragging longingly over her spine.

"I do," he answered, kissing her neck. Elarie bit her lip as she slipped into the heels. "And yes, this is for my benefit," Calix added when he ran his hand over the front of the dress, "watching everyone underestimate you is going to be my favorite pastime."

Favorite pastime, he says, *future queen,* he tells her, *when you are,* he muses. Elarie took a deep, clear breath. She hadn't felt this good in years. Even one night with him, now a morning, had done more for her than anything had in such a long time. Still, the god in the back of her mind again asked if she would kill him. Was it taunting her? Was it merely curious?

"Are you all right?" Calix asked, wrapping her in a hug. She closed her eyes, covering his hand with her own. "Please be honest with me."

"Ask me something else," she said, leaning into him.

He hummed as he thought of a question, accepting her avoidance. He'd gotten good at it, she thought, knowing when to stop and when to push. Stopping was best, though. Calix asked, "how old are you?"

Elarie turned around in his arms, holding the lapels of his jacket. "Twenty," she answered and gave him a kiss to interrupt his rebuttal. Elarie pressed against him, hoping to distract. She'd have to tell him, of course, that she *was* twenty and would always be twenty—until children—and that he was asking the wrong question of her.

He groaned, "fine," and pushed her into the chair. Elarie dropped onto the cushioned seat and he hovered over her, arms caging her in. "How long have you been twenty years old?"

She bit her lip and pulled him down so he bent for another kiss. "A long time," she answered before using him to stand again.

"Shall I guess?" He mused playfully, like age was a game. Still, Elarie was enjoying the press of him, the roaming of his hands over the dress he liked so much, and the exploration of his mouth. "How does five hundred sound?"

"Wrong," she answered when there was a knock at his door. Behind his head, Elarie switched the hand and finger the ring was on. She found it to fit wrong on any of her other fingers. A male voice called that *they* were ready for *you* on the training field. She doubted anyone was meant to be sent to fetch the prince, but perhaps they were impatient. Elarie pressed her face against Calix's cheek while he responded dutifully. Once the footsteps receded she asked, "are you ready to be entertained?"

He kissed her again and again as he walked her backward toward the door. "Say something for me," he demanded, sending tingles down her spine. "Say you're going to be my queen."

Gods, he was so happy. "I," Elarie smiled, "am going to be your queen. Your wife, your partner, all those words." If he survived. If the gods allowed it. If they felt like letting her be happy.

The training grounds were right next to Calix's garden, making Calix have to hold onto her arm so she didn't go there rather than the plot of land full of sweaty men and women. He promised *later* but she wanted *now* and he insisted *later*. She looked longingly at the garden and its fences and tall crops and the greenhouse in the back, making a point of showing Calix she was upset with him. He simply pinched her arm and forced her attention to the smelly men and women waiting for them.

A few were doing as they were supposed to—training—but most stopped to watch Elarie simply walk.

Macri came forward, her short hair pinned back. "You aren't dressed for the occasion," she said, leaning on a big stick. She was grinning, excited. She'd be one of Calix's guards soon, of course she was happy. "There's a changing room over there," she nodded to a small building that looked more like an outhouse. Next to it were the 'barracks' of their little training setup. Bows, arrows, and other weapons. More of the big sticks. And a familiar face with a board and paper, writing and inspecting.

"Bobo?" Elarie asked.

"Seriously?" Calix whispered more to himself. Bobo looked up, shocked at first. He then broke out in a grin that had Elarie walking over.

She said, "look at you." He signed the same, though with his brows raised and the shocked expression on his face it was more of a 'look at *you*.' Elarie laughed lightly and hugged him. Her arms stretched around his broad waist. "You look just like your father," she whispered just for him. He grunted and patted her back. "How have you been?" She asked as Calix approached. Elarie stepped away from Bobo as the prince touched her back.

"Bobo, how do you know Elarie?" He asked in such a good-natured way she couldn't help but smile.

Bobo signed that they knew each other years ago. Elarie was a child at the time, they had a little adventure together. And they did, but Bobo had been the child and the adventure had been breaking a pet hedgehog out of what Bobo had called 'illegal containment.' Elarie had been planning on breaking into the building herself to rescue a dragon. It had been a serious operation involving the capture of magical creatures for sale, one of the sellers had also taken Bobo's hedgehog. They broke in together.

"I would love to hear that story to completion," Calix said, "and I'm sure you would love to see how grown up Elarie bests your guards." He motioned to the group watching curiously.

He signed, *she couldn't possibly*, with a wink in her direction. Of course, he'd gotten a glimpse ages ago of what Elarie could do, but perhaps he had faith in his soldiers. Elarie was about to ruin that, even if Macri was half Fae.

Elarie walked back to the uneven stone ground and stood in front of Macri. She was still leaning on the stick. Staff, whatever. Macri looked to her left and right, her excitement boiling down to seriousness. Her career was on the line after all. Sensing the change, her comrades took steps backward. "Do you want a staff?" She nodded to the row of them behind Elarie.

"I'm fine."

"And all I have to do is... hold my own?" She glanced between Elarie and Calix. "Do you think I can't beat you?"

Elarie took her shoes off and bent to pick them up. She felt the earth beneath her, felt its hum of power. It was fresh here, even under the stones, feeding off the energy constantly stomped down on it. "You're welcome to try," Elarie said. She handed her shoes to Calix, who smiled warmly, gratefully holding them for her.

It seemed that Macri took Elarie's confidence to heart. She attacked without giving Elarie a chance to change her stance in any way. It was a good attempt, but Elarie still disarmed and knocked her down in only a few steps. Macri hit the ground with a thud, wincing and rubbing her hip while she stood. Elarie handed the staff back.

Bobo waved his hand for attention expectantly. He signed easily and a hint of guilt floated up Elarie's chest and to her throat. She stared at his scars, having been there when he received them. It wasn't her fault, she'd actually saved his life. The injury should've killed him. Still, part of her would regret it for the rest of her life.

And, hopefully, that would happen.

Would she have a 'rest of her life' or one of those fantasy-sounding 'until the end of my days' like in the stories? Elarie imagined what it would be like to regret something until she was old and dead.

His instructions and suggestions were sound. Elarie was now going to try to get to Calix. She would be attacking Macri to assassinate the 'King.' Elarie tilted her head and smiled at Calix, who now stood at the edge of the stone training square looking like he was very much in love with her. Elarie wished to kiss him for it. She had a dull sword in her hand, as did Macri. There were a few around them that wanted to jump at this challenge, but it was Macri's first.

Elarie walked forward, her desire making it easy to disarm the guard, knock her down, and assassinate Calix with a kiss. He whispered, "remember I *want* her to be my guard."

She chuckled and walked away, passing Macri again. She wiped dirt off her side and rolled her shoulders. Elarie said, "you can do it," and held up the sword. Macri surveyed her, suddenly a pretty half Fae sensing something was off about Elarie. She could tell Elarie wasn't human, probably guessed she wasn't Fae as she was. Her curious look discouraged Elarie. Was she moving too quickly? Was she too confident? Would Macri say something?

Elarie went forward again, this time allowing Calix to watch Macri move, see what she chose to do to defend. Each move should be calculated. The guard pushed Elarie back, concentrating. Her dark eyes moved and her mind worked. Elarie got past her again, of course, but Macri still managed to get a hit in.

Managed. Elarie gave her an opening. Now she gave Calix another kiss. "This is fun," she told him, "I like this game."

"Oh? I'm glad, you seemed so against it this morning," he said.

"That's because I wanted to have sex with you and you denied me," she said loud enough for the soldiers closest to them to hear. Elarie smiled when she felt the blush warm his cheeks, walking away.

Macri whispered, "I am so sorry."

"I'll get him alone later," Elarie shrugged. "Would you like to try again?"

"Do you think I got the job?"

She stepped close to her, "it's already yours, don't worry. Calix was very impressed with you." Macri brightened, a bounce in her now. "I am as well, I'd like to see you disarm me."

"Are you going to let me do that?" She raised a black brow.

Elarie flicked hers up and down a few times, stepping back. "Perhaps," she said, and she did. It wasn't really obvious, they knew Elarie was giving Macri a chance to show off her skill, so her ability to disarm and aim for the kill was something Calix would want to see.

She spent the majority of the afternoon 'battling' through soldiers to get to Calix, which meant many kisses for her, and before she began complaining about wanting more than kisses, Bobo interrupted. He dispersed them. Elarie smiled proudly.

"Look how grown up and superior you are," she said and Bobo waved her off. He walked away like the embarrassed boy she knew and Elarie wrapped her arms around Calix, placing her head on his shoulder. "Let's go tell a dragon some very special news," she suggested and he gave her a firm squeeze.

CHAPTER EIGHTY-EIGHT

KAELUM

He knew they'd show up eventually. This time they were hand in hand, the glint of a special red diamond shining on the wrong finger. She wanted to keep it private, then. Kaelum knew the kingdom would throw a fit once they found out. It made sense to keep something like this so secret.

"Hello, Kaelum, how are you?" Elarie asked in a sweet tone. She smiled.

"Well, how are you?" When she reached him he took her hand, looking at the ring and inspecting how it didn't fit right on her finger. "My future queen?"

She blushed, "it would seem so. Are you here about your stars? I thought I could teach you to track hidden ones."

He let go of her hand, smiling at Calix. He spewed joyous confidence. Kaelum said, "I can feel them all the time. I know Terry's in the shopping district, I know there are six that are on Rol's ship right now."

Elarie nodded, "maybe you should practice breaking things, then. Start with rocks in your hand, rocks from a distance. You'll need to form bursts around them, of course, but you can move up to breaking them without looking. Because you know where your stars are I assume you'll be able to target them and break them from a distance."

He had no desire to break them. He wanted them. He wanted to go to Rol's ship and get them back no matter the cost. They were *his*, shouldn't she understand that?

"Don't get addicted to them, Kaelum," she warned as if she sensed his feelings. "Come on, let's see how excited we can make a dragon or two." She took Kaelum's hand, not Calix's, and dragged him into the nest. Kaelum took a deep breath. She was preventing him from becoming addicted to magic that was his, magic that shouldn't be addictive to him. Elarie let go of his hand and turned around. How could she read him so well? "It's a god's magic. What do you think would happen to the average person—Fae, human, or otherwise—when coming into contact with magic that could destroy the world?"

He blinked rapidly. "I can do that?"

"Possibly," she said, now reaching for Calix. He took both of her hands. "Are you feeling powerful enough to destroy the world?"

Kaelum's brow slowly furrowed. Masha trotted forward, rubbing against their legs like a cat. He said, "no, not really. Should I?"

"Confidence is key," she said. Elarie then whistled softly, causing Masha to hop up onto her shoulders. "How was it?" She asked the dragon as she purred and rubbed her scales over Elarie's face. Elarie kissed her and Masha left for Calix, her human. "Well I am glad he didn't eat you, too."

Calix's eyes widened. "What? Why would he eat her?"

"You keep forgetting about territorial dragons with new babies," she shook her head at him. Kaelum smiled, liking their growing dynamic. Especially when she let go of his hands to switch where the ring was to the proper finger. "Come on, Greilor is waiting."

She walked away.

Kaelum looked at Calix and hit his arm. "She said yes?" He whispered.

"Yes," he grinned, "and we had sex!"

"Great for you, man," Kaelum shook his shoulder, much to the agitation of the dragon. "Way to go. How was it?"

Calix's eyes widened and he whispered, "the greatest of my entire life."

"I can hear you," Elarie said from inside the big cave thing. They walked over and found her smiling, squeezing a soaked sponge into Grey's mouth. She ran another over his face and Grey hummed appreciatively. Kaelum stayed back while Calix moved in slowly. Masha got off his back and sat on Kaelum's right.

"How are you, Grey?" Calix touched his big face, "you feeling all right?"

Elarie said, "he's just weak. But he's got help now," she nodded to a spot by the trough of water that was somehow always full. Kaelum had never seen Elarie carry water down, but Grey had to be drinking from it. Next to it was the little blue Frei, Gee, and one that was on fire. "That's Renci," she introduced. Renci waved proudly, straight-backed like he owned the world. "When Greilor goes to hunt and we aren't here he'll sit in the nest and keep the fire lit. Greilor will still worry, of course, and come back quickly, but this guarantees the eggs will always be on fire."

"Cool," Kaelum whispered, now leaning against the wall. "That's great."

"It really is and he knows it," Elarie agreed with a smile. "But there is something he needs to know." Grey snorted. Elarie then spoke in her own language, not Ceptareei. Thick steam floated from Grey's nose when Elarie made a ball with her hands, sparks floating around it made of different colors. She continued speaking, opening her hands to show the dragon a black ring. Grey lifted his head, looking between them. She took Calix's hand and slid the ring onto his middle finger.

Kaelum plugged his ears when Grey shrieked. Elarie did not, but Calix did, and suddenly—very suddenly—there was fire. Grey breathed fire on the two of them, the hot orange and red flames curling around them. Kaelum had to duck out of the nest area before he was singed.

Of course, Calix was laughing gleefully. A childlike grin was on his face when the flames finally stopped. He had a glow to him that Kaelum had never seen before. "That was amazing," he said, looking around the whole nest just to be sure everyone knew it. Kaelum grinned right back at him and Masha hopped up and down, also shrieking gleefully while starting a strange dance. "Amazing, amazing," he pulled Elarie in for a kiss, shocking her enough for her eyes to remain open for a moment before she adjusted to it.

Footsteps came from the entrance. Kaelum turned and smiled again, "what are you doing here?"

Terry said, "no one will come in here. They're looking for Calix, I came to see what Elarie's going to do about your stars."

"Calix!" Kaelum looked into the warm space. His prince looked up, "people are looking for you."

"Is Kolto here?" Terry asked, "they're looking for him, too."

Two people exited the room, equally glowing. Calix said, "no, he went to the House of Scholars for something." With a small glance at Elarie, Kaelum knew it had to do with her, but he could also tell she knew as well. Did she care? "Why?"

"Translation, probably," Terry shrugged.

Calix looked at Elarie, "can you translate?" She nodded, looking back and saying something else. It was a pretty language, Kaelum had simply never liked not knowing what people were saying. She opened her arms for Masha and the dragon jumped into them, accepting a warm, loving hug filled with dragon language whispers and purring. They waited for Masha to give Calix a hug, her tail wrapping around his waist. Finally, she jumped down to return to the front of Grey's space. Only then did they move to exit.

CHAPTER EIGHTY-NINE

ELARIE

Her gaze was on Calix's ring. It was a thin band of her obsidian, made easily and without issue. She hadn't thought of any consequence when it came to displaying the magic so closely, yet found no regrets as she watched it shine on his finger. His middle finger, the proper finger. Elarie had yet to move her red diamond. It was perfect this way, she thought, because they matched.

She hardly noticed anything at all until she came upon the throne room. It was a large rectangular room with a domed ceiling. On the rounded parts were different paintings. It was a fresco telling the story of the love between the Trec Princess and the Ceptarian Prince. The first to live in the castle. The first to sit on the thrones that were now occupied.

The king looked regal, of course, but the queen looked magnificent. Her hair was pulled back into a large bun, two combs of diamonds placed into it. She sat on her large throne with her knees facing her husband in a deep purple dress that sparkled in the daylight. Her husband, who had a council of people standing behind him, matched with a flower in his lapel.

"Calix," Ritan said, "I hadn't expected you'd bring your friends."

"It's fine, father," was Calix's reply. "What did you need?"

Elarie looked at the man in heavy furs. He was large and worried, his hands clasped together in front of him. His skin was pale, as was the silver hair on his head and face. "Muntaiins?" She asked gently, recognizing the wolf head sigil on his chest and the bag in his large hands. His soft eyes found hers and she smiled, "I can translate for you if you like." The Muntaiins' language was thick, the hearty kind that used the back of her throat, but she knew it well.

"I've come for my people," he swallowed nervously, looking from the king to the queen to the prince to Elarie as if he didn't know who to address. "I barely survived the journey."

She nodded. Elarie asked, "what is your name? I am Elarie."

"Brin, I am Brin," he bowed his head.

"His name is Brin," Elarie looked toward King Ritan. His firm, intense gaze remained on her. He had an elbow propped on the arm of the throne, his thumb against his lips as he watched. "He came on behalf of his people."

Brin said, "my people did not wish for me to come, they believe we will survive until the next growing season, but I know... I've seen what they are hiding." Tears filled his eyes, "none would survive through the winter."

"Why?" Elarie touched his arm gently. The overcoat he wore was warmer than any clothes she'd felt before. That was the Muntaiins, though. During the winter it was as if they lived in an icicle. People only survived and things only grew because of their magic.

"Our crop," he told her, "it's all gone. We were soon to have the final harvest, we have food now, but not enough. Nothing will grow, no seeds will sow in the ground, it is destroyed."

Elarie told the king, "their crop is failing, he says no seed will grow on their land." Her eyes went to Calix, "could it be the disease you were talking about? The one in North Reidle?" Suddenly he looked dreadfully guilty. The color in his face had paled significantly. He looked at two people. His father and his best friend.

"It seems it has struck a thirteenth place," the king said, then turned to the members of his council. They all leaned toward him.

"I have proof!" Brin suddenly boomed. Elarie jumped, shaking her head as he opened his bag. "This, this is how it looks now," he said desperately.

"Brin, you have no reason to fret now, they were merely discussing other cases of the disease—"

But he dropped a stick into her hand. He closed her fingers around the cold, ugly thing. "This was once a great branch," he told her, "now look at it. Tell them, tell them," he urged.

Elarie's brow slowly furrowed. "This was a branch," she said, doing as he asked. The stick was yellow, some nasty mustard seed color that made her want to vomit. It was fuzzy, almost, but had the rough edges of sharp sawdust.

"And this," he dropped his wolf seal bag and held a smaller one. Brin pulled the synch and grabbed her hand, dumping sand into her shaking palm. It piled and spilled to the tile floor below, smelling of rot. "This is the soil," he said, "nothing will grow in it, it is ruined. Lifeless."

"He says this is the soil," Elarie felt her voice quiet. A thrum of magic rolled through her as if it was asking her if she needed defending. As a child that meant lighting herself on fire. Nothing could touch her if she was on fire. No one could touch her if she was on fire. "It's ruined," she said.

The king grunted and his council stirred nervously. "So it seems the golden blooded monster strikes again. Why the Muntaiins? There's nothing there, it's not my land, what could it possibly want with them?"

Elarie looked at Calix. "What golden blooded monster?" She asked, a quiver in her tone. Brin was looking at them desperately, but she was only looking at Calix. Calix, who loved her and Calix who wanted to marry her and now Calix who lied. He lied or he omitted, but it was all the same when she was staring him down knowing he was wrong. "Calix?" Elarie tried keeping herself firm, but she couldn't. She was shaking.

"The humanoid one," said his father.

Her hand dipped and what once was a tree branch slipped from her fingers.

"I told him not to tell you," Kaelum said quickly. "I didn't trust you knowing someone else like you was here."

Terry didn't know either, it seemed, because he was shocked as well. He turned to the love of his life, but said nothing. He'd most likely be silent until they were alone.

"I need aid," Brin said, "please ask for aid, I do not want my people to die."

"My people died," Elarie said, but in Ceptareei so he did not understand her. Calix did. She watched the realization shine in his Lathin eyes. "My family died."

He started, "Elarie..."

She tilted her hand to the side, letting the sand that was once soil spilled to the ground. It collected with the rest, forming a pile of ruin and waste. Elarie stared at it, her throat tightening. Her entire body was being squeezed. The pressure was increasing. "This is what became of the Forgotten Lands," she said. Her lip shook, "he came and he killed everyone and he turned it to ruin and you didn't tell me."

"It was my fault," Kaelum said.

"I told you about my wings, I told you about my family, I shared my magic," she put her gaze on Calix, fixed on him because he had been her everything for such a short amount of time, "I said I would *marry* you, I had *sex* with you, and you didn't tell me?"

He swallowed, "I was going to."

"When?" She asked, her hands forming fists, "because you should've told me the moment you found out. I should've been the first person you told."

"I know you should've been," he said.

Elarie blinked tears from her eyes and tore her gaze away, looking at the king. "The People of the Muntaiins need your help. They will die without it."

"What are you?" He asked curiously. "A golden blooded thing, yes, but *what* golden blooded thing? Tell me and I'll help them."

Why would he hold that over her head? Why would he do that to her? Elarie wiped her hand against her skirt, still able to feel the disgusting sand she'd practically drowned in so many years ago. Her throat throbbed, she was blinded by the tears rolling down her face. Yet she wasn't the one to say it. Elarie wasn't sure if she would've been able to anyway, given how long she'd kept that secret. Could she even whisper the word? Calix said, "she's an Eneblood."

"And what is that?" Ritan asked with some sort of satisfied sigh. He sat back in his chair.

"An elemental. *The* elemental," he said, "without her we'd all be dead."

Elarie looked at Brin. He'd stared blankly at everything, though he took in the emotion rolling through each of them. "Eneblood," he said to her, "that is a thousand year name."

"A few thousand," she said faintly. He nodded, giving her a pained smile. "King Ritan will provide aid to your people, if he does not I will enact vengeance upon this terrible castle and those deserving."

He nodded again, his head moving and his neck bending into a low bow. Elarie just squeezed his arm lightly before she walked away. She wiped her hand again and again, but the stinging feeling had returned. Long ago she'd spent ages unable to rid herself of the feeling. It wasn't until she grew a whole new body that it did, and sometimes she could still feel the scrape against her head like sand in her hair. It followed her as her memory haunted her and now it had returned.

The throne room doors opened for her and closed behind her. She was blind now, stumbling and sparking, but she clearly heard the doors open again. Then her name. Her name on the lips of someone who loved her. "Elarie, please wait," he said. She considered going. Elarie could burn his wooden leg so he couldn't follow. She could flee as she always did. And yet she let him catch up to her, let him grab her arm. "Please," he whispered vehemently.

Elarie turned and shoved him weakly. Her weakness was still forceful for a human, so he stumbled. "You should have told me!" Elarie shouted. She blinked tears from her eyes. There were people in the hall, but what did it matter? Everyone could know what she was. Maybe they'd kill her and dump her body into the sea so she could be free of them.

"I know," Calix said, again stepping toward her. He didn't care about their audience either, he just held his hands out wanting to touch her. "I know."

"Why is it always blood?" She asked. He didn't have an answer. Elarie inhaled sharply, "he killed my family. He killed my *family*, Calix, and you didn't tell me."

He said, "I know."

Rage boiled inside her, so familiar. She was an inferno. She was a volcano waiting to erupt and he knew it, yet he wasn't trying to stop it. He wasn't begging, he wasn't pleading, he wasn't making excuses that would only make her want to explode more. Elarie sobbed, "he killed Matian."

Calix said once again, "I know. I'm sorry."

"My entire kingdom was turned to a pile of nothing because of him and even if you didn't know that," she said, "even if the only connection you feared was blood, you should have told me." He nodded, tears dripping down his face. "You know what I am, you should have told me."

"I didn't know that was how the Forgotten Lands disappeared," he said. His first excuse. "None of the artifacts we've been finding look like that, everything is just preserved." His second. "Elarie, I'm sorry." He was saying it like he didn't expect forgiveness. Calix just wanted her to know he regretted it.

She asked, "what were you thinking? That because he was evil with golden blood I shouldn't know? What if he was like me and I was a liar?"

"I wasn't thinking," he swallowed thickly, taking another step toward her. They were close enough now. Close enough to reach up and touch her. And he did, despite the burn she knew he felt because she wasn't pulling in her feelings or her fire. She saw him wince, saw the pain in his eyes, and finally felt the cool obsidian on his finger. It pressed against her skin, causing her to wonder how long he had known for and what made him come to the realization that she was an Eneblood. *How* had he come to that conclusion? If he didn't know what an elemental was in the dragon cavern how had he figured this out?

"Is this the part where you beg for my forgiveness?" She asked.

Calix shook his head. "Not right now. I'll grovel in a few days, you'll love it," he tried to smile, but couldn't, which had his joke falling flat. "I just want you to know that I'm sorry."

"We've been here before," Elarie reminded him, "when you said you just wanted me to come home with you and you weren't going to ask what I wanted you to do for my forgiveness, what do you want now?"

"For you to stay," he whispered, his thumb brushing over her cheek. "Just stay. It doesn't have to be here, it can be in the nest or by the river. Just stay."

She brought enough heat into her cheeks that he was forced to let go. "There is nothing you can do that will make up for this lie," she told him and pulled the diamond off her finger. Elarie dropped it at his feet and walked away.

CHAPTER NINETY

There was something he could do. He could find a way to kill a golden blooded monster. From what he already knew, it was like Elarie in two ways—the color of their blood and their ability to not die. The issue now was figuring out how to kill this new monster. In Elarie's case, she had to have children to age, hopefully it was different for this one. Maybe Calix just had to hit the right spot.

"We need to find where to get faerthorne," Terry suggested, lounging on one of Ryd's couches. He was seated opposite to Kaelum, who had done the groveling already. Calix hadn't yet. That would come soon. "He's a magical creature, right? Anyone with magic is stopped by faerthorne. So we just wrap a bunch around him and bury him."

"But how long will he stay dead for?" Kaelum asked. He was lounging the same way, only he was watching Ryd draw. Ryd had been angry with Calix. Everyone was. His father was for *allowing himself to fall in love with a golden blooded and potentially taint their line.* His mother was because he should've told Elarie. His sister was because *you ruined my chance at having a sister, I hate you go fix it.* Ryd was, only he hadn't actually said anything. Still, the kid was allowing the three of them in his space, which was a good sign.

Calix switched the brush in his hand as he said, "Elarie's been buried with faerthorne before. I think bugs and shit eat the thorns."

"So we kill him, wrap him in faerthorne, shove some down his throat, sew his mouth shut, sew his eyes shut," Terry paused, glancing at Ryd before he added, "shove some up his ass, sew that shut too." Kaelum laughed softly. Still, Terry wasn't finished. "Stuff him in a box, fill the box with faerthorne. Then we seal the box with magic. *Then* we add another layer of faerthorne before we box it up with stone."

"That might actually work," Calix nodded. He was on the floor below Terry, blowing gently on his poor painting job. "I'll have to ask. What do you think?" He held up the carving. It had taken him three days to get the wings of the butterfly thin enough, then it had been another struggle to paint light enough to not snap them. But there they were.

"It looks like shit, she'll love it," Terry said. He then held up the butterfly he painted using one of the ones Calix broke. "Like mine?"

Calix looked at them. The wings were blue and white. One of them was snapped in half. "I hate you," he said when he decided they were great. Terry chuckled and went back to painting whatever detail he wanted. Calix's had no details. They were childlike wings, green and black with the red and orange fire around the body. "Ryd, what do you think?" He showed his little brother.

Ryd looked at them and smiled. He then pushed his drawing toward Calix. There was a butterfly. *Her* butterfly. The one tattooed on Elarie's back, the one she spoke of before they reached the river. Ryd had seen them like he saw so many other things.

"Everyone is more talented than me," Calix sighed.

"I gave up on mine," Kaelum reminded him. He had. A broken butterfly was lying in a puddle of red paint on the table.

He set his down carefully while it dried, willing it to dry quickly. Calix stared at the butterfly. The orange interior of the wing seemed to flash before his eyes like sparks. Sparks like Elarie. Ryd had drawn her wings without ever seeing them or hearing her talk about them as far as Calix knew. Calix looked around the room at all the things pinned to the walls. Dragons and birds and bugs. There were so many of each he couldn't tell which were his wings and which weren't. Could all of them be?

"Is she still in Grey's nest?" Terry asked.

"How do you feel about her now?" Calix turned his head, looking at his friend. Who once was one of his closest friends. How had their relationship been repaired in these past weeks? Had it at all? Calix felt his and Kaelum's was much better, but he wasn't sure what to say about Terry.

Terry looked ahead. "Maybe I don't think she's a monster anymore," he said after a moment. It was a step in the right direction, then. "I want to know more. I still want to know about the Fae island. You know, what did that have to do with her blood or her magic? Where did something like that come from? I also want to know more about her magic."

"The Enebloods," Calix said. He looked away from Terry and back to the carving. "It's a name Kolto found when he was translating some of the Muntaiins documents. He did some more digging upon my request. We don't have much about them, just a few papers, so he went to the House of Scholars because he thought they'd have more."

"So what do we know?"

He sighed, "that Eneblood was the name of the Forgotten Lands. So if Elarie is an Eneblood that makes her..." he blew a breath through his lips, counting in his head and tapping his fingers together, "ten thousand years old? Possibly more. We've always had trouble identifying the age of the artifacts we find."

Kaelum whistled. "Ten thousand," he said, "imagine being alive for ten thousand years."

They settled into silence. Ten thousand. How could something live for ten thousand years? Calix thought back to the dragon attack when they were floating magically in the water surrounded by Dragonflame. She'd wished for a final death. She wanted to die. Ten thousand years was such a long time.

It was Terry who broke the silence. He whispered into it, "now I think I feel bad for her." Out of the corner of his eye Calix could see him lying with his head against the couch's armrest. He was shaking his head. "Sounds like torture," he said, "I'd hate to live that long."

"Especially if all you do is run and die," Kaelum agreed.

How much of it was from the golden blooded man?

Calix picked up his butterfly and stood, careful not to disturb the paint on the table or any of Ryd's artwork. "I'm going to go down there."

"Good luck," Terry grunted, "I believe in you."

He managed a smile, his chest warming. "Thanks, Terry," he said, hitting his friend's boot. Calix said goodbye to Ryd and Kaelum, headed to the nest. He knew Elarie was down there. She hadn't left as Calix requested. He received updates from guards, including Macri whenever she was posted on that side of the castle, and was told Elarie went inside the castle for food. She'd gotten her blankets and a pillow and some clothes. She was spotted with soap as well, so it seemed she practically planned on living there.

Calix hadn't seen Grey or Masha in three days, he felt empty without them. Would they be upset with him? He deserved it if they were. He deserved whatever was coming to him.

He walked into the nest with a shake in the hand holding the butterfly. Calix saw where Elarie was sleeping, with her pile of blankets in one of the alcoves she'd created for a dragon. It wasn't a mess at all. In fact, it looked comfortable. There were small fires around it, either for light or for warmth. It would be both for him given the chilly ocean wind, so perhaps it was for her.

Elarie appeared around the corner, her hand on the wall. Her eyes flicked over him, guarded as they should be.

"It looks like the golden blooded man was surrounding this area. He didn't go south, we don't know why. It was twelve locations at first, thirteen with the addition of the Muntaiins," Calix said. "When I went to North Reidle it was a wasteland. I got a sample of the soil there, it looked the same as what Brin brought." She leaned against the wall for support, staring silently. He pushed on, "they fought back and there was golden blood everywhere. I was told he kept coming back—the way you do." She nodded. "And he killed everyone but twelve people, none of which will ever be able to have children and further their line. The village is dead."

She pulled her lips into her mouth to stop the shaking. Elarie's brow furrowed and she crossed her arms defensively. "Greilor went hunting for the first time," she said, "it's just us and the Frei now. Masha went with him so they could talk privately."

His throat tightened. "I'm sorry, Ela—"

"Stop," she whispered, "stop apologizing." Elarie breathed in through her nose, looking away from him. "You should've told me," she said, her cheeks reddening. She sniffed, "you should've told me. You," her breath grew shaky, "*you should have told me*."

"I know."

Elarie swallowed, her intense gaze back on him. "It's a message for me," she said painfully. "I've been," again she took a breath like this was difficult and she struggled not to burst into tears. "I've been running because of my pain and because making attachments is... impossible," she shook her head, "but I've also been running from him. I think he hunts me."

Calix nodded. Gods, this was hard. He struggled not to clench his fist around the butterfly. His hand ached and trembled.

"I don't know how he found out I was here," she wiped under her eye, "but he isn't attacking from the south because he killed my family from the north. If he attacks again it will be north of here," Elarie shifted, her shoulder pressed into the rock wall she created. It wasn't just with fire magic. She'd used earth as well, he knew that now. "Twelve were left alive," she explained, "because that's how many seconds it took to destroy my kingdom. Twelve. A god told me," she shrugged painfully. Elarie grimaced, "and thirteen places were attacked because in the summer I will have been alive for thirteen thousand years."

He managed not to faint. "Thirteen..." Calix breathed.

"Thirteen thousand," she nodded. "I'm still twenty, my mind is a little wiser but I'll always be twenty. It's why I was fool enough to fall for you and fool enough to think you accepted, loved, and believed in me."

"I do all three of those things," he said firmly. "All three."

She winced, "but you don't trust me."

Calix was looking around now, spotting the leg she'd made leaning against the wall. Only this one was different. Newer and smoother. He went to it, quickly trading prosthetics. It was comfortable, more so than the last one, and bent at the ankle as well as the knee, seemingly for more mobility. Calix pushed his pant leg back down, ignoring his shoe. She was in the same place when he walked back over, only now she was crying.

He knelt in front of her and she whispered, "you're an idiot," without any cruelty or spite behind it.

"How many times has this happened? A prince on his knees begging like a fool?" Calix then held up the butterfly, "I thought I'd try this before I take the ring back out and propose properly."

Elarie choked out a sob and sunk down the rock wall, tears pouring down her cheeks. Her shirt ripped. She didn't care. Instead, she wrapped her arms around herself and stared at the butterfly. "I hate you," she said.

"What did I do this time?" He asked, "was this bad? I thought... well I wasn't thinking, I just wanted to do this. I wanted to tell you that you're still my wings, that I do trust you. With my life, with my heart," he looked from the butterfly to her. Paint had stained his fingers and smeared over the wood from his touch. "I think I trust you more than Grey," his brows pulled together. Calix lowered the butterfly, "and I know that's wrong, but I want you to know that you're my wings just as much as he is."

She reached forward quickly and covered his mouth. "You can't say that."

Calix pulled her hand down, "why not? You are my wings—"

She slapped her hand back over his mouth. Calix glared at her. "You don't know *anything*," she said angrily, "nothing. You are such an idiot and I hate you so much it hurts."

Again, he pulled her hand down. Calix took in her fearful eyes, a contrast to her angry tone. "I know absolutely nothing about your culture," he said softly, setting the butterfly gently to the ground. He reached up and held her face all over again. Her cheeks were warm, but not painful like they were before. "But I sense I've said something very important that you don't want to hear."

"I hate you," she said again.

"I am so in love with you," he replied.

She shook her head, "I don't forgive you. I'll never forgive you."

"Please marry me," Calix mumbled, "you don't have to forgive me, I'll never expect that from you, but..." he swallowed, "you haven't let yourself be happy for nearly thirteen thousand years. The golden blooded man destroyed your happiness and by running and hiding you're still letting him do it. Every day. You deserve to be happy and I know you're happy with me."

"You think you can fix all my problems if I marry you and have your children?" She asked with a hint of a snap in her tone.

"I think *you* can fix your problems if you stop running from them."

She said, "I don't forgive you."

"You already said that," he replied.

"I hate you," she said.

Calix shook his head, "you already said that, too."

"How am I supposed to stay and not run when he's here to kill me?" Elarie asked, which she had not said. "I'm not allowed to kill him."

"We don't kill him," he said, "we wrap his ass in faerthorne, put him in a box and wrap that in faerthorne, then encase him in stone."

"He'll come back," she said, "and you won't find enough faerthorne in time, he could attack any day he wants to."

Calix wiped away tears, arguing, "we have what Red used on you. We'll figure it out."

"Humans are so optimistic it's disgusting," she told him.

"You're trying to find excuses because you know I'm right," he shook her head just a little. "Listen to me, Elarie, please. Please." She said nothing. "You can be happy with me. You never have to forgive what I did. You can call me a liar and an idiot for the rest of our lives. You can say you hate me because I know you don't and it doesn't hurt. *Elarie*," he implored, "you can be happy."

She said, "you can make me happy?"

"You know I can."

"No I don't."

"I did before."

"You're such a matealn—"

Calix leaned forward and pressed his mouth to hers, shutting her up completely. Her face was wet and warm. She made a little noise of shock that paired well with a sharp inhale, but her breathing grew soft when he moved. Maybe they hadn't been kissing for very long. Maybe they'd only had sex one time. But Calix knew how to kiss her. He knew to drag his hand back. Cradle with one, move the other through her hair. He knew when to draw back and when to push in for more. "You're my wings," Calix whispered, his lips brushing hers as he said it. It felt like she was ready to argue. And she would've done it quite well.

Until the fateful, ever-present interruption. Calix groaned and Terry shouted her name. He tripped and hit the ground with a grunt, but looked at the both of them. "I got the faerthorne," he said, breathing heavily. He held up a vine and the two thorns that had been in her side. "He destroyed a field up north. No one saw him, but there's a road going next to it, a traveler just reported it to the guard. He said he didn't see anyone there."

"I told you," Elarie said numbly before she stood and left both of them.

CHAPTER NINETY-ONE

ELARIE

Elarie did not want to go north, but she could feel the disgusting magic coming from it, rising like steam floating up to the clouds. She stared at the tree line. Beyond it would be destruction. Beyond it would be ruin. Was she prepared for that? For this? For Calix's silly little idea, for Terry's faerthorne? No matter how much she may want to be happy, there was no guarantee this would work. Elarie had never faced him, she'd only seen him. She'd been *told* of his blood, she'd been taunted with him by cruel gods that kill her to have conversations.

Kaelum touched her arm, also breathing heavily like he'd run from town, not from the castle. "What do you want to do?" He asked, "we should have a plan."

"I can't hold the faerthorne for long," she said, "neither can you."

"We can," Terry said. Calix was next to him. "You can disable him, each of us will have the thorns. When he's down we poke him with it, wrap the vine around his wrists, and figure it out from there."

Maybe it was that easy. Maybe she had just been scared. He was just a man with magic. She could knock out a man with magic.

"Your Highness," Macri jogged forward clad in her armor. She looked at each of them, then addressed her future king, "your father is requesting your presence in his study."

"Noted," Calix said, then began walking north. "Let's kill a golden blooded monster," he smiled at Elarie, who just stood there. Terry followed and Macri began asking what was going on, also following.

Kaelum stood by Elarie. "We can do this, you know," he said, nudging her. "Here," he held a star out for her. Elarie took it from his hand carefully, catching the serious, gentle look on his face. He gave her a nod, "I doubt you'll need it, so think of it as a boost. I believe in you."

"Thank you, Kaelum," Elarie squeezed his hand and he pulled north. She slipped the star into her pocket, already feeling stronger and lighter with it. They were the most powerful things, of course. Raw magic that could be used for anything. It rubbed against her pants, but she felt it on her skin.

Elarie looked back at the nest. Gee and Renci were there, so the eggs would be fine. Perhaps she should wait and tell Grey. He already knew about the golden blooded man, shouldn't she wait and ask his advice?

But she was already being pulled north and the entrance to the nest was growing smaller.

Kaelum asked, "so did you say yes to marrying him again?"

"I can't think about that right now," Elarie shook her head. Why would she? Yes, it mattered, but in this situation it wasn't the most important thing. She needed to concentrate. She needed to pull her magic in, she needed a plan. "You'll help me, right?" She asked him,

"I know you aren't the best with the bursts, but maybe you can create one around him. It'll make for good practice."

"Practice," he repeated with a chuckle. They entered the woods, a place that was quiet and cold. Leaves were gone from the branches, blowing in the wind. "Elarie," Kaelum said in a low voice. She glanced at him, stepping over a fallen tree. He got over it as well. "I wanted to apologize. I told Calix not to tell you in the first place, yes, but you're also my friend. I should've told you."

She kept her eyes ahead. "I don't forgive you," she replied.

"I understand," was all he said. But she was still holding his hand, which should've counted for something. For both of them.

Macri was still talking ahead of them. It seemed that she didn't agree with Calix's plan. She was arguing against it, saying they should go back for more guards or soldiers. Calix felt that this was something a small group of people could do. He then had Macri try to hold the faerthorne, finding she could, so she was charged with the vine. The half Fae looked back at Elarie, holding it in both hands. Her eyes went to Elarie's wrists before quickly turning away. She attached the faerthorne to her belt.

"Should we be worried about that?" Kaelum whispered.

"She won't get anywhere near me if she tries," Elarie replied.

They walked. And walked. It took an hour, maybe more, but the scent was so strong she knew that another few steps and she would see it again. All over again. She'd never escape it.

Ever.

Calix had stopped, as had Macri and Terry. Elarie let go of Kaelum's hand and moved past both of them, stepping weakly onto the field. It was bare. Ruined, as she knew it would be. It didn't make it any less difficult, though. The pain was fresh again, rooted in her chest like a thorn. Spreading and spreading and spreading until she was full of it. Full of the shaking, aching thing.

The rot spread to the trees beyond, turning them just as yellow and shrunken as the branch Brin had brought with him as proof. Elarie wondered then why no one had been killed. Had the golden blooded man come in the night and destroyed their crops? Or was North Reidle the only village that lost people?

She took another step. Then another. What had once been grass crunched under her feet.

"Would the golden blooded man be here?" Macri asked. "Why would he stay here and not flee?"

Elarie began turning, her mind on something similar as she slowly went numb with the thought. He never stayed in one place, did he? But there was warmth in front of her, the warmth of a body, and a cracking nose. Elarie looked at Calix, then ahead. No one was there. Still, she pushed a burst of flames outward and something screamed. Her fire burned over something—some*one*—that thrashed and dropped to the ground with a thud.

Her neck was stabbed. Cold liquid seeped into her veins, fogging her vision as something was pulled from her pocket, though she wasn't sure what. Someone screamed her name and Elarie swayed toward it, her knees buckling. It was a familiar feeling despite the place around her not being so. She was being lifted. Carried. That was familiar.

Grunting sounded. A fight. That was also familiar.

What was in front of her? Sand? It was yellow, unlike any beach Elarie could remember being on. Could she remember anything at all? The pounding of hooves echoed on her right, followed by a laugh as another tube was stabbed into her neck. She could see who did it now. It was a Fae, one that sneered as he pulled the broken glass away.

The laughing continued. A man. Was he going to tell her what to do? Elarie looked at him, watching him move like he was walking above the yellow sand, not in it. The tops of his black boots were clean. The man grinned at her. He was ugly. His hair was a strange shade of yellow, as were his eyes. His skin was pasty, wrinkled, and aged. He had clean teeth, unnaturally straight. "Here she is," he said, his voice chilling her uncomfortably. Elarie tried to move away from his reach but he grabbed her face and jerked her forward. "Aren't you beautiful?"

Wasn't she supposed to be fighting, not receiving compliments from strange men with yellow eyes? The feeling in her, the thing coursing through her veins, it meant she needed to fight.

"Well, princess, it's been a long time, hasn't it?" He chuckled, grinning with his strange teeth. Elarie squirmed and he grabbed her throat. Callouses scraped against her skin, burning differently than fire. Elarie grunted, wrapping her hands around his wrist. "And you brought friends," he said, looking behind her, "how lovely."

Elarie tried to turn her head, wanting to know what he meant by friends. She couldn't remember having any.

The man jerked her head back, making her dizzy. "You and I are so similar," he told her. "I'll bet we've experienced all the same things. All the same deaths, all the same losses," he looked at the top of her head for some reason, then twisted his long finger through her hair. He dragged it down to her shoulder, then her collar. "There is one thing I've always wondered," the man said. His happy, condescending tone dropped as he asked, "is your heart as golden as your blood?"

Her brow furrowed. How was she supposed to know that?

The man's hand thrust into her chest. Elarie gasped, grabbing his other wrist. She dug her nails into his skin, her mouth hanging open as he gripped her heart. Her lashes fluttered. She trembled. This was not normal, this was not fighting, this should not be happening.

He pulled his hand free, taking her heart with it.

Elarie's body dropped to the yellow sand and she found herself in a lake. It was the color of crystals and surrounded by trees. There was a glow to the place around her, but Elarie wasn't given the chance to admire it. She was pulled back into the world, finding a hand gripping her hair and an ugly face bent over looking at her. She peered at him for a moment before he thrust a knife into her throat and dragged it to the side.

Elarie slapped her hand over the blood gushing from her body. She grunted, pushing him. A blast of fire sent him backward, giving Elarie time to turn over and crawl over the sand.

She didn't make it very far.

Surfacing again on the sand was hard. It ached.

Someone grabbed her head and snapped it to the side.

Elarie gasped, splashing in the water and sobbing before she was jerked back into her body. Back on the sand. Back where she did not want to be.

"Oh, I am going to have so much fun with you," said a scratching voice. Tubes were stabbed into her neck and she went numb, forced to her knees. Elarie should be standing. She was always standing when she felt the cold liquid move through her. "I set out to kill the Enebloods," he said. Elarie looked at him and he stabbed a dagger through her chin and into her mouth. Why was he doing this? What did he gain from this?

Water.

Sand.

Water.

Sand.

Back and forth. Elarie was not supposed to go back and forth.

"Destroy the Crosha, kill the little princess before the ceremony," he stabbed her gut. And stabbed her. And stabbed her. Elarie sobbed as she grabbed at herself like there was anything she could do but die. "And all the elemental magic stops. Right?" He held her jaw once she surfaced. Elarie was going to vomit. "Then nature kills the humans."

The next time she died her body spun around and she landed on her stomach. Waking up, she inhaled sand and coughed. There were people in front of her. Four of them, each of them horrified and trying to speak to her. They were all on their knees but one. One specifically was on his stomach. He was sobbing, pleading and shouting and squirming against the boot on his back.

Elarie knew him. She knew him, who was he?

"I become the gods' favorite," said the familiar voice. She was lifted again. Elarie was punched. She was kicked. "However," he said, "this is so much better." He laughed before a sword spilled her insides onto the sand. Elarie gaped at them weakly.

Stay under, stay under, please stay under.

She did not. Elarie looked at what was meant to be in her body that had been taken out of her body and vomited. Her body shook and she was crying. The man did not care. He killed her again. And again.

Elarie stared at the clear sky. She couldn't catch her breath. Her lungs were gone. They were ash, they were dirt, they were sand.

"For all of our never-ending lives," said the man pleasantly. He stood over her, breathing heavily and covered in golden blood. "We'll have each other. Isn't that perfect? Just you and me—"

Elarie threw her hand out and he went flying again, only this time it was upward. Air pushed him and pushed him and pushed him until he was a dot in the sky. She breathed quickly, everything around her blurred, but she could *feel* everything just fine. She pushed back the Fae coming toward her and found another. Half of one. Elarie's blurred eyes landed on the faerthorne at her belt and crawled toward her. She grabbed the vine, ignoring the way it dug into her hand as the man's body thunked on her left side.

The thorn went into his neck. She ripped her hand away, her body burning. No one could touch her if she was on fire. No one could touch her if she was on fire. He couldn't touch her if she was on fire.

But the man sat up.

He sat up.

Elarie sobbed, watching the faerthorne vine turn to the same sand she was covered in and surrounded by. "You and me," he said as he stood. "Your ancestors and your family will watch as I break you over and over. I can do anything to you. I can rip you to pieces and all they'll be able to do is watch." Elarie crawled backward. "You'll keep coming back to me. What torture that will be," he chuckled, "let's begin now."

Every movement hurt, but the faerthorne was so much worse. She'd been too focused on the man, she hadn't noticed the Fae working with him. Elarie hadn't felt the heat through the one on her body until it was gone. One silly thorn and it was gone. The man knelt in front of her and the Fae grabbed her.

"I'm so glad you tried to settle down with someone," he said as he wrapped his hand around her upper left arm. He squeezed it. "I knew you'd try it eventually, but this was too good of you." Suddenly his nails were sinking into her skin. Elarie jerked and moved, trying to push him. She'd never been weaker than someone, but he wouldn't move. She screamed, the sound traveling over the barren field, maybe even the ocean. Her blood poured down her skin and hissed against the sand. Elarie hit him again and again. Her bone cracked as he dug into her.

She hit him and kicked him and scratched him but he didn't move. He wouldn't move. Elarie tore at his throat, pushing her fingers around arteries and yanking them out of his body, but he didn't move. They stitched back together. Elarie sobbed and screamed. Her arm was splitting. It was *splitting*. He was *pulling*. He was *tearing*. He was *ripping*.

Elarie had never been dismembered before.

She'd never watched a piece of her body be...

There was so much blood that Elarie could hardly see any other color but gold. Gold was everywhere. It was all over her. It was all over him. When he yanked the last of the tendons apart he looked at her arm. A grin spread on his face.

"I could start a collection," he said and Elarie blinked slowly. She was losing blood quickly. She would die soon. "I could build a new *you*." She closed her eyes, but he grabbed her face and jerked on her so they fluttered back open. When she looked, it wasn't his hand on her, it was her own lifeless one that he was holding.

His laughter echoed in her ears. It echoed in the lake she took a breath in. It echoed as she came back to life, the faerthorne out of her body only momentarily.

Another dose of the cold, evil liquid was pressed against her neck. Then two more. "It's time to go home," he said smoothly. "Bind her wrists, put her on my horse. I'll see to the—"

A great roar came from the west. Elarie's head turned, familiarity prickling over her skin. She knew that roar. She had to know it. The dragon flew quickly, he flew purposefully. His wings were long and grey and beautiful. He roared again, telling her he was coming. He was coming.

"Interesting," said the man who told the Fae to put her on a horse.

Elarie's throat tightened. "He's alive," she realized. That was Greilor. That was her dragon. He'd died with the hatchlings, but there he was. Alive. "He's alive," she said again, fresh tears blooming in her eyes. Her voice was hoarse, barely there, but it didn't need to be, because his was there telling her to hold on and to fight.

The man sighed and looked behind Elarie at someone that was screaming. "I'll leave his body for you," he said. The screaming grew louder. Greilor was close now, so close Elarie could make out his whole, great body. She gazed at his wings. Her wings, as they had been years ago.

Leave his body? "Wait," Elarie whispered, "wait." She watched some sort of yellow spear grow from nothing. Then another. And another, until there were twelve of them. Elarie's eyes widened. She jerked against the Fae holding her arm. He was trying to grab both of them. "Stop, stop!"

The spears flew through the air and Elarie froze. Everything turned silent. Twelve of the spears. Twelve spears. Twelve seconds.

One. They soared.

Two. People screamed.

Three. Greilor dodged one, suddenly alert and trying to evade.

Four.

Five.

Six.

Seven. One spear tore through his wing.

Eight.

Nine. A second spear grazed his back leg.

Ten. Greilor screamed.

He *screamed.*

Eleven. A spear struck his chest.

Twelve. Greilor hit the ruinous sand with a bang that shook the ground. His body rolled. It twisted. It broke. He cracked and folded, staining the yellow sand red like she stained it golden. He was dead before he finally slid to a stop, his mouth open and spears sticking out of his back.

Elarie stared across the field. Blood began to pool around him. His wing stuck out at an odd angle.

There was sobbing coming from behind her, and now she knew who it was. She knew it was Calix, the Dragon Prince, who dreamed of yellow and black wings. Who rode a dragon. Who feared falling. It was Calix, who she bonded with because of their mutual love for a dragon. The dragon across the field. He called him Grey, she called him Greilor. Greilor loved him. He *loved* him.

He couldn't just be gone. That couldn't be him.

"Well," said the man with a sigh, clapping his hands and wiping them as if to say *job well done.*

Elarie twisted out of the hand of the Fae and grabbed his head, smashing it into the sand and pulling the faerthorne free. She dropped it, her hand in the Fae's pocket in search of a star. The smile on the man's face was gone, but that didn't matter to her. She was looking at Greilor, because he couldn't be dead. She'd find a healer. She'd become a healer. She'd give her life—she'd give a thousand lives, over and over until she got him back. He couldn't die. He couldn't be dead.

She stood and pocketed the star. Elarie's lips trembled as the man got on his horse with some sort of fresh gleeful expression, as if he couldn't wait for a fight the way the Messenger never could. He shouted something, she didn't know what, but something was stirring in the air. The star in her pocket burned against her thigh. She'd get Greilor back. She'd bring Greilor back.

Elarie ran forward, her body dizzy and aching. People were coming out of the woods that had been untouched. They shouted with a fury, they held spears and bows and swords.

Greilor was right there. He was right there.

The earth erupted when Elarie stumbled. It swallowed the Fae. They screamed as water rushed like a tidal wave and wind pushed them to drown. But it was fire, beautiful raging fire, that churned and funneled. It surrounded them, scorching the earth and burning the little army. Males and females alike ran flailing as their bodies burned. Some turned to ash or coals to stoke the flames higher. As all other elementals faded away, her powerful flames remained.

It was her element. It was her power. It was...

Greilor's.

Elarie stopped in front of him and the fire went out. Silence spread over the field. She stood by his face, swaying like she'd soon be unable to hold herself up. His neck was snapped, she was looking at him like he was upside down. The horn at the tip of his nose faced the ground and his beautiful black eyes were rolled upward. Blood stained his mouth, dripping from between his teeth.

His body was facing the right way, but one of his wings had been ripped off. The other was snapped.

Elarie dropped to her knees. She lifted her hand, but couldn't bring herself to touch him, to reach out far enough. When her family died, when it felt like the whole world had broken around her, she'd screamed. She had screamed and screamed until she had no voice at all. She couldn't touch the Keep. She was too afraid. And she couldn't touch Greilor. She couldn't scream. She couldn't even feel a tear. She had nothing.

No one.

But she felt him before she heard him. Calix. Calix, Calix, Calix.

Calix just lost his wings. He was standing away from her by just a few steps and she could feel him trying not to cry. He was shaking. His breaths were labored and sharp. Elarie stood, facing him. They mirrored each other. Both covered in the yellow sand, both covered in blood. Red in his case, gold in hers.

Elarie went to Calix slowly on shaking legs, only looking at him for a moment before she slowly took his hand. He clasped it tight, a quake rolling through him that caused her arm to tremble as well. It felt as if he'd lose his balance at any moment. That the shaking would cause his knee to buckle. She squeezed his hand he let her pull him to Greilor. His face was strained, turning red, and his eyes shined.

"Calix," she whispered and he sobbed. Tears rolled down his cheeks.

"He's gone," Calix said.

Elarie squeezed his hand. "He loved you so much," she said, now faced with her own sorrow. He was her priority, but it was there, surfacing. Calix nodded again and she pushed on, "when a rider loses his dragon—" an intense, horrifying sob came from him. It ripped through him, causing him to bend forward and fall against her. "We have a way of saying goodbye," she told him, rubbing his back. "We'll do it together, you and me, he'd want that."

Calix nodded and pulled away. He wiped his face, but it did nothing to stop the tears from falling. She faced Greilor, gripping his hand tight. "*Saera-a mesai, Greilor,*" she said softly. Elarie looked at Calix, "say goodbye and thank him."

He bit the inside of his cheek, trembling as he said, "goodbye. And thank you for—" his voice cracked and he cleared his throat, "thank you for everything."

"Deep breath," she nodded. He tried his best, and that was enough. She did the same, leading his hand to Greilor's scales. She pressed it flat and held hers over it. She focused on his fire. On the beautiful, powerful flames she'd grown up with. His scales warmed. "Just breathe, it's all right," she said and he was still trying. Behind them, Kaelum fell to his knee, lowering, and Terry did the same. Even Macri, and it looked like she might be crying as well.

Elarie took a deeper breath and Greilor's body warmed, concentrating on this one part the way her magic did inside her. Under their hands it churned, drawing inward.

"May your wings take you to the Clouds," she said, shaking on her own now. Elarie had never heard the prayer in any tongue but her own, but she didn't stop. Calix needed to hear it. "And the fire you breathe challenge the might of the gods. May your flight be never-ending and your watch upon us as great and as loving as the care you felt for us and we felt for you."

His body began to burn. From the wing that had ripped off his body to his tail and upward, sparks danced through the air coming to one location. Fire engulfed their hands, making Calix gasp. It covered both of them.

Calix closed his fist around a grey stone and held it between them. An entire dragon, fit into one rock. "This is his fire," Elarie explained, looking at the scale pattern she would never see again, "so he's always with you."

He stared at it as she was, breathing through his mouth because his nose was stuffed. Some of the scales shined as he turned it. "Can you break it? In half, so we both have a part of him."

Elarie took in a shaky breath, her lip quivering. She nodded after a moment, her head moving quickly. Elarie took the warm stone from him. It was heavy and solid, but if she tossed it into the air she was sure it would soar like a dragon. She squeezed it, feeling it crack. When she opened her hand the stone was in two. Inside was the same black, shining glass that covered the walls of his nest. Elarie handed one piece back to Calix. He continued staring at it as if it would breathe the fire he could feel was trapped inside it. She wrapped her arms around him. His knees buckled when she did and Elarie caught him in time to lower both of them to the ground.

Calix gripped her shirt and broke down.

Chapter Ninety-Two

Kaelum

A very small dragon screamed from the sky, flying from the same direction Grey had. They'd been together, then, and Grey must've been much faster than Masha was. Kaelum watched her fly over the yellow waste and launch herself right into Calix's arms. It was good that she was slower, though Kaelum hated the thought gracing his mind. Yet given what happened to Grey, Masha being late was a blessing.

The blood was gone. Elarie had managed to get rid of that as well when she burned Grey's body. She was standing now, everyone was, though while everyone was looking at the destruction or at their prince, she was staring at her arm. It was clean and pale. Gone were the years of scars and tanning. She blinked weakly, swaying. Even with her arm around Calix and with them leaning against each other she still looked like she was going to fall over. Had she ever died that many times? How many had it been? Over and over and over, Kaelum couldn't count.

Terry took a step forward, braving a good question. "What about his eggs?"

Calix looked urgently at Elarie, but she shook her head, "they're fine." She looked at Calix and nodded, "they're fine. Renci is still with them, I can feel the fire." Calix breathed a quiet sigh and put his head against hers.

Again, Terry asked an important question. "What are we going to do now?"

The question hung in the air. There was a weight to it. Even the soldier Kaelum didn't know seemed to be asking herself that. She was crying like everyone was, her cheeks just as wet as Kaelum's or Terry's. Not Calix's and not Elarie's.

"I can't kill him," Elarie said, "I was told by a god that I wasn't allowed to. There will be consequences if I do and I just..." she looked at the spot where it had all happened. She *had* killed him. More than once, technically. "I can't kill him," she repeated.

"I will," Kaelum said. "I'll do it. We just have to find him and you have to teach me, but I'll do it."

Terry said, "or we just lock him up like we planned before."

"The faerthorne didn't work," the soldier reminded him.

"There has to be something," he said.

Kaelum nodded, "there is something. I'll do it."

The soldier asked, "how?"

His eyes found Elarie's. She was scared and in pain. Kaelum figured the only reason she was standing was because of Calix and the only reason Calix was standing was because of her. "I have the power of a god," he said, "the ability to create magic, I just need you to show me how."

"This could end so badly," she whispered.

"He killed Grey," Calix said, his voice practically gone. He wasn't whispering, but there was little left of it. Masha whimpered and he dragged his fingers soothingly over her scales. "He has to die."

They looked at each other. It was her decision, really. Elarie knew him best, she knew how to get to him, she had the magic, and she had the answers for Kaelum. They couldn't do it without her. "Then we have to go to Eneblood."

"He's in the Forgotten Lands?" The soldier asked, "how did he even get there? How would *we* get there?"

She said, "it's just another thing I'll have to teach Kaelum," and looked at the star maker. Elarie said, "and he was going to take me home. That doesn't mean just anywhere. He won't live under someone else's rule and he's too rotten for the Faerie Lands, so he stayed in Eneblood."

"Are you prepared to go back?" Terry asked gently.

Elarie grimaced and shrugged. "He killed Greilor," she said as if that was a real answer. Calix understood it, he had the sad eyes like he'd ask her later.

The soldier asked, "then do you have any idea where in Eneblood he'd be?"

"Not the Keep, that was my home and he destroyed it," she pulled herself closer to Calix, "but there are plenty of places that would be vacant. The Center Castle is the biggest."

Terry sort of smiled, "princess, huh?"

"It's where I would go," Elarie said, ignoring Terry's comment.

"So we're going?" Calix asked her. She nodded, looking at Kaelum. It would all be on him, then. Kaelum would have to learn how to kill something that couldn't be killed and he didn't have long to do it.

"Then let's set sail for the land of ruin," Terry said.

They looked at Elarie once again. She stared down at her hand instead of at them. "To the land of ruin."

Made in the USA
Las Vegas, NV
17 January 2024

84519740R00412